DIVINE GRACE

Seize the Day

Divine Creek Ranch 1

Heather Rainier

MENAGE EVERLASTING

Siren Publishing, Inc.
www.SirenPublishing.com

A SIREN PUBLISHING BOOK
IMPRINT: Ménage Everlasting

DIVINE GRACE: SEIZE THE DAY

ISBN-10: 1-61034-228-3
ISBN-13: 978-1-61034-228-5

First Printing: January 2011

Cover design by *Les Byerley*

Vaughan, Stevie Ray Lyrics. “Honey Bee.” *Couldn’t Stand the Weather.* Epic Records. © 1984.

Printed in the U.S.A.

PUBLISHER
Siren Publishing, Inc.
www.SirenPublishing.com

DEDICATION

To my husband. Just when I think life with you can't get any sweeter, it does. Thanks for being my fantasy come true.

Thanks to Rebecca, Dana, Lisa, and Kayla for believing in me.

Thanks to Christi, Jennifer and Tonya for your contagious enthusiasm.

And a very special thanks to Diana and all the ladies and gentlemen at Siren Publishing for their patience, hard work, and belief in my manuscript.

Heather Rainier

Best wishes and Happy Reading!
Heather Rainier

DIVINE GRACE

Seize the Day

Divine Creek Ranch 1

HEATHER RAINIER

Chapter One

Grace Stuart carried two pairs of men's black trousers back to the dressing room where one of her favorite customers waited for her. Standing outside, she tapped lightly on the door and waited for him to open it. Jack Warner opened the door a crack and handed her the jacket, which was also too small.

"Darlin', maybe I've put on weight. That coat's too tight," he said in his sexy Texan drawl.

Grace bit her lip. His voice, even speaking of something so mundane, was like a velvety caress to her senses.

I'll get you whatever you want, just please keep talking.

"I think it's just the manufacturer, Jack. The shirt I gave you to try on is the same size you always buy. You're not gaining weight." *You're just as fine as ever, handsome.* "You're going to look really sharp in your new suit. Though I wish it was a happier occasion. Your mom was a really sweet lady. I'm going to miss talking to her every Saturday."

"Thank you, darlin'. I'm gonna miss her a lot. Dad's taking it pretty hard. She was his whole world. They were married over sixty years."

"You're so young. She must have had you later in life."

"I was her late-in-life baby. All of my siblings are much older than me. She used to say it was like having a firstborn all over again, but in a good way."

"I'll bet she spoiled you rotten." Grace pictured Jack as a little boy trying to sweet-talk his mother. Thinking of him at all always set her heart beating a little faster.

"She did, I suppose, but I was just as likely to get my ear pulled or my butt whipped as the others if I misbehaved."

She heard rustling around on the other side of the door, zippers zipping, and then he sighed softly.

"Jack? You okay?" She heard him sniff and felt like kicking herself for bringing up the reason for today's purchase. Jack's mother, Rose Marie, had passed away two nights before while she slept. She had been sick with chronic bronchitis, which had often turned into full-blown pneumonia for the last few years, and it had left her very weak.

Grace hadn't seen much of her in the store the last few months and had missed their Saturday morning chats. Rose Marie always made a weekly shopping trip to Stigall's department store. She was in the habit of stopping by the menswear department where Grace worked every Saturday. Grace would miss her dry wit and common sense advice. It was because of Rose Marie that Jack had become Grace's regular customer.

"Grace, would you mind getting my size in that other suit you showed me? I should have listened to you and gone with it to begin with. Sorry."

"Sure, Jack. I'll be right back."

After retrieving the other suit in his size, she returned and tapped on his door again. When he'd closed it before, it hadn't shut properly, and she was witness to her own red-faced mortification as the mirrored dressing room door swung open. He was busy hanging the pants back on the hanger for her and didn't notice at first. Evidently, underwear was optional today, and commando looked so *good* on him! He glanced up when she gasped, and his reflection made eye contact with hers. She slammed her eyes shut and quietly pulled the door closed.

"I'm so sorry, Jack. The door swung open when I tapped on it," she whispered, afraid of drawing attention to her embarrassing predicament. "Please forgive me?" She heard him chuckle behind the door. Her heart was pounding, and heat radiated from her cheeks.

"It's my fault for not making sure the damn door closed all the way. If it'd been up to me, darlin', I'd have at least taken you out for a nice meal before sharing that much *information* with you. I like that shade of pink you're wearing, though," he said softly with a chuckle. Even now, in this embarrassing situation, his voice affected her, her body reacting in all sorts of inappropriate ways.

"Huh?" She was dressed in blue today.

"Your cheeks, darlin'," he replied as he opened the door, now clothed in the dress shirt and pants.

His comment about the color of her cheeks made her blush even harder. She wanted to slink off quietly and hide under one of the clothing racks and give herself a chance to cool off.

She'd just seen her favorite customer partially nude. He'd had the dress shirt on, but it had been unbuttoned, and she'd seen his entire torso, completely bare in the mirror's reflection in the brightly lit dressing room. The image of his physique was burned into her retinas now, every beautiful, glorious inch of him. Of course, the next thought to pop into her dazed mind was if he's that long and thick when he wasn't aroused, how big is it when he's hard? *There* went her cheeks again! Hiding under a rack was looking like a better option all the time. She turned and put her hands to her burning face.

* * * *

"You okay? I'm sorry I embarrassed you, Grace," Jack said quietly as he came up behind her. He wanted so much to reach out and touch her, even if it was only to put his hands on her shoulders. He could see how embarrassed she was, and he was worried that she would withdraw back into the shell he'd been trying to draw her from for months. "Nobody saw, I don't think. It'll be our little secret, okay? These pants will need a hem put in. How quick can y'all do that?" He tried to distract her and give her a chance to regain her composure before anyone else walked up.

He felt bad that she was embarrassed by what happened. He wished he could feel the same. He could have gotten by with his other suit, but being near Grace comforted him in a way that he wished he could put into words. She had been close to his mom, probably not realizing just how much Rose Marie enjoyed visiting with her on Saturday mornings. This morning there were any number of things he could have done, but he needed to see Grace's beautiful face and hear her soft voice more than he needed to keep busy.

Even if he could only interact with her as a customer, she still eased him with her sweet presence.

"Let me check real quick." She picked up the phone at the sales counter and dialed the alterations department. They spoke for a moment, and she hung up.

"I'll put in a rush order for you since you need them for tomorrow. It's still early enough that we could have them ready by the end of the day, and you can wear them to the visitation at the funeral home tonight if you want to. Mona asked if you can you come by after five o'clock. We close at seven."

"Sure, will you still be here?" he asked wishfully. Was it too much to hope he'd get to see her again later? Her sweet blue eyes sparkled at his question. Maybe that meant she'd like to see him again also.

"Yes, I should be. Just come back here and I'll run and get them for you." She fished around in a drawer behind the counter, looking for something.

Grace was dressed in a long denim skirt, a loose red top, and white sandals on her slim little feet. She squatted down, looking in a lower drawer, and when she did, Jack noticed how the skirt clung to her luscious derriere. He could see how tiny her waist was as she stretched to reach the back of the deep drawer, muttering to herself. Grace tended to dress very modestly. Grinning, he noticed there were little white daisies painted on her pink toenails. She was shy about everything but her pretty feet.

"You take good care of me, Grace."

She finally found what she was looking for and stood back up.

"Don't be so quick to jump to conclusions, Jack." Grace smiled and then blushed a little more. "I still have to measure your inseam." She held up her tape measure.

* * * *

His eyes twinkled back at her, and he gave her that devilish bad boy grin that told her she'd be blushing some more before they were done. She almost melted into the carpet at the effect his eyes had on her composure. She had to remind herself that she might be only part-time help here at Stigall's, but she was still a professional. She'd measured lots and lots of customers, young and old alike, and Jack would get the same professional service everyone else got.

But somewhere between his bad boy grin and the moment she knelt in front of him to use the tape measure, something changed. Her hands hesitated, shaking with the fresh knowledge of what rested under those pants. She paused and looked up at him. He looked down at her, encouragement in his eyes, but the way he looked at her was different. She lowered her gaze and used her tape measure. He stood perfectly still, and she thought maybe he was holding his breath. She made a note of the measurement on the work order, and preparing to rise to her feet, she leaned forward and made eye contact with his erection.

Oh, my sweet heaven.

Now she *knew* the answer to her earlier question. *Great balls of fire.* Her mouth actually started watering!

Offering her his tanned, callused hand, he helped her rise to her feet and was slow to release her hand. She wondered if he could feel the heat coming off her cheeks, but the sudden dampness in her panties was even more disconcerting. He was her customer, and here she was lusting after him. Okay, so he was her favorite, very sexy, *very* handsome in a cowboy sort of way customer. But she also counted him as a friend, thanks to his mom. And that was the sobering thought. She shouldn't be thinking these thoughts, not when he'd just lost his mom.

He returned to the dressing room and changed back into the denim shirt, blue jeans, and boots she was used to seeing him in, most of which he bought at this very store. She even did the embroidery above the left breast pocket that carried his name and company logo. That had been her idea. Grace's full-time job was at a local screen printing and embroidery shop in their little city of Divine. All the local sports teams had their jerseys and hats printed there, and local businesses had similar items embroidered with their company names and logos. She'd asked him if he had a company logo, and when he'd told her no, she invited him to come by the shop with all the new shirts he'd purchased from her. She'd helped him design a logo and had done the embroidery herself. Thanks to Jack, they had received a lot of referrals for more work.

She wrote up the alteration order and attached it with a straight pin to the pants he handed back to her, neatly hung on the hanger. Jack was always a considerate customer. Lots of people left heaps of clothes littering the dressing room floors after trying on half the store or threw the wadded up rejects to her and left the hangers still hanging in the dressing room. He was always neat as a pin about things like that.

"Do you have any neckties, Jack?"

"Yes, but all the ones at home are old. How about you set me up with something that will look good for tomorrow?" He looked down into her eyes, giving her that winsome smile that made her heart do flip-flops every time she saw him. She walked over to the tie rack and came back with a dark aquamarine silk tie. She held up the necktie to his shirtfront to see if it was the right color.

"This one reminds me of your eye color. Your mom would have loved it. Did the jacket fit okay in the sleeves? Not too long or short?"

"No, the jacket was fine. I'll take the tie and the shirt."

"Jack, is there anything I can do? To help out, I mean?"

"No, Mom and Dad's Sunday school class is bringing over food to the house for after the funeral, and he's already got a refrigerator and freezer full of casseroles. But I appreciate the thought, Grace."

She knew he assumed she was asking if his dad was covered for food, but she'd meant for Jack. He looked like he could use a home-cooked meal. He paid for his purchases and promised to be back after five o'clock. The morning was slow, and at two o'clock her boss let her go home. She was disappointed she wouldn't see Jack but left word that he'd pick up the pants later that day.

She stopped at the grocery store and got everything she'd need to make a nice home-cooked meal for Jack and his roommates. Owen wasn't at home, so she was able to work in peace. She baked bread, made homemade beef stew, and baked a cake, too. With everything loaded on the front seat of her little Honda, she drove out to the Divine Creek Ranch.

Jack and two friends owned equal shares in the ranch. All three were self-employed. Jack was a general contractor and electrician, Ethan Grant was bartender and co-owner of a local night club, The Dancing Pony, and Adam Davis was also a contractor.

The opportunity to buy the horse ranch had come along, and they'd decided to sell their homes, live in the ranch house, and invest the money from the sale of the houses in the ranch. From the looks of things, their investment was paying off. She knew all this because Rose Marie told her all about them in extensive, glowing detail. Up until that moment, Grace hadn't met any of Jack's roommates.

The only associate of Jack's she knew personally was his ranch foreman, Angel Martinez. She liked Angel because he was always polite to her and made direct eye contact when talking to her, but she sometimes got the impression he was flirting with her.

She drove through the gated entryway, holding the lid on the pot to keep it steady as she drove over the cattle guard, and headed down the long gravel drive to the large rock-faced ranch house. Horses grazed on thick green grass in fenced pastures on both sides of the drive, and she noticed a couple of the dappled gray mares looked like they would be foaling soon.

She followed the drive around where it curved in front of the house and parked by the porch steps. She saw a truck parked on the side of the house, so at least one of them had to be home. She gathered up the box that had the cake and bread in it and climbed the steps that led up to the welcoming shade of the front porch. She rang the doorbell.

Half a minute later, the heavy oak door was opened by a gorgeous man dressed in faded jeans and an unbuttoned plaid shirt, which revealed his muscular chest and abdomen. He stood in the doorway toweling his shoulder-length brown hair dry. He must have been fresh from his shower, judging by the clean, masculine scent that followed the gust of cooled air that swept past her when he opened the front door. Her nostrils were filled with his spicy scent, and her mouth watered as she tried to pull enough brain cells together to form words into sentences.

He spoke in a voice that was like velvet, soft and smooth, with a slight Texan accent. "Hi. What can I do for you?" He smiled warmly at her, looking curiously at the box she held.

"I'm a friend of Jack's and wanted to bring him some food to help out. He told me that his father had plenty of food at his house, but he didn't say anything about at his own home. I have a big pot of homemade beef stew out in the car, and I made y'all fresh bread and a cake."

Smiling, he opened the door for her and stepped aside so she could enter. "Let me get my boots on and I'll carry in the pot for you."

It was then that she noticed he was barefoot.

He disappeared for a moment and came back with socks and boots. "Sorry, you caught me coming out of the shower," he said with a grin.

One moment she was thinking what a nice visual image he had provided her with, and the next second, she was wondering why she would think something like that. A small part of her knew for certain that though it might not go anywhere, she already had the hots for his roommate Jack. Where was her loyalty, even if it was only loyalty to a fantasy?

"I'm sure Jack will really appreciate your thoughtfulness—" He paused, waiting for her name.

"Grace! Grace Stuart. I'm sorry. I should have introduced myself properly before barging in your house." She saw pleased recognition in his eyes, and a big grin crossed his handsome face.

"You're Grace! I've heard a lot of nice things about you. It's good to finally meet you."

Had Jack told his roommate about *her*? The dawning recognition in his eyes mixed with a little surprise had her very curious. She wondered what exactly Jack had said about her. His roommate was already headed out the door. She followed him down the limestone steps to the car. The hot summer sun beat down on them as they left the shade of the deep wrap-around porch. He opened the front passenger door, and the smell of the stew wafted out.

"That smells really good, Grace." He lifted the cardboard box lined with a towel that contained the stew pot. "I have a feeling we're going to eat good tonight."

She followed him back into the house, still carrying the smaller box. "I know from experience that when you're dealing with the loss of someone really close to you, it's easy to neglect the mundane tasks like preparing meals. I'm still in shock that Rose Marie passed away. She was my favorite customer at Stigall's."

"Jack hasn't been home a lot since it happened. He's been trying to make arrangements and watch over his dad. He probably has missed a few meals. It'll mean a lot to him that you took the time to come all the way out here for him. I'm sure we'll all be singing your praises later." He placed the cardboard box on the black and gray granite counter top.

His compliments made her blush and feel self-conscious. She lifted the covered pot from the cardboard box and set it on the back burner of their stove. The beautiful kitchen had stainless steel appliances and granite countertops. The floors were all hardwood, with area rugs scattered here and there. Their dining table positioned in the breakfast nook was counter height and surrounded by four barstools. The walls in the kitchen were done in a beautiful rich, dark-colored wood, but the walls in the living room that opened out from the kitchen were done in a light cream color, giving the space a light, airy, and open feeling. The back of the house must have a deep covered porch as well, as she could see out the back windows to the shaded area where several rockers and an old-fashioned glider sat in shadow. The red horse barns in the distance provided a pastoral backdrop. She thought that glider would be a wonderful place to spend the evening, even in this heat.

"So, you work at Stigall's?"

"Yes, part-time in the men's department and full-time at Harper's Embroidery. I did the embroidery work for Jack's work shirts. Angel's, too."

"Yes, I know. He told me. Y'all do good work. I stopped in there myself the other day, but I must have been in on your lunch hour or day off. I'm having some shirts done for The Dancing Pony."

"Oh! So you must be—"

"Ethan Grant. I'm sorry, bad manners. I should have introduced myself when you got here," he said sheepishly, holding out his hand.

When he took her hand in his, she noticed how warm it was. He had tanned, callused working man's hands, just like Jack. Jack was just a few inches taller than she, tending toward a stockier, more powerful build, strong and sturdy. Ethan was taller, maybe two inches over six feet, and more wiry. Though callused, his hands were long and graceful and strong. He had a gentle but firm grip, and when he touched her, she felt a little tremor go through her body. This man set all her senses on edge in a good way.

"It's nice to finally meet you, Ethan. I'm sorry I haven't ever been into The Dancing Pony before. I don't have much opportunity to go out these days with working two jobs."

Yeah, and having a no-account boyfriend who doesn't ever take me out anywhere but probably knows the interior of The Dancing Pony better than his own home.

And that was all the internal griping she was going to allow herself. Thoughts of her loser boyfriend overshadowed the nice visit she was having with Ethan.

She really needed to sit down and take stock in her life, make some decisions and some changes. Owen was at the top of that list of things to change, but she hated the thought of upsetting him. It never seemed to be a good time, and she wound up putting off the inevitable. If she was truly being honest with herself, she was a little afraid to tell Owen to get the hell out of her house and her life, especially when he was drunk, which was often enough.

"Well, you are always welcome to stop by. I'll even buy you a drink."

"That's sweet of you. I really should be going. My boyfriend will wonder where I am." Damn. She watched as his smile faded a bit.

Awkward.

"You sure you don't want to hang around? Jack will probably be home soon. You could say hello." He seemed almost reluctant to let her leave.

"I can't, but I did see him earlier today when he came to get a suit for the funeral."

"That's right. He said he was going in to see you."

Grace was surprised by that comment. He'd come in especially to see her that morning?

Ethan walked her to the door and opened it. The gust of heat, even this early in the summer, was stifling.

"Ugh, I should have rolled my windows down. You could probably fry an egg on my hood."

"You know, Jack and I tried that once when we were boys, and it actually worked, but his mom was not too happy about the mess on the hood of her Lincoln Continental."

"Y'all have known each other a long time?"

"Oh, yeah. We're very distant cousins. Our families were all neighbors out here growing up, and all three of us have known each other since we were little bitty. I grew up just down the road from here. That's one of the reasons we bought this place. We love the area. We used to jump the back fence and swim and fish in the creek that runs through this property. Our Tarzan rope still hangs in one of the trees, I think."

"I'll bet y'all have some funny stories to tell."

"Yeah, maybe someday we'll tell some of them to ya," Ethan replied. He said it like he planned on it, and though she didn't understand why he would want that, she wished it could be so. She could just imagine the trouble and adventures three little boys could get themselves into roaming around the countryside. She looked up at Ethan to say good-bye and was mesmerized by the way the sunlight lit his angular features, and she thought he had the warmest sparkling blue eyes.

"Jack will be sorry he missed you, but I'm glad I finally got to meet you," he said softly to her. She had the feeling that there was a lot more to what he was saying than the words he spoke, but it was really time for her to go.

"See y'all tomorrow," she replied as she got into her car.

He closed the door for her, raised a hand to wave good-bye, and stepped away. She started the car and rolled the windows down a bit as the AC kicked on, and a blast of hot air hit her in the face before it finally started to cool off. As she drove around the circle and back up the long driveway, she called herself every kind of name in the book for the guilty attraction she felt toward Ethan.

Owen was a no-account loser, and he was probably unfaithful to her, not that she really cared. He hadn't laid a hand on her in months. She was surprised that thought didn't bother her the way it should. What bothered her was the way she was acting and thinking about Jack and *now* Ethan. At least for her part, she was already in a committed relationship.

She shouldn't be noticing other men, even adorable and gorgeous ones like Jack and Ethan, who were, truth be told, *way* out of her league. She could flirt and kid and lust all she wanted, but she was a realist, too. They were probably just being nice, making her feel good about herself by flirting with her.

She saw her reflection in the mirror every day. She wasn't paper bag ugly, but her features were plain and unremarkable. She had nice, long blonde hair that she took good care of. And her eyes were a nice medium blue color, but the shape of her face was too round, and her complexion was on the ruddy side. She blushed *way* too easily, so she felt like her face was always too red. The Texas heat didn't help with that at all. If she stayed in the sun too long, she turned as red as a lobster but never tanned. Whatever skin wasn't red or pink stayed pasty white, and she'd given up tanning early on.

Owen preferred to always have the lights off when they did have sex, and he often told her it was because he didn't want to see her body shape. Maybe he imagined someone else in bed with him who was skinnier, and it was easier for him to fantasize with the lights off. She was a plus-size gal but not morbidly so. At least she didn't think a size sixteen or eighteen was obese. She had a round, generous butt and big breasts, but at least her waist was small, which always made it difficult to find jeans that really fit right. She'd always hated her thighs but most days felt like she'd come to grips with her attributes, except on the days when Owen would start in on her, usually at meal times.

Most men would be grateful to have a woman around who liked to cook and bake. Not Owen. He expected all those things, but when they sat down to eat, he felt it necessary to question whether she should eat this or that because it might make her fatter. Not fat. Fatter. Often, when he was drunk, he'd even called her Fatty. She did her best to consider the source of criticism. He was out of shape himself. He didn't have a regular job. He worked odd jobs here and there but really didn't contribute financially all that much. When she did ask for help with groceries or utilities, he acted as if she'd asked him to open a vein for her.

He'd been her boyfriend in high school, and after graduation they just sort of continued on with the status quo. When her mom passed away a few years before, it seemed to make sense to let him move in and help out with living expenses. She felt safer with someone else in the house.

Lately, whenever Jack came in the store, which had been frequently, he teased her, asking when she was going to dump her boyfriend and go out with him. She'd always assumed he was just kidding around. What if she weren't encumbered with Owen? Would Jack seriously ask her out? Unless she made some changes, she'd never know.

She pulled in the driveway, and there Owen sat on the front porch, drinking beer with one of his buddies. Beer she'd paid for, not that she drank the stuff. He belched as she walked up. She cringed at the greeting she got, but his next words truly horrified her.

"AC ain't workin'."

Oh, no.

There went her emergency fund. She had scrimped and saved everywhere she could to build that fund up so she wouldn't have to use credit for emergency repairs. She hated to start over. What if she didn't have enough? She walked in the house and started opening windows. He must have just gotten home from who knows where, otherwise he might have seen that dinner was on the stove. They undoubtedly would have scarfed it up themselves, leaving her little, if any. She even knew what he would say. Something helpful and supportive like, "Have a salad," or "There's mealshake in the fridge." Salad was an appetizer, and she hated mealshakes. She hated him, too, sometimes.

She checked the breaker to see if it had been flipped. Maybe that was all that was wrong. No such luck. She turned the central AC unit off and turned on all the ceiling fans in the house. She fixed herself a bowl of stew, tore off a small chunk of the fresh bread and buttered it, and sat down to eat, pondering her next move. She had planned to go to Rose Marie Warner's visitation tonight at the funeral home in town. Now she didn't feel like she had the strength to get ready for it. She would pay her respects tomorrow. Plus, she felt if she went tonight that it would seem too much like she was seeking Jack out.

She got out the phone book and looked in the yellow pages for an AC repairman. She called a couple of them to see what their rates were and when they could come out. One repairman said he was booked ahead for three weeks. She couldn't afford the rates of the other repairman but told him she might get back with him since he could fit her in the following weekend. A week, in summer, in Texas, with no AC. What could be worse?

Just then, Owen came in. Oh yeah. Owen definitely made it worse.

"Got any cash on you? I need to get some gas. Me and Dave are goin' out." He saw the pot on the stove but made no move toward it. He undoubtedly planned on eating out because he made no move to fix himself a bowl of stew. She felt like giving him the money just to make him go away. But as luck would have it, she'd cleaned out her wallet at the grocery store. She hadn't stopped at the bank because she was anxious to get started cooking for Jack.

Jack. Right now she *really* wanted Jack. Even if all he did was sit there and flirt with her. She wanted him bad. There were decent men in the world. He was living proof. She knew *he* would never ever ask her for money. He would never belch as a greeting. And if he intended to go out, he'd take her with him.

"Sorry, spent my cash on groceries today."

"Didn't you get paid yesterday?"

"Yes, electronic deposit."

"Can I borrow your ATM card?"

"No." A girl had to have limits, dammit.

"No?" he asked petulantly, putting his hands on his hips, where his boxer shorts rested several inches above the waist of his jeans. That was not a good look for anyone, in her opinion, but on him it was positively asinine.

"No."

That's when his buddy Dave piped up. "Come on, man, we'll stop by my house." He lived in his parent's garage. They could go sponge off his family for a while. She felt exhausted.

"Thanks for nothin', Grace."

Back at ya, asshole, she thought but didn't dare say. "Sorry." *Yeah, for ever having let you into my life.*

The screen door slamming shut was the only response she got as he left. He never even asked her how they were going to solve the AC problem. It was her house, her problem, as far as he was concerned. What an ass.

Chapter Two

Jack left Stigall's that afternoon with the altered pants wrapped in plastic on a hanger. When he'd gone back to the store, he'd been looking forward to seeing Grace again. He was disappointed to find out her boss let her off early. He saw the note she had written on the work order and smiled to himself. It said, "Make sure pants are pressed and ready to be worn. Very special customer!" She was the special one.

He'd been making excuses to stop by Stigall's on the weekends because he knew she worked in the menswear department. He'd also recently decided that all his work shirts needed to be personalized with the logo she had designed at Harper's. He really just wanted to see her. He'd always teased her about breaking up with her boyfriend and going out with him. But somewhere along the way, he realized he wasn't really kidding with her. He'd love the chance to take her out and spend some time getting to know her better.

Her boyfriend had stopped by the store one day to ask her for money while she was waiting on Jack. What kind of self-respecting man asked his woman for money? Jack had taken an instant dislike to him when he'd patted her ass and made a show of kissing her good-bye, embarrassing her in the process. Jack recognized a man marking his territory like a cat pissing on a tire. If her boyfriend acted like that in public—at her job, for crying out loud—how did he act in private? It galled him to think of it. It made him feel protective of her.

She was over twenty-one and could make her own choices, but he knew she could do better, and he knew where she could start—with him. The idea of spending time with her was no longer a playful notion, something to tease a sweet sales girl about. He started really paying attention to her after that.

Earlier in the day, when the dressing room door had popped open, her cheeks had flamed adorably. He really couldn't find it in his heart to be embarrassed, at least not too much. When he'd showered and gotten dressed that morning, he gave no thought to the fact he'd be trying on clothes and would need drawers on. Commando was cooler in this heat.

But she had given him a raging hard-on when she picked up that measuring tape and snapped it between her hands and smiled that mischievous smile at him. When she knelt in front of him, it conjured an image in his mind of her kneeling for an entirely different reason. Man, the way she affected him by just looking up at him with those innocent blue eyes of hers. She'd unconsciously licked her lips, and a ripple of heat had shot up his spine. He'd been afraid for a second he might explode on the spot. Then he would have had some explaining to do.

He had all kinds of mixed feelings today. He was supposed to be preparing for his mother's funeral. The words of his wise and kind mother kept ringing in his head. She was the one who originally introduced him to Grace. Over the years, she always told him, "Seize the day, Jack, because you never know how long you have. Have no regrets in life. Take chances." And her most recent question? "When are you going to convince that darling girl to dump that chump and go out with a real man? Hmm?"

God love her, she was right. It was time to stop sitting on the bench where the lovely Miss Stuart was concerned.

He smiled, remembering how her warm, delicate hand had trembled when he helped her from her kneeling position. He wondered—no, he *hoped*—that she was as affected by him as he was by her. He hardened a little, remembering her faint womanly scent when it had risen to his nostrils as she stood with his help. He'd been reluctant to release her hand.

He parked his truck next to Ethan and Adam's and went inside the ranch house. The house was clean, and there was a succulent aroma coming from the kitchen. They were already at the table eating, dressed, and ready to go with him to visitation tonight.

"Hey, you didn't have to cook, Ethan. I would have sprung for supper tonight," he said.

Ethan had a big shit-eating grin on his face as he shook his head. "I didn't cook. A friend of yours brought supper over for you earlier. I tried to talk her into staying, but she said she had to get home."

He was stumped. “Did she mention a name?” he asked as he lifted the lid and looked into the pot. His mouth watered. Then he saw the fresh bread wrapped in a dish cloth and the cake sitting on the countertop.

“Uh-huh,” Ethan replied, filling his mouth with a big bite, enjoying himself, no doubt. He and Adam shared a quick glance with each other before going back to their meal.

“Who was it?” This food was homemade. Who would take the time to do this for him and then come all the way out here?

“Grace Stuart,” Ethan said.

“Grace did this?” He wasn’t all that surprised. This was the kind of thing she would do, and she had asked earlier.

“She said she could tell how distracted you were by taking care of arrangements for your mom’s funeral and that she knew how hard it was to do simple things like fix meals. She wanted to help out, not just pay lip service.”

“Did you meet her, Adam?”

In between bites, Adam said, “No, she was already gone by the time I got home. But I heard all about her from Ethan.”

Jack got a bowl and spoon and fixed himself a glass of tea. He brought the loaf of bread and the butter dish to the table. He served himself and then joined the other two men. After saying grace over the meal, he dug in.

Lord have mercy, that woman wasn’t only beautiful, she could *cook*, too. This wasn’t just a meal. This was someone caring about another person and wanting to help them through a rough patch in the road. Boyfriend be damned, he was going after this woman the first chance he got.

“What did you think of her?” he asked, curious as to how Ethan had reacted to her.

“Beautiful. Caring. Sort of innocent, in a way. Intriguing. She seemed to feel guilty for being here when she was about to leave, like she was doing something wrong. She said she had a boyfriend. Is that the one you told us about?”

“Yeah, total asshole, not near good enough for her. So you liked her?”

“Yes, she’s adorable, gorgeous. I can see why you’ve been going on about her. She said she’d be at the funeral tomorrow, so Adam can meet her then.”

“Did she seem to like you, Ethan?”

"I think it surprised her, but yeah, seemed attracted. That could explain why she appeared to feel guilty. What do you plan to do if she takes a liking to Adam as well?"

"To take this *very* slow and see how she feels about it. What we want is pretty unorthodox. I don't want to scare her off completely if the idea of being with the three of us is too much for her to handle. Let's just take it slow and see how she does. First thing we need to do is focus on Mom's funeral and taking care of Dad." He paused and felt a hitch in his chest at the mention of her name. He let out a long, shaky breath, and Adam reached over and put a hand on his shoulder.

"I can tell you right now, knowing Rose as well as I did, that while she would appreciate the sentiment, she'd expect you to seize the next opportunity that presents itself to get closer to Grace. You know how much she liked Grace, and that if we really wanted someone who could love all three of us, she felt like Grace might be the one. Remember what she said about her?"

"A heart as big as Texas," Ethan murmured.

Rose Marie had not necessarily understood their desire for a woman who wanted all three of them. However, she did admit to them in her candid, no nonsense way that the thought of being a woman whose every need was attended to by three handsome, charming men was enough to get even her aging heart pounding just a bit. They'd all laughed, a little red-faced, over that, but she'd given them her blessing, warning them to let Grace set the pace if the opportunity presented itself.

Adam continued, "So just pray for an opportunity."

Ethan added, "And hope the boyfriend is soon out of the picture."

"She saw me half nekkid today," Jack mentioned nonchalantly as he took a bite of his bread.

Both Ethan and Adam dropped their spoons, and they clattered to the table.

* * * *

Grace tidied up the kitchen, took her shower, and got ready for bed. It was early, but the heat wiped her out, and she didn't feel like watching any TV. She lay in bed and tried to read, but thoughts of Jack kept creeping into her mind. Even more disturbing were thoughts of Ethan, with his sparkling bedroom eyes gazing down at her.

He didn't treat her as though she was an acquaintance or friend of Jack's or even a possible girlfriend of his roommate's. He reacted to her as though he was interested in asking her out for a date until she'd mentioned her boyfriend, and then he'd backed off. That had fueled her own guilt but not for the right reasons. She should feel guilty for lusting after two men, neither of whom was the man she currently lived with. Instead, her heart ached for feeling that way while attracted to Jack.

What a mess. Owen had to go as soon as she got up the nerve. She wished she was as strong as her sister, Charity. Charity would tell Owen to get the hell out. She'd throw all his stuff on the lawn and call the law on him if he complained. Grace hated to make a scene. Charity wouldn't think that the deed had been done right unless the police *did* get involved. She'd told Grace this on several occasions and had even offered to do it for her. It began to sound like fun.

Her thoughts rambled back around to the incident in the dressing room. She hadn't intended to stare. She was used to averting her eyes in that area, delivering and taking away clothing her customers had tried on. But most of her customers wore tighty whities or at least Underoos, for Pete's sake. Looking away from Jack and that fine package was more than she was capable of until she'd snapped out of it and embarrassed herself even further while measuring his inseam. Coming face-to-face, sort of, with his erection through the fabric of his dress pants had brought her to one eye-opening conclusion.

She had been robbed. *Robbed!* All these years, she had foolishly believed that Owen liked the bedroom pitch black because of *her* physical deficiencies. He never wanted her to get a good look at how small his dick was. Owen was the first and only person she'd ever had sex with, so she'd never had anything to compare him to. No freaking wonder she'd never been able to get off with him. His tiny cock was *needing both a magnifying glass and a road map to find it* kind of small. All this time, she'd thought there was something wrong with her.

Oh, baby, some changes are coming!

The house cooled off overnight, and she got up early, showered, and dressed with relative comfort. It was the end of May, and the mornings were a little muggy but not too hot yet. The thermometer outside read seventy-five degrees. Owen had never come home, and that was fine by her. He could sleep off his drunk somewhere else.

She checked her outfit in the mirror, hoping it would do. She was dressed traditionally for a funeral in a lightweight skirt, with a black blouse over a black camisole. She opted to go bare legged, detesting the thought of pantyhose in this heat. She slid her feet into her favorite heels.

When the time came, she locked up the house, got into her car, and drove out to Warner Ranch, which was just a little farther down the road from the Divine Creek Ranch. She parked in the row of cars lining the long driveway. She was feeling a little sad, a little tired, and slightly wilted as she walked down the drive to join other friends and family in the house.

* * * *

Jack stood with Ethan and Adam, talking in the living room, when Ethan nudged Jack and gestured toward the window with his head. Grace walked down the drive, looking like an angel of mercy come to comfort them. Each graceful stride brought her closer to him.

The long black skirt clung slightly to her legs as she walked, her sheer black blouse rippling in the breeze over the camisole underneath. She was modestly dressed, but there was just something about the way she moved and the style of the clothes she wore that set off her feminine curves. The sight made him wish for a chance to see the bare, sweet flesh that filled out that outfit so perfectly. Sometimes showing less really was more. As she came closer, Jack noticed sadness around her mouth and wanted nothing more than to kiss those soft lips and make it better. Ethan nudged him again and nodded his head at Adam, who was also staring out the window. Adam was tall, greater in height than either of them, but he seemed to stand a little taller, and his eyes took on a fierce glint as he asked, without taking his eyes off of her, "That's Grace, isn't it?"

A wide, knowing grin spread over Jack's face. "Yes, that's Grace. Come on, I'll introduce you."

* * * *

By the time Grace made it to the steps, she felt her chin wobble slightly. On the walk up the drive, she had reminisced over many of the fun times she'd had with Rose Marie in the years she'd worked at Stigall's. Grace had waited on her frequently, but what she loved about Rose Marie was that she would stop just to chat with her. She'd even invited her to lunch on a couple of occasions. She had been so wise but not pushy in giving advice.

Once, Rose Marie had found an outfit she thought Grace would look good in and insisted that she try it on right then. She had told the manager she wanted to see what it would look like on someone else, and Juliana had sent Grace right into the dressing room so she could model it for Mrs. Warner. What a hoot she was. Rose Marie had bought the outfit just to cover for her lark and told Grace she looked so beautiful in it she should consider it for herself as well. Grace wound up buying it later on sale. It was hanging in her closet at home.

Grace paused at the bottom of the steps, feeling like she needed a moment to compose herself before joining all the others inside. She took a deep breath and climbed the first step up to the porch. As she looked up, three men dressed in black suits and black cowboy boots walked out the screen door onto the porch. One handsome cowboy would have been enough to make her salivate, but three of them?

Jack looked so handsome in his new suit. Ethan, with his shoulder-length dark hair and those sparkling blue eyes, looked like he belonged in the pages of a magazine. The other cowboy was a stranger to her, but she imagined this was their other roommate, Adam Davis. What startled her most about their appearance, though, was how genuinely happy they seemed to be that *she* was there, even the one she didn't know.

He never took his intense pale green eyes off of her, this giant of a man. His hair was dark brown like Ethan's but cut much shorter, so only a little showed under his hat. He was taller by two or three inches than Ethan, so they were like stair steps, but all three were so imposing in their own way. They were all muscular, but this stranger was broader through the chest, and she thought he'd probably had to order that suit coat-custom made to fit as well as it did. There she went again, thinking inappropriate thoughts at Rose Marie's expense.

Jack trotted down the steps, took her hand in his, and kissed her cheek. He led her up to the shaded porch. Her cheek tingled, and heat bloomed where his lips had touched her. Her hand trembled slightly in his big, callused hand. She found his work-roughened, capable, working man's hands to be incredibly sexy.

"Grace, you met Ethan at the house yesterday, I hear. I'd like to introduce you to my other roommate, Adam Davis. Adam, this is Grace Stuart." Jack sounded so pleased that she was there.

"Grace, it's a pleasure to finally meet you. I've been looking forward to it." Adam reached out to her, and his big hand dwarfed hers as he lifted it and bent down slightly to kiss her knuckles. She was surprised by the old-fashioned gesture but even more so by the undisguised interest in his eyes.

Ethan leaned in and kissed her cheek, shocking her completely. She was not accustomed to receiving so much attention but had a feeling she could easily get used to it. He leaned in and said, "Supper was really good last night. We enjoyed it so much we thought about stealing you and bringing you home with us. Maybe we can cook for you some time to return the favor."

Surprised at his words, her lips popped open, but she wasn't sure what to say.

Oh, my gosh. Steal me. Plunder and pillage!

"He's serious, by the way," Jack said, chuckling a little. "Maybe sometime soon, after things settle down a bit, we could have you out to the ranch for a nice meal."

She had no idea what to say. She wasn't stunned speechless because she thought their invitation was inappropriate, though it might just be at the moment. She didn't know what to say that would not come across as *overeager*. Then Owen reared his ugly head in her mind again. He was so out of there it was almost funny. Like Wile E. Coyote careening over a cliff with an anvil tied to his ass. He never should have asked for her ATM card.

Thoughts of Rose Marie came to mind, and she could almost hear the old woman say, "Seize the day, baby." It was a truly surreal moment.

She grinned back at him and bravely said, "That sounds like a fantastic idea, Jack. I'd love to. Just give me a few days. I have some *serious* house cleaning to do first."

Though she meant it figuratively and not literally, it did bring her current housekeeping dilemma to mind, which made her pause and frown.

"You don't know any reliable, and more importantly, *available* air conditioner repairmen, do you, Jack?" It seemed like a reasonable, legitimate question. She wasn't prepared for the mild surprise on all three of their faces. Or the grins that followed. What had she said? They seemed pleased and amused by her question, even Adam, who finally spoke up.

"What seems to be the problem?"

"My AC quit on me yesterday. I got home from dropping off your supper, and it wasn't cooling the house anymore."

Jack said, "You remember me telling you that one of my partners was an AC and heating contractor? Adam's your guy. He can fix whatever is wrong with it."

Adam quickly nodded and said the magic words. "I can come over later this afternoon if you'd like."

"Oh, I'd like that just fine," she replied, so relieved she wanted to cry happy tears. "I'm definitely feeling a little wilted."

Jack took her hand in his and said, "Why don't we get you inside and cool you off a bit."

The men brought her inside and stayed with her until it was time to walk to the cemetery, which was a short distance from the ranch house. She would have preferred to blend into the background with the other mourners, but Jack kept her hand securely clasped in his own as the preacher spoke.

At the reception afterward, Jack introduced her as a friend of his who was close to Rose Marie. She visited briefly with some of the other attendees and got some interesting looks, but overall, she felt accepted.

"Adam, why don't you ride with her to our house and then follow her home in your truck." Jack said something else quietly to him, to which Adam nodded in agreement.

"I'll need to change out of my suit, anyway."

Jack and Ethan walked them down the drive to her car. She'd sensed a shift in their friendship today, and she felt it strongly as she turned to Jack. For the very first time, he took her gently in his arms and hugged her to him. For once, Owen didn't come to mind. She slid her arms around his shoulders, not retreating or holding back. She pressed into him, inhaling his woodsy, masculine scent.

"See you soon, darlin'." Jack squeezed her briefly, then released her.

Ethan leaned in and kissed her cheek and thanked her for coming. He hugged her, too. She got into her car, a little breathless, and Ethan closed the door for her again, reminding her to buckle up.

Adam climbed into the passenger seat, dwarfing her little Honda, and buckled up as well. She was unused to being so close to someone so big and strong, so powerful and masculine. He made her feel tiny and feminine by comparison. She smiled up at him as she turned the key in the ignition. She could lose track of time gazing into those pale green eyes. Jack and Ethan waved to her and watched as she and Adam pulled down the drive.

"I feel a little guilty for taking you away from your family this afternoon," she said, glancing over at him.

"There is no need. Everything around the ranch has already been taken care of, and Jack's older sister, Anne, is going to be staying with Joe for the time being. Jack and Ethan will probably stay around to visit a little longer and then head on back to the house themselves."

"Maybe so," she said, "but I imagine you were close to her as well. I'm sorry to put you to work on a day you would normally spend with your family."

"It seems to me Jack is more worried about me seeing to your AC problem than he is about whether I follow funeral protocol, whatever that would be in a case like this."

When he asked her, she described the problem in detail to him on the way down the drive. He asked her a few questions to make sure he had whatever he'd need on the truck. When they got to the house, he insisted she come inside while he changed out of his suit. Their house was cool and neat as a pin, everything in its place. While she waited, she looked at the photographs that hung on the living room wall near the front door.

She especially liked a larger black and white photograph of the three of them as boys. It was an outdoor shot of them all piled into an inner tube floating on a river. She guessed they must have been in about first grade because they were all missing their front teeth. Their hair was wet and standing up in spikes, and all their toothless grins were a mile wide. The little boys looked like they were having the time of their lives.

Adam came up behind her. "Rose Marie took that picture on the Guadalupe River when our parents took us camping in New Braunfels. They let us have a tent all to ourselves. We swore we'd stay up all night, and our parents said we could if we wanted to. We were on the river all day, had a cookout that night, and we were all sound asleep by eight o'clock. The sun had barely even set.

"Did you notice we were all missing our front teeth? They all started getting loose about the same time, and we wiggled and worked them until they were barely hanging on. Then one afternoon on a dare, we pulled them all out at the same time. Our parents told us the tooth fairy was gonna go broke." He chuckled. "Ready to go?"

"Yes," she replied in a daze.

Listening to him tell that story in that deep voice of his, she felt like she was there watching it happen. His voice drew her in and had a sort of hypnotic effect on her. Her confusion over her earlier feelings for Jack and Ethan increased, and she was troubled by the way she was now responding to Adam as well. She should feel nervous about being alone with him, but she wasn't. She wanted to stay and listen to him tell more stories.

She took one last look at the photograph, then turned to find him gazing down at her. "You know, it meant a lot to Jack that you came today. I noticed he never let go of your hand. He was right. You have a very sweet spirit." He leaned down and inhaled as he kissed her cheek.

Surprised, all she could do was stand there and blush. Was he saying these things to test her reaction? His kiss felt like so much more than just a peck on the cheek. It felt intimate. If he was testing her reaction, he certainly was getting one because her cheeks were flaming and her panties were damp.

"He said you blush easily. I'm sorry. I didn't mean to embarrass you. I just wanted you to know we appreciate you, you know? You look very pretty in that outfit." His voice sent a pleasurable shiver up her spine.

"Thank you. I'm just not used to people paying so much attention to me and saying such nice things. It's not that I'm mistreated or anything, I'm just…not used to it."

Owen was *so* out of there. She was *too* mistreated.

"Well, be that as it may, what I said was true and not just flattery. Let's get on over to your house and see what I can do about the AC."

She followed him out, feeling all warm and fuzzy.

She cringed when she turned onto her street and saw Owen was home, his beater truck parked in the driveway. She pulled up to the curb, and

Adam parked behind her. She got out of her car and noticed the grim look on Adam's face as he climbed out and opened the toolbox on the utility camper.

She wondered if Jack told Adam what he had seen of Owen's behavior that day in the store when he'd come in asking for money. She felt embarrassed and ashamed that Adam was probably going to meet Owen when he was at his worst—hungover and mean. She gathered her purse and led Adam into the house.

Owen must have been home for hours because the house looked it. Where he'd gotten the money for pizza she didn't know, but the remains of one were scattered across the coffee table. He was lying back in the recliner scratching himself when she walked into the living room. He grunted when she introduced Adam and said he was there to check the AC.

"About fuckin' time. It's hot as hell in here. I was about to leave and go somewhere cooler."

She bit her tongue and showed Adam where the thermostat was. He went outside to check the compressor, and she busied herself cleaning up after Owen. He must have had company while she was gone. At least some of the dishes made it into the sink. When she turned around, she saw him standing in the kitchen doorway. She scraped the plates off and ran soapy water in the sink.

"Where have you been?" he asked sullenly, scratching again.

"At a friend's funeral."

"Who's that guy?"

"He is an AC repairman."

"No, I mean who is he to *you*? I can tell he's a fuckin' AC repairman." He threw his beer bottle in the trash can, where it struck something else and shattered. She cringed. He was working on another drunk.

"He's my friend. He offered to come over and check it out," she replied, hoping he would accept her answer and walk away. For once, not start in on her, not while Adam was here. *Please*, not while Adam was there.

"Maybe what he's really doing is checking you out. He must be blind or something." He belched.

"What?"

"Maybe he needs glasses. Or maybe he prefers fat asses like yours. It takes all kinds, I guess," he muttered with a shrug.

“Whatever, Owen. Go watch your game and let me get done in here.” She would not give in and start crying. In his current state, that was like blood in the water to a shark.

“Whatever?” he slurred. “That’s probably what he was thinking when he saw your fat ass. I’m going to Dave’s. I don’t want to be around for whatever method of payment the two of you have worked out. Of course, he may demand cash payment on the spot *after* fucking your fat ass or maybe even demand a refund from *you.* That cunt will probably disappoint *him,* too. There’s a paper bag on the refrigerator if he needs it, fuckin’ slut.” He grabbed his keys from the table and allowed the screen door to slam shut on his way out.

Grace had frozen as the evil filth flowed from his drunken lips. Each horrible word flowed over her like acid. She was such a chickenshit. That was her opportunity, and she'd passed it up. Maybe not the best opportunity because Owen was not a drunk she wanted to piss off.

In the next second, what she’d thought was the worst moment of her life became so, so, *so* much *worse.*

She heard a tool clank against the air conditioner compressor, right outside the *open* kitchen window. She listened to the crashing thud of her heart. She broke out into a cold sweat, and each rasping breath made her throat hurt. Adam had probably heard every despicable word Owen uttered, the names he’d called her, and the innuendo he had dropped. Her day was now complete.

When she started seeing black spots in front of her eyes, she realized she was holding her breath and turned to make her way to a kitchen chair. She sat forward, placing her elbows on her knees, her forehead in the palms of her hands. The black spots went away, but the mortification stayed.

He startled her when she felt his large hand sweep across her back. She jumped, but kept her eyes closed, not wanting to look into his. He pulled up a chair and sat down and gently rubbed her back.

“You heard?”

“Yeah.”

“How much?”

“Every ignorant word. Why do you put up with someone who treats you like that, baby?”

"I plan to throw him out. I just don't want to do it when he's drunk. He's mean when he's drunk, as you can see. I didn't want an ugly scene while you were here."

"You were trying to avoid a scene because of me, baby? I wish I'd known you want to break up with him. I would have personally kicked his stupid drunken ass for you and then helped you throw his shit out with him. Is *that* the house cleaning you told us earlier that you needed to do?"

She nodded as he continued, "Grace, all you have to do is call us when you're ready to clean house. All three of us will come whether he's drunk or sober, and your house cleaning will be *done*."

"Thank you, Adam. I'm really sorry that he was here, and I'm very embarrassed about the things you heard him say."

"Don't be sorry. I'm glad he was here so that I could see firsthand what an ass he is. You deserve better."

Grace finally opened her eyes, wiped the tears away, and hoped like hell she didn't look like a raccoon. He smiled at her, and she tried to smile back.

"I need to order a part for your compressor," he said, distracting her with the change of subject.

She grimaced. "Expensive?"

"No, but very necessary. I don't have it at the house," he said apologetically, "but I should have it by Tuesday morning."

"When can you come back?" she asked, afraid that he might not be able to come back to fix the unit till much later.

"As soon as I have the part in my hand." He laughed out loud when her eyes got big, and she flung her arms around his neck.

"Oh, thank you, Adam! I'm dying here!" She wiped her forehead on the back of her hand.

"Would you consider something for me?"

"Sure, what?" She felt giddy that at least one of her problems was about to be fixed.

"Would you consider staying with us, just until the part comes? You're going to be miserable here for the next day and a half. We have plenty of room, and the house is big so we wouldn't be underfoot. We'd all be perfect gentlemen, I promise. *Absolutely no strings attached.*" He emphasized the last few words and took her hands in his, gently stroking her knuckles and the tops of her hands. The simple action was sweet, as were his words, and kindled more complicated feelings in her heart. An invitation to stay at their ranch was completely unexpected.

"That is really sweet of you, Adam, and I admit I'm tempted. But I think it would be better if I didn't. Y'all are going to have family and friends popping in on you while everyone's in town, and I think it might be better if I just stayed home."

"What about Owen? Aren't you afraid he'll come back tonight?"

"No, when he's like this he usually goes to his friend Dave's house. I doubt I'll see him before tomorrow afternoon. By then he might be sober again. He's probably already forgotten that you were even here. I'll be fine, but I really appreciate the offer."

"Okay, but if you change your mind later, the offer still stands, all right?" he said, smiling down at her.

"You are a real sweetheart, you know that?" She placed her palms on his cheeks as she stood up. She was stunned when he leaned down, wrapped his arms around her, lifted her off her feet, and hugged her tightly. She couldn't help the tremor that went through her and did her best to ignore the reaction her nether regions had to being enfolded in his warm strength.

No one had picked her up like that since she was a little girl. His arms wrapped securely around her made her feel tiny. It felt really good, especially after Owen's cruel words about her weight. She was suspended there for a moment as he held her close and buried his face in her hair. Then he looked in her eyes for a brief moment. Her body responded to his nearness with a deep yearning. She smiled in thanks for his sweetness, wishing the quiet moment could last as he put her down.

Adam gathered all his tools and left her his business card after writing his private cell phone number on it. She walked him out to his truck. She felt such a sense of relief that the problem with her AC was fixable. Mixed with that was a sort of delirious happiness that he seemed to accept and appreciate her just the way she was with all her flaws. He looked over at her as he placed his tool belt in the truck and then reached out to gently grasp her wrist as she turned to go.

His eyebrows knitted together as he considered his words. "Grace, I want you to know something. None of what that son of a bitch told you is true. None of the hurtful things he's told you in the past are true, and I'm sure he's told you a lot of things to hurt you. You're not ugly, and you're not fat. You're beautiful, and your body is a work of art. You were really pretty in this outfit today, and we were all proud as hell to be seen with you. You deserve to be with someone who appreciates who you are and what you do for the people you care about. You deserve to be cared for and loved by a *man* who knows how to do it *properly*." He reached out and palmed her jaw, grazing her cheekbone with his thumb. "Make sure you lock your doors tonight. I'll see you soon."

"Thank you, Adam. I really needed that."

"Don't forget. The offer to stay at the ranch still stands."

"All right. Drive safe."

As he pulled away from the house, she went back inside and locked up. The uncomfortable heat of the day lingered, and eventually she turned off the TV and took a cool shower. She felt like a new person when she was done. She thought over all the things Adam had said to her. She was exhilarated at the thought that he saw her that way but confused, too. Why would he say those things if he understood and acknowledged that Jack might possibly have feelings for her?

Judging by the way Jack treated her today, he did. She was jubilant to know that the attraction was not one-sided. But the affection that she felt from Ethan and Adam was baffling to her, especially considering that she'd just met them recently. It felt right and easy being that way around them, and Jack evidently approved because they had been the same toward her around him as well as apart from him.

She climbed into bed, turned off the lamp, and curled up with a pillow. For once, she fell asleep not worrying what she was going to do about Owen and the general chaos that was her life. She had some house cleaning to do and three willing men ready to help her.

* * * *

Had he pressed her too hard? Adam thought about all the things he'd told her on the way home. After what that bastard told her, he knew he needed to tell her what *he* thought. He wanted to take the hurt away and open her eyes to the possibilities.

Trying to see the situation from her perspective, he could see how she might be confused and overwhelmed by the interest the three of them were all taking in her. He'd grasped her delicate wrist and stopped her from walking away. He didn't pull her to him again because he knew he'd kiss the daylights out of her, and that couldn't happen yet. Not while Owen was still a problem. Once she was free would be different, though. He planned to kiss her like he had a feeling she'd *never* been kissed before. The thought made him harden. It was difficult to keep his hands off of her, and he knew Ethan and Jack felt the same.

When he got home, he filled the guys in on her situation and what happened with Owen. They were ready to jump in the SUV and go hunt him down and beat the crap out of him. Jack and Ethan were more relieved she was dumping the jerk and were only too happy to be involved in plans that might help bring that about. He told them what he told her as he was leaving and asked them if they thought he might have said too much.

"How did she react?" Jack asked. "Did she cry or seem upset?"

"No, she seemed more surprised than anything. I think she's starved for affection. The hateful things Owen said to her were more embarrassing for her because she realized I'd heard him through the window. To be humiliated within my hearing seemed more painful to her than his actual words. He must criticize her an awful lot."

Jack nodded as he sat on the couch and put his feet up on the ottoman. "You did right in what you told her. She needs to hear the truth, so she'll stop believing his lies. When do you go back?"

"On Tuesday, as soon as the part comes in. She's going to need to replace that unit soon. It's limping along on its last leg as it is. I considered doing just that. What do you think?"

"Order it instead of the part. I'll write the check as soon as you can tell me the amount."

"I'll call my supplier on Monday morning. Y'all want to split the cost evenly, tack a big red bow on it, and call it good?"

Ethan said, "Count me in, too. I'd rather do that than make her wait an extra day for the part."

"Then it's settled," Adam agreed. "I'll call the warehouse. They can probably have it to me by Monday afternoon, if we're lucky." He wished she didn't have to wait even that long.

"I gotta say," Jack said, "I don't mind spending the money to see her happy and comfortable in her own home, but I hope we're lucky enough to have her living under our roof some day."

Chapter Three

"Clear your schedules, boys," Adam said Monday evening when they gathered around the dinner table. "Our lady is ready to clean house and needs some muscle."

"Hot damn!" Jack responded enthusiastically.

"Hell yeah!" Ethan added.

"I wish we could go over there now. I offered to, but she said to wait until tomorrow after she gets off work," Adam said, in the mood to go and hunt the little prick down that night. When he talked to Grace earlier in the day, she'd told him Owen still had not come home. "That son of a bitch won't know what hit him."

Angel chuckled and responded, "Man, I would hate to be in that idiot's shoes come tomorrow if he's got all three of you after him." Jack had brought home some thick sirloins from the meat market to grill that evening, and Angel had come over to join them.

Adam turned to Angel. "Where is your woman, Angel?"

"Pouting."

"Pouting? Why?" Adam wondered what was wrong now. Angel's woman, Patricia, seemed to pout an awful lot these days.

"She's still mad at Ethan and me, I suppose. It's the same shit as last time. She thinks by pouting she will change our minds. She went with her friends to The Dancing Pony. She probably thought you were up there working tonight, Ethan."

"Is she still after y'all for what I think she's after y'all for?" Jack asked, shaking his head.

"She heard Ethan shared a woman with y'all, and she still wants a threesome with him and me."

Adam cringed, grateful he wasn't in on that deal.

Jack joined them at the table and said, "I hope that blows over quick because if things work out for us like we hope they do, we're going to have someone new under our roof real soon."

"What do you mean?" Angel asked.

"You remember Grace Stuart? From Harper's Embroidery?"

"Of course. How could I forget *her*? Are you seeing her? The three of you?" At their nods, Angel sighed and shook his head.

"What?" Jack asked.

Angel laughed and said, "I knew I should have asked her out when I had the chance. Now, knowing her nature, she'll never notice another man ever again."

"What about her nature?" Jack asked.

"She's loyal and submissive," Angel said as he opened his beer and sat down at the table with Jack. "Have you seen how that chump treats her?"

"Don't even get us started about that asshole," Adam replied derisively.

"She has a strong loyal streak," Angel continued. "If she becomes yours and you treat her the way she deserves, she'll never stray from you or be unfaithful. Does she know all of you are interested in her in that way?"

Jack shook his head. "No, we haven't talked to her about it, but there is definitely chemistry there. We want to see if it might work for her."

"What do you mean by submissive, Angel? Like she's a doormat?" Adam asked, a little offended by that notion.

Angel shook his head. "No, not at all. Lots of people are confused by that word. I'm surprised Ethan hasn't said anything about it."

Ethan shrugged as he seasoned the steaks at the kitchen counter. "It was obvious in her demeanor when she brought the food. She puts the needs of others over herself, and she likes to be of service. Though she's not happy with him, she places a high value on being a loyal girlfriend. I don't see her as a doormat, but who hasn't found themselves in a situation where they lived with the status quo for a while? I think she probably was attracted to Owen in the beginning because he sounds dominant. Unfortunately, he's dominant in a bad way. It will take time to draw it out of her because she's been hurt, but I have an inkling that she sees the same quality in us but in a positive way. That's why she's responding so strongly to us."

Turning to Adam, Angel said, "Being submissive doesn't mean she's going to allow you to walk all over her or push her around, although you might be *surprised* where her limits truly are when she's in the hands of someone she can trust. Considering the arrangement you guys are hoping for, gaining her trust should be your only goal right now. Show her that any loyalty and trust she puts in you won't be betrayed."

"Is your mom submissive? Is that why your mom and dads have stayed together happily for so many years?" Ethan asked.

Angel had shared with them over the years about his rather unorthodox upbringing. His mother was wife to three husbands. Angel and his brothers thought of the three as their fathers, and all three husbands claimed them equally. In the nearby town, they were careful that she was seen as the wife of only the eldest of the three brothers, and only close friends and relations knew the truth about their family.

"No, but my dads *wish* she was! She's mellowed over the years, but she doesn't have a submissive bone in her body. She still makes them pay if she doesn't get her way, but she loves them all just as hard. They spoil her like crazy, but they taught her early on to not try to play them against each other."

"What do you mean 'taught her'?" Adam asked, though he had a feeling he knew the answer.

"She wanted something really bad. I don't recall what it was, if they ever told me to begin with, and when one of them refused her, she tried to play the others against him to get it. He found out about her game, and he spanked her for it. She tried that several more times but eventually learned to not do that again. She's very stubborn."

"Your dads spanked your mother?" Adam asked, cringing at the thought of it.

"A few times in the beginning until she learned she couldn't manipulate them into getting her own way."

"How did that go over?" Jack asked.

"Well, I wasn't there, as you can imagine, but the rare times they have ever talked about it in front of me, she always blushes and shushes them, but…not like she's embarrassed. I have a feeling whichever dad spanked her did it in such a way that she learned her lesson the hard way but enjoyed the process. Know what I mean?"

There was a collective groan around the table.

"So, submissive is a good thing?" Adam asked, a little relieved. How Angel described his mother didn't sound like Grace at all.

"Yes, as opposed to being manipulative or controlling. It's taken her a while to get around to dumping her boyfriend, but that goes back to her being loyal. She's hung on until there is no hope left. And now you lucky assholes get to swoop in and be her saviors."

"So, Ethan, how is it that you know so much about Dominance and submission and we never knew that about you?" Jack asked, grinning at Ethan.

Adam snickered when Ethan turned to Jack and pointed a finger at him. "If you're imagining me in a black patent bodysuit and whip, you need to stop, asshole. I have an acquaintance that comes in the club every so often that knows a little about it. He made a remark about a conversation he overheard between me and an employee at the club and pointed out that I had Dom tendencies but a 'caring and considerate' personality, ideal qualities for a good Dom. I was curious about the subject, and he answered my questions. I'm not interested in living the lifestyle, but it's always good to be self-aware, right? He comes in from time to time and we talk. It's very intriguing." Ethan opened another round of beers.

Adam arched an eyebrow, unable to resist commenting. "But not *intriguing* as in you'd like to pop our asses with a riding crop and ride us on the lawn right? Because we'd have to kill you and hide your body. It would be messy, and the police would get involved." He laughed and tipped the bottle to his lips as the others joined him.

"Sorry, guys, you can keep dropping hints, but you're just not my type. Assholes." Ethan laughed. "Have a little respect. Not all Doms go around dressed in leather, ready to wield a whip. There's way more to it than that."

"How did you know he knew something about that stuff, Angel?" Adam asked.

"Patricia overheard one of their conversations at The Dancing Pony. That's when all the damn talk about a threesome with Ethan started." Angel rubbed a hand on his face. "I guess she figured one kink was as good as another."

* * * *

Grace was carried to the bed by strong arms and gentle hands. Once he laid her down, he moved to stand at the foot of the bed. She lay back on the pillows, and warm hands fanned her long hair across them. Gentle lips seared the skin from her collarbone up to the sensitive spot behind her earlobe. A warm, wet mouth settled on one of her breasts, teasing the nipple with his tongue while gently rubbing and pulling on the other. Another gentle hand slid down between her breasts and over her abdomen to the blonde curls over her mound, teasing there for a moment before sliding over her damp pussy. Warm fingers spread her lips carefully, baring her to her lover's gaze as he stood at the foot of the bed. Waves of pleasure inundated her at the sensory overload of having so many hands on so many places at once on her body.

The long fingers between her legs stroked over her clitoris, rubbing on that sensitive nub. She writhed in their arms, feeling the first stirring and tightening as her orgasm began to build. The bed dipped between her feet, and he joined them on the bed. He gently palmed one thigh open to the side and then the other. She willingly spread them even more, reveling in the knowledge that his eyes were looking upon the most intimate part of her.

The long fingers that parted her lips slid into her pussy and dipped into the juices that overflowed there before returning to her clit. His fingers stroked over and around it, rolling it back and forth and alongside it. She couldn't keep quiet any longer, and wild gasps and moans escaped her lips as now two fingers thrust into her pussy, going a little deeper, before sliding up to her clit again. His mouth continued to lap at her nipples, which had turned as hard as little pebbles.

Another voice whispered about dark, erotic pleasures in her ear, and she felt the fanning flames as her body tensed, preparing for the coming orgasm. The fingers withdrew from her mound, and she was momentarily bereft of the beautiful sensation before it was replaced by another as he gently blew a stream of warm air across her heated flesh, then lapped the length of her mound from her opening, up to her clit, and back again. Her body clenched hard, on the precipice, waiting for that last little nudge that would push her off into the abyss she knew waited for her. His tongue, so warm and wet, delved in between her pussy lips and gained entrance, giving her what her body now screamed for. She—

Exploded. On wave after wave of pleasure. As her body rocked through each pulse, she came more and more awake and further away from the most erotic dream she'd ever had. She couldn't remember ever reaching orgasm in a dream before, but it left her panting, bathed in sweat. She trembled, clinging to the fading memory of what and who had brought her to that exquisite state.

All *three* of them. *Sweet merciful heavens.* Ethan, Adam, and Jack had all been in bed with her at once. Her heart pounded at the thought. She lay there quietly, listening to her heart return to a normal beat, trying to remember as many of the details as she could before they faded. She hardly ever remembered her dreams, but she wanted this one etched in her memory forever. It was the stuff her most secret fantasies were made of. Just then her alarm clock went off, and she was grateful she had finished the dream before it could be interrupted.

She was surprised by how fast the workday flew by. Jack came by to check on her while on his way to an appointment. He kissed her cheek and made her blush all over. When she thought of what he'd done with those lips in her dream, she blushed even harder. He told her he looked forward to that evening and left for his appointment. Her employers, Martha and Rose, let her leave at 2:30 p.m. so she had time to run to the grocery store before going home. She was meeting Adam, Ethan, and Jack at her house at 3:30 p.m.

After the house cleaning was finished, she planned to prepare them a fresh, home-cooked meal to thank them for their trouble, although she had a feeling they'd consider being allowed to give Owen the boot reward enough in itself.

Chapter Four

Owen sat on the front porch in her mother's wooden swing, eating straight from a half-gallon container of ice cream, when she pulled into the driveway. It was only 3:15 p.m. All she had to do was get through fifteen more minutes with this SOB. He was eating. Maybe that meant he had sobered up a little. She parked, grabbed the grocery bags from the front seat, and lugged them up the steps. Of course, he didn't offer to help with them. One time when she'd asked for help, he'd told her no, she needed the exercise, so she never asked for help from him again. He just sat there, digging his spoon down into the container and sticking it into his mouth. What an ass.

He followed her inside.

"I thought that son of a bitch was going to fix the AC. It's hot as hell in here."

"He had to order a part."

"When's it gonna be fixed?" he asked, shoving the open ice cream carton, spoon and all, back in the freezer. What a disgusting pig.

"He should be here with it in a little while," she replied as neutrally as she could while she put away the groceries. He was spoiling for a fight.

He'd left more dirty dishes lying around on the counter and table. She finished putting the food away and filled the sink with hot, soapy water to let the dishes soak before she washed them. This was the last mess of his she was going to clean up. The thought made her smile, and she turned away from him so he wouldn't see it.

"I saw that, bitch. Why are you smiling? You know something I don't? Huh, Fatty? You're planning on fucking him again later, aren't you? That's how you're paying for the AC repair, isn't it? Hell, if I was him and that was an option, I'd want cold hard cash. At least I might get a little satisfaction because it's for sure not to be found in fucking your ugly ass. Faithless, fucking bitch!"

"Owen, stop it!" she said firmly, checking her watch. 3:20 p.m. Any minute now.

"Why are you so dressed up today, huh, Fatty? Are you excited about seeing that repairman? I see you checking your watch. Think you might be able to turn him on in that tight-ass top? How do you like this? Fucking cunt!"

Then the right side of her face felt like it exploded. He'd come up behind her and slapped her open-handed over her cheekbone and ear. Her ear rang, so now she couldn't hear him, at least not very well. She turned to him, stunned. It was rare for him to actually strike her. He usually limited his abuse to the verbal and emotional variety. As if it were happening in slow motion, she watched as his right hand whipped around as he prepared to strike her again. Right before the back of his hand made contact with her left cheek, she caught a glimpse of Adam, Jack, and Ethan charging through the open screen door.

She couldn't hear them, so she wasn't sure if Owen knew they were there. His trajectory never wavered, and the back of his hand cracked against her left cheekbone. The shock of it, more than the force behind it, made her reel back against the sharp edge of the counter, over the sink, before falling forward to the floor at his feet. Pain bloomed in her cheek in a delayed reaction to the blow. She was hurt, but she was also happy because she had seen them run through the door. She knew pain and relief all in the same moment. Surreal.

She'd fallen to her hands and knees in front of Owen and was momentarily worried that this position left her vulnerable to him if he chose to kick her. She watched in amazement as his boots somehow both lifted off the floor at the same time. She either felt or heard a great thud from somewhere close by but wasn't sure where it came from. She put her hands to her cheeks. The left side of her face throbbed. She felt another thud and yelling, but she didn't worry about it. Her men were there, and they would deal with him.

Someone approached her, and she felt strong hands on her shoulders. She couldn't hear what he was saying over the ringing in her ear and the noise. She tried to stand up, but her limbs wouldn't cooperate. He lifted her into his arms, carried her to her bedroom, and sat on the edge of the bed, holding her in his lap, cradling her against his chest. Even in her shocked state, she recognized Ethan's spicy scent.

For the first time in years, she felt safe. Protected. She had become used to taking up for herself and gradually just learned how to take what Owen dished out. That was over. Emotion boiled up inside her, and she began to shake. She turned and wrapped her arms around his neck and bawled her eyes out, soaking the cotton of his red twill button-down shirt.

After a few minutes, she noticed the presence of more than one pair of hands on her back, arms, and hair, stroking her. The crying at an end, she looked up from Ethan's damp shirtfront to see Adam and Jack on either side of her. They both stroked her and looked at her with worried eyes. The ringing had subsided a little bit, enough that she was able to hear what they were saying to her. Through her tears, she smiled at them.

"You came. Hi!" She hugged each one of them before hugging Ethan again. "What did you do with Owen?" She grinned when she realized that was the last time she'd ever care about his whereabouts.

"Out cold on the living room floor, waiting to find out what we're going to do with him," Jack said as he gently lifted the back of her shirt. "Darlin', you've got a red welt on your back from the edge of the counter. It might leave a bruise, but at least the skin isn't broken. He hit you pretty hard." He frowned darkly as he gently palmed her cheekbone, which felt swollen and tingly.

Finally, this was her moment. Where before she had experienced everything in slow motion, now she felt invigorated, like it was the first day of fall and a cold front had just blown in. She didn't feel the stifling heat at all. It was time to clean house.

"Adam, there is a box of big black trash bags under the kitchen sink. I need them. Ethan, can you disconnect his video game console and bag it up with all the games and controllers? Also disconnect the black laptop computer and put it in the computer bag that's probably still right there with it. Jack, will you help me bag up his clothes and toiletries?"

"Sure, honey, sounds like you've had this planned for a while." Jack grinned, helping her to her feet.

"Well, I've been ready for a while." She found her cell phone and dialed her sister's number. After giving her the brief rundown on what had just happened, she asked her to come over.

Jack said, "I'll call the police to come pick him up. You're going to press charges, right?"

"How many times did you guys hit him?" she asked, looking down at Owen, who was still unconscious on the living room floor.

"A bunch. Enough to lay him out. Why?"

"That more than makes up for him slapping me twice before you could stop him. I just want him gone from my house and my life."

"Grace, I don't know. Any man who would strike a woman deserves to be in jail for it. Wouldn't it be better to call the police? He hit you hard enough to knock you down—"

"And you are my witnesses. Right now, I just want him gone. I'll call Dave. If Owen's still out cold when he gets here, just put him in his truck with the rest of his crap."

Ethan snickered. "Gracie said crap." Then he kissed her forehead and went to start gathering Owen's stuff up.

Grace and Jack hurriedly stuffed all his clothes and shoes in garbage sacks, setting them in the living room as they filled them. She called Dave and asked him to come over to pick up Owen. Ethan gathered all the electronics and piled them in a cardboard box. She looked around at his belongings, seeing the evidence of her foolishness in allowing him to move in with her.

Most of the things in the bags and boxes were purchased with money she earned. A few were birthday or Christmas gifts, but the majority were things he'd told her he wanted that she had willingly purchased. It embarrassed her to look at his collection of crap bought with her money. She felt the urge to kick him while he was down on the floor, but she resisted, wanting to kick herself even more for being so stupid all these years.

She picked up the laptop and looked at it, debating on keeping it. It had not been bought for him. She used it to check her online e-mail account and for using the Internet, but he had gradually taken it over. It was probably full of viruses. She placed it back in the box, knowing it would be more trouble than it was worth.

Fifteen minutes later, Dave knocked on her screen door. He had the good sense to look embarrassed for his friend. He grimaced when he saw the swelling over her left cheekbone and looked at her men in fear when he saw them waiting inside. Owen moaned and shifted on the floor. Ethan and Jack hauled the bags and boxes out the door and put them in the back of Owen's truck. Adam hauled Owen over his shoulder and carried him out and slung him into the bed of his truck as well. She handed Dave the truck keys.

Dave was barely able to look her in the eye. "You know he really loves you, right, Grace?"

"He's got a funny way of showing it. I hope you don't show your love to your girlfriend by backhanding her in the face."

"He's really going to regret this when he comes to."

"He's going to regret it even more if he comes *back*. My house is no longer his home."

"Where should I take him?"

"I don't know, Dave. You know more about his homes away from home than I would. Just tell him I said to not come back, ever."

"I'll tell him, but he's not going to be happy about it."

"Not my problem, Dave. I appreciate you coming to get him for me, though. Take care."

He walked down the front walk to Owen's truck, steering clear of her men as they cut the plastic wrap and cardboard shipping container away from something loaded in the back of Adam's truck. It must be the part Adam needed. It seemed rather large for just a part.

Dave handed his keys to an unknown friend who had waited in the car for him, got into Owen's truck, and drove away with Owen still moaning in the truck bed.

It felt so good to clean house. She smiled at her men even though it hurt her cheek just a little, ignoring the vehicles as they departed.

She walked over to Adam's truck to see what they were up to. As they cut away the cardboard and removed the Styrofoam pieces, she realized what she was looking at. A completely brand-new compressor unit. Her jaw popped open. She took a wild guess at how much something like this would cost.

"Stop," Jack said, jumping down from the bed of the truck. "I know what you're thinking. Adam said your compressor was on its last legs. We decided to fix the problem, long term, for you."

"But I can't afford this," she said, gesturing at the big unit.

"You don't need to worry about it. It's already taken care of." He put his hands gently on her shoulders and looked into her eyes. "We wanted to take care of it for you so you can be comfortable. Will you let us do this?"

Her eyes fill up with tears again.

"There are no strings attached, Grace. Your unit needed replacing, anyway. Now you'll be comfortable in your home."

She leaned into him and squeezed him. "I have an inheritance from my mother. I want to pay you—"

"Don't touch that money, darlin'. Your mom worked hard for it. Leave it invested where it is. This is taken care of."

"All right, but I'm going to make it up to you somehow."

"You are not obligated by any of us to do anything of the sort. Just enjoy your cool air. Okay?"

"Okay."

Once they had it loaded on the dolly, they moved it around to the backyard.

Ethan came to her and said, "Gracie, I'm going to run to the hardware store and pick up new locks for your house. Owen probably still has your house key, and it wouldn't be very safe for you to leave them unchanged and count on him to leave you alone. I'll be back in a few minutes."

Ethan leaned down and kissed her, this time on the lips. It was just a soft, gentle brush of his lips against hers but so unexpected. She was startled by how her body reacted. She wanted to lean into him for another kiss and felt a rush of dampness and a warm throb in her clit. She gasped and looked around quickly. Jack was out back with Adam, helping him.

Oh no! What was she doing?

"Don't be worried, Gracie. Jack wouldn't mind. Neither would Adam." His statement made her feel even more confused. His eyes twinkled mischievously, and his sensual lips spread in a sexy smile. "I'll be back in a few minutes." He climbed in the SUV and drove off.

She was having another surreal moment. Her mind was clamoring, "*Guilty! Tramp!*" But her body was screaming like a disgruntled toddler, "*Mine! All mine!*"

She shook her head, reaching up to feel her throbbing cheekbone. She was so relieved that it was done. She had just cleaned house. She turned and walked in her front door, feeling somehow as though she had just moved in.

She walked through the house to the back door and found them outside.

"Could I interest you in a home-cooked meal?"

They looked up at her and grinned, and she noticed the twinkle in Jack's eye. She might let him make a meal out of her. And…of course, her cheeks heated up at the thought.

"Need some help?" Jack asked as he came around to her. "Adam has this under control, so I can help you if you'd like."

"Sure, why don't you get the grill going? All the supplies are in the garage through that door there. I'll start in the kitchen."

Jack cleaned the grate with her wire brush, loaded the grill with charcoal, and got the fire started. The odor of charcoal, starter fluid, and smoke—smells she always associated with Texas summers—wafted in with him when he came in the back door to wash his hands.

"Will you let me do something for you?" he asked as he leaned a hip against her kitchen counter.

"That depends on what it is. You've already done so much, Jack," she replied as she sprinkled the rub on the steaks she'd bought earlier.

"Would you let me program all our cell phone numbers into your cell phone, so if you ever need us in a hurry, you can call us? We're not convinced that you've seen the last of that asshole."

"If that's what you want, sure."

"It's not the only thing I want, but it will do for now," he said as she handed him her phone. He'd said it so matter-of-factly, and she had no doubt in her mind what he meant. It was in his eyes. Again, her body clamored for him, wet heat gathered in her pussy, pulsing.

Mine! All Mine!

It shocked her, the way her body reacted so viscerally to all three of them.

He helped her in the kitchen, chopping vegetables to go in a salad. He got down a can from a high shelf for her and slid his big, warm hand around her hip as he handed it to her. He tucked a lock of hair behind her ear when it kept falling in her face. She could get used to that kind of attention on a regular basis. She bent over to get the big roll of foil from the drawer under the oven, and when she backed up, pulling the drawer open, she bumped into him.

"Sorry! Ugh, this drawer always sticks!" And then she felt his hand right on her behind, and it wasn't there to steady her, either. She looked back over her shoulder at him, and he grinned devilishly at her, his hand remaining on that spot. Now he was definitely caressing her.

"Who are you? And what is your hand doing on my sister's ass?" a laughing voice said through the screen door.

"The drawer was stuck again!" Grace said in reply.

"So is his hand, evidently!" Charity replied as she pulled open the screen door. Grace was relieved that Charity was here but wished she'd made her appearance just a few minutes later. Even though Jack had removed his hand, she could still feel his touch through her blue jeans. Her heart pounded a little, her body hoping for another opportunity to see what his caress might have led to.

Grace skipped into the living room and gave her sister a great big hug. Charity looked amused as she did. She had not felt this carefree and happy in years. Charity grimaced when she noticed the red mark on Grace's cheek.

"That son of a bitch! What did he do to you? I hope you paid him back double!"

She and Grace laughed together when she heard Jack say, "Triple," as he fiddled with the drawer mechanism under her stove, and a voice filtered in through the kitchen window, "Quadruple!"

"So you pounded his sorry ass?" she asked Jack as Adam came in through the back door.

"Yes, ma'am. Pounded him real good." He offered her the hand he wiped off with a dish towel. "Jack Warner. I'm pleased to meet you. You must be Charity."

"Trust me, the pleasure is all mine. If I never see that miserable rat again, it will be too soon. Thanks for throwing out the garbage. I've been waiting for this moment for years. And you must be?"

"Adam Davis, ma'am. Glad to know you," he said as he held out his hand to her.

Grace grinned as she observed her sister's reaction. Charity's eyes got big and round as she sized both of them up and looked over at Grace with obvious approval. "I'll bet you did pound his ass real good! Could he walk?"

"Nope," Adam replied, chuckling. "I had to carry him out, but I'm sure he'll survive."

"I hope he doesn't file assault charges," Grace said, suddenly very concerned about that possibility.

"He assaulted you first in front of three credible witnesses," Jack reminded her. "I doubt he would be stupid enough to do that."

Charity snorted. "His stupidity knows no bounds, but I'm more worried about him coming back to harass you, Grace." Charity gestured to the overnight bag hung over her shoulder. "That's why I'm staying with you for a few days."

"That sounds like a great idea," Jack said. "We'll put a steak on for you, too. I was concerned about Grace staying there by herself tonight and was considering offering to bring her home with us temporarily until things die down.

Just then, Ethan walked in the door. Grace noticed Charity eyed him appreciatively as well, turning a curious look on her. In one hand, he had a bag from the hardware store, and in the other, he held a shopping bag that contained a six-pack and what looked like a bottle of wine.

"Hi. I didn't know if you had any beer. You don't seem like the beer drinking type, so I picked up a bottle of sangria as well, if you like that sort of thing."

"She loves it! And who might you be?" Charity asked as she took the bag containing the beer and wine from him.

"Hi. I'm Ethan Grant, and you must be Charity. I'm glad you could come over. Grace was pretty shook up earlier." As Grace came near, he put his arm gently around her shoulders and drew her a little closer. His fingers stroking her shoulder sent warm shivers racing over her skin.

"I appreciate all of y'all looking out for her. Everything is going to be fine now that he's gone."

"I hope so," Jack said. "We've got a poker buddy who's a cop. I called him and told him what happened, and he said he'd drive by regularly tonight."

"I brought my shotgun with me. He'll get the message if he comes back," Charity replied sweetly.

Adam whistled appreciatively as he turned around and walked to the back door. "Remind me to never piss you off, woman. I'm gonna finish up out here before it gets too dark to see."

Everybody laughed.

Charity then set about tidying the house from their quick pack-up of Owen's belongings. Jack and Grace finished the food prep in the kitchen while Ethan replaced the deadbolts on all her doors. Jack joined Adam on the back porch, tending the heating grill, and Ethan joined them on the back porch after he was done.

Adam finished the installation and turned on the AC. He walked in the kitchen and said, "Baby, you've got air conditioning again."

"Oh, thank you, Adam!" Grace rose from her chair and gave him a great big hug and a kiss on the cheek. She enjoyed the gentle, loving way Adam wrapped his arms around her.

He released her after a few seconds, retrieved a beer from the refrigerator, and went out the backdoor to join Jack and Ethan.

"I'll be right back. I'm gonna shut all the windows." Grace left the room, and Charity carried the pan with the steaks out to the guys to put on the grill.

Charity came back inside and poured two generous wineglasses full of the sangria and sat down at the kitchen table with Grace. "So…Jack?" Charity eyed Grace devilishly and bit down on the heel of her hand dramatically.

"Yeah." Grace breathed out on a long sigh and nodded, ready for the interrogation to begin.

"And…Adam? Mmm-mmm-*mmm*!" She made clutching movements with her hands spread apart like his shoulders were between them.

"Uh-huh!" Grace replied, remembering what it felt like to be nestled between those big shoulders when he'd hugged her Sunday night. She closed her eyes, wanting to go there again and again.

"And…Ethan," Charity whispered, licking her lips. Grace had to giggle.

"Mmm…yeah," Grace agreed in heartfelt appreciation as they toasted her men.

"When did you meet them?" Charity asked, expecting details. Grace gave her all the basics—leading up to the funeral and how she'd only recently met Adam and Ethan. She told her about the funeral, the AC, Owen, and, more importantly, how attracted she felt toward all three of them, including her conflicted emotions, feeling that she somehow was acting like a tramp wanting all three of them.

"Sis, it looks to me like all three of them want *you*. Have you done anything yet?"

"*No*!" Grace whispered. "I'm scared to. How would I choose? I don't want to choose."

"You want them all, don't you?"

"Am I crazy?"

"No." Charity refilled their glasses again. "If they all treated me the way they treat you and I wasn't already married with a family, they'd have me eating out of their hands. All at the same time, too." She had a wicked gleam in her eyes.

"Bad girl."

"You have no idea, baby sister. If I were you, I'd be on them like white on rice, any way they wanted me."

"You would not believe the dream I had this morning, right before I woke up." Grace said.

Charity was only a couple of years older than she was, and they'd always been very close growing up, sharing and keeping each other's deepest, darkest secrets. So Grace had no compunction whatsoever about sharing every detail of her dream. The wine helped release any information she might have held back. She refilled their glasses, surprised to find that they had polished off the bottle, and told her sister all about it.

"What should I do now?" Grace finally asked.

* * * *

Charity scoffed. "What should you do? Seize the freakin' day! That's what you should do." Charity took their glasses to the sink to rinse them out.

Right before she turned on the water, she realized she was hearing the sound of crickets because the window over the sink was *wide open*. Making a job out of rinsing the glasses, Charity gazed out the window, smiling at the stunned faces on the men sitting in the lawn chairs on the back porch. Jack looked up at her with guilty eyes.

Her mama didn't raise no dummy. She wasn't about to mess up the once-in-a-lifetime opportunity that fate had presented Grace with by being tacky and tattling on the men for eavesdropping on their conversation. Charity prided herself on being a good judge of character, able to smell a rat at fifty feet. Owen had been a rat. These men were a whole different breed. What they all had in common was their obvious adoration of her baby sister. She looked down and caught Jack's eye again and winked at him, trying not to laugh out loud at the dismayed look in his eyes. They never moved a muscle, a captive audience.

It was time to lay it *all* on the line. Otherwise, there was no telling how long Grace might torture herself with these conflicting feelings and no telling how long it would take to extract the necessary green light they needed from Grace before they could tell her how they really felt. Grace had little experience with men, and if she counted Owen as a real man, she had *no* experience. It was time for the master to get to work.

Charity rejoined Grace at the table and laid her hand on Grace's arm.

"Can I ask you a question? Will you be completely honest with me?" At her nod, Charity continued. "Do you love Jack? I don't mean love to have a fling with him. I mean do you really love him, forever kind of love?"

"Yes, I think I have practically since his mother introduced us. When I look in his eyes, I see such tenderness and acceptance. He's a kidder and loves to tease me, but when I'm around him, I want to hold on and never let go."

"You said you only recently met Ethan and Adam. How do you feel about them? Do you think you can love them?"

"There is this raw, new attraction that I feel toward both of them. I love how loyal they are to each other and to Jack. When they look at me, I feel beautiful and sensual. Sort of powerful, you know, like I know they are attracted to me. When I'm near them, there is not a part of me that doesn't want their hands all over me. Ethan kissed me for the first time tonight right before he went to the hardware store."

"Is he a good kisser?"

"Wonderful. It stole my breath and got me all—" Grace paused, blushing profusely.

"—all hot and bothered? Wet? Horny?" Charity asked, grinning and laughing along with her.

"Yes, yes, and hell yes!"

"Don't you wish you could just sit down and have them tell you how they felt about you so you could do the same?" *Listen up, boys. Can't make it any simpler for you than this. Thank me later.* "What would you say?"

Grace rested her cheek in her palm, twirling her wineglass between her fingers. She looked into Charity's eyes and spoke with a tremulous voice, "I would tell them I love them *all*. I'm almost afraid to say it out loud even to you, but I adore them. I want them all, and not just temporarily, and not just because they were my knights in shining armor riding in to save me today. I want them and love them each in a different way. But I can't choose between them, and I don't want to. *Oh, my gosh, I do love them*. Charity, I must be crazy. What kind of person goes blabbing she's in love with three men, two of whom she's known only three or four days?"

"You're not. That's just the wine talking, making you think you're crazy. I'll tell you what would be crazy, though. You missing out on an opportunity to be happy just because what makes you happy doesn't fit into a nice neat mold like the world says it should. Sometimes you have to take the opportunities life presents you with and enjoy the love that finds you, even when it's a little unorthodox. It would be sad if those guys never knew you loved them because they were afraid to tell you *themselves*."

Hint, hint...

Grace looked up at the clock and said, "I wonder what's keeping those steaks? The grill must have taken a long time to heat up. I'm going to run to the bathroom. Why don't you check on them?"

After Grace left the room, Charity walked over to the sink and silently lowered the window and locked it tight. She stepped out the back door as Jack turned from placing the steaks inside the grill and closed it, checking his watch.

"We can never thank you enough for not ratting us out, Charity," Jack said. "Once you got started talking, we were afraid to move a muscle for fear she might realize she left the window open. It would really embarrass her to know we overheard that conversation."

"You can thank me by not breaking my sister's heart, Jack. She deserves the best. I think that might be the three of you. But I will hunt you down with my shotgun if I ever hear that you've hurt her or teased her about her weight. She is very sensitive about that, and Owen never had an ounce of mercy for her." She watched Jack's face fall as she spoke those words, and she listened to what he said next and knew she'd judged them rightly.

"I can promise you that will never happen. We heard some of the things Owen said to her when we got here tonight. I speak for the three of us when I say we think she is perfect exactly the way she is. From the top of her head to the tips of her toenails, we think she's perfect. Thank you for helping her express her feelings about us. It was *very* humbling to hear."

"Don't leave her hanging."

"No, ma'am," Ethan said. "You'd really hunt us down with your shotgun?"

"Damn straight. They'd never find your bodies either. I'm a big *CSI* fan. And stop calling me ma'am. I think I hear her in the kitchen. I plied her with your wine, Ethan, so she's kind of tipsy. Give her a chance to sober up a little."

"The food will help, I imagine," Adam replied. "Thanks again, Charity. You're the best."

"You have no idea!" she cracked as she opened the back door and stepped back inside. Grace had plates and glasses down from the cabinet, put out silverware, and was filling glasses with ice when Charity came back inside.

"The steaks should be ready in a few minutes. They got busy talking and lost track of time."

Grace smiled at her and said, "Imagine that." She rubbed her temples with her fingers. "I think I may be a little tipsy."

"Me, too, but you're safe with us," Charity replied, smiling indulgently at her, just like a big sister should. Grace went to her and hugged her. "Is everything ready? Nothing else you need me to help with?"

"No, Jack was a big help earlier."

"Yeah, I saw him helping himself first hand, remember?" Charity snorted loudly at her own humor. They made iced tea, and a few minutes later, the back door opened, and the guys brought the steaks back in, ready to eat. Charity spent the next hour watching the way Grace interacted with her men. Charity could see that they really were *her* men. They waited on her, refilled her tea glass, as well as Charity's, complimented her cooking, and bragged to Charity about the meal Grace had brought to their house.

"I'm really sorry to hear about your loss, Jack. It sounds like she was a wonderful mother to all of you growing up. How's your dad doing?" Charity asked.

"It's been really hard for him. I think if I was married that long I'd feel like I was missing half of myself," Jack replied sadly. "But just like tonight, life has to go on. We're doing our best to keep him busy, help him get back into the old routine. They went everywhere together, except Stigall's. That was Mom's one guilty pleasure, going shopping every Saturday morning while he met his buddies at the Dairy Queen for coffee."

"Yeah, Dad was hoping he might sit with them for a while and have a cup this Saturday," Ethan said, passing the sliced tomatoes to Grace before she even had a chance to ask.

Charity thought it was nice that they paid attention, trying to anticipate her needs.

Their conversation continued as she rose from the table, took her plate to the trash can, and scraped it off. The men rose from the table, too, and took Grace's dishes from her hands. When she would have shooed them into the living room to talk while she cleaned up, they turned the tables on her and shooed her and Charity into the living room. With the three of them working, they had everything tidied up in a few minutes.

Jack came into the living room. "Well, ladies, we know you two want to talk some more, so we are going to head on back to the ranch. If you have even the faintest inkling of trouble from Owen, one of you call 911 and the other one call us. We can be here in five minutes. Remember, our cop buddy will be driving by to make sure everything is okay."

Grace rose from the couch and stretched, arching her back, and tried to stifle a yawn.

Charity went into the kitchen to get herself a glass of water and to give them a chance for a more private good-bye.

Chapter Five

Grace looked at the three of them standing there, so handsome and strong. She looked in their eyes and saw acceptance, hopefulness, and desire. Charity had encouraged her to take her chance. Rose Marie had encouraged her to seize the day. If she didn't act on that advice right now, she knew she'd regret it later.

She went to Jack first, wrapping her arms around his waist and laying her head against his chest. He leaned down to her, almost tentatively, tilted her chin up, and kissed her lips for the first time. His lips were warm and gentle against hers, making her feel small and precious to him. She was enveloped in his clean, masculine warmth, and she felt a little dizzy as she returned his kiss enthusiastically. She felt his strong hands skim down her ribs and come to rest on her hips, pulling her to him ever so slightly but enough that the erection growing inside his blue jeans pressed against her abdomen. She felt that yearning warmth begin in her belly and spread down to her throbbing clit.

She longed for a time when this might be the beginning and not the end of the evening. She was aware of Adam and Ethan standing nearby. She surprised herself, subconsciously recognizing them not as observers but participants merely awaiting their moment. How odd to feel that way. She had so little experience with men and this sort of thing, and she should have felt self-conscious about kissing Jack in front of them, but instead she was contemplating having the two of them kiss her next. It was over too soon.

Jack cupped her cheek, looking down into her eyes. "See you soon. Be safe."

"I will. You, too."

He looked at her for a moment like he wanted to say more, then released her and went out the screen door to start the SUV, leaving the others to their good-byes.

He'd released her to Ethan, who gave her a knowing grin. He was anticipating his second kiss of the evening from her. He looked down at her with warm eyes as she rose on her tiptoes, and he leaned down to her. He caught her in a more passionate kiss than the first time. He pulled her to his hard, muscular chest, pressing her breasts against him, and she was sure he could feel how hard her nipples were and the way she trembled in his arms. Unlike the first kiss, she opened to give him access. As his tongue caressed hers, her body bloomed into full arousal for him. He rested his hands on her hips, pressing himself to her, making her aware of how she affected him.

He released her to caress her cheeks, drawing his thumb across her damp bottom lip. "Call us if you need us, Gracie, no matter how late, okay?" He nuzzled her cheek. "Sweet dreams."

"I promise. Thank you for changing the locks. I feel much safer now. I–I'm—uh," she stuttered.

He bent down very closely and whispered, "I love you, Gracie."

The words stunned her with their simplicity, and her breath caught in her throat. He smiled gently at her, and she looked up into his sparkling blue eyes and whispered softly, almost silently, "I love you, too, Ethan."

"See you soon." Then he, too, was gone, but not before she saw the hopeful, fiercely purposeful light filling his eyes.

She turned to her patient, gentle giant, Adam. She just reached for him as he leaned down to her, lifting her into his embrace. She wrapped her arms tightly around his neck as his lips brushed hers and returned his kiss with all the joy in her heart. His arms wrapped around her, one around her waist and one around her hips. She turned her head slightly into his kiss and arched her back, pressing her breasts into his chest. She heard a faint growl come from his throat as she brushed her tongue against his, and of their own volition, her legs wrapped themselves around his narrow waist, pressing her now very damp folds against his abdomen. One hand slid down to cup her ass, holding her tightly to him. The tightness in her belly increased, and she felt the muscles in her pussy clench uselessly. Adam groaned softly, and she might have moaned a little herself at that sensation. Thank goodness she was wearing blue jeans. Otherwise, she'd have gotten him all wet. As he put her down, she lowered her legs to the floor, and he slid her down his torso. His growing erection rubbed against her belly as she found her footing again.

He leaned down to whisper in her ear, "I want you so much, Grace. We want you so much. All of us. You know you can trust us?" His eyes, like Ethan's, were so hopeful.

His words stole her breath, and she held on to him tightly, looking into his eyes, nodding slowly.

"I trust you, Adam. I do. Thank you for saving me today." Her chin wobbled a little. All these powerful sensations were getting to her emotions.

"I love you, Adam. So much," she whispered.

She laid her cheek against his chest and felt such a profound peace steal over her. Not all of them had made declarations of love to each other, but she knew they loved her, especially Jack. Even though he hadn't said it tonight, she felt it.

"I love you, Grace," Adam murmured softly to her, wiping a tear from her eye that she didn't even know was there. "Sweet dreams, baby."

"You, too. Drive safe."

He released her, and she watched him go. She waved to Jack and Ethan, who pulled away after Adam started his truck. Watching out for each other, as always.

"Wow, that was way better than porn," Charity said as she came back in the living room.

"Charity!" Grace blurted out, laughing. Her cheeks literally throbbed with heat.

* * * *

On the drive home, Adam groaned as he remembered the little stretch and yawn she'd had when she got up from the couch. And the way she had arched her back into it. That little move made him instantly hard. The caveman buried inside him wanted to pick her up and carry her over his shoulder back to his cave and bury himself deep inside her. He could still smell her on him, the scent that was uniquely hers and all woman. Someday, hopefully soon because he was in agony, he was going to feast between her thighs and experience for himself what she tasted like, too. He needed a cold shower something fierce.

She took a huge risk and told him she loved him. That had to be a sign of trust. And Heaven knew he loved her, too. His heart lurched when he remembered the trusting way she'd reached for him and the sexy way she'd turned into their kiss, getting as close as she could to him. She had given as much as she could give to him, for now, in that kiss and held nothing in reserve. When he felt her wrap those long legs around him, the urge to turn and take her to the bedroom was a strong one, but he'd reminded himself that her sister was there. And knowing Charity, she was probably watching. His heart was a lost cause. Grace now held it in her hands. Those trusting blue eyes had done him in for good.

* * * *

Jack glanced over at Ethan as he drove out of Divine toward the ranch. Ethan had been awfully quiet since they left Grace's house. Jack was curious about the cause.

"What's troublin' you, Ethan?"

"Nothing's troubling me. I'm just thinking about Gracie. I told her that I loved her."

"Well, that's a good thing, right?"

"Of course it is, Jack. But I've only known her four days."

"When you told her you loved her, did you mean it? Or did you just want to make her happy? Or are you just hoping to get in her pants and thought she'd let you if you told her that?" He knew none of those things were true but figured playing devil's advocate might help Ethan work it out.

Ethan laughed. "You know me better than that, Jack. I wouldn't say something like that unless I was positive I meant it."

"Then why does it matter if it's only been four days? The way I see it, you're faster on the uptake than I am because I've known her for a couple of years. Sometimes it takes people a while to realize they love someone, and sometimes it only takes a day. I think Adam fell in love with her the moment he saw her walking up Dad's driveway."

"How do you feel about me telling her tonight that I love her? By rights you should have been the first one to tell her. Any stirrings of jealousy?"

In answer, Jack asked him a question. "How did it make you feel when she kissed me good-bye?"

"Honestly, it was a turn-on to watch her kiss you. Don't get me wrong, Jack. I ain't getting turned on by you or anything like that, but yeah, I liked watching the two of you. Maybe there's a little more kink in us than we all thought, or maybe it's different this time because she's the right woman."

"I wanted the two of you to have your moment with her, so I went outside. Maybe I should have stayed and watched, too."

"I have a feeling you'll get your chance before too long. Can I ask you a question?" Ethan asked.

"Of course." Jack knew the only way they were going to navigate through this is by being totally open with each other and putting her needs first.

"You heard her talk about that dream she had. If she wants the three of us at one time, do you feel comfortable with doing that?" Ethan asked, turning to look at his best friend's face illuminated by the dashboard lights.

"Can you deal with it?" Jack answered.

"Hell yeah. I already told you it's a huge turn-on for me, and we have to put her needs first. There is no jealousy there. That's not to say I won't want to spend time alone with her all to myself, and I would expect you to want the same thing, as well. Adam, too."

"I'm not sharing her with anyone else besides the two of you," Jack said.

"I feel the same, Jack. I'm willing to share, but only with y'all. She doesn't strike me as the kind of person who would want that. Man, that was some kiss. She is so responsive. I can still smell her scent. Mmmm."

"Cold shower?"

"Make mine a double," Ethan said, laughing. "And I still ain't doin' ya."

They laughed for half a mile.

Chapter Six

Grace placed her hands over her hot cheeks as Charity snickered and sat down on the couch.

"Grace, you are one hot mama! You've got those men eating from the palm of your hand. Did you see the way they were looking at you tonight? I felt like fanning myself a couple of times, it was getting so hot in there. They adore you! I wouldn't be a bit surprised if they told you they were in love with you."

"Ethan and Adam did tonight. That was also the first time I'd ever kissed Jack and Adam." Grace joined her on the couch, recalling the effect their gentle kisses had on her.

"Are they good kissers? What am I saying? Of course they were good kissers. It was obvious. They are really into you. If I hadn't been here, you might be in bed with all three of them right now!"

"It's like something out of my wildest fantasies. I wouldn't even know where to begin. They would have to figure all that out. How would they do that?"

"One of them takes you vaginally, one takes you anally, and you take the other orally, all at the same time," Charity said with a lecherous grin, laughing at Grace's shocked expression.

"Charity! I swear, sometimes you take pleasure in shocking me. I already knew how the sex works. I meant how do they decide who takes me first? I meant just regular, straightforward sex! Rock, paper, scissors? Girl, your mind is in the gutter!"

Charity snickered playfully, rubbing her hands together. "Yes, and I'm so glad you've joined me. You're much more fun now that Owen got the boot. You must be exhausted. I think you're probably running on nerves and adrenaline right now. You have to work in the morning, so why don't we turn in?"

"'Kay. I'm going to take a shower. I'll be in there in a few minutes."

The house was so nice and cool now. She'd sleep like a baby tonight for sure unless thoughts of those men and their hot kisses kept her awake. Just the thought sent a spear of heat to her clit.

Bad girl.

When she got out of the bathroom, she found Charity in her bedroom, stripping the bed and putting on fresh sheets and pillow cases. "Sorry, I could not take the chance he slept on the sheets I'm laying down on tonight."

* * * *

It was too much to hope she would get a good night's sleep tonight. Grace had been in bed less than half an hour when the pounding on the door began, startling her.

Charity angrily threw the covers back. "Shit a monkey! I'm going to blow his frickin' brains out," she muttered angrily as they put on their robes and slippers.

"Stay put for a second, Charity. Don't turn the lamp on yet," Grace told her over the continued pounding.

She peeked out the blinds to see if it was Owen and whether or not he had any of his hoodlum friends with him. His truck was parked out on the curb with two of his buddies still sitting in the cab. All of his stuff was still piled in the bed of the truck. She had to snicker at that. No one had offered to take him in. Some friends he had.

He was still beating on the door, and she was worried the noise would wake her neighbors. She handed her phone to Charity and told her to do as Jack said—use Grace's phone to dial 911, since it was registered to her address and the cops would have a faster response time, and use Charity's phone to call Jack, who had programmed his number into Charity's phone as well.

Good thinking, guys.

* * * *

Jack had just said goodnight to Adam and Ethan when his cell phone rang. The men exchanged a worried look. Calls at midnight couldn't be a good thing. Caller ID confirmed it.

"It's Charity's phone. Grab the keys," Jack said as all three ran out the door. Jack answered the call.

"Hello, Charity. What's happening? Are you all right?" Jack asked as he pressed the speakerphone button so they could all hear. Ethan jumped behind the wheel and started the vehicle.

"For the moment, we're fine. I've already called 911. I have them on the line now. Owen is banging on the front door and has been for the last couple of minutes."

"Has Grace opened the door?"

"No, she told him to go away several times, but he won't listen. He's drunk as a skunk and yelling at her about video games. He says he won't leave until she returns the videogames she stole from him. Can you hear him?" she asked, and they could indeed hear muffled yelling and thumping in the background.

"Yeah, I can hear him. We're already on the road into town. Did 911 say how far away the police officers are?"

"They said they were sending someone now, and we can hear the sirens coming."

"Is there anyone with Owen?"

"Yes. Earlier, there were two guys sitting in his truck. I'm looking out the window, and they are in the yard now trying to get him to leave. Oh, great! Now they are fighting in the front yard. They must all be drunk. Hey, Grace wants to talk to you. Here ya go."

"Jack?" All three of them heaved a sigh of relief when they heard her voice. She sounded tired. The pounding on the door started again, and so did the yelling. Grace was trying to talk, but they couldn't make out what she was saying because of the noise.

"Grace, whatever you do, don't open that door until the police get there and tell you it's safe."

"I won't. Charity wanted to, but I wouldn't let her. She has her shotgun with her. I see flashing lights out front. Charity, go look out the bedroom window to see what's going on. I hear them scuffling on the porch. Is it safe? Okay. Jack? She said they have him and one of his friends facedown on the ground outside. How far away are you?"

"We just turned onto your street. You'll see us pull up in a few seconds. Stay put. I'm going to hang up, baby." He stuck the phone in his pocket and jumped out of the SUV as soon as Ethan put it in park.

The police officers had Owen and his friends on the ground and were handcuffing them. Owen started to yell again, going on about his video games. Jack was in the lead and made it up the porch steps first. He called to Grace through the door.

She opened the door and reached out for him, for all of them. They surrounded her, hugging her, hugging Charity, thankful that they were both all right.

Jack wrapped his arms around Grace and hugged her close to him. "You okay, darlin'?"

She smiled up at him and said, "I am now that you're here."

The officers marched Owen and both of his buddies over to one of the squad cars and placed them under arrest for drunken and disorderly conduct. After a few minutes, one of the officers, Jack's friend Hank Stinson, came up on the porch and knocked on the screen door. Jack opened the door for him and shook his hand.

"Sorry, Jack. We swung by just a few minutes before we got the call about a disturbance over here. We were clear across town. We're taking them in for drunk and disorderly conduct. Is that his truck parked out in the road still running?"

"Yeah, it is."

"It's blocking the road. Do you want to move it, or should I call and have it impounded?"

"It's his vehicle. We don't want responsibility for it."

"I'll have it towed, no problem. Hey, Grace, sorry to have to pay a visit so late at night. Can I ask you a few questions?"

"That's all right, Hank. It's been a long day for all of us. Did your softball team like those new jerseys we printed for them?" Grace asked. Jack had forgotten about referring Hank over to Harper's for new softball jerseys. He was glad that if she had to speak to a police officer this late at night that it was at least someone she knew and was comfortable talking with.

They all sat down in the living room, and Grace answered all of Hank's questions regarding what had occurred as well as what had taken place earlier in the afternoon. Grace agreed to come down and press charges against Owen in the morning.

After they were finished, Jack turned to Grace and Charity. "Do you want to come back to the ranch with us?" he offered, still hoping.

"He's not going to bother me anymore tonight. Charity is here, so I know I'll be fine."

"I'd feel better if one of us stayed here with you. Would you mind?" Jack asked, reluctant to leave the two of them alone again tonight. He wished now that he had made the offer earlier.

"It's fine with me if it's all right with Sis," she said, not seeing the enthusiastic nod and thumbs-up signal Charity gave to Jack. He had to cover his grin.

* * * *

"It's up to y'all who stays, Jack. Don't make me choose," Grace said, then yawned.

"I can stay. My first appointment isn't until nine in the morning," Adam said, volunteering for duty. The other two nodded and stood up.

"Jack, Ethan, thank you for coming so quickly. Once again, you're all my heroes," Grace said.

Jack hugged her tight and kissed her forehead, and then Ethan hugged her and kissed her cheek. They both hugged Charity and thanked her for being well prepared. Adam shared a quiet conversation with them on the porch and then left.

"Can I borrow a blanket and pillow, Grace?" Adam asked. "I'll sleep on the couch."

Charity shook her head at Grace and pointed at herself, letting her know she could sleep on the couch. Grace shook her head firmly and mouthed a *no* to Charity when she followed Grace down the hall to the linen closet to get what Adam needed.

Charity whispered, "I don't mind, Grace."

"I do, Charity. I kissed him for the first time an hour ago. I'm not ready for that yet."

"Heh–heh. Yet is right." Charity snickered softly as she retreated down the hall to the bathroom. Grace went in the kitchen and put ground coffee and water in the coffeemaker and set the timer to start brewing early the next morning.

Adam slipped his boots off and lay down on the couch. Grace turned off all the lights except the one on the end table next to the couch. Charity said goodnight and excused herself. Grace knelt down on the floor by Adam's head and leaned in to lay her head on his chest. She hugged him as he wrapped his big, strong arms around her and gave her a little squeeze.

He turned onto his side and moved up against the back rest of the couch. He patted the cushion in front of him. "Come sit with me. I don't want you kneeling on the bare floor."

She moved up onto the cushion, and he wrapped his arms loosely around her waist.

"Are you going to be able to rest after all this excitement?" he asked. His warm fingers caressed her through the fleece of her robe.

"I'm one of those weird people who respond to stress by becoming groggy. My mom could always tell when something was bothering me or if I was upset because my response would be to want a nap. I'll be all right. To know you are out here trying to sleep on my couch may be a distraction, but I'll do my best. Will you be comfortable enough?"

He nodded and looked at her, his eyes partially hidden in shadows with the lamp lit behind him. His gaze was like a physical touch, warming her. He reached up and caressed her bruised cheekbone lightly with the backs of his fingers. His mouth hardened momentarily, even though his soft touch didn't hurt in the least. She had a strong urge to just lie down and curl up with him and not worry about the rest of the world. Let him deal with it.

"Grace," he began, speaking softly in a deep voice that made her quiver inside, "I think I fell in love with you when I laid eyes on you the first time. It took a lot of trust to tell me you loved me when we've only known each other a few days. We feel *very* protective toward you. Maybe a little possessive, too."

"I love the gentle way you reach out and touch me, sometimes in innocent ways, like when you tucked that lock of hair behind my ear tonight, taking care of me. But also when you touch me the way a man touches a woman he wants. My body reacts to you in shameless ways. I knew I loved you tonight when you proved you were willing to defend me and protect me. The outrage on your face and the determination in your eyes did it for me.

"I feel laid bare before you," she continued in a shaky voice. "Like there is not a thing about me that is held back from you. You asked if I could trust you. I trust you with everything. I trust you to protect me. Obviously, you earned that trust in spades the last few days, but I also trust you with my appearance, the way I'm built. I have learned to build up a wall around myself over my body image, and for you to call my body a work of *art...*" She paused, her voice catching a little bit. "It felt good to be accepted like that. You know, I was afraid to turn my back on Owen for fear of his remarks about my rear end. My rationale, I suppose, was the less I showed him, the less I provoked him. I don't feel like that with you. I even have the feeling that maybe you like it."

She giggled as she watched a naughty grin spread across his face like he *was* thinking about her ass. Confirming her suspicions, his hands slid down and stroked her ass through her robe and gown.

"Okay, I showed you mine, now you show me yours," she said, snickering when he rolled his eyes.

"You couldn't think of a less torturous way to put that?"

"Bad girl. What can I say? Tell me how you know you love me. How could you fall in love with me on sight? I'm dying to know." She stroked his arms, still wrapped around her.

"That's an easy one." He reached out and fingered a curl lying over her shoulder as he continued. "I looked out the window at the funeral and watched you walk up the drive to the house, and something in me just clicked. The guys were teasing me some, I suppose, because I couldn't take my eyes off of you. There was just something about you, your curves and your shape. The smooth, graceful way you moved made my mouth water." He grinned when her jaw popped open, and she tried to hide her hot cheeks. "I loved you on sight, baby, and everything I have learned about you since just convinces me more," he murmured, grazing her cheekbone with his fingertips.

"You are really good for a girl's ego, I'll tell ya, Adam," she said, beaming down at him before taking on a more serious tone. "I don't know what to expect from you or Jack and Ethan. I feel very confused when I'm with all of you. I'm still trying hard to process the fact that I am so strongly attracted to all three of you, that I'm *in love* with all three of you. My mind should be screaming at me that this is all wrong, but it's not. I'm also concerned about becoming more intimate than we already are too quickly. It's not that I'm afraid of y'all. It's just going to take some time to adjust to that reality. Plus, I need a little bit of time to get Owen out of my head."

He smiled up at her gently and asked, "Do you trust me, baby? Do you trust Jack and Ethan?"

She smiled and nodded quickly. "Yeah, of that I am certain. I trust all of you. I don't think trust is the main issue."

"Then everything is going to work out just fine. Talk to us and tell us what you're thinking. We'll be open and honest with you. You can bank on it when I say the last thing we want to do is rush you into anything you're not ready for. You're too precious to us for that."

She leaned down and kissed him, desiring the contact but not wanting to push him too much. His hands slid up her spine, then down her arms as she sat up.

"Baby, you're tired. Why don't you get some rest since you have to work in the morning? You keep kissing me like that and I'm never going to get any sleep. I'll be thinking about you in your bed, just a few feet away, all night."

As she got up, his callused hand slid up the back of her thigh. Her breath caught, and he groaned softly, then removed his hand.

"Bad boy," she whispered, smiling sweetly at him, appreciating even more that *she* didn't have to make a move to stop him because he did it himself.

Chapter Seven

Grace yawned as she pressed the start button on the coffeemaker. She looked out her kitchen window and heard soft movements behind her. Adam's large, warm hands slid ever so gently around her torso and pulled her into his immense, comforting embrace. One muscled arm wrapped around her waist, and the other crossed her shoulders, pressing her back to his front. He sighed sleepily and swept her long, tousled hair from her shoulder and pressed his warm lips to her throat, beneath her ear. Her head fell back against his chest, and she tilted her head and allowed his lips to traverse her throat to her shoulder.

"Oh, boy," she groaned softly. "I died and this is heaven." He chuckled deeply and squeezed her to him. A breathy shudder left her lips as she became aware of his large, fully erect cock resting against her lower back. It was a crying shame they had clothes on.

"Good morning, baby," he murmured.

"Oh, it is." She turned in his arms and gazed up into his sleepy green eyes.

He gazed at her silently for a few seconds, then whispered in a husky voice, "God, you're beautiful."

She felt a warm, languorous wave flow through her as she held his gaze. She didn't blush hard, which should have been her reaction. She could see in his eyes that he meant exactly what he'd said, that it hadn't been just flattery designed to get a reaction from her. To him she was beautiful, and she smiled happily at him, accepting his truth.

"Thank you. You make me feel beautiful." What would it be like to start every day like this? Oh, hell. What would it be like to start every morning like that *times three*? Her body bloomed with arousal, answering that question.

Whoa, horsey! Slow down.

"Did you sleep last night, Adam?"

"A little, baby."

"Want coffee? I hope you take it strong."

"The stronger the better."

Grace chuckled and got mugs down. He made himself a cup of coffee, and she poured one for her sister and took it into the bedroom.

She tiptoed to the bed and poked her sister while carefully placing the hot coffee on the bedside table. She sang as she poked Charity's shoulder, just like their mother had when they were little to wake them. "*Birdie with a yellow bill…*"

She heard a muffled, "No."

"*…Hopped upon my windowsill…*"

"No."

"*…Cocked his shining eye and said…*"

"Fuck off."

Grace fought laughter so hard she had tears in her eyes "*…Ain't you 'shamed you sleepy head!*"

Charity pulled the pillow up and looked at her sister through tousled, messy curls, and they both burst into a fit of laughter. "You're way too frickin' cheerful this morning for someone who didn't get laid the night before."

"Shhh!" Grace put her finger to her lips and looked at the bedroom door. "He'll hear you, idiot!"

Charity grinned broadly. "So the knight in shining armor is still here?"

"Yes. Get your ass out of bed and I'll make breakfast."

"You're bossy now that you're all liberated. Is this mine?" she asked, pointing at the cup of coffee.

"Yes. Strong the way you like it," Grace said as she left her sister to rise and get dressed.

Grace made Charity and Adam breakfast, then took Adam back out to the ranch so he could get on with his workday. She headed over to the police station with Charity to file a complaint and press charges against Owen. Hank told her Owen had gotten his phone call, but nobody had come to bail him out, and his truck was still in the police impound lot. Hank also asked Grace to consider the possibility that she might need to file a restraining order against Owen if he continued to harass her. Grace cringed on the inside at the thought of doing that.

People broke up every day. They got over it and moved on with their lives, and she hoped he'd do just that. Maybe the judge would sentence him to court-mandated drug and alcohol rehabilitation. She didn't know for sure if he was using drugs. She did know that he was having blackouts when he drank, and that was a bad sign. He needed to get clean before the alcohol killed him.

It dawned on her that Jack, Ethan, and Adam were the first men in her life since her dad passed away who made everything better just with their mere presence. She tried to think of a time when Owen did this for her—made it better—and she couldn't think of one time. She had a flash of insight then, realizing who she had truly been to Owen all these years. She'd been his mommy. Taking care of him and cleaning up after him. Buying him what he needed. She didn't know which of them had been a bigger dumb ass—him for using her like that or her for being so stupid.

The week progressed quietly from that point, and Charity went home on Thursday, promising to come back and go shopping with her on Saturday. They would make a morning of it and then have a girls' lunch together.

Thursday morning, Martha and Rose pulled chairs up to Grace's desk before they unlocked the front door.

"Honey, we want to talk to you for a second," Martha began.

"Uh-oh. What's wrong?" Grace asked hesitantly, laying her work orders aside.

Martha and Rose looked at each other and smiled broadly before Martha continued, "Nothing, honey. We want to ask you about something."

"Oh, heck! Is this about Jack, Ethan, and Adam coming by the shop?"

During the week, the men had made a point of stopping by to check on her. They only stayed for a minute or two when they came in, but she'd wondered what Martha and Rose made of it. One day, Ethan and Jack both came in at the same time and both kissed her cheek while Martha and Rose were in the room. Grace noticed after the men left that the women were both blushing and had big smirky grins on their faces, but they hadn't said anything. Maybe they were worried she was getting herself into something she couldn't handle.

Martha shook her head and grinned. "Um, no. That's not it. Although we are *dying* to know what's up with you and those three handsome hunks. Mind you, we're glad they're looking out for you because Owen's gonna be mad as a hornet when he gets out of jail." Grace had filled them in about the whole affair. "What we want to talk to you about is totally unrelated."

"Oh."

"Rose got a call from her mama's doctor in Florida. She's not doing well."

Grace reached out and took Rose's hand and said, "Oh, I'm so sorry, Rose. Is there anything I can do to help?"

Rose nodded her head. "Yes, honey. There actually is something you can do. If you're of a mind to, that is."

"Rose would like to move down to Florida to be with her mom and spend the time she has left with her. Now that the kids are grown and gone, there's really no reason for her to stay in Texas if her mama needs her. We've talked about your savings and investments before, and I know you've been very careful about the money your mom and dad left you. We were wondering if perhaps you'd like to buy Rose out of her partnership in Harper's Embroidery. I'd love to have you as a partner. You handle your responsibilities around here as though you were already invested. Of course, we'd hire somebody to take on your duties."

"Wow." Grace was floored. This was an opportunity for her to be self-employed. That was something she'd always dreamed of.

"Of course, we don't expect an answer now, honey. You take all the time you need to think it over."

"Yeah, Grace," Rose said, checking the clock and removing her keys from her pocket. "It'll be at least four months before I move. It's not an emergency situation or anything. I just know it's inevitable and felt like we might as well get the ball rolling."

Man, when it rained, it poured. "It's a very tempting offer."

Martha pulled her chair back over to her desk. "I'll sit down with you later and give you all the particulars so you have a clear picture of what we're talking about. We just wanted to get a feel for whether you'd be interested or not."

On Friday, Grace hand-delivered the work shirts they'd embroidered for Ethan to The Dancing Pony. Grace knew Ethan would be available to pick them up, and Harper's didn't normally deliver unless it was a big order, but Martha agreed when Grace offered to deliver his shirts to him that afternoon. Grace finished the work she had started, hugged Martha, and left with the shirts.

She pulled up to the club and parked in one of the front spaces. It was a little after six o'clock when she arrived, and there were already quite a few cars in the parking lot. She hooked the hangers over her fingers and carried the shirts in the front door. The cold air conditioning in the darkened interior of the nightclub felt good after the glaring heat and oppressive humidity outside. She stopped in the entryway and allowed her eyes to adjust to the dimmer lighting.

She saw Ethan, clipboard in his hand, behind the bar, where several patrons were already seated. One of the bartenders tapped his shoulder and pointed her way. It warmed her heart when she saw the happy grin that spread over his face when he saw her. He walked around the bar and hugged her, then kissed her on the cheek. She loved the feel of his arms around her and looked up into his twinkling blue eyes. He took the shirts from her and gave them to the bartender to put in his office.

"Are you thirsty? Would you like a drink? Or a soda?"

"I'd love a Coke. It's really hot today. But I'm not complaining. At least I have an air conditioner!" she said, grinning.

"Coke it is. Come sit at the bar." He stood there and talked with her, waiting on customers here and there as more came in. People were sitting at tables now as well, and the waitresses showed up for their shifts.

Someone came in and sat down in the seat to her right. She was telling Ethan about Martha's partnership offer and didn't really pay attention to the person as he sat down. More customers came in, and they started to get busy. Ethan left for a moment to use the cash register, and she looked around the interior of The Dancing Pony.

The club had a large dance floor in the center, which was surrounded on three sides by the seating area, and the bar ran along the opposite wall. Most of the tables were high-topped, surrounded by tall cushioned chairs. Against one wall near the dance floor, an enclosed DJ booth was set up on a raised platform. Ethan worked the end of bar where she sat, and the other bartender worked the opposite end.

Ethan was busy mixing a drink when the man who sat next to her finally caught her attention. She got a whiff of something. Stale sweat. She hated that. There was nothing wrong with a sweaty man in her book, not by any stretch of the imagination. But a daily shower and a change of clothes were prerequisites for showing up to socialize at a night club. He greeted her nicely enough when she turned to smile and nod at him, but there was something about the way he looked at her that made her a little uncomfortable. His hair was shaggy, in need of a trim, and there was something a little greasy about him.

He asked her to dance, and she kindly refused, wishing that Ethan could come and talk to her some more. He smiled and winked at her as he placed money in the cash register when she made eye contact with him. It made her heart do little flip-flops. He sauntered back down her way, delivering a beer to the customer on her other side.

Just then, the man on her right leaned way too close and said rather loudly in her ear, "I don't normally beat around the bush so much. I prefer to beat *in it*. What do you say we go somewhere a little more quiet?"

To say she was shocked speechless was an understatement. It wasn't that the words shocked her sensibilities all that much. Yes, he was incredibly crude, but Owen had been, too. His attempt at a come-on had left her at a loss for words.

Ethan stopped what he was doing and leaned both of his clenched fists on the bar in front of her and said, "So, Gracie, are we still on for tonight?"

Still shocked, she looked up at him and caught his wink. Whatever paralysis she had been suffering from released her, and she smiled back.

"I can't wait, Ethan," she said enthusiastically. Then she turned to look at the greasy man. He was already climbing down from his seat. He slunk around to the other side of the bar and sat next to another poor woman who looked to be a regular. She probably knew how to deal with a slime ball like him.

"Thank you for saving me, Ethan, yet again! Does he use that line with every woman he talks to in here?"

Ethan laughed and nodded. "Yeah, I hope he develops some better openers or finds a new stomping ground because that line is gonna get him decked one of these days." The customer to her left laughed when Ethan said that, and Ethan introduced her to him.

“Gracie, this is a good friend of mine, Bill Duggan. Bill, this is Grace Stuart. Bill is one of my *decent* regular customers.”

“Don’t go telling her that. I might have some lines I want to try out on her,” Bill said, laughing and shaking her hand.

“I’m sure they couldn’t be as bad as his,” Grace replied.

“No hitting on my girlfriend, Bill. I sat her over here with you so she would be *safe*.”

“Girlfriend, huh? Grace, you must be something really special. I can’t recall the last time I heard of Ethan dating anyone. I guess that comes from working in a nightclub.”

She chatted with Bill for a few minutes while Ethan waited on more customers and filled orders for the waitresses. She felt much better now, not as self-conscious. Bill was a much older man with black hair sprinkled with silver at the temples. He was still in his work shirt, but he looked nice and neat. He had a thick moustache and friendly eyes and seemed genuinely interested in their conversation and putting her at ease. Ethan spoke briefly to the sleazy man who then got up to leave, never making eye contact with her, not that she wanted it in the first place.

Ethan spoke to the other bartender and then came back down the bar. “I’m about done, Grace. How about a dance?”

“I’d love to.”

He came around the bar, held out his hand to her, and led her onto the dance floor where a few other couples were already dancing. She immediately went into his arms, and they two-stepped to the final verse and chorus of a Bob Seger song. They stayed, swaying as the song ended and the other couples left the dance floor. The strains of the next song began, an old song she loved, “When a Man Loves a Woman” by Percy Sledge.

She smiled, looked up at him, and laid her cheek against his chest, hearing the thump of his heartbeat against her ear.

* * * *

“I played this song for you. Do you like it?” Ethan could tell she did when she looked up at him with shining eyes. He wanted to do something nice to make up for what Brice Huvell had said to her. Brice used that raunchy line all the time, usually with the same result. How could anyone be so clueless? At least he'd come to Ethan and apologized. He hadn't known that it was Ethan's girlfriend he was hitting on.

"I love this song. You are such a romantic, Ethan. You are going to have me wrapped around your little finger in no time."

He chuckled. "You already have me wrapped around yours. All three of us, for that matter. I like seeing you happy and smiling. Have you had a good week?"

"It's flown by. I'm going shopping Saturday to celebrate cleaning out the house. Charity is coming with me, and then we're going to have a girl's lunch afterward."

"Do you have plans for after lunch?" Ethan asked, smiling at her. This was the opening he'd been looking for.

"No, why?"

"The three of us have a surprise for you. We'll meet you at your house after lunch. How about that?"

"Do I get a hint?"

"Not even an itty bitty one. You'll see tomorrow." He sighed softly at how good she felt in his arms and how smoothly she danced with him.

"I love surprises. I love you, too," she said, sliding her arms around his neck.

He leaned down and kissed her. "I love you, Gracie." He squeezed her tightly to him, loving the feel of her lush curves against him.

"I'm keeping you from your work."

"Nah, Ben, the other owner and bartender, just got here. I'm not even supposed to be working tonight. I was just covering for Ben because he was running a little late. Now that he's here, I can leave. Let me ask you, did you ever shop around online for your new computer?"

"I thought we might look at some tomorrow while we were out shopping. Why?"

"My laptop is in the office here if you want to take a few minutes and look around online tonight, so you can comparison shop tomorrow."

"Would you mind? I haven't had access to a computer to do that and was going in blind tomorrow. It would help a lot if I could."

"That's why I offered. Follow me." He took her hand and led her back to the office.

* * * *

Here and there, Grace noticed people watching them as they made their way through the crowd to his office. He greeted many of them and stopped to say hello, often introducing her as his girlfriend. Most were very welcoming toward her, but not all the faces she encountered were friendly. Several women at a table in the corner stared at her with outright hostility.

She made eye contact with several of them as they leaned in to whisper to one woman who literally stared daggers at her. It was hard to tell much about the woman sitting there clutching her drink except that she was very thin with a sharp, angry-looking face. Grace turned from her as Ethan spoke to a customer and leaned into him a little, glorying in the way his arm slid around her hip, his warm hand coming to rest above the swell of her ass. She was not used to that feeling of belonging to someone, that claiming hand on her body.

Deep down, she felt accepted by him and maybe a little possessive toward him. Tackily, she wondered what the strange but hostile woman thought of her hand as it slid in a slow caress over his back and around his waist. He never once let go of her, always including her in the conversation. Eventually, they made it back to the office door.

His office was neat and tidy. After closing the door to block out some of the noise, he offered her his desk chair and pulled up a stool that sat in the corner.

They looked at a couple of websites, and he printed out several price lists for different models that would meet her needs.

By the time they were done, it was eight o'clock. She promised to meet him and Jack and Adam at her house after lunch the next day, asking again for a hint. He just laughed and kissed her. He walked her out to her car and held her door while she got in and buckled up. He told her he was heading home, too, and asked her to call after she got home so he would know she made it okay. She said she would, and then he leaned in the window and gave her a sweet kiss, cupping the back of her head. He made her feel so cherished with his gentle ways.

"I love you, Gracie."

"I love you, too."

She asked herself on the way home if she was crazy falling in love with three men and wanting them all equally. No, she wasn't crazy. She was seizing the day, just like a wise friend had once advised her to do.

* * * *

Jack sat on the couch with his feet propped up on the ottoman, talking on the phone as Ethan walked in the front door. He and Adam had been watching a movie, which was now on pause. Adam looked over at Ethan as he came in the room and sat down in one of the overstuffed chairs and said, "It's Grace. Just checking in."

Jack finished talking, wished her sweet dreams, and then ended the call. He looked up at Ethan and said, "She promised you she would call and check in once she got home. She asked for a hint on the surprise we have planned for them tomorrow. Half the fun of doing this for her is teasing her about it. She's dyin' to know what we're up to."

"How did she like The Dancing Pony?" Adam asked.

"She came by to deliver the shirts I ordered for the nightclub, and I invited her to stay for a bit. She was having a good time until Brice Huvell hit on her."

"He *what?*" they both said simultaneously.

Then Jack asked, "What did he say? Did he frighten her?" Jack knew that Brice was basically a harmless idiot, but he'd like to beat him to a pulp for harassing Grace. He had seen that guy in action before and wondered how she reacted.

"I don't think he frightened her. It was more like he surprised her. You know how he tends to go for shock value with his pick-up lines? Well, he was in rare form tonight. I had to force myself to leave my hands on the bar and not reach across to yank him off his seat and punch his greasy face. He said it to her right in front of me, and for a second, I think I saw red. He apologized for it later to me."

"He needed to apologize to her," Jack replied.

"He offered, and I told him to stay the fuck away from her, in those exact words."

"Probably for the best. She said you danced with her and played a song for her."

"Yeah," Ethan said with a sappy grin on his face.

"It sounds like it made her feel special. Good job, man. She needs that more than anything right now."

Adam chuckled. "Wait till tomorrow afternoon. We're talking major brownie points."

Jack continued, "After she told me about your song, she asked how it made me feel to know that. Did it make me feel jealous when she told me? I think she needed reassurance tonight about how we feel about each other spending time with her. She surprised me and told me that she was okay with Ethan introducing her to his friends as his girlfriend and that she trusted us to work that out with each other. Her primary concern was that there is no jealousy between us."

Ethan nodded. "It felt so right to introduce her as my girlfriend. I think the reason this relationship will work is because we've known each other so many years, and we've talked about all the ins and outs and pitfalls. It's all still so new to her, and she's got some things she needs to work out in her mind."

"Both of you make sure when you're alone with her to talk with her. Help her work it out," Jack said. "She has her sister to talk to, which is definitely in our favor because Charity likes us and trusts us not to hurt her. I think Grace just needs time together with the three of us to see how good it's going to be. She'll see that earning her trust and making her happy are our highest priorities. Are we still making our little side trip after we drop them off?" He grinned at the smiles on their faces at being reminded of the little shopping excursion they were going on for Grace. The fiercely purposeful looks in their eyes mirrored Jack's own emotions. His heart was so hopeful about the possibility that they had a chance at a lifetime of happiness and love with Grace.

"I hope she likes it," Adam murmured.

"She's gonna love it. You'll see," Jack replied. "We just need to be patient and wait for the right time. Our order will take some time. We'll just use that time with her wisely."

Clay Cook was a local craftsman who would handcraft a special engagement ring for Grace with three diamonds to represent the love each of the three of them felt for her.

Jack had cautiously brought up the idea to see how Adam and Ethan felt about it, prepared to put such a purchase off until they felt like the time was right, but they'd jumped on the idea, wanting to go ahead and have Clay get started. They were going to his shop the next afternoon to look at some designs he'd drawn up for them. This ring was going to be a one-of-a-kind work of art. Completely unique, just like Grace.

"Man," Adam said, rubbing a hand on his chest, "does anybody else get this ache in their chest just thinking about her? I want to go over there and kiss her right now."

Ethan chuckled. "That's not all I feel like doing. Right now I can still feel her in my arms, smell her scent on my shirt. If I went to her now, I don't think I could settle for just a kiss. I can almost taste her." He groaned, closing his eyes. Jack and Adam exhaled, Adam growled softly.

"I can just imagine how she tastes, and I don't mean just her mouth or her skin. What a feast," Jack said, shifting in his spot on the couch to make more room for the erection crowding his fly.

"Heaven," Adam said softly. "Hope you guys find something to occupy yourselves. I'm going to linger a while there."

"Oh, we'll keep ourselves busy enough, I'm sure. There is a lot to love about Grace," Ethan replied as he rose from the couch. "Just make her feel good. That's got to be our focus. I need a cold shower."

* * * *

Grace poured herself a cup of coffee and watched a Saturday morning news program. Curled up on the couch, she reveled in the serenity of the moment. No grumbling to turn the TV down. No worrying when Owen would come home if he'd been out all night and no worrying about what state of mind he'd be in when he got there. She'd tidied the house the day before, and it was *still* tidy today. Life was beautiful.

She looked forward to buying fresh things for her home, which felt new to her all over again. She didn't know how long it had been since she'd spent time with her sister, gossiping and laughing instead of getting hassled over how Owen treated her. She looked forward to the surprise her men had planned for her afterward, whatever it was. She had some fairly good guesses but kept them to herself because it was obvious that the men were having a good time teasing her about it. That was okay. She'd let them have their fun because turnabout was fair play.

When Charity showed up a few minutes later, Grace prepared to leave and took joy in the knowledge that the way the house looked now was the way it would look when she came home. It was a small thing, but it made her happy.

Grace and Charity hit a couple of department stores she hadn't been to in a while. She picked out new bath linens in trendy colors that *she* loved. She and Charity laughed hysterically when Grace picked up a package of black satin sheets and waggled her eyebrows at her sister. Charity leered, hanging her tongue out and giving her a thumbs-up, but in all sincerity said, "Seriously, Grace, you don't want to get satin sheets for your bed. Trust me." She shook her head like she knew what she was talking about.

"Why not? Don't you think it would be sexy to sleep on satin sheets?" She shivered wondering what Jack, Ethan, and Adam would think about her buying sexy sheets for her bed.

"Oh, they are fine for sleeping on. But there is one problem."

"What?"

"No traction."

That *could* be a problem. "Oh. I see. How do you—Oh! Too much information! Never mind. What do you recommend, then?"

"One thousand thread count Egyptian cotton. Soft as silk. You'll love them. *They'll* love them!" she said, snickering and snorting. They drew some odd looks with their laughter.

Grace splurged and bought a new comforter to match the sheets and a new mattress pad and pillows. After finding a few other odds and ends that she could use, they went to lunch. They ate at a local Mexican restaurant. Without guilt or remorse, Grace ordered her favorite. They ate, talked, and had a really good time. Grace felt bad for how stilted their rare get-togethers had gotten over the years. All Charity ever did was gripe about Owen, and Grace would just look for ways to change the subject. Now, the three men were the main focus of their conversation.

Charity quizzed Grace about the men and the plans they had for the two of them. She told Grace that Jack had called her a couple of nights before and asked her to not make any plans for that afternoon and clear it with her husband, which she did. Hoping he would let her in on the secret, she had asked him about it, but he wouldn't tell her anything at all, saying the surprise was for her as well.

"Did I tell you I saw Jack nekkid?" Grace asked, laughing when Charity nearly blew tea through her nose.

"No! When? I need details, specifics, and statistics, dammit!" The couple at the table next to them looked askance at Charity as Grace shushed her. It was a good thing they weren't having margaritas, or the whole restaurant would be able to hear.

"Last Saturday at Stigall's. I was helping him with the new suit he was buying for the funeral. I tapped on his door to hand him a pair of pants to try on, and the door popped open. He didn't realize I could see him at first. He was going commando that day." Grace whispered the last words.

"Really? Yum. So how was it?"

"Embarrassing," Grace said, being purposely obtuse.

"No! I mean, yes, I can imagine you were embarrassed. How was the *package*? Did it have 'satisfaction guaranteed' stamped on it?"

"Well, it was hard to tell," Grace whispered because the couple next to them looked at Charity again, "because it was, you know…"

"Flaccid?"

"Shhh! Yes! You are going to get us thrown out of here if you don't lower your damn voice, Charity!"

"But you must have had some idea. I mean," Charity whispered, "you're not a virgin, after all."

"Well, up until last Saturday, I would have agreed with you, but after seeing that?" Grace murmured, her cheeks flaming with heat. "We may both be wrong."

Shivery warmth spread through her whole body. What would Jack feel like filling her? Or Ethan? Or, oh, heavens, her great big gentle giant, Adam. The thought of being pinned to the bed under any of them had her panting. She shifted slightly in her chair at the shot of fiery lust that went straight to her clit.

"Okay, for the sake of clarification only, because the Good Lord knows I *really* don't want to know, but…" Charity held her index fingers out in front of her like she was measuring something. "Owen?" she whispered, holding her fingers out from each other at a distance that would have surely boosted his self-confidence had he known they were currently discussing his package.

Grace pursed her lips and reached out her hands and moved Charity's fingers much, much closer together, then a little more, aiming for accuracy. Charity's jaw dropped. Grace lifted one hand and held her thumb and forefinger in a circle, indicating girth or shocking lack thereof.

Charity leaned in and said, "And he gave you a hard time about your weight? That little prick. Ooh!" She laughed at her own joke, and Grace laughed with her.

"So, he realized I'd seen him, and he was very gracious about it, but I was really embarrassed. I had to measure him to hem his pants. I was kneeling in front of him—"

"Grace, you were kneeling?" Charity snickered with a lascivious grin.

"It's what you do to measure an inseam, Charity. What was I supposed to do?"

"Okay, so you're kneeling…"

"And I looked up."

"Yeah?"

"I was eye level with…his…erection," Grace whispered, even though the other couple had already left their table.

"Well?" Charity asked, holding up her index fingers again, being very generous. She must really like Jack. She was being positively assumptive on his behalf. Grace reached out and moved her fingers slightly farther apart, making Charity's eyes bulge.

"Oh, Mama!" was all she said for a second, but then she became thoughtful. "He probably would anyway with a cock that big, but you may need to warn him to take it slow with you the first few times. I think technically you may still *be* a virgin, Grace."

"Eeek."

Chapter Eight

Grace took a moment to just sit there and admire the men as they strode over to her car. All three were so mouth-wateringly handsome in different ways. Jack was thick, strong, and hard-muscled, ever ready with a crooked little grin. Ethan was leaner, a little taller, but emanated a powerful inner strength that resonated with some deep part of her. Adam was immense and powerful in his height and muscular strength, but he projected such an aura of gentleness she couldn't help but feel secure in his massive presence. All three of them together were a woman's fantasy come to life. She chuckled when she looked over at Charity and caught her staring, too.

"Hmmm, they must be just as anxious to see you, Grace. I swear those men are just deliciously irresistible. I know you're taking everything nice and slow with them, which I can appreciate. I don't want to see you jump into anything before you're ready. But when you take the plunge…*I want details!*"

"Charity! You're shameless!"

"Yeah, your point? I'm your sister. You know you can trust me!"

"Shhh! Here they come."

"Did you just say come?" Charity snickered.

"You are so bad, Charity." Grace giggled as she hit the button to pop open the trunk.

Jack opened the car door for her and helped her out of the car. Adam grabbed the shopping bags from the trunk, and Ethan opened Charity's door for her. Grace rose from her seat, right into Jack's arms. He leaned down and kissed her. He tasted like mint and Jack. Reaching up a palm to his cheek, she offered herself for another one. She'd wanted to tell him she loved him over the last couple of days, but she wanted to be alone with him, and she wouldn't tell him the first time over the phone.

When he finally drew back from her, Jack said, "Adam and Ethan want to tell you hello, too. Let's get inside and you can unpack. We got over early, so we have a little time before we reveal your surprise to you."

"Did you have a good morning?" Grace asked as he put his arm around her shoulder and they walked up to the steps. She loved that simple little gesture, as if just walking beside her wasn't quite enough. He needed contact with her as well.

His hand traced a pattern on her upper arm, sending goose bumps over her skin. "It was fine. We had an errand to run." He held the door open for her, and she walked into a cozy double embrace.

Charity laughed. "They *are* impatient, aren't they? At least they share well. Wonder if they *play* well together, too?" She cackled and dodged as Grace reached out a hand to pinch her, but she was wrapped up in two pairs of warm arms.

Adam kissed her lips while Ethan swept the hair from her shoulder and kissed her neck in a sweeping line up to the hollow below her ear. She was literally sandwiched in between them. It was the hottest embrace she'd ever experienced after their kisses the other night.

"Hot holy hell! I need a cold shower, girl!" Charity quipped.

"How was your morning, Gracie?" Ethan asked as she turned in the embrace to kiss him, too.

"We had a wonderful time. I bought all new bath linens, new sheets, and a comforter for my bed. I also found a few others things I liked." She slid her arm around his neck and kissed him again. Adam's arm was now wrapped around her waist as he stood behind her, kissing her shoulder.

"Did you find a computer?" Ethan asked.

"We comparison shopped, but I didn't find what I was looking for. Maybe you and I could get online and build one just the way I want it and order it? I could really use your help with that. The salesman tried to be helpful, but I think I just got more confused."

"I'd be happy to help. Are you looking forward to your surprise?" he asked her, the teasing tone back in his voice.

"You know I am. That's why we're back early. We can't wait. What are we doing?"

"We are dropping the two of you off for a spa day at Madeleine's in about twenty minutes."

* * * *

Three hours later, Grace and Charity floated into another room to have their manicures and pedicures done. Almost every available inch of their bodies had been exfoliated, oiled, and massaged. Grace could not believe how loose and relaxed she felt, having never had a massage before. Charity had a massage on a regular basis and told her Jack had paid for the very best, and they'd gotten his money's worth.

Grace's thoughts turned toward her men, not at all unusual these days. She was wrestling with a dilemma, trying to reconcile her upbringing with being involved in a romantic relationship with three men. She worried about the cool, possibly even hostile, reception that news would receive. Society's views on such things had changed over the years, becoming more progressive, but she wasn't stupid.

This relationship would affect them socially. They might all lose friends and maybe even some family relationships along the way. It would affect them financially because that was one way society showed their disapproval, and they were all vulnerable as self-employed people, including her if she bought into Harper's Embroidery.

"You are awfully serious and quiet over there," Charity said from the next recliner. "You have a crease between your eyebrows. Stop it—whatever you are thinking about—right now and relax."

Grace smiled guiltily at her sister. There wasn't much she could hide from her, and she was thankful for her, crude though she might be at times. Charity was a great judge of character, and it helped that she thought so much of Jack, Adam, and Ethan.

After manicures and pedicures, they were ushered over to have their hair shampooed, cut, and styled. Jack had given freedom to Grace to do as much or as little as she wanted. She talked with the stylist about a new shape and cut, making an appointment for a later time to have highlights put into her hair. That was something she'd always wanted to do but had dreaded Owen's typical ugly reaction to any changes or improvements she tried to make over the years. Had she really put her life on hold for the last seven years? She supposed she had. Charity opted for updating her cut a little and having it styled.

They were almost done when Madeleine came in with a garment bag and what looked like a shoe box in her hands. Madeleine took them to a dressing room with large mirrors and left them to their fun. Grace looked over at Charity, who had a knowing look in her eyes.

"Charity? What are they up to now?"

"Jack called me and asked me for your sizes. They must have gone shopping for you. Maybe that was the errand they were running this morning. Looks like you're going out to me."

Grace's heart was filled with trepidation. What was in that garment bag? What were their expectations for her? Her experiences with people buying clothing for her were not good ones. Nothing ever fit her because of the way she was shaped. She couldn't just shop for one set size. She had to buy clothing and then alter it to fit. It's what she got for inheriting her mother's hourglass figure. And would the shoes fit? What about undergarments? She got more nervous. She was in her granny gear today, like always. What if what they got wasn't what she needed?

"You know, Grace, you can work yourself up into a tizzy over what's in the bag, as well as what's in the future, or you can seize the frickin' day. Stop with the deer in the headlights look and unzip that bag before I do it myself." She was bossy, but Grace sure did love her for bringing it all back into perspective.

"Jack had me try on the shoes while you were in the bathroom back at the house because I told him our feet were the same size. They fit perfect, plus they're comfortable. Very sexy," Charity said with a wink. "Open the bag. I'm dying to see what they got you!"

Grace unzipped the bag and removed the plastic-draped hanger inside, finding a smaller shopping bag in the bottom of it. The garment bag had a store label on it. A store more expensive than she would have felt comfortable shopping in.

"There's that frown again. Stop it. Allow them to indulge you today, okay?"

"All right, but where are the price tags?"

"It's a gift, Grace. They had the saleslady remove them. Let's see what they got you."

They tore the plastic bag from the hanger. The first item was a dress. It was made of black satin and had a leopard print mesh overlay. The dress had black satin shoulder straps and a black satin Empire waist. The underskirt was a slinky, snug black satin, and the mesh overlay flowed just a few inches beyond the hemline, giving a sexy peek of upper thigh

Charity lifted the shoes from the box. They were shiny black snakeskin sandals with three-inch heels. Each had a narrow upper across the tops of the toes, and two rows of narrow straps that criss-crossed in the middle over her instep. Totally impractical and very sexy.

"I told him you had really pretty feet that you didn't show off enough except for sandals. Either they've got fantastic instincts, or they know a really great saleslady. Dressing you up is going to be so much fun. What's in the bags?"

Grace opened the larger bag on the dressing table and gasped. A pleasant little shiver rippled up her spine before descending into a warm pool in her pelvis as several silky bundles slipped from the bag.

"Holy crap, Grace," Charity whispered. "They bought you sexy lingerie. You are *so* getting laid. Oh! I love this black satin bra. Look." She lifted something from the pile. "A leopard print G-string. I wonder who picked this out for you. Adam, I bet. That naughty boy!"

"I can't wear that! My dimples."

"Yeah, you can, with this dress. You don't need a slip or anything with this style. What else is there?"

Grace had never worn a G-string and hoped there might be another option. Not that she was opposed to them. She just wasn't feeling that adventurous tonight. There was also a pair of sheer black panties that had a pretty satin bow on the back and black mesh cheeky shorts that were laced up on the sides with narrow ribbon. She decided on the panties with the sexy black satin push-up bra, which was perfect for the V-neckline of the dress.

She stripped down to nothing and put on the panties, blushing at Charity's bawdy compliments. She was beginning to feel a little daring, a little hot, and not quite like herself. She loved the bra because it did absolutely amazing things for her cleavage. There were no stockings in the bag, so she moved on to the heels. When she slid her foot into the shoe, she knew they were expensive. No shoes that looked like these could possibly be comfortable, but these were. There were no hard-stitched edges to rub against her bare foot, and the arch of the shoe fit her foot perfectly. They were made from soft leather inside and out. She was going to cherish these shoes. After she adjusted the straps, she stood and caught a glimpse of herself in the mirror from different angles and gulped, slamming her eyes shut.

"You've have always had such great posture, you know that, Grace? All those years of Mom telling us to stand up straight really paid off. *Stop it*. I see what you're doing. Open your eyes and stop looking for flaws that aren't there. We were never ever going to be stick people, you and I. We are voluptuous and beautiful. You look absolutely stunning in that lingerie and those shoes. That is *real* power. I would totally do you." Charity smirked.

"You are incorrigible, Charity, but I love you," Grace said as she removed the dress from the hanger. Charity took it from her and helped Grace put it on, careful not to mess up her hair. The bodice was snug, accentuating her curves, but the fabric had a little spandex in it, so while she felt dressed up, she was also very comfortable. She walked to the mirrors and looked at herself from different angles, and she smiled in relief at what she saw. She looked good.

Charity opened the box in the smaller bag, which came from a different store, and turned to her with big eyes.

"Don't freak out. Okay? You'll ruin your make up. Sit down."

"Why? What is that?" Grace asked, afraid to know but also dying to know.

"I'm going to put this on you. Sit down."

Charity lifted a necklace out of the box. It consisted of small gold rings interconnected to form a random pattern. It was a larger piece of jewelry than what she normally wore, but it went well with the dress. The links lay flat against her chest, glistening under the lights. There were matching dangle earrings and a bracelet as well. Charity put them on her and closed the box, holding it in her hand.

"You're not freaking out. That's good. They look beautiful on you."

"Why would I freak out, Charity?" Grace asked with a sneaking suspicion because Charity kept commenting about it.

"Because that's not costume jewelry," she replied, handing her the box from the jewelry store. "Clay Cook doesn't sell costume jewelry. All his pieces are handmade. Oh, my gosh. I'm here for one of your life-altering moments, aren't I?" Grace gazed into Charity's wide eyes in the dressing table mirror. "Boy, talk about non-verbal communication. Only a man, make that men, in love would buy something like this."

Grace put her hand up to the necklace, the cool metal warming to match the temperature of her skin. The earrings moved as she did, catching the light, along with the bracelet.

"I don't know what to say. This is too much. How can they spend so much money on me for one evening?"

"Do you *really* think this is about one evening, Grace? Really? They want you to feel special and worthy of these things. They are trying to show you they love you, and don't you *dare* tell them it's too much. Tell them you love it, the whole outfit. Tell them you love them for indulging you like that and for being so sweet and thoughtful. Accept the gift and don't mess up their blessing."

"Yes, ma'am." Grace laughed tremulously. She got up and went to stand in front of the mirrors again. Just then, there was a light tap on the door. Charity opened it and let Madeleine into the room. She took one look at Grace and gasped, her hand going to her lips.

"It's perfect on you, Grace! Mr. Warner has great taste. He chose well for you."

"With a little help from my sister, I think." She smirked at Charity.

"Hey, I only steered him in the right direction and gave him your sizes, that's all."

"Well, you look stunning, Grace. I also came to tell you they're waiting for you out front. I was instructed to call Jack when I delivered the bag to you. I'll let Jack know you'll be out when you're ready."

Madeleine left the room, and Charity hung Grace's clothing in the garment bag. When she put in Grace's sandals, she found one other parcel in the bottom.

"We almost missed this!" It was a black sequined evening bag, just large enough for her wallet, lipstick, and cell phone. Switching Grace's things for her, Charity handed her the evening bag and put her purse in the bottom of the garment bag.

Grace looked at herself in the mirror, feeling like a million bucks, and noticed that Charity was gathering up the extra panties they had purchased for her and placing them back in the shopping bag. She held up a hand and stopped her. If she was going to go for it, then she needed to really *go for it.*

“Slight change of plans, Charity.”

She reached carefully under the skirt of the dress and carefully pulled down the sheer panties she was wearing. “Hand me that G-string, sis?” she said as the black panties hit the floor and she stepped out of them.

“Change your mind, Grace?” Charity asked with a sexy laugh. “I’m totally enjoying watching you emerge from your shell. It’s about damn time, too!”

Folding the panties, Grace handed them to Charity and sat down, carefully slipping the G-string on. The barely there, open, sexy feel of the strings as they slid over her hips and bare ass was an immediate turn-on. She blushed and smiled at her reflection.

“It’s time I seized the day. Don’t you think?”

Chapter Nine

Jack glanced at Ethan and Adam standing beside him, similarly dressed in their black suits, boots, and Stetsons, before turning his gaze to the doorway, where he could hear tapping heels approaching.

With measured, slow strides, Grace entered the waiting room. His breath left him in a gust of air. Stunning. Radiant. That saleslady at the department store was definitely going to see some repeat business from the three of them. Grace looked incredibly beautiful.

"You look gorgeous, darlin'." He approached her, and the others followed.

She placed a hand on the gold necklace and said, "Thank you. You are so generous. I love it all. I feel very…precious to you. It's all so beautiful."

Jack leaned in and kissed her cheek. Ethan kissed her forehead, and Adam kissed her other cheek, each of them whispering a compliment to her.

"We have reservations in Morehead for six o'clock. Ethan has a friend there who just opened a new restaurant we'd like to take you to," Jack said.

Charity asked, "Where are you taking her?"

"Tessa's," Jack replied. "It's off the beaten path outside of Morehead. We thought she might enjoy the atmosphere."

"I think y'all have great instincts." Charity sounded pleased with their choice.

Adam carried the garment bag and the box to the back of the SUV and put them in. Jack helped Grace into the front passenger seat, his hand lingering under hers for a moment before closing the door. The others climbed in, and they returned to Grace's house. After dropping Charity off with Grace's things, they headed out to the state highway and drove toward Morehead.

* * * *

Grace turned to smile back at Adam and Ethan and then reached out a hand to Jack as he drove the SUV, stroking his strong bicep through the sleeve of his coat.

"Thank you again for my outfit and the jewelry, y'all. We both loved the spa day. I haven't felt this relaxed in…*ever*."

"We wanted to make you feel special, Grace. I'm glad you like everything," Jack replied. "A really nice saleslady helped us at the department store. We told her about you, showed her the list of sizes Charity gave us, and she helped us find the right things. Ethan found the necklace for you."

"And what did you help pick out, Adam?" Grace turned to smile at him in the back seat.

He leaned forward and gave her a little kiss. "I picked out your lingerie, baby. Did you like it?" he asked, his voice laced with desire.

"Very much. You have good taste," she replied, tentatively reaching back to touch the hand resting on his knee. He briefly clasped her fingers with his before releasing her. She glanced up into pale green eyes full of purpose and promise.

Ethan chuckled as he leaned forward from his seat. "Uh-oh. He was planning on going back and doing more shopping with that saleslady if you liked the things he picked out. Obviously, we weren't sure what your preferences were."

She turned to him and said, "Oh, I like *everything* you bought me just fine, you two. You've all got great instincts. Jack, you're all going to spoil me rotten."

"I think you could do with some more spoiling. You just let us worry about all that, all right, darlin'?" Jack drawled as he held his hand out, and she rested hers in his gentle, callused palm.

"Mmm-hmm," she murmured and settled back against the leather seat. Her body felt like it hummed from the massage and pampering, as well as the slow simmer they had her on from all the attention she was receiving. She felt beautiful, and the way they looked at her, like they needed her, made her panties damp and her folds just a little swollen. The whole night lay ahead of them, and she might combust if she didn't get her hormones under control.

They arrived at Tessa's which, like Jack said, was just a ways off the beaten path on the way into Morehead. The restaurant was nestled back in a stand of oak trees, looking as though it had been there forever. The restaurant appeared to be expensive, and she imagined couples came here to celebrate anniversaries and other special days. It didn't look like the kind of place that had a kid's menu and high chairs stacked up in a corner.

Adam opened the door for them to enter, and Ethan led the way to the *maitre d'*, who checked his list and escorted them immediately to a private booth. Grace noticed that she couldn't see any other tables once they were seated in the deep, draped enclosure.

A beautiful woman in a sleek black dress came to their table as Grace settled between Adam and Jack. Ethan rose to hug the woman and then introduced her to them. He reached for Grace's hand as he introduced her to Tessa Morgan, the owner. She was tall and thin, with full, red lips and long, perfectly straight honey-blonde hair. Her body was perfectly stereotypical of a supermodel, almost too thin.

"Tessa and I went to A&M together. She and her boyfriend and I hung out a lot. She helped me through a lot of rough patches, and we crammed for lots of exams together. Do you ever hear from Rex anymore?"

"Oh, yes," Tessa replied softly, in a sweet Southern lilt. "He came in last month when he heard about the restaurant. He's married now, and his wife is very sweet. It is a pleasure to make your acquaintance, Grace. Ethan has told me wonderful things about you. I hope you enjoy yourselves tonight. I'd better check in with your waiter now. Enjoy." She backed away from their table before turning with the grace of a supermodel in four-inch heels to see to her business.

"She's gorgeous!" Grace exclaimed, totally unabashed.

"Yes, she is," Ethan replied as he took his seat at the table. "She broke up with Rex during our junior year, but we stayed good friends. I like what she has done with this place."

"I do, too," Adam replied.

A waiter came and lit a candle arrangement and dimmed the light that was located above their table. Drapes around the back of their booth were drawn, further dampening the sound of the restaurant around them. The waiter welcomed them and told them about the featured entrees for the evening and left to fetch the wine they ordered. He returned a few minutes later and poured their wine, then took their order. He handed a cell phone to Jack, then backed from their miniature private dining room. “Enjoy your time at Tessa’s.” He reached up and closed a heavy drape over the entrance.

Jack placed the phone in his pocket and took a sip of his wine. “I’m glad you suggested this place, Ethan. Tessa has created a one-of-a-kind atmosphere out here.”

“What’s the phone for, Jack?” Grace asked softly as she took a sip of her wine.

“When each course is ready,” Jack said, “they send a text to notify whoever holds the phone, then wait for a text back on their end to let them know we’re ready. Otherwise, they don’t come to the table unless we page them for something. We’re served a gourmet meal and allowed to enjoy our meal in complete privacy. No one will come to the table unless we page them.” She was alone with them in their own little world, with the promise of privacy and no interruptions. The thought made her heart beat a little faster and the G-string a little damper.

Ethan explained further. “This booth is reserved for us for the next two and a half hours until the next party arrives, so we have plenty of time to enjoy our meal and talk to each other.”

* * * *

Ethan carefully observed Grace as they told her about the restaurant. Now that the waiter had dimmed the overhead light and lit the candles, the jewelry he’d picked for her at Clay’s shop twinkled and shimmered softly in the flickering flames of the candles. He could just make out her fluttering pulse where the rings lay over it, moving with each beat of her heart. This was just how he envisioned her when he’d seen the solid gold set in a display case. Jack and Adam had agreed they should get it for her, even though the handmade set was worth a pretty penny.

His greedy mind also wanted to see her in the necklace and other pieces with nothing else on. He imagined her straddling him, her back arched as she moved, and he wondered how she would sound when she came. He couldn’t help thinking about her that way, even though he knew that it could be a while before she let them into her bed or went home to theirs. Some primitive part of him liked the idea of her in their bed even better. Cocooned by all their warmth, keeping her safe and cared for.

"This has been a wonderful day. I feel so blessed."

"Well, darlin', the evenin' isn't over yet, is it?" Jack asked, smiling at her playfully.

"No, it's not, but I feel in my heart like things are about to change between us," she replied softly, looking up at Jack.

"What do you mean, baby?" Adam asked, looking unsure.

"I mean change in a good way."

"You mean that you're ready to move on in our relationship, don't you?" Ethan asked, understanding her perfectly. "You want to see what happens next."

She nodded. "I'm not sure about the physical aspect…" She blushed all the way down past her neckline.

Ethan saw her blush and knew what she was thinking and had to stifle an audible groan. If she was fantasizing about them naked right now, the evening was going to be long, and no amount of cold showers later would help.

"We want to make you happy, Grace," Ethan replied. "That's our main priority where you're concerned. We won't make love to you until you're ready. Once you're ready, I promise it will be good. We're not in this for a fling with you."

There! One of them had *finally* addressed the big elephant in the room. Making love to Grace. *Now* they turned the corner in their relationship. He wanted to make sure she understood they wanted something that would last with her. They wanted her forever.

"You can be satisfied with things that way? For a little while? Allow me to get to know you?"

"Don't worry about us," Jack said. "We'll wait as long as we need to. You are worth the wait, and once you're done with waiting, we'll make sure you never regret giving us your trust. I promise we'll make it good for you, darlin'."

When the pager buzzed in Jack's pocket, he responded with a quickly typed text message back to them.

"Can I ask a question, just for clarification?" she asked, grinning. "Since I don't know anything about how this will work—I mean I do, I'm not totally naïve—I want to be clear on what happens."

"What would you like to know?" Ethan asked, enjoying her blush all over again.

"Charity said I should just get everything out on the table with all of you. Is that okay?"

"Of course, baby," Adam replied. Just then, the waiter tapped and came through the curtain, carrying a large shrimp cocktail on a tray. He smiled, asked if they needed anything, and departed just as quickly.

"This is all new, and I don't want you to be put out with me for any of my questions or the things that I tell you."

"Not if you need the answers and it makes you feel better to ask and get it on the table," Jack replied.

"Have you shared a woman before?" she asked.

"We tried once, briefly, but it didn't work out," Ethan replied, already anticipating she would ask about that.

"Can I ask why?"

"She was someone I'd known who dabbled in the poly scene. There was no chemistry between her and Jack or Adam, but it was a useful experience."

"How so?"

"We realized then that we wouldn't mind sharing the right woman at some point in the future. We didn't mind being in the same room naked and having sex with the same woman. She had a good time, but we could see that the chemistry was off and chalked it up to experience. Everyone walked away wiser." Ethan took a sip from his wine glass.

"How long have you wanted a woman that would accept the three of you?"

"We've wanted this all of our adult lives," Ethan said without hesitation. "As teenage boys, the idea titillated us, of course, and provided a lot of good fantasy for masturbation, but that threesome happened about ten years ago in our mid-twenties. Because we grew up together and talked about it a lot, it became an ideal end result for when we eventually settled down. It was just a matter of meeting the right woman. Falling in love with her *and* her falling in love with all three of us as well was non-negotiable."

"Was it Tessa?"

"No. Tessa was involved in a polyamorous relationship with another girl and Rex, but it didn't last. Tessa is very jealous by nature and couldn't handle sharing Yolanda with Rex. It was not a good grouping. There was a lot of jealousy and manipulation and hurt feelings. The group eventually broke up. Down the road, her path crossed with Yolanda's again, and they gave it another try, just the two of them, this time successfully. Tessa's is their joint business venture."

"Would she be okay with you telling me her story?"

"I explained the hopes that we have, and she gave me carte blanche to tell all if it helps you to hear the story of another."

"Have you ever been with Tessa, just the two of you?"

"No, she's just my friend. Were you going to worry about whether or not we ever had sex?"

"Yes."

Ethan grinned. "Then I'm glad you asked. I have never been in a committed relationship before. Only short-term ones that for various reasons didn't work out. *This* has always been what I wanted. No girlfriends are going to come out of the closet. Better?"

"Very much. How will the sex work?" she asked bluntly. "Sore subject?" They groaned, and she put her hands on her blushing cheeks as she waited for the answer.

Ethan knew this was probably a big obstacle for her, so he jumped right in like a high school health teacher, explaining, very dryly, the basic mechanics. Vaginal penetration, anal penetration, if—and he stressed *only* if—she was interested in it, oral sex, for her and for them, at the same time if she wanted it that way. Then he made the most important point.

"If you were content to make love with us individually and separately and that was the most you could handle, we'd be content. If you were willing to make love to us all and sleep all together in one bed, sharing oral sex and trusting us to make our experiences together good for you, we would be lucky bastards. If occasionally you wanted to let us all make love to you at the same time, we would know heaven on earth. The only way it will work is if we have earned your trust as well as your love."

She appeared to think for a moment. "I can tell you right now I'm *not* interested in musical beds. I haven't done much research but have read a few erotic romances, and I relish the thought of sleeping tucked in amongst the three of you."

"You've looked into this lifestyle before?" Ethan asked, intrigued.

"Read about it only. I have to confess, I am turned on by the notion of making love with you at the same time. It's only ever been a fantasy, and now I've been presented with a dream come true."

"We'd make it good for you, baby. You'd never be left hanging," Adam added.

"I do have some issues I need to bring up with you. I want to be as upfront as I can so there are no surprises later."

"What's the first one?"

"I know one thing about myself that will never change. So don't ever, *ever* ask it of me."

They all leaned forward, and Ethan was ready to deal with whatever bomb she was going to drop on them.

Chapter Ten

"You are all fine with sharing me, and I'm happy because of it. But I will never, *never* share you. You bring another woman to my bed or your bed, and it is over between us. *Finito. Finale.* I was never jealous over Owen, but when I think of you with another woman, *any of you*, it feels like I'm swallowing razor blades. If I'm asking too much of you by telling you this, you need to say something now."

There were pained expressions on their faces. Her heart dropped into her stomach, and she experienced such an adrenaline rush that it felt like frozen ants were crawling over her skin. Had they been hoping for that? To increase their little foursome eventually? She looked at them and began to pant, needing to get up, to get away!

Ever observant, Ethan put a hand on her shoulder and shook his head. "That's not where we were going with this. If you want us, we would have no other. We would never bring someone new into our bed, female *or* male. You are *it* for us, Gracie, the beginning and the end of what we want in our lives. Bringing anyone else into our bed would be like cheating. It's only you, honey. Okay?"

She heaved a big sigh of relief. That was a biggie. Okay. She'd been ready to bolt.

Thunder rumbled in the distance, and Grace could feel it tremble up through her body. She wanted to be sure of what she was doing before she gave herself to them physically. Her heart was already involved. There was no doubt of that. Once she flipped that switch, there was no going back. She had a feeling they would ruin her for all others, and if it didn't work out she would be shattered. There was no fear in her heart where they were concerned, maybe just fear of the unknown and some lingering trust issues that needed to be tested.

"Ready for the next one?" she asked, looking at their adorable faces, braced for whatever was coming next. They looked so concerned. She reached out to the shrimp cocktail and dipped one in the cocktail sauce. She fed it to Jack with her fingers, touching his lips with her fingertips as she did.

"I've never had anal sex before."

Ethan smiled at her with a seductive twinkle in his eyes. "You see that as an issue, Gracie, but to us that means we would be the *first* ones to share that pleasure with you. If it's something you want to try, we would be very careful with you and make sure you were ready and able to handle it. We would never make you feel obligated or forced."

She glanced at Jack and Adam, and they seemed equally pleased.

"Good. I'll let you know when I'm ready," she replied. "There is something y'all need to know. It has to do with Owen. I'm sure that Jack has probably told you that I saw him nekkid. Yes?"

"You going somewhere with this train of thought, darlin?" Jack asked, looking a little confused by the direction of the conversation.

"I learned something that day, Jack," she said with a big smirk. Jack chuckled. She picked up another shrimp, dipped it, and reached out to Ethan this time. He licked her finger as he took it from her without using his hands. When she felt his tongue, she literally felt her clit throb. At the rate they were going, she was going to get the seat wet.

"The first few times with me, you're going to need to be sort of patient while I get accustomed to you," she emphasized "you," holding up her index fingers as a reference, "because I am use to something a little *less than.*" She reduced her reference to one hand, a short distance between her index finger and thumb. Understanding dawned on all their faces, and she could see that they took this as good news.

"We'll take as much time as you need and stop if you say to," Jack said, the others nodding. "Hurting you is the last thing we ever want to do."

A ripple of excitement wove itself into the current of sexual tension that filled the air. They were happy about her news. Good.

She selected a shrimp for Adam and dipped it in the sauce, purposely getting a little on her fingertips. She might have gotten too much on them, but she saw the anticipation in his eyes, knowing it was his turn. When her hand got close, he closed his fingers around hers, taking the shrimp from her, then sucking her fingers into his mouth, paying special attention to each one, then releasing each of them with a little pop. The tremor started in her neck and went straight down her back, and she let loose a little moan as he tongued her index finger. *Merciful heavens.* The gleam in his eyes sent heat straight to her clit.

He leaned over to her and said, "I wish it was you I was tasting right now." He released her fingers.

She closed her eyes, her breath coming in a ragged pant at his erotic words and the imagery they conjured up.

She needed to focus. She still had other questions to ask. "I think I already know the answer to this one, but I need to make sure. Don't want any surprises when we're already nekkid, right?" They grinned, seeming to relax a bit. "You all want to make love to me, like I want you, but you're not…"

"Gay?" Ethan asked. "No. We don't go there, ever. We don't judge men for wanting that, but we do not love each other in that way."

"Fuck no," Adam muttered.

Jack just laughed and shook his head in the negative at her.

"But," Ethan said, "speaking only for myself, I can tell you that watching Adam or Jack make love to you will be a total and complete turn-on for me. I have no problem with them in the room, in the bed, or with you, just not in my ass. We love each other, but it is brotherly love, not romantic love like we have for you."

"Good because I'm not sure what I would do with *that,*" she stated simply, making them all laugh.

The pager went off in Jack's pocket. The entrees were ready. He texted them back to bring them to the table.

Grace remembered one other important issue. "Just so you know for your own peace of mind, I have yearly exams and get screened for STDs at every visit. My last doctor's appointment was in April, and all test results were negative. I was never sure how faithful Owen was because he went out a lot on his own. We always used condoms, and the last time I allowed him to touch me was back in February. I'm on the pill. You can relax now. I think I'm done." She laughed, crossing her legs and smoothing out her skirt.

"We always use condoms when we have sex," Ethan said, "and we will with you, if you want us to. We can make an appointment to be tested, if it would make you more comfortable. It's been a while for all of us since we were with anyone. Work keeps us pretty busy, and most of the women I spend my time around are not women I'm interested in dating. We've been looking for the right one for a while. I'll make a call, and we'll all see the doctor so that you know we're safe. Then maybe condoms would be completely unnecessary?"

She nodded at him gratefully, seeing that he understood her need without her having to make it an issue for them to be tested again. It was unromantic but necessary.

Ethan leaned over the table and kissed her, stroking her tongue with his. She could taste a hint of the cocktail sauce and his natural essence. Then he nuzzled the hollow under her ear as she picked up another shrimp, dipping it in the sauce for Jack and wetting her fingers because he might like the extra sauce, too. He opened for her, leaving his arm around her shoulders. She put the shrimp in his mouth, and he sucked the cocktail sauce from her fingers. The inside of his lip and his tongue were slick and warm. When his tongue rubbed against the pads of her fingertips, it tickled deliciously.

She closed her eyes and sighed shakily, wondering if people ever lost control of themselves in this booth and went ahead and took advantage of the privacy. Jack surprised her when, after finishing the shrimp, he swooped in for a kiss.

There was a light tap outside the drape, and moments later, the waiter brought in a tray loaded down with their plates. He served them efficiently and refilled their wine, then exited. Jack and Adam looked each other in the eye, and Jack nodded at her plate. Adam picked up her steak knife and fork and began to cut off a few pieces of her tenderloin. She turned to Jack questioningly.

He pushed the dinner table, which must have been on small casters, away from him just a little and patted his lap. She hesitated briefly, but the excuse never left her lips. "No regrets" was one of her new rules, starting tonight. She needed to take a chance with these wonderful men. She knew Jack would accept her excuse if it made her uncomfortable, but he *wanted* her in his lap. By damn, she was going in his lap. She knew she'd look back and regret it if she didn't do this.

He helped her get situated, and then Adam and Ethan pulled the table back to them and moved closer.

"Have you tried the shrimp, Grace? You've been so busy feeding them to us, you haven't had any," Jack murmured next to her ear. He picked up a shrimp and dipped it in the sauce. He held it out to her, and she opened her mouth for it, brushing her bottom lip against the pad of his thumb as she did. She held eye contact with him as she chewed, feeling very sexy as he watched her lips.

Adam moved a little closer, took another shrimp, dipped it, and held it out to her. As she finished chewing the first one, a little drip of the cocktail sauce on the second one landed on the upper swell of her breast, very near her cleavage.

She reached for her napkin, but Jack gently stopped her, placing a hand over hers. "Let me," he whispered huskily.

With a shuddering breath, she watched as he leaned down to her breast above her neckline and lapped the cocktail sauce right off of her with a slow, unhurried sweep of his warm, wet tongue. She was sitting in his lap sideways so that she faced the other two. The feeling of his warm tongue and lips on her breast forced a low moan from her throat. She hoped like crazy no one heard her from outside the booth because she couldn't help it.

The gentle, sensual care her men gave her reduced her to putty in their hands. If they suggested leaving and returning to the ranch right now, the only questions in her mind would have been whose bed was she going in and who was first. Jack's tongue did a very thorough job of removing the cocktail sauce, going above and beyond what was strictly necessary to clean her up. She felt sure that in such close proximity he must be able to hear her heart pounding. She leaned her head against his shoulder, closing her eyes, lost in the moment. She felt warm fingers clasp with hers on her thigh as she reached out and stroked her fingertips through Jack's silky black hair. Both of Jack's arms were around her, and she realized Adam must have taken her hand when she reached out.

Jack shifted in his seat, and when he did, she felt his growing erection pressing against her backside. For just a moment, she fantasized about turning in his lap and straddling him. Unzipping his zipper and sliding her wet folds up his warm, hard cock, then taking him inside of her swollen, needy body. He groaned as he sat back up, giving his head a slight shake.

"She must taste really good, Ethan," Adam said, like it was just normal table conversation. "What does she taste like, Jack?"

With another sound, like a growl low in his chest, Jack replied, "Grace tastes like oranges and cream. Did they use flavored massage oil on you at the spa today?"

Unable to give them a more detailed answer, she simply nodded and sighed in affirmation.

Answering groans were their only responses. She looked at them through hooded eyes, her head still against Jack's shoulder. Up until this point, his discussion of her taste was the single most erotic moment of her life, but it also felt like only the beginning of something far more powerful than she could have imagined. She was swept away in the emotion of it and felt her body respond to them all, feeling the wetness from her juices on her thighs. The faint stirrings of an impending orgasm hummed in her, muscles tightening and clenching. One touch and she'd come right on the spot.

"That sounds like dessert to me," Adam said, "but I want to know what her sweet honey tastes like. That's a dessert I'd take hours to feast on." His hand now trailed gently up her arm.

"Would you like that, Grace?" Jack asked. "Would you like to feel Adam's lips and his tongue feasting on the warm honey flowing from your luscious little pussy? I'll bet your wet right now, aren't you, darlin'?"

She looked up into Jack's ocean blue eyes, feeling completely vulnerable with him, and whispered softly, "Yes."

Ethan said, "Why don't we let our girl eat her steak?" He grinned at her when she cast him an evil look. "She's going to need her energy, and the food is getting cold. We have the whole evening ahead of us, plenty of time for playing in a while."

Dammit, the food could wait a few minutes! Grace caught her breath and sat up from her reclining position as Ethan picked up her fork and held up a bite of steak for her to try.

"Is it done to your liking?" he asked as he speared a small piece of asparagus.

She nodded. "Rare, just the way I like it. It's very good. Thank you, Ethan." She'd wanted to kick him earlier when he'd put the brakes on, but now she was grateful. They did have the whole night ahead of them, and she had been in too much of a rush earlier. She took the next bite from him, and they began cutting into their own steaks. They took turns feeding her bites of her steak and the vegetables while they ate their own. The filet was tender and cooked perfectly rare all the way through.

Adam was staring at her with that devilish grin in his eyes again. She wondered what direction his thoughts were going in as he chewed a bite of his filet mignon.

"You look beautiful tonight, Grace," Adam said. Jack and Ethan agreed enthusiastically. "But you know the question I'm dying to ask, don't you?" He grinned when she laughed and nodded.

She suspected Adam had been fantasizing about which pair of panties she'd chosen to wear. Giving her multiple choices gave his imagination room to speculate. "I wondered how long it would take you to ask."

She grinned up at Jack, his eyes twinkling at her because he already knew the answer to the question. He'd been caressing the string across her hip for the last few minutes ever since he found it, his erection getting harder still against her bottom.

"What does Adam want to know?" Ethan asked her, grinning at her as he took another bite.

"*Adam* wants to know what she has on under that pretty dress," Adam replied.

Nodding and noting she had their full attention, she said, "You were so generous with your purchases that I had several pieces of lingerie from which I could choose. It was hard to make up my mind, and I changed it once before finally deciding."

"Are they the panties with the little bow on the back?" Adam asked, going for the most modest choice first.

"Uh-uh," Grace replied, very glad she'd changed her mind just to enjoy this moment with them.

"Are they the little undies that lace up on the sides?" Adam asked as Ethan moaned.

"Uh-uh," she replied slowly, shaking her head, taking immense pleasure in the way Adam's eyes rolled back and his head fell back on the seat.

He closed his eyes and said, "You're wearing the leopard print G-string, aren't you?" He leveled his heated gaze at her, his eyes filled with lust. "This woman is perfect. Sexy. Daring. Perfect."

Jack shook his head. "We tried to talk him out of it, sure that you wouldn't want to wear something like that. We were stupid. Now for sure he's going back to that store to do more shopping. I think we've created a monster." He chuckled.

"What was that saleslady's name?" Adam asked.

"June, I think," Ethan replied.

"My guess is that she's wearing that black lace bra. The sheer one with the plunging neckline," Jack said, stroking her cleavage with a finger.

"You got it right on the first guess," she replied sweetly. *Sparky gets a gold star!*

"Does that mean I get a reward?" he asked playfully. She grinned and kissed his cheek. Ethan fed her another bite of steak, and she looked at them, wondering how she got so lucky as to be wanted by all three. It no longer felt strange to think that at all.

"This is the prettiest outfit I've ever worn. Do you want to know what my favorite part is?" she asked.

"What, darlin'?" Jack asked.

She lifted one of her sexily shod feet and rested her calf across Adam's lap, placing her foot very carefully in Ethan's hand as he reached for it.

"These shoes," she said, enjoying the feel of her foot in Ethan's hands as he stroked her arch through the straps. "They are beautiful and fit well. It's impossible to find shoes that feel this comfortable and also look this good without spending a fortune. I could dance all night in these shoes."

"Well, that can be arranged, baby," Adam said as his warm, callused hand glided up and down her smooth calf. His erection was hard against her leg. He made no move to remove it from his lap, however, so she added the other just to see what would happen.

Ethan continued caressing her insteps. "Even though June didn't make a commission because it wasn't her department, she helped us find the shoes, too. She showed us which ones she thought would work."

"I've got to meet June someday. She's got great instincts, I think."

"You have the prettiest feet, Grace. Has anyone ever told you that?" Ethan asked. "Look at her pretty little red toenails, Jack. Wouldn't you just love to suck on them?"

"I'd start there, but that's not where I'd stop," he replied, sliding his finger across the string at her hip again, sending a shiver straight to her clit.

There was that humming in her pussy again. She sighed and rested her head against Jack's chest. The pager went off again. Dessert was ready. He texted them back to bring it.

A moment later, the waiter tapped outside before bringing in their desserts. She had been so distracted by their attention that she had not eaten very much, but she felt filled and content as she nibbled, totally relaxed in their arms. She wondered what the waiter thought when he came in with dessert, but he didn't seem to notice or think anything of it to find her draped across them so casually. They shared theirs with her, feeding her little bites, and she fed them from hers, too.

Adam and Ethan had continued their caresses, growing more daring throughout the dessert course. Her breathing was more like panting now as she rested her head against Jack's shoulder again.

Jack had grown progressively bolder as well. He turned to look into her eyes. "They are done serving us for now and won't be bothering us again. We have this table for another forty-five minutes. We can take you dancing if that's what you want to do tonight, but if you'd like, we can stay here and enjoy some time together first. We love being with you, Grace." His voice was husky with emotion and desire.

Ethan leaned forward, caressing her cheek. "Would you let us make you feel good?" he asked, searching her eyes.

She knew what they meant because she could see the desire in their eyes, feel their hot hands on her legs. She felt her insides tightening up like a rubber band waiting to be released. She felt a rush of heat and wetness at her pussy just listening to his voice. Ethan's hand moved up to her calves, and one of Adam's rested on her inner thigh, stroking her.

She looked up into Jack's eyes. "Yes, I would, but…"

"But what, darlin'?" Jack asked, smoothing a lock of hair from her cheek, his movements slow and purposeful.

"What if someone hears?" she asked, blushing. She had no idea how far away the next customers were. "What if I lose control and they hear me?" The last of her inhibitions were being stroked away by Ethan and Adam's soothing hands.

"These drapes are very heavy, made to block sound. But trust us to take care of that, Gracie," Ethan said. "Jack will help you, won't you?"

“Of course, darlin’.” Jack nuzzled her throat. “Put yourself in our hands, and it will be better than you’ve ever imagined.”

Ethan quietly pushed the table away and knelt in front of her on the carpet.

“Are you wet for us, baby?” Adam whispered to her, his words sending little vibrations through her pussy. She loved that they were so verbal with her like this. She’d wondered if they talked like this during their lovemaking. His hand grew bolder, sliding up her thighs under the skirt, making her shiver in delight.

“Your skin is like silk, so soft and warm,” he whispered, his rough fingertips finding the edge of the G-string. “I can’t tell you how happy it makes me that you wore this. Do you trust us, baby?”

“You know I do, Adam. Please—” Her breath hitched, waiting for him to do something, *anything*. The need for their touch had become desperate.

Jack whispered in her ear, “Please what, darlin’?”

“I need your hands on me. I need you touching me, please,” she whispered. Her head fell back against Jack’s shoulder. Her hands reached back to his neck and his shoulder, tilting her breasts up to him.

Jack’s lips found hers, searing her with a passionate kiss, and his tongue swept over hers. Ethan’s fingers slowly caressed up her calves and parted her knees. He leaned toward the table and blew out a couple of the candles, reducing the light.

She looped her right hand back around Jack’s neck as she arched to receive his kiss, reaching out with the other and feathering it into Adam’s short brown hair. She’d grown embarrassingly damp in the last few minutes, and her breath stuttered, her abdomen jolting as she felt Adam’s fingers take hold of the G-string. She lifted in Jack’s lap with his help as Adam eased the G-string down her hips, groaning as he drew the wet scrap of silk from her.

“Oh, honey. You’re soaked,” Adam said.

“I ache, please, please, something—” she whispered with a little sob.

“Baby, we’re going to make you feel so good. I promise,” he whispered soulfully.

He leaned forward and kissed her, and her lips trembled against his. He slid his hand back up her thigh after handing the G-string to Ethan. Her breathing hitched as his fingers slowly made their way to the tops of her thighs and over her mound before sliding down into the damp blonde curls between her legs. She parted her thighs to give him better access, moaning softly in anticipation. His fingers slid down over her damp lips, barely teasing into the opening there. She gasped against Jack's neck as he leaned to kiss her again, covering her moan with his mouth.

"Baby, you're so hot and wet, I could slip right into you with no problem. You're going to love it when we make love to you, slow and easy, just the way you want it. Now I can finally know what you taste like." Adam stunned her by sliding the fingers that had just been in her entrance into his mouth. She hadn't believed he would really do that, would *want* to know what she tasted like. But his eyes slid closed as if he liked it very much, and she felt a fresh rush of moisture at the incredibly erotic notion.

"How does she taste, Adam?" Ethan asked, his voice sounding husky with need.

"Like the sweetest honey in the world," Adam murmured softly. "Like heaven. Like the woman we imagined we would love." His fingers returned to her hips, shifting her first as Jack began to lift her skirt up and out of the way.

Jack softly said, "Let us see all of you, this beautiful part of you. Ethan, isn't she perfect?" Jack's voice sounded reverent, and the knowledge that all three men feasted their eyes on her was unspeakably erotic.

She felt Adam's fingertips at her slit again, opening her gently and stroking through her wet folds. Her head fell back limply, her eyelids slid closed, and all she could do was breathe and feel.

"I can see how wet she is. Look how she glistens in the light from the candles. She's close already, Adam. Her clit is so swollen. Why don't you make her feel better? Give her what she needs from you?" Ethan's seductive words swamped Grace with such desire the muscles in her pussy clenched, and an orgasm loomed heavily over her like a tidal wave, growing taller with each word.

"Listen to her, Jack. She's so responsive. I love this woman," Adam said softly as his fingertips delved into her pussy, avoiding the one spot where she craved his touch the most. She felt his warm fingers slide a tiny bit into her cunt, swirling through her slick heat. Ethan shifted and came to kneel beside her, and she laced her fingers into his long brown hair. Jack held her, and they looked down to where Adam leaned over her. He looked up at her briefly, silently asking her permission. She nodded at him and panted with anticipation. He gently slid a finger into her as he leaned down toward her aching clit.

"Oh, Grace, you're so tight, even on my finger, so hot and tight. Can you imagine how it will feel when I slide my cock into you?" Adam murmured before his hot tongue delved into her entrance for the first time, then swirled its way slowly up to her clitoris, circling a few times.

Her head fell back against Jack's chest. Her lips opened as she panted in growing ecstasy. Her back arched as his tongue flicked purposefully over her clit, sending the orgasm crashing over her, continually lapping as her body rode each pulse. Jack claimed the long, soft moan, the only sound she made, as her body came down from the first man-induced orgasm she'd ever had.

"So beautiful, Grace. You are just incredible when you come. Making love to you is going to be like heaven," Ethan whispered to her.

Self-induced orgasms were more a means of relaxation for her and had never ever been this intense. This was the first time a man had ever brought her to such a point. She smiled euphorically as she caught her breath.

Jack kissed the crown of her head. "Darlin', we love you so much. We'll always do our best to make you feel good. Did you like that?"

She moaned softly as Adam continued to gently lick her. "We know that Adam liked it, judging by how much he's enjoying feasting on you even now. You may have a hard time keeping your panties on now that he knows what you taste like."

A small aftershock hit her as Adam's tongue lazily lapped her clit one last time, and his talented fingers caressed her mound before withdrawing. He looked like he was in a daze, almost drugged.

"That good, huh, Adam?" Ethan asked, smiling.

Adam nodded, his eyes heavy lidded.

It occurred to Grace that though he had just brought her to an earth-shaking release, he'd had none. She attempted feebly to rise to a sitting position and reached for him.

"Adam, that was…amazing, but you must be in agony, all of you," she whispered, looking at each of them. "I've had my release, and you've been left hanging. You promised to never do that to me, and I want to do the same for you."

She looked at them as they shook their heads. She reached out and laid her palm against Adam's cheek. "Why, if I am willing to do that, would you not agree? I know this is painful for you."

"Today and tonight are all about you, Grace," Adam explained, turning his lips into her palm to kiss it. "We want you to see what it could be like if you let us take care of you. If you let us love you. Believe me, if you accept us, there will be plenty of give and take among us, but tonight is about us giving to you and you taking for a change."

"We need to let Gracie sit up and take a little break," Ethan said, helping Adam with her skirt. She gratefully accepted their help because her legs had turned to jelly. "How do you feel?"

She looked at the three of them, one at a time, enjoying the humming sensation that still rang through her body. Their vulnerability showed in their hopeful eyes, and she knew she was theirs.

I want to be theirs. Completely.

In turn, she put her hands on their cheeks or their chins, reaching out to kiss them one at a time, sweet, gentle kisses not meant to entice them further but to thank them.

"I have never been loved like that before in my whole life," she started to say. Her chin wobbled, but she willed it to stop. "And if loving you and giving myself to the three of you is anything like what I just experienced in your hands, then I'm *yours*, all of me."

They beamed at her, hugging her all at once.

Ethan picked up the G-string he'd laid on the table earlier and said, "Let's take our girl dancing. What do you say, guys?"

They nodded.

"What about you and Ethan, Jack? I feel bad for leaving you unsatisfied." She knew that all three of them must be very uncomfortable. Maybe they'd rather return to the privacy of one of their homes. "Is dancing what you wanted to do?"

Jack cocked an eyebrow at her and smiled a crooked grin. "Evening's not over yet, darlin'."

She giggled softly.

The evening was definitely not over. Hell yeah! Carpe diem*, y'all.*

Feeling playful, Grace pulled her skirt up a little higher and raised a foot, carefully inserting it through the opening Ethan's hands made in the G-string. Hitching the skirt a still higher, she raised the other foot and leaned back slightly to insert that high heel through the other string, giving all three of them a perfect little peep show of what lay between her thighs. She grinned when their mouths all popped open, a little slack in the jaws.

She stood up then, the three of them before her, and waited as Ethan slowly eased the G-string back up her thighs. The strings were hooked over his thumbs, so when he slid it over her ass and hips, it was as if he was caressing her with his open palms. Once he had it in place for her, she adjusted it and gave a little wiggle before dropping her skirt into place. They knelt there mutely as she completed that little maneuver, looking like they were about to drool. It did a girl's heart good to experience that kind of power at least once.

She reached for her evening bag and then smiled at them as they rose to their feet. Jack held out a hand to her as Adam and Ethan opened the heavy drapes and led the way out. Jack and Grace followed behind them.

"Do I look all right?" she asked. She only had the small mirror in her evening bag to go by and didn't want to walk back into public looking like she'd just had a roll in the hay.

"You look beautiful, Grace, but the ladies' room is right here if you'd like to stop in for a second while we pay the bill." He gestured to a door down a short hallway.

She made use of the facilities and fluffed her hair a little. The three of them waited for her outside the hallway, Jack once more taking her hand as the others led the way. Tessa wished them a good evening, smiled, and nodded to Grace.

The sun had set while they'd been in the restaurant, and though she heard more thunder, it still hadn't rained. Lightning danced behind the clouds, making them appear red in some places. She paused in the dark parking lot to watch. Storms had always spooked her a little, but she loved to watch lightning. When it flashed brightly again, she could see how tall the thunderheads had built up. There was dangerous potential in that storm, but it was glorious to watch from a distance. Ethan helped her into the back seat before climbing in with her while Adam took the front seat.

Grace found it interesting and oddly comforting the way they orchestrated their positions in relation to her. She was glad they didn't discuss who got to sit where in front of her, much the same way they didn't discuss the fact that Adam was the first of them to be intimate with her, even if it was only oral sex. She didn't want to hear them work out those details and appreciated the way things seemed to happen naturally between them.

She scooted into the middle so she could be next to Ethan. As Jack pulled out of the parking lot, Ethan laid his arm on the back of the seat around her shoulders. She felt so warm and happy curled into his embrace. She could faintly smell his cologne and his own clean scent as she laid her head against him.

"I didn't tell y'all how handsome you look in your dark suits and cowboy hats, did I?"

"Thank you, darlin,'" Jack said as he caught her gaze in the rearview mirror. "We dressed up to make you happy. I'm glad we pleased you."

"You all look yummy."

"Same goes for you, baby." Adam looked back at her with a tender smile and reached out to caress her knee.

She reached out and covered his warm hand with hers for a second before reaching to place it on Ethan's solid chest.

She leaned her head back to whisper in his ear, "Thanks for answering all my questions and being honest, Ethan, and for the little things you did like blowing out some of those candles. I was nervous about y'all seeing me like that. You helped make it beautiful."

"You're welcome, Gracie. You were stunning tonight. I confess I can't wait for a chance to taste you, to see you come undone like that for me and know that you trust me. I love you." He slid his hand along her jawline, kissing her tenderly. His tongue swept against hers, and the passion of their kiss increased. He placed his gentle, callused hand over the gold necklace and her pounding heart. "Your heart is safe with me, Grace."

Chapter Eleven

Ethan felt energized and excited as he sat in the backseat with Grace. During the drive back to town, he thought back to the moment she'd come in Adam's embrace, his lips on her pussy, his tongue dragging on her clit. Ethan looked up at her face at the moment when it happened. Her head had been thrown back, her sweet lips parted with her faltering, gasping breaths as she climaxed, her hair falling back over Jack's coat sleeve in golden waves. Pleasuring her was going to be just exactly that—pure pleasure.

He couldn't believe she was there in his arms right now. So soft and warm, smelling sweetly of her shampoo and the orange and cream massage oil they used on her earlier. They really had come to a turning point in their relationship and then celebrated it with true intent. He looked forward to dancing with her. Any time he spent pressed up against her was time well spent.

* * * *

Adam looked back at Ethan holding Grace in his arms as they sped down the state highway. Ethan looked so content with Grace quietly curled up beside him. She was really something. She stirred feelings in Adam's heart that he'd always thought were silliness—thoughts of wanting to protect her and defend her against any who would harm her. A primitive part of him acknowledged that he could and would kill to protect her. He'd wanted to kill Owen on that deep primitive level because he had struck her. Adam had felt the murderous urge well up in him when the back of Owen's hand had made contact with Grace's precious cheek.

He was happy they had ordered her ring today even though they'd had no indicator she would accept their proposal. After talking to her and having the chance to pleasure her, he was very hopeful. He loved her so much his soul overflowed with it. He remembered the taste of her, and her scent still filled his nostrils. He was engulfed with desire for her all over again. Her taste was sweet, warm, and womanly. He felt happy for his brothers that maybe soon they would know that same luxury and feel the same pleasure of reveling in her like that.

He adored Grace and felt only gratitude toward Jack and Ethan for allowing him to know her intimately first. It felt right to see her in his brothers' arms, and he was happy they would soon know that same pleasure with her.

* * * *

Grace shivered lightly as Ethan stroked the back of her neck with gentle fingertips, noting that they were nearing Divine again, and wished the ride were just a few minutes longer. She would sit still for Ethan's petting all night.

Jack looked in the rearview mirror at them and asked, "The Dancing Pony, Ethan? Or would y'all rather go somewhere less crowded?"

"The choice should be Grace's, I think. Don't y'all?" At their nods, Ethan turned to Grace. "Everyone knows us at The Dancing Pony. Are you okay with being seen with the three of us together?" Ethan asked.

She wondered how they would handle situations like this out in public. If they were open about their feelings for her, people would talk.

"Are you okay with being seen with me?" she asked.

"Well, of course we are," Ethan replied easily. "We're proud to be out with you."

"I know we aren't going to get warm approval from everyone in there or in town in the future, for that matter. I'm not that naïve. But if I act like a lady and y'all do your best to act like gentlemen, *at least in there,*" she added with a smirk, "then what can they say about us? The only opinions that matter are yours. I'd be proud to walk in your club with you, Ethan, and you, too, Adam and Jack."

They pulled into the parking lot of The Dancing Pony, which was full to overflowing, and parked. She took Ethan's hand when he offered it to her, climbing from the back seat.

"You look gorgeous, Gracie," he said to her and led her to the front door.

Loud music and voices poured out as Adam opened the door. Jack and Adam entered first, Ethan and Grace right behind them. She felt Ethan's large hand at the base of her spine, just above her ass, and had to smile at the intimacy of it. He did it in a way that was possessive without being improper.

Jack led the way to a table, greeting several friends along the way. A waitress came and took their order as a loud country and western dance song thumped a fast beat. Couples twirled and two-stepped past their table at the edge of the dance floor.

She settled in her seat as Ethan held it for her, laying her evening bag on the table. Ethan put his hand on hers. "Why don't I lock that in my office so you won't worry about it since you're going to be on the dance floor tonight?"

"All right. How did you know I was thinking that?"

"I figured you would wonder what to do with it." He leaned down and kissed her, and she handed it to him. He made his way through the crowd to his office and was back by the time the waitress brought their drinks.

Grace took a sip of the sangria he ordered for her. That was his thoughtfulness showing again, in remembering that she liked the sweet fruit juice and red wine combination.

A new song came on at a slower, more romantic tempo, and Ethan held out his hand to her. "Dance with me?"

"I thought you'd never ask."

He pulled her gently to him and twirled off to the romantic words of Brad Paisley's "Then."

* * * *

Jack sipped from his beer while he and Adam watched Grace look up into Ethan's eyes and say something softly in his ear. The lights reflected from the mirrored ball overhead glinted in the waves of her pretty blonde hair. Jack remembered the silken feel of it against his lips as he'd listened to her sexy moans when she came earlier. Holding her precious little body as she shook with her climax and the way she moved in his arms was now committed to sweet, cherished memory. He remembered, too, the way the warm, sweet flesh of her breast had tasted and the sound of her heart pounding in his ear.

He watched as Ethan smiled down at her and kissed her. They moved well together. Jack was happy that she could dance. He could remember as a kid his mom and sister, Anne, had taught him and told him, “You’ll thank us some day.” He’d complained, saying he wasn’t any good at it. They’d encouraged him, saying that it took practice, like anything else. His mom had to be in heaven looking down on him, saying, “You’re welcome,” because she’d been right about so many things. She’d certainly been right about Grace. He knew it now. She was the one. They were all sure.

“Are you as smitten by that angel as I am?” Jack rested his chin in his hand as he watched her dance.

Adam sat next to him, so Jack could hear him perfectly, even over the music. “She’s ruined me for all others.”

He could hear his brother’s heart in his voice. “But you’re not complaining, are you?” Jack asked with an indulgent grin.

“Hell no. I’ve been to heaven tonight, and spending a little more time with her is all I want. You need to dance with her next time. You’ve been letting us have a lot of her attention. She needs some of yours, too, but I appreciate it, man, for not going alpha male on us.”

“I want y’all to have her attention right now because you have time to make up for with her. Y’all let me monopolize her time at the funeral. If I hadn’t had her to hold on to, it would have been much harder. She was a comfort to Mom in the last few years, and she was to me that day, too. I want us all to be happy together, loving her.”

“Yeah, but I still ain’t doin’ ya,” Adam said, laughing into his beer.

Jack laughed, too, and slipped his jacket off. When he folded it and hung it over the arm of the tall chair, he could smell the scent of her clinging to it. He sniffed it, smiling.

“I still smell her, too.” Adam’s eyes were focused far away.

“I’ll just bet you do, man,” Jack smirked. “Lucky bastard.”

“You have no idea how lucky, but hopefully soon,” he said quietly as Ethan returned her to her chair when the song ended. They couldn’t have picked a more perfect song, judging by her dreamy eyes.

Jack smiled at her and stroked her shoulder. “You having fun, darlin’?”

"I am. Will you dance with me, Jack?" she asked as she twined her slender fingers between his big callused ones.

"I'd love to, darlin'."

* * * *

Ethan sat back down in his chair, doing as Jack had done and removing his jacket, and hung it over the arm of his chair.

"What's up, Ethan?" Adam asked, knowing by the way Ethan scanned the room that something was amiss.

"There are a lot of faces in here tonight that I don't recognize and some that I unfortunately do. Plus, Patricia and her girlfriends are here, which just makes my night. I'm going to check in with Rogelio and Mike and have them watch that group at the end of the bar. I'll be right back. Don't leave Grace at the table by herself for any reason, and don't leave the drinks unattended. Shit!" he muttered as he was about to turn to go see the bouncers sitting at the front door. "Patricia is on her way over here. Tell her to fuck off for me, okay?"

"Gladly," Adam replied. His mother would beat him six ways to Sunday if he did that, but if ever there was a female who deserved it, it was this one. She gave whiny, clingy, bitchy women a bad name. How Angel could put up with her catting around with her slutty girlfriends was beyond him. She was easy on the eyes in her own way, but she was a gold-digging whore. Lately, her antics had been over the top, especially the way she pursued Ethan under Angel's nose. Ethan had also mentioned recently seeing her leave the nightclub with more than one man at the end of the evening. It didn't sit well with Adam, the way she cuckolded Angel, and he hoped she'd move on to greener pastures soon. Angel was a good man and deserved someone who would treat him right.

* * * *

Grace looked up at Jack as he spun her in slow circles on the dance floor. "I have something I want to tell you."

"What's that?"

"I love you. I love you. I love you."

"Times three, huh? That much?" he asked, kissing her gently.

"I feel so good when I'm with you. Plus, you brought Ethan and Adam into my life." She wrapped her arms around his neck. "I'm so grateful to your mother for introducing us. I wish she could see us now."

"We had her blessing, you know."

"You and me?"

"No, the four of us, all of us. She understood."

Her lip trembled, and she whispered, "Then it really is perfect, isn't it? It doesn't matter what anyone else says, does it?"

"Not to us. But *they* are another story." He gestured to the people who surrounded them on the dance floor. No one was watching them, so she assumed he meant *they* figuratively. She understood, and she kissed him again, anyway, enjoying the way he held her to him so securely. "I love you, too, darlin'. You're everything to me. You know that?"

She looked up at him and nodded, needing no words.

They returned to the table about the same time Ethan did. They all sat down and enjoyed their drinks and conversation while Grace caught her breath and cooled off a bit. She noticed all three men had removed their jackets. They looked so ruggedly handsome in their suits, although she'd have taken them in their faded denim shirts and blue jeans as well. Plenty of women ogled them around the club, one table in particular. Several overly made-up women in cleavage-baring tops paid particular attention to Ethan, and among them was the one who had watched her with hostile eyes the other night.

Jealousy stirred and wormed its way into her heart, followed by worry. What would her men do if a woman approached them while they were here tonight and asked them to dance? Did they expect that she might not mind if they danced while she danced with one of the others? She hoped the thought wouldn't get put to the test.

Another song started, and Adam distracted her from her ugly thoughts. Another old favorite "I Love the Way You Love Me" by John Michael Montgomery began. Those sweet guitar chords plucked at her heart every time she heard this song.

"Baby, come dance with me," Adam said, helping her down from her chair. She followed him to the dance floor and allowed him to pull her into his arms. She should have known he would notice her change in mood, as well as its cause.

"You have nothing to worry about where those women are concerned."

"What?"

"Those women that were watching Ethan. The only woman he sees is you, baby. The one who keeps giving you the evil eye is Patricia. I'm telling you about her only because she can't seem to take no for an answer. The worst part is that she is our foreman Angel's live-in girlfriend. She keeps pestering Angel to set up a threesome with Ethan, but they both refused her."

"Why would she ask her boyfriend for a threesome?"

"She thought he would be open to the idea because she found out about his family. Angel had a very unique upbringing. His mother is wife to three husbands." He seemed to study her carefully, looking for a reaction to that information.

"She is? How did they manage that?"

"She's married to the eldest of three brothers, and they keep a tight lid on their relationship in the small community they are a part of in the Valley. She's careful in public to portray herself as married to only one of them, but she is committed equally to all of them."

"And it's worked out okay for them?"

"She sounds like a firecracker to me," he said, laughing. "But, yeah, it sounds like it's worked just fine."

She changed the subject on him then. "So I have nothing to worry about where these women are concerned?"

Patricia and another of her friends were standing next to Ethan, talking to him. Not *with* him, but *to* him. He looked tense and unhappy, and Grace noticed him look her way a couple of times. Adam looked down at her, obviously able to tell she was unhappy. She did her best to smile.

"I know that he knows a lot of people and this is his business. He has to keep the customers happy. I also realize that at least half the people he knows are women, some of them of loose moral character." She narrowed her eyes and looked away when she saw Patricia put her hand on Ethan's bicep. With her luck, Patricia was probably bathed in perfume that Grace would have to smell the rest of the night on him.

"Does she know he is here with a date?"

"I *know* she knows," he said with a chuckle. "She's testing him and, unfortunately, baby, she's also testing you. He won't mind if you establish for Patricia's benefit that he's here with you because he knows you would do it in a ladylike manner. So, no hair pullin', all right?" He smiled down at her. His words went a long way toward making her feel better, and she smiled back up at him. "Now, thanks to that skanky bitch, you owe me another dance because she messed up the whole romantic sexy vibe the four of us had going. Deal?"

"Deal, baby!" she said, and she reached for his neck. He picked her up and kissed her there on the dance floor. That got them some attention because her feet were a foot off the ground, but most people smiled and went back to their dances.

Chris Young's "Getting You Home" began, a little more up tempo, but they made it into a slow dance anyway.

"You ready to go back to the table, or do you want to wait until she leaves?" Adam asked her as she looked in the direction of their table. Patricia and her friend were still at it. They stood next to the tall chair Ethan sat in, chatting with each other and looking like they were attempting to include him. Ethan did not look happy. Jack looked a little disgusted.

"Will she keep coming back every time I leave the table with one of you?"

"Probably."

"Is that table and its occupants what I *could* consider my territory?"

"Honey, that table and its occupants are *all about* being your territory."

"Then it's time I set some boundaries. And don't worry. I'll be a perfect lady. I don't want to make trouble for y'all with Angel."

"Oh, don't worry about Angel. He knows what she's like. Just cover your ears because she's a *whiner.*" He said the last word in a whiny tone, making her laugh right as they walked up to the table. Adam held her chair for her.

Ethan's eyes brightened when she sat down and smiled at him. Grace could plead a headache and ask to go home, thus avoiding the conflict. But she wasn't about to cut their evening short and ruin her fun because she was afraid of a confrontation. Rose Marie would tell her, "Seize the day, baby!"

She got up from her seat, straightened her spine, and approached the two women who had ignored her up until now. Patricia once again had her hand on Ethan's shoulder. Yes, testing her. The other one who was standing nearest Grace backed away and retreated to her table. Grace made direct eye contact with Patricia, and a quiet calm descended upon her. She read the challenge in Patricia's heavily made-up eyes.

"Why on earth would you and your girlfriend stand here hanging all over a man who clearly has no interest in you? You've chatted him up for the last ten minutes, and he hasn't said diddly to you in return. Catch the fucking hint. I'd appreciate it if you'd remove your hand from my boyfriend's arm."

She locked eyes with Patricia and waited as Patricia's hand slipped from Ethan's bicep reluctantly, and she backed away, a false smile on her lips and venomous hatred in her eyes.

"*Bye!*" Grace called out softly, with a small wave of her hand, as Patricia walked to the bar. Grace turned to her men and laughed at their expressions. "What?" she asked as Ethan turned to her and kissed her.

"Gracie, did you really say 'fuck'?"

Chapter Twelve

Grace turned her attention to Adam as he groaned. "I love it when she talks dirty. When she says that word my cock goes nuts."

Ethan turned to him and snickered. "That must be confusing for your balls."

She laughed with them, grateful for the tension breaker. Patricia may have backed off, but Grace was not fooled one bit. This was only round one. "She would have kept coming back here, and it needed to be me that established crystal clear boundaries for her, right?"

Jack chuckled as he waved at their waitress. "Well, darlin', she knows where you stand now, doesn't she?"

"Unfortunately, I doubt she's going to give up that easily," Grace replied. "'Hell hath no fury like a woman scorned.'"

"Yes, but now she knows you aren't a doormat she can walk all over," Jack said. "Grace, you should know that Ethan did explain to her several times that he was here with his girlfriend. She ignored him every time."

"Freakin' psycho," Adam muttered, then drank from his beer.

"Well, I did my best to keep our conversation private and ladylike. I didn't want to take a chance on messing up my pretty new dress and shoes by kicking her *ass,*" she whispered the last word to them, making them laugh again.

"Your sister would be so proud of you!" Ethan rose from his chair as Trace Adkins' "Hot Mama" started playing. He held his hand out to her, laughing. "I do believe *this* is our dance," he announced with a playful gleam in his eye. "And I hope you are ready to *dance.*"

She sashayed over to him. "Am I ever!"

He spun her onto the dance floor, and her skirt swished around her as she put those dance lessons her mom had put her and Charity through to good use. She swung her hips and even worked a few grinding, dirty dancing moves into their dance. The energy level on the dance floor rose, and many of the dancers stopped to watch them while others followed suit with some moves of their own.

Her derriere shimmied against Ethan's front as he held her hands, and she spun again, her skirt fluttering around her thighs.

"You sure can shake those tail feathers, Gracie. Mmm-mm."

When the song ended, everyone on the dance floor clapped for them, and they returned to their chairs, laughing and out of breath.

"She gave me a run for my money, boys! Did you see that? Grace *is* one hot mama!"

"Why, thank you, Ethan. You say the nicest things." She giggled, taking a sip from her fresh glass of sangria. "Patricia *really* hates my guts *now*." Grace snickered, looking past them to the bar. Patricia hatefully stared at her, now clinging to a man who had just come into the club with a group of friends.

"I'll have a talk with her." Ethan sighed. "I should have been more forceful before."

Jack raised an eyebrow and scoffed. "Ethan, you did everything short of telling her to fuck off. You could not have been clearer. Her friend already wanted to go sit back down before Grace and Adam returned from the dance floor. Patricia stayed at our table just to piss Grace off."

"Maybe she just needs time to cool off." Grace knew when a rattler was cornered she should not piss it off further. She didn't want Ethan to leave the table. She reached for his hand. He entwined her fingers with his.

Adam changed the subject. "Grace, you are one fine dancer."

"Thanks to my mom and The School of Modern Dance. Charity and I both graduated with honors, and we taught ourselves to grind watching *Dirty Dancing*. I'm glad you liked it, Adam."

"I sure did, baby. We'll make sure and take you dancing on a regular basis. I like seeing you have such a good time, too." He kissed her cheek, and his warm lips sent a shiver down her spine.

She blushed at his compliment. "It's been years and years since I danced like that. I'm really out of shape."

"Trust me, darlin', when I say you're in *fine* shape," Jack murmured in her ear, his hand sliding around her waist. "I can't do any of that fast dancing, but if you've caught your breath, I'd like to guide you around that floor a few times."

"I'd love to, Jack," she replied as he took her hand and helped her from the tall chair. He kissed the top of her head as she snuggled up to him, putting her arms around his waist and sliding a palm up between his shoulder blades.

"You know you shouldn't worry about Patricia. Ethan detests her and always has."

"Just so she keeps her hands and other body parts to herself."

"You're a jealous little thing, aren't you?" Jack chuckled as he held her close.

"Where the three of you are concerned, I think I am. It really bugged me to see her hand on his arm."

"I could tell. I thought you handled yourself very well, darlin'. You were a lot nicer to her than she would have been to you. Now, no more talk of Patricia."

She wiggled into him, holding him even tighter, with her cheek against his chest. "I love being with you, Jack. This evening has been fantastic."

"It's still not over, darlin'," he said, making her giggle.

"You make me warm and shivery inside when you say things like that in that sexy voice of yours."

"Warm and shivery, huh?" He nuzzled his lips against her cheekbone.

"Mmm-hmm." She nodded, his touch making her tremble slightly.

After the dance, he walked her to the ladies' room when she asked where it was.

Grace went in and headed to the mirror to check her makeup. The overhead lights glinted off the gold jewelry she wore. She closed her eyes for a moment and contemplated what she was going to do next.

The door on one of the occupied stalls opened up, and Grace heard high heels click sharply up to the sink beside hers. She looked in the mirror, straight into Patricia's dark brown eyes. Patricia was beautiful in her own way, if she kept her mouth shut. She was shorter than Grace and very thin. She looked Grace up and down with an air of superiority, as if Grace didn't measure up. Her lip curled.

In a whiney voice, she said, “Nice shoes.” Her eyes were full of hate, but she was still able to recognize a great pair of shoes. “Ethan is mine,” she murmured, casually checking her abundant mascara.

“Ethan is not a toy to be fought over.”

“We’ll see. Don’t speak to me like you’re better than me ever again.”

“I spoke to you the way I would to any woman who had the nerve to put her hand on my boyfriend’s arm.”

“I already told you, bitch. Ethan is mine.”

Grace rolled her eyes, fighting a grimace at the grating quality to Patricia’s angry, whiney voice.

“Fine. March your psychotic ass out there right now with me, and let’s see who he welcomes with a kiss and a smile. Let’s go ask him which one of us is leaving with him tonight.”

“Ethan is—”

“Mine.” Grace was a little surprised at the low, deep tone with which that possessive word came out of her mouth. The hair on the nape of her neck stood up, and she knew she was moments away from defending herself against this woman.

Another bathroom stall opened and a beautiful, tall brunette came out to wash her hands. She had to be all of five feet, nine inches tall. Her shiny hair fell to just above the belt of her jeans. The woman took one look at Patricia and rolled her eyes. She took her time soaping and rinsing her hands, obviously sensing that Patricia was waiting for her to leave so she could really lay into Grace.

The brunette finally spoke as she dried her hands with a paper towel. “Look at her with your hateful eyes all you want, Patricia. Your little game is over. Stop pouting and go find some other rich white man to hit on because it looks to me like Ethan is officially off the market. We’re all tired of you hanging around in here with your gold-digging friends, sponging off of the hard-working men who come in here to relax and have some fun. Get the fuck out!”

This woman was taller and heavier than Patricia, and definitely looked capable and willing to help out in a fight. Patricia glared daggers at Grace but hesitated, as if weighing her options. The brunette impatiently took a step toward Patricia as if she was going to help her from the restroom, and Patricia turned angrily and stormed out of the restroom.

Turning to Grace, the brunette held out her hand. "I'm Rachel Lopez, your guardian angel for tonight. I think you could have beaten her ass in a fair fight, but it would be a shame to mess up that pretty dress."

"It's a pleasure to meet you, Rachel, I'm Grace Stuart."

"I'll let you get back to your men, Grace," she replied as she turned to leave. "By the way, she's right. Those are nice shoes," she said, glancing down at them appreciatively. Surreal. "If you need a bathroom buddy later, come and get me. Decent girls have to stick together, right?"

"Thanks, Rachel." Grace returned to the table and sat down, noting the looks of concern on her men's faces.

"Everything okay, Gracie?" Ethan looked a little tense.

"I just had a little talk with Patricia in the ladies' restroom."

"Are you okay?" Ethan looked ready to go hunt Patricia down, so she put a hand out to him to stop him.

"I'm fine. Nothing happened. There was someone else in the restroom with us. She put a stop to whatever Patricia might have said or done. She seemed like she knew y'all. Rachel Lopez?"

"Oh, good." Ethan seemed a little relieved.

"Grace, do you want to go home? Did she upset you?" Jack asked, looking concerned.

Grace looked up at him and smiled. "I was having a good time until I laid eyes on that person. If I leave now, I will have allowed Patricia to run me out of here. I came with my three handsome men to celebrate a special occasion, and I'm not going to let her ruin it for me. Who would like to dance with me?"

Simultaneously they all said, "I will."

Grace laughed. "Don't make me choose. I'd dance with all three of you, and then we'd *really* get some unwanted attention."

Adam held out his hand to her, and she took it. He twirled her around and then swept her into his arms off the floor for just a second. She giggled as he put her back down.

Garth Brooks started singing "Shameless," and recognition dawned. She looked up at him hopefully and said, "Are you?"

"Shameless? You know I am, Grace, but I don't mind telling you. You're beautiful tonight. Earlier this evening was a fantasy come true."

As he said this, his hand slid down her back. He pressed her to him, his hand at the base of her spine, just above her ass, and his hardening erection pressed against her belly through the thin layers of fabric. As they danced slowly across the floor, a deep, slow ache began in her depths. The G-string was going to get damp again, and she felt a trace of moisture on her thighs.

"What happened at Tessa's was a completely new experience for me, and you made it perfect." He smiled down at her tenderly as she drew him to her and cupped her hand to his ear.

"Tonight was the first time I've ever been brought to orgasm by a man," she whispered softly, looking up at him trustingly.

His sharp inhalation of breath let her know he was surprised. He spoke softly so no one would hear them. "That was the first time you've ever come?" He gathered her to him even closer.

"No, that was the first time I've ever been brought to orgasm by a man. I've had orgasms before, but nothing ever even remotely resembling what I experienced tonight."

He seemed to ponder the meaning of her words. "Do you touch yourself, Grace?" he asked softly, latent heat burning in his eyes.

She nodded slowly, and whispered back, "Uh-huh, I have. Recently. While thinking of *you*." *Oooh.* She had a feeling she was playing with fire.

Her words seemed to cause him physical pain because she heard him groan softly, or was it a growl? She couldn't be sure.

"Do you like that I was thinking about you when I touched myself?" she asked softly, pressing her breasts against him.

He leaned closer, his voice almost vibrating with desire. "Yes, but I'd rather be with you than have you imagine me there. Did you come?"

The sparkle in her eyes and her sexy smile provided the answer.

* * * *

Jack watched Grace as she danced with Adam. They were locked in a tight embrace, and Adam looked like he was enjoying it a lot. It was good watching her emerge from her shell with them.

"That is one intense conversation they're having, isn't it?" Ethan asked, nodding toward Adam and Grace.

"They're probably talking about sex." Jack chuckled. He knew that look on Adam's face. He'd seen it a lot lately, which was one of several reasons they'd allowed Adam to be the one to meet Grace's needs earlier at the restaurant.

"We still need to wait until after seeing Dr. Guthrie. She needs this from us. It will be worth the wait if our first time together can be without a condom," Ethan said.

"I agree. I'm going to ask her for one more dance. What about you?" Jack asked.

"Yeah, one more for both of us, and then we should probably get her home. We don't want her to be exhausted tomorrow."

Adam guided her across the dance floor and held her chair when they returned to the table.

Jack rose from his chair and offered his hand to her. "Are you having fun, darlin'? Got a couple more dances in you, or are you ready to call it a night? It's way past your bedtime."

"I could handle a couple more slow dances, and then I'll be ready to go. Would you like one more dance, Jack?"

"Always, darlin'," he murmured as she molded herself to him and allowed him to lead her onto the dance floor. He buried his nose in her fragrant hair, loving the sensory feast of having her warm, fragrant body pressed so closely to his.

* * * *

Her arms were draped loosely around his broad shoulders, his hands on her hips as he guided her around the dance floor. They bumped into Rachel and her dance partner as they passed. Grace mouthed a "thanks again" to Rachel, to which she nodded and winked. She had a feeling she'd made a lifelong friend tonight. She rested her head against Jack's chest, enveloped in his warm strength.

"Will it always be like this?" she asked.

"Will what always be like what, darlin'?"

"Will I always feel so spoiled? So precious?" She snuggled up to him, breathing in his clean masculine smell, treasuring this moment.

"I aim to make that your reality, so, yes, that's what we want. It's what you deserve from us, Grace. You *are* precious. My hope is that it only gets better from here."

"What if you're disappointed by the reality of who I am?"

"Darlin'," he said, chuckling, "is there some deep dark secret you need to tell us? Do you have a split personality? Are you a phone sex operator? Porn star?" She answered no to all of those things, laughing by the end of the list. "Then we can deal with your minor human failings. We all have them. Mom always said, 'Don't borrow trouble. Enough will always find you on its own.'"

"You're right. I'm sorry for being a downer."

"Don't be. I want you to talk about whatever is on your mind, all right?"

"Yes. Love me?" she asked playfully, feathering her fingernails into the jet black hair at the nape of his neck.

"Always, darlin'," he said as the song ended and they came to a stop at the edge of the dance floor where Ethan stood near their table.

Ethan helped her into her chair and she observed her men while she sipped from her sangria and said, "Tonight has been wonderful. Barring the potential smackdown with Patricia, I've loved every single minute of it." She leaned in to kiss them as chastely as she could, one at a time. The next song started, and Ethan drew her out to the floor. For the moment, they were by themselves as people returned to their tables, refilled drinks, or made pit stops.

"When a Man Loves a Woman" was now officially Ethan and Grace's song as he entwined his long fingers through hers. They barely moved over the dance floor, and Grace felt everything else fade away. It was just her and Ethan and the song. There was no need for words, except for the lyrics. She was perfectly content wrapped in his warm, secure embrace, just as she had been with Jack and Adam earlier.

The past with Owen didn't matter. The problem with Patricia didn't matter. What mattered was the future, her future, and hopefully theirs together. Their love healed her and helped her move forward with her life.

She was ready to reach for the things she wanted and had been too timid to ask for before. Seizing the day had become a daily goal and not just a dream deferred.

Chapter Thirteen

Jack pulled the SUV into Grace's driveway and parked behind her little Honda. For a moment, they sat silently in the vehicle. Grace sensed the current of sexual tension that flowed between them. The ball was in her court.

"Would y'all like to come in?"

"Yes," Ethan replied. "But only if it's what you want. We know you must be tired."

"Come in for a little while. I don't want you to go yet," she added softly. Her men helped her climb out of the SUV. She noticed the appreciative glances they gave her legs as she slid from the seat. It did her heart a world of good, and she felt herself perk right up.

Grace retrieved her house key from her evening bag and handed it to Jack. The men entered first, turned on lamps here and there, and checked the rooms to make sure everything was in order. That simple action spoke volumes to her heart. Even subconsciously, they were protecting her. She turned on her stereo and turned it down to a low volume for background noise.

"Would you like some coffee or a snack?" she offered, at a loss for what else she should say. Her men paused for a few seconds before Ethan spoke.

"Gracie, why don't you sit with us for a few minutes?" He took her by the hand, and they all moved to the couch and upholstered chair.

Ethan stroked her hand reassuringly. "I know you invited us in, and maybe you're not ready for the evening to end. I'm not sure we're ready for it to end, either." He paused, the three of them smiled at each other and her. "We had no expectations when we came in that door beyond spending a little more time with you. We can do whatever you like, but we want you to take things slow."

She looked from one man's face to another and found the confirmation of Ethan's words in their gentle gazes as he continued. "We don't want to be presumptuous about moving forward into a greater level of intimacy, but we're standing by our promise to all get checked. When we do make love to you, we don't want any doubts lingering in your mind."

Ethan understood her needs again without her having to explain them. She was thankful that their offer to be tested wasn't just lip service. It meant a lot more to her than they realized. "I'm glad you said something, Ethan. I really needed to hear that."

Jack and Adam reached out to her and made simple, quiet contact, seeming content to let him do the talking. Ethan did have a way with words.

"Did you enjoy the loving that Adam gave you tonight, Gracie?" Ethan asked.

She blushed, and she knew they must feel the tremor that had just run through her body. She felt the yearning begin to build in her body for them to be closer.

"I loved it. You know I did," she said softly. Her gaze lingered over their faces, looking lastly into Adam's eyes, and saw such love and desire combined there, it took her breath away. Her body responded to him with a tingling rush, and she had the urge to climb into his lap and let them do whatever they wanted to her.

Ethan lifted her hand and brushed his lips against her knuckles and softly asked, "Would you give us a chance to love you like he did?"

Her breath came in little pants, and she felt a rush of moisture flood her pussy. It amazed her that just their words could have such an immediate effect on her body.

"I want that very much, but if you don't mind, I'd like to shower first."

Jack nodded. "Of course that's all right, darlin'. We want you to be comfortable. Take all the time you need."

"Do you mind if we turn down your bed, or would you be more comfortable if we stayed in the living room?" As Ethan spoke, she noted the hopeful expression on his face and nodded. Her bed was only a queen size, but it would be more comfortable than her couch.

"The bedroom is fine. I'll only be a few minutes." She went to her bedroom, removed the jewelry they'd given her, and laid it carefully on her dresser.

"Take your time, Grace. We're not in any hurry," Ethan said as he followed her into the bathroom. He put his arms around her and kissed her. He slid his fingers down her back as the zipper descended all the way to the G-string. He released her lips and gave her a slow, sultry smile, gazing at her with bedroom eyes. "Someday soon I'll undress you, piece by piece, until you're naked, and then bathe you myself. Mmmm. Heaven." Then he backed out of the bathroom and closed the door.

She started the shower, and her heart hammered as she pinned up her hair. She slipped out of the shoes and removed the dress and the lingerie they'd purchased for her.

She stepped into the shower and did her best to catch her breath and calm down. She dried off after she was done and heard soft voices and movement from the other side of the door. She took her hair down and combed it out. Her makeup was gone, and she hoped they were okay with the façade being removed. She slipped into her ivory lace-edged camisole and cheeky shorts and looked at her reflection in the mirror. She hardly recognized the woman she saw there. Her face glowed, and she looked happy. The woman reflected back at her was loved.

She took some deep, slow breaths and opened the bathroom door. The house was dark now. Only one dim lamp glowed in the living room, just enough light to navigate through the living room. The only other illumination came from the candles they'd lit.

With their jackets removed, ties gone, and the top buttons of their shirts undone, they were undeniably the sexiest men she'd ever seen in her entire life. Ethan leaned against the doorway, waiting for her. Adam sat at the foot of her bed. Jack sat with his back against her headboard. As they gazed at her, the lust and desire in their eyes was clear, but it was tempered with tenderness. She should have been intimidated by the idea of three big, virile men in her bedroom, but the slow, seductive throb began in her clit, and she knew there was no safer place in the world for her than with Jack, Adam, and Ethan.

Ethan held out his hand, and she allowed him to draw her farther into the room. His fingers slid up her arms to her shoulders and gently skimmed up her throat to each side of her jaw. He leaned down and brushed his lips against hers. His fingertips traced over her collar bones and lightly stroked down the sides of her breasts to her waist. She wanted him to touch her nipples but he teased her, bypassing them completely, and they puckered and throbbed with need. She felt his fingers at the hem of the camisole. In one smooth motion, he gathered a few inches of it up and knelt down on one knee in front of her to kiss the exposed skin of her belly.

The feeling of his warm lips on her bared abdomen sent a jolt of lust through her, and she grew wetter from that simple touch. As he continued kissing around her belly button and below it, his fingers hooked in the edge of the camisole and pushed it up to just beneath her breasts. She looked up into Jack and Adam's faces, now tense and filled with lust. She noticed Adam palmed his erection through his pants and was surprised by what a turn-on she found that to be. She gave him a slow, knowing smile that told him she understood and approved. The two of them audibly groaned at the indirect contact she had with them.

She focused on Ethan's skilled hands again, which were now sliding around to cup each rounded cheek of her buttocks. He grasped them firmly, and she wanted to scream in pleasure as he pressed his lips to her abdomen, just barely above her mound. His hot breath seared her through the thin fabric. He groaned as if he were being tortured.

He rose to his feet again and moved to stand behind her and swept the hair away from her neck as his lips kissed their way up from her shoulder to below her ear. "I can see your pulse. Your heart is racing, Grace. Are you excited?" he asked in a low tone that seemed loud in the quiet room. She nodded.

"You're not afraid?" Her head shifted back against his shoulder.

"Never. Not with y'all." She whimpered as his hands palmed her breasts over the soft camisole, her nipples so hard and erect they stung. They felt swollen, and she ached for him to touch them without the obstacle of the thin layer of fabric.

"I want you to wear the jewelry we gave you once I've undressed you. Would you do that for me? I want to see it on you as we love you."

"Of course, if it makes you happy."

"It would make me very happy, Gracie." He'd teased her so much by this point that when his hands finally slid the camisole in a torturously slow move over her breasts she thought she would come just from contact with his hands brushing over her nipples and the feeling of her breasts swaying free.

Adam murmured, “So beautiful. Perfect. Your breasts are gorgeous.”

“Darlin’, you were made so beautifully,” Jack whispered.

She felt tears tingle behind her closed eyes, and joy at their words suffused her heart. She was poised very close to the edge and struggled to catch her breath.

Ethan turned away to her dresser, retrieving the earrings, which she placed back in her pierced ears. He fastened the clasp of the bracelet on her right wrist, then placed the intricate gold necklace back above her breasts and fastened its clasp. The minute or two it took to do this gave her a chance to recover slightly so she no longer felt like a rocket ready to go off at the slightest touch.

“You okay, baby?” Adam asked her, obviously seeing the emotion so close to the surface on her face.

“Yes. I’m just not used to being told things like that. It’s hard to see myself that way.”

“Then just listen to us. Your trust is a precious gift, and in time you’ll come to believe us,” Ethan said.

He still stood behind her so that Adam and Jack could see. His hands slid down her rib cage again, his fingers hooking in the stretch lace of her cheeky shorts, and with agonizing slowness, slid them from her hips, revealing the blonde curls they’d hidden. The soft cotton pooled at her ankles, and she stepped out of them.

And there she was, laid bare for them, standing in the presence of three men who found her desirable. Her heart was irretrievably lost to these men, and she knew in the short time she had been with them, in love with them, that she was truly ruined for all others.

Ethan moved to stand beside her, his hands stroked over her shoulders. “You hold our hearts in your hands. There could never be another woman like you anywhere in the world, and we’ll do whatever we can to satisfy you and keep you happy with us.”

He reached out to her, his left hand palming her cheek before he brushed her lips with his again. Her body throbbed so fiercely with desire she knew now that she was uncovered they’d see how wet with need she was.

She realized that Ethan could see their reflection in the mirror that stood in the corner. She had bought that mirror to use for a practical purpose and, in another life, would have been put off by the notion of watching as Ethan undressed her and made love to her with his hands the way he did. Seeing their reflection in the mirror now brought a fresh rush of heat and moisture to her slit.

"Are you all going to leave your clothes on?" she asked haltingly.

"For now, but we may get more comfortable later," Ethan murmured. "We want tonight to be about you, Grace, giving you pleasure. Just close your eyes and feel." Ethan's lips descended to the sensitive spot above her collarbone. She shuddered as his tongue traced over her skin. "Mmm, you taste so good, Grace." His fingers slid over her shoulders, the tips barely touching her as they wandered down both arms, raising goose bumps and sending shivers racing over her supersensitive flesh.

His fingers slid in between hers and raised her hands to reach back to hold onto his shoulders. When she did, the motion tilted her breasts out, and she ached to feel his mouth on them. She cried out when she felt his callused fingers stroke her nipples. He gently pulled one while he teased and stroked the other. Another rush of moisture gathered between her legs at the pulling sensation.

Ethan squeezed each tight peak gently between his fingers, and a moan escaped from her lips. "I can smell her beautiful scent and how aroused she is. Can you, Adam?"

"She has the sweetest smelling pussy I've ever known," Adam responded, his voice sounding a little strained. "I recognized her sweet honey when you were putting the necklace back on her. Are you wet for us, baby?"

"I'll bet she is," Jack said. "Ethan, why don't you put those fingers to good use? Show us if she's wet." He leaned forward to watch with Adam as Ethan's fingers slid slowly down her torso.

It affected Grace in unexpected ways to hear her men refer to her using that word. Spoken softly from Adam's sweet lips it was just as much a surprising turn-on as watching him stroke his hand over his cock earlier had been. She gloried in the freedom she felt with them.

She glimpsed their reflection in the mirror. She panted in little breathy gasps as one hand stroked her nipple while the other hand moved ever closer to her mound. Feeling it happen and seeing it happen was sensory overload. Ethan's steely hard erection ground against her backside, and she couldn't resist the urge to play, too.

"Ethan, I can feel how hard you are. Does it feel good touching me?"

"Better than you can imagine, Gracie," he said. His fingers strayed closer to her mound. Her clit ached and throbbed for his touch. Dying for his touch, she rubbed her ass against his cock.

"I think Grace has a naughty streak," Jack said, chuckling at her words. "Darlin', you've got us all hard as baseball bats waiting to have a first taste of that pretty little pussy of yours. Are you looking forward to feeling us between those sweet thighs as much as we are?" He palmed his own erection.

She smiled at him and licked her lips, causing him to groan. "There's something else I'd like to get a taste of for myself as well. Would you like that, Jack?" she asked, showing no mercy.

"We'll see, darlin'. Let us make you feel good first, and then we'll see."

She whimpered when Ethan's fingers moved over her mound and into her slit, captured her clit between his index and middle fingers, and then slid down over her inner lips to her entrance. Her breath escaped her in a high-pitched moan.

"Oh, you are wet for us, aren't you, Gracie. Mmm, I'm going to want a taste in a minute. You feel like hot, wet silk sliding through my fingers."

Her breath sounded loud in her ears. Her head fell back to Ethan's shoulder again. His fingers slid up over her clit before sliding back down again. Over and over, he stroked her pussy, slowly working her into a frenzy. He gently teased her, sliding his finger a little farther into her entrance. He gathered her juices and spread them around, then rubbed her clit again until she was so wet and in need that one more touch would send her over.

"Look at us, Gracie." She made eye contact with Ethan in the mirror. "You are so hot to watch with my hands on you. You're close to coming, aren't you?" She nodded and he added, "Let me have a taste, and I'll give you what you need."

His fingers left her, and the touch she craved was gone. He pulled her to sit on the edge of the bed. He gently pushed her back and knelt between her thighs, his soft, warm mouth just millimeters away from the spot that needed him the most. He used his long, talented fingers to gently spread her lips as she felt Adam gently lift her leg and place it on Ethan's shoulder in a loving gesture of care to make her more comfortable.

"Can you see how sweet and pink her pussy is? It's beautiful, baby," Adam said as he stroked her hair and kissed her. "Why don't you lick her little clit? I'll bet she wants you to. Are you ready to give Ethan a taste of your sweet honey?"

"Yes, Ethan, please put your mouth on me. I need you. Oh!" Ethan growled softly and she gasped as the heat of his mouth covered her pussy and his tongue flicked gently into her entrance. She was so close, so achingly close.

He tortured her for a minute before he said, "Gracie, you taste so good. Adam was right, so pure and sweet. I could stay here for hours. I can't wait to fuck you, Gracie, to feel your pussy tighten on my cock when you come for me." He flicked at her clit with his tongue, and she knew she was seconds away from climax. "Does it feel good? Tell me."

"I need to come, Ethan, please!" she cried out, feeling the tightening in her walls again. Her panting grew louder as the pressure from his rasping tongue on her clit increased.

Adam whispered in her ear and stroked her nipple. Suddenly, she felt Jack's warm mouth on her other breast. She reached for them both, and they intertwined their fingers with hers. Ethan sweetly lapped at her clit and gently sucked it between his lips, and she came undone in an overwhelming explosion of ecstasy. Grace's back arched sharply, and her lips fell open in a scream of pure, unbridled pleasure. He continued to lick her pussy and feast on her tumultuous release, her hips rolling with each pulse. Her breathing hitched as all the tension released from her body.

Her thighs were still resting on his shoulders, and he wrapped a hand around one as he kissed her swollen pussy, rested his temple against her inner thigh, and whispered huskily, "Oh, Gracie." He reached out for Grace, placing his hand gently on her abdomen. The contact startled her and sent another aftershock through her quivering body. He stood, carefully repositioning her feet on the floor.

"Baby, was it good?" Adam was on one side, brushing her hair from her forehead, stroking her gently. Jack was on the other, still holding one of her hands, whispering sweet words in her ear. She looked into Adam's eyes and nodded languidly before looking at Ethan.

Ethan stood over her at the side of the bed, the look of vulnerability and openness in his deep blue eyes sending a spear of emotion to her heart.

Seeing tenderness in his gaze, she knew she mirrored those same emotions in her own and in her soft smile that felt as though it radiated from her. Her breathing finally slowed, and she reached for his hand. He climbed into the bed with them.

"How do you feel, baby?" Adam asked as he leaned forward and lifted her bodily into a more comfortable position on the bed. She smiled up at him, her heart throbbing so loudly with love for him she thought he must be able to hear it as he leaned down to kiss her again.

She looked at Adam, and said, "I feel loved."

Jack allowed Ethan to slide in beside her. His big warm hand spanned her waist before sliding down her bare hip. If he'd allow it, she'd let him make love to her tonight, thoroughly and completely. He laid his head gently on her breast, placing his ear over her heart, and the love for him welled within her.

Ethan leaned down to her and kissed her tenderly and she felt as if her heart were stretching as it tried to hold that much love for the three of them.

"Ethan, that was beautiful. You play my body as if you know what will make me feel the greatest pleasure."

He chuckled and lifted his head to look into her eyes, grinned wickedly, and said, "Oh, honey, the maestro has not even begun to play his greatest symphony for you. That was merely an overture." Her pussy throbbed at the thought of him stroking her body to a perfect crescendo, and he grinned devilishly and said, "You like that idea, do you?"

"Yes, very much," she replied simply. She lacked the energy to bandy words too much, but wanted to revel a while longer in this sweet embrace. She stroked Ethan's cheek as he nestled against her, serenity washing over her as she savored the moment. For a while, she just lay there accepting their sweet touches and caresses. The candlelight flickered, and the light reflected off the shimmering rings of her bracelet as she stroked Ethan's cheek. Every time she wore this jewelry, she would think of this night.

She asked Adam for a glass of water, and when he returned with it, he was barefoot. She noticed the others had removed their boots as well. She curled up in the middle of the bed, surrounded by them. She marveled at the contrasts between her men and how perfectly they all fit together. Ethan was her mind reader. Jack was her teasing lover, and Adam, her gentle giant. All of them were capable of heating her body with their words and could reduce her to smoldering ashes with their touch. It surprised her when the thought of Jack loving her as Adam and Ethan had done produced another rush of wet arousal to her pussy.

Heat radiated from her depths, and she felt her inner lips swell a little and grow damp again. She imagined him teasing her with his tongue as Ethan and Adam had done. She broke out in goose-bumps at the thought of when he would finally slide his cock into her. Then she could truly know the feeling of an orgasm with a man who could fill her and love her the way she desperately needed.

Adam lay down behind her, his back against her headboard. Ethan was on the other side of her, running his fingers through her hair, and said, “I think Gracie has been fantasizing about Jack.”

Jack was at the end of the bed on the same side as Adam, stroking her legs, every now and then sending a tremor through her as his fingertips lightly grazed her with a tickle touch, eliciting a sigh or gasp. “Is that true, darlin’?” he asked, giving her the crooked grin she’d loved since the day she met him.

“Maybe if we’re sweet to Grace, she’ll tell us about her fantasies,” Ethan said. “Maybe we can make some of them come true for her in the future. Are you excited about what Jack wants to do for you?”

She looked up at Jack and nodded eagerly.

“I’ll bet she’s drenched,” Adam said. “Maybe she’s even wondering what his cock would feel like. I can smell her sweet honey from here. Jack may have the sweetest feast of all of us tonight.”

“Is that true, darlin’? Are you imagining what all I want to do with you, *to* you, tonight?”

She sighed and said softly, “I don’t know, maybe you’ll need to find out for yourself.” She’d never felt sexier as she drew a knee up and allowed one of her thighs to slowly open and fall to the side, leaving her pussy open to his gaze. She arched her back for him and opened farther so he could see her juices glistening in the damp folds of her pussy. She heard low, rumbling growls coming from her men, who were evidently very aroused by the sight as she offered herself to Jack.

He reached out to lay his hand on her mound. His thumb delved into her opening, and he groaned softly as it slipped through her slick heat. She sighed and arched into him and took his finger deeper. He withdrew and set her on fire when he put his thumb in his mouth to suck her juices from it.

"Lord have mercy, darlin', but you're delectable. You really do have the sweetest little pussy."

She looked up into Jack's eyes and felt her heart throb along with her clit.

"It's for you, Jack," she whispered as she propped the ball of her foot on his shoulder, affording him an even better view.

Chapter Fourteen

"Heaven help me, I love this woman!" he muttered before he settled into the spot between her open legs. She reached out and ran her fingers into his silky jet-black hair. This man was responsible for bringing so much happiness into her life. So much joy.

She giggled and then sighed deeply as Jack dipped his tongue down into the juices between her lips and his warm breath against her pussy sent warm shivers through her. He swirled his tongue around her clit, and when she squeaked a little, they both laughed. She stopped him for a second, backed up against the pillows piled at the head of the bed, and crooked her finger at him. She looked up at Ethan and at Adam, now that she was in between the two of them, and reached for them as Jack claimed a kiss. She clasped her fingers in Ethan's and squeezed Adam's hand. She leaned up into Jack's kiss and wrapped her legs loosely around his waist. She sighed again as his kisses descended down her neck to her collarbone. She looked up at Ethan reclining beside her and tugged on his hand, pulling him to her for a kiss, and then she turned to Adam for his kiss. She wanted to feel a connection with them as well.

She released their hands and slid hers over Jack's tanned forearms and up his biceps. She loved Ethan and Adam, loved the feeling of being tucked safely between them, but a part of her also wanted to lose herself in this moment with Jack. Shutting out the world didn't mean shutting them out, but she had fantasized about what it would feel like to be in an erotic embrace with him for a long time. She ran her fingers through Jack's hair, enjoying the feel of his hot, wet lips above her collarbone. She turned her head and flicked her tongue around the edge of his ear, tugging on his lobe with her teeth. She wished they would let her love them, too. She wanted to give to them, not to make it even between them, but because she wanted them to feel what she was feeling.

"Darlin', relax and let me love you. There will be plenty of time for you to plan all the naughty things you want to do to us later. I want to do this for you." Jack leaned forward and kissed her again, and she marveled at how well they understood her.

Tension curled in the pit of her stomach, knowing that her moment would come. She imagined all of them naked in bed together, with Jack kneeling over her like this, her legs around his waist. When she imagined the tip of his cock pressed against her dripping wet entrance, forging slowly inside, she felt her pussy tremble, anticipating that reality. She wanted him so badly it was painful.

The fingertips of his right hand slid from her breastbone slowly down over her abdomen, dipping into her belly button and over her mound. As his fingers skated down her sensitive flesh, she alternately moaned and gasped.

"Are you feeling up to a little more loving, Grace? You're not too tired? I'd understand," Jack offered playfully, and she knew he was teasing her. Wild horses couldn't have dragged her away from him at that moment. She shook her head, never breaking eye contact, and the playful mood subtly shifted. She didn't want him to stop, and she didn't want them to leave. They had given her such an amazing gift tonight, and she wanted everything he had to give her now.

She heaved a shuddering sigh. "Just love me, Jack. Never stop. Please just love me." She felt her cheeks burning and a prickling of tears behind her lids as she closed them. Under Owen's thumb, she could never have imagined that she would someday be loved so sweetly like this. She couldn't help the welling of almost overpowering emotion than filled her heart, and felt as if she would burst with it.

She felt Ethan's warm lips under her jaw and could smell his clean, spicy scent. Adam's lips brushed against her ear as he promised her their love, then kissed her lips. Jack's hot mouth descended on one of her nipples while plucking softly at the other. Then he worked his way down her belly, alternately kissing and licking her. He was teasing her. He knew how much she wanted to feel his mouth and where. She lifted her knees higher, giving him greater access, and invited him in.

"Darlin', you smell so good everywhere. This soft skin beneath your nipple is like velvet." He demonstrated, teasing the area with his tongue. "And this right here, down your ribs. *Mmm.* All of it feels like the smoothest, warmest satin. I want to fall asleep sometime with my head right here." He rubbed his nose across the flesh of her belly, beside her navel. "But you know my favorite, don't you, baby? I love every part of you, but this right here..." He trailed two fingers down her mound, which was open with her knees lifted the way they were, and his fingers slid down past the curls to her lips. "This beautiful pink pussy I crave like a man dying of thirst wants water."

Feeling daring, she reached down, gently opening those pink lips to his gaze, her fingertips making the most vulnerable place in her body open and exposed to him. She felt so powerful and sexy doing it. She also experienced a deep, primal delight at the heat in his gaze as his eyes rested on her swollen pussy, dripping with the arousal his words and her thoughts stoked her to.

"You are a wild, wanton thing, aren't you, Grace?" Ethan said, stroking her nipple between his fingers.

Grace sighed. "Only with you. The things y'all say, the way you treat me. I want you to touch me, Jack, please." She trembled, watching Jack's face as he leaned into that part of her that wanted him so much. He touched the flesh she held open for him, and his fingers strayed to her entrance, dipping inside slightly, before trailing down past that opening to the puckered one beneath it, spreading her wetness down there as well. As his callused finger gently slid over that opening, she tensed and gulped, her breath coming in ragged, shaking gasps.

"Not tonight, darlin'. I just want to touch you. It's completely up to you whether or not we ever take you there. Just let me touch you."

He spread more of her secretions to that spot. Each time his finger slid across that opening, her belly clenched. It was driving her wild, and she would not have thought it would feel as good as it did. She knew she wanted them to take her anally at some point. She'd thought of it as a gift for them, something they would enjoy, but not anything she would find all that thrilling. The tight arousal that now raged within her at the thought of one of their cocks thrusting into her ass was wild, dark, and thrilling. She no longer wanted it just for them. She wanted it for herself as well.

She smiled at him and held her knees, giving him access to it. His finger and the area around her ass were now drenched from his teasing. She felt his index finger pressing gently, but persistently, at her asshole. She clenched involuntarily at the intrusion. He circled slowly, pressing down steadily, and the muscles begin to give in to him, just a little. She felt a mixture of slight pain and naughty pleasure as just the tip of his finger popped into her tight hole. She moaned and felt the distant stirrings of an orgasm within the pit of her belly.

She didn't object to the intrusion, so Jack explained, "Darlin', you're very tight here. If we ever took your ass, we would prepare you first. If you could relax and trust us, you'd love it, too."

The look of barely bridled lust in his eyes made her bold. "I trust you, Jack. I trust you all. Someday soon, I'll let you take my ass. But right now, I want your mouth on my pussy. I need to come, Jack. Please?"

"Your wish is my command, darlin'." He withdrew, shifted his weight, and once more delved into her folds with the fingers of his other hand, followed by his hot tongue. Her head fell back at the hot sensation as his tongue flicked into her cunt. She longed for his tongue or his fingers to touch her clit, to stroke it. Shifting again, he lowered her knees away from her chest and planted her feet wide on either side of his shoulders as he lay between her legs. He looked as though he were getting comfortable, like he was planning to stay a while. A shiver of delight shot up her spine at the thought.

His tongue slid up, straight over her clit, making her jump a little, before swirling around it in a circle and then sliding into her opening again. He licked her inner thigh and chuckled as she wiggled to get him to bring that talented tongue back to her clit, and she moaned happily when he returned. His lapping became more purposeful. The thrusting of his tongue caused her hips to flex into his movements as if it were his cock inside her.

Ethan and Adam leaned down to her, stroked her breasts, and kissed and suckled until she thought she might explode. One hand gripped the cloth of Adam's shirt, and the fingers of her other hand curled into Ethan's silky hair.

Grace felt his thick finger enter her tight, dripping wet pussy and slide in and out slowly. He painstakingly teased her to the very edge before he slid two fingers inside her, palm up. She felt the slight burning as just those two fingers stretched her inner walls. He moved his fingers back and forth in a strumming motion and she felt a strange, but pleasant pressure begin to build. This didn't radiate so much from her clit as it had with Adam and

Ethan. This was different, with a whole new level of wild intensity. His playing of her body never wavered or hesitated. She moaned and gasped with every breath as the sensation of pressure and impending explosion loomed over her.

"He's found your sweet spot, Gracie," Ethan said. "Jack is going to make you come like you never have, *ever* before. Feel his love, all of our love for you." He entwined his fingers with hers while Adam held her other hand, stroking her thigh. The tension in her body increased to an unbearable tightness, and *still* the wave rolled up higher and higher.

"You're so tight on my fingers, baby. So tight and hot. You're almost there."

Her body vibrated with the tension, and her moan gradually built to a howl.

"Yes, Grace, you've waited so long. *Come* for me, come for me, little darlin'," he urged.

Like a rubber band breaking after being stretched too taut, her body found sweet release and came in a rolling wave. Her screaming, gasping cries filled the room, and his fingers continued to stroke her as she came in a great warm gush. His tongue lapped at her sweet release that flowed from her. With each pulse of her orgasm, her hips flexed against him. Her body shook and trembled in their hands, her hair plastered to her forehead. Her lips were still parted as she tried to catch her breath, shuddering on an aftershock when Jack's tongue licked her one last time and he withdrew his fingers.

She had no idea, the lengths a man like Jack would go to please her when she met him two years before. Two years she wasted being faithful to that asshole Owen. Two years she could've been loving a real man. Real men. Now she was his. Theirs.

* * * *

Jack could feel tension building in her body again. He felt her shaking and glanced up at Adam and Ethan in concern. Their lips were on her forehead and cheek, soothing her. Great sobbing cries broke loose from her in heaving waves. He lifted carefully from his position between her legs, gently closing them, and placed a soothing hand on her silky abdomen, feeling the depth of her sobs as they broke from her. It wracked him with pain to see her cry so hard, and he began to wonder if he'd injured her in some way. The sobs came from somewhere very deep within her and showed no sign of letting up.

Ethan made eye contact with Jack in the soft candlelight of the room and smiled knowingly at him. He lifted a hand and gestured silently for Jack to come up and lay beside her as he carefully moved away from her and went around to Adam's side of the bed and sat down, stroking her leg. As Jack lay down with her, she reached for him, and Ethan gently pushed her hip so she could turn to face him and be cuddled in his arms, her sobs softened somewhat but continued. Jack stroked Grace's curving hip, down her thigh, and comforted her. She melted into his embrace, and he allowed her to cry as long as she needed without being interrupted or shushed. His only regret was that it had taken him two years to come to this moment.

After a few minutes, her sobs decreased and finally subsided. All the tension in her body abandoned her and left her limp and calm in his arms. He tilted her chin up to study her face and see for himself that she was all right. She made silent eye contact with him and her face showed nothing but relaxed serenity. Her eyelids were drooping sleepily.

"Tell me you're okay," Jack whispered.

"I didn't know that it was possible to feel *that* level of ecstasy until it hit me. I had no idea, and I feel completely undone by it. I love you, all of you, so deeply it *hurts*. I guess everything I've been holding inside all these years broke loose with it." Her breath hitched a little. Her eyes slid closed briefly before she struggled to open them again, trying to stay awake.

"Gracie, you need to sleep, sweetheart. Would you like us to stay while you fall asleep?" Ethan continued to stroke her hip.

"Mmm, please stay and keep me warm. Extra keys on the shelf by the front door. For y'all to keep," she murmured, her eyes sliding closed.

Ethan, Adam, and Jack arranged themselves around her, cocooning her with their warm bodies, stroking whatever part of her was within reach. Jack thought she'd drifted off when she whispered with a hitching breath, "I'll love y'all forever." Wherever they were situated around her, they kissed whatever part of her was easiest to reach.

"I love you, too, darlin'." Jack whispered.

"Baby, I love you, too." Adam snuggled closer to her back.

"Love you, too, Gracie." Ethan nuzzled the inner curve of her hip with his lips.

They stayed that way for a while to make sure she'd fallen deeply asleep. Ethan rose first. He gently slid the top sheet and comforter out from under her calves and covered her. Jack and Adam slowly climbed from the bed and tucked the comforter around her so she wouldn't be cold. Ethan blew out the candles, gradually darkening the room. Pale moonlight filtered through the blinds on her windows, and they stopped to gaze down on her one last time, the moonlight glinting platinum against the earrings that were still in her ears.

"Do you think we should remove the jewelry?" Adam asked.

"Let's take off the earrings and bracelet," Ethan said, "so they don't come off in the bed, but leave the necklace where it is. We'd have to disturb her too much to find the clasp, and I have a feeling she'd like to wake up in it, just this once. She'll remember how it got there."

They nodded, smiling in agreement.

Jack found a notepad and left a note for her by the coffee pot where he knew she would find it. Ethan found three house keys lined up on the shelf near the front door. She'd had one made for each of them. Jack locked the front door behind them.

As Adam drove home, Jack studied the clock in the dash. Four fifteen. Time flew fast with Grace. He hoped she'd sleep in that morning. He doubted he'd sleep at all. The deep, aching pain was heavy in his testicles, and he knew he'd replay the events of the evening over and over in his mind if he lay down. The sound of her orgasmic screams echoed in his mind.

"I think I know why she cried," Adam murmured from the driver's seat.

"Why?" Ethan asked in a muffled tone from the back. Jack *knew* Ethan knew the reason. He seemed to be able to read Grace's thoughts sometimes.

"You touched her soul tonight, Jack," Adam replied.

"*We* touched her soul tonight—all of us—in a different way," Jack said. She would want them to know that they all had.

"I think we've only scratched the surface with Grace. She is incredible." Adam's voice sounded like it hurt to speak.

Jack never did sleep that night. Thoughts of her kept him awake, wishing with all his heart she were curled up, warm and cuddly, cradled in his arms. It somehow seemed wrong to leave her home alone. He could still feel the smooth satin of her skin against his fingertips and the silky texture of her hair as he ran his fingers through it. The worst torture, though, was the clear, sharp memory of the lush, wet, silky feel of her pussy under his mouth. The memory of her trusting welcome as she opened that hidden part of her body to his touch had him aching for the feel of her hands on his body, her delicate fingers wrapped around his shaft. He'd masturbated in the shower, but the relief was short-lived, like he knew it would be. He felt like a horny teenager, unable to control his body's responses.

The irony of wishing she were in his bed, and not having her, in light of the fact that Patricia lived on their ranch, was not lost on him.

* * * *

Looking at caller ID, she answered Charity's call, wondering what she would ask her first.

"Are you hung over?" Charity was obnoxious, but Grace sure did love her sister.

"Good mornin' to you, too, sister."

"Did you get laid?"

"I hope the kids are not within earshot of this conversation."

"No, they're at Grandma's house. Justin surprised me last night with a kid-less house, a candlelight dinner, and then a moonlit ride on his Harley. I got laid. Did you?"

"Not very subtle, are you?" Grace said, grinning at her sister's audacity.

"Did. You. Get. Any. Dammit?" Charity laughed.

"No," she responded simply. She decided to make Charity work for it.

"Were you a good girl?" She sounded disgusted.

"I never said that."

"See any cocks? Have a new frame of reference? Shall I call Guinness?"

"No, but I had three amazing orgasms, two of them screaming orgasms, and one of them in a semi-public place."

There was dead silence on the other end for a few seconds, then a dark chuckle. "You are coming over for supper tonight. You cannot say no, and I'll even buy a bottle of that sangria you like. I need details, you naughty girl!"

"I have to work from two to five today, and I hoped to see my men."

"*Your* men, huh? Absence makes the heart grow fonder, remember? They'll miss you and be so happy to see you the next time. You should thank me. Justin is cooking, and the kids will be at Kathleen's until tomorrow. We can talk to our hearts' content, and you can tell me all about your evening."

"All right." She giggled. The truth was she really wanted to tell Charity all about it. She needed to confide in her sister. She knew her men wouldn't mind. "I'll be over after work, around six o'clock, but I can't stay late, okay? I have to work in the morning." She hung up

The low rumble of thunder in the distance made her smile. She laid her phone aside and stretched luxuriously, savoring the sound of the rain. She turned over to get comfortable and snuggled down to listen to the rain for a few minutes. When she turned, she felt the gold rings of her necklace shift and slide over her bare chest.

Her hand reached out to lie across the gold rings. Her body blushed at all the incredibly erotic images that came to mind. She thought of their mouths and hands and how all of them had taken their sweet time bringing her to orgasm.

She cried after Jack had given her that intense climax. The tears seemed to wash over her and erase all the hurt and mistakes she made. Her attitude was different now toward the last seven years. That experience brought her to the place she was in now, loved by three wonderful men.

She sat up and stretched her arms overhead. Her skin still felt warm and tender from being cocooned in the comforter. Her men must have tucked her in last night so she wouldn't wake up missing their warmth. She ran her hands over her arms and down her sides. Her skin still felt silky from the massage oils they used at Madeleine's. She slid her fingertips over her derriere, around her hips, and down her thighs. She felt different, changed. Well loved. Thinking back over the previous night, she doubted there was a single inch of her skin they hadn't explored. That thought sent ecstatic shivers down her spine, and her heart ached a little to be with them again. Her clit throbbed in happy agreement. She removed the necklace and padded naked to the bathroom. She'd never been one to prance about in the buff, even when she was alone. But she felt so good, and, truth be told, so sexy, she wanted to leave all the drapes and blinds closed and walk around naked all day.

She went into the kitchen to start her coffee pot. Her heart thrilled like a lovesick teenager's when she found Jack's note.

Darlin',

I hope you slept well. Wish I could be there with you so we could wake up together. You were beautiful last night. You've made us your slaves, eager to do your bidding. We'll call you later to see how you are.

Love, Jack

She smiled, reading his note twice. She closed her eyes, remembering the sound of his voice, the feel of his lips all over her body. The throbbing in her nether regions increased, and she shook her head and smiled. The effect that man, *those* men, had on her body. They didn't even have to be in the vicinity to turn her on.

After her shower, she dressed for work, casual on Sundays, in a nice pair of jeans, her sandals, and a dressy knit top that she felt pretty in. She finished drying her hair and pinned it up loosely with a hair clip, leaving a few tendrils around her neck and at her temples. She hardly ever fussed with her hair, but took the time this morning.

She looked at herself and felt beautiful. Sexy. Then it dawned on her. She no longer felt like hiding those things about herself. It was okay to show who she really was on the inside. She found her features to be only average in appearance, but the way she felt on the inside showed in her eyes and her glowing cheeks. It was a powerful feeling.

While she looked in her kitchen cabinet trying to figure out what to have for an early lunch, her phone rang again. She looked at caller ID, and her insides quivered in delight.

"Hello, darlin'." That sexy, deep Texan twang had her wet in a split second.

"Hi, Jack. How are you?"

He chuckled. "Needy. Did you sleep well?"

"I did. Like a baby, then I woke up to the rain this morning."

"How do you feel this morning? Worn out?" he asked.

"No, I feel wonderful." She drew out the last word, and she smiled when she heard him groan on the other end.

"What do you have planned today?"

"I'm scheduled to work the two to five shift at Stigall's, then I'm going to Charity's for supper."

"She dyin' for details?" he asked with a chuckle.

"You know her well," she replied, laughing.

"It's only eleven o'clock. Since we can't have supper with you, would you like to have lunch with us before you go in?"

"I'd love that. I was just wondering what to fix myself to eat."

"We'll pick you up in twenty minutes. Does that leave you enough time?"

"Yes, I'm ready for work now."

"See you in twenty minutes. I love you, darlin'."

"I love you, too, Jack."

She tidied up and went out on the porch to water her plants and wait for her men to arrive. She had just put the hose away when Owen's truck pulled up to the curb and he honked at her.

Chapter Fifteen

That set her teeth on edge. He did it to summon her to the vehicle like he had done a hundred times before. Only she was no longer at his beck and call.

He looked pissed off she didn't come when he honked. Dave sat in the passenger seat with the good sense to look embarrassed. Owen climbed out of the truck, slammed the door, and walked up to the porch. He looked like he hadn't bathed in a while, and his clothes appeared to have been slept in. The front door stood open behind her, so she knew she could retreat in time if she needed to.

"Why are you here?"

"I'm here for my stuff."

Grace sighed and looked over at Dave. He shrugged, holding up his hands helplessly. This could to get ugly. She glanced at her watch. They'd pull up any second.

"Owen, I bagged up all your stuff, and we put it in the bed of your truck. Do you not remember anything?" Seven years of her life, spent with this moron.

"The fuck you did. When I got in my truck this morning there was nothing in it."

"Who bailed you out?"

"Nobody you know. Don't change the subject. Where are my fucking video games and my clothes? Where's my computer?"

"I put all of that in your truck bed, along with you, on Tuesday afternoon." She pulled open the screen door. "It was there when Dave left with you shortly thereafter."

"What the fuck are you talking about? You threw me out for no good reason, and I know you've got my shit in your house. I swear, if you don't give me my stuff, I'm going to beat the crap out of you!" His eyes blazed as he yelled at her, and she wondered briefly if he was on something, not that it was her problem any longer.

Just then Jack's black SUV pulled to a halt behind Owen's truck. Dave slithered down in the seat, looking like he wished he'd stayed home in his parent's basement. Because Owen was yelling so loudly, he was ignorant of their arrival.

Trying to keep her voice down, she reiterated, "I don't have any of your things, and you don't live here anymore. I hoped you would move on, but if you keep harassing me, I'll file a restraining order. Is that what you want?" She backed over the threshold as he moved toward the porch steps threateningly.

"Snotty bitch, I oughta give you a pop for talking to me like—"

"I wouldn't recommend that, not if you want to go on living." Adam growled from directly behind him. His hand clamped down on Owen's shoulder and impeded him from climbing the steps.

What condition must Owen's faculties be in that he was unaware of them as they had moved up to stand behind him? Was he high or just plain stupid? His demeanor changed as he realized the three big muscular men had overheard what he just said. They all stared down at him, death gleaming in their eyes.

Ethan looked down at him like a king cobra, ready to strike. "You heard the lady. Your property was placed in the bed of your truck and was still there when it was towed by the police Tuesday night."

Owen squinted and rubbed his forehead. "Wait a minute. I recognize you, all of you." He had the nerve to sound outraged.

"I'm surprised," Ethan said, "considering how drunk you were, that you can remember any of it."

"What the fuck are you doing here?" Owen acted as though the property he stood on was his. Grace felt like decking him herself.

"We were going to ask you the same question, but the answer is obvious. You're here to harass and embarrass Grace, which we don't like." Adam tightened his grip on Owen's shoulder, turning him around. Disgust at Owen's unwashed state was evident in his eyes.

Jack and Ethan closed in around him, their arms across their chests.

"Boy, we need to educate you about some facts of life," Jack murmured menacingly. If asked, Grace would have admitted to being incredibly turned on by the sight of them defending her like this. The dampness in her panties would testify to this fact and so would her throbbing clit.

"I don't have to—" was as far as he got. He had turned away to go to his truck before Jack grabbed him by his shirt front and planted his ass easily where it had been seconds before.

"Yeah, you do." Jack shook him by his shirt front. "You struck Grace twice before we stopped you. Touch her again, and you'll live to regret it. She threw your sorry ass out. Your stuff was probably stolen from your truck while it was in the impound lot this week. Go to the Goodwill store, get some cheap clothes, and take a fucking *shower*. You reek. Maybe Dave there will take you in," Jack said, gesturing to the unfortunate passenger in Owen's truck and giving him a perfunctory wave. "Hey, Dave! Yeah, I *see* you."

"How'm I suppose—"

Jack shook his head. "Not our concern, son. Listen to me. Grace is being watched over and protected. Get your shit together and leave her alone. That's your only option."

The three of them escorted Owen bodily to his truck. He turned to look her in the eye, and she saw the anger burning there. She knew Owen better than they did. She hadn't heard the last of him. They closed his door and backed away from the truck as he sped off.

They walked up the driveway to her with concern in their eyes. She reached out to all of them at once and sighed as they enveloped her in their warmth.

Adam wrapped an arm around her shoulder and kissed her temple. "Are you all right, Grace? He didn't touch you before we got here, did he?'

"No, he didn't. You know what you just did?" At their uncertain expressions, she smiled up at them and continued. "That is every woman's fantasy, knowing that someone will ride in and save the day like that. To know she will be protected and defended that way. How did I get so lucky to have three knights in shining armor coming to my rescue? You have no idea how hot you looked, manhandling that jerk back to his truck, telling him all that." She kissed each of them, not caring if neighbors peeked from their windows.

"So, you're all right?" Ethan asked, relief showing in the smile he gave her.

"Yes, he'd only been here a couple of minutes. He never got any closer to me than he was when you pulled up. He's very angry now."

"Maybe he'll leave you alone now," Adam said.

Grace wasn't so sure about that.

* * * *

Ethan worked on sketches and ideas for a bed for Grace's future bedroom. This bed would be large enough for all four of them to fit comfortably. It was going to be an over-the-top romantic design that would be something straight out of Grace's fantasies. At least, that's what he hoped for. They were feeling more and more hopeful that Grace might choose to become a permanent part of their lives. If that hope became a reality, they wanted her to be comfortable and happy. Since Grace would be busy the rest of the day, they decided to sit down and start working out the plans for a possible home renovation.

They talked about transforming the upstairs into a huge master suite. They would keep their bedrooms downstairs and allow upstairs to be her space. She could be alone if she needed to, and she would be able to spend time alone with each of them or have all of them sleep with her at night. That way she had options. Until the renovation was through, she could use Jack's bedroom downstairs because it had the large master bathroom, and he would use the extra bedroom upstairs.

Ethan got in touch with a couple of friends, Wesley and Evan Garner, who owned a custom furniture business and talked to them about building the bed. Wesley invited them out to their house to eat and watch a baseball game that evening. They could talk about their plans and get the ball rolling. If it were up to Ethan, he'd move her in today, just so he could be sure she was safe. Like Grace, he was not convinced they'd seen the last of Owen. That was just expecting too much.

He told the others about his concerns, and Jack made some phone calls to a friend who might be able to help them. Jack's friend Ace Webster planned to arrive in Divine by mid-week after tying up some loose ends in San Angelo. Ethan wished he could come sooner but felt relieved they'd have somebody who could keep an eye on him now that he was out of jail.

They had promised Owen they'd be watching him, and it was past time to act on that promise. They'd just have to be vigilant until Ace arrived.

Before the game started, Wes took them out back to the big workshop and showed them what he was working on as well as pictures of what he'd made in the past. Ethan showed him the sketches of what he had in mind. Wes laid out some samples of wood and showed them a photo of another custom bed he'd made recently.

"We could add posters and a rail for a canopy with no problem," Wes dropped a transparency over the photograph and using a dry erase marker to show them what he meant. "If you'll call and let me know a time, you can bring her by and see if she likes it and pick out the wood for it. She can look at the other photos if she wants to. Did you want more than just a bed?"

Jack nodded. "That part's a surprise. She'll probably want a dresser or chest of drawers, as well. But we'll want you to build the other pieces that would go with it. She'll have plenty of space for them."

Wesley showed them some layouts to give them an idea and to get an estimate of how much wood they were going to need. Ethan looked on and pointed at the several different pieces he thought she would like and said, "Show her these pictures and see if there are any particular pieces she seems interested in, even if she doesn't come right out and say so. She won't want to ask for anything extra. That's why we're doing this."

"Make the lingerie chest a large one," Adam stated simply.

Wesley looked at them and laughed. "I have *got* to meet this woman. She must really be something! This is a big commitment you're making."

"Wes, this is nothing compared to what she's brought to our lives," Jack said. "We just want to make her happy. You let us know, and we'll pay your price. We might be able to bring her out next weekend or next week. Depends on how she likes our renovation plans."

"You're renovating, too? Wow. She have a sister?" Wes replied, half teasing. "She must really be something, judging by the goofy expressions on your faces." The three of them chuckled quietly but made no excuses.

"Sorry, Wes, her sister is already married with kids and a big biker dude husband," Ethan replied.

They went back inside to eat and watch the game. Ethan had a good time with his friends, but found it hard to ignore the little hitching ache in his chest when thoughts of Grace invaded his mind. He imagined her satin-soft body wrapped around him in his king-size bed.

During a commercial, Wesley muted the TV. "You don't worry about feeling jealous of each other?"

"I don't think it would have worked," Jack said, "if we hadn't known each other for so long. You would have to meet Grace to understand. She met Ethan and Adam and fell for them as hard as they fell for her. It came as no surprise to me when that happened, and I was already open to the idea she might be the one."

"You don't worry about being manipulated?" Wesley asked. "What if she played one of you against the others? I'm not saying Grace is like that. I'm just curious," Wesley said.

"I think your frame of reference is a little different from ours." Jack explained. "The women in town who go for uncommitted threesomes and one night stands might play those games with the men they latch on to, but that's not how we met Grace. She has no experience with a relationship like ours. We met through my mother."

Ethan returned from the kitchen with more beers and handed one to Wes. "She'd never even been in The Dancing Pony until last week. She's innocent to what goes on with those women. For her, and for us, this isn't about power, it's about love."

Wesley nodded silently. Evan had been listening intently and then spoke up. "Patricia still after you, Ethan? That's who you were referring to, wasn't it?"

Ethan replied, "Unfortunately, yes. Grace is a lady through and through, otherwise she might have kicked Patricia's ass for putting her hand on my arm last night at the Pony. Yes, Patricia remains very persistent."

"She's still with Angel?" Wesley asked, and at their nods, he said, "That's got FUBAR written all over it."

"Tell me about it," Jack said. "Her living arrangement is on shaky ground unless she backs the fuck off. Angel was disgusted today because she didn't come home until this afternoon. Of course, she claims she spent the night at a girlfriend's house because she had too much to drink."

"They don't like each other?"

"Grace wants to simply live and let live," Adam said, "but she's the jealous type, and Patricia doesn't play fair. Rachel Lopez caught Patricia in the bathroom with Grace last night, looking at each other like they were about to have a cat fight."

"Did she pitch a fit, Ethan?" Evan grinned. "Make you kick Patricia out of the club?"

"Naw, it's like Adam said. She's willing to live and let live if possible. She never said another word about Patricia and seemed determined to not let her ruin her fun. She loves to dance, and I think she had a really good time with us," Ethan replied, smiling, remembering the joy in her eyes as he spun her on the dance floor. "Grace is not the type to pitch a spoiled hissy fit."

"Nobody said anything about her being with the three of you together?" Wesley asked.

"Nobody much cared," Ethan said, realizing they were all but ignoring the game. "We raised a few eyebrows when she kissed all three of us. But she wasn't giving us tongue or anything like that. Like I said, she's a lady. When we went out for lunch today, she sat with us like we were all just friends, not like she was in love with us. She's aware people may talk."

"What if people get judgmental with y'all or her?" Evan asked. Ethan noticed he seemed very concerned about how this relationship would affect her.

"If you were in love with a worthy woman, would you let public opinion sway you?" Jack replied.

"No, but what about her? What if *she* can't handle the criticism?" Evan asked, pointedly ignoring the frown Wesley sent his way.

"We just have to make it worth her while to be with us. What do you really want to know, Evan?" Ethan asked, wondering at the burr obviously up Evan's ass tonight.

"Well, I remember when y'all first told us you wanted a woman you could share. Someone you could make happy together, have a family and everything. That was years ago, remember, back when we were teenagers? But then, seeing how most women are, manipulating and lying to get what they want, I just don't see how it could work. I mean, we all play games, we all manipulate, right?"

"I think your issues are with women in general," Ethan said, knowing that Evan's problems with women ran deep, "not a woman willing to try a polyamorous relationship specifically. Not all women are liars, Evan, and not all people manipulate. You're still not over Rita, I think. Ruling and using the men in her life is not the goal of every woman out there. What if there was a woman who has so much love in her heart that she falls in love with Wesley, meets you, and falls just as completely for you. Would you let your past keep the three of you from being happy?"

Ethan watched Evan's reactions, noticing that Wesley watched him just as closely. Evan didn't respond, so Ethan pressed on.

"Do y'all want the same kind of relationship?" He looked from Wesley to Evan and saw the fleeting look of hope on Wesley's face. Ethan glanced at Evan and saw several emotions cross his face. He smiled weakly, but the look in his eyes was doubtful. Dubious. Then he realized exactly who this was all about.

They were interested in how Grace was handling loving them because Rosemary Piper was back in the picture. They'd always had a soft spot for her, even if she was a bit of a spitfire. They obviously did not want to go into details. Maybe it was a sore subject, and here they were with all their sappy puppy love vibes.

Ethan made eye contact with Wesley and grinned knowingly. "We're here for y'all if you want to talk about it, okay?"

Wesley nodded almost imperceptibly. His phone rang, and he checked his caller ID before excusing himself. Evan hit the mute button on the TV remote, thus ending that conversation. Adam caught Ethan's eye and shrugged at him.

They were yawning by the time the game was over and left soon after. Wesley and Evan never brought their earlier topic of discussion up again, and neither did the guys. After so much lost sleep the night before, they were ready to call the evening done. Jack called Grace on the way home to see if she'd made it back home all right. She was just preparing to climb into bed. Jack put the phone on speaker so they could all say good night to her.

She sounded sleepy and sexy. "Hey, guys, did you have a good time this evening?"

"We did. What are you doing, Gracie?" Ethan asked, hearing rustling sounds coming from the phone.

"Gettin' ready for bed," she said, lapsing into a drawl.

"What are you wearing?" Adam asked playfully.

"Can you guess?"

Adam chuckled. "That skimpy outfit you had on last night?"

"Nope." Grace giggled.

"Flannel pajamas?" Adam asked.

More giggling. "Nope. Too hot."

"A T-shirt?" Ethan asked.

"Nope."

"How about a nightgown?" Jack asked

"Nuh-uh."

"A babydoll nightie?" Adam asked.

"No," she replied.

Ethan leaned forward to the phone and asked softly, "Gracie, are you wearing what I think you're wearing?"

"Uh-huh," she said, giggling with anticipation.

"Really?" He laughed at the confused looks on the others' faces. "Jack and Adam still haven't figured it out. Why don't you tell them, honey?"

The interior of the SUV got very quiet as she let them wonder a few seconds more, and then he heard a small, slightly breathy voice say, "I'm nekkid, well, almost."

Adam almost stuttered. "R–Really? What's almost?"

"I was thinking about my men, and I decided to put my necklace back on."

"Holy fuck," Adam whispered.

All Jack could manage was a low moan.

Ethan asked, "You're wet, aren't you, Gracie honey?" Even though he was exhausted, his hardening cock volunteered for duty.

"Yes, Ethan, a little."

"Do you need us?" Jack asked.

"I'll always need you, honey, but it's been an exhausting weekend for all of us, and you have busy schedules this week. If you come over, you know you won't leave for hours. I'm kicking myself for saying this, but I want you to have your rest. I'll be fine."

"We wouldn't mind, Gracie," Ethan's cock was now sitting up and begging.

"I know you wouldn't, but I don't want to worry about you being tired behind the wheel tomorrow. Get your rest."

"Will we see you this week, honey?" Adam asked.

"If you want, yes."

Jack picked the phone up off the console. “We’ll call you, darlin’.”

“I love you.”

“We love you, baby, sweet dreams,” Adam said.

“’Night,” she whispered before hanging up.

“She is the sexiest woman I’ve ever met,” Jack said as he ended the call.

“I’ll bet she’s touching herself right now,” Adam muttered, sounding like he was in pain.

“Maybe, but I doubt it,” Ethan said, grinning, his cock threatening mutiny. He palmed it to the other side, trying to get more comfortable.

Jack looked over at him curiously. “Why do you say that?”

“Because things changed last night. I know Gracie. If she can’t have what she wants, she’d rather wait than settle for a substitute. She just subjugated her needs for ours. *That’s* Grace.”

“You’re right, not that it helps right now,” Jack muttered.

Chapter Sixteen

Grace had a full day at Harper's on Monday. She was sitting in the break room eating her lunch when her cell phone rang.

"Hi, Ethan." She giggled into the phone.

"Hi, Gracie," he said. "Guess where we are." He snickered.

"You're all together? Shouldn't you be working? Are you playing hooky?" She tried to sound scandalized.

"Nuh-uh. We're at Dr. Guthrie's office, waiting for our appointments," he replied.

"All three of you?"

"Yep."

"Thank you, Ethan, for understanding. You're a peach."

"You're worth it, babe." She heard a feminine voice in the background say, "Ethan Grant?"

"Time to go, Gracie, love you."

"Love you, too." Then he hung up.

They were really going through with it, for her. They really wanted this very badly if they got into the doctor so quickly. They must have waited to be worked in.

"Good news?" Martha asked her, coming in to get another cup of coffee. "I heard you on the phone and now you're blushing and smiling. You seem to do that a lot lately."

"Yeah, that was Ethan."

"Oh? As in 'Ethan, Jack, and Adam' Ethan?"

"Yeah. He loves me."

"I'd have to be a dummy not to see that."

"Grace?" Rose said, slipping into the break room. "Owen is out front asking for you. You want me to call Jack?"

"No, I'll deal with Owen. Don't call Jack. If Owen gets ugly, call Hank. I'll get rid of him." She walked up front to the counter. Owen waited there by the door, looking very agitated.

When he saw her approaching, he stepped to the counter and got straight to the point.

"Grace, I need some money."

"What?"

"I need some money. I know you have some from your mom."

"Why?"

His face got red and he bellowed, "*Hey*! Because of you, all my stuff is gone. I need some money. Now, today."

She noticed that his demeanor was different. Something was wrong with him. He looked bad, but a different bad. He didn't act drunk, slurring his words. He was talking too fast and his eyes darted around. She was willing to bet he was on something. She didn't recognize the clothes he had on, but they didn't look new. He must have taken her men's advice and gone to the Goodwill store. He'd been angry with her the other day, but today he seemed worried, apprehensive, and ready to jump out of his skin.

She looked at him through narrowed eyes. "Who bailed you out the other day?"

"None of your business. I need the money."

"I'm not giving you any money."

"Grace, I'm not fucking around with you. You owe me."

"I owe you *nothing*, Owen. If anything, you owe me." She heard Rose talking on the phone to Hank. "Jack, Adam, and Ethan told you to leave me alone. They were serious, and they will not overlook your little visit to me today. Even if I could touch my investments to help you out, I wouldn't. My days of enabling you are officially over."

"Are those their names? Your fuck buddies? Don't kid yourself, Grace, they're just using you. Once you've paid off that AC repair, they'll move on, and I'll be around to pay you back for all this fucking trouble you've caused me!"

"What trouble have I caused you? You got yourself arrested."

"I need to pay the person back who bailed me out. I *need* that money, Grace." He was still angry, but there was a desperate quality to his anger.

"If you couldn't pay your bail back, you should have stayed in jail. If you keep pestering me, I'm going to file a restraining order. Now go."

"You're going to regret this, Grace." He growled, taking a step closer.

She didn't back down. She placed her hands on the counter and leaned across it slightly. "Not as much as you're going to regret coming here today. I was the best thing that ever happened to your sorry ass, and you screwed it up. I have a feeling Rose is on the phone with Hank Stinson right now. Do yourself a favor and pull your head out of your ass before your stay in jail takes on a more permanent quality. Now *get!*" she yelled at him, pointing toward the door, satisfied at the glimpse of surprise she saw in his eyes. He yanked on the door handle, slamming it as he left. A few seconds later tires screeched outside as he tore out of the small parking lot.

"Well done, Grace. I wish you'd have stood up to him years ago," Rose said as she entered the front room.

"I wish he'd stay away. I'll have to get the restraining order if he doesn't stop this."

* * * *

Jack was the last to exit the doctor's exam room. Each of them had blood drawn and made good on the requested samples. The unpleasant part was over—the gloved and lubricated finger. Doc had insisted they do this.

"It's not my favorite exam to perform any more than it's your favorite to be on the 'receiving' end of. Look at it this way, Jack. At least I don't have to stick a cold metal speculum up your ass and crank you open to do your exam."

Doc laughed hard at Jack's full body shudder and the look on his face. "The nurse will let you know your test results when they come in. I think it's really nice you're doing this for Grace. Your relationship is a very unconventional one. Grace is a favorite patient of mine, a real sweetheart, and she deserves to be happy. Don't you break her heart, okay?"

"You can keep a secret, can't you?" Jack asked with a grin.

"Sure. Patient confidentiality and all that. What's your secret?"

"We've ordered her ring. I'm proposing to her when it's ready."

Dr. Guthrie clapped her hands enthusiastically. "Congratulations! You're a lucky man, men—oh, you know what I mean! I think y'all are going to be very happy. Will you remind her I'm here if she needs me, if she has questions or she needs to talk?"

"Sure. I promise we'll take very good care of her."

"I know you will, and thanks for being so candid with me about your relationship. You'd be amazed at the vital information my patients sometimes withhold from me."

Jack left the office with Adam and Ethan, ready to get on with the rest of their day. He was glad to have that behind them, both literally and figuratively. Jack called Grace from the parking lot to let her know they'd been seen by the doctor.

"Did you have a prostate exam?" she asked sympathetically.

"Yes, we feel like we need to take showers now," Jack said, shuddering.

"I'm sorry baby. I sort of know how you feel." She sounded sympathetic, but he had the feeling she was covering a giggle.

"At least it's done now, and we'll have our results in a few days." Jack said, opening the door on the SUV which was hot as an oven inside.

"Thank you, honey. Are you done working for the day?" she asked.

"Yes. I miss you. You get off in a few minutes?"

"Yes. I'm going to the grocery store, then home. Something happened that I need to tell you about. Could you put me on speakerphone, please, honey?"

He gestured to Adam and Ethan to come closer and listen as he switched to speakerphone. "You're on, what happened?"

"Owen came by the shop asking me for money."

Jack looked at the others in disgust.

"Are you all right?" Ethan asked.

"Yes, I'm fine. I told him no, of course, and Rose called Hank for me. He came by and took my statement, and I told him I would tell you myself. Owen looked like he was on something, and he was very agitated, almost scared."

"Did he threaten you, darlin'?" Jack asked, itching to take action of some kind instead of talking on the phone in the parking lot.

"Yes, I suppose he did. He told me I'd regret not giving the money to him. He told me I was responsible for his things being stolen from his truck bed. He said he needed to pay back the person who bailed him out."

"I imagine that he does," Jack said. "We did some checking on Owen after his visit to your house yesterday. Hank told us he's made some new friends while in jail and mixed up with some potentially dangerous people. He could lead them to you as a possible means of paying his debt. What they really want is for him to begin dealing for them, but they'll extract their pound of flesh, with interest, however they can. I don't think it's safe for you to stay alone."

When they hired the private investigator to watch Owen, Jack had let Hank know about it. Hank said the individuals Owen was hanging around were under surveillance, and that his investigator should hang back so he didn't jeopardize their ongoing investigation. Jack planned to have Ace assist them in watching over Grace when he arrived. Today's confrontation just proved to him that Grace needed protection as much as Owen needed watching.

"I agree, Gracie," Ethan said quickly.

"Me, too, baby," Adam agreed.

"I refuse to be run out of my house," she replied firmly.

Jack couldn't fault her for feeling defensive. She had been at Owen's mercy for a long time. Now that she finally had some power and control back, she was holding on to it with tooth and nail. "Darlin', Adam has an appointment he needs to go to, and Ethan needs to get over to the Pony. Why don't you go on to the store, and I'll meet you at your house. We can talk about your options and figure out what to do, all right?"

"Okay. I don't want Ethan and Adam to be late. I'll be about thirty minutes, Jack. See you at the house." Bidding them all good-bye, she hung up.

"She didn't sound very happy," Jack said as he put his phone away. "It's better if only one of us talks to her. Otherwise she'll feel like we're ganging up on her."

"I want her in our house where she's safe," Ethan said as he climbed into his truck and lowered the windows, "but not if she feels like she's there under duress. Let me know how it goes."

Adam turned and looked at Jack seriously. "You know, you could offer to stay with her. That way, she's in her home, but we know she's safe. It's okay with me if you two sleep together. I would understand under the circumstances."

Ethan nodded in agreement. “Same here, Jack. If she offers to let you stay the night, do it. I’d rather that when she moves in with us it’s because she wants to and not because she feels pushed. I’ll understand, too.”

Hands on his hips, Jack shook his head. “No, we agreed the first time for all of us would be together. If she lets me stay, we’ll watch a movie and I’ll sleep on the couch. But thanks for telling me that.”

“Okay, see y’all later. I’m running late,” Ethan said as he rolled up the windows now that the truck interior had cooled a little and drove out of the parking lot.

Adam’s phone rang, and he nodded and waved to Jack, answering the call. It was probably his last appointment of the day wondering if he was still coming. Jack got in the SUV and drove out to Grace’s house. No point in dawdling. He sure hated to make her unhappy, and she was not happy at the moment.

* * * *

Ethan breathed a sigh of relief as he entered the dark, overly cool interior of The Dancing Pony. Happy hour was well under way, so a few of the regulars were there already, including Patricia. He spoke with Ben briefly and fixed Patricia a mixed drink. They left the patrons at the bar in the capable hands of the other bartender, and brought it over to her table where she sat alone and joined her. She smiled flirtatiously, but seemed confused by Ben’s presence.

This was primarily Ethan’s problem, given Patricia’s behavior toward Grace on Saturday night. But Patricia and her friends’ behavior in the club in general were an issue for both Ben and Ethan, and the nightclub’s reputation as well.

“We need to have a talk, Patricia,” Ethan began.

“About what?”

“About your behavior Saturday night. And about what you and your friends have been up to.”

“What did I do Saturday night?” she asked defensively.

“I’ll put it simply for you, if that’s how you want to play this. This is a place of business and not your territory. The decent hard-working men who come here are not your territory. *I* am not your territory,” Ethan said, leaning toward her a little so he couldn't be overheard. "You will stop threatening the female customers—"

"I didn't threaten anybody," she muttered angrily, looking down at her drink, tapping her long nails on the rim.

"—stop threatening the *ladies* who come in here to unwind after a hard day *working* and want to have a good time visiting with their friends."

Ben spoke softly, "The ladies' room has a lock on the door so that our waitresses can change clothing if they need to, not so you can use the restroom to have quickie sex."

"I don't know what you're talking about!"

Ethan was repulsed by the innocent act she put forth, having seen her in action slipping into the ladies' restroom with a male club patron a time or two. He'd heard rumors from other reliable sources as well.

"Patricia, we've all seen it, so please just listen," Ben said reasonably.

Ethan kept his tone even as he continued. "You're to leave Grace alone. Regardless of whether or not she is here, you will keep your hands *off of me*. You did that the other night just to get a reaction out of her, and she bested you."

As he said those words, her eyes narrowed to black slits. Her mouth turned down into an even bigger pout. She opened her mouth to say something further, and he cut her off.

"The little stunt that you tried to pull in the bathroom backfired on you when Rachel caught you eyeing Grace for a shiner. Grace *works* two jobs to earn a living. She's taller than you, and I can tell you she's a lot *stronger* than she looks." Ethan could not stifle the grin that thinking of Grace inspired. When she saw it, Patricia glowered at him and looked about ready to come unglued.

Ben took a sip from his glass of soda before saying, "Patricia, if you are *that* into a regular threesome or foursome experience, you really need to move to a bigger city where they have private clubs *devoted* to that kind of entertainment in a safe setting.

"For now, we are not banning you from The Dancing Pony," Ben continued. "Some of our customers enjoy your company. But if we get any more complaints or more fallout from you and your girlfriends' shenanigans, we will reserve the right to not serve you further. *Comprende*?"

"Yes," she said through gritted teeth.

"And you understand about Grace?" Ethan asked.

"Yes. No!" she whined, her face flushed under her heavy makeup. "I *don't* understand. How am I any different from Grace, who was in here openly kissing the three of them, flaunting herself with *all* of them?" she asked, looking at Ben.

Ben sighed. "Patricia, the difference is that she came in with them and left with them and didn't cause *problems* while she was here. She acted like a lady. Now you're welcome to stay if you'd like. Nobody else knows what we're talking about over here. But you're going to behave yourself." Ben stared at her until she nodded.

As Ben and Ethan got up to return to the bar, Patricia reached out a hand but didn't go so far as to touch Ethan. He paused and nodded at Ben as he turned and walked away. Ethan looked at her hand, then into her eyes, a little curious to hear what she had to say.

"Why don't you want me? Why her? Why not me? You could have shared me with Angel. I would have let you share me with Jack and Adam. I would never have refused you. Why not me, Ethan? I could please you in ways she can't even imagine. Why do you want that cow and not me?"

As she spoke, any compassion he might have felt for her situation dissipated. Her words turned his stomach and gave him a glimpse into her black heart.

He stood there and crossed his arms over his chest, contemplating his answer. "Why her and not you? You have an itch for multiple penetrations that has nothing to do with love, Patricia. You don't want to *share* with me and Angel, you enjoy cuckolding him. You get off on it." She opened her mouth to interrupt, but he cut her off.

"Jack and Adam would remain celibate rather than have anything to do with you. You say you can please us in ways Grace can't imagine. To me that means I can *only imagine* how you got that experience. And as for your reference to her being a cow?" Ethan shook his head and looked at her with distaste.

"She's fat, and you could do so much—" she whined, which made her even less appealing than she already was.

"She's absolute stunning *perfection* to us because some men prefer a woman who isn't obsessed with her weight and can love a man into slow, sweet oblivion, as opposed to taking a chance on having to pick bone splinters from his cock after fucking a thin, angry, and malnourished spiteful witch. You have some odd notions about what men find appealing in a woman."

"I hung around all this time waiting for you."

"Patricia, you are supposed to be Angel's girlfriend. You live with him, for crying out loud. You didn't wait for anyone or anything. You were just biding your time fucking every man who looked your way in here. If you were waiting on me it was in vain because I would never have agreed to have any sort of contact with you."

"Why?"

Ethan wished he'd walked away with Ben when he had the chance.

"You're not making this any easier by asking me questions like that, Patricia."

"Why, Ethan? I would take it however y'all would give it to me."

Didn't that just paint a rosy picture in his mind?

He shook his head and rubbed a hand over his face. "And that's why you can't have it. You're desperate to fill a void that can't be filled with sex. You need to take a few steps back from what you've been doing and get some help."

His words served only to anger her, and he watched a deep flush come over her overly made-up face. Her mouth clamped down into an ugly frown.

"Seriously, Patricia, get some professional help. We'll let you stay tonight, but no shenanigans."

As Ethan returned to the bar Ben said, "Well, that was interesting."

"This problem isn't going away," Ethan muttered in disgust. "We're going to have to keep an eye on them. They might behave for a few nights, and then they'll be up to their old tricks again. We better tell the waitresses so they can watch for trouble. Watch both restrooms, too, I guess. We should have just banned them for all the trouble we'll have to go to watching them. Shit."

"Well, they've been warned, so they can't complain if they get banned later."

"Once her friends get here, I'll check in with them myself. She may not tell them anything out of spite, just to cause trouble. I'll let Rogelio and Mike know also."

"It's a shame she caused all that trouble for Grace. It really backfired on her, seems like," Ben said. "I'm gone if we're done."

"Later. Enjoy your evening." Ethan turned his attention to one of the regulars and opened a beer for him.

* * * *

Jack parked the SUV in front of Grace's house, finished the phone conversation with one of his sub-contractors, and climbed out. No sooner had he put the phone in his pocket than it rang again.

"Hi, it's Grace. I'm at the store right now. Is there anything you need before I join a checkout line?"

"No, I'm good, darlin'."

"I'm going to fix you a steak dinner. I'm sorry for snapping at you earlier," she said apologetically.

"There's nothin' for you to be sorry for, darlin'. You just got your house back to yourself, and you don't want to lose that. We can talk about it when you get home."

"I love you, Jack."

"I love you, darlin'."

"Bye."

He pulled his key out and went inside her house. He opened the back door and put charcoal in the grill and started it up, then went inside. He set the table and had a thought. He pulled out his phone.

"Yeah!"

"Hey, Adam, how's the last service appointment going?"

Adam whispered into the phone, "Like a bitch. I'm in an attic. This is not going to be an easy fix."

"We're grilling steaks for supper. You want us to grill one for you?"

More muffled, juicy cursing. "Probably not. I'm going to be a while, and I'm filthy and covered in insulation." This was not Adam's day. "Looks to me like you've got our girl to yourself tonight. Lucky bastard. I've got to get this fixed tonight for Mrs. King. She's got two little ones, expecting another, and the AC quit on her. After I get this up and running for her, I'm gonna take a nice long shower, drink an ice cold beer, and eat. Tell Grace I love her. And thanks, man, for thinking of me. It means a lot."

"No problem. I'll tell her."

"Hey. I meant what I said earlier, about tonight. It's okay with me, you know. If something happens between you tonight. She's…hard to resist."

"Thanks, man. Regardless, tonight she's sleeping safe. Something is bound to happen soon with that investigation."

Jack turned on her stereo and looked in the refrigerator for fixings for a salad. He was slicing a tomato up when she walked in the door, laden with bags. He went running, taking them from her.

* * * *

She'd loaded up like a pack animal to save herself trips out of habit, but she'd forgotten that this man was eager to help with the heavy lifting.

"Thank you, Jack," she said, and gave him a kiss as he took them from her.

"I didn't hear you pull up, otherwise I would have helped you. I'll get the rest," he said, as he put the bags on the counter.

She began to put the groceries away, and then she noticed he'd set the table and had sliced a tomato for salad. His thoughtfulness in helping with the prep work was such a change from what she was accustomed to. In contrast, she remembered the last time she had hauled groceries up those front steps. Owen had belched by way of greeting, eating straight from a half gallon of ice cream. She'd promised herself that after she'd kicked him out she was going to deal with the carton and spoon he'd thrown back in the freezer but had forgotten all about it. She opened the freezer and there it was, still sitting there with the spoon frozen into the contents, jutting out of the half closed lid. She pulled the spoon out, ran it under hot water, and tossed the entire container of ice cream in the trash. Gross. She shuddered, remembering what came next, her hands becoming fists at her sides.

Strong arms slid around her, and that memory, so powerful for a moment, slipped away. She felt his lips on the back of her neck as he said, "It's just us now, darlin'. He's nothin' more than a bad memory. No one's going to mistreat you anymore."

She turned in his arms as the tension slipped away and put her head on his shoulder. "I was having a moment."

"I could tell." And that was all he said. "I started the grill for you. Do you want to marinate the steaks or just season them?"

"Let's just season them and get them on the grill when it's hot enough. I'll go change into something more comfortable. Be right back."

She changed into some soft knit capris and a T-shirt and returned barefoot. The steaks were on a plate in the kitchen, ready for the grill. Jack sat on the couch, and when he patted his lap, she didn't even hesitate. She cuddled into his lap and allowed him to draw her close for a long, slow kiss.

"Will you stay with us until we know you're safe from Owen?"

Grace sighed and rested her head on Jack's shoulder. "It's not that I don't want to. I just wanted for the first time I spent the night at your house to be under different circumstances. I wanted to keep that kind of sacred, you know?"

"Of course, and I feel the same way. But our desire to keep you safe comes first for us. We promise that we would behave ourselves—"

"But that's just it. I don't want you to *behave yourselves* when I come to spend the night with you." That shut him up right quick, for a few seconds, anyway. "Why don't you stay here with me?"

"That I could do, but with some limitations that we need to agree on," he replied, caressing her hip.

"Okay? What kind of limitations did you have in mind?" she asked. She already had a good idea, but decided it would be best to get all of that out in the open, up front. His fingertips caressing her through the soft knit capris were doing magical things for her. The spot one of his fingers was currently stroking made her back arch and her abdominal muscles tighten involuntarily and she had to hold back a little squeal. After all, he was trying to be serious.

"No lovemaking tonight. Ethan and Adam told me they understood if it happened, but I want to start out on the right foot. I think it would be unfair to them."

"I can understand that. You are a good and decent friend to them. You know they'd do the same for you, right?" The dynamic between them would never work if they were into serving themselves if it went against the best interests of the group. She already knew none of them would violate that ideal. That didn't mean she wasn't going to at least try to *give back* tonight.

"Without a doubt. So let's eat supper, watch a movie, and try to behave. If you want to fool around a little, that would be okay. Torture for me, but if you need it, I'll be happy to oblige." His words reawakened the needy ache in her pelvis as she imagined them all together in bed, warmed up and ready to take their relationship to a deeper level.

"Only if you let me give you a blow job."

"Let's just wait and see on that, all right?"

"I can work with that." She smiled because he had not given her a definite no.

He patted her ass and then squeezed her thigh and said, "Why don't I fix you a glass of wine, and we can sit out on the back porch while the steaks cook?"

"That sounds wonderful, honey." She hopped up. "It's nice now that there is shade on the back porch. I know Ethan is working tonight. What is Adam up to?"

"He is unfortunately still on a service call. He has a soft spot for damsels in distress, in this case an expectant mother with two toddlers. Her husband is currently serving in Iraq, and her AC is on the fritz."

"Poor baby!" she said sympathetically, taking the glass of wine he offered her.

"Which one?" he asked with a chuckle as he picked up the plate the steaks were on and held the door open for her.

"Are you kidding? *All* of them. I miss him, but I know how they feel without AC. To be pregnant with no relief from this heat? I'm glad he's so soft-hearted. We damsels in distress need guys like him," she said, sitting down in a lawn chair.

As the steaks cooked, he lifted her bare feet into his lap and gave her a foot rub while they talked. He shared Dr. Guthrie's take on his squeamishness over his prostate exam when compared with her yearly exam, much to her amusement.

"Having to submit to an exam and Pap smear is nothing compared to what I'll go through someday if I have a baby." She giggled, making bulging eyes and motioning over an imaginary pregnant belly with her hands.

"Is that something you want some day?" he asked, grinning at her.

"Absolutely, with the right man—or men, that is." She rested her hands over her abdomen.

"Speaking of babies, you need to come out to the ranch sometime real soon and see the new foals we have scampering around. There are two of them, born just a few days ago. Cute as they can be."

"I'd love to. But—"

"What, honey?"

"If I go out there, to the back, I mean, around the horse barns…Doesn't Patricia live back there? Do you really think it's a good idea, especially if I encounter Angel? If she finds out I know Angel, she's going to go apeshit on him, on me, on everybody."

"Darlin', you have more rights out there than she does. She is there by our good graces alone. She doesn't work out there or anywhere as far as I can tell. She is Angel's woman for as long as he tolerates her attitude and habits, coming and going like a cat in heat. If you want to see the babies, just let us know, and we'll take you out to see them, then there would be no risk of a confrontation."

"I'm not afraid of a confrontation with her. I'm worried about the trouble she will make for Angel and y'all. I don't want to be the cause of bad feelings between y'all."

"Don't worry. Angel can handle her. He's no dummy. He knows how she is. I wish he'd find someone decent that he could settle down with."

"I know someone who thinks Angel is the most irresistible man on the face of the earth," She giggled when he tickled the bottom of her foot, before continuing to rub them.

"Who?" Jack asked curiously.

"I work with her at Stigall's. She was helping me in menswear one day when he came in to buy new blue jeans. She stuttered and blushed for ten minutes after he left before she finally told me. I'm used to his flirtatious ways, but she was completely smitten with him."

"Maybe you and I have some matchmaking to do, darlin'. Is she pretty? What's she like?" Jack asked enthusiastically.

"Her name is Teresa Palacios. She's my age, maybe a couple of years older. She lives here in town, and she works there full-time. She normally works in the jewelry department. She's petite and very pretty. As I recall, your mom liked her a lot, too."

"Now there's a resounding endorsement. Mom liked her, too, huh? Well, maybe I need to run some errands in town with Angel one day and conveniently remember that you hinted around about something you liked at the Stigall's jewelry counter."

"There's just one catch, Jack. She's a single mom. She has a little boy. He's two years old and sweet like his mommy."

"Angel is a great guy, grew up in a big family. I don't think that would put him off too much. We may get in trouble for matchmaking. Are you up for it?" She lifted her feet from his lap when it was time to check the steaks.

"I think she'd go out with him if he approached her right. She feels very shy around him because he is so direct. If he could just get her to open up to him, it'd be fine, I think. You're really anxious to get rid of Patricia, aren't you?"

"Aren't you?" he asked

"Only in a *huge* way," she quipped.

He removed the steaks from the grill, and they went back inside.

They ate their supper at the kitchen table, talking and laughing, and then watched their movie. She got up to take her shower after the movie was over. After she finished, she came out of the bathroom with her robe on over her pajamas. She decided to show Jack a little mercy by not parading around in revealing night clothes. She came to him and sat in his lap again on the couch.

"Where are you sleeping tonight?" she asked him, sitting carefully as she noted the erection that pressed against her hip.

"I think on the couch might be best, Grace." Jack sounded resigned, almost reluctant. "Quite frankly, I want you so much it's painful right now."

"All right," she said softly, neutrally, "I'll get you a pillow and a blanket. You should keep pajamas here or something."

"I'm hoping you and I get to a point real soon where pajamas become unnecessary." He smiled when she blushed, allowing her to get up from his lap.

She felt bad, thinking of him being aroused to the point of pain, and though she wasn't ready for the night to end, she felt like she needed to leave him alone so he could get some rest. She retrieved what he needed from her linen closet.

"There is an extra towel hanging in the bathroom if you want a shower. It might help you relax."

She was coming out of the bedroom with a glass when he emerged from the steamy bathroom in his knit boxer shorts.

"I was just getting some water," she said softly. She'd already removed her robe.

"I hope you don't mind. I mean, that I'm in my boxers."

She smiled and wanted to say more, but only replied, "Not at all."

He unfolded his blanket and got his makeshift bed ready. The unfulfilled sexual tension between them was thick, and rather than draw it out to see what would happen, she went to him and softly said, "I love you, Jack. Sleep well."

She hugged him, careful not to rub him or to overtly take notice of the erection standing proudly and reaching the waistband of his snug knit boxers. *Sweet merciful heavens.* She wanted him so much. Going to bed like this just wasn't right. Neither one of them would get any rest. She tilted her head and looked up at him. His fingertip held her chin in place, and he gave her a sweet tender kiss that melted her knees and had her stomach doing flip-flops.

"It won't always be like this, darlin'. We can do this, just for now, until we know you're safe. I love you, Grace. Good night." And that was her signal that he needed her to help him out by going on to bed.

"Good night," she whispered and walked to her bedroom, glancing back to see him reclining on the couch, his arm flung over his head on the armrest, arranging the blanket so he was covered decently. His tanned chest was bare, and she could just make out the tops of his hips above the edge of the blanket. He was like a jungle cat stretched out, looking languid, but the trained eye could see the coiled tension in each muscle, ready for action with a second's notice. He was beautiful to her in that moment. She stepped into her room, and in a daring move, she stripped to her bare skin and climbed into bed naked. Sleep wasn't going to come easily to either one of them.

Grace felt adrift in her bed. When she moved, the cotton of her sheets slid across her thighs and her abdomen, teasing her nipples into erect peaks. Every once in a while she heard Jack's soft sigh or the sound of him shifting like he couldn't get comfortable. She hadn't touched herself, but she was drenched with need for him. She wished he was pushing that big cock into her that very second.

Her hand drifted to her hot, wet slit, and a shuddering breath escaped her. She was afraid for a second that he might have heard her and then chastised herself. This was silly. Climbing from the bed, she padded naked down the hall. He lay there in the dark except for a faint glimmer that shined across his chest from the light outside. He heard her in the doorway and turned to look at her. She didn't care that she stood there naked, but she did care about his pained expression.

She wanted to honor his request, and she planned to, but she knew in her heart that what she wanted from Jack would be okay with Ethan and Adam. On silent feet she went to him. Standing over him, she held out her hand to him. He hesitated for a moment before reaching for her hand, a shuddering sigh escaping his lips. Rising from the couch, she saw in the dim light that he was still erect and even larger, if that was possible.

She led him back to her bedroom and pulled back the covers. She opened the drapes on the window nearest her bed, letting the moonlight stream in. She returned to him, her fingers sliding down his muscled chest to his waist.

"I wanted to be able to see you," she whispered in a trembling voice as she eased the waistband over his erection carefully. She knelt at his feet, looking up at him as he stepped from the boxers. The last time she knelt at his feet a new chapter in her life had begun. He reached out and gently palmed her cheek.

She stood and climbed into the bed and beckoned him to lie down with his head on her pillows. She slid a hand under his knee to lift it aside and climbed between his powerful thighs. His breathing had become shallow and rapid. Wanting. In the moonlight, she got her first good, leisurely look at his magnificent cock, simply beautiful, fully erect, and tremendously thick.

"I want to suck your cock for you. Will you let me do that?"

Chapter Seventeen

Like he would say no?

"Yes, darlin', please." His voice shook with anticipation as he lifted his heavy, hot erection off his belly for her. His cock throbbed and wept a drop of cum for her. She leaned down and turned her head and he could see her face as she prepared to take the head between her lips, her sweet blue eyes locking with his.

Jack watched Grace's angelic face as her full, pink lips parted, opening to receive his cock. He couldn't stop himself from crying out at the sweet sensation of her hot mouth. Her tongue flicked out, laving back and forth over the sensitive underside and down to the base. The feel of her silky tongue was almost enough to undo him by itself. She worked up the head again, her lips parted and he watched in utter rapture as his cock slid inch by inch into her warm, wet mouth.

Agony and ecstasy washed over him at the feeling of his cock being engulfed in her hot little mouth. His breathing was nothing more than low, ragged moaning. She hummed quietly in response over his cock, sending vibrations down through him as she suckled up and down with her lips drawn tightly over him. She wrapped her soft hand around the base of his penis and began to slide it back and forth in the same rhythm as her lips, squeezing and pulling on him gently. The need to thrust was irresistible. She closed her eyes as she continued and took her sweet time torturing him until he knew his release was close.

"Darlin', you're doing that so good, I'm not going to last much longer."

She looked up at him, her blue eyes illuminated by the moonlight, and she smiled at him. Even with his dick in her mouth, he could see the smile in her eyes—eyes so full of love. His balls drew up and the muscles began to tighten in his back and his legs. He knew he was about to come but she showed no signs of backing off.

"Oh god! You're gonna make me come, darlin'. You've got to let go!" He was stunned when she held on to him, instead of releasing his cock. A searing bolt of lightning shot down his spine and gathered in his balls, ready to explode. She increased her suckling just a little. It was too much and just enough to send him over the edge. He let out an agonized yell as he came, surrendering his cum to her mouth. He couldn't take his eyes off of her face as she received each pulsing stream and swallowed every drop.

Licking gently, she cleaned his sated cock. Her angelic face was a picture of blushing ecstasy. From beginning to end, that had been about him, his need being filled. He lay there slack-jawed. Awestruck.

When he was finally able to speak, his voice was rough. "That was— You are amazing, Grace. Amazing." He couldn't believe she hadn't stopped, had swallowed his cum.

"Thank you. I'm glad I did okay. I'm not very experienced with blow jobs." She sat up, a soft, lovely blush still evident on her cheeks.

"Well, I'd never be able to tell. Damn. I'll do whatever it takes to make you happy, darlin'."

"Just love me and spoil me," she said teasingly as she grabbed a pillow and lay down at the foot of the bed, spreading her soft thighs so he could see her warm, wet pussy glistening in the moonlight. Beautiful.

* * * *

She was filled with wanton boldness as she spread her legs for him. A shiver ran through her as he sat up and his face was hidden in shadow.

He reached out a hand and slid it down her inner thigh. "Would you like to come like the other night?"

What a silly question. It was like asking if she could use a million dollars.

Of course! "Make me come hard for you, honey."

And he did. Twice.

She experienced another first that night—the joy of quality time alone with Jack. "I feel happy and torn, all at the same time," she said with a shiver as he slid his fingers up and down her torso in a tickling touch. His fingertips sent waves of chills and goose bumps up and down her abdomen.

"Why, sugar?" he asked and grinned at her gasping cry when he touched a particularly sensitive spot.

She chuckled softly with him at the way her body involuntarily responded to him. "Because I'm so in love with all three of you, and I'm enjoying this time alone with you so much. I just want to wrap myself around you and stay that way all night. Those feelings are having a conflict."

"None of us expects you to be able to share all of our time, the four of us together. But just because you spend an evening alone with one of us, like tonight, don't think that you're going to be on the outs with Ethan and Adam until they get the same amount of time with you to themselves. That would be a childish attitude for us to adopt and tiresome for you to keep up with."

"I'd need a day planner just for *that* schedule." She giggled.

"Yeah, and we'd prefer to be a little more spontaneous than that." He trailed his fingers over a little spot that, when he touched it right, made her back arch ever so slightly. He chuckled when it happened again, making her shiver.

"Darlin', just do what feels most natural and comfortable for you. If we begin to feel a need to be alone with you, we'll let you know. The same applies to you. You have a different relationship with each of us, and your body responds to each of us differently. There may be something that you need that only one of us can give you. You seem to like the way I strum your sweet spot to orgasm. If that skill was something you wanted from me on a particular evening, you could ask for it from me, whether we were alone or all together. The same goes for that talented tongue of yours. Once I tell the others how generous you are, they will want you to show them as well. Would that be all right with you?"

"I think I could handle that."

"We would also understand if you don't feel like swallowing every single time. You may spoil us by doing that, but we'd understand if you didn't always feel up to it. The same goes for when we're making love to you. You are not obligated to make love with all of us every night. We won't let you push yourself like that, especially in the beginning. You'll need some time to adjust to our sizes, but that's what lubricant is for," he said, grinning devilishly at her.

"Jack," Grace whispered, thinking about that subject, "your cock is very big and beautiful. But…It's so *large*." She covered her cheeks and felt how hot they were. She was glad the light was dim.

"You say the nicest things, darlin'," he said, kissing her before continuing. "I'm glad you like it, but don't worry, I'll make sure you're very ready for me, and I'm positive it will fit just fine." He pressed against her hip. She breathed a sigh of appreciation, reaching out a hand to glove him.

"Are Ethan and Adam similar in size?" she asked in a breathy whisper, listening to his rough breathing as she continued to slide her closed hand back and forth over him.

"We are all unique. I think you'll be very happy with your *options*." He moaned as her tongue descended on his head, licking at the droplet that glistened there.

"This is an option that I think I'm going to be very satisfied with. Did you know I fantasize about what your big cock will feel like the first time you slide it into my pussy? I think I'll come right on the spot from the feeling."

She grinned wickedly when he gulped and moaned right before her mouth descended over his head again. She slid as far down his cock as she could, sucking gently as she slid back up, swirling her tongue around the ridge again before releasing him with a slight popping sound.

She felt a range of emotions as she watched him receive what she offered. She experienced a rush of primitive and possessive lust, like he was *hers*. And she felt the tenderest of love feelings for him that he *needed* this from her, placing that power in her hands.

Her mouth descended over him again, and he cried out, "Sugar, your hot little mouth is like heaven."

She giggled and moaned a little in response to his reactions and verbosity. She didn't break contact again to say anything else. She took her time, learning every solid inch of him, in no hurry to bring him off. She did this for him to thank him for the explosive orgasms he'd given her a little while ago.

At least this time she hadn't cried when he brought her to her release. She realized that bout of tears had been building up in her for years before he finally burst the dam on them. She sucked on the head, sliding her wet lips back and forth, and gradually worked up to a steady rhythm, torturously slow at first, listening to his encouragement as she continued with a slight increase in pace.

His fingers gently cradled her head as he whispered beautiful, erotic words to her. He cried out in a hoarse voice as he came again, her mouth receiving each spurt of his cum.

She was happy she'd discovered something she could do for him that no one else had. On an analytical level, she failed to see what the big deal was about swallowing his semen. He feasted on her, seeming to especially enjoy when he made her come hard, and took all of it in like it was the sweetest honey. He seemed to love it and took a lot of masculine pride in wringing it from her with his talented fingers and mouth.

Gone was all the sexual tension between them, replaced by a comforting serenity. She was entwined in his arms, enjoying the feeling of his lips as they kissed and nuzzled each other, lazily stroking.

"Why don't you go to sleep?" Jack murmured. "After you drift off, I'm going to return to the couch, so if you wake up during the night and I'm not here, you'll know I didn't leave."

"Why? You're already comfortable." She laid her hand over his on her breast, squeezing it.

"Because, darlin', I have a feeling I'll wake up at full attention. With your warm, tender body snuggled so sweetly to me, my cock may act for its own benefit before I'm fully awake. You're so sweet and warm, I'm hardening again at the thought of slipping into that silky wetness between your thighs. I still want to save that for later."

"I understand, Jack. Do you need—" she began to ask, very impressed with his stamina and his ability to get her wet and warm with mere words.

"I want you to rest. You're going to be a zombie tomorrow if I don't let you sleep, and so will I. My cock will have to behave. Try to sleep." He kissed her temple.

She drifted off, her head pillowed on his bicep, breathing in his masculine scent, clean and unique to him. His strong but gentle fingers stroked over her shoulder and down her spine. Cuddled so closely in his embrace, she felt peaceful and secure. She prayed for a lifetime of nights drifting off just like this. She burrowed a little closer to his shoulder and kissed his chest and sighed softly as she felt his lips against her hair.

* * * *

She awakened the next morning to the alarm clock on her phone chiming. As she turned it off, she heard the shower running and remembered that Jack spent the night and he was still there. She stretched and yawned, then realized she smelled fresh coffee. Now *that* was something she could get used to, a man who made the coffee in the morning. Grace was not a morning person and had to have her coffee before she felt like herself. To have it waiting for her when she awoke was love on a basic level. She looked over, noticing he'd left a steaming cup on her nightstand. She grinned. If making the coffee was love, then this was surely *foreplay*. What a man!

She sipped from her steaming mug, propped up in bed, when he came out of the bathroom fully dressed. He gave her a crooked little grin, and she felt her heart do flip-flops. She was so smitten with this man. He sat down next to her, a cup of coffee in his grip. When he sat, the comforter fell down from where it had been covering her breasts. He leaned over and kissed her. His gentle callused hand slid from her cheek, down her throat, and over the swell of her breast. He cupped the globe in his hand, and his thumb gently rubbed over her nipple. Her eyes rolled a little, and she sighed in pleasure. His touch communicated itself to her pussy with a rush of heat and moisture. His gaze was so sweet and tender, so in love, it made her eyes prickle slightly with tears. He spoke after a few moments.

"When I think of you today, which will be often, this is the image I'll have in my head. You, all sleepy-eyed and warm from being under the covers, your beautiful breast in my hand," he murmured as she drew a shaky breath. She knew she needed to get up, but this moment was too precious and fragile to break. He leaned in and kissed her sweetly on the lips.

"What's on your agenda?" she asked as he sipped his coffee.

"I have to visit a couple of jobsites today, see if they are on track after all the rain the other day. Then I'm going to work with Angel. Will you be at Harper's all day?"

"Yes, we have a big job with a deadline. I may need to work a little late, depending on how busy we are during the day."

"I'll check in with you around lunch and see how you're doing. Don't pack a lunch. I'll bring you something, okay?"

"You spoil me rotten, Jack," she said, to which he chuckled.

"I think you are the one doing the spoilin', darlin'. I'm just looking for reasons to see you during the day."

"Well, then I must be doing something right because I love the attention." She leaned forward and put her arms around her knees.

"One of us will come and stay with you, depending on how things go today and schedules. I've got to run home and change into fresh clothes, but I'll see you in a bit. Will you be all right here?"

"Yes, it'll only take me a few minutes to get ready. You don't have to worry. Owen was never an early riser. He won't be around."

"Then let me kiss you, and you can get started. Be safe." He leaned forward on the bed to kiss her. Her palms came up to hold his whiskered cheeks, and she kissed him back sweetly.

"I love you, darlin'."

"I love you, Jack."

* * * *

Grace stopped to take a couple of Tylenols before lunch because her head was throbbing.

"It's the barometric pressure, baby," Martha said when Grace came back to the break room for a bottle of water. "It will get better in a little while. You need to take a break?"

"No, it's not that bad. I'd rather push through and get this order finished."

Martha patted her back. "I think we'll be done before we close. I'd like to be home and hunkered down if storms are gonna blow through. Are you going straight home after work?"

"Yes, I did my grocery shopping yesterday," Grace said as she returned to the work room.

"After the storms hit, I'll bet your head will feel better, honey. Oh, look, you have company." Rose pointed out one of the windows.

Jack's SUV had just pulled up. He looked particularly handsome in his denim work shirt, jeans, and work boots and wearing his straw cowboy hat. He must have just come from one of the local Mexican restaurants because he had two big plastic bags with their logo printed on them.

"He told me he'd come by for lunch." Grace held open the door for him. He smiled when he saw her and kissed her full on the lips, lingering just a second before he came through the door.

"Hope y'all are hungry because I brought lunch for everyone."

Grace chuckled as the ladies made a fuss of Jack's kindness. His phone rang as he sat talking with them after they were finished. He looked at caller ID and then said, "It's my sister. I'd better take this."

Grace watched him walk out of the break room and saw a hint of worry on his face.

Jack's sister, Anne, was still staying with his dad, watching over him, making sure he ate properly and got out enough. Grace knew they were worried about him isolating himself and his health going into decline. Jack had told her that he'd been doing fairly well, going every morning to drink coffee with his good buddies at the Dairy Queen on Crockett Street. Doing that gave Anne a chance to grocery shop, run errands, or have some time to herself.

Jack returned to the break room. "That was Anne. Dad had a little fall. She's taking him to the ER to get some stitches and get checked out. I'm going to meet them there."

"Did she tell you what happened?" Grace got up from her chair. An elderly person falling could be a very serious thing, becoming complicated very quickly.

"He took a tumble from a step ladder," Jack looked worried. "He was outside painting shutters and lost his balance. She didn't know until he came inside looking for a paper towel to blot the blood off his arm. It sounds like he got banged up a little, and she wants to make sure he's okay. She'd rather be safe than sorry, and I agreed."

"Let me know if I can do anything, Jack. Will you call me when you know more?"

"I sure will, darlin'."

She walked him out to the vehicle and kissed him good-bye.

"That's a good man, Grace," Rose said when Grace returned to the break room. "You've really been blessed with him in your life. Hold on tight. It's too bad about his dad. I know how he feels because I worry about my mom, too."

They went back to work and managed to be done by closing time. Jack called during the afternoon from the hospital. His dad had needed some stitches for the big gash on his arm and a cut on his head. They were giving him fluids because he'd been a little dehydrated.

He told her Ethan would come stay with her that evening. Even with all the worry over his dad, he took the time to arrange that. She understood their concern and knew they needed to be sure she was safe, although she thought it might be a little overkill. She couldn't complain too much because she was enjoying the time spent alone with them. Maybe she'd have the opportunity to make it worth the trip for Ethan, she thought with a smile as she headed home.

The sky grew dark, and thunderheads were piled high in the atmosphere. Before she left work, she listened to the weather radio and caught the announcement of a severe thunderstorm warning and a tornado watch for their county. It started to rain as she pulled into her driveway, great big fat drops that stung when they hit. She popped open her bright pink umbrella and ran up the steps under the porch. As she turned around to close her umbrella, she saw Ethan pull up in his truck. Perfect timing.

He ran up the front walk, the rain plastering his black button-up shirt to him in seconds. She looked up into his sparkling blue eyes as he reached for her and kissed her on the porch.

"Hey, hot stuff! Have you heard any more about Jack's dad?" She loved the feel of his hot skin through the damp sleeves of his shirt, his muscles firm and solid under her fingers.

"They plan to release him later this evening. Of course, he's not happy about it. He wanted to get home and batten down the hatches before the storms hit. I just checked on things at his place."

Grace unlocked the front door and let them inside.

"Was everything all right? Jack said he fell while painting shutters."

"Yeah, I put away the ladder and tools. I picked up some smaller things that might blow around, moved what needed to be moved over into the barn, and closed it up. I'm sure everything will be fine over there. Now I'm here to batten down *your* hatches." He pulled her to him with an evil grin. "I heard something good about my Gracie." He waggled his eyebrows.

Chapter Eighteen

"Oh?" she asked innocently. "And what did you hear? That I'm a good cook? That I'm in love with three smokin'-hot cowboys?"

"I heard from Jack that you have a gifted little mouth and can give a blow job that could make a grown man weep with joy. High praise. Wonder if it's true."

"Did he tell you everything about it? All the details? What makes it different from just any old blow job?"

"He said you finished what you started and didn't leave him in the lurch, that you took every drop of his cum. Is that true?" With each word he spoke, she got hotter and hotter, and he got harder and harder.

She looked straight into his twinkling eyes and said, "Every last drop. I took it all and loved it, too."

His eyes burned with lust for her. She wrapped her arms around him, and he lifted her from the floor.

"All right, hot mama!" He set her down on her feet again. "Let me check the back porch and move anything that may blow around back there. You stay inside, okay?"

"Can't I help?"

"You might want to bring that hanging fern in off of your front porch. They were warning of possible straight line winds on the radio, and there's a tornado watch for the whole evening."

He went outside and opened the back door to her garage. The storm had picked up in the last few minutes, and lightning flashed all around them. She went out to the front porch and hoisted the fern from the chain. Luckily, it wasn't full of water yet. She opened the garage door, getting whipped by the wind and soaked in the process. She carried the fern into the garage as Ethan guided her barbeque grill through the back door. Her lawn chairs and patio furniture were already brought in.

“Let me have your keys, and I’ll pull your car in the garage. You run in through the back door. You’ll be protected better by the back porch roof. Stay inside, okay? I got it all.” He ran out to her car, jumped in, and started it. She ran to the storm door and noticed that her headache was gone. Just as Rose said it would be.

The wind blew hard, and the rain flew past the house sideways. It sounded like the house was being scoured with it. The tree branches blew at extreme angles outside. She closed and locked the front door when she heard him close the back garage door and come through the storm door in the kitchen. She got him a towel and then plucked stray leaves from his hair.

He dried off as well as he could, standing on the mat and wiping his boots. She went to the front windows and became a little concerned when she watched a trash dumpster be blown by the wind down the center of the street. She watched the storm and jumped when she heard a branch hit the roof. She turned to look at Ethan, who stood next to her at the window.

“I wish we’d had time to pull your truck into the driveway closer to the house.”

“It’ll be fine. It’s just a work truck, and it’s insured.”

Something crashed against the side of the house, startling her again. The wind began to scream loudly over the house. A chill went up her spine at the sound. He wrapped his arms around her and calmly said, “I want you to go into your bathroom.”

Straight line winds.

“I know where Jack is right now, but have you heard from Adam?”

“No,” he said as he ushered her to the bathroom, “but don’t worry about Adam, honey. He’ll seek shelter if he needs to.”

He went to her bedroom and brought her pillows and her comforter. He helped her into the old enameled cast-iron tub and put the pillows and comforter in with her. He left and came back a few seconds later with the cushions from the couch and her purse. Thoughtful Ethan. She backed up and made room for him in the tub as he closed her bedroom door and the bathroom door.

He climbed in with her, turned her so she was underneath his body. He pulled the comforter and cushions over them, and they hunkered down to wait. The cushions and comforter might not protect them from falling debris, but would at least provide some cover from flying glass. The wind outside continued, screaming insanely. Lying in the solid old tub, she felt the house vibrate. Somehow it felt like even the air in her lungs vibrated. She started to pray and couldn't hear her own voice over the noise. She tried to stay calm as he held her protectively. His weight on her comforted and grounded her through the storm.

She focused on her breathing and willed herself to calm down. He clasped his hand in hers, kissing her cheek. He must have noticed her attempt to contain the hysteria that threatened. The kiss and the contact helped. They were in the safest place in the whole house.

Impossibly, the wind grew even louder. The walls vibrated, and then she heard a tremendous shattering sound. She shook and trembled under him as she listened to her windows blowing out. Whatever they found when they got up was going to be a real mess.

Suddenly, there was a tremendous crash against the tub, at their feet. She couldn't imagine what that must have been but was thankful she hadn't replaced this old tub with a newer one over the years.

Ethan's lips were at her temple. Beyond their tiny sanctuary, all hell broke loose, but inside the tub, clasped tightly in his arms, she felt safe. She wasn't alone to deal with this latest disaster the way she always had been before. She knew there would be plenty of wind damage. Her house had minor wind damage in the past, and this did not sound minor.

She felt Ethan's body relax a little. The winds were still loud outside but losing intensity because she could make out what he was saying.

"I love you, too, Gracie. I love you, too." Somehow he'd heard her over the cacophony of the wind.

Filled with relief that the storm was passing, her body went limp after being so tense in fright. She wondered about Jack and Adam and hoped they were able to take shelter. Jack was probably still at the hospital, in which case she knew he was safe. Adam could have been at a customer's house, or worse still, on a construction site.

Ethan turned on his side to take some of his weight off of her, and she turned to face him. They were like sardines in the tub, and she giggled when she realized she hadn't even noticed because she'd been holding on to him for dear life. Ethan left the cushions where they were for the time being and peeled back the comforter to look out of the tub. She heard the tinkle of broken glass from the window above them as he shifted. The dim room had begun to lighten a little as the storm passed.

"Grace, stay here for a minute. I'm going to go see how bad the damage is. The storm may not be over yet. I'll be right back."

"Be careful."

"I will, I promise."

She lay back and listened to the sounds as he moved from room to room. The wind and rain had calmed considerably. She heard her front door open and glass fall to the floor. The large glass panel in her storm door must have broken. She heard his boots crunching in places. He came back in the bathroom, and she heard a soft curse. She pushed back the comforter and peered over the edge of the tub. Ethan squatted down at the foot of the tub, holding half of a red brick in one hand and felt the dent it'd left in the end of the tub with the other hand.

"That was close," she said. "I wonder where it came from."

He held out his hand to her and said, "The façade on State Bank, two blocks over, is made from this kind of brick. I think it's safe to come out. The rain has even stopped. You lost a few windows, and I'm willing to bet you're missing a few shingles, too. There may be more damage on the roof."

She took his hand because she needed help rising from the tub on her wobbly legs. "You're really shaking. Come here, honey." He helped her stand and wrapped an arm around her waist. She laid her head on his shoulder and heaved a sigh of relief.

"Feeling groggy?" He gently rubbed her back.

"It'll pass. I'm just relieved that we're okay, that the house is still in one piece. Thank you for protecting me and keeping me safe, Ethan. I was terrified."

He squeezed her in his strong, solid arms. "Stay right where you are. I've got you. I'm calling the guys to let them know you're okay."

She waited as he dialed Jack's number first.

"Hey. Yes, she's fine. You want to talk to her?" Ethan smiled and handed her the phone.

"Hello?" Grace said.

"It's Jack, darlin'. You okay?"

"Yes, just a little wiped out."

"I'll be there in just a few minutes. I'm already on my way."

"Good. Be careful, honey."

"Hold on to Ethan. I'll be there as soon as I can. I love you, darlin'. I was so worried about you."

"I was worried about you, too. I love you. Here's Ethan."

"Hey," Ethan said, "it's the stress. She said it would pass. We've got some damage here. Plywood and maybe a tarp. I've got a drill in my truck. Okay, I'll call him."

Ethan hung up and then said, "Wait here for just a second. Don't come outside." When he returned, he was dialing Adam's number. He handed her a stick of gum.

"It's Juicy Fruit. The little bit of sugar might help you feel better."

She took it and popped it in her mouth.

"Hey, Adam, it's me. Yes. She's all right. It was pretty scary. A little wiped out but I think she'll be okay. Yes, we do have some damage. Are you still at Jack's dad's place? I need the plywood and the big tarp if you can find it. No, I have a drill, but bring screws. While it's still light enough I'm going to have a look at the roof. Here she is."

He handed the phone to Grace.

"Hello?"

"Were you scared, baby?" His soft, husky voice comforted her deeply.

"Yeah, but I feel better now. Are you coming?"

"I'm going to get plywood and a tarp, and then I'll be there."

"Be careful, okay?"

"Okay, I love you, baby."

"I love you, too, Adam."

She handed Ethan his phone. He put it in his pocket and looked at her. She felt like she was bouncing back a little. She smiled at him.

"Better?"

"A little." She smacked her gum and grinned at him. "Okay. Game plan time. I'll sweep up as much of the glass as I can then mop. With no power, I really don't want to close up the house with it wet inside."

Ethan said, "I'll check the outside and climb up on the roof and take a look. You sure you're okay?"

"Yes. I'm okay. I can handle this part. It really helps that you're here." She hugged him hard.

"I'll have a look outside, and then I'll come back in and help you." He went out the front door and carefully stepped over the broken glass from the storm door, and she went in search of her work gloves, broom, and mop.

She brought the trashcan into the living room and got started, working as fast as she could. She had the room swept in a couple of minutes and poured the glass in the trashcan. She moved through each room, sweeping as efficiently and quickly as she could. Ethan returned and began to mop. They had no electricity, so they couldn't turn on the fans, which would have helped a lot. After she swept, she found her old sponge mop and helped with the mopping.

Jack arrived, found her in the bedroom, and hugged her firmly. He heaved a big relieved sigh and then another. His body trembled before he finally spoke.

"I called several times and kept getting your voice mail. I'm so glad you're all right."

"I probably didn't hear the phone ring. It was so loud I couldn't hear anything. I was worried about you, too." She hugged him, and he kissed the top of her head.

"Adam is bringing plywood. We'll board up the windows and secure the house. Will you come and stay with us?"

After all she'd been through, trying to stay independent, refusing to leave her home, she had to laugh. She finally nodded.

"Yes, Jack. I seemed destined to it, no matter how hard I try to remain in my own place. I'll go home with you. But I love you so much I may never leave." It wasn't that she didn't want to stay in his house. She *knew* once she got there she'd never want to leave again. She still didn't know if she was ready for this step.

Jack's eyes twinkled as he kissed the tip of her nose. "It's more likely we won't *let* you leave. Let's just see how things work out. I hear Adam. I'll finish mopping in here. He's probably looking for you, too. Go see him, and let him know you're okay."

"Okay." She left the bedroom and walked through the living room to the front door, following the sound of Adam's voice as he talked with Ethan on the front porch. She overheard Ethan say that she seemed like she felt better. They were sweet to be concerned over her odd reaction to stress. Now that they were all here, she felt so much better. She pushed open the framework of the storm door, and Adam turned to her at the bottom of the steps. He held his arms out wide, the big grin on his face showing his relief to see her. She flung herself into his arms and wrapped her legs around his waist. He hugged her tightly and chuckled.

"I see you're feeling better, baby."

She nodded and hugged his neck. "Yes, now that you're here, now that you're all here with me. The wind was horrible. Ethan made me get in the tub and kept me safe. Now you're all here, and I feel much better." She knew she probably sounded a little hysterical, but she thought they would understand.

"Are you coming home with us now?" He sounded so hopeful.

"Yes, I told Jack I would. I'll go home with all of you. If that's what you want."

"Gracie, you know it is. You don't ever have to doubt that's what we want. We may never let you leave."

"Jack said the same thing."

They got the house mopped dry, and Adam and Ethan screwed the sheets of plywood over the broken windows. Several sections of the roof were missing shingles, so they spread the blue tarp over the worst areas and secured it in place. The power eventually came back on, so Jack set the ceiling fans on high and left the AC on. Drying out the interior and keeping it cool were her highest priorities. She could not afford to give mold a chance to start growing.

Grace packed her clothing and other items she would need during her stay at the ranch, and put things in as much order as she could. She packed the gold jewelry set and other valuable pieces from her jewelry box into a small compartment in her suitcase. Ethan and the others came and stood in the hallway outside her bedroom door. "We're ready to stop for now, Grace. It's late, and you must be exhausted. Do you have everything you need?"

She walked to the door and handed him the garment bag.

"Yeah," she said, looking at each of them tenderly, "I really *do* have everything I need."

This house was where she kept her stuff, slept, and where she got her mail. Real independence was making up her own mind about how she lived her life. It was clear to her now that she was making a liberated choice, and that was so much more valuable than living on her own in an illusion of independence.

Adam and Jack lifted the other pieces of luggage and carried them into the living room as she said, “I may have over packed, but that way I have what I need until we can sort things out here.”

Jack nodded and opened the door. “One of us will come back in the morning to see if the house is drying out all right. You feel okay to drive?”

She grabbed her purse and pulled out her keys. “Sure, I can drive. That way you won’t have to chauffeur me. But I am beat. Let’s go.” She turned off the lamp in the living room.

“Darlin’, you sound happy to be come home with us, almost eager. What changed?” Jack asked as his hand smoothed over her shoulder.

“I wanted to be independent. Be in my own place for once. More and more I feel my place really is with the three of you, regardless of the circumstances that put me there. I love you, and I want to be with you. Now my actions line up with my words.”

“No more doubts?”

“No, not doubts. I didn’t doubt you. My only worry is Patricia making life difficult for y’all.”

“Ethan and Ben had a talk with her Monday night,” Jack explained. “She knows she is on thin ice. If there is trouble, she’s already been warned. Angel knows about it as well. Come on home with us. It’ll all work out.”

Ethan had her car backed out of the garage with the AC already on when she stepped out of the front door. Would they grow bored with looking after her like this? She hoped not. It wasn’t the things they did that made her happy so much as it was the fact they put thought into what would please her. She knew what Rose Marie Warner would say. “Seize the day, baby!”

Yes, ma’am.

Chapter Nineteen

She parked next to Ethan's truck and Jack's big, black SUV. Adam pulled in beside her and walked Grace up the front steps to the wraparound porch. He stopped her when she would have walked in and picked her up, gently, into his big muscular arms and carried her over the threshold. Still holding her, he kissed her.

"Welcome home, Grace."

Being cradled like that sent a delighted thrill through her. He made her feel like she was as light as a feather.

He put her down carefully and took her hand. "Let me show you which room is yours."

"Y'all already have a room picked out for me?"

"We were optimistic, baby, that's all." He led her back to what must be the master suite. Jack and Ethan were already there, their faces boyish and hopeful.

"Do you like it?" Ethan asked.

She looked around the room, surprised. She could smell lemon furniture polish and knew they had cleaned and vacuumed it recently. The room was simply furnished with a king-size bed against the wall opposite the doorway. There was a wide dresser topped with a mirror, a chest of drawers, and lamps on small tables on either side of the bed.

"It's wonderful." Grace looked at the three of them smiling at her. "But who gave up their bedroom so I could have the master suite?" Some planning had gone into this move.

"Jack did," Ethan replied. "He wanted you to have a walk-in closet and the master bath. We want you to be comfortable and happy here. We gave you the best room because we hope you'll stay forever."

Grace turned and looked up at them. "Jack? Adam? Is that what you want, too?"

"More than anything," Jack replied.

"With all my heart," Adam said, kissing the hand he still held.

Ethan added, "We didn't expect you to make a decision tonight, especially not under these circumstances. We want you to rest and feel at home with us. Your closet is here through this door, and your bathroom has a separate shower and tub."

"I'll go put something together for supper," Adam said. "None of us ever ate anything tonight. Baby, get settled, take a shower if you want, and we'll get supper on the table for you. Want me to bring you something in here?"

"No, I'll come in the kitchen. I won't be but a few minutes. Right now a shower trumps food, but not by much."

They left her alone. She unpacked her luggage, found the bag with her toiletries in the bathroom, and started the shower. She had a feeling that if she got in the tub right now, she'd fall asleep and drown. She was that tired. It had been a long and over-stimulating day.

She wondered how Harper's and Stigall's had fared in the storm. She'd know how Martha and Rose were tomorrow, and she would call Ms. Meyer from work and see how things were at the store. It was too late to call anyone tonight, and she was just too tired.

She bathed in the shower, which was big enough for the four of them, then walked into the bedroom and retrieved her night clothes and put them and her robe on. She toweled her hair and brushed it out, then went straight to the kitchen.

Her men were gathered around the table. She joined them and accepted the plate Adam had prepared for her. Leftover spaghetti, green salad, and freshly made garlic toast. It was simple quick fare that hit the spot. The hour was late, so she only ate a little of everything but savored it nonetheless. They looked at her questioningly.

"Grace, is that all you're going to eat?" Adam asked.

She hoped he wasn't offended. "I have to be careful about eating this late because it gives me indigestion if I overdo it. Plus, eating this late will pack the pounds right on my hips. I don't want that."

"We'll have to remember not to make such a heavy meal at night again," Ethan said. "We didn't know you get indigestion."

"That's all right. I ate what I needed, and y'all can enjoy the rest."

"As for your hips," Jack said playfully, "we love your hips, don't we, guys?"

"They're like works of art," Ethan said, grinning at the others. Adam just smacked his lips, making Grace's cheeks tingle with heat.

"Are you happy with your room, Grace?" Ethan asked.

"I love it. I'll get spoiled with such a big bathroom. That tub has my name written all over it. And whoever bought new linens," she looked directly at Ethan and paused for effect, "did a great job. I love blue and white. Very soothing."

"I'll bet she loves that mattress," Jack said. "Like sleeping on air."

"Did you give up your mattress for me? What if you're uncomfortable?" she asked, appalled that she'd kicked him out of his comfy bed.

"I had one delivered for the bedroom upstairs when I moved out of the master suite. Believe me, darlin', it's money well spent to sleep that good."

"Well, y'all, as much as I'm enjoying the conversation, I really need to lie down before I fall down. See you in the morning?" She rose from her chair.

They all came around to hug and kiss her goodnight. She stumbled back to her room. She vaguely noticed for the first time that the room was a little warm. She would check the thermostat in the morning.

She was too tired for any siren songs tonight. She slipped off her robe and night clothes then turned off the lamps.

* * * *

Adam cleaned up the kitchen, watching as first Jack and then Ethan went quietly down the hall to her bedroom to check on her. They each returned to the kitchen with satisfied smiles on their faces. Adam dried his hands on a towel and said goodnight as they went to their bedrooms. He hung the towel and turned off the lights then stepped silently down the hall to look in on her.

He leaned against her bedroom door and drank in the sight before him. The room must have been too warm because she'd gone to bed naked and left her night clothes and robe draped over the foot of the bed. She'd pushed the covers back in her sleep, so the sweet curve of her nude back and hip were clearly visible, and the blanket just barely covered her delectable ass. She was finally under their roof. He hoped she never left.

* * * *

Grace gasped, and her eyes flew open at the sensation of a warm mouth and the light flick of a tongue on her shoulder. Ethan? She stretched and yawned as she turned onto her back. She gazed up blissfully into his sparkling blue eyes and watched as they roamed over her naked form. She must have thrown the covers off during the night because she was completely exposed from the hips up. She smiled at him, feeling that familiar ache begin in the pit of her belly. She stretched again.

"Good morning, beautiful," he murmured, packing an awful lot into those three simple words with his eyes and the sweet smile on his lips. "Were you comfortable last night?" He was dressed in faded blue jeans, work boots, and one of his work shirts, dark green twill with The Dancing Pony logo above the pocket.

He held two cups of coffee in his hands. He held one out to her. She sat up and took it from him. It was made just the way she liked it. Creamy and sweet. Perfect.

"I think I was asleep before my head hit the pillow. It was a little warm in here last night, though."

"Ah, that would explain why you're naked, wouldn't it?" he said playfully. He walked over to the thermostat on the wall by the armoire. "I can fix that. It's set on seventy-nine. No wonder you were warm. How low do you want it?"

"Set it on seventy-three, and we'll see how I do tonight. I forgot to put out my phone last night. Am I running late?"

"No, it's early. Not quite seven o'clock. You don't have to hurry. Adam and Jack are cooking you breakfast." He sat beside her, sipping his coffee. "I made your coffee. Is it the way you like it?"

"Yes. You're good that way, Ethan. You know that? You notice all the little things about me, like the way I take my coffee. Thank you for bringing it to me."

"I couldn't resist. You left your door open last night, and we noticed you were naked when we came to check on you. I went to bed thinking of waking you with a kiss." He reached out a hand to caress her cheek.

"You did? You say the sweetest things, Ethan. Y'all checked on me last night? I must have been slept really hard. I never heard you."

"We didn't want to wake you. We noticed you left your door open and, to be quite honest, couldn't resist peeking in on you. You were sleepin' purty, but we left the door open for you in case you were too warm."

"Sleepin' purty, huh?" she whispered, her heart doing a little flippity-flop.

"Mmm-hmm," he murmured softly, leaning in to give her a chaste kiss before getting up.

"I'll leave you to get dressed. Breakfast should be done soon." He grinned at her as she reached for her robe, before walking from the room.

She got up from the luxurious bed and walked into the closet. She felt sexy and daring this morning, so she put on her favorite cleavage-baring bra, the black lace cheeky shorts, blue jeans, boots, and her favorite body-hugging knit top. She brushed out her hair and left it down around her shoulders in soft waves and applied just a little makeup and lipstick. After making the bed, she found them in the kitchen. Adam scrubbed a pan in the sink, and Jack was wiping down the stove and counter. They'd waited for her to join them before they sat down to eat.

"Good morning, Sleeping Beauty," Adam said when he looked up and saw her. She knew they were neat and tidy but marveled as she watched. Men who cleaned up after themselves. How lucky was she?

"Good morning," she said as she refilled her coffee cup.

"Did you sleep well, darlin'?" Jack gave her an admiring once over, his eyes lingered admiringly on her top. "You look beautiful this morning."

"Thank you." She blushed, warming under his prolonged gaze. "I slept like a baby last night."

He came up behind her to give her a kiss on her cheek and to nuzzle her neck. She turned to him, irresistible in his denim shirt and jeans. He smelled wonderful, like spicy soap. She wrapped her arms around him and breathed him in.

"Did y'all sleep well last night?" she asked as Jack released her to finish stirring the sugar in her coffee.

"I've had better." There was a rather melodramatic tone to Jack's reply.

"Me, too." She had to stifle an indelicate snort at Adam's whiny reply.

Ethan yawned as he joined them in the kitchen. "Me, three." She detected a definite pout.

"Well, what happened, boys? Bad dreams?" she noted they all looked very pathetic suddenly. Adam was dressed in a bright red twill work shirt similar to Ethan's. He looked really sharp in his freshly pressed clothing.

"It was really hard to fall asleep with the knowledge there was a beautiful, nekkid nymph sleeping in our home just a few feet away."

"Oh!" She giggled, delighted at the way their faces lit up at her laughter. Adam gave her a big bear hug and motioned her to the table, bringing her cup of coffee to her as she sat. "Thank you! If my being here is going to keep you from getting your proper rest, I should go. I don't want to torture you." She snickered.

"If that's torture, baby, chain me to a wall," Adam said.

"When are your test results coming in?" She grinned at them over her cup of coffee and winked at Ethan.

"Not frickin' soon enough," Adam muttered, and the others laughed, too.

They ate breakfast quickly. Grace was ravenous after foregoing most of the meal last night.

"I called the glass company," Jack said as he rose from the table. "They'll come either tomorrow or early Friday to replace your glass."

"Thank you for taking care of that, Jack. I wondered who I should call about the glass."

"It's handled. I know a guy," he said. "I'm just glad he could fit us in. They are going to be busy this week. There are lots of windows blown out and trees down all over town."

"I feel very lucky it wasn't worse. Did Ethan show you the brick?" Grace asked as she rinsed her plate and put it in the dishwasher.

"Yes, he did." Jack shuddered. "Good thing y'all were in that old cast-iron tub and not one of the newer fiberglass models. You would have been seriously injured if you had."

She reached out a hand to him as he stepped around the marble counter top, gathering his phone and planner.

"Do y'all have time to talk for a minute? It won't take long." She smiled at her men. They looked hopeful but uncertain. A little worried. She hoped they would understand where she was coming from with these next words. She was done settling for half measures and good enough. She wanted her dream, and she was going to ask for it. That didn't mean she wasn't a little freaked out about taking the bull by the horns. The breath shuddered in her throat, and she had to stop and take a few quick breaths. Her heart started pounding.

"Gracie, honey, breathe," Ethan said, looking worried. He got up from the table, came to her, and put his arms around her. "Whatever it is, you can say it. We love you, and we can work out whatever it is."

She felt sheltered in his arms, reassured. She took slow, calming breaths. A little voice said "Seize the day, baby!" That made her smile.

Yes, ma'am.

"I am so in love with the three of you," she began, holding on to the arm Ethan had wrapped around her from behind. "I never would have believed I could feel so loved, so cherished. It overwhelms me to think of it sometimes. I'm going to tell you what I need, if you want me to stay. I don't expect things to be perfect or to work out overnight, but my heart tells me to trust you. Some of this is not easy for me to ask for.

"I just came out of a miserable live-in relationship. I'm not sure what type of arrangement you had in mind, but I'm not looking for another live-in situation. You don't strike me as the kind of men that would expect that from me, but it's important that I tell you that I need a long-term commitment in order to move forward."

They seemed relieved and quietly listened to her, allowing her to get it all out.

"Additionally, I find Patricia's presence here very uncomfortable. Because Angel is your friend, this places you in a difficult position. I don't expect you to kick her out onto the street. But as long as she lives on your ranch, I won't be able to let my guard down. I'm not going to seek her out looking for trouble. Just don't expect me to make nice with her."

So far, so good. No unhappy faces and she'd pretty much said what she needed to say. Almost.

"I want to become partner to Martha Harper at the shop. I'd appreciate your support and guidance because you have so much experience. I just want you to know how I feel. I love you, and I want to stay, if you still want me."

Ethan squeezed her gently, resting his forehead against her head, and spoke softly in her ear, "*If* we still want you? Gracie, we'll take you any way we can get you. We'd do just about anything to keep you. We'll drop-kick Patricia over the fence today. We'll invest in Harper's, too, if it's what you want. You can work, or you can stay home." They had all gathered around her, hugged her. Adam lifted her off the ground and kissed her soundly, then handed her over to Jack.

This was what she needed. A sign that things would work out. They knew what she needed and accepted what she said. She didn't have to have all the answers today. She just needed to know they could move forward from there. She'd seized the day, and it had seized her right back.

Jack turned her to him and said, "We have something special planned for you, but you're going to need to be a little patient with us. Can you do that, darlin'?"

"Of course. I just needed you to know how I feel." She laughed and cried a little at seeing how pleased they were. "I need to get to work, although how I'll be able to concentrate is beyond me."

"We'll bring you lunch. Would that be okay?" Jack asked.

"All of you?"

"Yep," Adam replied.

"I'll walk you out to your car. Do you have everything?" Ethan asked.

She picked up her purse and keys. He walked her out, and Adam and Jack, like exuberant school boys, followed them out to kiss her good-bye. Adam lifted her off her feet again and swung her around. They all laughed when she squealed as her feet went flying. "I love you all so much. See you at noon."

As if on cue, they heard a car pull up the long driveway that led past the house to the barn and other outbuildings. They all turned to look in time to see Patricia, just coming home. She did not look happy to see them or to be seen, as she drove past without stopping, and continued on to Angel's home.

Suddenly serious, Jack said, "Some changes are comin' around here."

Adam grunted affirmatively. Ethan was silent, only holding out his hand to her. She refused to allow Patricia's arrival to mar her morning. She smiled and reached out to him.

* * * *

Jack opened the door to climb out of his vehicle as Angel opened the front door of his house and stepped out. Jack was immediately sorry he'd done that because he could hear Patricia screaming at Angel in Spanish. Unfortunately, Jack spoke Spanish fluently and understood what she was yelling. Angel threw his hand up in the air like he was waving good-bye without looking back at her. He pulled the front door closed on her diatribe. He came over to the passenger door and got in. If Jack didn't know better, he'd say Angel was amused.

"Trouble in paradise?" Jack backed the SUV and swung around to head out the driveway.

"She's pissed."

"The saddle?"

"Mmm-hmm. I might have mentioned we're shopping for a woman's saddle. She might have put two and two together."

"You told her it was a woman's saddle we were looking for?"

"I may have, yes." He buckled the seat belt.

"So basically you told her you were going shopping for Grace?"

"I suppose she might have drawn that conclusion." He chuckled, looking over at Jack.

"Did you tell her just to piss her off?"

"Might have."

Jack shook his head. He really didn't understand their arrangement at all. "Why don't you just tell her to leave?"

"She'll get upset and cry. I can't stand to see a woman cry."

"If she's pissed off about the saddle, how is she going to react when she finds out about Grace living here?"

"She may already know."

"You can't stand to hear a woman cry, but the screaming doesn't bother you?"

"Not when it leads to the makeup sex."

"I don't think you're gonna get any makeup sex off of this, amigo."

"That's okay, haven't been seeing much action lately, anyway. She's hardly ever home. Speaking of Grace, how is she doing? I heard she had some damage."

"Yeah, but I think it's going to be a relatively easy fix. Everything looked like it was good and dry this morning, just have to keep it that way and get the roof checked out. Ethan and Grace were in the house when it hit. Sounds like they had a wild ride. I was never so relieved to hear her voice."

"I'll bet, man. Is she happy to be staying with y'all?"

"I think so. She has some reservations, but she said she'd stay."

"Is Patricia one of those reservations?"

"Yeah, unfortunately, she is, Angel. Sorry. You heard?"

"From several different sources. One of the hands was at The Pony for a little while Saturday night, heard the girls talk about her, plus I ran into Rachel at the vet's office. She told me all about it. She says y'all are a cute couple, grouping, or whatever." He used air quotes over the last words, chuckling.

"I appreciate you coming along."

"That's what I'm here for, but what did you really want to talk about?"

"We're already talking about it," Jack said as he followed the winding curve of the road that led into Divine.

"Let me guess. She knows Patricia hates her, she wants Patricia gone, but she's afraid she'll hurt my feelings. Was I close?"

"That pretty much sums it up. How do we deal with this?"

"Patricia is difficult," Angel said, to which Jack quietly chuckled.

Yeah she was difficult, all right. Like a busted water pipe during a hard freeze was difficult. He'd had root canals that were more fun to deal with than Patricia.

"Okay, Patricia's a bitch, no denying it." Angel laughed. "I'm surprised she hasn't moved on by now, if you want to know the truth. She doesn't come home until late at night, most nights, sometimes not at all. I know she ain't staying with her girlfriends those nights. We have no exclusivity to each other. It's convenience for both of us. She has a place to stay, and she never turns me down. I've heard she seldom turns anyone down, for that matter. She still after Ethan?"

"She was until Grace had a little heart to heart with her last Saturday night. Ethan had a talk with her Monday night at The Dancing Pony. I'm not sure how much good it did or if it just pissed her off more"

"If she needs to go, she needs to go. She's like a bulldog. I could see that she was more than a little fixated on Ethan. I never should have brought her out here, wouldn't have except she had nowhere to stay. I'm sorry she's made things difficult for y'all with Grace."

"Grace is torn because she considers you her friend, and she doesn't want you to be upset, but she won't be comfortable with Patricia out here. How attached are you to her, Angel? That's what this boils down to." Jack hated to have this conversation with his friend.

"I'm more attached to the friendship I have with y'all. I consider Grace a friend, too, and her happiness is tied to your happiness. I'll tell Patricia she's worn out her welcome as soon as we get back," Angel said with a sigh.

"Somewhere out there is a decent woman who'll honor you, Angel. With Patricia gone, maybe you'll find her," Jack reassured him as they pulled into Cheaver's Western Store parking lot. Jack didn't mind being the means to possibly help him find her, maybe even this afternoon.

"Maybe so. Let's go find your lady a saddle."

The midday sun beat down on them, blasting them with heat as they climbed from the SUV.

"Why don't you come out with us some weekend to The Dancing Pony? Grace loves to go dancing. You've been working a lot of hours and not getting out much."

"Do I get to dance with her if I do? I heard she knows a few dance moves."

"Hell no! Find your own woman!" Jack laughed as they entered the store.

An hour later, they left the store with a new hand-tooled leather saddle for Grace. It was of good quality and workmanship, and it had a floral design that Grace might like. All in all, Angel said, until they knew how much riding Grace would actually be doing, this was a good, comfortable saddle for her to start off with.

Angel had stopped him from ordering a custom-made saddle. If she really took to riding, then Jack could spend seven thousand dollars on a custom saddle, if that was what he wanted to do.

"Speaking of spending money on Grace, do you mind if we make a quick stop at Stigall's? I want to surprise her with a little gift."

"No, I need some new blue jeans, anyway. I tore a hole in my best pair the other day."

Jack smiled. That was easy. With a little luck, Teresa would be there working. Angel went over to the menswear department to get his jeans, and Jack headed for the jewelry department. He stopped at the ring of counters and started browsing. As he looked into a case that displayed jewelry with different gemstones, he heard the click of little heels approaching. He looked up and grinned. The pretty, young Hispanic woman walking toward him smiled in greeting. He noticed her nametag. Teresa. Perfect. Now all he had to do was make this transaction last long enough for Angel to come find him.

"Hello, I'm Teresa. May I show you something?" she asked softly. Just as Grace had said, Teresa was petite, with curling black hair that hung past her shoulder blades, pulled back from the front. She had sweetly rounded cheeks and warm brown eyes.

"You sure can, ma'am. I'm looking for something for a special lady. I think she's a friend of yours. I hope you can help me."

"Who is your friend?" she asked with a twinkle in her eye.

"Grace Stuart."

"You must be Jack," she said quietly. "I was so sorry to hear of your mother's passing. She was a very sweet lady. Grace has told me much about you." Her voice was soft and feminine, and her speech was very proper with little accent.

"Thank you, ma'am. Has she really?"

She nodded conspiratorially. "She said you helped her *clean house*. I'm glad. Owen was not good to her. Are you shopping for a gift for her?" she asked helpfully.

"I heard her tell her sister there was a pair of silver filigree hoop earrings she wanted. I'd like to surprise her with them. If you still have them."

"Yes. I know exactly which ones. Come down this way."

She led him to a small locked display located on top of one of the glass-topped jewelry counters and unlocked it. Inside were a selection of silver and gold hoop earrings in various sizes and designs. Teresa pulled out a silver pair, with filigree etching, two inches in diameter.

"Grace admired these a couple of weeks ago," she said, handing them to him. They were pretty with the way the light sparkled off of them.

"I think I'll take them, Teresa, but I'd like to look at some other pieces, too. I don't want to keep you from other customers." He looked around for Angel. Where the hell was he? He'd have to stall for a while, have her show him some other jewelry.

"No, sir. You're my only customer right now. Was there something in particular you'd like me to show you, or…would you perhaps like to see some other things I know Grace liked?" Jack had to chuckle. He'd been taken in by her shy, quiet demeanor, but he had a feeling he was dealing with a hit-and-run saleslady. By the time his wallet knew what had hit it, it would be too late.

"I knew I came to the right lady. Why don't you take me shopping for Grace, Teresa?" Jack noted the way Teresa smiled behind her little hand and blushed. Grace had told him Teresa was shy and got embarrassed easily. "If you have time, that is."

"Of course. Come with me." She led him back to the case that displayed the gemstone sets. This was more like it. She removed a velvet-covered jewelry display board. Attached to it were a pair of amethyst earrings and a necklace with a large square-cut amethyst pendant accented with very small but brilliant diamonds.

"Grace's birthday is in February, so amethysts are her birthstone." February? That was good to know. "She's tried this set on before, and I know she likes it but wouldn't consider it because of its cost." Teresa pulled out another display board when Jack heard a paper bag crinkle and Angel walked up to the counter. Perfect. Angel could help him decide. Interact with the beautiful saleslady.

Teresa laid the other display board on the glass counter, and as she did, Jack noticed her hand shook the tiniest little bit. He looked up in time to see her glance away from Angel and blush. She was suddenly very quiet. Maybe Jack could get her talking a little. Angel laid his bag on the next counter and came over to see what Jack was looking at.

"Hey," Jack said nonchalantly, "find what you needed?"

"Yeah, you?"

"Teresa was kind enough to show me some pieces that Grace is partial to. Now what is this, Teresa? A garnet?" Yeah, use her name, jog Angel's memory. Keep her talking. *Breathe, sweetie, breathe.*

"That's a ruby pendant. The choker is solid silver. It looked good on Grace but not as good as the amethyst." She blushed as she glanced up at Angel. Jack watched Angel as he recognized her. He wanted to do a fist pump as he watched the flirtatious smile spread across Angel's face. She was in for it now.

"How are you, Teresa? Do you remember me? You and Grace sold me some clothes a few weeks ago."

"H-hello. Angel, right?" she asked, blushing again very sweetly, saying his name with the traditional Spanish pronunciation.

"Yes, that's right. How have you been?" Angel asked.

"Very well, thank you. You are shopping again today, I see," she said, indicating his shopping bag.

"Yes, I'm hard on clothes, needed more jeans."

Jack noticed he never broke eye contact with Teresa, who looked ready to topple over. Time to redirect and let the girl breathe.

"What about that bright blue stone, Teresa. What is that?" Jack asked, pointing.

"This is a blue topaz. The ring, necklace, and earrings come as a set. I can have the ring sized for you if you know her size. The same set is also available in a pink topaz." Good, she was breathing again, focused, but glancing at Angel. "Of the two, Grace would prefer the pink. It's her favorite color."

"Pink is her favorite color?" At Teresa's affirmative nod, he replied, "I never see her wearing pink."

"She thought it made her look fat. That's what Owen once told her. To tell you the truth, I think he told her that because he didn't want her to wear a color that might draw attention to her."

Angel said, "Her boyfriend told her she was fat? Blind bastard. Grace is perfect. No offense, Jack. Pardon my language, Teresa."

Jack chuckled. "None taken." He smiled down at the pieces on the counter. Teresa was no longer blushing, and it sounded like she was breathing again. Moving right along.

"Teresa, is that a sapphire ring? I can't tell in this light."

"Yes, Jack, but Grace wouldn't care for this setting. Everything would snag on it. She uses her hands so much, something that has inset stones, like that amethyst there, would be much more practical, and she'd wear it more often." Turning her attention to Angel, she bravely asked, "Angel, are you shopping for jewelry today as well? May I show you something?"

Jack had to fight his grin. *Good girl.* Teresa had just gone fishing and was about to land a whopper. Angel looked her straight in the eye and said, "No, not today, Teresa, I don't have anyone to buy such things for. Maybe someday I'll get lucky, like Jack, and find a good woman. For now, we shop for Grace." Smiling, eye contact. More eye contact. Still more eye contact. And…redirect!

"Teresa, which do you think Grace would like better? The amethyst set, with the ring you just showed me added to it, or the pink topaz set?"

Teresa smiled and proved what a good friend she was to Grace. She glanced at Angel for a split second and made her pitch.

"Honestly? Buy the topaz, along with the silver earrings she likes for your surprise today, and come back for the amethyst for her birthday. She will look beautiful in both."

Angel chuckled. "Jack, that was quite a sales pitch. Do you work on commission, Teresa?"

"Yes, Angel, I earn a commission on all my jewelry sales," Teresa said. She laid one small hand on top of the other and added, "I can lay the amethyst aside for you if you'd like to think about it for a day or two." It was then that Jack remembered Grace telling him that Teresa was a single mom with a small son to take care of.

"Can you wrap them up for me, Teresa?"

"Which ones?" she asked with a grin. "The topaz?"

"No. You're a good saleslady. I'll take them all. You're right. She'll be beautiful in both. Don't wrap the amethysts, though. I want to show those to Adam and Ethan tonight. Angel, I left my wallet in the SUV. Why don't you stay here and talk to Teresa while she wraps the other pieces for me, and I'll be right back."

Angel grinned and nodded as Jack sauntered off, too pleased with himself.

As he walked away, he heard Angel say, "I noticed you don't wear a ring. Is there a man who spoils you the way Jack does Grace?"

Way to go, smooth operator.

Grace was going to flip over the jewelry. So was his wallet, but it was worth the cost to hear Teresa's soft, negative reply as he moved out of ear shot. "No, there is no one."

He took his time as he went to the truck, opened the SUV, checked his cell phone for missed calls, piddled around looking for a stick of gum, found one, popped it in his mouth, wadded up the wrapper really, really good, patted his back pocket where his wallet had been all along, and went back inside the store to close the deal. Angel *had* to have her phone number by now.

He walked back in, spying them at the counter over the racks. Angel was leaning against the counter, chatting easily with her. She had a slightly dazzled, but happy, look on her face, and her cheeks glowed. When Jack returned to her counter and handed her his debit card, she turned her full attention to the sale. She glanced every so often at Angel, who never took his eyes off of her, ogling her soft, rounded curves when she turned her back to him to use the register. She returned with the slip for him to sign and gave him his copy.

She brought a small, handled shopping bag to the counter along with the boxes. She placed the amethyst set and the amethyst ring in the shopping bag. She wrapped the pink topaz necklace earring and ring set and the silver earrings in pretty paper and placed them in the bag as well. She handed him the bag and said, "I know that Grace will love them. She deserves a nice man like you to spoil her." She glanced again at Angel, whose eyes never left her.

"Thanks for all your help, Teresa. I really appreciate it." Jack shook her little hand and stepped away from the counter. He pretended not notice as Angel softly said good-bye as well. He returned his wallet to his back pocket, satisfied with a job well done. It was well worth it to see the interest and intensity in Angel's eyes, to see the chemistry that had developed in that short conversation they had shared while he'd gone on his goose chase.

Grace was going to be thrilled. Mom would be so proud.

Chapter Twenty

As Grace climbed the front steps, Jack came out the front door. She showed him the two lightweight bags in her hands, which contained a loaf of bread and a carton of eggs. She smiled up at him and shook her head.

"This is all Ethan will let me carry."

Jack chuckled as he stood there looking unassumingly sexy. "We enjoy doing things for you, darlin'. Get used to it."

Oh, gosh, twist my arm.

"It's not what I'm used to, but I'm trying. Did Ethan tell you I'm cooking y'all supper tonight?" *Yep, we're gonna eat, and then I'm going to have y'all for dessert.*

"Yes, I'm looking forward to it."

"I hope you like chicken. I promised Ethan I would keep it simple."

He gave her a wolfish grin filled with lust and heat. Her panties were damp in a warm flash.

He grinned irresistibly, with a wicked little twinkle in his eyes. "I'll eat *whatever* you feel like serving me."

She paused and looked up at him, started to walk past, then gasped and turned to look at him again, her jaw popping open in shock. *Oh, mama mia!*

Two could play that game. She grinned back at him and blushed. "I can't make up my mind between quick, hot, and spicy, or slow, rich, and creamy." She licked her lips provocatively as she added, "I guess it will be a surprise for everyone tonight."

"Does this mean we're talkin' dirty over dinner?" Ethan asked as he carried grocery bags up the steps, having overheard them. "Because I'm all in for that."

Jack brought the rest of the bags in, still chuckling. He helped Ethan put away the groceries while Grace got started with the sauce. She chopped several green onions and threw them in a skillet with a little olive oil, added a crushed garlic clove to it, and set it on medium heat. She opened a couple of cans of crushed tomatoes and added them to the skillet. She put Jack to work slicing Roma tomatoes for the salad and kept Ethan busy making a pitcher of iced tea and setting the table.

As they moved around the kitchen, she noticed they were in constant contact with her, brushing up against her to get the pitcher, leaning around her to get a salad bowl, pressing against her when getting the salad tongs from the drawer, trailing a hand across her ass as they asked her a question.

She opened the large package of chicken breasts and heated olive oil in another skillet. Her hands were full, trying to season the chicken, when she felt Ethan's hands slowly slide around her rib cage and up to her breasts, cupping them gently in his hands. She leaned back against him as he pinned her gently to the counter, his tall, hard body intoxicatingly warm behind her. His lips slid along her neck up to her jaw line. All she could do was stand there and receive because her hands were messy.

"I love your breasts, Grace, did you know? They fill my hands, just slightly overflowing, begging to be nibbled on. I can feel your nipples through the fabric. They're getting even tighter right now. Can I reach inside?"

She dreamily nodded, and he unbuttoned the top buttons of her shirt and slid his fingers inside her sheer ivory lace bra. He squeezed her breast gently, which drew a hot, rushing response from her pussy. He groaned softly, pressing his erection against her derriere.

"Yes, baby, so warm and lush."

Grace was hardly aware when Jack took the platter with the chicken breasts on it and used a fork to place them in the heated oil as she stood there enjoying Ethan's attention.

"Couldn't you just feast on them, Ethan?" Jack asked as he moved the chicken around the skillet.

"That I could, Jack. Do you think Grace would like it if I did?"

"I think you would do it *just* the way she likes it. I'll bet she's warm just thinking about it."

"Getting warm, Grace?" Ethan whispered then brushed his lips against her earlobe, sending a pleasant shudder up her spine.

With a loud gulp, she replied, “Very. You say the sweetest things to me. You feel so good holding me like this, but I can’t touch you. I need to wash my hands.”

Ethan released her slowly, and she moved to the sink. Jack came beside her, cupping one cheek of her backside in his hand as Ethan tended the chicken. She scrubbed her hands clean and shivered as the tip of Jack’s tongue tickled the outer edge of her ear. He nibbled her lobe, which made her giggle and shudder deliciously again. A soft wave of happiness wove itself into the currents of desire between them as she reveled in the easy way they allowed her to move from one man to the other.

“I love that sound, darlin’.” She turned to look up into Jack’s eyes and kissed him. Her hands slid up his chest as she gently undulated her pelvis against the bulge at his groin. He groaned softly and said, “I’m so glad you’re here, Grace, so happy you want us, this. I love you.” He leaned his forehead against hers.

Just then they heard the squeal of tires and a car engine rev as a vehicle flew past the ranch house. She glanced out the front windows in time to see Patricia’s car shoot down the driveway at top speed, barely missing Adam’s work truck as he returned home.

Jack sighed and shook his head. “Angel must have told her she’d worn out her welcome. He told me earlier today that he would. He also wanted me to tell you his decision had as much to do with her habits and behavior as with your presence here.”

She bowed her head a little. Regardless of how much she disliked the woman, she still hated being the reason she was now homeless. Jack slid his fingers into her hair and tilted her head back to look into his eyes.

“You are not responsible for her unhappiness, Grace. Please don’t be upset.”

“Because of me she has no home now. And Angel will be lonely.”

“Angel would not have sent her away empty handed. She will go to one of her girlfriend’s houses or show up at the home of whichever of the men she’s been hooking up with is most likely to take her in.”

“But I placed Angel in a very uncomfortable situation. He’s probably unhappy with me right now.”

Jack shook his head and grinned. “Your need for Patricia to be gone helped him more than it disappointed him. Now he will be free to find a woman who is worthy of him. As a matter of fact, he seemed mighty interested in one today."

Grace giggled in delight. "Jack Warner, did you play matchmaker today?"

"I sure did, darlin'." Jack grinned, winking at her.

Adam walked in the door, two shopping bags from Macy's and a plastic garment bag hanging from his fingers. "I hope that female tearing out of here like a scalded-ass dog is a sign that she won't be back unless it's to pack up her stuff," he said hopefully.

"Angel told her this afternoon she'd worn out her welcome at the ranch. She can't have been too surprised." Ethan stole a peek in one of the shopping bags and grinned.

Adam's eyes immediately found Grace at the kitchen counter, where she still stood in Jack's arms. He laid the garment bag over the back of one of the chairs in the living room, put the shopping bags down, and lifted her up as she came eagerly into his arms.

"What have you been up to, big boy?" She wrapped her legs around Adam's waist.

"Is it just me," Ethan asked with a soft groan, "or is that move one of the sexiest things you've ever seen?"

She kissed Adam tenderly, then laid her head on his shoulder and smiled at Jack and Ethan.

"You mean the way she wraps those long legs around his waist? I could hammer nails with my cock right now just watching her. Feels good, Adam?" Jack asked.

"Mmm, a nice and warm welcome to come home to, baby." He cupped her ass and pressed her pussy to his groin. She squealed when the position caused close contact with her clit, and the men chuckled.

She turned her head and whispered softly in his ear so only he could hear, "Just wait until after those test results come back, honey. Then I'll give you a whole new definition of a warm welcome."

She flicked his earlobe with her tongue and then nibbled lightly. She giggled delightedly when a very clear growl rumbled from his chest, setting off a flurry of pulses in her pussy. His strong arms squeezed her gently and then put her down. She drew him into the kitchen.

"What are you up to, Grace? It sure smells good in here," Adam said as he lifted the lid on the sauce, sending a fragrant cloud of steam into the air.

"I'm cooking supper tonight. Just something simple," she said, turning a chicken breast. "I want to let this simmer for a while. You know what they say. Anything worth doing is worth doing *slowly*." She looked straight at Jack, licking her finger after sticking it in the sauce.

"There she goes again with those sexy food innuendos," Ethan said, tasting the sauce. She turned the heat off under the chicken breasts in the skillet and put the lid on to keep them warm.

"So how's June?" Ethan grinned as Adam brought the Macy's bags to the marble counter top.

Adam looked pleased with himself. "She was glad to hear everything was to your liking. She was happy to help me find some more things for you. I hope that's okay, baby, that I went shopping for you. Next time I'll take you with me, but I wanted to do this and knew that June would steer me right." He watched her face as if he was worried she would think he was being presumptuous.

After going shopping at an expensive store for her? *Puh-lease!*

Adam's eyes were hopeful as he looked down at her and reached out to tuck a lock of hair behind her ear. "Anything you don't like, we'll take back and exchange. June said that wouldn't be a problem."

She peeked in a bag playfully. "Whatcha got in there?"

She had him pull it out piece by piece and hold everything up to show her. Adam seemed to like her in bright, clear colors and jewel tones. There were jeans, dressy tops, casual tops, skirts, a couple of dresses in different lengths, and an array of bras, panties, thongs, and other lingerie, some of which made her positively blush—a black shelf bra, matching garter belt, and G-string. Wow!

"You're going to spoil me."

"That was my plan." Adam kissed her again. "You haven't seen the shoes yet."

She squealed and clapped her hands. Adam had hit her hot button. Shoes. There was a pair of dress boots with a very stylish heel trimmed with straps and buckles, another pair of elegant dress shoes in a silver strappy design, and a pair of the shiniest, kinkiest black platform Mary Jane pumps she'd ever seen with a half-inch platform and at least a four-inch heel and straps over the instep. Grace had never owned shoes like that but knew what they were called and what they would look good with. These were "fuck me" shoes, and she imagined wearing them with the shelf bra, garter belt, and G-string.

She lifted one out of its box and held it up in the light, turning it. She heard one of her men gulp audibly and glanced at them. Their eyes were on the shoe, but they weren't seeing the shoe. They were imagining her in it. Yeah, they knew what it would look good with, too.

Now that would be a fun evening.

Wait till Charity got a load of these!

"I'm not sure I have the ankles for these, but I'll give them my best shot, Adam. Thank you for everything, baby. I love it." She smiled at his relieved look, kissing him sweetly.

They helped her carry it all back to her closet, and she put all of it away. When she was done, it was time to put the chicken into the sauce and serve supper.

"We have something we want to show you and get your input on," Ethan said as Jack went into the office and brought back a sheaf of large pieces of paper and laid it on the counter. They served themselves from the stove and brought their plates to the table.

While there were no overtly sexual comments made, gradually over the course of the meal, the mood between the four of them changed. One would stroke her hand or arm occasionally, while another would gently caress her back. She couldn't look into their eyes without seeing the desire and love shining there.

"What did you want to show me?" she asked as they cleared the table and wiped it clean. Jack brought the plans and the blue bag to the table. She recognized the logo on the bag and smiled. Jack laid the sheaf of paper on the table and opened it to show her architectural blueprints. Unsure of what she was supposed to be seeing, she looked up at Jack, confused.

"We are going to remodel upstairs into a master suite for you, with a large bedroom and sitting area, a combination dressing room and walk-in closet, and a master bath with large walk-in shower and king-size Jacuzzi tub." She sat speechless as he pointed out what they planned to do upstairs then told her when they would start, how long it might take, and what elements they were going to need her input on. She stopped him when he mentioned a fireplace.

"A fireplace? In the bathroom? Really?"

"Sure, can't you picture yourself lying in the tub, gazing into the flames from the fireplace? It would be open on the bedroom side of the suite, also, so that you could enjoy it from the sitting area as well. What do you think?"

"I think my men take spoiling me to not just another level, but another universe. You can afford to do this?"

"We wouldn't do it if we couldn't. But we want you to understand it's all for you. Upstairs would be your space. We would hope to spend as many nights there as you'll let us, but you can also have time totally to yourself, or with just one of us, that would be fine, too."

She thought back to her night alone with Jack and quivered at the notion of spending time alone with each of them there. Plus, with all that space, there would be plenty of room for the four of them, except for one thing.

"I am concerned about one thing, guys. Jack, I know your bed is a king-size, but I don't think a king-size would be big enough for the four of us. It will get crowded, and I'd want us to be able to *sleep* comfortably, too."

"We have something else for you to look at." Ethan slipped more print-outs over to her. They were illustrations of a beautiful bed in a medium-toned oak. The stylized posters that mirrored the sleigh bed's curving silhouette and the canopy with gauzy drapes were incredibly romantic.

"Our friends, Wes and Evan Garner, build custom furniture. You can change the wood or the color if you'd like something different," Ethan said, showing her a few other options. "Your bed is a one-of-a-kind creation. There won't be another one like it."

"Y'all designed this bed?" She was in awe they would go to that much trouble for her.

"Ethan drew the plans with our input," Adam said, "and we gave them to Wesley to work on. This is what he came up with. The design looked like something you would enjoy."

Breathlessly, she replied, "It's perfect. It's just what I would want my fantasy bed to look like. The canopy is a beautiful touch. I've always wanted something like that. Romantic but not prissy. I love it."

"Wesley said he can also make a dresser or chest of drawers, or whatever you might need to go with it," Jack said.

"You spoil me, boys! This is all such a shock. A fireplace in the bathroom? A custom-made fantasy bed? What's next?"

"You tell us. We're ready to spoil you some more," Adam said, rubbing her back.

"Remember I told you that I might stop by the jewelry counter at Stigall's while I was in town with Angel?" Jack grinned at her obvious excitement.

"I'm dying to know how that went. Did you see Teresa?" she asked eagerly, wanting details.

"Yes. She helped me find the perfect thing for you. Angel helped, too. She's quite a saleswoman and a great friend, I think. Angel and she seem to have developed a little chemistry." Jack quickly filled Adam and Ethan in about his matchmaking expedition earlier that afternoon.

Grace rubbed her hands together, eager to see how things turned out between the two of them. "I knew I saw a spark between the two of them that day."

"I have your earrings, plus something else she thought you might like." Jack placed the bag in her hands.

She lifted out the smallest box first and opened it. "I love these. Thank you. What's in the other box?" She suddenly felt nervous.

"Open it and find out. It's all right, darlin', I just wanted to surprise you a little bit. We didn't realize we'd be double-teamin' you with all the gifts. I think it will look beautiful on you."

Grace's hands shook a little as she unwrapped the box. Once the paper was off, she set it gently on the dining table. She hesitated briefly before she gently lifted the lid on the velvet box and gasped.

She stuttered and looked up at him in surprise. "The pink topaz! You bought me pink! You bought me pink!" She ran around the table to him, threw her arms around his neck, and covered his face with little kisses. "You bought me the pink topaz set!" She kissed him some more and hugged him.

"Dang, this is how she reacts when we buy something pink," Adam said.

"I'll make a note." Ethan chuckled.

"I take it you like the pink topaz, yes?" At her teary nod, Jack handed her his handkerchief and said, "You can have the ring sized to fit whichever finger you want to wear it on. I'm glad you like it so much. I haven't seen it on you yet, but I can tell you this, Grace. You will look beautiful in pink, *any* shade of pink. Haven't I always told you I like you in pink?" he asked, teasing her now.

"Yes, but you were always referring to my cheeks. I never wear this color."

"I know, and we want to see you in it more."

"Or less." Adam gave her a crooked grin. "Oh, look, there go her cheeks again!"

She blushed even hotter. She went to all of her men and kissed them tenderly, one at a time, on the lips. She took her time and stoked some embers in all four of them.

"I'm blown away by all of this, guys. You *really* want me to stay if you're willing to do all the remodeling." Reaching for Jack's hand, she said, "You understand what that pink topaz set actually represents to me, Jack, and I appreciate what you're trying to say to me with it. I've been wrong about a lot of things, and I've wasted a lot of time worrying what other people think about me."

Jack drew her to his side and squeezed her waist. "I think it's time our little darlin' relaxed a little. Why don't we fill up the tub for Grace?"

"That sounds like a good idea." Ethan got up to attend to that task. She kissed Jack and winked at Adam then went to her bedroom. She heard the rush of water as the tub began to fill.

She put the dark blue velvet box on the dresser in her bedroom then went into the bathroom. Ethan reached into a drawer and pulled out her hairbrush. She unbuttoned her top and slipped it off, leaving it on the counter. He stood behind her as she faced the mirror, and she watched him as he brushed her hair out, gently stroking his fingers through it. The repetitive action was almost hypnotic. He made eye contact with her in the mirror and smiled. Not his usual playful, mischievous smile. This smile was warm and radiated from his heart, and vulnerability was in his eyes. She was mesmerized. Finally he placed the brush back on the counter.

She took a clip from the drawer, deftly twirled the length into a knot at the back of her head, and clipped it into place. As she raised her arms to do this, he reached in front of her. She gasped at the jolt of heat his gentle fingertips speared through her. He slid them down her abdomen, and she leaned back against him and slipped her fingers around his neck and into his hair. He maintained eye contact with her the whole time, loving her with his eyes as he loved her with his fingertips. His warm, sensual lips brushed lightly over her shoulder as his fingers slid to the waistband of her jeans.

He lowered her zipper then parted the fly, his fingertips searing hot through the thin fabric of her thong. The humming in her clit increased to a decadent rhythm, singing in her blood. His fingers slid down inside her jeans to the tops of her thighs, pushing the denim down a little. His fingers glided back up around her curving hips, along the waistband of the thong, then back down over her ass. He pushed her jeans down with the backs of his hands, getting the job done but guaranteeing maximum contact with her skin. His fingers gripped both cheeks gently but firmly, and she inhaled sharply and felt a rush of damp warmth to her pussy. She watched him in the mirror through half-lidded eyes and could see clearly the heated desire on his face and the caged strength in the rippling muscles of his arms as he stroked and squeezed her.

He knelt behind her, lowering the jeans, tickling her when strands of his hair whispered against the backs of her thighs. He held the bunched up jeans down as she stepped out. This was Ethan, caring and yet so intense at the same time, doing the little things for her. Ethan, the lover, knowing the catastrophic effect his fingertips were having on her. Her heart pounded, and her body ached for his touch.

She trembled when she felt his lips glide up the back of one of her thighs, and she cried out softly when she felt his teeth gently nibble one of her ass cheeks. The throbbing between her legs increased exponentially, and she had no doubt that an orgasm was imminent if he continued. He slid his hands up over her ass and her back, standing as he did. He reached out and unhooked her bra, looking into her eyes in the mirror, a sexy, seductive smile spread across his sensual lips. His heated blue gaze was awash with unfulfilled desires, speaking his heart to her from their depths. His lips parted as she watched in the mirror, and his tongue extended to the sensitive skin below her ear. When his warm tongue made contact with her skin, she gasped again, and her head fell back to his chest.

“Oh, Ethan! If–If you keep doing that, I–I’m going to embarrass myself. You don’t know what you do to me.”

“Gracie, you respond to my touch so quickly. The way you sound when I touch you, every little thing about you makes me crazy.” His fingers rolled a nipple and pulled gently before squeezing her breast. "The way you arch your back when I touch just the right spot, the way you breathe when you're about to come, oh, yes, that soft panting!" His fingers skimmed in a slow glide down her abdomen, and her high-pitched panting increased as his fingers found her slit.

The sensation of his fingers as they slid into her wet pussy was compounded by watching it in the mirror's reflection. She saw the desire and lust in his hooded eyes, in the set of his lips.

Glancing in the mirror, she noticed Jack and Adam silently watching. They had done nothing to make their presence known. She knew it was because they didn't want to break this magical moment between Ethan and her. She closed her eyes and gave this moment to Ethan as his insistent fingers slid over her swollen clit. His touch, and the unfulfilled sexual tension between the four of them that grew daily, sent her to the crest of a wave. Her voice raised in breaking sobs as she teetered there, waiting for that last little push into the abyss.

"Come for me, Gracie. Let go for me."

His beautiful, velvety voice and his long, stroking fingers sliding into her opening sent her crashing into orgasm. Her lips fell open on great panting sobs as she uninhibitedly rode out each wave of the orgasm. Once the pulses stopped, his lips slid up and down her throat and kissed her as his fingers withdrew, and he allowed her to recover. He wrapped his arms around her waist and held her to him. Opening her eyes, she could see the tension in his face and knew he must be close as well.

He went to the large tub, which was very full now, turned off the water, and started the whirlpool jets. He held her hand as she climbed into the tub and held on to her until she was seated, then unbuttoned and removed his shirt. Once she was settled, Jack and Adam entered quietly. They seemed sensitive to her need to quietly bask in that moment. Ethan rolled a hand towel and put it beneath her neck as she leaned back against the tub. The suds rippled and parted around the upper swells of her breasts.

Ethan picked up a washcloth, wet it, and poured a little body wash on it, lathered it, then gently rubbed it along her upper chest, shoulders, and arms before sliding it under the water. The scent of orange blossoms filled the room, and her eyelids slid shut as she feasted on all the sensations.

The shower turned on, and she opened her eyes in time to see Adam's tall, athletic form slip into the shower. For the first time, she saw him fully naked, well, *almost* all of him. He'd had his back to her, but what a glorious back it was. His broad shoulders tapered to a narrow waist and hips, which were cut so perfectly she wanted to nibble on them. Her fingers clenched unconsciously with the desire to squeeze his tight, muscular buttocks. His powerful legs were sprinkled with dark hair.

Jack knelt beside her, bare-chested, and reached in the tub for one of her legs and gently lifted it. Using another soapy washcloth, he tenderly scrubbed from her thigh to the soles of her feet. He said nothing, only gazed at her, loving her with his eyes and hands. Ethan's hands and the washcloth delved deeper into the water, down over her breasts and torso. Ethan's hands and Jack's hands met in the middle.

Ethan whispered in her ear, "Lift, baby, for a second. Let us finish, then you can soak and we'll take a shower." She did as he asked, and they finished the task of bathing her, paying gentle attention to her sensitive pussy and then her ass. She would have thought she'd be embarrassed by having someone else bathe her so intimately, but she wanted them to do it. She wanted them to know she trusted them and welcomed their attention to every part of her. She shuddered and moaned softly as Jack's fingers and the washcloth swept over her rear opening, sending shivers racing up and down her spine.

Adam left the water running but climbed out of the big walk-in shower with a towel already wrapped around his hips. *Damn it, he must have had a towel in there.* He grinned at her, probably guessing her thoughts, and ran a hand towel over his dripping wet hair.

He squatted down beside her and said playfully, "Just a few more minutes, baby, then I'm going to feast on those sweet breasts of yours."

She sighed and smiled up at him. "Just a few more minutes, and I'm going to taste that great big hard cock of yours," she said in her most sweetly seductive voice.

"Holy shit, I love your mouth, baby. I can't wait." He gulped hard. "I'll be right back." He left the bathroom for a minute. She watched in growing arousal as Ethan and Jack removed the rest of their clothing and stepped into the big walk-in shower and made use of the multiple showerheads. Her body responded shamelessly to the sight of both men, nude and highly aroused as they bathed. Her mouth watered at the sight of their cocks standing proud and stiff as they lathered their muscled torsos. She looked forward to taking a shower with her men, maybe later.

"Jack, it sounds to me like Gracie has some big plans for us tonight."

"So I heard. Scrub it good, Ethan. She's worth the extra trouble. Mmm-mmm." Jack smiled back at her through the glass wall. "I'll bet her body is still singing from that climax earlier, which was glorious to watch, by the way. I love the way she cries out when she comes. Like she wants to die and sing and cry all at the same time. I'm hard as a rock just remembering it."

Smiling, Grace said, "Thank you for the things you bought from Madeleine's, Ethan. It makes tonight even more perfect." She lifted a long leg out of the bath, sluicing water and bubbles back into the tub. She glanced up in time to catch them watching her with hungry eyes.

Jack grinned. "The evening isn't over yet, darlin'."

"Well, I sure hope not. I have big plans for both of your wickedly handsome bodies. I've been fantasizing about tomorrow, after the doctor's office gives you the all clear. Then you can show me what you've been fantasizing about all this time." She felt beautiful and powerful in the hungry, lusting gazes they gave her.

These men brought out the wanton in her. She'd let them do anything they wanted to her, even take her ass and fuck her all together if they wanted to. She had absolute trust that they would not take her where she could not go safely.

Adam's warm hands swept over her arms and shoulders, and sensual lips slid along her jaw line.

"There you are. Where did you go?"

"Brushed my teeth."

Adam kissed her, and she noticed he tasted minty and smelled woodsy clean, that Adam smell she loved.

"We'll go do the same," Jack said as they left the bathroom, their hips loosely draped in towels, their hard-ons proudly erect. "Why don't you help our woman from the tub, Adam?" Ethan said as he stopped at the door, giving Grace a wink.

Adam stood and held her hand as she rose from the tub, the warm water running down her body as he watched admiringly. He held an open towel out to her and wrapped her in it, then lifted her from the tub. While she stood on the bath mat, he took the towel from her and patted her dry with it. He took particular care with her breasts and the juncture between her thighs. The humming in her pussy returned. She was fresh out of the tub, but she knew she'd be damp again soon.

Grace could clearly make out the silhouette of his cock through the towel. She licked her lips, looking at it, and it grew even larger.

"You keep looking at me like that, and I'll embarrass myself like a teenager," Adam murmured, kissing her shoulder.

"Not before I've had a chance to love on your cock for a bit. It's so big, Adam. Will you take your time with me? Make sure I'm ready?" she asked as she rested a hand on his shoulder while he knelt and dried her ankles and feet.

"Baby, I promise I'll take really good care of you." He rose to look down at her, cupping her chin in a gentle hand. "And if you need me to slow down or stop, I will. Trust me?"

"You know I do." She turned to pick up her toothbrush. Adam went into the bedroom.

After brushing her teeth, she removed the clip from her hair. She stepped out of the bathroom, carrying her hairbrush, and shut off the light. Her men had lit the candles in her bedroom while they waited for her. She walked to Ethan and held out the hairbrush to him. He took it from her and carefully brushed her hair before laying the brush aside on her dresser.

Jack said, "Tonight you're in charge, darlin'. Tell us where you want us."

She didn't even hesitate as she turned to Jack and Adam. "Y'all lay on the bed right there where you can see. I want to thank Ethan for the way he touches me and talks to me. I want you to watch me thank him and know you're next."

As she turned to Ethan, she thought she heard one of the other men growl softly. Her pussy responded to the sound with another rush of heat and felt her juices seep to her inner thighs.

Chapter Twenty-one

She placed a pillow on the floor at Ethan's feet. She positioned herself so that Jack and Adam would see everything. She took Ethan's hands to steady herself and knelt on the pillow. At first Ethan seemed unsure about her kneeling on the floor.

She reached out and laid her palms on his insteps. Yielding to her instincts, she leaned forward and loosely wrapped her arms around his legs and rested her cheek against his thigh. Her eyelids slid closed as a feeling of utter peace and joy flooded her as she knelt there. She stayed that way for a few seconds and held onto him. A wave of adoration for them shook her with a light tremor before she released her arms and trailed her hands up the light layer of brown hairs that covered his legs.

Her hands slid under the towel, and she looked up at him. She wanted him to see the utter…surrender in her eyes. What he saw must have pleased him because his chest swelled, and his features radiated with intense pleasure. His gentle hands reached out and caressed her cheeks. Her heart lurched in her chest at the overwhelming love she felt for these men. She reached to his hips, slowly unfolded the towel and removed it, and then allowed it to fall to the floor.

His erection sprang free, proud and stiff against his belly, extending to his navel. He palmed it and held it out to her. She took it in both hands, sitting up off her heels just a little. Adam and Jack were silent, unmoving, maybe even unblinking. She savored the moment, not diving right in. She wanted to savor and remember it. She licked her lips, and she heard a slight motion from the bed, maybe a groan. She parted her lips and looked into Ethan's blue eyes as she took her first taste, swirling her tongue around the head. His loud moan filled the room, and he sounded as though he were in pain. Were it not for the look of sheer ecstasy on his face, she'd have believed she had hurt him somehow.

“Holy fucking hell.” He groaned as she licked her lips again.

Gently grasping his cock at the base, she slid the head into her mouth and then sucked lightly. She could taste the droplet of fluid that had seeped from the opening. Ethan tasted salty and wild, and the humming in her cunt increased, but it was accompanied by something else. She felt a languor stealing over her body that she’d experienced only once before as she’d served Jack in this way. She relaxed into it, and all she wanted was to rest in this position and feel his cock in her mouth. All she wanted was to love him.

She thought of the sweet things he did for her. Like the first night when he’d turned her to Jack so that he could hold her when she cried. She recalled earlier when he’d shown her the drawings of the bed. She knew those romantic designs had come right out of his head.

She remembered his fingers searching her body, finding hidden places, sending her to perfect, ecstatic heights, and then holding her as she came down from them. She was perfectly content to kneel before him with her lips around his cock. She wanted nothing more than to love him and let him use this part of her for his pleasure as long as he wanted to.

His fingers slid into her hair, setting a gentle rhythm in and out of her lips. She cupped his balls and played with them as she slid his cock farther into her mouth, bumping the back of her throat.

“Her mouth. It’s so hot, so fucking good. I could die right now,” he grated softly. “I love that little bit of suck—that’s it, right there. Damn, you’re so good at this. I’m going to make you so happy you’ll never want to leave. I love you so much. Fuck! Tomorrow night is going to be heaven! I’m going to come soon, honey, if you don’t want—oh! Gracie, I’m coming!”

Ethan cried out harshly as she embraced his thighs while his cum streamed into her mouth in hot jets. She swallowed it all as his moan rasped in his throat. When he was finished, she continued to very gently lick him clean of every drop of his cum, watching his face the whole time. He opened his eyes, making eye contact with Jack and Adam and muttering softly, “Yes, Gracie.” His hands were warm and gentle at her shoulders. Finally, she released him and settled back onto her heels.

“Amazing, isn’t she?” Jack asked, and she noticed him palming his cock through his towel.

Ethan unsteadily helped her rise then made his way over to the edge of the bed and flopped down. "You are unbelievable. Jack, now I see what you meant. Fuck." He lay down on the bed and put his arm over his eyes.

She crawled across the bed and lifted his arm to look at him. "Are you still alive?"

"Yes, I just need a moment. My mind is blown." He laid his palm against her cheek. "Jack, could you help Grace lie down on the towels? Adam, would you grab that oil from the bathroom? The orange-scented one?" Ethan asked as he caught his breath and shook his head a little. "We wanted to give you a massage after your bath, Gracie. Just one little thing we want to do for you, then we are all yours to do with as you please, honey."

"A massage, huh?" she said, filled with renewed anticipation. "Will this be a nice full-body massage like the one I got at Madeleine's? Or will it have a different rating?" she asked with a soft giggle.

"How would you rate the massage you had last weekend?" Ethan asked.

"It was wonderful, but I wouldn't give it more than a PG rating, and that's only because I was nekkid under the sheet."

"I see what you're getting at, Gracie," Ethan replied, evidently getting into the game. "Well, *this* massage is going to go quickly from PG-13 to R because you're definitely coming at least once or twice, if not more. For the triple-X massage, you'll have to wait until tomorrow."

In a husky, needy voice, she asked, "What's the difference between an R-rated massage and triple-X?" Hotly turned on by the whole idea, she was on her hands and knees, lowering herself to the towels layered on the bed sheet.

Ethan chuckled darkly. "In an R-rated massage, you come at least once. In a triple-X massage, you get at least part of the massage with one of our cocks in your pussy. No thrusting, just held inside of you. We'll massage you, filling you to bursting while you try to stay still and just experience all the sensations, and you can't come until after the massage is done. Think you want to try that sometime soon?" He grinned devilishly at her.

"Say the word, Ethan, and I can be ready in two minutes." She held up two fingers, looking over her shoulder at him. "Is this how you wanted me?" She laid her head down.

"You're perfect, darlin'." Jack moved up beside her.

Ethan retrieved her clip from the bathroom and did a fair job of twisting her hair up and pinning it out of the way so they wouldn't get oil in it. Adam climbed up on her other side. Ethan positioned her ankles loosely together, and she wondered what he was about to do to her when he crawled over her feet and straddled her calves, her ass positioned within easy reach.

"You just lay still and relax, baby, okay? We're going to give you a good rubdown," Adam said, palming a shoulder blade.

Jack slid a warm hand down her spine to the curve of her ass. "If anything we do doesn't feel good to you, tell us right away, darlin'. If we do something you like, tell us, and we'll make sure and do that more. We're learning what you like tonight so we can do this for you on a regular basis. Would you like that?"

"I'd love it, Jack. Y'all take such good care of me." They moved her arms to rest at her sides.

"It's because we love you, baby. You deserve to be taken care of," Adam answered for the three of them. His warm hand slid up her thigh and over her ass, sending a warm tremor up her spine.

Grace said nothing more as she concentrated on the warm hands touching her. She was already wet with need for them. Her pussy was drenched and swollen with desire. They warmed the oil in their hands first and then applied it to her skin. Adam and Jack mirrored each other with their motions. Each worked out an arm, a shoulder, and part of her back, down to her hips. Ethan focused all his energy on her hips and ass, gradually working his way down her legs to her feet. Then he massaged her back again himself. She trembled a little when she felt his hard erection brush against the cleft of her ass and smiled when she heard him hiss softly.

Adam and Ethan switched places, and Grace gasped in arousal when Adam gently parted her thighs. She knew that her pussy was now exposed to him, and he'd be able to see that she was wet and warm with need. She moaned in anticipation.

"Gracie sounds like she wants to come, Adam. Even over the orange scent I can smell her sweet, wet pussy," Ethan said in a deep, husky tone. "Do you think she would like it if you made her come?"

All she could do was moan in affirmation.

"I think she'd like it if you used your fingers on her," Jack murmured. "Show her how skillful you are with that sweet spot of hers, Adam."

Grace trembled with the rapacious need to feel him stroke that place in her that responded so explosively to Jack the other night. Her sweet spot had sung in gushing waves for him and wanted to for Adam as well. She felt another throbbing rush of lust in her pussy and wanted to feel his fingers in her, on her, touching her. She tilted her ass slightly to him.

"Damn, what an invitation, Adam!" Ethan murmured. "I love how she offers so sweetly." All of their words served to further inflame her. Finally, with a groan of appreciation, she felt Adam's big, roughened hands rest on the backs of her thighs, slightly above her knees. He slid them up, over the massage oil, to the juncture between her thighs. She heard rustling and looked back to see Adam wipe the oil from his hands on a towel, and then Ethan poured a little of the lubricant on Adam's fingers.

She sighed in gratitude when she felt Adam's large fingers spread some of the lubricant on her lips, slide a thick finger into her opening, then around her sensitive, throbbing clit. He teased her like that, sliding into her then over her clit for several torturous minutes. Such sweet torture. He had her so wet, she was sure the lubricant had been unnecessary. Her pussy tingled in rapture when he slid two big fingers into her. Adam had big fingers, and for her, this was a bit of a tight squeeze. The slight burning sensation made her want to scream for release.

He leaned close to her ear. "Am I hurting you, Grace? Please tell me. I don't want to hurt you." Even in this erotically charged moment, her wellbeing was uppermost in their minds.

"No, baby, really. I love it. Don't you dare stop!" She undulated on his hand as he stroked.

"Fuck. She is so tight on my fingers, so sweet and hot. Baby, I'm going to love sliding into your sweet little pussy. You are so beautiful, so perfect. Mmm, so wet for me."

She felt like she might pass out from the pure pleasure of the sensations, and the words he used to describe her made her dizzy with need. She wished he could slide it in right now. She felt her pussy gush and clench at the thought.

"Mmm, more sweet honey for me. I feel you gripping me with your pussy. You want it, too, don't you, baby?"

All she could do was moan ecstatically. His pace and rhythm changed. His fingers slid deeper into her and started a slow, hypnotic stroking in her cunt. That familiar pressure began to build. She spread her legs, uncaring of how shameless she might look. She arched her back and ducked her face into her hands as he played her body. She felt Ethan or Jack's hand on the small of her back, which kept her centered. Adam slowed the pace, and she moaned in need and frustration then gasped in surprise as she felt his lips make contact with one of her ass cheeks.

"I love this ass. I just have to taste it." He licked and nibbled at her as he continued to strum her sweet spot, picking up the pace again. His other hand slid under her mound. One of his fingers found her clit and rubbed it in rhythm with the internal stroking he was using to drive her insane. The tension began to coil tightly inside her. His warm lips and tongue moved over her ass slowly, as he made his way to her cleft. Her tension skyrocketed.

He set a steady, intentional rhythm and played her body gently but purposefully. The crest of the wave grew and sent her higher. She wanted to scream as her walls tensed up impossibly tighter.

His tongue slid down her cleft, and his lips nuzzled her ass as he moved ever closer to her rear opening. She wailed at the sensation and couldn't believe what he was about to do as Jack or Ethan's gentle hands held her hips tilted up to him. She screamed as his tongue slid in gentle, slithering strokes around the tight ring of muscles in her asshole, while still stroking her sweet spot. The sound was cut off as she gathered a lungful of air, and he swirled his tongue around her opening again. She screamed again, louder this time, and an explosive orgasm slammed into her. She wailed loudly in their arms, and her body convulsed on his fingers and rode each wave. After he was done, Adam's fingers and tongue retreated, his hands moving to caress her ass as he kissed her there and nibbled some more.

It felt so perfect and right for him to want this position of control, or dominance over her, to love her in this manner, and it made her desire for them to try anal sex with her even stronger. She felt completely unafraid to leave herself so open and vulnerable to Adam or the others, and they were big men, too. Her ass should be clenching at the thought, but here she was, wishing for it in the very near future. She gasped and trembled as she tried to catch her breath.

"Grace, let us help you turn over, sweetheart, so we can do your front. We're only half done." Jack grinned at the obviously incredulous look on her face as she turned over. *Only half done?*

She'd die of pleasure. Or so she thought. Adam excused himself for a minute to clean up so he could continue with their play. They left her breasts and her mound for last to tease her some more. Finally, Adam and Ethan very gently massaged oil into her breasts, tenderly licking at her nipples, sending shards of white-hot desire straight to her throbbing clit, making her moan incoherently. Jack wiped his hands on the towel and used lubricant to massage her mound and paid gentle attention to her swollen clit.

"Darlin', can you come for us again? I want to make you feel good," he murmured to her as he looked up from between her thighs.

How could she refuse in the face of such love? She reached for it. His tongue slid into her pussy and over her clit in quick succession. She was amazed by how quickly the blistering hot orgasm came upon her. He continued to lick her and love her, and she felt the pressure build for another right on the heels of the last one. She moaned in surprise that another one raced closer and closer.

"Oh! Jack, please don't stop, oh, god! Please don't stop. Harder, just a little hard—ooohh! Jack!" She keened and sobbed as the orgasm washed over her like a waterfall, dragging her into its depths. Their lips caressed her, and their hands slid all over her body. This, this was ecstasy. She had felt it as she knelt before Ethan, and as they sent her repeatedly into an abyss of joy, and in the feel of their sweet caresses. It was ecstasy. And they hadn't technically made love to her yet.

Then she remembered a cruel fact. Adam had been the first to make her come, and he would be the last to come for her. He had waited so long, and he wasn't going to wait any longer.

* * * *

Adam stroked her damp hair away from her forehead and kissed her temple as she lay among them and caught her breath. He smiled as she closed her eyes for a moment in bliss and sighed. Her cheeks were a rosy hue and very warm under his fingertips. She smiled dreamily and pressed her cheek to his hand as she turned to look into his eyes. She focused on him intently for a moment and then gave him a devilish smile.

She rose from their midst and reached for him as she unceremoniously straddled his chest. He growled in pleasant shock as she kissed him passionately while Jack and Ethan looked on, grinning. She pressed herself to him, from her bountiful breasts peaked with hard nipples all the way down to her sweet, wet pussy, which felt like a hot brand against his chest.

“Adam, she looks like a woman on a mission. I think you’re about to get thanked, *but good*!” Jack said, amused.

“Oh, I think she may be about to torture him a little bit first. See what she’s doing?” Ethan asked.

She inched down his chest, and he groaned at the sensation as her hot pussy rubbed her warm, sweet honey over his abdomen. She sat up, and he could see she was drenched with the juices that flowed from her pussy as she reached down to touch herself. She gazed seductively at him and moaned.

Oh, fuck!

She’d told him the other night at The Dancing Pony that she’d brought herself to orgasm while thinking of him, and she must have known how much it would turn him on to watch her. She rubbed her clit, sighing shakily, and her juices coated her delicate fingers. She settled her pussy dangerously close to his cock. He went silent. Motionless. Waiting for her next move. The urge to thrust the tiniest little bit toward her was strong, almost undeniable. He fought to control that urge.

She looked down at him with playful lust in her eyes. “Trust me?” She looked over at the guys and then back at him, waiting. All three of them nodded at the same time. What the hell was she going to do?

She shifted carefully down his torso, bracing her little hands on his chest. She reached for the bottle of lubricant, and Jack handed it to her. Hot fucking hell. Whatever she had planned was going to be good.

“Let me do this, honey. I promise I won’t leave you hanging. Be still for a minute, okay?”

He’d be as still as a fucking statue if that’s what she wanted. She poured some lube in the palm of her hand and spread it all over her pussy and then on his cock and balls. His cock twitched in delirious excitement as realization of what she planned dawned on him.

"Baby, you'll need to be still as you can. Just enjoy, okay?"

Adam knew she was taking a big chance here, especially with as much lubricant as she'd used. One misplaced move and he'd be inside her. His cock rebelled with another twitch, reminding him that was *supposed* to be the *fucking* plan. She braced a hand on his chest and reached the other hand down as she rose slightly, spread her sweet inner lips, and settled her hot pussy on the painfully hard length of his shaft.

"Oh, fuck!" he groaned loudly as she sat fully on his cock.

Chapter Twenty-two

The sensation was so good he nearly lost control, grabbed her hips, and impaled her. But he didn't do that. He lay still just like she'd so sweetly asked him to. He pressed his head back into the pillows as he fought for control.

She began a slick, soft rhythm, sliding over him as he did his best not to thrust. His breath left him in a rushing exhale as she did the next best thing to letting him slide his cock into her. She was hot and wet and so incredibly soft as she moved on him. He slid his hands over her thighs, needing to hold on to her somehow. Her breath had turned to soft panting, and he watched her face as she took pleasure from this, too. Her hips flexed against him as she rubbed her little clit along his stiff shaft. He groaned again when she switched to a sinuous grinding motion and gave him the hottest, most erotic lap dance he'd ever had.

She stopped for just a moment, motioning Jack and Ethan closer. They must have been stroking their own cocks as she'd been doing her thing. He watched in awe as she took each of their hands and touched them to her literally dripping-wet pussy. They went back to stroking as she settled back on him. She smiled seductively and continued her grind as Jack and Ethan lubricated their shafts with her juices and stroked themselves to shouting orgasms. He held on to his own release by the thinnest of threads.

Grace shifted from her straddled position and moved between his thighs and used her little pink tongue to lick up and down his cock, coating her lips with all the juices there, then parted her lips and looked up at him as he watched his rock-hard dick slide into her sweet little mouth. Her eyelids closed, and she moaned softly as she took him to the back of her throat. The vibration almost undid him like a horny teenager with his first girl. Then she started sucking him.

"Oh, baby! You're killing me! Oh! Your mouth, oh, you *angel*! Yes, suck me, baby, oh, yes!"

She popped his cock from her mouth like a lollipop, making him shudder and cry out. She softly sucked his balls into her mouth, tonguing them, too. She gently grasped his cock at the base and slid him into her mouth, sucking him in again.

She swirled her tongue around the head of his cock before taking him in deep again, over and over, until he was shouting and whimpering. His release gathered to explode, his shaft hardened even more, and his balls drew up, the tension is his body reaching seismic levels until he felt his control begin to slip.

"Baby, I'm going to come soon! Damn you feel so good. I'm—I'm coming, oh!"

He howled as his release exploded in hot streams into her welcoming mouth. She increased her suction just slightly and held on to him. She didn't release him, or pull back, or slow down. She suckled gently and swallowed every drop of cum that erupted from his cock into her hot mouth, drawing on him until he whimpered for mercy. Then she licked him until she'd gotten it all, and he lay there unable to move, speak, or think. Hell, he was doing good to remember to *breathe* at this point.

She climbed carefully back up his chest and settled with her head under his jaw. Her sweet little body molded itself to him as he laid there in tingling satisfaction, trying to catch his breath. He brushed a lock of hair from her face and wrapped his arms around her adoringly as she snuggled closer to him.

Her head was turned so she could look at both Jack and Ethan, who now sat on the bed. Jack stroked her thigh, and Ethan caressed her warm cheek.

She sleepily murmured, "Love you," then he watched as her eyelashes fluttered closed.

He lay there for a few minutes and allowed her to rest. He was in complete awe of Grace. Where did she find the energy for all of them? His thoughts wandered back to the moment when she was kneeling in front of Ethan with her arms around his legs before she took his cock in her sweet mouth. He thought he understood now what Angel and Ethan had meant about Grace being submissive in nature. Intuition told him that she was content to stay in that position, adoration obvious in her sweetly flushed face, with Ethan's cock in her mouth for as long as Ethan had wanted. Her willingness to serve them unreservedly with trust was her submission to them.

A while later, Jack rose and turned on the shower in the bathroom. Adam carefully sat up with her and carried her into the bathroom. She roused a little, and Adam stood her on shaky legs and helped her into the shower.

With Ethan and Jack's help, Adam used the body wash to gently cleanse her, being careful of her sensitive little pussy. They bathed themselves, as well, then rinsed her thoroughly before turning the water off and wrapping her in a towel.

Ethan dried off then went back to the bedroom to strip the bath sheets they'd used earlier from the bed and got it ready for her. Adam and Jack patted her skin dry, found a gown in her dresser, and slid it over her naked, sleepy form. Adam smoothly lifted her and carried her to the bed. He laid her on the sheets, and they tucked her in.

Kissing her tenderly, he paused to watch her, curled up, motionless, in her slumber. Her golden curls were spread out over her pillow, shining in the dim light. Finally, they left her room and stopped in the hall outside the closed door. Adam leaned back against the wall, his hips wrapped loosely in a towel like the other two. He tried without much success to walk away from her bedroom door. He leaned his head against the wall, looking at Jack and Ethan, before closing his eyes on unshed tears. He felt complete. Sated. Speechless. Utterly speechless. The way she loved and trusted him, the three of them, blew him away.

He walked across the house with them, and each man went to his own bedroom. Adam didn't even bother to turn on a light, just climbed straight into bed. He contemplated the depth of the love she showered them with. His chest ached with love for her. He looked forward to tomorrow night with eager intensity, but this feeling went deeper. He wanted to make her his permanently, to satisfy a lifetime's worth of nights spent in her sweet arms. He knew Jack and Ethan felt the same way because it had been in their eyes when they stood in the hall outside her bedroom.

* * * *

Grace stretched and felt deliciously languid as she recalled the events of the previous night. Had all that really happened, or was it another erotic dream? Her pussy felt sensitive when she stroked her fingers through it. She was a little damp, and her clit throbbed when she touched it gently, sending fresh moisture to her slit. She stretched again and recalled the feel of their hands and tongues on her body. She barely remembered they had bathed with her afterward. She smiled as thunder rumbled and raindrops splattered on the window panes.

Her bedroom door opened quietly. She rolled in the bed to face Adam, and a slow smile spread across her lips as she reached for him. Adam came to the bed, his heart in his beautiful green eyes. He sat down next to her. The sheet slid down when she rolled over until only the very tips of her breasts were covered. She stretched, which offered them up to him, and he happily obliged her. He still hadn't said anything, just bent down to lovingly suckle one nipple, then the other, before he kissed her lips. His eyes loved her and spoke to her as though words from his mouth were unnecessary. She ran her fingers into his hair before she pulled him to her on the bed. He was shirtless, dressed only in blue jeans.

She nuzzled her nose against his chest and allowed him to gather her in his arms, squeezing her gently. He sighed, and she heard his heart thud in his chest, increasing in its pace as he kissed the top of her head.

"Are you sore this morning?" he asked as he tilted her chin up to look into her eyes. His green eyes searched hers.

"A little but not in a way that is unpleasant. I feel like I've been with you, and I love that feeling. I want to feel that way even more tomorrow morning. Was last night all right, Adam? Did I please you?" She felt self-conscious as she recalled her impromptu attempt at pussy-jacking him. His chuckle rumbled deeply in his chest as he rubbed his hand over his face.

"Did you please me? Oh, baby, honey, angel, you nearly *killed* me with pleasure. I'm probably not going to get much work done today. I'm going to be hard and cranky all day. Your pussy on me last night was a little taste of what heaven will feel like tonight." He brushed his lips along her jaw line. "I can't wait."

She heard someone else in the hall.

"Good morning, Gracie." Ethan entered with a mug of coffee for her. "I thought I heard Adam's voice. Y'all sleep well?" He leaned in and kissed her as she sat up, and she took the mug from him.

"Thank you, Ethan. I slept very well last night. I think I was sound asleep even before you left the room."

"You were," Ethan chuckled. "I'm still not sure you were entirely awake in the shower. You were sound asleep when Adam tucked you in."

Placing her palm on Adam's cheek she said, "Aw, you tucked me in? Y'all are so sweet. I don't know if I'll ever get used to it."

Ethan reclined on the bed, resting his head in the palm of his hand. "It's supposed to rain all day, Grace. Jack is a little concerned about you driving your Honda into town this morning and back home this afternoon. There are two low water crossings you have to go through to get back to the ranch. The ground is really saturated right now, and it wouldn't take much rain for flash floods to occur."

"I noticed those crossings, but I'd be careful to not drive through one if it had a lot of water in it." She didn't want them to worry that she would take unnecessary risks.

"I know you would, but one of us can take you to work and bring you back home, then we won't worry about you being stranded in town. I could take you in this morning, and Jack said he could pick you up this afternoon. He had to leave early, otherwise he would've talked to you himself. He wants you to call him."

"I don't need to be chauffeured. I know when not to drive through a low water crossing. I'll be very cautious." She saw the determined looks in their eyes. "But if it will make you *happy*, I'll let you cart me around today. It's a good thing it doesn't flood that often around here, otherwise y'all would get sick of me!" She sat up, laughing at the way they ogled her breasts. Ethan looked like he wanted a bite.

"Oh no, honey, we won't get sick of you." Adam leaned forward to kiss her shoulder. "We'd just buy you an Escalade or a Hummer, and then we'd know you were safe. No driving into walls of water or anything like that, of course."

She held up her hands in surrender. "Let's hold off on buying Grace anymore stuff until she settles in a bit, okay?"

"Okay," Adam said, "but you may need to adjust your expectations a bit, baby. We love to buy you stuff. It makes *us* happy." He got up from the bed. "Well, now that my warm, fuzzy moment has been disrupted, I'd better get myself ready for work. What time do you have to go in, baby?"

"Not for another hour or so. Would you like me to make you two some breakfast?" She looked for her robe but didn't see it.

"Nope, we already have breakfast ready for you, honey." Ethan replied. "Jack made you French toast and eggs. He left just a little while ago."

"I wish he would've come and kissed me before he left." She was pleasantly surprised he'd cooked for her but a little disappointed that he was already gone.

"He peeked in on you and said you were still sound asleep. He didn't want to disturb you."

"Y'all kissing me good-bye will always take priority over disturbing my sleep. I'll miss his kiss all day now."

"Aw, but you'll only have to wait until noon." Ethan tugged playfully on her sheet and chuckled. "He's going to bring you lunch. Maybe Adam and I can tide you over until you see him later." They advanced on her when she rose naked from the bed.

"Let me brush my teeth first. I don't want you to kiss me with morning breath. Give me one minute." She held up one hand to halt them and one over her mouth.

"Yeah, like it would be possible for Grace to have morning breath. She's *perfect*." Adam snickered from the doorway of the bathroom as she looked askance at him and just said, "Humf!" as she scrubbed her teeth at the sink. She rolled her eyes when she caught them both ogling her naked breasts as they swayed and jiggled with her movements. "Eefin, mer my wobe?" she mumbled over her toothbrush.

Reluctantly, Ethan got her robe from behind the door and helped her into it as she continued brushing her teeth. After she was finished, she went to both of them and kissed them soundly. She reveled in the feel of their warm hands through the thin, semi-sheer blue mesh of her new robe. She felt sexy in it knowing that her men would be able to make out just a hint of her nipples through the thin fabric. Damn, but Adam had good instincts!

"What should I wear with my pink topaz today, boys?" She thought they might like to pick out her outfit.

They picked out a pair of blue jeans, which was what she preferred to dress in at Harper's, and a multicolored print top that was made from a slinky fabric that draped sensuously over her breasts. It revealed just a bit of her cleavage.

"Ah!" she gasped, shocked as she looked first in the mirror, then down at the front of her top. "Would you look at *that*?" Both men came closer, looking for something wrong.

"What?"

She grinned crookedly up at them. "If you stood *right here*," she said as she beckoned them close to her sides, "you could see down the front of my shirt!" she said in a shocked but teasing tone.

"Here, let me come closer and see." Ethan drew her against him and looked down her shirt with a naughty grin. "Yep, Adam, I can see right down Gracie's top. You chose well!" He fist bumped Adam as he came closer and took a gander also.

"I like this top, and I love those smiles." She giggled as she exited the closet and returned to the bathroom to finish getting ready. She applied a little makeup, fixed her hair up in a clip, and put the pink topaz jewelry on. She stood back and admired the effect. The top was a lot brighter colored than she normally wore, but she loved the way it felt on her. The men sure seemed to like it.

She slipped on her shoes and went out to the kitchen to reheat the breakfast Jack had made her. Ethan had already done it and was setting her a place at the table, along with theirs. While she was in the bathroom, they'd also finished getting ready for work. Adam was dressed in his standard denim shirt and jeans with work boots. Ethan was in his cowboy boots, jeans, and another of his twill work shirts, sapphire this time. It made the blue of his eyes an even more intense shade as he took in her appearance with appreciation.

"Do you have to work this evening?" Grace asked him, hoping he didn't because tonight was important.

"I have ranch business today, and then I'll be going in to The Pony for a while this afternoon. I've cut back some on the late night hours so we can have more time together. Ben and I have talked about hiring another bartender to pick up some of the slack. I'll still need to spend some evenings there to make sure things are run smoothly. You can come with me on some of those evenings if you'd like."

"Only if I won't be in the way."

"Not at all. To have you up there would make it more fun for me. I'd seat you next to Bill, and he could keep you company if things got busy."

They finished their breakfast, and Adam went on to his first appointment after giving her an enthusiastic kiss good-bye. Adam was looking forward to tonight if the bulge in the front of his jeans was any indicator. She hoped he wasn't really going to be like that all day. She'd feel awful if he did. When he left, he was smiling.

Ethan helped her into his work truck and drove her into town. They drove through the first low water crossing, which already had water in it this early in the day.

"Good thing you didn't take your Honda, Gracie. I'd have been worried about you driving through these."

"If it keeps raining like this all day, I probably would have been stranded in town."

"I'd rather err on the side of caution where your safety is concerned, honey." He reached out and caressed her cheek. She tilted her head into his touch.

"I love you," she whispered. Her heart ached with a longing to stay near him, to not be parted from him even if it was only for the work day.

"I love you, too. I can't wait for tonight. I'll be hard all day just thinking about you in my arms."

She felt warm and safe and turned on all at the same time. "Will you call me when you hear from them, Ethan? I don't think I'm going to be able to concentrate on anything but fantasies, myself." He nodded and took her hand in his warm one. "Thank you for waiting for me and for going to all this trouble for me."

"It's worth it to start with a clean slate."

They quietly rode into town. He pulled up in Harper's parking lot and helped her climb out of his truck. The warm breeze blew a few wisps of her hair into her face. As he brushed them from her cheeks, he gazed into her eyes.

He wrapped her in his strong embrace, his lips pressing against hers tenderly. She heard a low rumble in his chest as he kissed her with increasing passion. Tension vibrated in the muscles of his back and she could hear it in his breathing. His kiss made her knees feel like they were about to melt, and she was glad he held her so snugly. Otherwise she might have become a puddle on the hot asphalt. Just like with the other two men, his gentle, passionate kiss made her panties wet, and the growing bulge at his groin made her wish he was picking her up instead of dropping her off. He chuckled deeply when she moaned softly, and he finally released her lips, punctuating his kiss with a little flick of his tongue against her bottom lip. He sighed softly and shook his head as if to clear it, and smiled at her.

"Remember, Jack will bring you lunch. I'll call you when I hear from the doctor's office, and I'll see you this evening." When he said it, the sound of his sexy, velvety voice made her pussy tremble in excitement.

"Okay." His kiss had robbed her of intelligent speech. He hugged her one more time and walked her to the door and opened it for her. He waved at Martha and Rose inside as they tried to look busy, but grinned widely.

"Hi, Martha! Hi, Rose! Have a great day, honey." Ethan gave her a quick kiss and was gone.

"Oh my goodness, girl! Was that kiss as hot and sweet as it looked?" Martha fanned herself. "I may need to go home at lunch and see my husband! Wowee!"

"Grace, you're glowing. You look like we could knock you over with a feather! Was it that good?" Rose smirked.

"Uh-huh." Grace sighed and nodded to them.

"The way he *looks* at you, oh, honey!" Rose rhapsodized, "He is *so* in love with you. Those blue eyes!"

"Those biceps!" Martha made squeezing motions with her hands, like she was squeezing his thickly muscled arms.

"That hair!" Rose replied rapturously.

"Look at her pink topaz! Did they give that to you?" Martha admired the necklace and earrings and held Grace's hand up to look at the ring.

"Jack surprised me with them last night, among other things. I'm still in shock I think."

"Those men know how to spoil a woman." Rose admired the ring as well.

"I'm going to be utterly useless today if we don't focus. My legs still feel like rubber." Grace chuckled and sighed as she poured herself a cup of coffee and sat down with the stack of work orders for the day.

Monogramming had to be done on more work shirts for local businesses. There were hats that needed company logos embroidered on them, fresh baseball jerseys in need of screen printing, and a large box of children's hoodies needing their school name embroidered on them.

Grace did her best to throw herself into today's orders and make them her best work ever. She purposely did not look at the clock unless she absolutely had to. She was at the front counter when Jack walked in with lunch. His eyes twinkled with mischief as he put the sacks down and hugged her.

"I understand I'm in big trouble." He was unable to hide his grin as she came around the counter and gave him a hug.

"Big trouble, mister. Huge." She snickered as he tried to look guilty and failed miserably.

"I promise to never leave the house again without kissing you first, asleep or awake." He slid his big, warm hands up and down her ribs, starting a warm vibration in her clit with his touch.

"Well, all right. I'm glad we got that worked out. I missed you this morning." She glanced around and stole a kiss from him.

"Oh! Hello, Jack," Martha said as she came into the front room. "How are you today?"

"I'm better now," Jack drawled as he picked up the lunch bags. "I picked up lunch for everyone."

"I see that! We want to buy you lunch sometime to thank you for treating us so often," Martha replied.

"It's my excuse to get to see my girl." He kissed Grace's cheek and followed her into the break room. "I brought y'all sandwiches from Rudy's today."

They ate their lunches quickly, and then Martha and Rose left the break room to give Jack and Grace some time alone. While Grace finished her lunch and Jack told her about his morning, his phone rang. He answered without looking at the caller ID.

"Jack Warner. Hey, Ethan! You did? What did they say? Really? Good. I know, right? Yeah, she's right here. You wanna talk to her? Sure." He held out the phone to her. Each word from Jack's side of the phone conversation made her heart pound faster.

"Hello?"

"Honey, you are *so* getting laid tonight," Ethan said. She felt the warm flush in her cheeks spread all the way down her throat.

"Am I?" She giggled, smiling at Jack, who looked like a man with a new purpose in life. "How is your day so far?"

"Better than it was five minutes ago. How about you?"

"Ditto."

"Is Jack feeding you lunch?"

"With his own hands?" she teased. "No, I ate what he brought me."

"Do you like the idea of us feeding you with our hands?" Ethan asked softly.

"Yes, very much. It's kind of sexy."

"You're making me hard."

"Am I? I wish I was there. I could help you with that." She heard him growl. She asked in a sultry voice, "Do you like the idea of me helping you with that?"

"I'm imagining you on your knees in front of me, the way you were last night, your lips around my cock." He snickered at her stunned gasp.

"Please tell me you are alone right now."

"Of course I am. I only talk dirty for *you*, honey. I'm in my truck."

"I'm looking forward to tonight. A lot."

"Are you wet from thinking about it?" His sexy, deep voice did *that* all by itself.

"Yes, I have been all day."

"I can't wait to slide into your hot little body, hear you moan my name." She gulped at his suggestive words and felt a fresh gush of moisture between her thighs. "Gracie? You there?"

"Uh-huh."

"Are you ready for me right now?" he asked softly.

She felt her pussy clench involuntarily at the thought of it. "You know I am, Ethan. Just the sound of your voice, the things you say. It's going to be a *long* afternoon." Jack held out his hand for his phone. "Jack wants to talk to you. I love you, Ethan."

"Hey, thanks for getting her all hot and bothered and leaving her with me. Were you talking dirty? Because she is fifty shades of pink right now. Well, enjoy your afternoon. Thanks for the information. Later." He looked at her hungrily after he pocketed his phone. "Well, that was a hell of an interesting conversation to hear only one side of."

She whimpered and laid her head in her hands. "This afternoon is going to last *forever*." Her last word was punctuated by a nearby boom and crash of thunder, followed a few seconds later by another. Startled, she jumped a little both times. He placed his warm, comforting hand on her back.

"Thunderstorms must be moving into the area now. We're under a severe thunderstorm warning until seven o'clock. Unlike our friend Ethan, I'm not going to sit here and torture us both with fantasies about tonight. I've already done that for the last several days. I'll check back with you in a few hours when you know what time you'll be done."

She rose from her chair, and he wrapped his arms around her. She laid her head against his chest and could hear his heart pounding. He might not say anything to her, but she heard it in his heartbeat and felt it in the hardened cock pressed against her belly. She nestled into him for a few seconds and enjoyed the feel of his strong arms around her and his fresh, clean scent.

"Y'all are so sweet," Martha said as she came into the room to refill her water glass. "I hope you're not working outside in this weather today, Jack. It's looks nasty outside."

"No, ma'am. I have a couple more stops to make, but they're all indoors, thank goodness."

"That's good. Grace, we're probably going to be done early this afternoon because it's been so quiet. Jack, if you want to pick her up around four, I think she'll be done."

"But what about customers?" Grace hated to leave early when Martha and Rose had to stay because they had set hours of operation.

"Nah! Like I said, it's really quiet. We'll be done early, and all I'm going to do is putter and clean. We can handle the customers, too. You two can enjoy your evening," Martha said with a wink.

"All right," Grace conceded. "If you really don't mind."

"I wouldn't suggest it if I minded. Just be careful if you get out in a storm. I'm still a little leery after Tuesday night. We'll listen to the weather radio this afternoon."

Grace walked him to the door and whispered, "Jack, I'll look forward to a little alone time with you if I get to leave early."

"What's up, darlin'? You okay?" he asked, grazing her cheekbone with his knuckle.

"I'm fine, Jack. I just woke up this morning and realized something."

"What's that, darlin'?"

She leaned in to him and softly said, "*Everyone* came last night but you, and I want to make that up to you, honey."

"It's sweet of you, darlin', but I *did* come last night, if you'll recall, thanks to that *sexy* little move of yours. If you want to fool around a little when I get you home, I'm up for that, but don't feel like you have to keep it all even to make us happy. Now I'm as hard as a baseball bat."

He gave her a long kiss that sent a spear of desire straight into her clit before going out the door into the rain. She sat at her desk and tried to focus on what needed to be done next.

"Wow," Martha said as she and Rose came in the front room and watched through the window as Jack pulled away in the SUV.

Grace looked up as she paged through work orders. "Huh?"

"Nothin', just *wow*."

"She means that's a hot cowboy you got there. Damn, you're lucky, Grace." Rose chuckled, going back to work.

The weather radio posted an update saying that thunderstorms were moving in their direction as the afternoon got steadily hotter. Martha, Rose, and Grace did finish their work early, as anticipated, and Grace kept an eye on the window as she swept out the shop. The afternoon sky had taken on a funny color that made her nervous, and the air seemed charged.

Jack showed up at four o'clock on the dot, helped her gather her things, and made sure the ladies had safe transportation home because parts of town were experiencing flash flooding. A block from the shop, a deluge slammed into them, and Jack had to slow down to a crawl because visibility became so poor. Hail began pelting the SUV as they reached the edge of town. It was mostly marble-size hail stones, but being in the midst of it was really loud. The hail lasted about two minutes then suddenly stopped and turned back into a downpour. Grace was grateful there was very little wind.

The low water crossings were getting full but remained open, and Jack drove through them with no problem. The rain came down harder as they pulled into the ranch entryway and started slowly down the drive.

"I'm glad you listened to Ethan and allowed him to drive you to work. We would have been worried sick."

"I'm glad I listened, too. Storms scare me under normal circumstances, and I think I've already met my fear quota for the week on Tuesday evening."

"You did, darlin'. We'll get you in the house, and you can relax. We'll have to make a run for it, though. I don't have an umbrella. I'll pull as close as I can to the front steps."

She opened the door and hopped out and ran straight up the steps, glad she was in athletic shoes and not sandals. It didn't matter that she was only on the steps for a few seconds. In that short time, she was soaked to the skin. Jack ran the short distance from the parking area on the side of the house to the porch, also getting soaked. The hail and the heavy rain cut the oppressive heat somewhat, but she felt like a steaming, drowned rat.

Jack unlocked the door and opened it for her to go in. The frigid air inside the house blasted them as they entered, and they both started to shiver.

"Come with me, Grace. There are some bath sheets in the laundry room. We can take off these wet clothes in there." Jack pulled her with him as she shuffled along behind. Nothing felt as gross as soaking wet blue jeans unless it was soaking wet, suddenly cold, blue jeans.

Jack led her into the laundry room and turned on the light. He grabbed two big fluffy towels from a cabinet over the countertop and threw them in the dryer to warm them up. Then he started to shuck clothes fast. She stood there and watched for a few seconds.

"You need help, darlin'? Because if you do, I'm volunteering," he said with a playful grin, reaching for the hem of her top. "I really like this little top you're wearing. I like it even better soakin' wet on you." She lifted her arms so he could gently pull it over her head.

"I like it, too."

"Let's get you out of these wet jeans, darlin'. You're shiverin'."

He unbuttoned the snaps for her, and she shimmied out of them as he watched appreciatively. That particular move caused her breasts to bounce and jiggle in the confines of her now-transparent wet bra. She grinned at him, liking this bra more and more all the time.

June totally rocks.

He finished undressing right down to his skin, and she noticed his cock was stiff and erect. He was completely unselfconscious around her and did not bother to hide his arousal, smiling over at her with desire in his eyes. He reached in the dryer, took out the warm towels, and dried himself off quickly. He rubbed his hair with the towel until it stood up in spikes, reminding her of the black and white framed picture in the living room of him with Adam and Ethan on the Guadalupe River.

She stepped from the jeans, slipped out of her thong, and reached behind her for the closure on her bra. She peeled it off and laid it with the thong on the counter so they could dry. Jack wrapped the towel around her and rubbed her dry. She shivered again as he squeezed the water from her hair with the towel.

"I have a good idea, Grace. Why don't we take a nice, warm shower together? It'll warm us up, and we could have some fun in the process, you reckon?"

She nodded as she took his hand, and he led her to the master bathroom. They left the towels on the bathroom counter, and he started the warm water in the shower. He turned to her, held out his hand, and stepped in as she followed him. The hot water streamed over her hair and down her back, warming her quickly. She heard the click of a lid, and then Jack was shampooing her hair. He worked the soapy suds through her hair and massaged her scalp with his fingers. She sighed happily, leaning against him.

"Let's rinse your hair, darlin'."

She turned into the spray and tilted her head back, letting the shampoo rinse from her hair, then applied a little of her conditioner. While she did that, she noticed that his cock was very stiff and fully erect. Her hands were in her hair, letting the water fall on it before squeezing the water through to remove the conditioner. She closed her eyes when the water ran in her face and jumped and giggled when she felt his warm mouth close over one of her nipples. She loved the playful lover in Jack. In bed, he was the most likely to make her giggle, at least early on. When it came to lovin', he was as serious as the others. She gasped when he suckled on it then released her with a pop, setting off a tingle in her clit.

He picked up the bottle of body wash and poured a little on his hand. He created a little lather before he spread it over her breasts and palmed them gently. He flicked his thumbs slowly over her nipples then trailed down her rib cage to her belly. Her heart pounded as his fingers slid around her hips to her buttocks and gripped her ass in his slippery hands. He pulled her to him, and every inch of his cock pressed against her bare, slippery skin. She arched her back and rubbed against him. She took the washcloth and poured more of the body wash on it and lathered it well, and then she *seriously* took to the task of bathing his body, paying particular attention to his balls and, of course, his beautiful cock.

Because she got on the job and actually did bathe him, he did the same for her, scrubbing every inch of her gently and thoroughly. He discovered a new ticklish spot, directly over the cleft of her ass, when he ran the washcloth very lightly over it. She squealed a little when he did it again as he chuckled deeply.

"Now we're havin' fun, aren't we, darlin'?" He nuzzled her ear when they were both rinsed off.

"We are, Jack." She rose on her tiptoes to kiss lightheartedly him on the lips. She held one of his hands to steady herself as she knelt in the shower. His breath caught when he saw what she was doing, and the mood changed instantly.

She came to him and gently lapped his balls with her tongue. She laved and sucked on them, then swirled her tongue around them, playing. She grasped the base of his cock and gently tilted it into her mouth.

Leaning forward against the tile wall, he groaned, bent over her, and spoke softly to her. "Grace, I love when you do this for me, the way you take your time. Your mouth feels so good."

She slowed her strokes and sweetly tortured him as she gazed up into his eyes and listened to what he said. When he was no longer able to speak, she closed her eyes so she could concentrate on him as much as possible. He had brought so much love into her life, starting with his own, then Adam and Ethan's. If this one act could demonstrate for him how much she loved him in return, then she'd make this the most mind-bending blow job he'd ever received.

Set to remain here a while, savoring his cock, she started a slow, steady rhythm with her hand at the base and her mouth gliding over the head. She relaxed her jaw muscles and regulated her breathing, taking him into her mouth, running her tongue along the underside of his cock. She felt his hand sink into her damp hair to help her establish the rhythm he needed. He moaned in pleasure, his head on the arm that braced him against the wall in front of him, the sound echoing off the tile.

* * * *

She hummed softly in response to him and the vibration against the tip of his cock had him hissing and groaning. Jack basked in the outpouring of her love, content to go slowly if that was what she wanted, but each time she suckled, his urgency increased. He wallowed in the decadent knowledge that she had no intention of stopping until she was good and ready. He was at her mercy, and he knew instinctively that was powerful for her as well. No other woman could satisfy him the way she could. He gazed down at her beautiful face. He cupped her cheek as his testicles drew up, signaling his imminent release. She opened her eyes and looked into his and commanded him to come from those blue depths. He howled as his release blindsided him. Never had he had such an explosively powerful orgasm from a blow job. *Never*. And he knew it was because he had never loved anyone the way he loved her.

Receiving his cock in her mouth like that could be viewed as a one-sided act, since she received no mutual stimulation in their current position. That might be true, but it spoke volumes to him of the love Grace felt for him. After she released him, and he'd caught his breath, he knelt in front of her. He pulled her languid body into his embrace. Words were unnecessary. He kissed her and noticed with a flare of renewed desire that he tasted himself there. A wild, possessive part of him was smugly pleased that his essence was inside of her and now a part of her, and even more would be later after they'd made love.

He helped her rise to her feet and shut off the water. When they stepped from the shower, he heard voices and realized Ethan and Adam were home and, from the sounds of it, were setting the table for supper. Ethan had told him earlier he planned to bring home some Chinese takeout food. After she dried off, he went into her closet and retrieved her sexy, blue mesh robe and helped her into it.

* * * *

Grace squeezed as much water from her hair as she could and combed it out before blow drying it a little. Jack returned in his own robe, a jet-black fleece that looked very warm and soft. He came to her, palming both cheeks, and kissed her tenderly, the way she loved for Jack to kiss her, like she was so infinitely precious.

"Ethan and Adam have picked up supper and have everything already on the table. Are you hungry, darlin'?"

"A little." She was so excited her stomach was the last thing on her mind.

"Well, you need to eat something because you're going to need all your energy tonight," he whispered. The light of desire shone plainly in his eyes. "We have big plans for you."

They walked to the kitchen where she was greeted with a hug and a kiss from Ethan and Adam. Their hands glided down her back and palmed her ass as they led her to her seat.

"How long have you been home?" She watched as they served her from the containers of Chinese food.

Ethan poured her a glass of tea. "About twenty minutes. We saw that you and Jack were busy in the shower and decided to check on things at the barn and see how Angel is doing."

"How is he?" Jack asked.

"Great. Patricia came and got all of her things this morning while we were at work, and no one has seen her since. I checked in with Ben a minute ago, and neither she nor any of her friends are at The Pony yet. She didn't make any trouble, just came with empty boxes and left with full ones." Ethan sat back down and started eating. She noticed he used chop sticks to eat while everyone else used a fork.

"I sure am glad to be home, baby. It's been a long, long day," Adam said, looking at her appreciatively in the robe. "I picked that robe because it reminded me of your eyes. Do you like it?"

"I love it. It feels very sexy on, like I'm not wearing anything at all." She looked him in the eye and caught the glimmer of lust and desire reflected there. He leaned down and kissed her gently as his fingertip stroked her erect nipple. Its rosy color was slightly visible through the semi-sheer mesh fabric.

"You look beautiful in it, baby," he replied, smiling as she sighed happily at his gentle caress. "Did y'all get rained on coming home?"

"We got soaked to the skin. That's how we wound up in the shower. We both got chilled when we came into the air conditioning and needed to warm up." Grace smiled softly at Jack.

"You looked pretty warm when we got home and found you in the shower."

"Yes, it was wonderful," she murmured dreamily and blushed a little. She looked up to catch Jack watching her lovingly.

"*Look* at that beautiful face and those cheeks." Ethan put his fingertips to her cheek. "We're going to love you so well tonight, Gracie. I hope you walk around with that dazed expression for a week. I don't know how we ever got lucky enough to be with you."

From her seat beside him, she leaned her head against his shoulder and sighed in contentment as he wrapped his arm around her. What she was experiencing now was deeper and more profound than just an afterglow.

She ate a few more bites and said, "I'm done. Take your time and finish. I'm going to go brush my teeth and get ready for bed."

Ethan released her, and she smiled at them then sauntered slowly back to her room.

* * * *

Jack watched hungrily as she walked away, her hips swaying invitingly.

Food was now the last thing on their minds as Jack cleared the table, and Ethan and Adam went to quickly shower and prepare for the evening to come. Jack rinsed the dishes and put the leftovers in the fridge. He locked up the house and turned off most of the lights, leaving only a very dim light on in the living room.

He returned to Grace's room to find her lighting candles. He turned down the top sheet and blanket to the foot of the bed and arranged the pillows against the headboard. He watched her as she moved around the room, the candlelight glinting off her golden blonde hair. She looked at him and smiled a happy, serene smile. He'd worried she might be nervous, but their time together earlier seemed to have left her in a relaxed and languid frame of mind. She turned and looked to the door as Adam and Ethan entered the room.

Chapter Twenty-three

Standing within reaching distance of Grace were the men who loved her most in all the world, and they wanted to love her, make love to her, and please her. A little orgasmic shudder went through her as she thought about it. They reached for her, love and concern in their eyes.

"Are you all right, darlin'?" Jack caressed her shoulders then his warm hands slid down to her elbows. He was still in his robe, and Ethan and Adam were dressed in robes as well. She smiled up at each one and drank in the sight of them.

This was their turning point. Up to this point, their relationship was based on attraction, desire, and a hope that they were *right* for each other. Now was the time to find out, to turn another corner.

"I've never felt so all right in my entire life, Jack. What should I do now?" she asked simply, unsure of how he wanted to proceed.

Jack leaned down and kissed her. She felt his warm hands move up to the neckline of her robe and gently slide it from her shoulders. Either Ethan or Adam had already pulled the tie at the waist loose. Jack slid the robe down her arms, and it disappeared. She didn't feel exposed. Having already spent intimate moments with all of them, she felt covered and protected by their nearness.

"Beautiful," she heard Adam reverently whisper.

She felt Adam's hands sweep her hair from her shoulder, then he began to kiss her throat while he gently caressed her arm. He sucked on her shoulder, and the pull of his mouth sent a throbbing jolt to her clit. She felt swollen and needy already.

Ethan lifted her left hand and kissed the palm then worked his way up her arm to her collarbone. He moved on to her breast and brushed his fingertips over the nipple, teasing it as it peaked and sent little white-hot pulses to her pussy. He slid his hand to the underside and held it, gently squeezing. She shuddered and moaned a little as Adam's hand slid over her abdomen, and she grew wetter and wetter, aching with need.

Jack released her lips, and as if on cue, Adam and Ethan stopped their advances to look at her as Jack spoke.

"Darlin', this is another night of firsts, and we want it all to be as perfect as we can make it for you. We'll only go as far as you're able. You're not obligated to make love with all three of us tonight. We want to make you feel good, not used, and we never want you to feel obligated if you're not in the mood. Would you like to lie down?"

She nodded, and he led her to the bed. She climbed into the middle of it and waited to see where they would end up. She noticed Jack make eye contact with Ethan and give him an almost imperceptible nod.

* * * *

Ethan's heart pounded as he removed his robe and climbed up onto the bed with her. She knelt there with her little hands rested on the tops of her thighs. She waited for him to make the first move, to take the lead. Her shining, long blonde hair hung down around her shoulders, a wavy drape that framed her luscious, round breasts. He was vaguely aware of Jack and Adam moving onto the bed on either side of the center, where she would soon be.

After discussing it in advance, both Jack and Adam agreed that Ethan should be the one to go first. Jack was reluctant to be the first and risk making her too sore to continue if she wanted to. Of the three of them, Jack was, without a doubt, the thickest. Adam was the longest of them, and though he would have jumped at the chance to go first, he was worried about her inexperience with a normal-sized penis and opted to let Ethan go first. Adam and Jack shared a mistaken belief that somehow she was more attuned to Ethan, and they thought that it would help her if she could experience the first time with him.

He personally doubted that she was any more attuned to him than she was to the others, but the size issue did win out. Although he'd been tapped by the cock fairy's wand more than once, he was the closest to average in length and girth. Of course, his voracious cock was *all* for doing the right thing and being the first to take the plunge. Greedy bastard.

Ethan came to her and reached out to caress her face. Her eyelids slid closed at his touch, and a soft smile spread over her sweet lips. He slid an arm around her and leaned into her. She reached out to him, grasping his biceps for balance as he laid her back on the pillows Jack piled up for her. He sat back up and ran his fingers along her silky inner thighs, spreading them gently, until her beautiful pussy was exposed. His fingers trailed back and forth over her smooth flesh, which made her sigh shakily as he gazed at her. Her damp curls glistened, and her womanly scent beckoned to him. Moving slowly, he watched her face as he came to her. For an instant, she seemed to brace herself a little, and he smiled reassuringly down at her. He slowly lowered himself into the cradle of her body, groaning softly as he settled against her warmth then gave her a slow, searing kiss. His cock throbbed incessantly as he pressed it against her pussy.

There were no words for how it felt to be in such a simple, intimate position with her, her supple thighs spread so that he could lie comfortably between them. He rose up on his elbows and kissed a trail down past her tightly peaked nipples to her mound. His tongue delved into her slit as he trailed his fingertips through her wetness, brushing against her slick inner lips. Her body trembled under his touch, and a soft, sexy moan slipped from her parted lips.

"Mmm, you're so wet for me, Gracie, so sweet and wet," he murmured softly, looking up into her trusting blue eyes. "Is this what you want, Gracie? What you've been waiting for? I'm going to lick you till you come, and then I'm going to finally make slow, sweet love to you. Do you want that?"

Her eyes rolled a little in her passionate response, and her cheeks blushed warmly. "Oh, Ethan, you know I do. Please, please—"

"Please what, Gracie?" He kissed her inner thigh. "Tell me what you want, and I'll give it to you."

"Please put your mouth on me," she whimpered. "Make me come, Ethan, please."

He tilted his head so he could see her eyes and lapped her clit with his tongue, enjoying the sounds of her pleasure as he played her body. He teased her with slow strokes through her wet entrance and up to her clit, laving it with his tongue before dipping into her pussy again. Her arousal was already at a fever pitch, so it didn't take him long to have her panting and sobbing for release, a release he gladly gave her. He didn't hold back as he greedily licked and then suckled her clit between his lips, sending her into bliss. She cried out his name as she came. He gloried to hear it falling from her lips, saying it with such love and passion.

Jack murmured in her ear and brushed her hair from her cheeks as Adam suckled her nipple and soothed her with his hand on her abdomen then moved up to kiss her temple.

Once she'd caught her breath, Ethan leaned forward again and kissed her lips, responding to her satiny, stroking tongue. He backed away a bit and looked in her eyes.

"Let me make love to you, Gracie." He gazed into her softly dazed eyes.

"Fill me, make love to me, Ethan." She reached out to draw him close to her.

He knelt between her thighs, parting them and laying them over his as he sat back on his heels. He looked over at Jack, and he handed him the bottle of lubricant. Ethan quickly applied some to her cunt and his cock. She uttered a soft sigh and nearly blew his self-control as she reached down with her delicate fingers and parted her pussy lips for him. She smiled at him seductively when he gasped in disbelief at her beautiful invitation. He leaned forward, balancing on one hand at her side. His cock brushed against her damp pussy, sliding his length through her sweet, soft warmth. Then he angled his hips to position the head at her fragile, wet entrance. His abs shuddered at the feel of her wet heat kissing the head of his cock. He glanced at Jack and Adam and saw the hunger and pure lust that was mirrored in their faces. He locked eyes with her, and she licked her bottom lip and nibbled on it.

He settled over her, bracing his weight on his arms. He closed his eyes and flexed against her gently, keeping a tight rein on the urge to plunge in. The lubricant made it easier, but he could feel for himself how tight her pussy was. He watched her face for any sign of pain as he thrust in gentle waves against her. Her body resisted, and he paused to give her time to adjust.

"How are you doing, Gracie?" Ethan kissed her as she softly moaned, evidently needing a moment to voice her feelings. "You're so tight, honey, so hot. Damn, it's hard to hold back."

He took a few deep, shaky breaths. He laid gentle kisses in a line on her throat, feeling his calm returning somewhat. She turned her face to him and kissed him, and he could tell she was breathing deeply and trying to relax and open for him as well. There was no trace of pain in her expression as she looked into his eyes.

"You're very big," she whispered, and he chuckled deeply, feeling some of the tension leave him.

"You say the nicest things, Gracie." He gazed into her eyes and stroked a lock of her hair.

"Ethan, you're big, but you're not hurting me. You're just way more than I'm used to. If you go slowly to give me time to adjust to your size, I'll be fine."

Ethan leaned forward over her, and as he did, she tilted her pelvis and rocked a bit. With a gasp from them both, he slid in a tiny bit farther. He kissed her and smiled down at her, then pulled out just a bit and thrust again. Damn, she felt so good, but he could tell as he continued moving against her that it was starting to hurt. He could see it in her eyes and the way she gulped. The tension began to build in him, and he knew he would soon reach the point of no return. It was either stop altogether or plunge forth. His thrusts slowed, trying to gauge what she wanted in this moment. Jack and Adam were quiet and seemed tense. She looked over at them and then back at him, with determination in her sultry gaze.

"Ethan, I can't wait to feel your big cock pumping into me, really fucking me," she whispered softly and seductively, her vulgar words and sweet tone contrasting in a shocking way.

His head came up sharply, and he was sure he saw Jack and Adam's jaws drop open in his peripheral vision.

"I love feeling you slide in and out of my pussy, and I'm getting wetter and hotter." Her little tongue flicked out and stroked his lower lip then tugged it between her teeth gently. "I love you so much. I want to feel your hot cock slide all the way into me. Later, I want to get on my hands and knees and find a mirror so I can watch you fuck me from behind. I want to be able to see your cock pumping into me until you make me come, and *fu–ck! Oww!*" She yelped as Ethan plunged into her. The resistance to his intrusion suddenly gave, and his cock sank to the hilt within her.

Dammit all to hell, fucking *caveman*! He really *hurt* her! Fucking *Neanderthal*! Son of a *bitch*! She was still a *virgin*! Oh, *god, it felt so good!*

Then sanity returned to him as he remembered the way she'd cried out in pain. She looked into his eyes and surprised him when she wrapped her legs tightly around his waist, determined to keep him right where he was, buried deep inside of her. She caressed his shoulders and nuzzled against him. He rose up on his elbows to look in her eyes. He didn't see pain or hurt, only love, as she touched him. The little minx knew he was about to pull out and took matters into her own hands.

He knew she was all right the moment she slowly and gently flexed her hips, moving with his cock inside of her, tenderly stroking him with her body. A soft, breathy moan came from her lips.

He let out a soft groan. "Gracie. If I had known, I would have prepared you better. I would have made sure you were ready."

"Honey, I *was* ready. I didn't know," she replied, then gave him a cheeky grin as she flexed her hips against him again. "Am I in trouble?"

"I'll have to remember you don't fight fair. I hate that I hurt you."

She shook her head. "You didn't hurt me. *Owen* hurt me. *You* saved me. Please stop worrying and love me. Make slow, sweet love to me just like you wanted to." She moaned softly as he flexed his hips and thrust his cock gently inside her. "Yes, do that. I love the way it feels, you sliding into me. It's the most beautiful thing I've ever felt."

"Darlin', you think it feels beautiful? It *looks* beautiful, too," Jack whispered, then sat up so he could watch Ethan pump his cock slowly into her little pussy.

She stroked his shoulder and said, "Please, I have to see, Ethan. Help me."

Ethan stopped his stroking, and Adam gently lifted her while Jack piled the pillows a little higher behind her. Ethan moved into an upright position and groaned as the sensation changed with her new position. She lifted her knees, and both Jack and Adam held them back gently for her. Moving her knees changed the way their bodies were aligned, and Ethan's cock began stroking her sweet spot.

Ethan growled as Grace lost herself in the sensations, her pussy drawing on his cock. He looked down where their bodies were joined, able to watch her pussy take his cock in this upright position. His greedy cock slid slowly into her cunt, then back out, coated in her juices, glistening in the candlelight. As it disappeared inside her, he could feel how tightly he filled her. He stroked her G-spot steadily, and she whimpered again, louder.

"Do you like it, Gracie? Watch my cock fill you. You like to watch while I make love to you, don't you?" Ethan asked her, looking into her deep blue eyes. Her expression was so vulnerable, her eyes revealed the pleasure his cock gave her.

"Oh, baby, I do! It's the most *beautiful* thing I've *ever* seen."

He thrust harder and growled when her pussy went slick with her juices.

"Yes, faster! I *want* to come, Ethan! I *need* to. Please don't stop."

Ethan pumped harder and faster, stroking her sweet spot some more. He leaned down to her and kissed her ravenously, never missing a beat. She writhed beneath him as her pussy gloved him tightly. More of her cream coated his thrusting cock. "*Yes,* baby. Give me that sweet cream. That's what I want to see. *Look at you*, baby. You're so hot and so tight. Is that the spot?"

She wailed, "Yes! Ethan!"

"Right there?" He concentrated on her sweet spot and gave her what she panted and whimpered for.

"Yes! Oh, yes, yes, *yes!* Ethan, I'm gonna come, I'm coming, I'm—" Her body went motionless and as tight as a spring, one millisecond away from shattering and releasing all that pent-up energy.

"Yes, Gracie, come for me, hard!" He roared as his release shot from his cock, streaming into her in hot bursts as she screamed.

"Ethan! *Ethan*! Oh!" And her body released all its tension with a gush as she came harder than she ever had before. She looked down at where their bodies were joined together, then up at him with a rapturous look on her face. "Oh! Beautiful! Oh, *look*! I never knew, oh, my goodness. I *never knew*." She whimpered, then fell back in Adam and Jack's arms, still connected with Ethan. He slumped forward into her arms, completely limp, and his breath came in heaving pants.

"Holy. Fucking. Hell," Adam growled. "Grace, you are really something, baby. I think I've died and gone to heaven, except I'm still hard."

Ethan chuckled because now he did know what heaven felt like. Heaven felt like Grace coming all around his cock, screaming his name in utter ecstasy. He lay there for a minute, just catching his breath, while Adam and Jack stroked her neck and kissed her temples and her throat.

"How do you feel, Gracie?" Ethan asked, concerned for her, but also in awe of her. He had just shared the most erotic experience in his entire life with the people he cared about most. This moment was the stuff his dreams, aspirations, and hopes had been built on—for them to find the right woman, for her to love them, and for them to be able to be like this together.

"I'm feeling real good right now. How about you, honey?" She looked up at him.

"I'm about as satisfied as a man can be, baby. Are you worn out?" Ethan was unable to fathom how she had any energy left after the wrenching orgasm she'd just experienced.

"I feel alive and energized. Give me a few minutes to catch my breath and I'll be ready. What?" She looked from one man to the next. Ethan grinned at her, awed by her enthusiasm for them. "I'm fine, I promise," she said. "Let's just take a few minutes to recover. Can I ask a favor of y'all tonight?"

"Whatever you want, baby." Adam kissed her temple.

"Don't leave me tonight?" She reached out to stroke them individually as she spoke. "Will you stay with me? That is, if there is enough room for you to sleep comfortably. Four people in a king-size bed will be a bit tight, I know. But I miss you when I wake up after I've had your lovin' and you're not here."

"Of course we'll stay with you, Gracie. We'd love to." Ethan gently kissed his way down her throat. She laced her fingers through his hair and reached out to lick his earlobe, and he groaned as he felt her inner muscles gently stroke his sated cock like a private, loving touch just for him.

Playfully, she added, "Of course, I wouldn't want you to feel obligated and risk you getting tired of having me around."

A chuckle rumbled deeply in Ethan's chest as he murmured, "Gracie, may I say, from my current enviable position, that you are a joy to have around, and make no mistake about that. We find that we *intensely* enjoy your company."

He slowly pulled out of her sweetly stroking pussy and sat back. As his cock slid from her, he could see his seed there in her opening, filling her and overflowing.

It did something to him deep inside to see her that way. His seed dripping from her. It was a feral, primitive sort of possessiveness that he felt for her. Although it damn near killed him to cause her pain, the notion that he had just claimed her only added to that intense primal feeling. There were slight traces of blood mixed with his cum. That was finished, and there would be no more pain for her, only pleasure from this point forward.

Ethan went to the bathroom to clean up a bit. After doing so, he returned to the bedroom on the tail end of Jack saying, "We thought to ease you into handling the rest of us. Of the three of us, Ethan is—"

"The smallest? But his cock is *enormous*! You're all enormous! I noticed that the other night, and I love your cocks—"

"Well, thank you, Gracie!" Ethan chuckled as he came back in the room, still naked. You say the nicest things, don't you?" He knew she'd been more than satisfied with his prowess, but he liked a compliment as well as the next guy. "What's the discussion?"

"We're not sure we should continue." Adam looked like he wanted to kick himself for saying it. "I don't want to hurt her, and neither does Jack. She's probably going to be really sore in the morning."

"We have lubricant, which in hindsight I *should* have used more of," Ethan said. "I thought that if I brought Grace to orgasm she would be plenty wet enough and ready for me. This was as big a surprise for her as it was for us. Use the lubricant if you're worried, but if Gracie wants you, she should get you." He climbed up onto the bed.

He wrapped his arms around her warm, luscious body, his chest to her back. He swept her hair away from her neck and kissed his way from her shoulder up to her ear. "I haven't told you tonight how good you taste, have I, Gracie? You do taste good, *everywhere*." His hands slid from her breasts down her abdomen. He loved the way she felt, so soft and tender in his arms, and had to squeeze her again, his fingers trailing down over her mound. His questing fingers dipped into her sheath, finding her hot and soaking wet with her juices.

"Well, all this anti-climactic talk hasn't slowed you down any, has it, honey? Hot, wet, and wanting more?" Ethan murmured in her ear. "Do you want another cock?"

"Mmm-hmm." She closed her eyes and sighed, then gasped as his searching fingers teased her clit. Ethan kissed her then switched places with

Adam and reached for the bottle of lubricant. He placed it within Adam's reach.

She turned to Adam. "Tell me how you imagined our first time would be, Adam. What did you fantasize about doing with me?"

* * * *

Adam hissed softly when she wrapped her delicate little hand around his aching cock and stroked back and forth. In length, Adam was a little longer than Ethan, but they were roughly the same in girth.

"To be honest, baby, when I imagined our first time together, I always pictured slow, sweet lovemaking in the missionary position, maybe with your legs thrown over my arms, holding you wide open. I'm glad you like to watch us make love to you because you'll be able to watch in that position. Jack, maybe we should get Grace some freestanding mirrors for her bedroom."

He grinned at Jack's indulgent nod and hum of affirmation.

"Later, I want to try every position you can imagine, especially rear entry, with your knees spread wide while I stand behind you and pump into you and play with your clit. Would you like a mirror in here so you could watch me do that?" He helped her lie down on her pillows again. She opened her thighs to place a foot on either side of him on the mattress. When she did, he could see that she was wet with need, and the sweet scent of her desire filled his nostrils.

"Mmm, you like what I'm telling you, don't you? I smell your sweet cream. You must be flooded with it." Unable to resist, he reached out a hand and trailed his fingertips gently over her mound. A fingertip slid into her slit, lightly grazing over her clit, and she moaned in need. "You know, a chaise lounge near the fireplace in your new bedroom would be a nice piece of furniture to have. If we found one just the right height, I could bend you over the back of it and you could take my cock from behind while you suck on Ethan's or Jack's cock as he kneels on the seat."

"I like the way you think, man." Ethan palmed his cock as Jack agreed, doing the same thing as they watched.

"But for tonight, baby, I just want to make love to you the sweet, old-fashioned way. Man on top, missionary. I'll use the lubricant and take it real slow for you." *Please, help me take it slow!*

"Good luck with that, dude. Wait till you feel how tight, hot, and slick she is." Ethan handed Adam the lubricant, then reached out to suckle and lick one of her nipples. Adam wanted her to be as ready as she could be for him because he knew his size was going to push her limits.

"Baby, how do you feel about us going down on you when one of us has already come inside of you? Would it bother you if I went down on you right now? Because it won't bother me."

"No, Adam, I would rather have taken a shower if you wanted that, at least tonight. I think I will probably lose my inhibitions about it in the coming days, but for tonight, if it's all right with you, I'd rather not."

Adam nodded as he leaned down to kiss her. He poured a generous amount of lubricant onto his hand and fingers, which he reached down and applied to her pussy. He poured more in his hand and applied it to his cock. The fact that she watched him hungrily as he did this only made his insistent cock even harder.

He wiped his hands on a towel and positioned her the way he wanted her, her legs spread, knees only slightly bent. Jack and Ethan caressed her arms, mirroring each other, and then caressed her breasts, before leaning in for a taste of her tight nipples. She moaned, and her back arched. It was beautiful, the way she responded to all of them together like this. She never shut anybody out but allowed them to touch her and love her as they were able. He knew he was ruined for any other woman.

When he was satisfied that he had her the way he wanted her, he moved into position between her thighs.

He growled softly as he saw the evidence of how highly aroused she was, dripping from her inner lips because she was so ready for him. He was pleased beyond measure when more seeped from her opening at his low growl. Damn, but she responded beautifully, so sexy. He parted her inner lips and pressed the head of his penis to her wet, quivering entrance. The heat felt incredible.

"You look so beautiful like this, baby. Spread wide for me, parting like a little flower, letting me in so sweetly. The lube is helping already, isn't it?

I want to slide into you so bad, baby. Ethan, you were right. It's gonna be hard to hold back."

Ethan and Jack released her nipples so they could lean forward to watch, but his little sweetheart stayed exactly as he had positioned her. He lifted her knees and spread her thighs wide over his forearms, giving him his fantasy, though he could tell she wanted to move badly as she clutched at Jack and Ethan. She allowed him complete control of the moment.

He rested his hands on the tops of her inner thighs, and he looked down into her eyes. The entrance of her pussy clenched on the head of his penis. This was their moment, their dream coming true. He pressed his slippery cock into her an inch or two. He groaned softly as her slick pussy accepted him easily. He'd been genuinely concerned. She moaned in pleasure.

"Oh! Adam," she whispered softly. "It's so sweet, just the way I imagined it. So big, filling me." He groaned deeply as her pussy stroked his cock with her inner muscles, and she flexed against him, trying to take more. "Baby, it won't take much. I'm going to come easy for you." He felt engulfed by her warm, slick sweetness. He thrust against her gently and gained ground with each stroke. She became restless, and her cunt began to tighten around him.

"Good, then maybe I'll make you come twice." The lubricant helped so much, and it was a good thing because he felt like he might even be increasing in size inside her, she felt so fucking good.

"You doing okay, baby? Want more?"

"Yes, give me some more, Adam."

He held on to her thighs and flexed his hips a little, struggling not to slide all the way home. His cock slid in easily another couple of inches.

"Damn, that's hot." Jack groaned. "That is a beautiful pink pussy. I just can't say it enough, darlin'. Your pussy is the sweetest, prettiest pink I've ever seen. Mmm, you start that slide in and out, and she's going to come quick. Listen to her breathing. How does it feel, darlin'?"

"Like heaven." She sighed.

Adam kept to the slow, steady rhythm, giving her a chance to adjust to his size.

"Does it hurt at all, darlin'?" Jack asked as he caressed her cheek.

"No, do you like it, Adam? Do I feel good?"

"Oh, baby, you do, so hot and tight, like you were squeezing me. Are you okay? Can I give you more?"

"Why don't you give it *all* to me? Slide it in slow and easy, oh, baby! That is amazing!"

He didn't ask if he hurt her because he could see the happiness radiate from her face and hear it in her voice. He really wasn't hurting her, and he had worried for nothing. He'd thank Ethan later for remembering the lube.

He was all the way in. He released her thighs and lowered himself to her torso, suckling on each breast before kissing her. He loved the feel of her delectable little body snuggled under his as she took every inch of his cock inside her, holding on to him so sweetly. She slid her palms up his chest and wrapped her arms around his neck, turning her head into his gentle kiss. She stroked her tongue against his, her natural womanly fragrance filling his nostrils.

"I love you." Adam looked in her eyes as he kissed her face.

She shifted position slightly, lifting her legs to curl them around his thighs. She flexed her hips, and he moaned.

"Baby, that felt so hot. I can feel every little muscle spasm rippling over my cock." He kissed her gently and said, "I want this to last for you, baby, give it to you just the way you want it. You want me to make love to you?" She shuddered and gasped as he flexed his hips, thrusting into her.

"Yes, Adam, I want it all. Everything." And she only had to ask once. They both moaned as he slid nearly all the way out before plunging back in.

"Ethan, can you see her cream all over him?" Jack asked from beside Adam. "He must be stroking all the right spots. Grace is so responsive. I can only imagine how it must feel sliding into her sweet body like that."

"I love those little pink lips of hers," Ethan murmured softly, "stretched over Adam's cock. You're gonna love it, Jack. She's so hot and sweet, tight as a vise. It sounds as if she likes listening to us. She's dripping wet. Listen to the way she moans. That sound gets me hard just hearing it."

Judging by how flooded with her cream she had become, she must have really enjoyed listening to them talk.

Adam leaned down to her, propping up over her on his elbows as his hips began to piston, pumping her harder, sliding his cock home, over and over. She held on to his arms to keep herself in place. She lifted her head, trying to see his cock as he slid in and out.

“Take her knees, help her, she wants to see.” Adam growled as he rose up onto his hands, pressing back on her knees gently. “Isn’t that right, baby? You want to see my cock fucking you? You like to watch us pumping into you? Tell me.”

“I do. I love to watch you slide that great big cock into my pussy. I love the way you fill me so full. You’re so big, Adam! Can you give it to me harder?”

Jack and Ethan supported her from behind with pillows again so she could watch him as he pulled almost all the way out and then plunged back in to the hilt. He groaned when her pussy rippled and gripped him tightly as she teetered on the edge.

“I can tell how close you are. You’re getting even wetter. You want to come, don’t you, baby?”

“Yes! Adam, make me come! I’m—I’m so *close*!”

He grabbed on to her ass cheeks, gripping them hard as she moaned and whimpered. Ethan’s free hand slid down to her swollen little clit and very gently began to rub right beside it in a steady, gentle rhythm similar to the pace Adam had set. The moment his finger made contact, her whole body tensed, tightening like a rubber band about to be released.

“I love her swollen little clit, begging to be touched,” Ethan said as he bent down and took a nipple into his mouth, laving it with his tongue. He added another finger and carefully stroked her clit between the two fingers, then pinched gently but firmly. The twin sensations of Adam’s cock thrusting and Ethan’s fingers were too much, and she went off like a rocket, wailing and sobbing her release.

“Oh, yes, Adam! Oh, that’s so good, Ethan. Oh, I love you. Yes, fuck me, fuck me, Adam! Fuck me!”

Adam continued his pace, charging for his own release, as Ethan continued strumming her clit. On the waves of the last orgasm, she came screaming again, and her hips rolled convulsively with Adam’s, slamming into him. His body tensed, and his release poured forth into her as he yelled at the top of his lungs, holding tightly to her. He thrust one final time into her depths and shuddered and moaned as he filled her with his seed.

She went completely limp under him and scared the shit out of Adam.

“I think she passed out.” Ethan sounded calmer than Adam felt. “Stay where you are, Adam. Let’s just give her a few seconds.”

She came around finally, looking confused.

"Are you okay? Was I too rough on you?" Adam asked gently. "Please tell me, baby."

She rubbed her forehead. "You weren't rough, Adam. You gave it to me just the way I wanted you to. It was perfect. I think I might have fainted at the end. That's never happened before."

Jack chuckled. "I guess it was just that good, Adam. Damn."

They reclined on the bed as Adam carefully withdrew from her and lay down with his head resting carefully on her abdomen.

She sighed in contentment, one hand resting softly on his cheek. The other stroked through his short hair at the base of his skull. He nuzzled and kissed her right above her mound.

"Can I tell y'all something?"

"Anything, darlin'," Jack replied.

"I know without doubt that I am living the happiest moment of my life right now. Lying here with you. I'm the happiest I've ever been."

Jack turned to her with a grin. "The evenin' isn't over yet, darlin'."

"What would you like to do, Jack?" she asked, her eyes lighting with invitation.

"I think you need a little break. Guys, I want to shower with our girl. Grace didn't eat much earlier. Why don't y'all warm up some of that Chinese food for her? She must be a little hungry now. What do you think, darlin'?"

"I could use a little break, and I am sort of hungry, Jack, thank you." She rose onto an elbow and smiled down at Adam. He looked up at her and grinned as he kissed her mound one last time before rising.

"Thank you, Grace. Making love with you was worth every bit of the wait. I love you."

"I feel the same, Adam. Thank you," she whispered back as he kissed her lips.

Adam and Ethan threw on their robes and watched as Jack helped her from the bed. She must have felt their eyes on her as she stood up. Still holding Jack's hand, she looked up, motionless.

"Grace, you amaze us," Adam said, wishing he had a way with words like Ethan. "You rule our hearts with your loving touch. We'll always adore you, even when we're old and gray."

Chapter Twenty-four

Ethan went with Adam to the kitchen to reheat what was left of the Chinese food and heard the water start in the shower. Adam stood with the refrigerator door open, staring blindly into it. Ethan grinned, recently familiar with the dazed look in Adam's eyes. He came around him and removed the containers from the top shelf. He passed his hand in front of Adam's eyes.

"Earth to Adam," he said and placed the containers on the counter and opened them to see what was inside.

"That was unbelievable." Adam rubbed his hands over his face. "Making love to her…"

"When she takes you in, it's more than just your cock she's taking, right? Making love with her feels soul deep, I think," Ethan replied as Adam nodded at him.

"Yeah. You think she's really okay or just not letting on how sore she is?"

"She's definitely going to be sore in the morning. She just doesn't realize it yet. We'll make sure and give her a couple of ibuprofen before she falls asleep. That will help. I wish I'd used the lubricant more liberally. She started that dirty talk, and I lost all control. If she's sore, it's my fault. I hated that I did that, but…" He rubbed his face hard, trying to sort out the memory of that sensation and the confused rush of feelings that came with it. "But I *loved* it, too."

"Knowing you were the first to go there?"

"Exactly."

"Understandable. But I think it happened the way it did with you for a reason. If we had known there was any remnant of her virginity, I still would have preferred that you take it. You have a different connection with her than Jack and I. I think she loves that you seem to know what she's thinking sometimes. It comforts her to be understood like that."

"That wasn't the *remnant* of her virginity, Adam. I felt it tear. She said she had sex regularly with Owen up until the last few months when he started treating her so badly. She said he had a little dick, but she told us herself she didn't have anything to compare his size to. We're on the large side, in one sense or another, but his dick must have been as small as my pinkie. It wasn't just a case of me being big and her needing time to stretch to accommodate me. She lost her virginity in *our* bed tonight. I hated hurting her, but God help me, I loved taking it, too. I feel like some fucking Cro-Magnon throwback."

"Then the past doesn't matter, does it? She truly is our perfect woman."

"You got that right. I'm hard now at the thought of making love to her again."

All the leftovers were in bowls, either already on the table or heating in the microwave when they heard Jack exclaim, "Oh, Grace!" from the bathroom. It wasn't a good sound. He sounded like he was in pain.

They bolted from the kitchen and ran to see what was wrong. They came to a skidding halt in the bathroom. The room was steamy, and both Grace and Jack were in the shower together. Her hair was pinned up on her head, with tendrils streaming down, damp and curling from all the steam. They could just make out Jack, kneeling at her feet, his arms wrapped around her thighs. His face was turned away toward the wall, the muscles in his back, shoulders, and arms knotted tightly.

Ethan had a feeling he knew what had happened. They watched silently as Jack's arms shifted and slid up her thighs, over her ass, his hands coming to rest on her lower back and across her ass. He squeezed, then released her and looked up into her eyes with a pained expression.

"What's wrong?" Adam asked.

Jack looked up at them and picked up the white washcloth to show them the red-tinged cloth. Blood. "She's bleeding."

Grace looked at Ethan, her cheeks pink, and said, "I…guess you really did take my virginity. Every last little bit of it."

Ethan and Adam both gave a low, guttural growl, and she gasped and blushed even harder. Jack rose to his feet, and she looked up at all of them as Ethan and Adam came to the doorway of the shower. Her lip trembled, but she smiled at them.

Her heart in her words, she looked at Ethan and softly said, “I’m so glad it was you. If I had known, I would have told you. I’m sorry.” She moved under the showerhead to rinse the soap off of her tender pussy as they watched her hands. Jack took down the shower massage and held it for her to help her get the soap off. She smiled at them as her next words tore at Ethan’s heart.

“Owen told me once he only wanted to have sex with me in the dark, that it bothered him to see the way my body jiggled when he fucked me. He didn’t want to see my dimpled behind. All these years, I thought I’d given that part of myself away on a whim to keep him happy.”

She giggled some more. Even though her words were not happy ones, she seemed truly happy. Ethan knew then she really had moved on from Owen. She reached out to him.

“Now you know I’m yours, *all* of me.” She laughed and cried as Ethan pulled her into his arms, soaking wet, and hugged her tightly.

“Yes, honey, you’re all ours, and we take good care of what’s ours. We’re keeping you forever,” Ethan said in a voice that he couldn’t keep from shaking. He reached up to wipe her tears away. “Adam, you wanna take a shower real quick while we get everything on the table?”

“You don’t want to feed our princess her snack in bed?” Jack asked. “It could be fun. We might spill food on her, especially if we used chopsticks. We’d have to clean her up.”

Adam snickered. “Yeah, with our tongues.”

Ethan said, “As sexy and fun as that sounds, man, to feed Grace while she’s lying in bed will probably only lead to indigestion. I’ll bet she could handle *breakfast in bed* with you, though. You know how messy syrup can be sometimes.” He waggled his eyebrows, which made Grace giggle. “But if she’s going to sleep later, she probably should sit up to eat. What do you think, Grace?”

“He’s right, Jack, I’m sorry. It sounded like lots of fun, though.”

From the shower, Adam grinned at Ethan over Grace’s pinned up curls, tapped his head, and pointed at Ethan. Ethan smiled and got a towel to wrap her in. He patted her dry while Jack retrieved their robes from the bedroom and helped her into hers.

* * * *

Grace sighed happily as she walked into the kitchen. Her body tingled and hummed with the new knowledge of what true *love*-making was all about. She looked at her men and felt like her world consisted of the four of them and the warm bubble they were wrapped in. Jack sat down in his chair as Grace came to the counter-height table and saw that there were only three places set. She looked at him in confusion and then smiled when he patted his lap for her to sit upon. She giggled and let Adam help her into Jack's lap in the tall chair.

She settled there with one arm around his shoulders, facing Adam and Ethan. She turned to look into Jack's eyes and said, "Are you still upset about earlier, in the shower?"

It embarrassed her to discover she was so clueless, that she had mistaken Owen's awkward thrusting and humping as actual sex. She'd been every bit as shocked as Ethan when she'd felt the sharp tearing and pain inside her when he finally thrust home. More distressing for her had been the way Jack reacted when he helped her bathe and discovered blood on the white washcloth. He assumed they'd harmed her because he hadn't realized the significance of her pained yelp. After all, she'd *told* them she'd had sex before with Owen.

Jack caressed her back and shook his head. "Everything worked out the way it was supposed to, I guess, darlin'. I think I can speak for all of us when I say that it was really cruel of Owen to insult your body to cover for his own deficiency. If we're making love to you and parts of you *aren't jiggling,* we're not doing it right. You're a beautiful, voluptuous woman, and we love every part of you that jiggles or sways when you move." He nuzzled her lips as he palmed the ass in question while Adam reached out and cupped her breast, running a thumb over her nipple, which made it peak instantly. She shuddered and sighed in Jack's arms and smiled dreamily at Adam.

Ethan and Adam served the plates from the bowls they'd heated and remembered to put nothing too spicy on Jack's plate.

Adam spoke up and had his say on the issue. "As for your 'dimpled behind,'" he said, using air quotes, "you don't have that many dimples, and I love its winsome, little upside-down heart shape." He grinned as she blushed at his description. "Having gotten to know your ass up close and personal, I can honestly say it's the perfect size for my hands to grab on to, and I want you to remember that what you've got back there is just fine with us."

Jack picked up his fork and speared a bite of Moo Goo Gai Pan for her and fed it to her.

"That also explains why Gracie likes to watch while we make love to her. She's never seen what a real man fucking a real woman looks like," Ethan said, amazing her with his insight. "We're buying mirrors for every room in this house!"

Everyone laughed.

Ethan gathered a bite of chicken and broccoli in his chopsticks and fed it to her as he gazed into her eyes. "Do you like it when we feed you, Gracie?" he asked softly. "Does it make you feel cared for? Safe and looked after, like we'll give you what you need, just the same way you give us what we need?"

"Yes, Ethan, it shows me you care, and it feels sexy. It's an elemental need, just like making love and then sleeping together. When you sleep with me, I feel safe, guarded. I love that you are all so protective of me and in charge. I know it's not a popular view today in our culture, but I don't *want* to kill my own scorpions or change my own tire or my oil. None of those things make me weak."

Adam fed her a bite of his shrimp with Chinese vegetables and said, "Baby, the last thing you are is weak, and you never have to worry about scorpions, tires, or oil changes ever again."

"Thank you, Adam," Grace replied as Jack handed her his glass of tea. "I'm so happy I feel like I could burst." They all looked at her with misty-eyed smiles.

"What are your schedules like for tomorrow?" she asked as Jack fed her another bite.

"I have two service calls in the morning and two more after lunch. It should be a light day," Adam replied.

"I'm not going in until 3:30 p.m., but I'll need to hang around for a while tomorrow night. I'm interviewing a bartender at four o'clock and another bouncer at 4:30 p.m. Rogelio and Mike have a friend who has experience and wants to work at the club. I think we could use the extra help, and Ben agreed."

"Why don't Adam and I bring our girl by for a while during the evening?" Jack asked.

"Is it safe, Ethan?" Grace asked, not really relishing the thought of another run-in with Patricia.

"With Jack, Adam, and me there watching over you? You'll be as safe as you would in Sunday school," Ethan replied. "Besides, I'm about ready for more dancing with my sweetheart. I hope you wear that sexy pair of shoes with one of your new outfits."

She gave him a crooked smile. "If you mean the Mary Janes, I think I can manage that. I'll have to surprise you tomorrow night." She had to laugh out loud at Adam's facial expression. "Y'all are imagining me nekkid, wearing only those shoes, aren't you?"

Ethan rolled his eyes and groaned. Jack cleared his throat and nodded.

Adam said in a guttural groan, "Damn, I love the way she says 'nekkid.'"

"How about you, Jack. Do you have a busy day scheduled?" she asked, then received another bite of chicken from Ethan.

"I'll be at a construction site all morning, then I'm coming back at lunchtime, and I'll be working around the ranch after that. You know, I think I may invite Angel to come along with us to The Pony. He needs to get out some, especially now that Patricia is out of his hair."

"Wouldn't he worry about running into her at The Dancing Pony?" Grace asked.

"He knows how to handle her," Ethan replied. "It has been a long time since he's been out to the club."

"The more the merrier. Jack? I have one more question." She nuzzled into his neck.

"What's that, darlin'?" He handed her his glass again.

"Are you going to make love to me tonight?" She slid her hand under the lapel of his robe, the heat from his warm skin tingling into her fingertips.

"How do you feel? Be honest. Are you sore? Because if you are, it's going to feel worse in the morning if I make love to you now. I would really rather you eased into fooling around with all three of us in one night. Your work day will be miserable if you overdo it tonight."

"I'm a little sore, but I want you right now, very badly. I won't be happy until I've been with you, too. Please?" she asked, not begging or wheedling or, heaven forbid, whining. Just wanting. Thinking about making love with Jack set her pussy to quivering and swelling. She squirmed a little in his lap and could feel fresh moisture gathering there for him.

Jack sighed. "I'm stopping at the first grimace or wince. Understand?"

She hugged him and kissed him passionately. "I promise, Jack. I know my limitations. If it hurts, I'll stop you. Thank you. I'm done eating. I'm goin' back to bed."

Jack helped her down from his lap, and she sashayed back to the bedroom. She removed the clip for her hair and brushed it out. They must have left everything where it sat on the table because they were already waiting for her when she came out of the bathroom. Naked. She sauntered to the bed, dropping her robe from her shoulders, and left it in a silken puddle on the rug.

"Jack, will you tell me what you fantasize about when you think of fucking me?" she asked, sweetly, seductively. "Tell me what you want, and I'll do it for you. Whatever you want, honey." She climbed onto the bed and went to him where he lay at the foot. She brushed her hair back behind her ear and kissed him, then reached out to caress his incredibly thick cock. He hissed and growled as she wrapped her hand around his girth, and she noticed her fingers didn't meet, he was so wide. Her pussy clenched and seeped as that realization sent a bolt of heat through her. He stayed her hand and rose to stand at the end of the bed and crooked a finger at her. Cheekily, she turned and backed her ass toward him and looked over her shoulder to see what he would do next.

He came up behind her on the end of the bed, and she panted when she felt his cock brush over her cleft. He parted her knees as she was knelt on the bed, opening her. He lifted her torso so she was upright and no longer on her hands so Ethan and Adam could watch what he was doing. The knowledge they were watching and the touch of his gentle hands sent warm shivers all over her body. His fingertips blazed a heated trail down her abdomen.

"I'm going to start with having a taste of this sweet, tender pussy." He slid his fingers over her mound, into her slit, and gently stroked her sensitive clit. Her breath left her in a rush, and her pussy clenched in eager anticipation. She leaned back against him, and he slid his other hand up and cupped one of her breasts, tweaking the nipple. “And after I’ve had my fill of your sweet pussy, I’m going to position you on your knees like this at the edge of the bed. You’re going to spread your legs as wide as I want them, and I’m going to slowly and gently fuck you from behind until we’re both screaming.” He nuzzled her throat, and she felt like her heart might literally pound out of her chest. “And then we’re going to get comfortable and fall into a coma-like sleep, all of us tucked around you, all night. How does that sound, darlin’?”

“That sounds perfect.” *Ooh, I can’t wait!*

She lay back on her pillows as he came to her, settling between her thighs. She raised her knees to give him better access. The thought never occurred to turn him down. He’d told her what he wanted. Ethan and Adam leaned in and began to kiss her and suckle her breasts, multiplying the sensations she felt.

Jack gently spread her lips and licked with an upward swipe of his tongue, making her hips flex involuntarily. She moaned. He licked her again. This time he swirled his tongue around her clitoris and chuckled softly at her panting cries.

“Grace, you sound wonderful when you moan softly like that. I love it almost as much as I love this pretty pink pussy.” Jack gave her another gentle glide of his tongue and then delved into her cunt. He growled deeply. “You want some more, darlin’?”

“Yes, yes! I want it!” she cried desperately.

He became serious about pleasuring her at that point. He mercilessly stroked her clit with his tongue and pushed her right up the precipice. Through shuttered eyes, Grace watched as he put just a bit of lubricant on the index and middle fingers of his right hand. She knew what that meant! Her G-spot!

His fingers slid very carefully into her and found that hidden place in her that responded so volcanically to his touch. Her body vibrated with passion as he strummed her to the point of unbearable tension, and her pussy clamped down impossibly tight. She was poised on the very edge when he deftly flicked her clit with his tongue and sent her screaming into her orgasm. She cried out and sobbed as he licked her pussy to his heart’s content, feasting on her cream.

"Mmm, she's so beautiful when you make her come like that, so sweet and wild, but innocent, too." Ethan kissed her cheeks as she caught her breath.

Jack rose from between her legs and reached for the bottle of lubricant. He helped her sit up, wrapped his arms around her, and kissed her tenderly. He quickly spread lubricant over his fingers and smoothed it liberally into her throbbing entrance. She gasped when he touched her clit, causing a little aftershock. He quickly smoothed a generous amount up and down his cock.

After wiping his hands on a towel, Jack caressed her hip and said, "Come here, darlin'."

He helped her to the edge of the bed, and she turned on her hands and knees so he was behind her at the end of the bed. Ethan and Adam climbed off the bed and stood beside Jack. The knowledge that they would watch from behind as he entered her had her pussy contracting tightly, ready to come at the first touch. She took several deep breaths and tried to slow her heart rate a little. She wanted to make it last, but it was going to be *too good.* Grace knew she'd come before he was even in all the way, just as she had in all her fantasies. This was her fantasy coming true right now.

She felt his hand on her tailbone. "Spread your knees a little wider. Wider, darlin'. Perfect."

When she positioned herself to please him, she felt her wet lips open up and knew that Jack, Ethan, and Adam could see how hot and ready she was. Her pussy pulsed in need as she waited for the first touch of Jack's huge cock, ready to fuck her. Just the anticipation made her want to scream and come right then. She'd never last.

"Man, that is a beautiful fucking sight." Ethan's voice was deep and gravelly with arousal. "Gracie, you are a goddess. Mmm! Look how she arches for you. She wants you so bad, Jack. It must be torture for her. Hell, yeah, I'll take some of that lube. No way could I not come from watching this. Give it to her, Jack, before she comes undone."

She felt Jack's hands at her hip bones as he pulled her back. She began to whimper and moan, begging him to take her as her arousal spun out of her control. She didn't know what she said or if any of it made sense. She just knew she *needed.* She tilted to him and tried to entice him as she looked over her shoulder at them.

"Damn, that's hot, Grace, the most beautiful thing I've ever seen." Adam's breath rasped, and he panted as he stroked his cock. "The way she arches her back like she's dying for your cock. Jack, you've got to give it to her before *I* come!"

Jack stepped in closer behind her, his gentle hands at her hips. She felt the head of his huge, thicker-than-the-others cock at her quivering cunt. With his fingers, he gently spread her pussy lips, and the head of his cock slid in easily. He cried out in pleasure, and her pussy suddenly seized around him, trying to draw him farther in.

"Oh! Oh! Oh, Jack!" She couldn't stop herself from crying out for him. His big, stiff penis filled her slowly, completely, and felt so good. She did her best to hold her orgasm back, but the sensation was just too much.

His gentle, callused hands trembled as they swept over her hips and held on to her. His voice revealed the strain he was under. "Oh, darlin', you're so sweet and tight. Fuck! Don't hold back, baby, *don't*. If you need to come, then come *hard* for me. *Fuck*!"

He was only a few inches into her when his words, the sensation, and the knowledge that Ethan and Adam avidly watched caused her pussy to clamp down on him, and she screamed his name.

* * * *

Jack tried to hold her still. He didn't want to push her tender body too hard, but she reared back on him, and he slid in another couple of inches. She came again and howled when the second one hit her. He breathed deep to control his own release, not satisfied to have it end this soon. Her warm, silky pussy squeezed and milked his cock and almost undermined his control.

Incredibly, her orgasm rolled on as she worked herself against him. He realized what she needed and helped her efforts, thrusting into that spot. He felt her sleek muscles begin to quiver and ripple around him again. His head, both of them, actually, felt like it might explode from the pleasure he found inside her.

He felt his release begin to build and gather and knew his control was almost at an end. He began to thrust into her as gently as he could, which, under the circumstances, wasn't very gentle at all, not that she seemed to care at the moment. Her pussy milked his release from him as he came with a roar, like a beast in the jungle. She wailed his name and climaxed in a hot gush.

Her hips flexed against him as her orgasm came and receded. He pressed tightly to her, buried as deeply as possible. He wanted to wallow in the sensation of her torrid, wet depths. He stayed that way for a few moments and took in huge gusts of air as he tried to catch his breath.

"That was insane, Jack." Adam sounded breathless himself. "Damn, I'll be right back." He went into the bathroom and returned with several warm washcloths. He and Ethan must have finished, as well.

Jack was reluctant to remove his sated cock from her sweet warmth, but he did finally pull out, growling softly at the feel of her tight pussy drawing on him. He gently caressed her ass and her back and then helped her lie down. He lay down beside her and brushed his fingers along her rib cage.

"That was my fantasy come true, darlin'." She turned her face to him and looked up with dazed eyes and parted her lips as he kissed her deeply. "You are absolutely amazing. Incredible."

She smiled tenderly at him and kissed him back. "You made my fantasy for our first time come true, too, Jack." She snuggled closer, and he squeezed her to him tightly. "I knew I wouldn't be able to hold my orgasm back once you started to slide in. I *knew* your first touch was going to make me come, and it did. I'm so glad you said yes. I'd hate to have missed out on this. Thank you." She sighed and kissed him slowly, lingeringly.

"Now that was a perfect evening." Jack glanced over at Adam and Ethan after seeing her wide smile.

"Damn straight," Adam replied.

"Hell, yeah," Ethan said.

"Carpe diem, my dirty-talking sweethearts," Grace murmured, then giggled. She was awake and alert, but so serene.

Ethan got up and went into the bathroom and turned on the shower. Jack and Adam helped her to her feet. Jack smiled as Adam lifted her into his arms and carried her the short distance to the bathroom with obvious satisfaction. Jack understood that Grace loved it when Adam carried her like this. Intuitive as ever, Ethan handed her some ibuprofen and a glass of water. She thanked him sweetly and took them after Adam gently set her on her feet. She pinned her long golden curls up in her hair clip. Yawning deeply, she stepped into the shower, allowing the warm spray to stream over her body. She lathered a fresh washcloth, and Jack noticed she was very careful when she washed between her thighs.

"Everything all right?" Jack asked as he joined her, along with Adam and Ethan. She showed him the washcloth with a smile. No blood.

"Everything is perfect, Jack."

They all bathed quickly and then helped Grace for the sheer fun of it. They knew she would be sore, so there were lots of kisses, but no real hanky-panky. They helped her from the shower, and she dried off.

"Do you want a nightgown, baby?" Adam asked.

"No, honey, I'm going to bed nekkid every chance I get from now on," she replied as she brushed her hair. She grinned at him in the mirror's reflection.

"Baby, baby," Adam chuckled as he came up behind her and wrapped his arms around her, "I like the sound of that." He nuzzled her throat. "I love the way you smell, like soap, oranges, and Grace. Sweet and clean."

Jack and Ethan went to the bedroom and quickly stripped and replaced the fitted sheet, then pulled the top sheet and blanket back into place. They fluffed her pillows and added a few from their own beds.

They helped her into the center of the bed, and she got comfortable on her back. Jack curled to her left side, and Ethan curled to her right, Jack's forearm draped warmly under her breasts and Ethan's across her waist. Adam somehow slid in alongside her legs, his head at her abdomen.

Grace giggled as she offered him a pillow, but he turned his cheek to her belly and kissed her there, saying he was perfectly content. Jack chuckled in amusement as he noticed Adam's feet definitely hung off the end of the bed. She draped a long, sexy leg over his ribs, and Adam wrapped his arm around it like it was what he'd expected her to do.

* * * *

Grace was slowly aware of two gentle, warm mouths, each suckling a nipple, and the scratch of their morning whiskers. What assailed her next was the feel of Adam's warm tongue lapping at her cunt. His gentle fingers parted her lips, and his tongue leisurely explored the entrance of her pussy before trailing up to her clit.

He murmured one word reverently. "Woman."

The stunningly erotic effect of that moment made her careen in seconds toward orgasm as her body clenched at his tongue and his gentle exploratory fingers, which struck just the right chords in her responsive body. Her head fell back, and she moaned twice as the waves built and crested. She came as she rode the soft waves.

Ethan and Jack leaned forward and kissed away the tears that she hadn't even realized were there as they rolled from her eyes onto her temples. She sobbed as her body shook with an aftershock. She reached down to cradle Adam's cheek, and he nuzzled her hand.

Jack chuckled. "Now I understand why you were willing to sleep down there, rather than beside one of us. That was sweet to watch."

Adam sat up slowly, stretching. "It was totally worth sleeping with my feet dangled off the end of the bed to be able to wake up and nuzzle against her. But we definitely need to order that bed…and two freestanding mirrors."

"I second that motion." Jack laughed with them.

While she got herself ready for work, the men made breakfast. She sat down slowly and with care at the table, and Adam poured her a cup of coffee. Ethan placed two ibuprofen in her palm then leaned down and kissed her. He tasted fresh like toothpaste and smelled like his shaving gel. It lingered in her nostrils after he sat in his chair.

Adam placed a plate of scrambled eggs, bacon, and toast in front of her and put the grape jam by her plate. All three laughed and cringed when she put a spoonful on her scrambled eggs to soften and melt as she stirred them a little.

Grace laughed and said, "This was the only way my mom could get me to eat eggs. It turns them green, see? You remember *Green Eggs and Ham*, don't you? It's still my favorite way to eat them, but I promise not to do that in public if we ever go out for breakfast."

"Darlin', if that's how you like your eggs, then that's how you'll get them. Nobody else's opinion matters to us but yours."

"How bad was the flooding last night? You know, once we got home, I honestly didn't pay attention to whether we got any more rain. I was consumed in other activities." She smirked.

Her men chuckled a little, and Ethan told her, "According to the gauge, we got three more inches. I think we were all oblivious to the rain. I'll take you to work again today, provided we can get through the low water crossings. I'll be ready whenever you are, Gracie."

Adam returned to the living room, dressed and ready to go on his service calls. She went to him as he reached for her, sliding his hands up and down her rib cage. She pulled him down so he could hear her whisper only for him as she caressed his cheek. Jack and Ethan gave them their space.

"Adam, I know you think Ethan is the sensitive one and that you miss a lot of the finer points about loving me. But I need you to know something really important, okay? You made me believe I was worthy of a real man's love when you said those beautiful things to me the day of the funeral. You were the one to calm me when I saw Patricia make a move on Ethan and helped me to keep my sense of humor. You were the one who wanted to sleep entwined with my legs last night because you wanted to be close to me and to wake me this morning, giving me that beautiful orgasm. So *please*, baby, don't think for a minute that you're just the big, tough, strong guy to me. I won't lie. I *love* that part of you. I love it when you pick me up, and I loved when you fucked me hard last night, but I love your tender heart, too."

She caressed his neck. "I didn't want you to think I overlooked that part of you." Grace wrapped her arms around his neck and kissed him tenderly. He slid his hands from her rib cage and around to the small of her back, pressing her to him as his hands slid down to palm her ass cheeks. She moaned and sighed and then said, "I'll miss you."

"Baby, I'm going to miss you, too. I hate to leave right now. I'd much rather spend this day with you, especially after last night. I'd just want to stay near you, not *do* anything, because you must be sore. I wish I could tuck you in my pocket and take you with me." He buried his nose in her hair and inhaled.

"We'll have this evening, Adam. That's what I'll look forward to, and I feel fine. Only a little sore, just a heightened awareness, knowing that you've been inside of me. Really, Adam, I see the doubt in your eyes, but you saw me this morning sit down at the table with no real problem. That's all behind us now. I'm going to look forward to dancing with you tonight."

"If you feel up to it. Why don't you take a nap after you get home?"

"Are you going to nap with me? I love a good nap. Bet I'd like it even more if I could cuddle up with you."

"Yeah, but the question is, would you get any sleep?" He gathered her in his arms and lifted her off her feet, and she squealed. She heard Jack and Ethan laugh quietly from the kitchen, probably watching.

Adam finally made it out the door, still obviously reluctant to leave, but he couldn't keep those customers waiting. Jack promised to be there in the afternoon when she got home.

She walked Jack to the door as he said, "Ask one of the hands, and they should be able to tell you where I am. I want to show you the new foals now that you'll feel more comfortable roaming around the place. The ranch is your home now, and you have free run of it. Plus, I'm sure Angel will be glad to see you again."

He was out the door and down the drive a few minutes later. She sat down with Ethan and had another cup of coffee. They talked about the bed and what dimensions would help to solve their problem of four in the bed, although Adam hadn't seemed to suffer too badly last night as the odd man. They decided that an increase of three feet in width and length would probably make things more comfortable. Ethan called Wesley and let him know they'd be over Saturday evening. He showed her a couple of websites that offered custom bed linens that could also make her canopy drape and the window treatments for the master suite, as well.

"Ethan, I need to know something. Will y'all expect me to withhold my affection for you when we are in a public setting, like at the grocery store, or restaurants, or the movies?"

Ethan seemed a little reluctant to broach that touchy subject. "We talked about it a bit before we asked you out. How would we treat you, which one of us would be allowed to show affection in public. Divine is a small city, and we have greater anonymity than Angel's parents, but we're all self-employed, including you soon. Unfortunately, that means caring about public opinion. Because you conduct yourself like a lady, there are only a few situations we need to be careful in. Bear in mind that we don't have all the answers, okay? But I think you would agree that, outside The Dancing Pony, public displays of affection need to be limited to just Jack…"

"Meaning I can't show affection to you and Adam?" She felt bereft at the thought.

"You've known Jack the longest. It would be all right with me and Adam if you treated Jack as your boyfriend. Just try not to tease us too much with not being able to touch you. I know that there are other similar relationships in the area, but they all either maintain a roommate or marriage façade, like Angel's parents. At The Pony, you acted like such a lady that no one really thought anything of it if they saw you kissing us during the evening. Most of the regulars who come there are decent people who mind their own business. We'll deal with any situations that arise while we're there. Ben feels the same way, by the way. He thinks you're a peach."

"Really? That's sweet! So, in the grocery store?"

"You can hold Jack's hand, act like his girlfriend, but you need to let us push the cart and do the heavy lifting. I know it's a lot to get used to, but all of us are committed to making you happy, so we're willing to be flexible. Let's just be careful until things settle down."

"I wouldn't want to harm Jack or Adam's business. Keeping it a secret is probably for the best, but at least the people closest to me—Charity, Rose, and Martha—have all been totally supportive. They adore you three."

Ethan grinned and kissed her forehead. "We can sit down and have a talk together this weekend and see how we all feel. For now, it can keep. But remember what I said about The Dancing Pony. You're *our* date, okay? I feel like I've upset you." He reached for her hand, and she leaned her forehead against his shoulder.

"You haven't upset me, not really. I'm already pretty careful when we're in public. I'm just afraid I'm going to unconsciously take your hand or Adam's because I feel so comfortable with you. I don't want to mess up."

"You know what we all have in common? None of us wants to hurt the others. If you catch yourself and have to withdraw a gesture of affection, don't feel like we take it as an emotional withdrawal. I'm more worried about the love that shines in your eyes than I am about you accidentally taking my hand at the checkout line in the grocery store."

"Then you'll have to blindfold me because I don't see how I can hide it."

Chapter Twenty-five

She loved days like this when the shop hummed with activity. Filing the last order she'd just taken, Grace heard the door open and turned to help the next customer. It was Fred from Merritt's Florist making a delivery. He set the large, heavy crystal vase containing one dozen blood-red, long-stemmed roses on the sales counter and smiled at her politely.

"These are for you, Miss Stuart."

"Wow! Rose! Come look!" Martha shouted loudly, startling both Grace and Fred.

Grace sniffed them appreciatively as she removed the card from its clip. "They're beautiful, Fred."

"Who are they from?" Rose asked, almost bouncing on her toes.

"I'll be right back." Fred said as he turned to the front door.

"The card says they are from Ethan," Grace said dreamily after glancing at it. There was a handwritten note as well.

"Why did Fred say he's coming back?" Rose asked.

Martha peeked at the card. "I see his handwriting, Grace. What did Ethan write? Read it!"

"Y'all, it's *private*!" Grace laughed, holding the card to her breast. "Did Fred say he was *coming back*?"

"Oh, my gosh!" Rose said in a stage whisper as another dozen long-stemmed roses moved past the front window.

Fred came inside bearing an arrangement of the most vivid yellow roses she'd ever seen, also in a heavy crystal vase. No expense had been spared on these arrangements. Fred set the yellow roses next to the red roses, still smiling sweetly. The women were shocked, awed into silence as Grace took the card and looked Fred in the eye.

The elderly man blushed and said, "I'll be right back, Miss Stuart."

Evidently unable to contain herself, Rose screamed. The poor man cringed as he turned for the door again. Grace had a feeling she was about to be the talk of the town.

"Dang, Rose! Who are they from, Grace?" Martha asked. This time she positioned herself so she might be able to read what was written on the card.

Grace opened the card carefully. "Adam," she whispered. Her body hummed, and her heart pounded.

Another rose arrangement passed in front of the window. This one held a dozen long-stemmed roses in a deep shade of rosy pink in another heavy crystal vase. She felt beads of sweat forming on her brow. As Fred walked in, his face split in a wide, happy grin, but he glanced at Rose in anticipation of her next reaction.

"The gentleman said I was to tell you he picked each one of these pink roses himself so he knew we'd send the *right* color. All of the vases are Waterford Crystal, the best and largest we had, according to his request."

"Who are they from?" Martha asked.

Rose gawked at her. "Like we don't already know." She practically snorted. "Open the card, missy."

"These are from Jack." Grace sniffled, misty-eyed. "I don't have to open the card to know that."

Fred added, "Mr. Warner also asked that you open his card last. Ladies, you have a great day. Y'all sure made mine." He smiled as he left, shaking his head.

"I wonder why Jack felt the need to handpick those pink roses. Pink is pink, right?" Rose asked.

Grace was seeing black spots. "I think I need to sit down." She went to her desk chair behind the counter.

"Get her some water, Rose. Here, honey, put your head between your knees," Martha said, taking charge. She steadied Grace as she put her head down. "Slow, deep breaths, sweetie. I don't want you to pass out and hit your head."

Grace clutched the cards to her breasts, obeyed Martha, and breathed in slow and deep.

"Here, sweetie, drink up." Rose swept in with a glass of water like a mother hen fussing over a chick.

They pulled up chairs to hers as she sat up. "How do you feel?" Martha asked. "Don't get up yet. Give the blood a chance to circulate back to your brain first."

"Those men are so in love with you, honey. I take it you had a nice evening last night?" Rose smiled conspiratorially.

Grace blushed. "Yes, we did have a nice evening. I'm so in love with them, my heart aches with it. Thank you, Martha, Rose, for not judging me for loving three men. They are so sweet and so good to me."

Martha patted Grace's shoulder and sagely said, "In this life, honey, you have to take true love and hold on to it for dear life, even when it doesn't come in the usual ways. If three men loved me like they *obviously* love you, and I loved them in return the way you obviously do, I would frickin' go for it."

"Martha, did you just say 'frickin''?" Grace laughed.

Martha grinned and rolled her eyes. "I'm just saying, is all. Go for it, honey."

"Yeah! Seize the day, sweetie! Beautiful, hot cowboys are in love with you! Ride 'em, cowgirl!" Rose whooped.

Martha turned to give her a shocked and disgusted look.

"Oooh!" Rose gasped when she realized what she'd said, turning five shades of red. "Why that particular shade of pink?" Rose asked once she'd recovered. She tilted her head in curiosity. Grace put her hands to her flaming cheeks and said nothing, but her thoughts were almost singing. *Because it reminds him of my pink pussy!* Her cheeks tingled with heat.

"Let's leave Grace alone to read her cards, Rose. It's none of our business," Martha said, shooing the curious Rose from the room.

Grace drank from the glass of water and opened Ethan's card first. He'd written it in his own hand.

For the woman I adore—
Red, because the heart that beats in my chest beats for you.
Red, for the love in your wantonly innocent invitation.
Red, for the sweet yet seductive words that flowed from your lips.
Red, for the blood and the pain that is in the past.
Red, for the pounding of my heart when I think of a future with you.
Your Ethan

She laid his card on the desk and looked at the red roses. His note was sexy and straight from his heart, just like him. The phone rang in the back room. She heard Martha answer it. Grace laid her hand gently on the card. The love that flowed in those sweet words was like an arrow straight into her heart.

She wiped the tears as she opened Adam's card next, also written in his own hand.

For you, Grace,

The flower I love the best in the entire world. The roses are nice, but they can't compare to your beautiful face, your beautiful heart, or the love that shines in your eyes. Thank you for seeing my true heart. I loved you the moment I first saw you, my angel. You *are my true heart.*

Love, Adam

His true heart. She pressed her lips to the note and wiped her eyes again. She heard the overhead door open and assumed UPS must be here. Martha and Rose talked with the driver, quietly. Grace undid the seal on Jack's card. His script was economical and to the point, just like her Jack.

Darling,

I think I got pretty close on that shade of pink, don't you?

Look up and say yes.

Love, Jack

Confused, she looked at the back of the card. There was nothing else written on it. Wiping the tears from her eyes, she read it again and heard a sound from the door. She looked up and expected it to be Rose or Martha checking on her.

It was Jack. And Ethan. And Adam. Their hearts in their eyes, tender smiles on their faces. Her eyes overflowed with tears, and she noticed their chins wobbled a little, too. Martha and Rose were doing their best to peek around them since there was no point trying to see over their tall shoulders. The ladies were grinning from ear to ear.

Her men came to stand before her, and her heart pounded as she looked up into their sweet faces.

Jack knelt down in front of her, on one knee, and reached out to wipe away a tear. "Darlin'? Marry me?"

A sob wrenched from her throat.

Adam knelt at Jack's side. "Baby? Marry me?" Adam took her hand and pressed it to his cheek, love glowing in the green depths of his eyes.

Ethan knelt, too. "Gracie? Marry me?" He kissed her other hand.

Her heart felt like it would pound from her chest. She fell from the chair into their arms, sobbing. Martha and Rose quietly sniffled and sobbed.

They gave her a minute to settle down before Jack said, "Darlin', you would make us the happiest men in the world if you would say yes." He offered her his handkerchief and helped her back into her chair.

"*Yes*, with all my heart. Yes, yes, and yes. I don't know how this will work, but yes!" She did her best to stifle the sobs that threatened. "The roses are stunning. Your sweet cards," she held them to her breast again, "are priceless beyond words. I'll save them forever." She held out a hand to Ethan's cheek and gazed into his damp, sparkling eyes. She placed the other hand on Adam's damp cheek, and he looked up into her eyes, so vulnerable and happy. Then she placed both hands on Jack's cheeks and leaned in to touch her forehead to his. "Thank you, Jack, for bringing me into your lives. Nothing could make me happier than to marry y'all. You really surprised me." She smiled as she wiped away her tears.

"Your ring won't be ready until next Wednesday. Clay is rushing it but couldn't have it ready any faster than that," Jack said. "I'm sorry. I really wanted to have it in hand when we proposed, but we decided we couldn't wait that long."

"Couldn't wait, huh?" She kissed him, and then she sat up straight. "Clay Cook? Clay Cook is making a ring for me? When did you order it?"

"Last Saturday while you and Charity were at the spa." He chuckled at her gasp of surprise.

"You boys *do* work fast! You knew back then you were going to propose? When we were at the restaurant? And my necklace?"

Ethan reached out and tucked a stray lock of hair behind her ear. "All those things were for our future wife, Gracie. Yes, and we *knew* that night in the restaurant we had been right to order the ring. Every moment we've spent together only confirms it. We wanted to propose and give you the ring before you came to live with us, but then the storm happened. We've been in love with you since the day of Rose Marie's funeral, at least Adam and I have. Jack's been in love with you forever, I think. We couldn't stand to wait until Wednesday."

"I love my flowers, and the crystal vases are lovely, too. You must have spent a fortune, and the roses are beautiful colors."

"How'd you like that pink, darlin'? Did I do good?" Jack asked softly.

"Well," she whispered with a crooked grin, "I think Ethan, Adam, and you are probably a better judge of whether it's the *exactly* perfect color." She blushed.

"I'm hard just looking at them and thinking about it." Adam snickered.

"Me, too!" Ethan waggled his eyebrows at her as she put her finger over her lips.

"Shh! That's too much information for Martha and Rose," she whispered, laughing.

Martha returned to the front room. "I found my camera. Why don't I take your picture?"

"I look awful!" Grace wiped under her eyes and mopped her nose with Jack's handkerchief.

"You look beautiful!" all of them said at one time, and then they all laughed.

Martha took charge. "A girl wants to look good for pictures. Here's your purse. Go powder your nose." She handed Grace her purse, and Grace went to the restroom and fixed her face, then returned. Martha had arranged the roses and her men at the sales counter. She positioned Grace amongst her men and took several pictures. Then she surprised Grace by saying, "Now y'all go enjoy your afternoon off."

"You're giving me the afternoon off?" Grace asked in surprise.

Martha nodded and put her hand on Grace's shoulder. "Honey, you need to adjust your thinking. You're a self-employed woman *taking* a well-deserved afternoon off."

"That's not official yet."

"Go, before I have them carry you out. Enjoy your evening. Go dance, go eat, go make out, go have fun. We love you, honey. Congratulations," Martha said, kissing her cheek. "Consider it our gift to you."

"Martha, you got a box and some padding we can use to get these arrangements home in?" Ethan asked.

"Why don't you leave them here until after lunch?" Martha said. "You could take her out then just swing by and pick them up on your way home."

"I'm starving for a good steak," Adam said. "What do you think, baby? Can we take you to lunch?"

"Sure, I'm hungry, and it is noon."

"That settles it. Ladies, we'll be back."

In the SUV, she told them, "I am so happy, I may have a hard time not showing my feelings to y'all. I feel like I could burst with it." She was trying to get her emotions under control.

"We'll ask for a quiet table, and you can sit with your back to the room if you're worried, but we're not concerned. I think it will be fine." Ethan took her hand as they climbed from the SUV.

They asked for a quiet corner table, and Rudy was able to accommodate them. They seated Grace so she wouldn't feel so self-conscious. Jack sat next to her and held her hand. She wished she could show equal affection to all of them. Trying to see the humor in the situation, she imagined ways she could be sneaky with her affections with them in public.

"Grace is up to something, I think," Ethan said softly as Adam and Jack looked on in confusion. "Let me guess. She's thinking up ways right now to be sneaky in public."

Jack looked over at her and chuckled, "I think Grace can do whatever she sets her mind to do. Far be it from me to curb her from showing affection to the two of you. I mean, it's not like we have to worry about her crawling under the table and sucking one of your cocks or anything."

"Oh, no. *That's* for when we're at Tessa's," she said enthusiastically, giggling at the smirks on their faces. "*Yum*." Then she licked her lips and grinned.

Adam shifted in his seat and smiled at her, saying, "Now, Grace, there's a difference between showing affection and teasing us."

"I wasn't teasing you. I was giving you a sneak preview of a *coming* attraction." She giggled some more. Their mouths popped open for a second, and they *all* did a little shift in their seats.

"I've been meaning to give Tessa a call and make reservations." Ethan smiled at her. "Would you like to go back sometime soon?"

"Tessa's was a major turning point in my life. I'd love to go back." She squeezed Jack's hand and looked at all of them. "I'm still reeling. That was quite a proposal."

"We can't wait for your ring to be ready. I hope you like the design." Jack rubbed her knuckles soothingly.

"I'm sure it's beautiful. If the three of you designed it, I wouldn't change a thing about it. Can he put an inscription inside of it?" she asked.

"Yes, I think he could. Is that something you would like, darlin'?" Jack asked. "Ethan said you might like that."

"Very much. It just seems like a very romantic thing to do. Like wearing a love letter." She hoped they didn't think it was silly.

"Did you have something in mind that you wanted inscribed inside it?" asked Ethan.

"No. No. I'd leave that up to you."

"I'm glad you said something, darlin'. We want it to be perfect for you," Jack said as their waiter delivered their steaks. Grace thoroughly enjoyed her filet mignon and salad and did her best to behave herself during the meal.

Ethan turned to her and said, "Are you looking forward to dancing tonight?"

She reached out and placed her hand over his upper thigh and replied, "Oh, yes, I'm—" *Dammit!* She looked down at her hand and looked up at him, then over at Jack and Adam before glancing at the tables nearby. She slowly withdrew her hand and finished her statement. "Yes, I'm really looking forward to it, Ethan." *This is gonna take some getting used to. Good going, dunce.*

Ethan and the other men smiled at her, understanding in their eyes, but that only made her blush harder. She sighed and looked at her hands in her lap and tried to calm the fast pace of her heart. Now she was afraid to look around and see if anyone else had noticed. She sat back in her chair and breathed calmly. Jack reached out and took her hand, clasping her fingers in his, and smiled encouragingly at her. The rest of the meal was uneventful, but her lapse and resulting embarrassment tainted the celebratory occasion.

The waiter brought the check, Jack paid him, and they got up to leave. She headed to the ladies' room for a few minutes, and the three of them waited in the foyer for her.

* * * *

Ethan muttered softly in disgust, "It's bullshit that she has to stop herself from doing something loving for someone else that comes from a pure heart. There wasn't a single person in that dining room that doesn't have one type of skeleton or another in their closet, and they're all still mostly decent people. She looked down like she was ashamed that she'd messed up already."

Ethan hated seeing the embarrassed blush creep over her cheeks when she reached for him. What was even worse to him was that he knew she would eventually learn to curb those expressions publicly. It seemed a terrible loss to him. She could be as circumspect as a saint, but all anyone would have to do is take one look in her expressive eyes when she gazed at him or Adam and know the truth in an instant. The depth of her love for them glowed in her eyes.

"If you want my opinion," Adam shoved his hands in his pockets, "people get hot enough and need their AC fixed, they don't really give a shit what circumstances surround my marriage. If they do, I don't want their business. There's plenty of holier than thou AC repairmen around. She's a lady through and through, and she'd never shame us with her behavior. Even at The Pony, where she can let her hair down, she acts like a lady, and she treats us like kings. I don't want to see that get messed up."

Jack nodded. "I saw her reach out for you, Ethan. She blushed like she'd done something wrong. It's not right to expect it of her. If I lose a contract from someone who judges me over our marriage because they don't understand, that's something I can live with. I *can't* live without her. We'll tell her this afternoon when we show her the foals. But you do know there is a downside to this. People probably won't say anything to her when she's with us. They'll wait until she's alone and offer her their opinions then, when she's *defenseless. Dammit.*"

Ethan growled softly. They were no closer to a solution over that issue than they were before they met her.

She rejoined them a few seconds later, red-cheeked, furious, and looking ready to kick someone's ass. She angrily wiped tears from her eyes, and as she made eye contact with them, her chin started to wobble. She reached with both arms for Adam, who immediately caught her and wrapped his arms around her protectively.

Chapter Twenty-six

Adam held her as she trembled violently in his arms. “Baby, what happened? What is it?” he asked quietly. Her body quaked, and she was trying hard to contain sobs.

Rudy came hurriedly into the foyer, which was thankfully empty by this point, wringing his hands. He spoke in a soft voice so no one would overhear.

“Miss Stuart, Miss Stuart, I am so, *so* sorry, I heard what happened. He is stupid, *ignorante*, *maleducado!* I will fire him. *Please* forgive me. I will fire him today. Please do not cry. If word gets out about this, no decent women will come to my restaurant. *Please* let me take care of this!” The poor man looked like he was about to cry. His words sank in, and Adam felt a dull rage begin to develop in his gut.

“Is there somewhere quiet we can talk, figure out what happened?” Ethan asked. The restaurant had gotten very quiet even though they were not visible from the dining room.

“Of course.” Rudy nodded and pointed to a nearby doorway in the foyer. “My office is right here.” Rudy unlocked the door and held it open for them.

When the door was closed, Adam hugged Grace and then released her and looked into her flushed, tearstained face. The hurt in her eyes fanned the flames of rage that had ignited in his chest. “Can you tell me what happened, baby?”

“One of the busboys accosted me on the way into the r–restroom.”

“*What?*” All three men growled at once. Rudy hung his head and looked mortified.

Adam moved toward the door, ready to deal out some retribution, but Ethan stopped him. “Let her tell the whole story first before you go kicking someone's ass. Then I'll go with you and help. Go ahead, Grace." Ethan folded his arms across his chest.

"He said one of the waiters saw me with y'all at The Dancing Pony, pointed me out to him, and told him that I was one of the girls that hangs out at the club that is interested in group sex and told him I participated in group sex in the bathroom that night with two other girls and the three of you. He followed me into the ladies' room when I tried to get away from him. He pinned me against the wall and put his hands on me. He had a filthy mouth."

"Now he's dead," Adam said.

Rudy cringed.

"He evidently mistook the *utter shock* on my face for eager interest and thought he'd see what my breasts felt like."

"No, *now* he's dead." Ethan growled.

"I popped him one in the eye and flattened his balls with my knee. He said he heard I was nothing but a whore, *bad move* when you're in *that* condition, and that I was just playing h–h–hard to get. I punched him in the nose when he wouldn't let go." She looked anguished for a second, as if she were in trouble, then burst into tears.

"Rudy," Jack asked calmly, "are either of those men family?"

"No, Jack. What can I do to make amends? Please?"

"We want two minutes alone with both of them, the busboy *and* the waiter."

"Are you going to—?"

"*No*, we're not going to kill them, just *educate* them. I proposed to Grace today, and now her day is ruined because of their behavior. Satisfaction is all I'm asking for. Nothing more."

"Three against two?"

"No, only one of us will do the honors." Adam hoped like fucking hell he got that duty as Jack continued, "Unless you have any other smarmy assholes working for you that need a lesson in manners to even it out. Two minutes, and it's forgotten. If it's okay with you, Grace?"

"Do I get to watch?"

Adam had to grin down at her. She was a bloodthirsty little thing! It was good to see her recovering, though. He was impressed she'd been able to defend herself so capably.

Jack chuckled in amusement. "No, sweet thing. I want you to wait for us in the SUV. Rudy?"

"Again, Miss Stuart, I apologize for my *former* employees' ignorance. I will fire them *both.* Congratulations on your engagement. Gentlemen, follow me. You may use the alley."

Quietly, they followed Rudy down a hallway that led back to the kitchen. Jack caught Adam's eye. "I want to talk to them first."

Adam grinned evilly, crackled his knuckles, and nodded at Jack. "I'll try not to break any bones." Rudy pushed the door open to the kitchen.

* * * *

Grace walked out to Jack's SUV and used the remote to unlock it. She started the ignition, turned up the AC as the June heat blasted her, and then climbed into the backseat to wait.

All in all, she was rather proud of herself. At first she had been so shocked she didn't know what to say, almost slipping into Owen-mode, which was *avoid and escape*, but opted instead for Charity-mode, which was more of a *kick-butt-and-take-names* sort of maneuver. She really had moved on from Owen. It felt good.

What she really wanted now was a shower and clean clothes. She could still smell the busboy's greasy food odor mixed with sweat on her clothes. His hands must have been dirty or wet. She hoped they both needed to go to the hospital after her men finished with them. She wished she'd kicked him, too. Fucker. Then she burst out laughing. Her mindset had certainly changed in just two weeks.

A couple of minutes later, Adam climbed into the backseat of the SUV with her, and shortly thereafter, Ethan and Jack climbed into the front seat.

Grace took Adam's hand and gently inspected his split knuckles. "What happened?"

"Jack and Ethan let me have the honor of making them really, really sorry for molesting and upsetting you. You really did a number on that busboy, baby. I was proud when Rudy kicked him out the alley door with his buddy. The job was already half done, at least on him. His waiter friend was another story, but I fixed 'em up good."

She leaned in between the front seat to look at Ethan and Jack. They both shook their heads and pointed back at Adam with their thumbs. Jack said, "We just watched. Turns out those assholes were neither lovers nor fighters. But they *are* really sorry. Don't worry, darlin', Adam taught them a lesson but didn't do any permanent harm."

Ethan looked at her and smiled. "Rudy fired them, I banned them from The Pony, and I'm also banning Patricia and her friends. It's because of their antics that this misunderstanding happened. I already called Ben, and he's on it. We're real proud that you defended yourself, Grace. We wish it hadn't been necessary."

"I won't go around picking fights, but it sure felt good to stand up for myself."

Jack said, "Rudy told me he'll host our rehearsal dinner for free to thank us."

"He doesn't have to do that. I don't even know how much that would cost. But it must be expensive."

"Honor among gentlemen, darlin'. Those two would have eventually screwed up with the wrong person and caused Rudy even more trouble if we hadn't called them on their bad behavior. It's all good."

"Thank you for defending my honor, sweethearts. Adam, I'll clean and bandage your knuckles for you when we get home."

"I'm going to swing by for your flowers real quick. You stay put, darlin'." Jack pulled into the shop's little parking lot.

Ethan popped the hatch on the SUV and got out to help him load the flowers. She waved at Martha and Rose but stayed in the SUV. The ladies would have taken one look at her red eyes and known something had happened and wanted full details. Right now, she just wanted to get home. A minute later, they were heading down the road to the ranch.

Sitting next to Adam, she picked at the fabric of her top and pulled it away from her skin. "I need to get these clothes off. I can still smell his greasy, sweaty odor on them. Ick," she muttered in disgust.

"Take them off, then," Adam said to her as Ethan's head swiveled around to look at her and nodded encouragingly. She saw Jack's eyes flick to her in the rearview mirror. "Seriously," Adam continued, "the windows are tinted real dark, so no one would see you, and one of us will run in and get your robe and bring it out to you, so there is no chance anyone would see you naked but us."

"It's really just my shirt I wanted to change, but I would like to take a shower as well." She snickered suggestively.

"Well, *see*? You'll be ready to just walk right into the shower when we get home. Might as well be thorough," Ethan added so helpfully.

Jack muttered. "Dammit, I'm driving here. You want me to wreck? Shit, *go ahead*, honey."

She carefully peeled the shirt over her head, avoiding her face and hair.

Adam sighed happily. "Now that's better already." Her breasts, encased in the pink lace bra, bobbed free when she released the back closure. The sensation inspired a sudden deep, hot ache in her pussy. Adam reached out to caress her breasts. "Damn, but you're beautiful in *or* out of pink."

"You say the nicest things, Adam."

Then she slipped her shoes and socks off and left them on the floorboard. Next went the jeans, which left her in a pretty pink thong that matched the bra. *Thank you, June!*

"Adam, I need help with the thong. I hurt my hand when I popped him in the nose. Could you help me? Please?" She was so enjoying this game.

Adam slid his big, warm hands up her thighs and over her hips, hooked his fingers in the elastic waist of the pink lace thong, and slowly pulled it off of her as she knelt on the seat next to him. She lay back so he could get it past her knees and off completely.

"Baby, are you wet?" Adam asked softly, palming her thigh open. She nodded, biting her lip.

"We're still a few minutes away from the house, Adam, if you want to show her how much we love her," Ethan said in his velvety, sexy voice. "I'll bet she'd love it, wouldn't you, Gracie?"

"Yes, I would." She allowed her thigh to lay open on the seat, the other against the back of Ethan's seat.

It would be an understatement to say that Adam dove in and went to town. She moaned and panted as he used his tongue, lips, and fingers. She was close to climax within a couple of minutes. Ethan caressed her thigh and whispered words of encouragement and inspiration to her and Adam both. Adam seemed to know she was getting close. When the moment was right, he gently sucked her clit just as Jack drove over the cattle guard. His stimulation, plus the abrupt vibration of the pipes over the road, sent her over. She moaned Adam's name as she came.

"Beautiful," Ethan whispered.

"She is somethin' else," she heard Jack say.

"Mmm, I could never get tired of this sweet honey of yours, Grace. Or the way you sound when we make you come," Adam murmured as he kissed and licked her slit. "I love you so much."

"I love you, too, Adam."

He sat up as Jack pulled up to the steps. Ethan climbed out and returned a minute later with her blue robe. Adam helped her sit up and put it on, and she tied it at the waist and accepted Ethan's hand when he helped her down from the SUV as she held the robe closed at the knee. She hurried in the house, followed by an amused Adam and Ethan, while Jack pulled around to park.

They inspected her hands, seeing that one of the knuckles of her right hand was a little red and swollen.

"Gracie has a mean jab, I bet." Ethan kissed her red knuckle. "If it swells more or the pain gets worse, we may need to have it X-rayed, but I think it's okay."

Grace got the first aid kit from the pantry in the kitchen and tended to Adam's split knuckles. Adam had a particularly deep cut on his right hand that looked like it might have been caused by a tooth. "Keep an eye on this one. It may get infected. His disgusting mouth was probably full of all kinds of bacteria." She cleaned the wound out. He never even flinched.

"Are you going to be my nurse?" He grinned mischievously at her. "Take good care of me?"

"Just call me Nurse Grace."

Ethan came up behind her and palmed both cheeks of her behind. "Mmm, Naughty Nurse Grace." He nuzzled under her ear. She leaned into him and closed her eyes, smiling.

"Great, I have to go to two more service calls before my day is done. Y'all are going to be here this afternoon, and I'll know what you're doing," Adam said, going for the pout.

"But Ethan will have to work tonight, and you and Jack will have me all to yourselves. When do you have to leave?" She grinned wickedly.

He looked at his watch. "Ten minutes. Why?"

Grace turned to Ethan and kissed him. “Honey, can you spare me for a few minutes?”

“Sure, Gracie. I’ll be in my bedroom.” He kissed her again and left the kitchen.

Grace turned to Adam, took his least damaged hand, pulled him down the hall to her bedroom, and shut the door behind them. With the drapes drawn, the room was dim and cool. He wrapped his arms around her.

“Thanks for picking me, Grace,” Adam said as he nuzzled her throat. “Jack and Ethan didn’t mind, but it meant an awful lot to me that when you were so hurt and upset it was me you reached for.”

She sighed happily in his arms. “Adam, I love all of you equally, but for different qualities you possess. I feel safe and protected with all of you, but you’re my dragon slayer.”

She left it at that and reached for his belt buckle. After she had it undone, she unbuttoned his jeans, reached inside the waistband of his boxers, and found him completely erect. He hissed and shuddered when her fingertips found the head of his cock. She worked his jeans and underwear down his thighs to his boots.

With her right hand, she grasped his cock and slowly stroked him. She slid her other hand up to his neck, pulling him to her for a deep kiss. His big, strong hands cradled the back of her head, his fingers threading into her hair. The sweet romance quickly heated up, however, when she held his forearm, knelt in front of him, and guided him to sit on the edge of the mattress behind him.

He sat and propped himself up with his arms behind him, his massive shoulder muscles rippling. A look of anticipation crossed his tense facial features as he watched her lick her lips. She parted her lips over the head and gazed into his pale green eyes as the head of his cock pressed against her lips softly before sliding into her mouth.

His voice was a deep rumble in his chest. “Baby! Oh, those sweet lips, so warm.”

His breath left him in a rush. With a soft moan, his head fell back, and his abs flexed in the dim light of the room. She ran her tongue back and forth in soft, slow strokes on the underside of his cock from the ridge at the head, down the shaft to his balls, then back again in slow, torturous, lapping waves. She licked the tear that formed at the slit as she sucked his cock back between her lips again. In up and down strokes, she worked him slowly to the back of her throat, enjoying the groans and gasps that came from his mouth. She hummed and giggled in response, which made him moan even more at the vibration.

"I love it when you do that!" He shifted on the edge of the bed and moved with her. He brought one hand forward and cupped her cheek, looking down at her with such tenderness she wanted to cry. She wasn't doing this because Adam had given her a release in the SUV earlier. She was doing this because she loved and adored him and wanted him to go back to work with the knowledge that she hadn't missed the opportunity to show him that love. "I'm a lucky man, honey. I'd do anything to make you happy."

She replied with a soft, breathy sigh, and her other hand came up to grasp his wet shaft, sliding back and forth.

"Baby, I'm gonna come soon, mmm." There was a new urgency in his tone. She kept a steady rhythm, slowly increasing the tempo as she listened to his breathing. She increased the suction a little each time he slid from her, leaving just the head between her lips, then allowed him to thrust back in. She lovingly suckled and stroked him with her tongue and thanked him for being her dragon slayer.

His breath came in all-out panting as he began moving in concert with her. He begged her not to stop and then threaded his fingers gently into her hair.

"Baby, I'm gonna come. Get ready, Grace! I'm coming!" He gasped in great heaving waves as his seed shot forth from his cock into her mouth, and she swallowed. More and more came, and she took it all as he cried out her name. A rippling shudder shook his body, and a moan slipped from his lips.

"Angel," he whispered.

She finished licking him as he lay back to rest a minute. She crawled on the bed and carefully laid her head on his chest under his jaw and listened to his heart rate gradually slow.

"You're *my* angel," she whispered to him, stroking her fingers through his dark chest hair. "I just love you."

He stroked her hair from her cheek. "You do things like that to me and make it nearly impossible for me to leave. I'd like to curl up around you and stay that way for a whole day." He turned to her, his fingers across her tailbone, tucking her into him.

"We'll make time to do things like that, just the two of us, I promise," she said as he tried to sit up, sighed, and laughed softly. Finally, a minute later, he sat up successfully.

"I'm going to feel this in my legs for the rest of the afternoon," he said as he rose and redressed.

"Shaky?"

"Yeah. But in a good way. I'll look forward to tonight. I'd better go. I don't want to run late."

She walked him to the door and then got a drink of water. She made her way down the hall to Ethan's bedroom. She hadn't spent much time in their bedrooms. She liked his room on the east side of the house. It was a little dimmer than hers, the windows already in shadows. He lay on the bed as she walked in and closed the door. He was dressed only in his jeans, his chest and feet bare.

"Hello, beautiful," he murmured in his husky, velvety drawl. His sexy voice always did wonderful shivery things to her.

He was lying on top of the black and dark red paisley comforter. His room was done all in muted and darker tones, and it felt cozy but nice and cool all at the same time. The dark plush rug felt rich between her toes as she walked to his king-size bed. The bed frame was higher than on her bed, so she had to climb as much as crawl onto it. She went to him and curled up against his side.

"How do you feel?" he asked. "Tired?"

"A little, but it's mostly passed now." She slid her palm up over his abdomen to his chest. He turned to kiss her and rolled onto his side, facing her.

"How do you feel after last night? Sore?"

"A little, but not like I expected. Ethan? Will you make love to me?" She looked into his vivid blue eyes. "I want you."

She felt like her heart was in her throat. She was so lost to all three of them. She felt tears prickle behind her eyelids.

"Just slow and easy, honey, then would you nap a while?" he asked tenderly. "You can stay in my bed and nap for as long as you want. They'll wake you when it's time to get ready."

She nodded as she untied the belt of the robe she still wore. Ethan got up and pulled back the comforter and top sheet and then undressed while she watched. He got back onto the bed and helped her out of her robe. When they were both naked, he pulled the comforter and sheet back up over them.

"I love snuggling under the covers with you, Ethan," she said with a little shiver. She must have gotten chilled because his body felt like a heated brand against her skin as he wrapped his arms around her and cuddled her. He nestled in between her thighs and settled there for a few minutes, teasing her with soft, brushing strokes of his lips against her throat and collarbones. His weight felt good over her as she raised her knees and wrapped her thighs around his hips. His hard length was pressed against her pussy, and she reveled in the feel of his masculine warmth and strength as he held her to him and kissed her slow and deep. He was hard and muscled but not sculpted like he spent time in a gym. Grace had a passing thought.

"I'm keeping you from work, aren't I?"

His lips nuzzled a trail from the sensitive spot below her ear down to her nipples. "No, Jack, Angel, and the ranch hands keep things running smoothly. Sometimes you have to make time for more important things, like the people you love. This is time I set aside for you. Jack and Adam will do the same. We've worked hard to get the ranch where it is, and Angel does a great job of staying on top of everything. It's all good, honey. I'm right exactly where I want to be right now."

"You're just about where I want you, too." She nuzzled his throat and licked him.

"Just about?" he teased as he rose up and reached for the lubricant. This time he applied it only to his cock as he sat back on his knees. She enjoyed watching him handle his big, hard shaft as he smoothed the lubricant up and down the long, thick length. She eyed it hungrily and felt her pussy tighten at the thought that soon it would be inside her.

Her body hummed with desire as she watched his hand curl around his cock. She licked her lips when she saw the drop of fluid that seeped from the tip. She heard him growl and looked up into blue eyes that glowed with desire. She had a feeling that the notion of slow and easy had just gone out the window. She lay back on his pillow and opened her thighs as he came to kneel in front of her. He looked down at her pussy, which throbbed and yearned for him. As he knelt there, his cock was ramrod straight, seeping another droplet. A wave of goose bumps passed over her, and she knew she'd remember this moment forever. Perfect.

He pointed to her right with his index finger. "Look, Grace."

She looked in the direction and noticed that he'd repositioned his dresser and its attached mirror, so she would be able to watch everything as he made love to her. Her heart lurched at his thoughtful gesture, and she couldn't believe her body's primitive response. Her pussy flared with burning arousal as she looked in the mirror and imagined watching as he fucked her good and hard.

Liquid heat pooled in her cunt as she gazed at their reflection. He was poised over her, palming his erection, and she lay there, legs open and relaxed, waiting for him to slide his cock inside of her. Maybe he would take her from behind on his bed so she could watch in the mirror. The wetness increased between her legs.

Smiling, she looked up at him and said, "Thank you, Ethan. That is so thoughtful. I love it."

He moved over her as she lifted her feet and slid her thighs onto his, like last night. He hooked his right forearm under her left thigh and lifted it gently and held his shaft so the head was poised to press into the throbbing wet heat between her thighs. She slid her right hand down her abdomen and into her slit. She heard the evidence of how wet she was for him as she wickedly delved a finger into her entrance before using her fingers to part her lips for him.

"Can you see how wet I am for you, how much I want you, Ethan?"

"Mmm, Gracie, you make it hard to control myself when you do things like that. Do you want to feel me inside you? Want me to slide inside your sweet, hot pussy?"

"More than anything, honey. Give me your cock." A sensation of hot expectancy inflamed her pussy. "I'm burning for it."

He gripped her hips and tilted them a little as he positioned his cock at her entrance and flexed gently against her. She sighed in pleasure when her pussy lips stretched around his cock, and he eased in a bit with great care. He felt huge in the opening to her pussy, but not painful at all. She looked in the mirror and could see his cock, only partially lodged inside her, as he held her leg up. She watched as he flexed his hips and the muscles in his back, legs, and tight buttocks rippled as more of his cock slid inside her.

Watching brought a fresh rush of wetness to her pussy, and his cock slipped through it, then he pulled out with a soft moan. He paused briefly and groaned.

Grace wanted to scream with ecstasy even though she wasn't coming quite yet. She could tell it was close, though, because she felt that internal flexing and tightening. She rocked her pelvis instinctively, taking another inch as he thrust gently.

He kissed her neck and whispered, "You're so incredible, Grace, tight and sweet around me. I love you."

His words escalated the rise of the wave she rode, and she rocked again as he slid home, seated to the hilt in her pussy, every inch buried deep inside her. He released her leg and slid an arm under her hips, pulling her under him more, and slid the other arm beneath her shoulders, so she was a captive in his arms, and began to thrust gently into her pussy.

Grace could feel the climactic wave building. The sensation of his cock and the sight in the mirror of his muscles rippling as he thrust was incredibly erotic. The angle at which her pelvis rocked, thanks to his hold on her, aligned her clitoris with his pubic bone in a series of devastating collisions that made her writhe and plead.

"Oh, Ethan! You feel so good! I'm going to come, Ethan, just a little harder, honey. Oh, yes! Oh, yes, that's perfect!"

He pulled farther out now on each stroke but thrust a little harder. Her moans became cries as she continued to watch in the mirror.

"You feel so good, Grace. Oh, fuck, you feel so good. You're going to make me come! Come with me, Grace. Let go!"

His words and his need to come with her sent her over the edge. She heard him come, too, growling her name as he drove into her. His body stilled suddenly over her, and he groaned loudly in relief. He pressed into her body as he kissed her lips, tenderly stroking her tongue with his own.

He released her hips and shoulders. Resting his weight on his elbows, he gently brushed his fingers across her lips. "Mmm, baby," he sighed softly as he rested his cheek between her breasts, "your heart is racing. I love that sound." He stayed that way as she caught her breath. After a few minutes, he leaned back and pulled out of her slowly, watching as his now softened cock slid from her. He smiled blissfully and closed his eyes for a moment.

"What is it?" she asked.

He bowed his head, then hesitantly said, “It touches a deep primitive place in my soul when I pull out of your body and see my cum filling you, seeing it leak from your pussy. It satisfies me in a way that’s hard to express.”

She smiled languorously, understanding completely. It was the other half of the way she felt, receiving him like this, feeling filled by him.

“When the time is right and we’re all ready for that step, you’ll make love to me, and we’ll make a baby together. I want your baby someday.”

Judging by his reaction, her words pleased him a lot. “You can’t imagine how happy that makes me, Gracie. I’d love to make a baby with you.” He kissed her deeply. “Do you need to shower?” he asked.

She looked at him and smiled softly. “No, I’m satisfied to stay just like this and fall asleep in your arms,” she murmured, stretching in sweet contentment as he watched. “I’m perfectly content to sleep here in your bed even after you leave to go to work, with your cum still filling my pussy, just the way *you* like it.”

“Damn, you’re amazing, woman! You can’t begin to understand how deeply that image affects me. I may have to fuck you again before I leave.” His stiff cock testified to the fact that he was ready for another round. Her pussy bloomed with a corresponding needy ache.

“And I would not complain even a little. I want to fuck you again right now, too. I’ve managed to get myself all hot and bothered just thinking about it. Will you?” she asked as she rose up, filled with a sudden feral sense of urgency. She needed him now. She shocked herself, feeling more moisture flooding her cunt, her folds growing swollen and hot again. “From behind. I want to see you fucking me from behind so badly.” She almost begged as she got on her hands and knees for him.

He moved into position behind her, angled so she could watch what he did to her. She watched as he knelt behind her, spread her knees farther apart, and positioned his long cock at her wet entrance. Her pussy clamped down, and her breath came out in keening moans as she watched his cock slide all the way home in one smooth stroke.

“Seeing your cock slide inside me makes me crazy. I know I won’t last, so fuck me hard, baby!”

“Yes, ma’am.” He punctuated each word with a firm thrust into her clenching pussy.

Chapter Twenty-seven

Her cries started out soft, like sobs, and built with each thrust as the muscles in her cunt grew tighter and tighter as she neared her orgasm. His breath sawed in and out as he struggled to hold back from coming before she did. He pumped harder, and her arousal escalated as she watched him bury every inch in her. He reached forward, found her swollen clit, and firmly stroked it between his thumb and forefinger.

"Come for me, honey!"

She flew apart at his touch and screamed loudly, unable to contain her ecstasy. Her arms collapsed under her, and her hips gyrated convulsively on his cock as he joined her, as he roared out his release. Every exhalation was a hitching sob from her lips as she tried to catch her breath.

"Damn," he groaned blissfully, "I think I saw stars."

When they could finally move, he slowly pulled out of her once again. She could see him watch as he withdrew, the pleasure evident on his face. She felt a wet rush and heard his soft growl of satisfaction.

"The caveman like that?"

"Enough to want to throw you over his shoulder and take you back to his cave," he said good-naturedly. "I'm glad you understand that part of me."

"I love that part of you, Ethan."

He helped her lie down in a more comfortable position. She was truly exhausted now. He got up and went to the bathroom for a warm washcloth and gently cleansed her thighs and her pussy. She was half asleep already when he returned and lay down beside her. He pulled her back against his chest, with her head on his bicep.

"I love you, Gracie."

"I love you, Ethan."

* * * *

Ethan pushed the button on the side of the phone to stop the soft alarm so it wouldn't disturb her sleep. The shadows had deepened in the room. The small amount of muted light that came through the bedroom window illuminated her blonde hair, fanned out over his pillow. He lay there for a few minutes and quietly watched her in slumber as the upper swell of her breasts rose and fell with each soft breath. Her lips were slightly parted, her right forearm tucked under the pillow, the other arm resting at her side, her hand lying on her belly. She gave a soft sigh.

He felt the same sense of primal satisfaction as earlier watching her slumber peacefully. He was still tired, but there was a very deep feeling of contentment that overrode the fatigue. He had deeply satisfied his woman, and she was unbelievable when she came, screaming her pleasure, uncaring if anyone heard. They might have. Now here she lay, sleeping as peacefully as an angel, an incredible contrast to the tigress she'd been earlier.

He pushed the comforter to her so she wouldn't miss his body heat behind her. He wanted to touch her, but he sensed that she was not deeply asleep and resisted the temptation. He didn't want to wake her yet. She'd missed out on some sleep last night and had a lot of excitement today. He knew, where they were concerned, she would push her limits in order to please them. He hoped she would slip into an easy routine with them without exhausting herself first or sacrificing sleep and her health in an attempt to meet all their needs.

He quietly removed a fresh, pressed shirt and jeans from his closet and grabbed socks and underwear from his dresser. He carried his boots and clothes from his bedroom down the hall to the bathroom. Showered, shaved, and dressed, he emerged a little while later. Quietly checking on her from the hallway, he found her still sound asleep. In her sleep, she'd shifted to the other side as if she had turned to him.

The sheet had slipped down to her hip, baring her breasts and her smooth, soft abdomen, one arm flung over her head, the other resting across his pillow. His chest ached with the love he felt for her, combined with the satisfaction of seeing her lying in his bed. He thought of what she'd said to him earlier. She was content to fall asleep lying there in his bed with his seed still between her thighs, the way *he* liked it. She loved the caveman inside him.

Silencing the deep rumble of pleasure in his chest, he gently pulled the door to within a few inches from the jamb so she wouldn't be disturbed by any other noises. The house had been quiet while they slept, but he knew Jack would be in soon. Ethan left through the back door and went in search of him. He found him at the corral behind the first barn, where he was currently leaned against the fence, talking to Angel.

The two new foals in the corral followed their mothers around the pen, exercising their long, spindly legs. Ethan walked up and looked into the pen, staring at the new additions to the ranch, but didn't really see them.

"Hey, Ethan," Angel said quietly. "Jack, I'll see you later up at the house. Seven?"

"Yeah, I'm glad you'll come with us." Jack pulled off his leather gloves and slapped them against his pant leg to remove the dust and dirt.

"You're sure you wouldn't rather just meet me at The Pony?"

"No, have supper with us first," Jack replied. "I know Grace will enjoy a visit with you while we eat. We're gonna keep her on the dance floor once we get her to the club."

"Later." Angel walked away from the pen to finish the work day.

Jack and Ethan stood at the pipe fence. "You goin' in now?"

Ethan nodded, feeling about a million miles away. "Yeah, I have those interviews. If they work out, they can start learning the ropes tonight."

"Good. What's Grace doin'?" Jack asked.

"She's asleep right now. Has been since 2:30 p.m." Ethan replied in a low, deep voice.

* * * *

"She okay?" Jack was well aware she was very okay but needed to ask him. He knew when he'd left the house that Ethan intended to spend his free time that afternoon making love to Grace. It's what he would have done.

He would never mention it to Ethan because that had been a private moment between the two of them, but Jack had heard her glorious, climactic scream an hour and a half ago. He'd been up at the house returning the water hose to the faucet in the backyard. He'd heard them both but had grown painfully hard at the wild, rapturous ecstasy he'd heard in her voice. Judging by the look on Ethan's face, it had been passionate in the extreme.

Ethan nodded as he rested his forehead on his arms braced on the fence. Damn, it had been so good it robbed his best friend of the ability to speak.

"We'll let her sleep as long as she wants. We'll probably go to O'Reilley's for supper. Want us to bring you something? We'll head over to The Dancing Pony about eight o'clock."

"Yeah, bring me something back. If the new guys work out, we should have things situated by then. I'll take a quick break to eat, maybe even dance with Grace a little." Ethan finally turned to look at him. "Jack, I really…*love* that she's in our lives. I will never be able to thank you enough. Sounds trite, but she's a dream come true."

"That she is. I wonder what she's wearing tonight. She said she wanted to surprise us." Jack smiled at the look of deep contentment on Ethan's face.

"She never stops surprising us. Gotta go, don't want to be late." He grinned. "Have fun."

"See ya," Jack called. It was good to see his brother so happy, so content. He went back to work, throwing more bales of hay in the back of the pickup bed. He'd give her another hour or so before returning to the house. He'd still have plenty of time to show her the foals and get ready. By then Adam would probably be home as well.

* * * *

Ethan laid the pen down on the desk in his office. Satisfied after rereading it, he took out an envelope, folded the sheet of paper, and placed it inside. He'd lock up her evening bag for her tonight and slip it in then for her to find later. It was time to do the interviews. He left the envelope labeled "Gracie" on his desk.

Ethan believed strongly in first impressions and listening to his gut. Ben and Phil were bartending for the two or three regulars already there. When Ben saw him, he came out from behind the bar to meet him.

"Quinten got here ten minutes ago." Ben handed Ethan the man's application and gestured over to a table in the corner. "Looks like he's dressed and ready to go if we like him. He's clean-cut and looks strong. He just moved to Divine. He has five years experience tending bar in Fort

Worth at a club called Chaps. I took a look at their website. It's a bigger place than this, so he can probably handle whatever comes his way here. I talked to his former boss. They hated to lose him and said he told them he wanted out of the big city. He said the same thing. They say he took good care of his customers and did his share of the grunt work."

"Married?" Ethan asked.

"No wedding ring."

"Okay, thanks." He approached the guy sitting at one of the high-top tables. He looked to be in his mid-thirties, roughly about Ethan's own age. Military style haircut, high and tight. He seemed strong and hardworking. The guy looked up as he approached, made eye contact, and maintained it as he rose from his chair. Ethan held out his hand.

"Quinten Parks? Ethan Grant, good to meet you. Have a seat." Ethan shook hands with him. He had a good, strong handshake.

"Good to meet you, Ethan." Polite but not subservient.

"A few questions for you. You had good recommendations from your former employer, so a lot of my questions are answered, but I need to know a few things." Ethan detailed what the starting bartenders' wages were, plus tips, and detailed other particulars. "We expect bartenders to do their fair share of the grunt work cleaning up. If you were used to salary plus tips with no grunt work, I need to know that because you wouldn't be happy here."

"I came to Divine because I got tired of the big city. I made more in Fort Worth, but the cost of living was also a lot higher, especially rent. I've found a house to rent here that is less than half what I was paying for a small apartment in Fort Worth, and I live alone. What you're willing to pay works for me."

"Okay. One other question. Tell me how you would handle this scenario. We have a lot of regular female customers. A woman comes in and sits at the bar. After serving her, you notice that a guy is hitting on her. She does not appear happy about it and looks like she may be about to leave. What do you do?"

"Is there a cordless phone behind the bar?"

Ethan tried to hide a grin. He liked this guy. "Yeah."

"I'd go get it and hold it out to her, make eye contact with her, and tell her that her boyfriend or husband wanted to talk to her. Provides her with an out if she needs it, plus it's something she could get out of if I read the situation wrong and she enjoyed his attentions. If she's someone I know, and he's really harassing her and she looks genuinely unhappy, I might approach her and ask if we're still on for our date on Friday night as the jerk is standing there. Either way, she has an out."

Ethan was happy with that response. He was glad the guy didn't make some excuse about letting the bouncers handle it.

"What if two guys begin fighting over the same woman?"

"See to her safety if I can and let the bouncers deal with the guys." Good enough. He knew his role concerning keeping the female customers happy and safe from unwanted attention, as well as when to back off and let the bouncers handle the fights.

"Is there anything else you want to tell me or something about you that I need to know?" Ethan had gotten all kinds of responses to that question over the years. Propositions, confessions, it varied.

"This looks like the kind of place I can fit in. I'm all about the business of drawing people into The Dancing Pony. If you're making money, I'm making money."

"I'm going to talk to my partner. Hang tight for a minute," Ethan said. "You need a Coke or something?"

"Sure." The guy nodded. Cool, not overeager.

Ethan returned to the bar and asked the waitress for a Coke for Quinten. She filled his glass from the soda gun and put it on a tray and took it to him. Ben came over.

"Maintains eye contact, good, strong handshake, and good instincts for watching over the ladies. I say we give him a shot." Ethan was relieved.

"Lots of experience, hardworking, *not a diva.* See if he can start tonight," Ben replied.

Ethan headed back to Quinten's table, where he sat drinking his soda.

"Can you start tonight?"

"Yes, I can."

"You're hired, then. You can start at five o'clock. That gives you time to run and get some supper. Three things you need to know that are non-negotiable in our nightclub. No dating, flirting with, or fucking the waitresses. No drugs." Quinten nodded. "And absolutely no domestic strife. If you get a girlfriend at some point, no fighting in The Dancing Pony. Do that at home, or preferably not at all." Ethan grinned and reached out to shake their new bartender's hand. Quinten looked at his watch and said, "I'll be back in twenty minutes. That should be time enough to get home, make a sandwich, and get back."

"See you then."

Hot damn, one down, one to go. Ben brought him the other application. This one he was really looking forward to. It was 4:25 p.m., and Mike and Rogelio had just walked in with a guy who had to be every bit of six foot nine. He was easily pushing two seventy-five and wore a black leather biker jacket. He had long, straight black hair that looked like it reached more than halfway down his back, pulled into a ponytail, and black shades, which he removed. The first thing he did was scan the interior of the club, which did not escape Ethan's notice. He removed the jacket, revealing a powerful physique, and looked like he could easily take on anyone who might cause trouble. With his pretty face, he was going to make quite an impression on the ladies.

Mike and Rogelio had both recommended this guy. If they felt comfortable with him watching their backs, that was enough for him. He looked very capable of handling the job. They just needed to cover the basics.

"Eli Wolf?" At the man's nod, Ethan held out his hand. "Ethan Grant."

"Good to meet you, Ethan." Good, strong handshake. Not a pissing contest, just a handshake. Good.

"Mike, Rogelio, you feel comfortable with him watching your back?"

"Abso-fuckin'-lutely," Mike replied without hesitation, but only because no ladies were nearby.

"Ditto." Rogelio didn't talk much, but he saw everything.

He covered the wage particulars with Eli, which he readily agreed to, then covered the three rules for working at The Dancing Pony.

"Can you start tonight?"

"I can start right now."

"Go have supper with Mike and Rogelio. Come in with them at eight o'clock. They can show you the ropes and answer your questions. See me or Ben if you have any other concerns. Good to meet you, Eli."

"Same here, Ethan," he said, shaking his hand again. He left with Mike and Rogelio, and a few moments later, Ethan heard the familiar throaty growl of a Harley starting.

Ben and Ethan had already discussed hiring Eli as bouncer, and the biggest plus Eli had going for him was that Mike and Rogelio were comfortable with his abilities. Ben had already given his approval. Ethan had just needed to meet him. Same criteria. Eye contact and handshake.

"That went well," Ethan said as he sat down at the end of the bar next to Ben. These two new hires would take a little of the heat off of them, hours-wise. The club was a huge success in Divine. They could now afford to hire more personnel and just hadn't done it up until this point. He was glad to have more flexibility in his hours. Grace was certainly a motivating force as well.

"How are things going with Grace?" Ben asked.

"Good. Jack and Adam are bringing her in tonight after eight. Angel is coming with them. How's the situation with Patricia and her bunch?" Ethan asked.

"I have not seen her or any of her girlfriends. It's a real shame you traced that waiter from Rudy's and that rumor he spread back to Patricia." Ben replied.

It turned out the waiter and Patricia were *friends,* and she had shared that false tidbit, pointing Grace out to him while she sat with her men last Saturday night. The information had not been that difficult to extract from him as he quivered and pissed himself in Adam's clutches. What a pussy. All Adam had done was tap him a little. Patricia must have thought the rumor would not be traced back to her, but that little mistake cost her and her girlfriends their welcome status at The Pony.

"Mike and Rogelio know about their new status?" They were working the door and so were essentially the key to getting inside The Pony tonight.

"They know all of them and will politely turn them away at the door with as little attention drawn as possible. They appreciate the break from having to watch the women's restroom so closely," Ben laughed, "especially Rogelio." The women's restroom was on the opposite side of the bar from the door, which meant they had to divide their time going back and forth. That was cool during the week, but on the weekend they needed to be at the door and on the club floor, not babysitting the ladies' room.

* * * *

Jack quietly entered through the back door. The house was cool and peaceful, and he went to her bedroom first. She wasn't in her room, so he went to check Ethan's bedroom, which is where he found Adam. He was leaning silently against the door jamb. Jack stood beside him and looked in and understood the sappy, smitten look on Adam's face.

Grace lay amidst the comforter and top sheet on Ethan's bed. She must have gotten overly warm under the heavy comforter because she'd flung it off of her and was only partially covered in the sheet. She lay on her back, one arm lying back over her head, the other arm also up but with her hand tucked into her cheek. With both of her arms up, her full, round, pink-tipped breasts were offered up invitingly to them. The sheet barely reached the top of her mound, and Jack was sure if they came closer they would be able to see her blonde curls there. Her skin was the palest ivory in contrast to the black bed linens. Because of the cool air, her nipples were tight, pink points that rose and fell with each breath.

Jack moved to enter the room, but Adam held up a hand, stopped him, and held a finger to his lips. Jack smiled, and they stood there for several minutes, drinking in the sight of her peacefully supine form.

Finally, Adam shifted from the door frame and whispered to Jack, "Why don't you go wake her up? I'm gonna take a shower, a cold one." He grinned.

Jack entered the room and left the door open. As he approached the bed, he knew he'd been right. There were curls visible, and he could even see the top of her slit. Her breathing pattern had shifted and had become shallower. He realized she was dreaming as her breaths became more audible, but she didn't awaken. She sighed softly, shifted a little, and a blush came to her cheeks. He quickly drew a conclusion about what she must be dreaming when she raised her knee slightly, and a soft, panting moan escaped from her lips.

She was having a sexy dream. There was no way he would awaken her now and interrupt such a beautiful vision. Her body bloomed with arousal. She was utterly beautiful as her blush spread down from her cheeks all the way to her breasts, and her nipples became even tighter. Her bent knee fell to the side, and her mound was completely revealed to his eyes. He drank in the sight of her moist pink flesh, her lips slightly parted, wet with her arousal and slightly swollen.

His cock was erect and twitching for action at the sight of her in this condition. He was going to need a cold shower, too, but he could bring her to release if she needed it. One of these days, she'd awaken from such a dream with his cock planted deep inside of her, but today was not the day. There was something sacred about finding her in Ethan's bed, fresh from making love with him. He couldn't take her in his brother's bed. But he looked forward to the day when she would awaken to the feel of his cock sliding home.

She softly panted, and her body filled with tension. He laid a warm hand at the warm curve under her breast and slid his hand down her silken abdomen to her mound as he listened to her sweet sounds. She reacted to his touch in the dream, arching into him as his fingers splayed and slid over her mound. His fingers slid through her wet curls into her drenched slit, delved into her opening, and slid easily into her satiny warmth. She was very aroused, judging by her sounds and the warm honey that coated his fingers.

She arched and groaned as he slid his fingers deeper inside her before sliding them out, then slipping them in again. Her body began to move on his fingers, flexing against him as he slid two fingers in to the top knuckle. He could feel her shake. The muscles of her cunt rippled around his fingers and began to contract and tighten. The moisture flowed from her slit, coating his hand as he slid his fingers in and out, slowly increasing the pace.

He continued the motion and wet his thumb in her juices, then slid it very lightly, like a feather, over her clit. She reacted to the light touch with a breathy moan and began bucking in earnest as his thumb brushed her clit again and again. He made no move to awaken her, content to watch her dream play out. He enjoyed the sight of her uninhibited passion and wondered which of them was making love to her in her dream. Her breath burst from her in quick, successive pants. He rubbed her clit more firmly, still fucking her with his fingers as she came on a wail, crying his name, her hips pumping on his fingers as she suddenly opened her eyes.

Another orgasm on top of the first hit her hard, and she sobbed. "Jack! Oh! Jack!"

She arched and threw her head back, coming undone as her body danced on his fingers. As she came down, he caressed her breast with one gentle hand while running his fingers over her wet, pink lips. He loved the feel of his fingers sliding over this intimate part of her, wet from the double climax he'd given her, both in her dream as well as in reality. Calm now, she reached for him with warm hands, her eyes closed, and an angelic smile on her face.

"Hey, sleepyhead." He smiled at her as she stretched like a contented feline. "You were really worn out. Did you get a good nap?" He brushed his fingers over her warm breast, the skin still flushed and heated, blushing from her orgasm.

Bleary-eyed, she smiled sweetly up at him and yawned again. "I feel wonderful! Like I slept all afternoon. What time is it?"

"Just a little after five."

"Really? Now I'll probably be up all night." She stretched again, and the sight had his cock throbbing and trying to burst through his fly.

"That's kind of what I'm hopin' for, darlin'. Did you have sweet dreams?" He playfully ran his damp fingers up and down her abdomen in a light, tickling touch. She shivered and giggled.

"You know I did. You were the star in the one I woke from."

"So I heard. You've really got your men looking forward to tonight. Why don't you throw some clothes on and let me show you the foals? Then we can come in and get ready for tonight. Angel is coming over at seven to go out with us."

"That's good. I'll be ready in just a minute." She sat up from the bed. She came to him, and he wrapped her in his arms. "Thank you, Jack. That was wonderful. I'll never grow tired of waking up in your arms. Never. No girl's as lucky as me." She leaned into his embrace and kissed him unhurriedly. "Now, I'll get dressed, and I have to *pee*! Be back in a minute." She threw on her robe and hurried from the room.

He just barely made out her cute tush wiggling as she moved before the robe covered it completely. He grinned like an idiot. There wasn't a part on that woman that wasn't delicious.

Adam stood in the doorway with a towel wrapped around his hips, drying his hair with another. "Was that Grace flashing down the hall half naked?"

Jack chuckled. "She needed to pee and change clothes. I'm gonna show her the foals. You wanna come?"

"I need to make a couple of calls before we go out. Has she picked out her outfit yet?"

"She's keeping that one a secret. All I know is that she's promised to wear those sexy, black schoolgirl shoes you bought her. I've really enjoyed all the visual rewards of that little shopping trip you went on for her."

"I did good, didn't I," Adam said proudly. "June told me about a website that sells all kinds of sexy lingerie in Grace's sizes. She secretly told me that they have a much better selection than Macy's does, which is a shame because I'd have bought one of everything in Grace's size. What do you say we visit the Hips and Curves website and do some more shopping for her?"

"Gee, twist my arm. Do they have corsets?" *Mmm, Grace in a corset. What could be better?* His small brain provided the answer. Grace in a black satin corset, G-string, garters and stockings, and those sexy, black high heels. His cock *had* started to settle down a bit until that image popped into his mind.

"June said they have *everything*—lingerie, bras, panties, garters, corsets—even *leather* and patent. Do you still have your list of sizes Charity gave you?"

"Yep, I carry it in my wallet, just in case. I'm dyin' to see our little darlin' in a corset."

"Mmm-hmm!" Adam replied hungrily.

"Hey, baby!" Grace came down the hall, fully clothed in fresh blue jeans, a top, and sneakers. "I think I left my clothes and underwear in the SUV this afternoon. I need to remember to bring those in. Wouldn't want anybody else to see them, now would we?" She gave Adam a hug and a kiss. "You smell good! Yummy!" She grinned up at him.

"Why don't you go see the new foals, then we can all get ready? I have to make some quick calls. Okay?"

"Mmm-hmm. Let's go, Jack. I want to get ready. I can't wait for you to see what I'm wearing."

* * * *

Grace put her arm around Jack's waist, and he considerately matched his pace to hers. They walked through the backyard gate and out to the driveway beyond it that led to the barns. As they approached, she heard neighing in the barn and voices, the sounds of the work day finishing.

"Remember how you were concerned about showing affection to us in public? Ethan told you we thought we should keep that to a minimum, but we've reconsidered. If you want to reach out to one of us, don't stop yourself like earlier today, okay? Seein' you blush and look down like you let us down already just about broke our hearts. It's more important to us that you not be hurt or embarrassed than whether or not you reach out to hold one of our hands."

She nodded and leaned into him as he kissed her temple. "I would try to refrain from kissing Adam and Ethan in public places, although Ethan told me I could in The Pony. Under any circumstances, I'm not likely to lay a wet one on any of you in the middle of the grocery store. That's just not my way."

"We know it's not, and that's why we decided to give you a little more freedom. Just try to prepare yourself that some people may not be very nice about it, especially if they encounter you when you're alone."

"I know. I've been thinking about that lately. I'll always do my best to honor you and never embarrass you in public. At home, in the bedroom, anything goes, though," she said, giggling.

"Hot damn, I hope so!" He squeezed her ass.

As they entered the barn, Jack and Grace saw Angel at the other end. He waved and approached them.

"Hey! I was just wondering if y'all were still coming out. Hello, Grace, it's good to see you again." He returned her friendly hug. "I sure am glad you're out here with these guys. They deserve a good woman like you. I hear wedding bells are even ringing."

"Yes! I'm still in shock. They really surprised me today." She remembered Fred's face as he delivered those arrangements.

"You want to see the new babies on the ranch?" Angel asked her.

"That's why we're here. I've been looking forward to it. I remember seeing their mamas still carrying them the day I brought supper over here for y'all."

Grace walked with them as Angel led the way back to the second barn, where the foals were kept.

"They're here in these two stalls right next to each other." Jack led her to the row of horse stalls. She looked in through the windowed openings at them and marveled that their spindly little legs could hold them up. Even at only a few days old, they were already very sturdy on their feet and growing rapidly, nursing on their mamas. After she'd seen her fill, they returned to the house to get ready for their evening out.

As she walked with him back to the house, Jack said, "We got a saddle for you the other day when I was in town with Angel. I meant to show you, but we ran out of time. If you'd like to go for a ride sometime, we have a very gentle mare that I think you'd take a liking to. Have you ever ridden?"

"Years and years ago, but I really enjoyed it. I don't know anything about horses, but I sure would like to learn. Thanks for the saddle. I hope it wasn't very expensive?"

"No, no, Angel said it was a good saddle at a good price and that it would be comfortable for you, starting out, until you decide if that's something you might enjoy doing. Then I'd order you a better custom-made saddle. I'd love to teach you about the ranch and the breeding operation. I know we'd enjoy having you involved in the workings of the ranch if that's what you want."

"You spoil me rotten."

"I could say the same thing." He leaned down to kiss her as they walked in through the back door.

* * * *

Right before seven, Adam heard her bedroom door open down the hall. He and Jack looked up eagerly at the sound of clicking heels. She floated into the room, serene and beautiful. Her beautiful blonde hair hung in thick bunches of curls down her back and over her shoulders. She looked radiant, absolutely stunning to him.

"Come see?" She beckoned them to her, back to her bedroom. "I want you to *really* see my outfit before Angel gets here." There was a devilish twinkle in her eyes.

They both followed her back to her room. Adam eyed her voluptuous beauty hungrily and with appreciation. She was wearing the wild zebra patterned red and black top that he'd had purchased for her. The cut and style of the top made her breasts look gorgeous. The sexy, silky fabric skimmed down her rib cage, accentuating her hourglass waist, which was the reason June had recommended it to him.

She wore a black skirt that reached just past her knees. Adam gulped loudly as she turned for him, and he saw the seam running up the back of each leg. He had purchased a satin and lace garter belt and silk stockings for her. A shot of hot lust jolted straight to his cock, just like he knew it would if she ever decided to wear them. She had strapped on her platform Mary Janes, which were a sexy mixture of naughty and nice.

"Want to know what I have on *underneath* this lovely top Adam bought me? By the way, thank you, honey. I love it. It's very camouflaging."

"What could you possibly want to hide from us, baby?" Adam asked in a strained voice, his erection threatening to burst the seams in his zipper. Damn it, there was no time for a cold shower!

"There is nothing I want to hide from you. I want you to know what's underneath. It's the world that doesn't need to know. Come closer."

She took their hands and placed them at her rib cage and slowly slid them up over the silken fabric. Their hands encountered the underwire of her bra and slid up over it. No surprises there, then the bra…just…stopped, but *she* didn't. Adam realized their hands were now sliding over Grace, just pure, unadulterated, sexy Grace, and he could feel her hardening nipples through the fabric. She bit her lip and moaned softly at their touch, and his cock jerked in response.

"Oh, baby." Adam groaned at the sweet torment.

"Darlin', you are somethin' else. I'm going to be hard all night just thinking about your sweet little nipples pressing against us as we dance."

Adam's hand stroked the underside of her breast. "Baby, you are absolutely gorgeous tonight. You know what I want to know, don't you?"

Her eyes sparkled with a playful twinkle. "Mmm-hmm. You want to know what *undies* I'm wearing, don't you."

"Yes, baby, what's under that garter belt?"

"Show or tell?" *Cheeky wench.*

Adam glanced at Jack. "Show us."

Chapter Twenty-eight

Adam's mouth practically watered as she slid her hands down her hips and clutched a handful of the skirt and began gathering it a little at a time until she reached the hem. Then she began to lift and slid it up her thighs. She slowly revealed the lace tops of her stockings and teased them with the length of bared leg and garter straps until she finally reached the tops of her thighs. The bows of the garters were exposed and so was her mound. Between her legs lay an almost non-existent layer of sheer black mesh that left nothing to the imagination, as he could see her slit though it. Then she turned to show them her bare ass, winking at him cheekily over her shoulder.

"That's the black G-string with the side ties, isn't it," Adam said in a shuddering whisper. "Hot fuckin' hell. We can reach inside your waist band and untie that without anyone knowing it."

"Yes," she whispered, her eyes filled with a kaleidoscope of emotions—love, lust, joy, amusement, and pleasure—as she lowered her skirt again.

Around her neck, at her wrist, and on her ears was the gold ringed jewelry they had given her.

"Did I choose well?" she asked hopefully.

"You chose perfectly, but we have to tell you something." At her questioning gaze, Adam continued, "You know you only get to dance with your men, right?"

"I knew that even before I picked the outfit out. You're the only men I *ever* want to dance with. I'll be able to feel my nipples brushing against y'all as we dance. Just putting the bra and G-string on made me a little wet, if you want to know the truth." She giggled at Jack's soft growl.

"Wait till Ethan gets a load of you. He's going to be taking the evening off," Adam predicted. "Angel should be here any minute. Are you ready, honey?"

The moment of truth had come. Either they got out of that bedroom or the outfit was coming off and Angel was waiting in the living room for an hour, or two, or three. It was a *hard* choice, but he wanted her to have the full evening to enjoy herself.

"Let me get my bag. Remember I'm not used to these heels, so I'll be holding on to you a lot tonight," she said as she went into her closet.

She could hang on to him *all* night long. Judging by the sexy sway of her hips she wasn't doing too badly.

"We're your willing slaves, darlin'," Jack said as she returned and put the things she needed in the small black evening bag.

Angel showed up right on time in a white western dress shirt, blue jeans, black snakeskin boots, and fresh straw cowboy hat. They made a pretty dapper bunch. Angel was waiting in the living room for them when she walked in. Adam watched as his friend reacted to her appearance. His eyes went wide open, and he glanced at Adam and Jack, then looked back at her and smiled appreciatively.

He cleared his throat and said, "You look stunning in that outfit, Grace, absolutely gorgeous. Everywhere we go tonight you'll turn heads." Adam thought he saw a hint of mild regret in Angel's eyes and noted the trace of territoriality that rose up inside him.

Too late, dude.

"It's after seven. Why don't we head out?" Adam asked as Jack offered his arm to Grace, which she took happily. It was safe to say that Grace glowed tonight. Adam's efforts in shopping for her had a profound impact on her. He loved the way she blossomed under their loving and careful attention.

* * * *

Adam held the door for them as Jack escorted Grace into O'Reilley's. They were shown to a table in the center of the dining room, and Jack held her chair as she sat. Jack appreciated the dignity and class with which Grace handled herself as he noted the eyes that followed her through the room.

O'Reilley's was the most popular restaurant in town. People chose it because of its excellent food and service, but also because it was a place people went to be *seen*. This was Grace's debut as his fiancée and the starting point for questions that would be asked about the nature of her relationship with him and his friends, who were all known in Divine as well-reputed, hard-working businessmen.

Additionally, Angel was with them, well-known as the foreman of the Divine Creek Ranch. That might lend itself to more fanciful rumors by those who were jealous. The more people around to observe the ladylike dignity that permeated Grace's demeanor, the fewer wild rumors would fly. But, after tonight, the questions *would* begin. Grace had proved she was able to handle unwelcome advances, at least to a point. Jack didn't worry about that quite as much as he did the women. Women were catty and subtle. Women were sneaky and so much more likely to be cruel. Could Grace handle it? Could they love and support her enough to make it worth it to her? The answer to the first question would be proven with time. The answer to the second question was a no-brainer. He was her rock, and he knew Ethan and Adam felt the same.

Jack noticed the heads that turned, the admiring glances that came her way as she situated herself and he, Adam and Angel joined her at the table. A few people raised hands to wave, others nodded to them, and Grace even saw a few people she knew and waved at. Jack asked her before they entered if she wanted him to request a corner table. She had declined his offer.

"I've got nothing to hide. If they sense you shielding me it will only make them more curious. I'll sit wherever they seat us and be proud to be seen with y'all."

Now, there she sat, at center stage.

* * * *

Grace smiled warmly at Jack as he politely held her chair and waited for her to sit down. Jack took the seat on her right, Adam was opposite of her, and Angel sat to her left. She would have been perfectly fine with Adam sitting next to her but understood his preference. The set of his shoulders was a little tense, and she felt the eyes on her and knew he wanted to make this dinner as easy for her as possible. She smiled sweetly at him as he winked at her, smiling back. The lights were dimmed slightly in the dining room, and they settled into their conversation while they waited for their food to be prepared. An older man approached their table to say hello, shaking hands with all the men. He turned to Grace to be introduced as he was joined by his wife. She had her purse, so they must have been on their way out.

"Darlin', this is Alan Cunningham and his beautiful wife, Sophie. They own the feed store and co-op in Divine. Alan, this is my fiancée, Grace Stuart."

Sophie spoke first. She was a vivacious little white-haired lady, probably a real looker in her heyday. "I remember you from Stigall's, honey, and of course, the funeral recently. It's good to see you again, and *did you say she's your fiancée*?" Sophie asked, completely unaware that her voice had increased slightly in volume as she said the last few words. She sure could project. Grace blushed and noted the room had gotten quieter and felt the eyes on her again. She sat up straighter and smiled, shaking Sophie and Alan's hands.

Jack spoke up. "Yes, ma'am! I proposed today, and she did me the honor of accepting me."

Grace did her best to ignore the butterflies in her stomach. "It's a pleasure to see you both again, Sophie, Alan. I'm glad it's under happier circumstances this time. You look well."

Alan greeted Adam and Angel. They all made small talk for just a few more seconds before congratulating them again and bidding them a good night.

They went back to their conversation as Jack squeezed her hand and looked at her as though he was making sure she was doing okay. She nodded to him and squeezed his hand gently. His fingers stroked her palm. For some reason, the memory of how he'd awakened her earlier popped into her mind. She felt a little flush return to her cheeks, and she shielded her eyes with her lashes as she remembered the feel of Jack's fingers on her, in her, just as he'd been in her dream. Jack saw the flush and looked over to Angel to ask him a question about the ranch. Adam joined in the conversation, giving her time to sit quietly and just enjoy the moment.

Grace noticed a woman staring at her from across the dining room. She rose from her table and approached, leaving her husband sitting at their table eating. The woman's eyes were narrowed and filled with voracious curiosity. Grace smiled politely at the woman, while inside she braced herself. The woman's demeanor might have been curious, but she could tell it was not friendly. Grace noted that the woman's eyes were on the necklace and knew this was no social greeting but an information-gathering trip. She glanced over at Jack, and he soothingly stroked her palm as he watched the approaching inquisitor.

She heard Adam take a slow deep breath. "Uh-oh, here comes a member of the frozen chosen," he uttered softly.

"Was that necklace made by Clay Cook? I remember seeing that necklace with the matching bracelet and earrings on display at Clay Cook's showroom downtown."

Wow. No introduction, no small talk, just straight for the throat.

"Yes, ma'am, I do believe it was created by Clay Cook." Grace kept it simple and polite.

"There's *only* one like it," the woman commented loudly. Her eyes narrowed. "Made in *solid* gold." *Way to be tacky!*

"Yes, ma'am. It's my understanding all Mr. Cook's pieces are one-of-a-kind originals."

The woman folded her arms across her chest. "*I* heard *Ethan Grant* bought that set."

Say it a little louder, the cook and the bartender didn't quite catch that. Jack cleared his throat, and it sounded as if he was preparing to intervene. Grace gently squeezed his hand. This is what they worried about, and she needed to learn to deal with people on the issue from the get go.

"Yes, ma'am, he did."

"Ethan gave it to *you*?"

"It was a gift, yes."

"But I just heard that Jack proposed to you today."

Yeah, from across the room. Grace was willing to bet this woman didn't even know any of her men, yet somehow made it sound as if she were on a first-name basis. Perhaps she thought to make trouble by pointing all these facts out in Jack's presence.

"Yes, I *am* engaged to Jack." Grace smiled over at him and squeezed his hand. She had this.

"And his *roommate* gave you a gift made from solid gold?" Grace heard a female gasp from the table behind her.

"Ethan is a beloved friend whom I care very deeply for. He gave me a beautiful gift because he loves me and wanted to make me happy. He succeeded admirably, wouldn't you say, Jack, Adam?" Grace asked in a very congenial, non-defensive tone. Both men responded in the affirmative and nodded quietly. She kept her voice as friendly as she was able to. She knew adopting a defensive posture here would only encourage this woman.

The woman sputtered. *"But you're engaged to Jack."*

"And he is friends with Ethan?" Grace posed it as a question.

"Yes!"

"Do you ever receive gifts from people other than your husband? Who is finishing his supper alone now, by the way," Grace said, gesturing with a hand toward him.

"Yes, but—" She swiveled her head to check on her husband, who was looking mortified, gazing into his plate as he finished his meal alone. Grace noticed a lady at another table look at the strange woman and curl her lip in disgust.

"I'm sorry, what was your name? We've never even met, but here I am chattering on, answering *your* questions." Grace studied her closely and thought she might have seen her in Stigall's on occasion but had never come into direct contact with her.

"But I don't understand—"

"The concept of gift giving?" She was amazed that she was able to keep her tone conversational and nonchalant. The *new* Grace was a badass! Charity would be so proud. "He bought a gift for me because he cares about me. Jack has no problem with this and was there when I received it, weren't you, honey?"

"But such a costly gift implies—"

Grace cut her off smoothly, "I didn't ask him how much it cost when he gave it to me because that would be *tacky*." Grace whispered the last word. "But a costly gift would imply that he cares quite a lot about me, doesn't it? Oh! Here comes your husband."

The man nodded to Jack and Adam and spoke softly to his wife, "Elizabeth, I think you've said what you wanted to say. People can hear you, and you've bothered this kind lady long enough. Let's get home to the baby, now," he said firmly but trying to be circumspect. They were definitely the center of interest in the room.

"But our date night—"

"Is *over,*" he said firmly, his patience at an end. Handing her purse to her, he quietly apologized to them for interrupting their evening and led his wife from the room.

Grace looked over at Jack and shrugged, then looked at Adam and smiled. All three of them looked at her with admiration. She picked up her tea glass with a hand that shook ever so slightly and took a drink. Luckily no one else approached. She refused to allow that woman to ruin her evening. She hadn't made any ugly outward accusations, but the implications had been clear. Grace was confident she would get good at deflecting those kinds of questions because she knew this was only the beginning.

The men conversed like they normally would and looked her way every so often to see how she was doing. Their food came a few moments later, and they were able to eat in relative peace. Grace thoroughly enjoyed her grilled salmon and shared a bite with Adam and Jack so they could try it, too.

Angel cut into his bacon wrapped filet as he said to Grace, "Lady, you are one cool customer. Jack, Adam, I hope you know what a prize you have in Grace. She handled that situation with finesse that my mom still does not possess today. She just pretends she can't speak English and lets my dads handle it. Otherwise she gets too pissed off and loses her cool."

"You did make us proud, darlin'. You handled that woman's rudeness about as well as could be expected." Jack leaned over to kiss her cheek, which did make her blush a little. "You really are a fine lady."

"You keep sweet talking me like that, and you're going to make me cry," she whispered back. "I wonder how she knew that Ethan bought the necklace."

"No telling," Adam answered. "She may have been in the shop that day Ethan bought it or heard it through the grapevine. Maybe she wanted it for herself and recognized it on you after hearing it had been sold to Ethan. I know Clay is not one to share that kind of information with people. She was just snooping. I thought you handled it well, too, baby."

Jack gave her a bite of his veal scaloppini, smiling indulgently as her lips closed over his fork. Adam later offered her a bite of his Australian lamb chop with truffle potatoes. Everything was delicious, and Grace could see why this establishment was so popular.

When the waiter came back to check on them, Jack ordered something for Ethan for supper, settling on the grilled shrimp and vegetables. After they'd ordered their dessert, one of Grace's regular customers came over to say hello and congratulate her. Grace rose from the table to greet the elderly Mrs. Barrows and introduced her to the men. Mrs. Barrows greeted them politely and shook Jack's hand, admonishing him to take good care of Grace. He grinned and promised willingly. After Mrs. Barrows made her exit, the desserts arrived. Angel had black coffee, Adam had a blueberry crisp with ice cream and coffee, and Grace shared a tiramisu with Jack and ordered coffee as well. Jack fed her from his fork. A couple of times Grace looked up to Adam as Jack fed her and winked at him. Adam chuckled and mouthed, "Bad girl."

"Pssst. Pssst!"

Grace ignored it the first time because it sounded so far away, but the second time was louder, directed at her back. She turned to face the person behind her who was trying to get her attention. She hazarded a guess that this was the woman who had gasped at the woman's ugly remark. Grace looked into the twinkling violet-blue eyes of a bubbly young woman with curly black hair, sitting with her friends, having a girls' night. Admiration showed in their eyes.

The brunette whispered, "Great shoes! Where did you get them?" Almost as an afterthought, she looked over at the men and chirped, "Hey guys," then looked back down, admiring Grace's shoes.

"Hey, Rosemary." Jack chuckled as the girls continued on about the shoes.

"They came from Macy's." Grace told them about another website she'd seen them at and mentioned it as well. The brunette and two of her friends at the table would probably go for the cute and trendy plus-size fashions they offered on line. "They had them in white and also in ruby glitter." The girls all giggled.

"Beautiful necklace," the tall, voluptuous redhead seated to the right of the brunette said admiringly.

Grace put her hand gently to it and said, "Thank you. It's very precious to me." The redhead nodded and turned back to the table so that Grace could enjoy her dessert in peace.

"I'm Rosemary Piper, by the way. You handled that witch with real style, Grace. Congratulations on getting engaged."

Grace blushed, "Thanks, Rosemary. It's nice to meet you."

Rosemary winked at her and returned to the conversation at her table, allowing them to finish dessert.

Adam looked right at her when she turned back around, a crooked grin on his face as he leaned forward and whispered, "Ruby glitter, huh?"

"Uh-huh!" She nodded with another suggestive wink before turning to Angel and making small talk with him. With the exception of Elizabeth's rudeness, the dinner out had been enjoyable for Grace. She thought she had done well answering the woman's rude questions. She hoped she would develop a thick skin rather quickly and be able to respond without getting emotionally invested in every conversation.

Jack talked to a couple of friends who were also in the construction business. He told them they were all headed to The Dancing Pony and introduced them to Grace. After politely greeting her, they said they might stop in there as well.

In the SUV, Grace told them that she would be giving her two weeks' notice at Stigall's the next day. She told them she knew what she wanted, which was more time with her men.

Sitting beside her on the back seat, Jack nuzzled her neck. "What Grace wants, Grace gets. Darlin', you smell so sweet I could eat you right up. You're making my mouth water," he whispered softly.

"You say the sweetest things, Jack." She shivered at the feel of his soft lips brushing against her ear. Lowering her voice she said, "By the way, where are my clothes from earlier? I don't want Angel to see them."

"I put your clothes and shoes in the laundry room while we waited for you to get ready. I knew that would bother you if he saw them."

"Thank you, Jack. You look very handsome tonight." He was irresistible in his cowboy hat.

"I love you, darlin'."

"I love you, too. Thank you for taking me to dinner. The food was delicious. I hope Ethan likes the shrimp."

"Did we remember to pick up the to-go box with Ethan's supper in it?" Jack asked Adam.

"Yeah, I have it up here," Adam said as they pulled into the parking lot of The Dancing Pony. Once again, the parking lot was overflowing. Jack helped Grace down from the back seat.

"I'm never going to grow tired of y'alls' good manners," Grace commented as she climbed down carefully. The night was humid, and heat still emanated from the sidewalks and pavement.

"We love looking after you, darlin'. Our mamas raised us right," Jack replied, sliding his arm around her hip as they walked to the night club entrance.

Chapter Twenty-nine

Ethan stood near the door, talking with Mike and Eli as Rogelio checked IDs and collected cover charges from the customers who milled at the front entrance, waiting to come in the night club. The Pony was really thumping tonight, and Ben and Ethan had both been relieved to find that Quinten lived up to the recommendations of his former employers. He was fast, neat, and clean behind the bar. The waitresses took an instant liking to him because he hadn't screwed up any of their orders.

Eli was doing fine as well in his new capacity, although the real test would come later in the evening if any customers got rowdy. As Ethan predicted, the ladies took an immediate shine to him, and he noticed several had approached Eli at the front as he tried to learn the ropes. He was always sweet to them but never encouraged the attention. He was more intent on listening to Rogelio and Mike as he learned the ins and outs of the club. Ethan had a good feeling about both of the new hires.

Ben and Ethan enjoyed being able to move around and mingle with customers. Patricia and her bunch had made themselves scarce again tonight, so far. Ethan hoped it stayed that way. The music thumped loudly, and the dance floor was full. As he checked his watch, he heard Eli make a soft comment, looking over the heads of the people who were crowding the doorway.

"Hot damn! She is *fucking* gorgeous. Come to Daddy, honey," he said, grinning when Ethan scowled up at him.

"Sorry, boss, I know I'm working. Wait till you get a load of the *woman* walking through that door."

Ethan looked up. The group having their IDs checked finally moved off into the club to get a drink. Ethan saw whom Eli had been referring to and couldn't help the shit-eating grin that plastered his face as he leaned over to him.

"You think she's gorgeous, huh?" Ethan asked. "Look at that *body* and that beautiful *face.*"

"Bet she's sweet as candy, too," Eli said admiringly in a lower voice.

"Sweeter." Ethan watched appreciatively as Jack released Grace's hand and she sauntered seductively up to him. She slid her hands up his chest and into his hair before wrapping her arms around his neck and turning her head to kiss him open mouthed. *Holy crap*, what did she have on under that outfit?

"I brought you something to eat," she said simply, then smiled playfully at him.

Ethan chuckled deeply at her innuendo. "I want to introduce you to someone." He glanced over at Eli as he schooled the "Did I just lose my job, boss?" look on his face.

Ethan grinned good-naturedly at him and said, "Grace Stuart, meet Eli Wolf, the newest member of the team. Eli, meet Grace Stuart, my fiancée."

"Grace, it is a pleasure to meet you," Eli said with perfect manners, holding his big hand out to shake hers.

"Likewise, Eli. Welcome." Turning to Ethan she said, "We brought you some grilled shrimp. Are you hungry?"

"Yes, *very*." He gazed into her eyes. Her blush told him she understood his innuendo.

Ethan introduced Adam and Jack to Eli as well. They all shook hands. More people came in the door and stood waiting to have their IDs checked.

"We'll let you eat, Ethan. I'll go see about a table," Adam said.

"I had a waitress reserve our table from the other night over by the dance floor. Otherwise you probably wouldn't be able to get one this time of the night," Ethan told them as he slid his hands around Grace's hips, pressing her to him just a bit, enough for her to know she had an effect on him. He whispered in her ear, "Gracie, honey, what are you wearing, or *not*, under this outfit?"

Grace rubbed her delectable body against him as he held her and murmured, "Take me to your office so I can put up my purse, and I'll let you in on a little secret." She was careful that no one else could hear her.

Ethan turned to his new bouncer. "I'm going to seat my friends and go eat real quick, Eli. If y'all need me, I'll be in my office for a few minutes. Hold down the fort."

"Okay. Boss?" When Ethan turned aside to hear Eli, he said, "Sorry, boss, didn't know she was your fiancée. No offense?" He held up his hands.

"None taken, Eli. I react that way *every* time I see her."

* * * *

Ethan turned the envelope over on the desk as soon as he flipped the light switch on in the office. He placed his supper on the desk and turned to Grace as he closed and locked the door behind her. "I need another kiss like that last one, and then you can show me what's under there." His lips plundered hers.

The wild part of Ethan wanted to push her skirt up over those satiny thighs and slide his cock right into her hot, wet cunt. But his conscience wouldn't allow him to do that and then send her out to Adam and Jack that way. He was not a caveman, for crying out loud.

The kiss finally ended, and he asked, "How was dinner?"

She encouraged him to go ahead and eat. She sat down on the edge of his desk as she told him about what happened at O'Reilley's and Jack's talk with her concerning not withholding public displays of affection anymore.

"I loved that public display of affection you gave out there just now. That made my night, sort of like the glowing smile on your face right now."

While he ate, she mentioned to him that she planned to give her two weeks' notice at Stigall's when she went in the following day.

"I'm torn because I love the people I get to work with there, but I need that time back on the weekends to spend with y'all."

He knew she'd have more fun shopping at Stigall's than she did working there. "I'm sure you'll be in there on a regular basis, and who knows? If Jack the matchmaker has any luck, we may start to see a little of your co-worker Teresa around the ranch in the future."

"I would really like that. How was your shrimp?"

"It was good. Thank you. I was starving." He closed the container and beckoned her to come to him.

"Would you like me to show you?" she asked, smoothing her hands down her hips.

"I'd love for you to show me." His cock wanted a peek, too.

"Are you gonna behave?" she asked, giggling as she approached.

"As much as I am able when I am in your sexy presence." He laid his hands on her hips and slid them up her hourglass waistline to her full, round breasts. "Oh, damn! You're wearing that black shelf bra," he said, discovering her deliciously bared nipples. He gently strummed them with his teasing fingertips to tight peaks. "Mmm, Gracie, I'm going to be able to feel these when I'm dancing with you, aren't I?" His cock twitched at the sound of her stifled moan.

"I hope so," she murmured with a shudder. He gently slid his fingers into the deep overlapping neckline of her top and stroked the satiny swell of her breasts.

* * * *

"Can I see what's under here?" He knelt in front of her when she silently nodded, enthralled by his heated blue gaze. His warm fingertips traced over the lace tops of her stockings. She gathered up the skirt in her hands as she heard him softly sigh. "You're wearing a garter belt? Another of my fantasies coming true. May I?" He smiled as she let him lift the rest of the skirt up and felt her pussy melt at the deep growl in his chest when he found the transparent G-string. He fingered the delicate silk ties at each hip and rested his forehead against her thigh for a few seconds. She slid her fingers into his hair at the nape of his neck, and he looked up at her. She smiled at him, waiting.

"Just a taste?"

"I'll never turn you down, honey. Never."

He pulled the tie at one hip to loosen the G-string just a tad. He swept it aside and ran a finger down her very wet slit, making her gasp. His tongue gently followed, delving into her wet entrance, searching for and finding her throbbing clit. The beat of the dance music outside the office door punctuated his movements and the pounding of her heart. Gripping his desk behind her, she allowed him to lift one thigh and ease it over his shoulder. She imagined how decadent they must look at that moment. Pure, lustful enjoyment was written all over his face, but the lust was tempered by the love that also shined in his eyes. He communicated his pleasure to her with a deep groan and she felt the vibration against her clit. She gazed into his eyes and thought to herself what an amazing turn her life had taken, to be loved like this, times three. It boggled her mind. He slowly lapped at her, then gently suckled her clit until she came undone, trying to stifle her high-pitched panting moans. She felt sure it was not possible to get off that quickly, only…it *was*. He helped her tie the string back properly after she tidied herself, then lowered the skirt to where it should be. He tipped her chin up and looked in her eyes.

"Woman. You amaze me with your love."

"I can say the same about you," she murmured as he kissed her sweetly one more time.

He released her to fix her lipstick and powder her nose, then she handed him her evening bag for safekeeping in his office.

After they were done, he guided her from the office and escorted her to the table where Adam, Jack, and Angel sat, smiling as she walked up with him.

"Was sangria all right, darlin'?" Jack asked, sliding it in front of her when Ethan held her chair for her.

"That's just fine, thank you, honey," she replied, kissing him sweetly.

"So I see the interviews went well. That the new bartender?" Jack nodded toward the bar, where an unfamiliar man worked rapidly.

"Yeah, he seems very capable. The waitresses aren't complaining, and you know how they fire off the drink orders. Eli is doing well, too. He has good instincts. We'll see how he does later tonight. He's made quite an impression on some of the ladies."

As Ethan spoke, he reached out to caress her cheek. Her eyelids slid closed, and she leaned slightly into his hand. A woman laughed loudly across the club, bringing her out of her dreamy little haze.

Suddenly, a thought occurred to her, "Oh, shoot!"

"You forget something, baby?" Adam asked as people milled around, trying to get to and from the bar and the tables.

"I didn't call Charity! I could kick myself. I should have called before I left work to tell her the news. How self absorbed am *I*?" She suddenly felt lonely for her sister's company. The laughter she'd heard reminded her of Charity's laugh. She *could* have called her this morning, but she knew the reason behind that. It had been because she wanted to keep last night with her men all to herself just a while longer. She *should* have remembered to call when they proposed.

Then she noticed the grins they were trying unsuccessfully to hide. She gaped at them in surprise. "You already called her?"

"Darlin', I wanted to ask her permission to propose to her baby sister," Jack said.

"And to invite her and Justin to come out to The Pony to help us celebrate tonight." Adam added as he waved at someone he knew across the room, nodded, and pointed at their table. Grace looked in the direction he was waving and saw Charity and Justin approaching.

Justin was in his riding leathers, snug white T-shirt, and jacket. Charity was dressed in her biker babe outfit, thigh-high boots, zip-down skirt, leather corset, and leather jacket. Her long, curly blonde locks were in wild disarray, but not the "I just spent half an hour on the back of a motorcycle" sort of disarray. No, her hair fairly shouted, "My hair looks like this because up until just a few minutes ago he had his hands in it as I gave him the blowjob of his *life.*" Of course, Charity was tall and a little on the voluptuous side herself, especially after two kids, but she carried it well and was looking very sexy tonight.

Charity saw Grace and sauntered over to the table with Justin at her side. "Grace, you look like sex on a stick tonight! Congratulations, honey!" As Charity hugged Grace, she uttered a stunned whisper, "What in freakin' hell are you wearing tonight, bad girl? I want to see later in the girls' room. You *cannot* deny me. You know I need all the details, but not here. Every eye in this place is on y'all."

Grace scoffed and shook her head. "No, honey, every eye in this place is currently on you and Justin. Talk about hot! Pull up a couple of chairs if you can find them." Before they could go in search of one for Charity, Adam got up and offered her his seat. Grace made introductions for everyone with Justin. Grace sipped her sangria, and Jack ordered drinks for Justin and Charity when the waitress came to check on them.

Speaking to Jack but looking at all three of them in turn, Charity said, "Congratulations on Grace accepting your proposal. She is very precious to me, and I hope you take as good a care of her as she deserves. One look at her tonight and I can see just how happy you've made her. She loves y'all very much, and I can see that y'all love her, too. Remember I have that shotgun."

"Yes, ma'am." Jack laughed as she winked at him.

"Enough of the mushy bullshit." Charity tossed a curl. "Justin, I need to dance with you." He took her hand, and she slid from her chair.

"This is a really nice surprise, y'all. Thank you for calling her. I still can't believe I didn't call her myself." Grace watched Justin pull Charity against him and move flawlessly over the floor with her.

Jack got up and held out his hand to her. "When I talked to her I explained that you'd had a really full afternoon and had been too busy to even think." She laid her hand in his warm palm, and he spun her onto the dance floor.

"I love you, Grace. I'm gonna love you forever," Jack said to her, dancing with her to a Brad Paisley love song. Swept away by the emotion in his voice and the love in his eyes, she was unprepared for the deep passion of his kiss. He usually kissed her with short, sweet kisses when they were here, but this kiss was like he was dying of thirst and she was the only drink that could satisfy him.

With his kiss he claimed her, clutching her to him, uncaring about what others thought. She was enveloped in this tender kiss, cocooned in his sheltering arms, and she loved the way they felt around her. She pressed into him, moving smoothly and allowing him to lead her.

* * * *

Grace clung to him, passionately receiving his kiss. Her sweet fragrance filled his nostrils as she took all he gave her, just as she always did, never turning away from him. She pressed her luscious curves to him as they danced, and held nothing back.

He could feel the luxuriant, soft firmness of her breasts as they perched in the top of her brassiere, offered up to him. Her tight nipples teased him through the fabric of his dress shirt, brushing against him. Her head tilted to the side as she continued to kiss him, and her fingers twined in the hair at his nape, beneath his hat, before slipping down to caress his neck. Her right hand was held in his big one, so delicate and soft. His right hand rested on the swell of her hip and her lower back, his fingers lightly strumming the back of what he was sure was her G-string.

Her lush curves pressed against him had him hard and needy. He wished for the warm, wet *easing* her delicious body could give him, as well as the release that went beyond the physical into a more spiritual plane with her. The kiss was so exquisite, their bodies moving so fluidly together, he was surprised when the song ended.

"That has to be a record for me," Grace breathlessly said. "That was the longest, hottest, sexiest kiss I've ever had. I thought your fingers rubbing against my hip were going to be my undoing."

"No, darlin', your undoing comes *later,*" he murmured in her ear, careful no one could hear him. He felt her soft little intake of breath at his words because she was still pressed against him. She laid her cheek against him and made the most delightful moaning sound just for his ears. "Does that thought make you warm?" She nodded, plastered against him still. "Wet?"

"So wet," she whispered. "I ache for you, it's so strong." He leaned down so he could hear her small voice. "I'll never stop loving you, Jack. Please don't break my heart. I'd die." Her lip trembled.

"Darlin', I'd never break your heart. It's too precious to me. Your trust and your love are the most valuable possessions I have. I promise I'll take very good care of your heart. You know Adam and Ethan feel the same exact way. We'll devote ourselves to you, honey, I swear it."

* * * *

She slipped her arms around his neck, fighting tears, and kissed him again.

"Get a room," she heard Charity say as Justin two-stepped her past them. They had stopped on the dance floor, and everyone was dancing around them, including Angel and Rachel Lopez. Jack offered his arm and escorted her from the dance floor. Ethan had excused himself to mingle with customers and keep an eye on the door. Jack helped her into the tall, cushioned chair, and she sipped from her glass of sangria. So far Patricia had not shown up at the club, and Grace was relieved. She'd had more than enough drama for one day.

Just then Jack's acquaintances from the restaurant arrived and struck up a conversation, greeting Adam and Grace again before ordering beers and standing at their table to talk a bit. Grace reached out a hand to Adam's broad, hard chest, and he covered her hand with his palm and helped her down with the other hand. She caressed Jack as she stepped away with Adam, and he looked over to her and smiled, momentarily losing focus of his conversation, watching them. "I Melt" by Rascal Flatts began to play as they moved to the dance floor.

Adam's right hand slid down her spine until just his fingers reached the top of her ass, not too far down but far enough to set her body to humming. Adam seemed to pick up right where Jack had left off, arousing her to a greater level. She slid her hand into his big callused one and put the other around his waist and pressed herself to him. Her body warmed even more at the sensation of her nipples brushing against his linen dress shirt, a slight groan from him letting her know he noticed the hard peaks pressing against his chest. She wondered if he imagined what it would feel like to have those peaks pressed against his bare skin.

"Can you feel them?" she asked.

"With every *inch* of my body, I feel them, Grace." Adam growled, gripping her waist for a moment. "Your slightest touch sets my body on fire, woman." His words sent another spear of desire to her pussy, which wept in response.

"I love you, Adam. I love the things you say to me. Later, I'll do whatever you want me to do, *anything*. I love you so much, baby." She laid her palm on his cheek. "I'll do my best to make you happy, Adam."

"You make me happy just being with me right now. I'm proud to be seen with such a fine woman. I'm the lucky one that you accept me and love me." He kissed her tenderly as they danced. The song was over too soon, and Adam escorted her back to the table. He murmured to her, "I'm lovin' those shoes on you, by the way. Very, very sexy, baby."

"Thank you." She leaned her head against his shoulder before she settled in her chair again.

"Come on, bathroom buddy," Rachel said as she walked up to their table. "I'll bring her back, gentlemen. Looks like there won't be any smackdowns in The Pony tonight. Be right back."

As Grace walked with her, she said, "I saw you dance with Angel. You looked like you were enjoying yourself."

"Oh, yeah, I've known him for years. We've been friends a long time, but he stopped coming in here when Patricia started in with her games. It's great to see him have a good time."

"I think so, too. He works very hard at the ranch." Grace waved Charity over. She introduced them as they went in the restroom together.

Charity eyed Rachel with admiration. "I knew when she told me about you that I'd take a liking to you. Thanks for watching my sister's back."

"Decent girls have to watch out for one another," Rachel replied. There was nobody else in the ladies' room at the moment, so Charity pulled Grace into the handicapped stall, giving them a little privacy but leaving the door open.

"Okay, show me what you got going on under there, sister."

"Charity!"

"I wanna *see*. Just a peek!" Charity whined.

Rachel laughed and came over and peeked in the open stall door. "What is goin' on in here? Show her what?"

Grace and Charity grabbed Rachel's arms and pulled her into the handicapped stall with them, giggling. Both girls' eyes bugged when Grace carefully lifted her blouse to show them and then pulled it back down very quickly.

Rachel let out a gasp. "*Holy shit*! Grace!"

They all giggled loudly, and when Charity pointed at her skirt, Grace put out both hands in a swiping motion. "Uh-uh! No, no! I have on a G-string and a garter, and, no, you can't see. I'm bein' bad showing you my bra!"

"I love that bra!" Rachel said. "Where did you find that?"

"Adam bought it for me at Macy's."

"Adam bought that for you?" Rachel smirked. "I'm impressed!"

"He bought the entire outfit I have on, even these shoes."

"I want a man who knows how to shop for me," Rachel said as they left the stall and she fluffed her hair in the mirror.

"He's out there somewhere," Grace assured her.

"I wish he'd get his fine ass to Divine," she quipped, reapplying her lipstick.

Charity stepped from the stall and washed her hands, and they left the bathroom. Everyone had returned to their table, even Ethan, when the next song started.

Grace squealed happily and looked at her men who were suddenly mute. Charity looked resigned and rose from her chair alone, and Rachel was already headed to the dance floor, looking back to see if they were coming as "Save a Horse, Ride a Cowboy" began to pound through the sound system. The guitars started the heavy beat. Bodies swarmed the dance floor.

"Oh, hell girl, come on!" Charity yelled. "We'll dance together and give *them* a show!" She unzipped a couple of inches on the zippered slits of her leather skirt.

Justin just shook his head. "This is where the torture begins."

Lots of people headed to the dance floor as the song by Big and Rich began to play. Grace grinned cheekily at her men as she slipped away with Charity and followed Rachel onto the dance floor.

"Come on, Grace, let's see if you still know how to shake that moneymaker!" Charity hollered and cackled. Grace decided she'd *show her* and shut her up right quick.

Chapter Thirty

Ethan and six other men stood speechless, watching and drooling. Some with their mouths open. Charity and Grace proved that two-steps and waltzes weren't the only thing they learned at the School of Modern Dance. Rachel kept up with them just fine, showing her own natural sense of rhythm. When the hips started dipping and rolling, Ethan reached over to close Adam's jaw.

Angel's eyes were bugging slightly from his head, and he left the table to get another beer from the bar. Ethan watched with utter amazement at the sensuous, carefree way Grace danced with the other girls. The way she moved set his blood racing like a wildfire through his veins. His cock stood up tall and erect, howling for immediate action. Grace's blonde curls bobbed and danced around her shoulders. Her arms moved in graceful arcs as she led with her luscious hips. Hips he remembered dancing and gyrating just for him this afternoon.

She looked up and caught his eye and smiled seductively. *Damn*, could she read *his* mind? For someone who wasn't sure about walking in those heels, she sure looked confident in them out on the dance floor. She kept eye contact with him and turned and wiggled her tush for him. He'd remember forever the joy and sass in her eyes, the playful sensuality in her dance moves. The song was over much too soon. No one made a pretense of having carried on a conversation when the girls returned to the table.

Justin reached for his wife and said, "You still got the moves, woman." Whatever he whispered in her ear afterward made her laugh and giggle. After Charity took a sip of her drink, Justin pulled her back to the dance floor for a slow dance. David, one of the men who had been talking to Jack, asked Rachel if she'd like to dance, and she nodded, smiling.

* * * *

"Where's Angel?" Grace asked, looking around for him.

"He went to the bar for another beer while everyone was on the dance floor," Jack said.

Grace sipped from her sangria and looked at her men. Their eyes were glazed with passion. "Did you enjoy our dance?" Grace asked and then added more softly, "I was really dancing for y'all." She heard deep growls from all three of them and felt a responding rush in her pussy. More moisture pooled there, soaking her G-string this time.

"Would you like to dance with me, Grace?" Ethan's voice was like a sweet caress.

"Always." She took his hand as "Bring It on Home" by Little Big Town played.

He wrapped her in his arms and spun her onto the dance floor before settling into a two-step. She loved to dance with all three of them. But when she danced with Ethan, it was like two people becoming one.

"I loved watching you dance, Grace. I couldn't take my eyes off of you. You look stunning tonight, and dancing for us like you did made us want you so much it's painful." His strong hands slid up and down her ribcage, and she tingled inside at his touch.

"What time will you be done tonight?"

"Around one or so. It'll be late when I get home."

"Not too late for me, honey. Come to me when you get home, will you?"

"If you want me to, but I won't wake you if you're asleep."

"Fair enough, but I won't sleep until you're home."

"You should. You have work tomorrow," he admonished gently,

"We'll see." She tucked her head against his shoulder, bringing her arms up to his thickly muscled shoulders. His hands slipped around her hips and his fingertips brushed the top of the cleft of her ass. Intimate and so sweet. He leaned into her and kissed her deeply, not a friendly kiss, but a lover's kiss.

"The necklace looks good on you tonight. It flickers when the lights reflect off of it on the dance floor. Someone is waving at you." He pointed at someone on the dance floor. Rosemary, the cute little brunette from O'Reilley's, was dancing with Steve. Grace smiled wide at the friendly young woman and waved back before she disappeared in the crowd on the dance floor.

"I met Rosemary in the restaurant tonight. She and her friends were sitting directly behind me. They complimented my necklace and shoes."

"Those are some sexy shoes on you, Gracie."

"Thank you. Maybe I'll wear them for y'all at home, too," she murmured seductively. "What are you thinking about?" She giggled, wiggling slightly against his insistent cock.

"All the different ways I might take you, including with those heels still on."

"Oh!" She giggled softly. "Can you tell me? What are you imagining?"

"Well, besides fantasizing about you in those heels with the lingerie you have on and nothing else, I get really hard at the thought of making love to you outdoors. Maybe we'll build you a gazebo in the backyard. We'll install nice deep benches inside it. At night, you and I can slip out there and get naked. We could also take a couple of blankets out to the glider rocker on the back porch, you could straddle my cock, and I'd rock you until you come for me."

"Oh, mercy." She felt her cunt clenching and swelling. "What else?"

"We might also use one of the saddle stands in the barn. I'd put a nice soft saddle on it and bend you over it, spank you if you've been naughty, and then fuck you from behind while I play with your clit." Oh, merciful heavens! She was feeling *very naughty*! When he said fuck and clit, he whispered them softly into her ear so nobody could hear, and she felt moisture seep between her thighs.

She turned to whisper closely in his ear, "Keep talking like that and I'll come on this dance floor. What else?"

"I thought I might tie you to my bed with your legs spread wide and introduce you to a sweet little vibrator and dildo I bought for you." As he spoke to her, his muscular thigh slipped between hers. His leg brushed rhythmically against her mound as they danced. His fingertips subtly stroked her ass and her tailbone, sending warm shivers straight to her clit. Oh, goodness, he didn't know *how close* she was, and if he kept *talking*…

He maneuvered them to the darkest corner of the dance floor as he continued speaking. She knew he could feel her gasping breaths against his neck.

"I'd use nice soft rope, and tie you up, and get you good and hot with my tongue. Then I would put your vibrator right between those petal-soft lips against your little clit and let it strum you until you came hard." As he said the final words, he ground his erection against her aching clit, and at the same time, he brought one hand forward, maneuvered her so his back was to the wall and tweaked one of her throbbing nipples.

She gasped as the tightening in her pussy began. *He* knew he almost had her when she missed a step in the dance, but he carried her through it and never stopped moving against her. She felt herself slide ride up to the edge and teeter, waiting for his word. "Then I'd take the nice soft dildo I bought for you, Gracie, and I'd slip it into your sweet-tasting little pussy. I'd slide it in and out while I push the vibrator against your clit, and I guarantee, just like *now*, that you'll *come for me*." He tweaked the other nipple.

Her eyes slammed shut, her lips pressed together, and she locked her jaws to prevent the yowl that wanted to escape from somewhere deep inside her. She tilted her face toward his neck as he angled his head down. No one could see her face or they would have seen the ecstasy evident there. He kept them dancing smoothly as her tense body, struggling to betray no sign, rode pulse after pulse of her orgasm. Trying to hide her response only intensified her climax. She felt hot cream smearing her thighs as her pussy quaked and pulsed, drenching her G-string. She rode the wave down, and he clutched her tightly to him as she experienced her first public orgasm. "Then I'd lick the honey from your pretty little lips after I'd untied you. Then I'd cuddle you to me and hold you till you fell asleep in my arms. How was that?"

"Oh, goodness, did anybody hear me?" She looked around, panicked.

"No, not at all. No one could see your face. They would assume I was kissing you. It's a good thing that everyone is wearing cologne, though."

"Why?"

"Because it masks the scent of your sweet honey that I can smell now, like the sweetest perfume in my nose and mouth. Did you come hard?" he asked, nuzzling her.

"So *hard*. That was amazing, Ethan. Thank you," she said in a shaky voice, her legs weak, her hands shaking a little as she held on to him. Boneless and languid.

"Do you need a break, Grace?" he asked as she began to melt in his arms.

"Maybe the ladies' room, for a minute. I'll meet you at the table. Will you walk me? My legs are shaking."

He turned to escort her to the restroom. "I'm going to check the front, and then I'll be back waiting for you here," he said as he pushed the door to the ladies' room open for her.

"All right." She needed to sit down somewhere private for a few minutes. She walked in and went to an unoccupied stall and locked herself in. After taking care of cleaning herself up a bit and using the facilities, she put her outfit back together and just sat for a little while longer, catching her breath.

She was in awe of Ethan. He had a verbal power over her that astounded her. She knew her relationship went very deep with him and could not account for it. She was just as close to Adam and Jack, but in different ways.

Grace stayed another couple of minutes, allowing her body to come down from the orgasmic high, the tingles gradually fading back to a soft hum.

She needed to get back out there before Ethan and the others wondered if she was okay. She stepped out of the stall and checked her outfit in the mirror. Looking closely at her reflection, she realized she needed to touch up her lipstick. Her color was still a little flushed, but she could attribute that to dancing as much as anything else. Ethan said nobody had noticed, and she hoped he was right. After fluffing her hair, she left the restroom to find Ethan and ask for her evening bag.

Another lively dance song was playing, and the club was very noisy. She returned to their table but declined when Adam stood to help her into her seat.

"I need to get my evening bag from Ethan's office." She put her hand on Jack's shoulder as he started to rise. "My lipstick is in it. Have you seen him?"

Adam pointed toward the front, and she looked that direction and saw him at the bar talking to Ben and a customer.

"Want me to go with you, baby?"

"No, Adam, I'll need to return to the ladies' room after I get it. Stay here, I won't take long." She patted his chest in assurance and he returned to his seat.

She carefully made her way through the thick crowd. When she looked to the bar across the club, Ethan was no longer standing in the same spot. She paused and looked around, then saw him talking with Angel and two other men nearby. She made her way through the people milling around and looked up just as he was called to the front by Rogelio, one of the night club's bouncers. Ethan quickly excused himself from the group, and she admired his strong, muscular physique as she followed him to the front entry where the bouncers stationed themselves. She thought it odd that Angel followed closely on his heels.

She paused, wondering for a second if it would be okay to follow, in case he was dealing with one of the girls who had been banned from the club. The fewer witnesses to that the better, she supposed. She glanced over at Rogelio and noticed that his eyebrows were drawn together as if he were watching and listening to whatever was being said. She drew closer as Rogelio put his hands on his hips and shook his head in disgust. Then she heard Patricia's voice.

Grace stepped to the entryway and took in the scene. Eli Wolf stood near the door behind Patricia, looking down at her with a frown on his face. She could tell it was Patricia but only by the sound of her irritating voice. Ethan's body blocked Grace's view from where she stood.

"Patricia, you and your friends have been banned from the club. You know the reasons why. Please don't make a scene," Ethan said in a neutral tone.

Grace stepped toward Ethan and Angel, but Rogelio gently touched her arm and held her back.

"Ma'am, I wouldn't. Why don't you wait back here with me?" Rogelio spoke in a soft, polite voice.

Ethan heard Rogelio speak and turned to see who was behind him. He smiled at her and was about to speak when he was interrupted.

"Yes, Ethan, you have your reasons for not wanting me here. But I have my reasons for being here, anyway."

"Boss," Eli barked, "gun!"

Grace watched as Patricia leapt away from Eli and toward the wall by the door. Angel reached for the gun, and Patricia pointed it at him and shot him in the midsection. She turned and pointed the gun at Ethan, and before Eli could reach her, she fired another round. The mirror on the wall behind the bar shattered in a great crash and fell to the floor. All hell broke loose in the club. Patricia looked beyond Ethan at that moment and spotted Grace where she stood with Rogelio. Her heart froze in her chest as Patricia aimed the gun directly at her.

"No!" Ethan roared and jumped in front of her, blocking her view of Patricia's hate-filled eyes. A third shot rang out, and Ethan toppled back into her, knocking her to the ground with him. Grace's head hit the floor hard, and everything went black.

She returned to consciousness with the sound of someone screaming insanely nearby. The back of her head throbbed, and she felt slightly nauseated. It was hard to breathe, and she realized why a moment later when a great weight was lifted from her.

Ethan!

"Oh, no. Ethan! Angel!" Grace whimpered and reached clumsily for Ethan as she tried to sit up but her limbs wouldn't cooperate.

Strong hands lifted her gently to a sitting position. The disoriented feeling faded quickly and was replaced by panic. She looked up and realized it was Adam who had lifted her up. Beside her, Jack tore at Ethan's shirt as a bartender brought a stack of bar towels. He began wiping blood from Ethan's chest, trying to find the wound.

"Let me through. I'm an ER doctor. Let me through."

Never had she heard more welcome words. A man came and crouched beside Ethan and swiped at his chest, locating and applying pressure to the wound in Ethan's shoulder above his collarbone. The doctor looked up at her.

"Are you injured?"

"I'm all right. I just banged my head."

The doctor lifted Ethan's shoulder up, located another wound, and seemed relieved by that as he pressed another towel to that one. "Y'all hold these towels to the wounds. We need to stop his bleeding. I have to go see to the other victim. Ma'am, tell the paramedics you hit your head, so they can check you out, too." He tilted her head down. "You're gonna have a good-sized knot, but there's no bleeding. Ice it," he said rapidly and was gone.

They did as he instructed. She gathered Ethan's head into her lap, and they pressed the towels firmly to both wounds. She thought she could hear sirens in the distance, but it was hard to tell because Patricia was still screaming.

"It's all right, Grace, don't cry. I'll be okay," Ethan murmured softly to her, putting a bloodstained hand on hers. He reached up to wipe away her tears. Weakly, he grinned at her. "Sorry our evening got cut short."

"It's all right, Ethan. Please be still. I hear the sirens. I'll bet that's an ambulance."

She could still hear the scuffles and screams directly in front of the door in the foyer, which had gone on far too long.

"Ow! She bit me. Bitch, I told you to stop fighting, but you wouldn't listen." The screaming was cut off by a meaty thunk. Lights out.

She could see blue and red lights bouncing around on the walls of the entryway to the club, illuminating another person lying in the entry hall.

Grace looked at Jack, who had followed the doctor to help if he could. She caught his eye, and the look on his face was grim. Grace realized Charity and Justin were still there when Charity reached out and placed her hand over Grace's hand holding the towel. She didn't speak, just squeezed Grace's trembling hand.

Adam turned to Grace. "What happened, baby?" he asked in a shaking voice.

"Patricia," Grace replied softly.

Grace noticed the bouncers, Eli and Rogelio, stood over Patricia's prone form. Neither one of those guys looked like the type to willingly strike a woman. She'd sounded insane. The police arrived, and the bouncers pointed to the weapon she'd used lying on the floor, untouched.

The paramedics came in shortly after, and Adam helped Grace rise from her knees and back away as they took over treating Ethan while another team helped the ER doctor. Angel was lying still as Jack returned to her side. "She shot Angel in the abdomen. He's semi-conscious."

"Will he be all right?"

"Doc didn't say," Jack replied quietly. She went to him, and they wrapped their arms around each other. He looked as pale as she felt.

He wiped tears from her face. “Did you see what happened?”

“Patricia came in trying to get past Eli, I guess. Ethan tried to reason with her. She shot Angel and tried to shoot me. Ethan jumped in front of me. She was going to shoot me.”

Jack and Adam closed their arms tightly around her and held on to her that way for a minute.

While Grace waited with Jack, Adam, and the others, the police organized the club patrons. Those who hadn’t seen what happened were allowed to leave through the emergency exit. The front entry was now a crime scene. The police talked to all the witnesses, including Grace and the bouncers, and took their contact information.

Grace stayed near the foyer where Ethan and Angel were being attended to. The paramedics moved Angel onto a gurney to transport him to the hospital in nearby Morehead. Angel looked so pale, not at all like the flirtatious and dynamic man she knew. He caught sight of her as they raised the folding gurney to roll it out to the ambulance. He reached out to her, and she took his hand and squeezed it. He smiled then released her as they wheeled him out.

She turned to Ethan as he was eased onto a gurney, protesting that he could walk to the ambulance. He grimaced when he lay down but smiled weakly for her. He asked one of the paramedics to look at her head, telling him that she’d struck it on the floor in their fall. The paramedic examined Grace and recommended an ice pack and pain killer, but otherwise she checked out fine.

Patricia regained consciousness, spitting mad and acting crazy. Hank handcuffed her, put her in the police car, and took her to jail. There had been many corroborating witnesses and it did not look good for her. Watching her now, Grace would have agreed if her lawyer decided to enter a temporary insanity plea.

Jack got her an ice pack from the nightclub’s ice machine and helped her into the ambulance with Ethan. Angel was already in surgery by the time they got to the emergency room at the Morehead Medical Center. Ben, Quinten, Mike, Rogelio, and Eli arrived a while later and waited with everyone else. Ben and Quinten both needed a few stitches from minor lacerations they received when the mirror shattered.

Ethan's bullet wound went all the way through cleanly and had not nicked any arteries or struck bone. They would clean the wounds thoroughly before stitching them both closed and then he'd be admitted overnight for observation, just to be on the safe side.

Adam and Jack both chuckled when someone came through the swinging doors that led into the trauma rooms. They could hear him with whoever was cleaning his wound and sewing it up.

Grace frowned and looked at them. "Is that…Ethan I hear singing?" She didn't have it in her to laugh, but it registered as funny that he knew all the words to "Thank God I'm a Country Boy" by John Denver.

Jack chuckled softly, also seeming to feel at a loss for how to react. "Yes, darlin', they must have given him Demerol for the pain. This is how he reacts to it. Whatever comes into his mind goes right out his mouth. You'll see."

Adam handed her a fresh ice pack, and she frowned, wondering why the comical sound of Ethan singing didn't inspire her to at least smile.

Grace prayed for Angel as they waited for word on how his surgery went. His parents arrived and took up vigil with everybody else. Her men introduced her to his parents, Maria, Eleazar, Marco, and Ricardo, and they sat together and chatted until finally a nurse came and got his parents and ushered them down the hall to a private office. When they returned, they looked weak with relief.

Grace reached out to hold Maria's hands. "Is he all right?"

Maria nodded, tears flowing from her eyes. "Yes. The surgeon said they had much damage to repair, which explains why it took so long. There were many repairs to make. He is worried about infection but was very careful and thorough. Now we wait. She turned to her husband. "Eleazar," she said in her thick accent and then proceeded to rattle off several tearful phrases in Spanish, totally losing Grace. Eleazar nodded indulgently to Maria and held out his arms to her, and she went to him.

Jack smiled at them and said softly, "She's asking to be taken to Angel right now. She's telling him she wants him to 'fix it' so she can stay with her firstborn, Angel. She wants her baby. That's basically it."

Eleazar spoke with a nurse and then ushered Maria through the swinging doors that led into the hospital, followed by Marco and Ricardo. Maria turned at the last second and blew a kiss to Jack and Grace.

"Angel looks just like his father. Eleazar, right?"

"Yes. Eleazar is Angel and Joaquin's father."

"Joaquin?"

"Yeah, he's planning on coming to visit for a while soon. You'll like him. We're trying to talk him into staying on at the ranch to help with the breeding operation."

A smiling nurse walked up to her and said, "Grace Stuart?"

"Yes, ma'am?"

"Mr. Grant is asking for you. Would you like to come with me?"

Grace looked at Jack and Adam. "I'll see if they'll let y'all in, too."

"Take your time, darlin'. We'll be right out here," Jack said.

When the nurse opened the door, she heard loud singing coming from a cubicle at the end of the walkway. She also heard giggling or snickering from some of the private, curtained-off cubicles as she passed by.

"Walkin' through the front door, Seein' your black dress hit the floor..."

Grace felt her cheeks heat up as she recognized the words to the Chris Young song "Getting You Home".

"Honey, there sure ain't nothin' like you lovin' me all night loooooong...And all I can think about..."

If he wasn't high and recovering from a gunshot wound, she'd be inclined to say he sounded pretty good. She flung the curtain aside when the nurse gestured with a smirk to his cubicle, as if Grace couldn't tell which one he was in.

"Is gettin' you home."

"Me, too, cowboy," she said softly as she allowed the curtain to swing closed behind her.

"Gracie! Here's my honey pie, right now! Come just like an angel of mercy to nurse me back to health." He ogled her breasts and waggled his eyebrows. Then he adopted a pouty look and said, loudly, "Come here, Gracie, you look plum tuckered." He beckoned her with his good arm.

Hesitantly, she sat on the edge of his bed. He grinned at her, pulled her to him, and kissed her affectionately. Gingerly, she laid her arm over his chest and snuggled as close and tight as she could until she trembled. The tears came, and she quietly wept for a few minutes, wiped out with relief that he was not more seriously injured and that Angel would be okay.

One of the nurses sweetly brought Grace a set of hospital issue scrubs because her skirt and the knees of her stockings were covered in bloodstains. She laid them aside until Ethan had sobered up a bit more, so he didn't give their audience a blow by blow description of her stripping, or worse.

She cuddled back up with him and stayed that way while he talked on and on, asking questions and singing to her, softly this time. He really did have a beautiful singing voice when he wasn't singing obnoxiously at the top of his lungs.

An hour later, he began to sound like his normal self, so she took the opportunity to change in the cubicle after letting the nurse on duty know so no one else would come in while she was undressed.

"Maybe I should just throw this out." She eased the top up. "There's blood all over the whole outfit."

"Don't throw it out just yet," Ethan said. "I love that outfit. Hold off and see if it won't soak out. I was hoping to see it on you again sometime." As her nipples came into view, he growled. "*Yummy, yummy*."

Hmm, maybe he wasn't as sober as she thought. She tried for a disapproving look and shushed him.

She lifted her top over her head and laid it on the bed. Ethan broke into an appreciative smile at the sight of her breasts perched in the shelf bra. "I feel better already," he said softly, licking his lips.

"Yeah, I can see that," she said, noticing the stiff cock making its eager presence known under the hospital gown. She started to feel her sense of humor return as she smiled at his enthusiasm. She slipped the skirt down her hips, letting him watch her get undressed but not encouraging him. She was still afraid he'd start bleeding again. The side tie G-string would have to stay in place, for now. As she put the scrub top on, she was especially thankful it was a printed fabric. The print would hide the silhouette her body created in the bra, since she was not about to go braless. If it had been a solid color, everyone would have been able to see her nipples poking at the fabric.

"Just a taste?" he asked softly, trying to sweet-talk her.

"No, I'm sorry." She gestured with her thumb to the cubicle they were enclosed in. "That's a *sheet*, not a wall. It's just not private enough. If someone walked in, I would die of embarrassment. Plus, I don't want to take a chance of your wound bleeding again." She pulled the elastic-waist pants on over the G-string. She slumped in the chair, feeling an adrenaline crash coming on as she rested her head in her hands. "It's late, or early, or…whatever. You should be resting."

Ethan reached for her again with his good arm. "I'm sorry, sweetheart. Come here. My other brain was doing the thinking there for a minute. Come up on my good side and let me hold you some more. Are you feeling woozy?"

"Like a zombie." She carefully climbed up onto the side of the bed with him. He slid his good arm down her back to her buttocks as she settled against his side, perched on the bed. "For a second, I thought I'd lost you. Ethan, she meant to kill me, didn't she? She could have killed you." The memory of Patricia's enraged face filled her mind.

"I stopped her, though. We're all okay." He soothed her with his lips against her forehead. "Besides, it's going to be harder than that to get rid of me. I love you." He squeezed her ass.

She carefully placed her right arm across his abdomen and snuggled to him. "Thank you, Ethan. It sounds ridiculous and trite, but…you're my hero."

"No, I'm hardly red-cape material. I just couldn't bear the thought of her harming you. There were no other options."

"You're still my hero, honey. You're all my heroes, in fact. What time is it?"

"It's almost four o'clock. You should go home and get some sleep."

"I'm not going anywhere until you leave here. How do you feel? Are you in pain?"

"I've had better days, but the pain meds are helping a lot."

"Knock, knock, guys." It was Adam and Jack, who swept aside the curtain and came into the cubicle.

"I talked to Charity a few minutes ago and gave her an update," Jack said, "and I talked to Angel's parents. They were with him in the recovery unit. I saw Angel for a few minutes, too. He was conscious but groggy, already flirting with all the nurses and one of the doctors. That's encouraging, right?"

"He'll be back to himself in no time," Ethan said. "Honey, are you sure you don't want to have Jack or Adam take you home?"

"No." She yawned so hard her jaw popped.

"That's all right, darlin', we understand. We're reluctant to leave, too, but there's stuff that needs doin' back at the ranch. Ethan, if you know where your truck keys are, we'll swing by the club and check in, then pick up your truck and take it home for you."

Pointing to his jeans folded on a counter top, he said, "Should be in the pocket. Grace's evening bag is on my desk. Would you get it for her?"

Chapter Thirty-one

Jack and Adam brought breakfast and a change of clothes for her and Ethan when they returned. The morning progressed rapidly from there. Grace called in to work to let them know what happened and that she wouldn't be in. Ethan was released, but before they left the hospital, they stopped at Angel's room to check on him. His mother was fussing and cooing over him like he was a four-year-old on his death bed. His dads just rolled their eyes and smiled. Angel was her firstborn, so she was entitled.

Grace and her men headed home. On the way there, she called Teresa to let her know what happened. Teresa asked her if Grace thought she should go visit him while he was in the hospital, and Grace told her that she thought it was an excellent idea.

Once they got home, Jack and Adam convinced Ethan and Grace to go straight to bed. The fact that she was weaving on her feet made it fairly easy to convince her, especially when Ethan started in on her as well.

She changed into a nightgown and helped Ethan get comfortable, then curled up carefully next to him. Jack closed her bedroom door, and they fell asleep snuggled together and stayed that way for hours.

She awoke to a warm hand on her shoulder, stroking her gently awake. She opened her eyes and looked up at Jack. He gestured to Ethan, who was also stirring. "We went and got some smoked brisket and sausage from the market smokehouse."

"What time is it?" she asked blearily.

"Six o'clock. The food's all hot if y'all want something to eat."

"Okay. Be right there." She stretched and turned on her side to Ethan as he rubbed a hand over his eyes. "Hi. How do you feel?" She stroked a hand over his good shoulder.

"Groggy as hell."

"It's probably time for pain meds."

"Not the Demerol. We've got some Tylenol. I'll take that. The Demerol makes me loopy."

She grinned and snickered. "It also makes you sing."

Ethan got a far-off look in his eyes like he was trying to remember, then groaned loudly. "Oh crap, did I sing 'Thank God—'"

"'I'm a Country Boy'? Yeah, you did. Impressively, too. You know all the words to that one." She giggled.

He grinned at her and managed to be sexy, even all bandaged up and in pain. "Did I sing to you?"

"Oh, yes. It was sweet, too. I'll let you sing to me whenever you want." She went to him and kissed him, then climbed from the bed and put her robe on. "Hungry?"

"I could eat, I think." He sat up, and she helped him get his robe over his shoulder. He'd refused the sling the hospital offered him.

After helping him put his robe was on, she wrapped her arms around his waist and hugged him gently.

"I'm sorry our evening got ruined, Gracie."

"Up until it ended, it was wonderful. I'll take the good with the bad, honey. That's just life. Truthfully, I feel like celebrating because you're still here."

"I'm *feeling* in the mood to celebrate, too," he said, nuzzling her ear with his lips. His erection testified to his willingness.

"Ethan! You're recovering from a gunshot wound." She giggled as his right hand squeezed her derriere.

"I still have one good hand. I say we eat and see what *comes up*."

She breathed in the warm masculine scent that lingered on his robe and chuckled softly. "Oh, I think I already know. Come on." She took his right hand and pulled him from the room before he got her horizontal on the bed again.

The delicious smell of smoked brisket wafted through the air when they came down the hallway. Adam was setting the table while Jack cut up the sausage links and placed them on a big plate with the sliced brisket.

Jack looked up as they came into the kitchen. "It's not as good as yours, buddy, but it's close. Y'all hungry?"

They sat down at the table and ate while Jack and Adam filled them in on everything that was happening. Angel was expected to be out of commission for at least two weeks and then slowly get back up to full capacity again. Of course, that was provided there were no complications along the way.

"Of course, that means we'll be filling in for him while he's laid up." Jack turned to her. "Darlin', if you're still interested in learning about horses and the inner workings of the ranch, you might want to hang around with us on Wednesday, if you can get away from work for the day. Some friends of ours, Bill and Maureen Travers, from the Houston area are bringing out a couple of mares for stud service. I think you'd really like Maureen. The horses belong to her. She's brought mares out to us before, and her husband tells me she won't take her mares to any other studs to breed with when they're in heat."

"Does she have a particular liking for one of your stallions?"

"No, there are two or three that would do. We'll decide later which ones. They'll stay in town a few days since we may need to try a couple of times."

"It's okay for people to be milling around when they do that?"

"The horses don't care, and neither does anybody else. Horse breeding is a big part of what we do on the ranch. It'll take some getting used to, but it would be a good place for you to start learning."

"So why does she only want your stallions?" Grace had a feeling there were vague sexual undertones growing in this conversation. It was horse breeding, for crying out loud, but she felt a slight arousal at the topic of discussion.

"Horse breeding can be very dangerous for both horses. The mare can kick at the wrong time and turn a stallion to a gelding in a heartbeat if she's not ready or doesn't want to breed. Also, the stallion can be too rough on the mare. It can get ugly quick. Angel has trained our stallions from the time they were young to be gentlemen and wait for the command. This gives both horses time to be fully ready."

Her cheeks bloomed with heat, and her panties were now decidedly damp. "Whoa, I'm blushing here. Your stallions wait until the mares are ready? Does that mean what I think it means?"

Jack gave her a sexy, knowing grin and told her, "We can show you some videos so that you can have a comparison for Wednesday if you like.

You're blushing because you're not used to discussing the topic, or at the thought of being around when it happens?"

"Both." They had horse porn?

"Horse farms need to have videos of their stallions mating on their websites as proof they are viable studs. It's good advertising," Ethan explained. "And if their studs are well-behaved, that helps to raise the standards in the industry. In many parts of the country and the world, natural horse breeding is done in a very haphazard way, and horses have been harmed needlessly through injury or through poor hygiene."

"Poor hygiene?"

"Not controlling the mare's tail, not washing the mare beforehand."

"The mare gets a bath?"

"No," Ethan said as he returned to the table for the rest of the dirty dishes, "we or the owner, if they are responsible, use a mild soap and wash the mare's vulva and anus right beforehand because the mare's reproductive tract is very susceptible to infection."

Jack continued, "This is a large part of what Angel does on the ranch, and we would put it off until later, but the horses keep to their own fertility schedule, and later would not be convenient for Bill and Maureen. Maureen can probably also teach you a lot if you'd like to learn from an expert horsewoman. The three of us and Angel can teach you, but women sometimes have a different perspective, especially on issues like breeding. It only takes one really bad breeding experience to ruin a good broodmare, and Bill and Maureen and all of us are dedicated to raising the industry standard for natural breeding to a higher level."

"Are the videos rough?"

"Rough?"

"Awful? Violent? I've never seen anything like that in real life before."

"No, just negligent at times. We'll show you. There are several videos that are good representations of how horse breeding should be."

"Like that cremello stallion?" Adam interjected.

"Exactly," Ethan said enthusiastically. "That horsewoman maintains a very high, and unfortunately very rare, standard for gently breeding a mare. You should see that one. Are you all right, Grace? You're very flushed all of a sudden."

"I must be a very sick person."

Ethan laughed. "Why do you say that?"

"Should I be getting mildly aroused by all this talk about horses mating and watching videos of horses breeding?"

Jack caressed her shoulder reassuringly as he spoke. "Sex is sex, even among animals. I wouldn't be put off if you were turned on by it. We're pretty matter-of-fact about it because we've been around it all our lives, Grace. You're new to all of this, and I'd be surprised if you were unaffected by it. Plus, knowing your tendency toward visual stimulation, I can imagine how you feel. Let us show you tonight, then at least when the horses get together it won't be so shocking to you. Horses are big animals, and all their anatomy follows suit."

Grace gulped audibly.

"Honey," Ethan said, leaning toward her, "if you enjoy what you see on the videos and you want to fool around with us afterward, there is nothing abnormal about it. It'd be the same as having sex after watching porn."

"Only horse porn." She squeaked a little when she said it. *Ooooh*, if they only knew how much that conversation was turning her on. *Bad girl.*

Ethan wiped the table down quickly, and Adam brought Jack's laptop from the office. He pulled up videos on YouTube for her to watch, some of which were of poor quality, grainy, and not well done, with lots of noise in the background. But she began to get the gist of what Jack was trying to say.

Some of the videos showed handlers who did not control the horses as well as they could have. Some allowed the stallion to try to mount before it was truly ready, potentially injuring the mare in the repeated attempts before finally getting down to business, which only took a few seconds.

She felt sorry for some of the mares and wondered herself why the handlers didn't hold their tails for them or at least wrap them up. She could see how the bacteria on the hairs could cause infection if a tail hair got shoved up in there during penetration. Plus, tail hairs were usually very coarse. *Ouch.*

"Thank you so much for showing me these, guys, so I know what to expect *size wise*, I mean. Their…parts are huge. I would have shown what a greenhorn I am by being surprised at how big their cocks are."

"Now show her the video of the cremello stallion, if it's still up," Ethan said. "Angel has raised our three stallions using the same basic method as the horsewoman in this video. You'll see what we mean about the stallion being a gentleman in a minute. Here it is. You'll love this, Grace." Ethan stood behind her chair, his hand on her shoulder. She reached up to stroke his hand absently as the video began.

Well-behaved was an understatement. The stallion in question was a solid creamy off-white color. She noted that the video was several minutes long. She understood why as the video played on. This wasn't just straightforward horse sex. She watched in amazement as the stallion utilized skilled foreplay to tease the mare into a more receptive state.

She hit pause, blushing, and turned to Jack. "Is he sliding his tongue in her entrance?"

He just smiled and nodded. "Horse foreplay, you could call it."

"*Mercy*," she whispered.

She clicked play. She was really getting turned on, and now they all *knew* it. She could tell when she glanced at them.

"Watch, Grace, you'll miss it."

Grace's lips popped open, and she could not suppress a gasp. She hit pause again.

"She *came*, didn't she?" Merciful heavens, she felt like coming, too.

"Yes, she did," Jack replied, not even bothering to hide the desire burning in his eyes.

"He made her come first."

"That's what a worthy male would do," Ethan remarked, and Grace did not miss the lustful gleam in his eyes. Her pussy felt warm and wet when she shifted in her seat.

"Do you mind if I back it up and see that again? I wasn't expecting that!" She watched in unabashed curiosity as the video continued to the normal conclusion.

"That was amazing! I didn't know that horses would do that for each other. Very beautiful." Arousal hummed through her, and she wanted only one thing now.

"Yes," they all murmured, love and desire shining in their eyes as they gazed at her.

"Watching that has turned me on, can we go to bed please?"

Chapter Thirty-two

Grace went around the house and dimmed lights while her men took their showers. She lit the candles and turned off the lamps. After turning down the sheets, she slipped out of the robe and night gown and brushed out her hair. She noticed her evening bag sitting on the dresser and opened it to remove her wallet and other items to transfer them back to her purse. She found an envelope. She didn't have to wonder who it was from because it was labeled *Gracie*. Only Ethan called her that. She slipped the piece of paper out of the envelope and opened it. He must have slipped it in there at some point while they were in the office together with the door locked. That memory further stoked the fire in her pussy.

My Gracie,

You made me the happiest man in the world today when you said yes. I want you to know I'll devote myself to you. Do everything I can to make you happy. My memory of you asleep in my arms and in my bed fills my mind now. The thought of you, your belly swelling with my child, looking up at me with love in your eyes, brings tears to my eyes right now. There has never been a woman who could hold my heart captive the way you do. Even if I had all eternity to hold you close in my arms, I'd still want you more. You're my whole life now. I love you.

Your Ethan

His Gracie, her Ethan. It was no wonder she cried so much. They were constantly doing things like this that touched her heart.

She returned the note to its envelope and laid it on her dresser and climbed into bed. Her body was singing with arousal, her pussy wet and throbbing. Adam entered the bedroom first. He stopped at the foot of the bed and watched intently as she bent her knees slightly, placing her feet flat on the mattress and spreading her legs invitingly for him.

"Are you ready for me?" he asked in a soft, deep voice, palming the long, thick cock that stood straight out from his body.

"I'm burning for you," she answered, sliding her fingers down to her pussy lips. "Watching that video with you made me wet, wanting to feel your big cock sliding into me. Do you want me to suck it for you?" She loved watching Adam react to her words. He looked like he was about two seconds from jumping her.

"Yes, baby. I need you to use that hot little mouth on me."

She rose up on her hands and knees and met him at the end of the bed, parting her lips and taking his big cock in her mouth. He groaned as she began sucking and sliding on him. His hand was gentle as he helped her set the pace he needed.

Adam groaned and rubbed her arching back as she sucked him. He reached down to her wet slit and slipped one finger inside her. She moaned and clenched on his finger, riding it and wanting more. "Baby, I can't wait to slide into you. Mmm, you're so wet. You're dripping with honey, aren't you?" She murmured in agreement against his cock. "You want to feel me slide it in there, baby?" She murmured her agreement a little louder. "You want me to fill your pussy with my cum?" She was imagining the stallion for a second and was practically screaming her agreement against his cock when he pulled from her mouth.

"Turn around, baby. Let me fuck you like that stallion. You want it? I guarantee you I'll last longer."

Oh, she loved him so much! He was going to go with her on the stallion fantasy.

"Yes, Adam, but first I want your tongue on me." She turned and backed to the edge of the bed with his help.

"Oh, *hell* yeah, baby." He growled. "Are you gonna come for me like this, baby? I'll get that sweet spot humming just right, and I bet you'll give me your cream just the same way the mare did for her stallion." He got down on his knees behind her, parting her legs more, so he could reach all of her with his tongue. He tilted her hips up so her lips were parted and right on his face.

"Adam, I love it when you talk like that. It really gets me going. Let me feel your tongue, honey." She gasped when his tongue slid straight into her. Each time her body tightened more and more on his tongue, so she felt every delicious, hot inch of it. She was trembling and soaking wet when he removed his tongue and slid two fingers into her pussy, palm down, and stood behind her so she felt his cock against her ass.

"Are Jack and Ethan watching yet?" she asked desperately, wanting them to be here to see them like this.

She heard Jack's voice, soft and deep behind her. "Yes, darlin', we're both here. Do you like it that we're going to watch him make you come?"

"Yes, I do. I need you here, want you to see." She was almost incapable of speech as Adam found her sweet spot and began to strum her gently. The pressure built, and her muscles began tightening. There was nothing in the world like the sensation of that impending orgasm as he played her body, stroking that small spot that had the ability to make her see stars.

One hand held her gently in place, wrapped around her upper thigh, while he used the other hand to stroke her. This moment between the two of them—no, the four of them—was the fulfillment of pure lustful fantasy. But the tenderness and undeniable love in his touch let her know this was more than just fucking and getting off to Adam. Her body reacted to the combination with volcanic intensity.

She felt her entire body tighten exponentially and then explode. A raging white-hot inferno ripped through her body as she screamed rapturously and her cum gushed wetly from her pussy for him.

Breathlessly, Ethan said, "Damn, that was amazing. She came so hard!" One of them groaned deeply. "Gracie, we could see it stream from you, perfect and beautiful."

Urgently, she looked back at him, her whole body quivering. "Fill me, Adam, give it to me. I don't want to come down yet. Make me come again." She backed toward him as she felt him take hold of her hip and position his engorged cock at the opening to her pussy. She was wet and ready, and he slid every glorious inch of his cock into her.

He was still a tight squeeze and so very long inside her that it made her think of the stallion again, and, *oh*, but her pussy clenched at that thought.

"Mmm, baby, that was amazing. Your hot little pussy likes when I give you every long inch, doesn't it."

"Yes, baby."

He slid all the way out and then back in as he reached around to her sopping wet clit, swollen with need, and began rubbing it. Adam slid her clit back and forth between two fingers, and she begged him to fuck her harder.

He took shorter strokes and fucked her faster and harder. She spoke sweet, dirty words to him, thanking him. She was aware of murmuring behind her from the men but couldn't concentrate on their words. Her pussy ran slick with her juices, and he began to move even faster. Wetting his fingers in her juices, he stroked her clit some more. She began to wail, softly at first but gradually growing louder as the intensity of her orgasm built. It felt like a storm breaking inside her.

He maintained the same rhythm, not changing a thing because it was right where she wanted it. She rode his cock, bucking on his length as the wailing got louder. Her entire body suddenly ceased moving, her pussy clamped down on him, and she screamed. He thrust a couple more times, and with each pulse that rocked her body, she felt him filling every inch of her to the brim. She loved the glorious, full feeling Adam's cock gave her and the strength of his hands clenching her hips, holding her to him tightly so every inch of him was in her, not a bit left out.

He stayed there, rocking into her gently, breathing in deeply. When he finally slid his softening cock from her, Ethan and Jack came to help her move to the center of the bed and lie down on her back.

"Grace, you are indescribable." Ethan spread her hair gently over the pillow, then leaned down to her and kissed her forehead. "The unreserved way you love us and take us into yourself. Watching you come undone like that was…magical. There is not a bit of yourself that you don't give to us. Your body, your trust, your love, you give it all." He settled carefully on his right side.

"Because you do the same for me," she replied, her fingertips touching his cheek before drifting down his throat to his chest.

Adam climbed on the bed with them, claiming his spot at her abdomen. "Baby, did I hurt you? Was I too rough?"

She shook her head. "No, Adam. Even when you were thrusting hard at the end, I could tell you were holding back and trying to be gentle with me. Thank you. I'm going to get used to your length in time, and you won't have to worry about hurting me. I *loved* that position with you, with all of you."

She would take her men in whatever position they wanted to try, but there was something about rear entry sex with them. It made her feel like they were the ones in control and all she could do was submit to their desires.

Jack lay down at her other side and kissed her gently. "Would you tell us, darlin', if we asked if you were imagining the stallion was Adam and you were the mare?"

She blushed and nodded. Her men smiled at her, and she didn't think she imagined the low rumble that came from deep inside one of them.

"I love that visually you are very easily stimulated," Ethan murmured, smoothing his hand over her belly.

"I've always felt like an undercover freak, but I think that the image of a hardened penis inside a wet vagina, whether it's imagined or visible, still or in motion, is the most beautiful, most erotic and heavenly thing ever created. Even though they were animals, fundamentally, it's the same anatomical union. When that beautiful stallion slid that two-foot long cock into his female and she took all of it, I felt it in my pussy, like one of you were stroking into me." She had complete and utter trust that they understood her.

"That doesn't make you a freak, baby," Adam said. "It just shows us that you are very empathetic, you feel very easily. It's also why you're so compassionate. We'd never change those things about you. I don't think you could separate the two and still be Grace."

Grace grinned, turning to look at Ethan. "Talk about *feeling* easily, did you tell Jack and Adam what happened on the dance floor?" she asked Ethan.

"No, I didn't know if you minded if I share what happens between us when we're alone." He gave her a crooked grin. "Although, technically we *weren't* alone." He snickered as he rubbed his knuckles against the underside of her breast.

Adam and Jack groaned. "What were y'all up to on the dance floor, darlin'?" Jack asked.

"We were talking. And Ethan was whispering in my ear all the different ways he was imagining fucking me. I loved all your ideas, by the way."

"And?" Jack prompted.

Ethan chuckled. "Grace liked my ideas so much, the thought of it—and a little discreet touching and prompting from me—had her coming on the dance floor. It was so hot to watch and listen to her come and fight for control not to show it at the same time. She never once made a peep. Nobody even had a clue. Grace has amazing control. That spells for a lot of fun in the future, honey." He nuzzled and kissed her. She figured he must be imagining other places he wanted to try to bring her to orgasm. Her pussy pulsed once with enthusiasm at the notion.

"Amazing," Adam chuckled. "We were all watching y'all the whole time you were dancing, and we never would have guessed. I just thought y'all were kissing a lot."

"That explains why you were in the restroom afterward," Jack said.

"I needed to recover for a few minutes. Everyone would have thought something was wrong with me, and I didn't want the evening to end." She stopped herself from thinking about the fact that the evening *did* end right then. It was now past tense, and everyone was going to be okay. She was blessed.

"Y'all are free to talk about what happens between us when we're alone with each other, unless I specifically ask you not to. I can't imagine why I would need to do that, but I reserve the right, if you don't mind." She stroked Jack's hip, watching as his previously softening erection jumped to life.

"If that's what you want, you're entitled, Grace," Ethan murmured. "You have a deep, private relationship with each of us and are allowed to have moments that are completely private, things you don't want to share. That's not withholding." Grace watched in fascination as Ethan's cock hardened and twitched as he watched her stroking Jack's very thick cock with her fingertips. He maintained eye contact with her as he reached down and took hold of his hardening cock.

She blissfully sighed, and a wave of soft desire flamed through her whole body. "I really enjoy watching you do that, guys. Seeing your strong, tanned hands stroking your cocks, and especially when they get even bigger when you do it, really sets my body to humming. You, too, Adam! Wow! Can we try something?"

They stopped what they were doing. All eyes were on her, waiting for her instructions.

Jack said softly, "We told you we'd give it to you however you wanted it, darlin'. Command us."

The thought of commanding them in how they pleased her and in how they touched themselves was a heady sensation. Would they really let her? When she thought of what it would be like with all of them together, an image of what she wanted had come to her mind. Maybe they would let her try it now.

Ethan held up a hand. “Wait, Gracie, are you sure you’re up to more fooling around right now? We would all understand if you wanted to stop now. Last night must have been very traumatizing for you, and I’m not sure you’re up to another round. I know I encouraged you, stroking like that, but we don’t want to push you too hard.”

“I had that nice long nap with you, Ethan. And I feel like I’m mostly dealing okay with last night. I’d rather not have gone through it, of course, but I feel like celebrating that you’re still with us. Doing what I have in mind would certainly be celebrating.”

Ethan glanced at the others, then back at her and said, “Okay, Gracie. I can understand that. But go easy, okay. I’d like to see you get some more rest.”

She smiled and nodded. “I promise I’ll be very good. We’ll have plenty of time to rest later.”

She retrieved the lubricant from the nightstand drawer and gave it to Adam. “Adam, will you come up on the bed beside Ethan? Get your cock good and wet for me with the lubricant.” Adam did as she asked, and Grace straddled Ethan, right where he lay in the center of bed.

“Tell us what you want us to do, Gracie.” Ethan sounded breathless as her pussy brushed against his cock.

She gave him a crooked little grin and said, “You, my angel with a damaged wing, stay right where you are. You’re perfect. I’m going to suck your cock until you come.” She giggled softly when he growled in pleasure at her words. She held up a finger as she continued, “But you have to come before I do. Jack, honey, take some lubricant and stroke your cock until I give the signal, then I want you to enter me from behind and start thrusting. Remember Ethan has to come first, so please back off if you start to feel me losing control. Adam, I want you to stroke yourself until you’re ready to orgasm. I want you to bring yourself to orgasm, but come along with us, not before. You can come on me if you want to, on my breasts or my back or my ass, and rub it in, too, if you like. Afterward, we can take a shower together. How does that sound?" She looked at their smiling, amazed faces.

"Damn, Grace. You have no idea, do you," Ethan said, new admiration in his eyes. He looked up at her, his hands sliding gently from her hips, down her thighs, and then back again, sending a trail of goose bumps tracing over her abdomen and her breasts.

She softly shuddered and grinned back at him, reveling in the awe in his eyes, anticipation filling her for him to tell her what put it there. "What? Do you like my plan?" she asked, trailing a fingertip down his ridged abdomen, making him shudder and gulp hard. A drop of semen seeped from his cock at her touch.

She gently swiped his seed from his cock and then licked her finger. She hummed in pleasure at his taste, and he gulped as she slowly shifted down his thighs. Jack moved into position behind her, placing a warm hand on her backside so she would know he was there.

"*You* are so fucking hot right now I think I may explode the minute your lips touch me." Grace silently beamed at Ethan before lowering her lips to his cock. She nuzzled his length with her lips, torturing him sweetly the same way they all did to her. They elevated nuzzling to an art form, finding and tormenting all her sensitive spots. It was empowering listening to Ethan groan and shake as she brushed her lips over his shaft, feathering up and down his length, then licking her lips and running them in smooth strokes along the underside of his distended cock. When she neared the head, his cock twitched and bobbed with anticipation, begging for her to take him into her mouth. She softly licked and retreated, denying him momentarily.

"Gracie, I'm begging." He moaned aloud as she wrapped her hand around his twitching erection, noticing another drop of semen gather on the head.

His words energized her in unexpected ways, and she wanted to do her best to make the scene work out the way she planned it. She arched her hips and looked back at Jack, smiling and nodding, offering herself to him. Jack glided to the hilt in one smooth stroke, crying out, and she suddenly wasn't so sure it would take long at all to come. She panted as her pussy stretched to take his very thick cock. When he slid home, she knew she was going to be well and truly fucked.

She parted her lips and licked the head of Ethan's cock. Ethan cried out and went tense all over as her lips parted and she slid down over his cock. She glanced up and could see the immense tension in his face, as well as the euphoric rapture. Talk about power. She felt filled with it to be able to make him feel *that* good. The scene was going to be his dream come true if she had anything to do with it.

She took him to the back of her throat, then backed off and wrapped her hand around the base and stroked him. She glanced over at Adam as she sucked and caught his eye. He used the lubricant to stroke his erection, kneeling beside her on the bed. His hand slid up and down that long hard shaft, groaning and watching her with adoration in his eyes, waiting for the moment she specified. Jack slowly began pumping into her from behind, stoking the fire that was raging in her cunt, and she loved every tightly squeezed inch of him moving inside of her. He tilted her hips a bit more and rubbed the secret spot inside her, his head strumming back and forth over it in a rhythm that was guaranteed to please her.

Grace increased the suction on Ethan's cock as she continued stroking it in time with her suckling, loving the masculine, ecstatic sounds he made. She knew he was close. Some instinct made her release him with a pop.

"Not yet, Ethan," she commanded, grinning deviously when his eyes opened, wide as saucers.

Ethan moaned and gulped in huge breaths, trying to do as she asked, and a soft growl rumbled in his chest. She had a stray thought that she might pay for her domination of Ethan's release later. The thought made her giggle. *Bring it on, bad boy.* Jack increased his tempo, bringing her closer to her orgasm.

Jack chuckled deeply as he thrust with renewed purpose, probably trying to push her into releasing Ethan from the edict. "Damn, I *fucking love* this woman. Naughty and angelic all rolled up into one."

Adam growled, "Yeah, looks like Ethan's getting a taste of heaven *and* hell. I'm holding it for you, baby. Say the word." He added in a deep, gravelly voice.

Grace began to feel her muscles tightening involuntarily, signaling her impending release. Jack found her sweet spot, which brought her perilously close to the edge. She was there. She released Ethan from her suction for a second. "Come for me, Ethan," she gently commanded in a soft but steely voice before immediately sucking him back in and swirling her tongue.

He came with a loud roar. "Oh! Fuck! Yes!" He released into her mouth and cried out again as she swallowed his cum, murmuring her approval even as her own orgasm swelled.

Jack squeezed her hips, thrusting harder. "Darlin', I can feel you're about to come. Please let it go, Grace. Let us come!"

She released Ethan's cock, finally crying out as the orgasm blindsided her with its intensity, screaming, "Come! Yes, come! Oh, Jack! Yes, come for me, Adam."

She felt Jack's release jet into her hot slick cunt. Adam came as well, shooting his cum in streams across her back and her ass. Then she felt his warm hands smooth his seed over her skin, rubbing it in, marking her as his. Jack gripped her hips tightly, groaning as his release continued to stream into her. She was shocked by the length and intensity of his orgasm as she took everything he had. She kissed Ethan's cock, then rested her cheek on his abdomen. Smiling, she turned to Adam, who had laid down right next to her, and bent down and licked his cock clean as well, smiling at his awed expression as she did so. Adam tasted different than Ethan, but wonderful nonetheless.

"That was perfect. Exactly what I wanted. You did it perfectly, guys," she murmured, sighing as Jack slipped his cock from her pussy. She sat up and looked down into Ethan's sleepy blue eyes.

Ethan's face was a picture of perfect bliss as he said, "I think I can speak for the three of us when I say our future wife is perfect. We're your willing, adoring love slaves." His words sent what could only be described as a post-orgasmic wave through her body as she slumped over on her side with a groan and softly sighed. Seeing their concerned faces, she met their gazes from her slumped position on the bed.

"That's the first time any of you has referred to me as your wife. It sounds so right, so wonderful. I'm overflowing and running over with your love. I may burst. Baby," she murmured as she stroked Adam's thigh, "will you lay aside the comforter and untuck the blanket and top sheet? I want all three of you under the covers with me."

She curled on her side as Ethan and Jack smiled, getting into bed with her, lying beside her, while Adam did as she asked. She pulled the sheet back for him so he could take the position in the bed that he'd had two nights before, with his head on her abdomen, her thigh resting against his ribs. She grinned in the dark, having a pretty good idea of how she was going to be awakened in the morning.

* * * *

Early Wednesday morning, Jack stirred when he heard Ethan sit up. It was still early, and he wanted Grace to sleep in a bit. Jack was an early riser, and so was Ethan. Adam, not so much. Grace slept on peacefully, unaware they were awake. Adam stirred briefly, and Jack handed him a pillow because Grace had turned during the night onto her hip, effectively removing his. Jack grinned as Adam moved up higher in the bed and cuddled Grace to him and buried his nose in her hair then drifted back off to sleep as Jack and Ethan left the room.

It was 5:30 a.m., and they had three hours before Bill and Maureen Travers would arrive with her mares. Time enough to see to chores and make breakfast. Adam would wake Grace in a little while. She'd been able to take the day off from Harper's and was enthusiastic about being invited to observe the day's work. She still blushed when she talked about watching the breeding but seemed to have gotten more comfortable with the subject. Ethan gingerly stretched his arm and shoulder as he readied the coffeemaker while Jack removed eggs from the refrigerator. Ethan was still sore but feeling better every day.

After checking in at the barns, Jack gathered the renovation plans and the specifications for the bed. He got online and ordered the special mattress and the canopy drape Grace liked. He e-mailed Katie Grasso, the interior designer Jack preferred for business, to help Grace find the materials and colors she wanted to use. While he made arrangements for a crew to begin work upstairs, Ethan added to the order Jack and Adam had begun the previous evening after Grace went to bed.

Adam had shown Jack the website June had recommended, Hips and Curves, which Ethan had a feeling was going to get a lot of repeat business from them if the quality of the first order was good enough. Jack and Adam had picked several things they thought Grace might like.

Jack had considered ordering her a red satin corset but thought better of it. The lingerie was supposed to be for her enjoyment as well as theirs, and he didn't want for her to think she'd have to get laced into something, nipped and tucked, so to speak, in order to please them. When they showed her the website later, she could look at the corsets for herself and see if she'd like to try one out.

Ethan browsed around the website, checked the shopping cart to see what Adam and Jack had ordered, and then made his selections.

Jack was beating eggs for breakfast and had bacon going in the skillet when they heard a long, moaning cry from her bedroom, a sound they were blessed to be well acquainted with.

Chapter Thirty-three

Ethan and Jack grinned at each other. Jack groaned a little as his cock hardened, envisioning what they must be doing in there.

"Gracie's up," Ethan said, before groaning a little himself.

"We need to go easy on her for a few days. She's going to wear herself out trying to please us all equally." Even as he said it, Jack tried unsuccessfully to imagine himself turning her down.

"I agree," Ethan replied.

As Jack finished putting the food on the breakfast bar, Adam joined them, dressed in his bathrobe, looking pleased with himself. He went to change clothes while they waited on their bride-to-be. Grace came out a few minutes later, dressed in her jeans, boots, and another brightly colored top made of that slinky knit fabric that looked so good on her. It had a round neck, and Jack could see just a hint of cleavage that still blushed pink from her earlier climax.

She went to Ethan as he closed his laptop and laid it aside, reaching for her. Jack watched as Grace went to Ethan and kissed him. He'd never be able to explain why contentment and not jealousy flared in his heart at the sight. They'd lived as bachelors in this house for a few years, just the three of them, and it sure was nice to have a woman's presence to warm it, and them. Ethan whispered softly to her, then kissed the upper swell of her luscious breasts above the neckline of her top before he released her to come to Jack.

"How are you feelin' this morning, darlin'?" Jack asked as he served her a plate. She took it from him and slid the plate onto the counter as he drew her in for a kiss. He wrapped his arms around her waist and held her to him. Her kiss tasted of peppermint, and her lips were soft and sweet. Her breasts were even softer, pressed against his chest.

"I feel wonderful, thank you." She gave him one more quick peck.

"You sure do, darlin'," he agreed and then slid his hands up and down her ribcage, circling her waist. She giggled and took her plate and sat down after he released her. He got the grape jelly from the refrigerator and put it in front of her on the bar, along with the soft butter. Adam returned and poured them each a glass of orange juice, and they made quick work of their breakfast.

"Bill and Maureen will be here within the next half hour or so," Jack said. "How about we take you back to the barn and acquaint you with Languir and Esperer since it's them you will be observing later?"

"What do their names mean?" she asked as they cleared the dishes from the breakfast bar and rinsed the skillets.

"Yearning and Hope."

"What romantic names for two stallions," Grace said as she brought her plate to the sink. "This is going to be a very…interesting morning. I hope I don't make an idiot of myself showing my inexperience."

"You are going to do great, baby," Adam said. "And since stallions can be unpredictable, one of us will be with you at all times. You won't always feel nervous about stuff like this. It's just fear of the unknown." He put their plates in the sink and rinsed them before placing them in the dishwasher. "Maureen is really looking forward to meeting you."

"How much are you going to tell her?" she asked.

"She already knows about us." Adam replied, then hastily added, "I hope that's okay with you?"

"It's fine. But it would be good for me to know who *doesn't* know and more importantly *wouldn't* understand."

"The best thing to do is assume anyone you meet doesn't know about our relationship," Jack suggested. "If you were to encounter someone who knew about us, like at the grocery store, they would not expect you to talk about it. The people who have known us a long time, and knew this kind of relationship is what we wanted, knew that we were just waiting for the perfect woman to come along."

"Don't you mean the right woman?" she asked as they went out the back door onto the porch.

"No," Jack said as he closed the back door, "we were waiting for the perfect woman because three men needed to fall madly in love with her in order for it to work. With you, it really is perfect, darlin'."

"And what about when I disappoint you, or God forbid, hurt you or don't live up to your expectations? I can't be your perfect woman. That's too high a standard to expect me to live up to."

"We don't mean perfect, as in flawless. We mean perfect as in just right for us. Just what we need." Jack nuzzled her neck.

"Oh, I see! Well, back at ya, baby!" She giggled as she gave him a bump with her shapely hip. "So Maureen knows that I am engaged to all three of you?"

He nodded, "Yeah, she's known our families forever. When we bought the ranch, she developed a professional relationship with us, bringing her mares for stud service. She's known us since we were little boys. It was Mom that told her about what we were hoping for."

* * * *

Grace felt like Jack's words were a confirmation of Rose Marie's approval. "Seize the day, baby!" Maybe that was what Rose Marie had meant in those last few months. Grace had always thought Rose Marie was speaking of life in general. Maybe she'd been trying to maneuver Grace in their direction all along. "Did your mom encourage you to take more than a friendly interest in me, Jack?"

He grinned at her while the other two sort of snickered. "Daily. She adored you. Thought we'd be great together, and she was right."

Finding him irresistible, she drew him to her by hooking her fingers in his belt. His big strong arms wrapped around her felt delicious, and the hard muscles in his back were solid as an oak.

"When Rose Marie and I would talk, she used to tell me something all the time. After that interesting encounter you and I had at the dressing rooms, and again when I first met Ethan and Adam, and many times since, the words she used to say would pop into my mind. It felt like I was being encouraged by her to take a chance because there might be something that would last between us. Something worth taking a chance on."

"I'll bet I can guess, but what did she tell you, darlin'?" Jack had a big sappy smile on his handsome face. He leaned against one of the thick posts that supported the back porch, and the sun shone on his black hair as he ran a hand through it before he put his straw cowboy hat on.

"'Seize the day, baby!'"

Her men smiled at each other and then at her, gathering her into a group hug. "If that's not confirmation, I don't know what is," Jack said, bowing his head. "Miss ya, Mama." His voice sounded shaky. Grace wrapped her arm around his waist as she went down the steps with him, allowing him to tuck her to his side. He turned to her and kissed her temple softly. "I'm glad you told me that, darlin', so glad to hear it."

"I love you, Jack."

"You're my heart, darlin'."

Chapter Thirty-four

"Remember," Jack said, "stay near one of us when we have the stallions out of their stalls and when you're near the fence. They can be unpredictable sometimes, especially when there are mares in heat around them. We don't want to take any chances with your safety."

"I will," Grace said. "I promise. Thank you for protecting me."

After peeking in at the foals, her men walked her down the row of stalls, and she got her first look at the two Andalusian stallions. They were large animals and truly majestic, their dappled gray coats a contrast to their dark manes. They looked almost identical.

"Twins?" she asked softly, looking back and forth between the two.

"Same sire, different dams…mothers," Jack explained.

"And they sired the two new foals?" she asked, wondering about the difference in coloration.

"As the foals get older, they'll lose that dark coat and gradually become dapple gray like the ones that created them."

Languir was removed from his pen and taken to the empty corral. Several of the ranch hands had shown up to help where needed after they finished the multitude of chores that needed to be done. Everyone pitched in, covering for Angel while he was laid up. His parents must have already left for the hospital because their truck was not parked in front of the foreman's house. Grace turned to look back through the barn at the sound of a pickup truck and horse trailer coming down the driveway.

"Is that Bill and Maureen?" Grace asked as Jack turned to look as well.

"Yeah, that's them. You okay?"

"So far, so good," she said with a smile, wiping her hair from her forehead as the wind kicked up a bit.

"Come with me. I'll get you a hat. It'll help keep your hair back and protect your pretty face from getting sunburned. We're going to have to make a trip to Cheaver's for a properly sized hat for you sometime soon." Jack walked her back into the barn as Adam and Ethan followed. He went into the office to get her the hat he'd left in there the day they'd brought her saddle home.

"By the way, this is your saddle if you want to go riding with us." He placed his work-roughened hand on the brown, tooled-leather saddle. She approached it as he looked for the hat, mindful of the company that had arrived. He found it, brushed it off quickly, and put it on her after she brushed her hair away from her face.

Jack took a step back to admire her. "Perfect. For now anyway. Don't worry, it's mine."

"That's okay. I have it on good authority that my cooties like your cooties. It's loose, but not very much. Thanks, honey," she said, kissing him. "And the saddle is beautiful. I'd love to go riding. Just break me in gently." She gave them a cheeky grin as her men groaned and rolled their eyes.

"We should have seen that one *coming*!" Adam smirked as they laughed.

Jack took her hand. "Let's introduce Grace to Maureen and Bill. They're probably wondering where we disappeared to. Come on, darlin'."

Bill and Maureen had pulled the pickup truck and trailer alongside the first barn. Grace was grateful to have the hat now that the wind was really kicking up. They walked around to the two occupants of the truck as they climbed out. They made small talk for a moment about the trip over as Grace smiled and observed. Maureen was in her mid- to late-forties and very shapely. She had on a cowboy hat also, and Grace noticed twinkling brown eyes under the brim, looking her over as well. Maureen was a very pretty woman and seemed to exude contentment. It was in her manner, the way she held herself so confidently, and the way she spoke with the men. Straightforward but soft spoken, she had a sweet laugh.

Jack squeezed Grace's hand and said to the couple, "Maureen, Bill, I'd like you to meet Grace Stuart, soon to be Warner. Grace, meet Maureen and Bill Travers, from Conroe."

From the barn and the corral, they suddenly heard loud neighing. Deep, throaty, he-man neighing, Grace supposed. The others didn't seem to pay much attention.

Bill reached out and shook her hand, and Maureen said, “Grace, I have heard such nice things about you. It is a pleasure to finally get to meet you. I would have met you at Rose Marie’s funeral, but we were cross country hauling some horses to a buyer and we couldn’t get back in time. I watched these boys grow up from little kids, and I’m so glad they’ve found the love they hoped for. Did they tell you I used to babysit them when I was a teenager? Let me tell you, those were some hard-earned dollars.”

“Oh, you loved watchin’ us, Moe, and you know it!” Ethan laughed. “We were angels, Grace, don’t let her fool you,” he said to Grace, putting a hand on her hip.

“I imagine you were, honey, but I’m well acquainted with your dusty little halos, too.” That drew a loud cackle from Maureen. “But I will agree you are all definitely angels. Mmm-hmm.”

Maureen chortled and said, “You’re right, Jack. She *is* perfect! Sweetheart, we’re gonna be *good* friends!”

Maureen drew Grace around to the trailer to show her the Andalusian mares she’d brought with her. They were pretty things with sweet eyes and dapple gray coats, just like Languir and Esperer, only slightly smaller.

“Maureen, they’re so pretty,” Grace said admiringly. “I’m really glad I could get off of work to meet y’all today. I have no experience with horses at all, but I want to learn. The guys thought that this would be a good opportunity for me to start.” Grace patted one of the horses.

“We have to head back to town to see family after we’re done here this morning, but we’ll be here again for the Fourth of July. I’ll give you my e-mail and website address, and if you’d like, I can steer you toward some good resources. Listen to the guys because they have a lifetime of experience with horses, and you and I can talk about *whatever* you want to talk about. So things are all right with you and those cowboys?” Maureen giggled when Grace couldn’t help the big smile that spread across her face. “I’ll take that smile as a resounding *yes*.”

More neighing erupted, alternating from the barn and the corral. The stallions were evidently ready to get the show on the road.

“Better than I could have ever dreamed, Maureen.”

Maureen’s gaze shifted for a moment beyond Grace, and she murmured, “They’re looking over here wanting to know what we’re talking about so animatedly. Let me tell you about my mares. Did Jack tell you anything about horse breeding?"

"The guys told me a little and showed me some videos last weekend, but I've never been around horses when they breed."

"Well, the horse porn will help with understanding the mechanics, but it's going to be a little different from most of those. It won't be as rough, easier for the mares. Angel has worked magic with their stallions, and I've gotten to where I won't take my horses to anyone else for stud service. For one of the mares, Peaches, this will be her third time breeding, if we're successful. The other one, Coco, is being bred for the first time. I think we're going to let Peaches go first with Languir. Since you're new to this that would probably be best."

Grace thought she was doing okay so far with all the breeding talk until Maureen told her Coco had never been bred before. She felt oddly dismayed for Coco, sympathetic. Maureen was obviously a very caring owner and had the best interests of her animals uppermost in her mind.

"Grace, you okay?"

"Coco's never been bred before? This is her first time?" Grace felt a blush spread across her cheeks and hoped Maureen would attribute it to the heat.

"It'll be fine, honey, you'll see," Maureen said as she patted Grace's shoulder. "Esperer is wonderful. She'll be fine."

Bill came around, and they unloaded both horses. Coco was led into a separate holding pen outside the barn in the shade while Maureen led Peaches around to the front of the truck, Grace walking with her. Peaches was a lovely, well cared for animal, her coat clean and glistening.

"I already washed them and wrapped their tails at Dad's, Jack. Come look, Grace." Maureen demonstrated as they strapped the hobbles on.

Cushioned hock straps were buckled around each back leg, with a rope assembly attached to a strap that was fitted around the base of the mare's neck and connected between her front legs. She would have no difficulty walking in the simple but effective assembly, but would be unable to kick the stallion while he was behind her.

When Maureen and Jack were done, Maureen said, "Jack wouldn't appreciate it if my mare turned one of his stallions into a gelding with one well-placed kick." She patted Peaches and checked one of the buckles on a hock strap. "It's very effective, but it won't keep her from moving comfortably."

Maureen showed her how they wrapped the tail and indicated the area that had been carefully cleaned at Maureen's parents' ranch just a mile and a half away.

"She's already had her vaginal exam. The test results are here," Maureen said, handing Jack an envelope.

He looked the papers over carefully before returning them to the envelope and handing it back to Maureen. "Well, let's give them a chance to get acquainted. Grace, darlin', it goes pretty quickly from this point forward. Do you have any questions?" Jack asked quietly, and thankfully didn't make a spectacle of her lack of knowledge. Grace's heart was touched by Jack's show of respect.

She turned to Jack and softly asked, as she looked directly into his eyes, "Coco will be all right?"

Jack smiled tenderly at her. "Yes, the doctor's exam notes an insignificant hymen. The vaginal tissue of a horse is extremely elastic in order to accommodate a foal. She'll be just fine, Grace, you'll see. Anything else?"

Grace shook her head.

Jack nodded at Adam, who came and took Grace's hand while Maureen led Peaches near the corral. Jack and Ethan entered the pen and untied Languir's lead rope, leading him away from the entrance to the corral as the very loud neighing continued. It was a very earthy, aggressive sound. He stamped his hooves, but he went willingly with Jack and Ethan. The area around the pen was quiet except for his loud neighing and whinnying from Peaches. Maureen entered the corral with Bill and the mare.

Adam led Grace to a spot at the fence that was a safe distance away but where she would still be able to observe. Languir didn't try to break free from Jack and Ethan, but it was evident that he knew the mare was ready to be bred because his previously flaccid penis was quickly becoming erect and lengthening. Grace blessed Jack for letting her watch the videos the other night because this sight would have been more than she could handle otherwise. She resigned herself to the fact that her cheeks were going to be bright pink the rest of the morning. *It has to be all of two feet long, seriously!*

Grace thought she was handling things fine so far, but the sight brought to her mind the memory of Adam fulfilling her fantasy last night. Adam helped her climb onto the fence but kept his arms around her as he stood beside her. If the stallion got out of hand, he could quickly remove her from harm's way. She felt safe in the circle of his arms and she slid her hand over his. He'd placed her at the edge of the group, a slight distance away, and positioned himself so he blocked her from view with his tall body, but in a way that was not obvious.

Peaches' lead rope was loosely tied to the fence post. Jack and Ethan led Languir around the corral to Peaches. Esperer continued neighing, but Languir seemed intent on approaching Peaches with caution. He sniffed at her muzzle, and she whipped her head away from him, making a high-pitched noise like she wasn't the least bit interested in Languir.

Languir sniffed her, continuing with the soft nickering, while Jack and Ethan held his lead. He no longer made any aggressive noises. His body tensed as he approached her, continuing to sniff and make soft noises to her. Overtures. Conciliatory sounds. He slid his muzzle along her mane, nipping here and there. She whinnied shrilly again, whipping it away from him. Bill and Maureen stood aside, observing as he slid his muzzle down her mane again and over her back, nickering softly.

Softly, Adam said into her ear, "He's been trained to not lead with his cock. He will continue to do this for her, waiting for the command to mount her from Jack or Ethan. Doing okay, baby?" he asked softly, concern in his voice.

She turned and looked into his green eyes, nodded, and smiled. "Yes, I'm glad you wanted me to be around for this. It's beautiful," she said as Languir continued his soft sounds. She continued observing him, seeing that he was now sniffing and nuzzling at her mammaries as she made soft sounds of her own, responding to his gentle attention and no longer turning from him. Her body language had changed and no longer seemed to reject him.

Jack allowed slack on the line, and Languir accepted the signal to move around to the mare's hindquarters, attending still to her mammaries. After a minute, his muzzle slid up her flank, and the side of his head rubbed across it several times before moving to the other, stopping and nuzzling at her hips above her tail as well. She whinnied softly, sounding needy, and raised her tail. She was readying for the stallion. He lifted his nose to sniff her hindquarters and then moved to her vulva, rubbing his muzzle there, licking her.

He raised his head and neighed loudly. Grace noticed his previously hardening penis was now completely ramrod stiff, well up to the task, and had lengthened further as he sniffed and nuzzled her vulva, neighing loudly again. In taking time to serve her first, he was becoming well prepared to perform his service.

He licked her vulva, moving down her elongated slit to her clitoris, and Grace's heart pounded when she noticed the mare's breathing changed, and she made soft noises. Maureen made a soft comment to Bill, who nodded sagely. Jack looked at Ethan then over at Grace, checking on her. She smiled tenderly at him over the stallion's back as he continued ministering to the mare, licking and sniffing the mare's vulva, his tongue sliding down to her clitoris and licking there more.

How did they train a horse to take the time to do this when his driving need was to mount her? Amazing. Up close, Grace noticed the slight flexing of the mare's hindquarters as he licked and a sudden increased tension in the muscles of her flanks. Languir backed away when the mare gave a low guttural whinny and threw her head back fleetingly. Two streams of milky fluid ran from her vulva as she breathed out sharply and began backing toward the stallion. Her stance became wider, her tail pulling aside.

The signal came from Jack, and in a sudden, powerful concert of motion, Languir reared up proudly behind Peaches. His long, stiff, engorged penis pointed straight toward its destination. No fumbling around or trying to flop it into position, he just moved in behind her, the head of his penis sliding up her vulva and straight home. His huge body was an incredible sight to watch as he thrust all the way in, and she stood completely still for him. His front legs rested over her flanks, thrusting into her hard for a few seconds before becoming very still.

Like the stallion in the video, the only visible sign that he was ejaculating was the flexing up and down of his flowing, dark tail. He stayed inside her that way, snorting and breathing hard, for several seconds before pulling out. Semen seeped slightly from her vagina, trickling over her vulva, and a little flowed from his quickly softening penis. She glanced up to notice Ethan watching her intently. She blew him a kiss and placed her hand over her heart, which was pounding. He nodded at her, a small playful smile on his lips.

Adam squeezed her waist and turned to her. His face was shaded from the sun by his hat as he looked down at her. "What did you think?" He gazed into her eyes.

For a moment, she was dazzled by his light green eyes, reveling in the sweet love mirrored there. "I think he reminds me of another strong stallion I know," she murmured, blushing hotly for him. His eyes slid closed and he groaned softly.

"Baby, we still have one to go, and you've got me hard as a steel pole saying sweet things like that. You doing okay?" He nuzzled her neck.

She turned to his ear and whispered very softly as Maureen and Bill moved nearer, leading Peaches so she was nose to nose with Languir. "Tense, wet, and very, very ready, baby. I wouldn't miss this for the world. But when we're done, I'm going to need to be alone with you, Adam. Your arms around me feel so good, so strong. I love you." She held her hat on her head as she kissed him, her lips quivering a bit, sighing softly as he deepened the kiss before releasing her lips.

"I love you, too, baby. Oh, look. They'll load Peaches up in the trailer and give her some feed, then bring Coco out. Can you hear all the noise Esperer is making? He can sense a mare in heat, and that's why he's making all that racket. He'll change his tune when he enters the corral. Of the two stallions, Languir is the more aggressive, which is why we paired him with Peaches, who has been bred before. Coco may be more nervous, but Esperer is the lover of the pair." At the dubious look she gave him, he grinned broadly.

"Esperer is the *lover* of the two? What was that?" she gestured to the two horses in the corral enjoying a little post-coital nose-rubbing. "I gather a gentle stallion like Languir is very rare, but you say he is the *aggressive* of the two stallions? Oh, this is going to be *good*."

He gulped.

"When will you know if she's pregnant?" Grace tried to distract him, realizing the effect her words had on him. She fought the urge to rub against the erection pressed against her hip, which would be cruel. Later, she'd rub all she wanted.

"Within two days. If she's pregnant, her hormone levels will change, and her body will begin preparing to carry a foal. Her cervix is open during estrus to receive his sperm, but if this mating takes, it will close up tight, and an embryo will implant in her uterus. If she didn't get pregnant today, we can try again on Friday, if she's still in estrus. That's why Maureen and Bill are staying in town for a couple more days. Sometimes it takes more than one try. If you'd like, and our schedules allow it, maybe we can go out to visit Moe and Bill when it's time for the mares to foal. Would you like that?"

She turned to him enthusiastically and said, "That would be perfect! I'd love to." Then she looped an arm around his broad shoulders and squeezed. "By then I'll be your wife," she said softly as she stroked his back. "Maybe I'll be pregnant with your baby, too."

She watched as a faraway, yearning look came into his eyes. A soft, dreamy smile stole over his sensual lips. He swallowed hard and grinned slightly, but she saw the slight tremble in his lips.

"You're imagining it, aren't you? Me with your baby?" Her chin trembled a bit as well at the emotion in his eyes.

He nodded, hanging his head for a second. He cleared his throat and swallowed. He gazed adoringly at her. "Yes, a little baby girl, beautiful like her mama." His voice cracked a bit on the last word. "I'd be so proud." He seemed unable to say more and looked over as Maureen and Bill led Coco to the same shady spot in the corral that Peaches had been brought to earlier.

"I think you would make an amazing daddy. Will she have you wrapped completely around her little fingers?"

"I'll spoil her just as thoroughly as I plan to cosset her mama, but only in the best ways. She'll have her mama's sweet nature."

"And her daddy's tender heart." She placed her hand over his chest and felt the heart that pounded there.

Esperer's turn in the corral came as he was brought in on his lead rope by Jack and Ethan. "You'll see the difference between the two stallions in just a minute, baby. Esperer is a little older and farther along in his training. See?" They removed his lead rope and guided him with their hands. "I'll be quiet so you can watch." He slid his hands to her hips and steadied her on the fence as Esperer slowly approached Coco, who seemed nervous. Grace felt nervous for her, too.

Esperer seemed just slightly larger than Languir, maybe due to his age or lineage. Though he was larger, there was a perceptible sweetness in his nature, strange as that seemed in a randy stallion. She glanced at Adam, and it struck her so hard she gasped. Esperer reminded her of some*one* else, another gentle giant who was sweet at his very core. Her Adam. He smiled at her but didn't say anything.

She watched as Esperer finessed the nervous and hobbled Coco. Maureen spoke softly to her, rubbing her muzzle and scratching her forelock, speaking gentle words to her. Esperer's posture was cautious, respectful as he moved closer to her, responding to her as Languir had responded to Peaches. He nuzzled her and nickered to her gently. He was not as direct as Languir had been, and he took his time.

Coco whinnied and jerked away from him, staying close to Maureen at the fence line. She moved side to side as he approached her very carefully, steering clear of her rear entirely. Bill helped Maureen onto the fence and lifted her over it. Grace realized that was the reason Bill went in with Maureen, not to see to the horse, but to see to Maureen's safety. He held her arm and steadied her until she had secured her footing on the second rung outside the fence while she whispered to Coco and stroked her forehead.

Jack and Ethan remained in the corral as the drama continued. Coco was fighting a losing battle to convince Esperer his attentions were not welcome as he continued to lick and nuzzle at her mammaries and her flanks. He turned to her head, sniffed her muzzle, nickered softly some more, and started the process over again.

It was incredible to watch. There was no lead rope and no way, really, to control him or stop him if he had chosen at that moment to simply rear up and plunge in, but he didn't. He waited for the command, evidently knowing it would come after he had finished serving her first. He still hadn't even made it back to her rear. His penis was fully engorged and elongated. He was longer, even at this early point in the courtship, than his brother, a solid two and a half feet already. The parallel between Esperer and Adam was not lost on Grace as she perched with his arm wrapped around her hip. *Sheesh! Will I always blush like this?*

Coco seemed to relax under Esperer's persistent, but not aggressive, attention. After a few minutes, he very cautiously moved back to her hindquarters, steering clear of her hooves even with the hobbles on. He sniffed her hindquarters, going straight down to her clitoris and staying there.

Grace turned to Adam and whispered, "Her clitoris, yes?"

Adam smiled at her and nodded.

"Nice stallion. So considerate," she murmured softly, resting her chin on her palm. She heard Adam make a sound that was a cross between a groan and a sigh and smiled at him.

Coco panted as he continued his attentions and moved up to her vulva again. He nuzzled her flank and her hindquarters, nickering soft and low to her. Grace noticed the flexing in Coco's flanks as with Peaches and watched as her stance became less rigid. His muzzle slid to her vulva again as he stood directly behind her, his posture very cautious. She made soft whinnying sounds, and Grace had a feeling he was teasing her into a more willing state of mind.

Coco's breathing was harsh, and she whinnied again. The muscles in her flanks bunched fiercely as he continued at her clitoris. Esperer nuzzled and licked insistently before suddenly pulling away as Coco climaxed in three rushing streams from her vagina. Her stance immediately changed to one of willing acceptance. She raised her tail, and Jack gave the command.

Esperer reared up in all his massive glory, the cock that had previously engorged and elongated had grown incredibly thicker and was a darker color. Balancing on his rear hooves, he neighed loudly as the head of his penis slid into her opening. His proud, muscular flanks bunched with incredible power and strength as the entire shaft of his thickened penis slid home. His immense body balanced at her hindquarters, his forelegs resting lightly over her flanks. He began a wild, powerful pumping rhythm.

The sight of Esperer's massive penis pumping into Coco's hindquarters was so blatantly erotic to Grace that she felt her pussy throbbing. She thought momentarily she would come right on the spot, but she held it at bay, wanting to save that for Adam.

Esperer continued for longer than any of the stallions she had watched in the videos last night and even longer than Languir. He pumped into her hard, neighing as she whinnied fiercely. More fluid gushed from her, as he stilled and began to ejaculate in long streams, judging by how slowly and repeatedly his tail flexed.

Finally, he pulled out of her, his penis softening and already beginning to reduce back into the sheath it had slid from. She didn't understand the anatomy or the mechanics of it, but it seemed that Coco had climaxed a second time while he was pumping his shaft into her. Maybe she had a sweet spot, too, Grace thought with a smile. She hoped so, thinking she had a different kind of sweet spot for the stallion Esperer. He was quite a lover, big and sweet. Just like Adam, she thought, giving him a big crooked grin.

Grinning and chuckling at her, he asked, "What?" as she hugged him.

"I'll tell you later, baby. That was absolutely amazing," she said, unable to hide her enthusiasm. Maureen and Bill climbed back into the pen, untied Coco, and allowed Esperer and her to be loose in the pen for a few minutes. He stayed near her the whole time. Maureen came over to Grace and Adam, where she was still perched on the fence.

"Amazing, huh," Maureen said, bright eyed and with enthusiasm.

"I have never seen anything like that. My mind is blown," Grace said.

"We're going to hang around for a few days, make sure it took, and visit with my mom and dad. We're going to gather her now and get out of y'all's hair. If you'll give me your number, I'll call you tomorrow, okay?" Maureen handed Grace a small pad of paper and pen. Grace wrote her phone number and e-mail address down and returned it.

Bill came over, leading Coco. "Grace, it was a pleasure to meet you. I talked to Jack and Ethan, and we're going to go out to supper with y'all tomorrow night, if that's all right."

"That sounds great. We'll look forward to it." Grace climbed down from the fence with Adam's help.

"We'll see you then, Bill, Moe," Adam said as they walked Coco from the corral. Maureen waved to Grace, who waved back.

The ranch hands took over, handling Esperer and Languir for Jack and Ethan as they walked over to where Grace and Adam were standing. The ranch hands took the horses into the barn, leaving the four of them in partial privacy.

"What did you think darlin'?" Jack leaned down to kiss her. "Careful, I'm all sweaty," he said as she put her arms around him.

"I don't mind sweaty men." She turned to Ethan and kissed him as well.

"Yeah, naughty girl, but we're sweaty *and* smell like horse." He removed his work glove to palm her cheek and kiss her again. "We're going to stay out here and get some work done. That will give you and Adam some time alone together. We'll come in for lunch in a while. Then you and I are going to work on ordering a laptop computer for you. Wes called a little while ago and invited us all over for supper. We'll take the measurements for the bed and show him what we picked out for the wood and stain. I love that smile. Are you excited about ordering the bed?"

"I'm excited about ordering anything that brings me and my men together and more comfortable. I don't like Adam sleeping with his feet hanging off the bed the way he does. But I can't get him to sleep any other place, it seems." She grinned up at him and noticed he was still big and hard against her hip.

"Speaking of bed and favorite places to lay my head, we're going to head inside, guys. Thanks for the time alone with her. See you in a little while." Adam drew the conversation to a quick conclusion as he pulled Grace to his side, picked her up in his arms, and carried her away as she giggled.

"You're welcome!" Jack called after them as Adam carried her to the house. She looked back at them, waved, and blew a kiss.

Adam put her down on the porch, and they both shucked their boots before going inside. She turned to him and unbuttoned his jeans as he unbuttoned hers. She shimmied out of her jeans on the spot, right in front of the back door. She allowed him to remove her top, and he laid it on the dining room table with her hat. She unbuttoned his shirt and helped him with his jeans. Once they were off, she reached into his boxers and wrapped her fingers around his rigidly hard cock, and he hissed in pleasure. She stroked him, gently pushing him toward his big overstuffed chair in the living room.

"Adam, you're so big and hard! You've been hard for a while, too, haven't you, poor baby? I think you need some extra attention right now. I don't think it can wait until we get back to the bedroom, do you?"

"No, baby, I need you right now," he said in a soft, deep voice.

Gone was the aggressive Adam of last night who wanted to make her come hard with his tongue and fingers and then fuck her from behind. This was her gentle giant, the one who wanted to make love to her. Tenderness replaced the wild animal in him and gentled his baser instincts.

He lay back in the comfortable chair and groaned deeply when she licked her lips and took his cock deep into her mouth. He moaned as she suckled on him and established a rhythm that had his hips rocking. She gently gripped the base of his cock and stroked with her hand as well as her mouth. She gazed into the needful green depths of his eyes and saw the love that flowed from his heart reflected there. She pushed him to the point of rapture, and his groans and moans were like music in her ears. She released him, stood to remove the pink lace bra and thong she wore, and climbed into his lap, straddling his hips.

He stopped her, his hands gripping her hips. "Are you sure you're ready? I haven't made you come yet." How sweet and considerate he was. He was so aroused his pupils were dilated, yet he still expected to make her come before he took his own pleasure. His self-control was amazing.

She shuddered as she reached down, ran her fingers through the copious juices that wet her pussy, and then slid them between his open lips. "No, but I'm going to very soon, baby," she whispered in a shaky voice as he groaned.

"Stop, baby."

Breathlessly, she looked at him, waiting. He sat up, with her in his arms and still straddling him. In a powerful move, he lifted them both from the chair. She clasped her ankles at his back, and wrapped her arms around his strong shoulders, her head tucked into his neck.

* * * *

Adam walked into the hallway, placed his palm between her delicate shoulder blades so she'd have a cushion, and leaned her against the wall. With his other forearm supporting her buttocks and hips, he positioned himself. He delighted in her sharp, high-pitched gasp as her control began to slip. In one smooth-as-silk stroke, he slid gently into her warm, clenching pussy. She wailed in a keening, frantic voice as she came ecstatically undone around his pulsating cock.

He held her tightly as she relished every single pulse that went through her. It was heaven holding her like this and being engulfed in her satiny warmth. Her head fell back against the wall, her full lips parted, as she tried to catch her breath. He buried his lips at her throat, inhaling the scent of her skin, and willed his cock under control, not wanting to come just yet.

"I love you, Grace. I love everything about you, the way you smell, the way you cry out when you come, your beautiful mouth, the way you look at me with love in your eyes. I love you."

Her breath was hitching gasps, her hands grasped him, and her arms tightened around him. "I love you, honey, all of you, everything about you. Please never leave me. I'd be lost without you," she weakly responded.

"Don't worry about that. I'm not going anywhere, beautiful woman," he murmured against her throat as he gently held her to him and carried her to her bed, still gasping and moaning, as he moved inside her with each step. He pulled out of her honeyed pussy reluctantly, thankful for a woman with such an incredible capacity to love others, and helped her to climb into the center of the bed. He came to her and settled over her. Cradled by her body, he slowly slid back inside her silken cunt. Every inch of his overeager cock settled inside her warm, tight pussy He kissed her warm lips as she arched and undulated beneath him, already on the verge again. He began a slow, sweet rhythm, thrusting into her, feeling her body quivering and trembling under him as her orgasm took flight again. She rode his cock in a hard, fast rhythm that mingled with his own, coming again in his arms. Her whimpering moans in his ear were like a symphony as he helped her ride the orgasm to its finish.

He changed the angle his cock penetrated her with by sliding one forearm beneath her hips. With each thrust of his cock, his pubic bone collided with her clitoris as he sought the sweet spot inside her. Her second orgasm had not even faded before she began reaching again. He watched her sweet, blushing face as he stroked her. She was so beautiful and uninhibited in her pleasure.

He whispered words of encouragement, turned on by the sounds she made in her ecstasy. A euphoric smile passed over her face, and he groaned deeply when he felt her pussy go slick around him with her gushing juices. She sobbed in rapture as he drew the sweetest rippling orgasm from her. She drenched them both in the juices that flowed from her.

She breathlessly told him, "Roll over, let me ride you as you come, Adam."

Chapter Thirty-five

He didn't know what reserve she called the strength from after that powerful orgasm, but she managed somehow as he gathered her to him and rolled them over so that she was on top of him, still joined to him. She placed her palms on his pecs and rose over him, sitting up, putting her weight on her knees and shins. She began a slow pumping rhythm, her hair falling around her shoulders and breasts in blonde waves.

She arched her back, and her lush breasts swayed with her movements. If he hadn't felt the release rushing through him like a wildfire, he could have stayed that way for hours, just enjoying the sight of her sensual movements. Rising and falling over his hard cock, drenched in her copious juices, she raised her arms slowly over her head in lissome arcs. She tilted her head back, and he was spellbound by the grace and beauty with which she made love to him.

"Beautiful," she whispered as she clasped hands with his and rose up on her knees and began riding his cock in a hard, unrelenting rhythm, her muscles clenching as he moaned and cried out, so close to coming himself.

She tightened on him, riding hard and fast. He thrust into her with powerful strokes in a perfect concert of movement, his orgasm boiling through his body like a volcanic eruption, until she sent them both over the edge. Adam roared in pure primal abandon beneath her, his hands holding her hips tightly as she rode every short, explosive pulse of her fourth orgasm to utter satiation.

When he came back to himself, his hands slid to her breasts, lovingly cupping them, and then up her chest to her throat. He softly drew her to him in a blissful kiss before he pulled her down to lie on his chest. She was still joined to him, her hair now fanned out over his shoulders like a mantle. With gentle care, he held his hand across her luscious ass and pushed on each knee one at a time, prompting her to lower and straighten her legs to his so they were entwined. He didn't want to leave her lush, pulsing warmth, but he wanted her to be comfortable. Her sweet body felt languid and utterly satisfying as she melted over him.

She never lifted her head or moved as he reached for and pulled the sheet and blanket over their limp bodies. He laid an arm across her ass and laid the other hand on her back, and that was how they fell asleep. Satisfied and exhausted.

She woke to the feel of Ethan's warm hand on her back, sliding gently back and forth.

"Hey, Sleeping Beauty, we have lunch ready on the table when y'all are ready to join us." He left the room, giving them a minute to wake up.

She still lay in the position she'd been in when she drifted off to sleep earlier, lying on top of him, their limbs tangled together. She looked up to find Adam watching her through luminous green eyes.

"Hi, sleepyhead." Adam slid his warm hand over her bare ass under the covers, squeezing gently.

"Hi, how long have you been awake?"

"A while, but I couldn't bear to wake you up. I love to watch you when you sleep, and you're so warm. I was enjoying the moment, I guess."

She shifted on him, and as she did, she felt his softened cock finally slide from her body. Her head fell back to his chest, and they both groaned a little. "That was interesting." She giggled.

"We'd better get up before my cock takes a notion to return there and we miss lunch altogether." He helped her to sit up and climb off of him. She hated to move away from his tantalizing warmth. She felt serene and quiet as she went into the bathroom and turned on the shower, quickly pinning her hair up she peeked out at him. "Join me?"

He came to her in the shower, bathed quickly, then took her washcloth from her and carefully washed her. He was quiet, too. Contented. After they finished, he took her in his arms and kissed her long, slow and tenderly. She adored this gentle lover in Adam as much as the wild one.

Adam left the bathroom with a towel wrapped loosely around his hips as she slipped into the closet and got dressed in a pretty red demi bra and panty set, then put on blue denim capri pants and a bright red form-fitting V-neck top and strappy sandals.

Jack had made barbeque sandwiches for everyone. They must have napped a long while because both Jack and Ethan had already showered and dressed, besides having lunch ready. She was surprised when she saw the time. One thirty.

Ethan kissed her neck as he came to the table and pulled out a chair. "Why don't you eat and then we'll see about ordering that computer," he said as Jack slid a plate in front of her.

"How does your arm feel, Ethan?" she asked, kissing him.

"Not as stiff. My wounds are healing well. I didn't have any trouble with them at all this morning."

"You heal really fast. It's only been five days."

"That's what my mom always said. I'd be healed up from one misadventure, and before she knew it, I'd need to go get stitches or have a bone set. The stories she could tell you."

As he said the words, it occurred to her she only knew Jack's dad. She had not met Adam or Ethan's family yet. Jack's dad and his sister, Anne, were just down the road, but what about the rest of them? Would they approve of her? Did they know? Would they like her? She ate her sandwich in silence, wondering how she'd ever be able to keep straight who knew and who didn't. As usual, Ethan took one look at her and knew exactly what she was thinking.

"They'll love you, Grace. They're in the RV traveling right now. They wanted to drive up around North Carolina and see what it's like this time of year. They left last week, needing to get away for a while. They left right after the burial. I called them and told them, and they're very excited. Mom flipped when I told her about getting shot, but like I said, she's used to me and my misadventures. She said she can't wait to meet you, officially, and, yes, they know about the four of us. They've known that's what we wanted for a long time. I think you're going to be surprised by how supportive our families are. Jack has a couple of older siblings who don't approve, but ask him if he gives a rat's ass."

"Adam, what about your parents? Are they all right with all of this?"

"They are better than all right. They were also at the funeral and remember you. Mom said you've waited on her a couple of times at Stigall's when she's gone in to shop for Dad. They're just trying to give us a little breathing room from everything that's been going on. Give the dust a chance to settle."

"And your dad, Jack? What about him?'

"Dad agreed with Mom about that subject. One of these days, we'll take you to visit the cemetery at the ranch and show you around. I think it will explain why it's so easy for them to accept you. Don't worry needlessly, darlin'."

"Can't you tell me?"

"I'd rather show you. It'd be better. It's not a big deal. It'll just explain a lot."

"Now you've made me curious."

* * * *

After lunch, Grace ordered her laptop computer. Ethan helped her build one that would meet or exceed her future needs. She told him someday she might like to take up writing, and he made sure she had the word processing program that would meet that need. The option to order her computer in a color came up.

There was a time when she would've shrunk from ordering anything that might draw attention to her own sense of style, fearing negative input. She looked at the array of colors, and spotted a swirling flourish design in a pink that brought out the naughty girl in her. She bit her lip and pointed at it, then glanced at him, wondering what he would think.

He chuckled at her choice color and encouraged her. "Go for it, Grace, you know you *want* to. This is your time, your computer, and your money. Nowadays everyone expresses themselves with their laptop design and color scheme. Look, there's even a matching carrying case and all sorts of accessories in that color. Jack, Adam, come look at what we found. Gracie's trying to decide. It's just right, isn't it, Jack?" Ethan asked as Jack and Adam came up behind them at the dining table.

"Looks pretty close to me. What do you think, Jack?" Adam said, chuckling at her color choice.

"It looks about right to me, too," Jack agreed.

"You're right. I should go for it," Grace said.

"No one but the four of us would even know the significance of that color, and you know you'd enjoy using it." Ethan said, stroking her shoulder. "We'd enjoy seeing you use it. It would be our inside joke. Maybe it even might inspire you to write trashy novels someday. When you're old and gray and a famous author, someone will interview you, and you can tell them about the laptop you wrote your first novel on and how it was pink. But not just *any* pink. You can tell them it was your husbands' favorite color because it reminded them of your—"

Click. "Okay, I did it!" She grinned, laughing as they tickled her and kissed her. "And they're *not* 'trashy novels,' they're erotic romances!" She shrieked then giggled as they tickled her.

"I don't know, Ethan," Adam said playfully, nipping at her neck and making her chortle. "We checked the flower, but maybe we should check the main source of that particular shade of pink. It might be more of a rose or mauve color. It pays to be *accurate*."

"Now see?" Ethan slid a hand over her hip. Her body literally sang with joy at the way they played and teased with her. "Aren't you glad you did that? You love pink, and you've never indulged yourself in buying something in an impractical color before. Now you can afford to. I'll throw in all the accessories in the same shade *and* that fancy frickin' pink crocodile carrying case that has *Gracie* written all over it! Let's finish this order up." Ethan wrapped an arm around her as they placed the order. It was a big deal to her that he'd helped her. She wasn't sure she could have waded through all the techno lingo on her own.

After they finished placing the order, she went into her bedroom to tidy things up. She stripped the sheets from the bed, and Adam and Jack put fresh ones on for her.

"I'm spoiled."

"Uh-huh," Adam put a fresh case on one of her pillows, "just like we want you to be."

She tidied and threw out the used up candles. "I should go check on the house. I need to pack all my stuff and figure out what to do with it."

"I checked the house early Monday morning," Jack said as Ethan joined them, having heard her comment. "The workmen were finished. The blue tarp is still on because we need to have a few shingles replaced. The only thing left to do is decide if you want to replace the tub, since it has that big dent in it now. The workmen even cleaned up after themselves. I've arranged to have the roof taken care of and whatever you want to do about the tub."

Ethan picked up a pillowcase and began putting it on a pillow. "If you'd like, I can get boxes for you one day and we can all help you pack up next week. If we all help, it shouldn't take long."

"I feel like I've taken up a lot of time that you would normally devote to your businesses. I hate to keep imposing upon you."

"You know, there really is no hurry," Ethan reminded her. "It's not like you're vacating on a deadline. Why don't I help you one day this week if you can find the time? We'll go over there and pack up all your clothes and shoes and other necessities and empty out your refrigerator. When things have settled down some and you've had a chance to decide whether you want to sell it or rent it out, then you can pack up and clean it out. No need to get in a rush."

Grace thanked him for being the voice of reason. They finished making the bed for her and then went into the living room.

"Jack? Have you thought about when you'd like to get married? Do you have a date in mind?" She sat with him on the couch. He lifted her feet onto his lap, slipped her sandals off, and began gently rubbing her feet.

"How much time do you need to plan a wedding?"

"Do you want to go to the courthouse or get married in a church?"

"Darlin', the courthouse would be the easiest and quickest way, but it's not really what any of us want for you. You're only getting married once, and we want it to be special and romantic for you. If you want to keep it small, that's fine, but we'd like it to be in a church or outside, maybe, and as soon as you can comfortably pull it together."

"I know you are worried about all the details, Gracie." Ethan brought his laptop and sat down in the overstuffed chair across from her. "But Charity already said she'd help, and I think if we all sat down together, we could come up with a plan that will include all the things you want for your wedding, and as few of the hassles as possible. And you have all of us to fall back on."

"I wish I could be legally married to all three of you."

"We do, too, baby," Adam replied, sitting down and letting her rest her head in his lap. He spread her hair out over his legs, running his fingers through it and massaging her scalp.

"That feels good."

"You and I will be legally married," Jack explained, "and then a good friend of ours will perform a binding ceremony, just like the traditional marriage ceremony, that includes the three of us as your husbands. We'll do it in private right after, when everyone thinks we're taking pictures before the reception."

"When you picture me walking down the aisle, what do you imagine my dress looking like?"

Ethan replied first. "Simple and classic, but not informal, definitely a long dress."

Adam added, "Not a lot of petticoats and fluffy stuff, something with pretty trim around the bust. You know us, babe, we love your breasts." He grinned down at her.

Jack said, "Something you could feel comfortable and beautiful in. I'm with Adam. No big poofy skirt with too much material, and Ethan is right, too, not an informal dress. We can afford to get you anything you want, within reason."

"You know we can always look online," Grace said. "I'll bet I have better luck finding a good selection of plus-size gowns online than I will shopping in stores. A lot easier on the feet, too."

Ethan laughed as he typed on the laptop. "Good luck getting away from Charity. You know she's going to drag you to every bridal shop in a one hundred mile radius of here. Come here, sweet thing. I Googled some plus-size wedding dresses." He patted his lap.

They found a couple of the big online superstores that carried plus-size wedding gowns. He scrolled through a few. "It's too bad they advertise plus-size gowns and then show it on a model that is built like a stick. Not a good way to sell gowns, I would think."

They both said "Ooooh!" at the same time, pointing to the same gown, then laughed. Adam and Jack grinned and came and stood behind the chair and took a look. It was a strapless A-line organza with pale pink beaded embroidery at the bust, scattered around the skirt, and then at the back.

"You'd look beautiful in something like this in a softer, more flowing fabric. Soft and silky with some movement to it," Ethan said pointing at the screen.

"I think you're right. Do you want to help me pick it out, or do you want to be surprised?"

"I want to help," Ethan said, grinning.

"I want to help, too," Adam said.

"I want you to surprise me, darlin'," Jack said. "I want to see it for the first time when you're coming down the aisle."

"Ooooh! This is going to be so much fun!" Grace squealed, rubbing her hands together. "It's going to be perfect! But we're not fooling around in any dressing rooms, boys, got it?"

In unison, Ethan and Adam said glumly, "Yes, ma'am."

"This was how I was hoping it would be for you, to have fun putting it all together." Jack kissed the top of her head.

"I'll have y'all to help me keep it together. It's when a bride takes on every little detail that she loses her ever-lovin' marbles."

"We'll sit down soon and make some plans, set a budget, and *most importantly*, set a date." Jack knelt in front of her, and she leaned forward to kiss him.

She turned to look back at Ethan as she sat in his lap, then at Jack and over to Adam. "There is something about you guys that makes all this so much easier for me, and I want you to know I appreciate it. Earlier, I was with you on the couch when you were rubbing my feet. Then Adam came and laid my head in his lap and ran his fingers through my hair. You released me to go to Ethan, without any reservation or jealousy. You didn't mind."

She placed a palm on Adam's cheek as he came and knelt in front of her, too. "If I had even an inkling that you minded, it would make me feel guilty. Because you release me to each other like that, I don't hold back at all from showing you affection. I think that if I felt guilty for leaving one to pay attention to the other that I might not go to you to kiss you and love on you as often. You make it easy for me to be with all of you. Loving all three of you is freeing for me." She lay back in Ethan's arms and breathed out, "I live in heaven."

"Gracie, we work at loving you as a group and not only as individuals. We feel like if we keep you satisfied and happy with us, we make it easier for you to love us." Ethan clasped his fingers in hers. "Guilt could throw a relationship like ours out of balance, with you constantly trying to make it up to us. If we make time to be alone with each other, whatever needs we have that are individual needs are met, and everyone is happy. We feel like *we* live in heaven."

"We do, baby. You make us so happy." Adam stroked her leg.

"It's true, darlin'. You bless us so much," Jack added, squeezing her knee before rising. He and Adam went into the kitchen and she heard the refrigerator open.

"What time are we supposed to go over to Wesley's?" Grace asked. Looking into Ethan's bright blue eyes, she felt a tingle of desire for him.

"He said –5:30 p.m. or six o'clock."

"Were we supposed to bring steak or beer or anything?" Grace asked him. "I think we'll need to stop at the store if we do."

"It's three o'clock right now. If you'd like to bring steaks over, they won't complain, I'm sure. We can go ahead and pick up some beer, too. Don't worry, honey. They'll like you just fine," Ethan assured her, and she hugged him.

"How do you do that?" She rested her head against his chest, under his jaw.

"What?" he asked, settling back deeper into the chair with her.

"Read my mind like that." She stroked her fingers through his chest hair showing through the open placate of his shirt.

"When I look in your eyes and watch your face when you talk to us, I understand you. I sort of…feel what you're saying. I don't know how to explain it better than that without being too girly." He shrugged.

She slid her hand up his tanned forearm to his warm and thickly muscled bicep. "Ethan, trust me when I tell you there's nothing *girly* about you, honey. You are *all man*." She snuggled to him, feeling another soft wave of desire flow over her. It ought to be against the law for a man to smell and feel that good.

"Jack and I can run to the store for whatever you need, Grace, if you want time alone with Ethan," Adam suggested, watching them from the kitchen.

Grace looked up at Adam and then at Ethan, "I would love that, if y'all wouldn't mind." She turned to look at Ethan, "Would you like that?" she whispered. He grinned at her and rolled his eyes.

"No, I wouldn't mind a bit."

Jack got a pad and made a short list. "We don't mind, darlin'."

After Jack and Adam left for the store, Ethan and Grace went to his bedroom. He put on some soft music, and she lay down with him on the bed. She allowed him to slowly undress her and love her. Finally, when they were both naked, he positioned her so she could see in the mirror and made slow, searing-hot love to her, bringing her to a blissful, sweet climax before finding his own release. They lay in each other's arms afterward and talked quietly, their conversation intermingled with tender, loving kisses. Her heart felt again like it was being stretched, she felt so much love for them, for him.

* * * *

Adam drove while Jack looked at their shopping list. Adam noticed that Jack seemed distracted, looking at the pad but not really seeing it. The silly grin on his face probably looked just like the one that Adam knew must currently perch on his own face.

He contemplated his morning and afternoon spent with their gorgeous woman. Her effect on him was powerful, both her words and her touch. They'd talked earlier about visiting Moe and Bill in Conroe when the foals came, and she'd mentioned that she would be his wife by then. The bliss in her voice and on her face made his heart palpitate. He wanted to dedicate his life to keeping that look on her face, that soft velvety tone in her voice. She'd totally blown him away when she mentioned that it might be possible that she would be pregnant with his baby by that point. Prior to meeting Grace, he hadn't really dwelt on what it would be like to be a dad, much less envisioned a wife pregnant with his child, beyond the "one of these days" kinds of daydreams. Since meeting her, his cock had been in overdrive, so all he could think of was being with her. But she'd brought the future front and center to his mind that morning.

He imagined Grace sitting in the glider on the back porch at sunset, wrapped in his nice warm robe, one dainty bare foot tucked under her, the other pushing the glider to rock. Wrapped in a fluffy pink blanket in her arms was a beautiful infant girl with fuzzy blonde hair the same color as her mama's. Grace sang softly to her as she held the baby to her full, round breast, nursing her. Grace's delicate fingers gently caressed the baby's tender cheek. The vision made his heart throb and ache with love for her.

"Earth to Adam?"

He blinked once, and grinned over at the understanding look on Jack's face. "I'm her slave."

"I know, man. Me, too."

* * * *

She could definitely tell two bachelors lived here. There were a couple of young Monterey Oaks in front and more on the side that looked like they'd been planted after the house was finished being built but no other landscaping, just bare mulch around the foundation of the house. A deep porch wrapped around the front of the Garner house, and Grace wondered if it continued all the way around. There were no plants in clay pots or baskets hanging from the porch eaves. The house was beautiful, but it needed a woman's touch.

Ethan had reassured her that Wesley and Evan would like her just fine, but as Jack and the others introduced her to them, she couldn't shake the feeling that they had more than a passing interest in her relationship with her men. With Evan especially, she felt like she was being observed. Wesley was as friendly as could be, asking questions about her work and what she thought of the Divine Creek Ranch. He was sweet and good natured, very open. Evan was much quieter, more reserved. There were times she caught him watching her when she was close to one of her men. She didn't feel judged by him but rather like she was under a microscope.

She treated Jack, Ethan, and Adam the same way she normally would, paying attention to each of them as the opportunity presented itself. With a touch here, a kiss there, teasing with Adam, or scratching Jack's back. Jack had told her she could be herself around Wesley and Evan, and she wasn't planning on pulling back from her men just because Evan had issues.

"Thanks for bringing steaks to grill tonight," Wesley said. "You spoil us bringing such fine cuts of meat. We baked some potatoes earlier today, and I have vegetables in the refrigerator for a salad, if that sounds all right to you." He showed her the baking pan in the oven with the hot potatoes still in it.

"That sounds great, Wesley. Why don't you show me where you keep the knives and cutting board, and I'll chop the salad for you."

He showed her, telling her she didn't have to do that. She said she preferred to help out and not just stand around. She washed the vegetables in the sink and went in search of a colander and a serving bowl in the cabinets. The cabinets all had organizers in them and slide out drawers on the shelves, but they could have stood a little organizational work. The rest of the house was neat as a pin, but the kitchen? *Sheesh.* Everything was helter-skelter in the cabinets. *Bachelors.* She grinned, fighting the urge to organize just one or two while she searched. After preparing the salad, she covered it and put it back in the refrigerator.

The men came and went out onto the back deck where the grill was located, preparing the steaks and heating the grill. Someone turned on the stereo, so Stevie Ray Vaughan played in the background both in the house and outside over the outdoor speakers. Grace had been a Stevie Ray Vaughan fan since she was a little girl. Her dad always enjoyed his music, and she could remember dancing to "Mary Had a Little Lamb" when she was a little girl. They turned it up when "Voodoo Chile" came on, and she didn't mind a bit. Some music was meant to be enjoyed loudly. She was washing the knives and colander and other dishes in the sink when "Honey Bee" started. She had to laugh. She loved that song when she was little and had called herself "Daddy's little honey bee," but the song had some seriously grown-up connotations, listening to it as a woman.

She couldn't resist bobbing and swinging her hips to the tune, just enjoying herself, singing along softly. Suddenly, she felt a tall hard body press gently against her, pinning her to the counter's edge. Large warm hands slid down to cup her ass. *Adam.* She couldn't suppress a throaty laugh as he sang along softly.

"'Cause the way we kiss just can't miss,
Don't make me wait to feel your warm embrace,
Each and every time that we get the chance,
Come on, little baby, let's make some romance."

She giggled as he sang to her. She bobbed and swung with his hands on her, careful to not rub too hard against him, not wanting to start something she couldn't finish just yet.

"Yeah, you really groove me, baby, when you move your hips,
Shake it all around—"

"It's a good thing I came in here and got to see that, baby. You just made my day." Adam chuckled as the guitar played on. "I didn't know you were a Stevie Ray Vaughan fan."

"Ever since I was little. My parents loved his music. They couldn't see me dancing outside, could they?" she asked as she picked up the dish towel.

"No, baby, I'm the only one who got that pleasure, I think. You have great rhythm." He nuzzled her neck with his warm lips, kissing her there.

She chuckled softly. "Thank you, baby. Y'all make me feel like dancin'. Are the steaks almost done? I'll hunt down some plates and silverware and make some tea."

"Good luck with that," he said wryly. "I'll send one of the guys in to show you where they have that stuff hidden." He kissed her again before heading back out.

"That's okay, I can find it!"

She got on her hands and knees, mumbling, "With a hunting dog and a flashlight." She searched for a pitcher she'd seen earlier in the jumble but couldn't remember where. She heard him close the screen door and continued the search for the pitcher and found the salad tongs as well. In a cabinet? She shook her head and backed on her hands and knees away from the cabinet, right into another tall male body. Startled, she looked up at Evan.

Great. On her hands and knees, ass stuck up in the air. She plunked it down and smiled timidly. She handed him the pitcher and tongs and took the hand he offered her. She dusted off and took the found items from him.

"Adam said you needed help finding stuff." His face was a carefully blank page.

"Yes, plates, utensils, and glasses, tea, and a measuring cup."

He found her the measuring cup and tea first. She filled the cup with water, popped in three tea bags, and put it in the microwave while he got down the dishes.

"Do y'all like your tea sweet?" She reached for the canister marked sugar. It was empty.

"Yeah, but we keep the sugar in the pantry. I'll get it for you." After he handed it to her, he stood there watching her. It made her a little nervous.

She filled the pitcher with water, added half a cup of sugar, and stirred it until it was dissolved, then removed the measuring cup from the microwave when it dinged. Dipping the teabags up and down in the hot water, she waited for the tea to darken before pouring the hot liquid into the pitcher of sugared water. She found a long spoon and stirred it and looked over at him still watching her.

"Ice for the glasses?" she asked, trying to distract him a little. His staring seemed to have a purpose. He acted like he was thinking or trying to figure something out.

He took the glasses and filled them with ice while she removed the pan of potatoes from the oven and put it on the table, then searched the fridge for whatever they could put on baked potatoes and put the items on the table. She set six places at the table, lamenting the fact she hadn't thought to make a dessert. She turned to see he still watched her and caught a confused look on his face.

Enough of this bullshit.

She tried unsuccessfully to look into his hooded eyes. "What is it you want to know, Evan? You are Jack, Ethan, and Adam's friend. If you have a question, why don't you just ask me?" Rose Marie would be so proud to see her facing a daunting situation head on.

Seize the day, baby!

He seemed surprised by her direct approach. He surprised her in return. "Don't you worry at all what people will think of you being with three men?" His tone was not judgmental, merely curious.

Way to lead with the tough questions there, Evan, she thought. Her answer came straight from her heart as she paused, able to finally look directly in his eyes.

"Of course I am concerned by what people think, Evan. I'm only human. But I've lived *enough* of my life worrying what people think of me, only to discover they're too busy thinking of themselves. I care what Jack, Adam, and Ethan think. I'm not a whore, and they know I'm not a whore.

They know what is in my heart. With them by my side, I can deal with anything that comes at me. What else do you want to know?"

Evan took the opportunity. "So…what? You just decided you loved all three of them?"

"That's a very complicated question, Evan. What do you really want to know? How can I love all three of them? Or are you curious how it came about?"

"How did it come about?"

"Jack's mother introduced us some time ago. I was involved in a terrible relationship, so Jack would not ask me out, and I could not show that I was interested in him. Through a series of events, I met Ethan and Adam as well. They rescued me from that bad relationship and, quite literally, saved me from an actual beating."

She thought she saw his eyes narrow and a fleeting angry look, but he schooled his features just as quickly. "You might think it's convenient that I fell in love with the men who saved me, but once I was free, I realized that the feelings that were growing for them were reciprocated by them. In the face of such care and devotion, how could I not fall head over heels in love with them? Before they came into my life, I was convinced I was ugly, fat, and hopeless." At her words, his face registered surprise and disbelief. "Only love can make that kind of change in a person's heart. Did I answer the question you were trying to ask?"

"What's in this for you?"

"Are you asking if I'm a gold digger?" At her question, his face showed surprise again but also a grudging respect. Maybe also relief that she did not appear offended.

"Maybe?"

"What's in it for me is love, a chance to belong, to make a difference, and to belong to three men who adore me as much as I adore them. Beyond that, I have not the slightest clue."

"You don't know how much they are worth, collectively?" he asked incredulously.

"Beyond what I see in their hearts and their eyes, I have no idea. Sorry. I know what you're asking, and I'm doing my best to not be offended by the insinuation because I know you're their friend, and you seem to have more than a passing curiosity about our relationship." She tried to maintain a neutral body posture because she had a feeling she was being observed from outside.

She sighed before she continued, "Evan, you've presumed on the budding friendship between you and me, and so I'm going to do the same. I'm not going to pry and ask intrusive questions, just tell you something you need to be reminded of. Not *every* woman is a gold-digging whore, not every woman is going to break your heart. And not just any woman is going to wait around while you try to make up your mind. You won't know if you never take a chance. And *that* would be a crying shame, Evan, because some of us aren't *just* good, we're *damn* good." She hoped her streak of intuition was right and that this was about a woman.

"I think they are coming in. If you want to ask me any other questions, now or later, feel free, but I'd keep the gold-digging insinuations to a minimum. *They* won't appreciate that, and I still need to talk to Wesley about our bed. No sex questions, either. Ask the guys that stuff when you're alone. Could you bring the tea pitcher and the salad from the refrigerator?" she asked as the French doors leading out to the back deck opened.

The men came in bearing a platter of bacon-wrapped filets and a grilled onion, wrapped loosely in foil. Wesley commented, "Grace, your men tell me you like your steak rare, very rare, is that right?"

She laughed. "As in 'wipe its nose and threaten it with an unlit match' rare."

"I seared the bacon on the grate, that okay?"

"Perfect, Wesley." She took the platter from him and put it on the table. "That onion smells wonderful."

"Thanks," he said as they all washed their hands.

Ethan approached Grace with curiosity and concern on his face. She *knew* it was him watching her. He'd be the one to pick up on any tension in her posture if he was observing her through the window.

"Is everything all right in here, Gracie?" He leaned down to kiss her quickly, shielding her from the others for a moment. She looked up at him and smiled tenderly. They were always watching out for her, protecting her.

She nodded reassuringly. "Yes, we were just talking. Evan had a few questions about how things worked out for us. I was just answering his questions. Helping him understand women." She chuckled as she kissed him again.

"Lord, help him. I don't think he has enough time for that conversation!" Ethan softly snickered.

"All he needs to do is talk to you, honey, and he'd learn a thing or two about women." She stuck her fingers through his front belt loops. "I love you, Ethan."

"Love you, too, Gracie." He pressed his forehead to hers gently.

They lingered over the meal, enjoying the steaks and the conversation. Evan's demeanor seemed to relax somewhat, and Grace enjoyed chatting with him and Wesley. After the meal, Jack, Adam, and Evan cleaned the kitchen while Wesley, Ethan, and Grace looked at the sketches of the bed Wesley had made using the clear overlay and the drawings Ethan had already showed her. Wesley made note of the dimensions and the type of wood, stain, and finish. Ethan looked at Wesley over Grace's head and nodded at the catalog, which showed the different pieces of furniture he could make that would go with her bed.

She loved their designs and really enjoyed looking at the other pieces available but was careful to only ask for the nightstands, dresser with a mirror, chest of drawers, and additionally asked for a wardrobe or armoire she could store quilts and other large items in. She commented on the big heavy padded rocking chair and footstool and asked if Wesley ever made picture frames from the leftover wood. He said he'd be happy to make her some in standard sizes.

"Well, Grace, now that I know what you like and I have your measurements, I can place an order for the wood and get started right away. Have you already ordered the mattress and linens? They'll take a while to be custom-made as well." Wesley wrote down her choices and then put away the catalogs.

"I ordered the mattress this morning," Jack called from the kitchen, "and Grace is going to be meeting with an interior designer to pick out linens."

"I am?" She was surprised by this news and turned to Ethan.

"Yeah, Jack knows a designer who does a really good job. Katie can help you find what you want and help you pick paint colors and stuff. He also ordered the canopy drape for the bed this morning. I found a company that makes them completely by hand."

"Thank you, honey," she said, awed at the way he paid attention to the little things.

It was nine o'clock when they finished. Grace showed Jack and Adam what she picked out. Wesley promised to get a color copy of the bed drawing and furniture he'd be making for her to give to the interior designer.

Wesley's phone rang just then. He pulled it out of his pocket without checking caller ID and answered, "Wesley Garner."

Grace heard a faint feminine voice come from the phone and smiled. Wesley smiled and said, "Hey," like only a man in love could say *hey*, meaning a lot more than what that one word could convey. Coming from him it meant "I've been thinking of you, I miss you, might even love you, but I'm mostly glad to hear your voice." Wesley's *hey* spoke volumes. Grace pretended to look at the sample catalog.

"Thanks for calling me back. Yeah, we ate a while ago, just getting done looking at the drawings and catalog. Sure. Yeah, he's home. Maybe, I think it helped. Yeah, perfect. I'll ask them. I think they'd enjoy that. I'll let you know. You headed home? Be careful. All right. Sweet dreams, honey. I love you, too."

Grace glanced over at Evan. The look on his face was troubled, the face of someone who was confused by his feelings. *Ah-ha.* It spoke volumes to her heart, and answered any lingering questions about their earlier conversation. He was in love with whoever was on the other end of that conversation and didn't look very happy about it.

"Y'all remember Rosemary Piper, from Cheaver's?" Wesley asked, after he'd put his phone away. Grace smiled widely. She definitely remembered the bubbly little brunette.

"Yeah," Jack said, "she helped me and Angel with Grace's saddle last week. Why?" He had a knowing grin on his face.

"Well, we've sort of been dating, off and on. She hoped maybe we could all get together and have a cookout sometime in the next few weeks. I think she was kind of hoping to visit with Grace. I think you'd like her, Grace. She's a little sweetheart."

"I met her last weekend at O'Reilley's. She's just gorgeous. I'd love to get together, Wesley. Just tell her to set a date and let us know. Isn't that right, guys?"

Evan got up abruptly and went to the kitchen to get another beer, returning to find them all grinning at him. "What? Fine, okay? A cook out sounds great." Wesley rolled his eyes, and Grace made big eyes at Adam and smiled.

"It's getting late. We've all got to work in the morning," Ethan said, thanking Wes and Evan for the hospitality. After a few more exchanged words, they made their way out to the SUV and headed home.

"There's a heated conversation going on at the Garner house right now," Jack said.

"Evan didn't look happy." Grace tucked in a foot under her on the back seat, leaning into Adam a little as he put his arms around her.

"That's a complicated deal, right there," Adam replied, threading his fingers through her hair, rubbing the base of her skull gently. She practically purred.

* * * *

Jack took Grace to bed alone that night. Adam and Ethan had come to her and kissed her lovingly, wishing her sweet dreams, before going to their respective bedrooms. Jack and Grace made slow tender love to each other, whispering gentle, loving words, finding joy in unhurried time spent stroking each other into a state of sweet bliss. Jack showed her that he could stroke her to orgasm without the fiery explosion and have it be no less mind-blowing. She shed a few tears from the joy of it before slipping into an unfortunately restless sleep. After a couple of hours of tossing and turning, he told her he'd get Adam and Ethan. Relieved, she thanked him.

Adam was awake, reading, when Jack tapped on his door, wearing his robe. "Grace can't sleep."

Adam rose from the bed, throwing on his robe. They stopped at Ethan's door and found him reading as well. They went to her and cuddled around her, and she finally drifted off into a deep slumber.

Chapter Thirty-six

At lunch time the next day, Grace went to visit Angel at the hospital. She was pleasantly surprised to find Teresa sitting at his bedside. She was blushing as Angel spoke very softly to her when Grace walked into the room. Teresa was happy to see Grace but quickly made her excuses to Angel and bid Grace good-bye, saying her lunch hour was almost over and she needed to get back to Stigall's.

Grace turned an amused gaze upon Angel, who smiled boyishly and held his arms open for a hug. They must still have him on pain meds, she thought. "All right, lover boy, how are you doing? Are they treating you well here?" She hugged him carefully before she sat down in the seat Teresa had just vacated.

"You know me, just trying to be a good patient. I'm feeling better and better all the time."

"I'll bet. I hear you've been flirting with all the nurses. You must be in hog heaven around here with women fawning all over you." She took his hand and paused for a long moment, then said, "Angel, thank you for trying to help Ethan, for trying to stop Patricia. I couldn't live with myself if we'd lost you. I'm so glad you're going to be okay." Her chin wobbled as she her eyes welled up.

"Grace, please don't cry. I'll feel terrible if you start crying. I helped Ethan because it was the right thing to do. It was my fault for bringing Patricia out to the ranch. It was my responsibility to do what I could to stop her. I'll be back to my old self in no time." He swiftly changed the subject and chuckled in amusement. "So I heard from Ethan and Jack yesterday that you got to see Languir and Esperer in action. They are something, aren't they? I've worked with them since they were little colts, teaching them to be gentlemen."

"They were that, Angel." She put her hands to her cheeks as they heated up. "I've never spent much time around horses before. It was an amazing experience. I think when y'all have time that I'd like to learn more about the ranch and the breeding operation. Maureen Travers has also offered to help steer me in the right direction."

"Moe is a good horsewoman. She'll be a good one for you to learn from, and of course, I'd be happy to help however I can. Not to change the subject, but can I ask you a question?"

"Sure, Angel. About what?" *Like I don't already know.*

"Teresa." In all the time Grace had known him he'd always been very comfortable dealing with women, maybe because his mom was such a little spitfire. He possessed the ability to have women eating out of the palm of his hand. For once, he seemed a little unsure of himself.

"What would you like to know?" she replied cautiously, anxious about sharing too much information about Teresa. She was a very private person.

"Have you known her long? Can you tell me about her?"

"I've known her a couple of years, since she came to work at the store. She likes being around other people, but she's a very private person. She's new to the area, so she doesn't know very many people except through the store. You've seen for yourself that she's very shy and embarrasses easily. I think she may have had a hard life. Sometimes she seems…fragile, but she has a very sweet, tender heart."

"She's not a *dating* kind of woman," Angel said very intuitively.

"You're right, and that would be hard for her at any rate."

"Because she's a single mom?" he asked. She was reluctant to offer that information, but if he already knew, maybe it was because Teresa had told him. She stuck to information about Michael and didn't share anything about Teresa's history. If this relationship progressed, there were things Angel needed to hear from Teresa and not someone else.

"Yes, her little boy, Michael, is two years old. She has very little time for dating, and like you said, she's not the dating kind, not the type to bring men home, either."

"She said she might bring Michael with her tomorrow evening after work to visit me again." He smiled triumphantly, like he knew that was a big deal.

"*She did?* She was willing for you to meet Michael? How many times has she visited you here in the hospital?"

"Today was the third time. Why?"

"Wow. She is very shy, Angel. I'm surprised she worked up the nerve to come visit once, much less three times. She was very worried about you when I told her Saturday that you had been shot. Angel?"

"Hmm?"

"Please don't trifle with her. It would break her heart. I think…" she hesitated, "she has had enough hurt in her life. Do you feel attracted to her?"

He didn't hesitate at all in his response. "Yes, very much, but—"

"What?"

"I lived with someone like Patricia. Why would Teresa be interested in me?"

"She never knew Patricia, and she wouldn't judge you for your mistakes any more than you would judge her for her mistakes."

"Yeah, but I feel like it goes deeper. If she knew about Patricia, how she was, she would view me as tainted."

"*Tainted*? Wow. Were *you* participating in anonymous group sex with her every Saturday night? Or going home with strange women and not coming home until all hours of the night and morning? All you did was have a woman living with you who turned out to be a psycho. That's not your fault, either. She would no more view you as tainted than you would her for having had a child out of wedlock." *Crap!* She popped her hand over her mouth. *Crappity-crap!*

"Stop, sweetie, she told me that much herself when she told me she'd never been married. All you have to do is talk to her to know how innocent she is. On the other hand, I've been around the block a time or two."

"Angel, that makes you experienced, not a whore," Grace said laughing, shocking herself with her own words. They laughed about that, which helped to ease his tension.

"Do you think she might be attracted to me?" He sounded so hopeful.

"Yes, I think she's very interested in you, but your teasing nature makes her nervous. She's very loyal, Angel. I think she would be very good for you, especially because of Patricia. I was a little worried how you would feel about things since Patricia's little trip to temporary insanity land.

"You mean like there must be something wrong with me to allow Patricia anywhere near my friends and for not seeing through her? Yeah, you'd be right, Grace."

"Give it time, Angel. Get through Patricia's trial, if there is one, and put that behind you because Teresa *for sure* will not want to be involved in that whole mess. Maybe visit her at the store or take her to lunch. Meet her son, absolutely. That she is willing for you to meet her little boy is huge. But let me warn you, once you meet Michael, you'll be a goner. He is a precious little thing and *all boy*. He gets around faster than any kid I've ever seen."

"Really?" Angel grinned, seemingly undaunted.

"Yeah, maybe she'd come to our wedding as your date?" Grace suggested, smiling at him. "If I could, may I give you one cautionary piece of advice?"

"Sure."

"Never tease her about being shy. She hates to be teased. Gentleness is the way with her, not funning around."

"I will take those words closely to heart, Grace. Thank you for talking to me about her. I respect you for trying to protect her, being careful what you shared."

She returned to work soon after and spent the afternoon monogramming uniform shirts for one of the local restaurants. The afternoon was quiet, so she came home a little early and took her shower and washed her hair. After getting herself ready for the evening she went into her closet to choose her outfit. That's where she was when Ethan found her, standing in her sheer turquoise mesh panties and matching lace push-up bra, one foot perched on top of the other.

"What do we have here?" He came in to stand behind her, and his hands slid up her arms to her shoulders. His fingertips brushed over her collarbones and sent a warm thrill down her spine.

"Oh, I love it when you do that." She leaned back against him. "When you run your fingertips like that over me, it makes me quiver all over." Her voice was shaking slightly, the ache in her pussy sudden and demanding. "Make love to me?" She turned her face to look at him, dazzled by his sexy smile.

He caressed her cheekbones. "But you've just finished getting ready. We'll mess up your hair and makeup if we go to bed now. We need to be at the restaurant by seven o'clock and—" He nuzzled her throat, then glanced at his watch. "Its six thirty now." He chuckled when she pouted a little. "But we also can't have you unhappy now, can we?"

"No, you're right, a few minutes isn't long enough, and I don't want to make us late, but you've got to stop touching me like that. You make me melt when you do that, Ethan. Oh!" As she spoke, his hands slid down over her collarbones to fondle her breasts, rubbing his thumbs over her nipples through the sheer mesh of her bra. "Ethan, your hands, what you *do* to me. I can't—oh, no! Don't stop!" His hands had begun to slide down over her abdomen and then stopped at the band of her panties, just above her mound. "Please don't stop there, Ethan."

He grasped her hips, turned her, and gently guided her to the wall behind her, then knelt down in front of her and looked up at her. "I don't want to mess up your pretty hair or your lipstick," he slid her panties down, "but I can do this for you, honey." He looked up at her with his sexy bedroom eyes and pressed her back against the wall.

"What about you, Ethan? It's not fair."

"I'll be fine, and we still have later tonight if you want to do a little something for me."

As she opened her mouth to debate the fairness more, he put his mouth on her, effectively ending negotiations. He gently parted her lips and slid his tongue through her slit. He flicked over her clit, then round and round it. He repeated the move into her entrance, then in and out.

He changed it up a bit and began licking her clit in smooth up and down strokes, then wrapped his hand around one of her ankles and began sliding it up her calf, over her knee, then up her inner thigh, building the anticipation and tension in her body. He teased her slit with soft, gentle, featherlight touches, licking her clit at the same time. As she began panting, he slid a finger into her pussy, sliding in and out, then slid two fingers into her opening, stroking gently, working his way up to her sweet spot. Once he was there, he began licking voraciously at her clit. He kept her suspended on the edge like that until she began to teeter over.

"Ethan, oh, don't stop. I'm going to come, I—oh, honey, I'm, I'm, Oh! Ethan, I'm coming!"

He gently stroked her through every pulse as her fingers slid into his hair. When he touched her like this, he was so slow and gentle with her. Not at all like he had a goal and wanted to move on. Regardless of the clock, he took his time sweetly pleasuring her, not rushing her. He nuzzled her inner thigh and the curve at the juncture of her hip and upper thigh.

"Oh, Ethan, that was wonderful, thank you, oh! Honey." She tilted her head back against the wall, trying to catch her breath. She looked at him as he rose to his feet and gave him a wicked smile. "I don't mind reapplying my lipstick."

A look of speculation crossed his face then was replaced by a crooked little grin. "I *really* wish I was a bigger man, able to tell you no, so we won't be late, but that smile has made me weak, Gracie."

She knelt in front of him and made really quick work of his pants and boxers. She slid his cock into her mouth, and sucked him like a lollipop. She grasped the base of his cock and took him to the back of her throat. Relaxing her jaw, she allowed her eyelids to slide closed. This was her Ethan, and they could afford to be a little late. She took as much of him as she could comfortably, palmed the rest, and stroked back and forth.

Mimicking his earlier move, she slowly slid the backs of her fingertips up his inner thigh and then cupped his balls in her hand, stroking and caressing them carefully. Her other hand stroked his cock, squeezing gently, as she continued to suckle his shaft. His cock became harder and a little longer in her mouth, making her moan in admiration. The vibration sent him roaring over the brink, growling out her name, as she swallowed the cum that jetted from his cock. She licked him clean before she finally released his cock. He leaned against the wall and caressed her jaw as she looked up at him when she was finished.

"Thank you," he murmured in a hushed tone.

"My pleasure."

"We'd better get you dressed and ready for tonight, honey. We're going to be late now," Ethan said softly, sighing as he redressed. Grace looked up at him, watching his face.

"What is it, Ethan?" She rose with his help but made no move to get dressed. Her hands slid up over his muscled chest to wrap around his neck. She hugged him, enjoying the feel of his warm arms around her. He kissed the top of her head.

"I wish I could stay with you all evening, but after supper I'll have to go in to work for a little while tonight, make sure everything is running smoothly. The last several nights have been slower than normal for the club. Ben said Saturday night was really soft."

"I'm sure things will return to normal. Do you have to stay till closing?"

"No, I'll just go in for an hour or so, and then I'll come home."

"Would you like me to come with you?"

"That's sweet of you, but I'd rather you rested. I'll be home before you know it."

"What should I wear? Help me pick."

He released her and turned to her clothing hanging on a lone bar in the closet. "I'm going to get boxes and pick you up one day at lunch. We'll go pack up the rest of your clothing, okay?"

"Sure, if you don't mind. I need to bring my hanging fern over here, too. It's probably thirsty."

He removed a turquoise blue top from its hanger and handed it to her. She slipped into it as he pulled a snug-fitting pair of jeans off a hanger and held them out to her. He got out the boots Adam had bought for her while she slipped on the jeans and a pair of socks. Fully dressed, she stood in front of him and struck a pose.

"That looks good on you. Naked and in my bed would be better, but this is good, too." He smiled at her with hungry eyes, sliding a hand over her ass as she walked from the closet. He checked his watch. "Shit, we're busted. It's 6:55 p.m. We've got some explaining to do." He chuckled as they walked into the living room. Adam and Jack were seated, watching the news.

"We've already called Moe and Bill to let them know we'll be a little late. Look at this." He pointed at the TV then turned up the sound.

"Federal authorities were able to arrest eight suspects at the home of the well-known drug dealer, all in possession of narcotics and large amounts of cash. The drugs seized in the bust had an estimated street value in excess of one million dollars. The house was also being used to manufacture methamphetamine and grow marijuana. Three children were found in the house in one of the back bedrooms with another young juvenile. In other news…"

Grace had heard reports like this, but what stunned her was the image of Owen being led from a rundown looking house in handcuffs. His head was down, but she recognized him instantly. He didn't fight the officer who escorted him and said nothing, only hung his head and got into the police van without arguing.

"Did you know this was going to happen?" Grace asked.

"I spoke with Hank several days ago to let him know we were having Owen watched by a friend of ours. He told me to back him off a little because the dealer who bailed Owen out was under investigation. They had an agent undercover in the house and didn't want the leader getting suspicious. He let me know they'd be springing this trap sometime soon."

"You had someone watching Owen?"

"Yes. After he showed up at your house harassing you and then again at the shop, we had someone watching him who could provide support if needed, mostly while you were still at home," he explained. "Are you upset because we did that without asking you?"

"Why didn't you tell me?"

"We didn't want to worry you. We just wanted to make sure he stayed away from you, then the storm came, and it was no longer necessary. The guy is a witness to Owen being involved in several small drug deals and is going to be giving his account when they go to trial. That would explain why Owen finally backed off. The guy didn't want money as much as he wanted willing, obligated dealers selling for him. I hope he cooperates with the judge because Owen is going to have a very hard time in the system. Do you still feel like going out, darlin'?"

"Sure I do, Jack. I'd really like to see Moe and Bill before they go home. I knew that Owen would get himself into serious trouble someday. I'm just glad I extricated myself from his clutches before this happened. Actually, y'all extricated me. No, I'm not mad, Jack. I appreciate that you went to such lengths to protect me, and I'm sorry it was necessary. But you're right. I hope Owen cooperates with the investigation because he'd never survive going to prison."

So it was decided. They met the Travers at O'Reilley's and had a wonderful supper. A couple of Jack's friends approached him to congratulate him on becoming engaged, and he introduced them to Grace. Other than those two encounters, nobody said anything or approached them. It was a different experience than last Friday night when she'd felt so on display.

* * * *

After supper, Ethan left to spend a little time at The Pony. The mood in the club felt like that of a typical Thursday night, and Ethan and Ben put their heads together about doing some special events on weekends to draw more people into the club.

The lights were still on when he returned home. He walked in to find Grace sitting on the couch, wrapped in his robe, drinking a cup of cocoa with a legal pad full of scribbles balanced in her lap on a pillow. He put his hat on the hook on the hall bench before he came and sat down with her, leaning in for a kiss.

"The guys already go to bed?"

"Yes, I was too keyed up to sleep, so I decided to stay up and do something productive with my time."

"What are you working on?"

"I've been thinking of every wedding I've ever been to, remembering the things I liked about them. I've made a list of the people I want to invite. I also made lists of the elements I can't live without, as well as some of the stuff I'd like to skip altogether."

"What's something on your list that you couldn't possibly live without?"

"Dancing with all three of you, one at a time, in whatever order you want me." She chuckled and her eyes twinkled. He rolled his eyes and groaned, realizing the connotation of the words.

He grinned at her. "And what's something that is absolutely unnecessary?"

"The removal of my garter while everyone watches. Not because I'm shy, but because it excludes you and Adam. I'd prefer to spend that time with the three of you alone, trying to get me unlaced from my white satin corset and G-string. I could also totally do without throwing the bouquet so I don't have to watch my girlfriends go all WWF over it."

Her words had him laughing and smiling. She had a point about the garter. He liked the way she thought, but he knew who would win that bouquet toss. His feisty sister, Erin.

"I'd rather give them all flowers than do that," she continued, picking up the list.

"When are you and Charity going wedding shopping?"

"We set a date for Friday after next. She really is planning on taking me to every bridal shop within a hundred mile radius of here. Thankfully, that's not that many. At least she's calling around to see if they have plus-size gowns in stock for me to try on, so we don't waste a trip."

"Do you want one of us to go with you?"

"No, if I find anything that I really love, I'll put it on hold and have the two of you take me back to try it on again. Charity and I will have a fun girls' day. We'll probably have lunch in some prissy tea room, but the actual wedding attire I'm going to purchase with y'all.

"My lingerie will all come from an online source because even if we shop for lingerie in the mall, the chain stores won't have much in stock for someone with curves like me. You can shop online with me and help me pick that out, too. Y'all can plan the honeymoon while Charity and I go out. I'm really looking forward to those shopping excursions. But it's all just the means to an end for me. I want to be your wife." She quietly looked into his eyes. The warmth in her sweet blue eyes was like an actual physical touch. The soft lighting from the lamp beside her left her partially in shadow, and he thought she was the most beautiful woman he'd ever known.

"I want to be your husband. Are you sleepy?"

"Yes, writing it down, then talking with you about it really put it all in perspective. I want it to be as simple as possible and still make your moms and grandmas happy. I want to start off on the right foot with all of them."

"You've already done that by making their fondest wishes come true."

"What's that?"

"By falling in love with their sons and being a woman who could make all three of us fall in love with her. By being a real lady and loving us all unreservedly. You have no idea how precious and rare you are." He palmed her blushing cheek and kissed her. "They will all adore you."

"Adam called all of your parents and invited them over this Saturday evening. Jack also said y'all have something to show me that afternoon. I work the early shift from ten until two, and I'll be free after that. Juliana doesn't have me scheduled for Sunday at all." She tried to hide a yawn.

"We've booked a touring band to come play at The Dancing Pony next Friday night. They are supposed to be the next big thing in country rock music. The following Friday is going to be ladies' night, complete with male dancers. We've never done anything like that before. If it goes over well, we may have to do another one sometime."

"Strippers, hmm?" she said with a smirk as she rose from the couch, stretching her arms over her head. His robe fell open to reveal she had nothing on underneath. She smiled softly at him, when he caught his breath at the sight.

"Bad girl. I love seeing you in my robe. The caveman likes it, too."

"I wanted it because I knew it would smell like you. I wanted it around me, warming me. Does the caveman like knowing that, too?" She smiled seductively and reached for him, not bothering to close the robe.

"He's practically pounding his chest, roaring 'Mine!'" he replied as he lifted her up in his arms.

"My gosh, you are strong, Ethan Grant! I love it when y'all do that!" she said in a shaky voice as he carried her to her room.

"Is it just us tonight?" he asked, noticing the empty bed as he entered.

"For now, at least. We'll see if I can sleep. It didn't take me long to get used to having y'all snuggled all around me."

"I'll get them later if you need them. They won't mind. I know I didn't last night. Anything for my woman. I'm going to shower real quick. I'll be right back."

"I'll warm the bed for you." She giggled as she climbed under the covers.

"The caveman likes that, too." He pounded his chest a little.

When he returned, she had the bed warmed up, and she was as well. Ethan took his time with her, making her come twice before she ever even saw his cock.

* * * *

True to his word, Ethan picked up boxes and took Grace to her house during the week to pack up her clothes, shoes, and other necessities. They even had time to empty out the refrigerator and put the trash out. She thought the house looked great, except for the blue tarp, which would be removed on Wednesday when the workmen returned to do the shingle work. Angel came home from the hospital on Saturday morning. When she pulled up beside the ranch house after work on Saturday afternoon, she saw him in the barn walking around and inspecting everything, albeit at a slow pace. She went down to the barn to visit with him briefly and he told her how happy he was to be home. He mentioned to her that Teresa and Michael had been by the day before to visit him. Grace noted happily the sappy smile on his face when he talked about them both.

After returning to the house, Grace changed into more casual clothing—blue jeans and boots—at her men's request. Once she was dressed, they hopped in the SUV and drove out to the Warner ranch. Jack had gone into town while she was at work and picked up a bunch of pretty silk flowers, literally bunches and bunches of them. She understood once they made it out to the Warner family cemetery. They wanted to put flowers at all the women's headstones. Grace sat on a bench, removing tags and fluffing the bouquets, while Jack took a trash bag and started collecting the old faded ones from the vases and flower holders at each grave.

She watched her sweet men as they tidied up the cemetery and placed flowers in each vase, securing them with small rocks so they wouldn't blow away when the wind kicked up. She noticed that Jack had purchased all bright jewel tones and vibrant colors, which would look more cheerful than pastels, but need to be replaced more often because the sun would fade them.

They must do this on a regular basis.

The grass had been cut and a weed eater used recently, so when they were done, the small cemetery was a very cheery place. Once they were finished, they dusted off their hands and knees and came to collect her.

They took her around and told her about the ancestors and grandparents that now rested in that small plot of land. The ranch had been in their family for *five* generations. After the tour and the rich history her men told her about, she understood why their families were so excited.

"You are all very distantly related, aren't you?"

"Yes," Jack said. "Our great-great-great-great-grandmothers and one great-great-great-great-grandfather all came from Ireland together on a boat with their parents, Adam and Rebecca. All three of them settled on this land. I don't know if you knew that all three of our family's ranches adjoin on one side, but they do. This is the reason why. They bought the land together and divided it between the three siblings, Rachel, Ethan, and Eve, wanting each child to have a piece of land to raise their families on and make a life for their future children."

He led her over to a large headstone. She read the names, Caleb, Rachel, and Thomas, and the dates of death all hovered close around the late eighteen hundreds and early nineteen hundreds.

Jack said, "These are my great-great-great-great-grandparents."

Adam led her to another large headstone that read Adam, Mary, and Ethan.

Adam said, "These are mine, same generation, Ethan and Rachel were siblings."

Ethan led her to another headstone—Charles, Eve, and Titus.

Ethan said, "And these are mine."

They took her around to other headstones in the cemetery, but she quickly got confused because of all the different last names.

"We have it all written down at home," Jack said. "One day, when we were young kids roaming around on our summer breaks, we played in the cemetery and discovered all the multiple headstones. We knew we were distantly related. We didn't know about our families' histories of polyamorous groupings. We asked our moms and dads and grandparents, and they told what they knew of the family history. Traditionally, each woman married the older of the two men. Some of our ancestors were real characters. A few died very young. Some lived to be over one hundred. We became intrigued with the idea that there might be one woman out there that would want us."

Looking for common ground, Grace asked, "Are there any women in your family tree that were wife to three husbands?"

Jack replied, "Adam had two brothers who died in Ireland. Rebecca was married to him, but was wife to all three. Life was hard back then, and a full widow on her own with children and no man to take care of her and provide for them was more than our ancestors could bear to think of. In several cases, the husbands were brothers. If one of them died, she still had a provider and husband to watch over her and the children. They were a long way out here back then, and it made life easier for everyone. The family unit was more likely to survive if there were two men to look after the family. Financially, it also made life easier, since more providers meant more stability."

"Why no multiple wives?" she asked.

"Their purpose was to protect the women and children," Ethan said, "not have a harem to serve their needs. More women would have meant more children and more need for support and protection. Plus, they believed it might lead to jealousy among the women. The only men who became part of such a marriage were men who were close friends or brother to the other man in the group and able to share with no rivalry. You see how we are with you, and you said yourself how you would be in a grouping with another woman. I remember you saying it would be like swallowing razor blades to see us with another woman. We believe that it's in our nature to be like this, just like that inability is part of your nature, overriding even your submissive tendencies." Ethan removed his hat and ran his fingers through his long brown hair before he put the hat back on.

She chuckled. "Yeah, there's no way I could be happy with another woman in the house. I remember having a mental image of another woman walking from one of your bedrooms, fresh from having sex with you, and just like then it makes me feel nauseated and cold to think of it. If that's what y'all had wanted, I'd have run from you screaming the first day."

"For us, there's no way we could be happy without sharing you," Jack said. "We might each have individually found a woman to be happy with, but it wouldn't have been the same, and it wouldn't have been what we dreamed of all these years."

"So there is a history of polyamory in these parts I never knew about?" she asked.

"This area was very sparsely populated back then. None of our parents were polyamorous. Neither were my grandparents," Ethan replied. "Either because they were worried about the social stigma attached to polygamy and bigamy, or because the right people never came along or were too scared. Jack and Adam's grandparents and my great-grandparents were the last groupings we know of. None of the polyamorous groupings were exclusive to bloodlines, so we believe there were many other polyamorous groupings from those times in related families throughout the area.

"Because we had so many family members all together in one place I think is the only reason we put two and two together. Nowadays, family members are spread out and don't know much about their ancestors. Outsiders probably would have thought that a triple headstone meant a wife who had two husbands, married to one, widowed, and then married to the other. It's not the kind of thing that could have been listed on a marriage certificate."

"What about cousins, and…you know…"

"Inbreeding?" Ethan answered, chuckling.

"Yeah."

"They were very fastidious about not intermarrying between cousins and viewed intermarrying too closely the way any other normal person would. There is none of that in our family, and you'll notice," he indicated two very small but carefully crafted headstones situated side by side, "the only infants in the cemetery both died in 1918, during the Spanish influenza pandemic, so there were no babies born with birth defects or abnormalities that died from them and no one that we know of that lived who was deformed. Our three bloodlines are very distinct and separate. There is more likelihood that we're closely related to you than to each other." He slipped a hand around her hip and kissed her cheek.

"So how often do you come here to make the cemetery look so pretty?"

"It's always been done two or three times a year, plus sometimes seasonally," Ethan replied. "My mom loves poinsettias, so she comes at Christmas and decorates the headstones with bunches of bright red and white poinsettias. Jack's mom loved lilies, so she always decorated at Easter. What's your favorite, Gracie?"

"Roses, of course."

"If you wanted to decorate on Valentine's Day or Mother's Day," Adam told her, "that's how it would work, if you wanted to. Not everyone likes to come out to the cemetery. For some people, it's just too painful. We do what we can."

They came to stand in front of the still freshly covered grave of Rose Marie Warner. They had removed all the dead flower arrangements that had been left after the funeral, and the mound of recently turned earth looked bare and somehow raw in the summer sunshine. Only the profuse and brightly colored silk arrangement Jack had placed at it remained. It reminded her of a fresh bandage on a quickly healing wound for some reason. Life went on.

"I wish I knew more of Rose Marie's story. Did she know your dad's grandparents or Adam's grandparents, Jack?"

"She was very good friends with Rose, Adam's grandmother, and even vaguely remembered a very elderly Callie Grant, Ethan's great-great grandmother. Mom and Dad lived with his parents right after they got married. Mom's mother died when she was little, and so my Grandmother Regina was like a mother to her, and grandfathers Robert and Daniel treated her very well, better than her own family did. She loved being a part of the Warner family."

"Now I really wish I knew more of her story."

"Ask Dad sometime, and he'll tell you what he knows of it," Jack replied, smiling. "We'd better get home soon. People are going to start coming over at six."

* * * *

Ethan had smoked a ham and a brisket, and her men had assured Grace that everyone else was bringing food. If she wanted to make tea, and maybe a dessert, that was all she was to do since she was the bride-to-be. The night before, she'd baked three homemade peach cobblers. The men had already dipped into one. She knew they would, which was why she made extra. They'd all enjoyed it with Blue Bell Homemade Vanilla ice cream after supper the night before. After tasting her cobbler, they told her she would be an instant sensation in the family. She made it the old-fashioned way, from scratch, with rolled-out pie dough, not store-bought.

Kathleen and Paul Grant were the first to arrive, with Ethan's sister, Erin, who was in her early twenties. Now Grace could see where Ethan got his blue eyes and handsome good looks. He was the image of his father. Erin was a peach, but feisty as well, giving Ethan a hard time about getting shot. She was a medical school student at UT and had to see his wound.

Grace remembered Ethan's parents vaguely from the funeral. She'd stayed so close to Jack the whole time that the opportunity had never presented itself to meet them. They warmly welcomed her to the family, and Kathleen offered to help in any way Grace might need with the wedding. Grace told her once the plans were set she would contact her.

Sue and Richard Davis, Adam's parents, arrived next with Sue's mother, Rose, who was in her early nineties. Surprisingly, Sue was a tiny little thing with dark brown hair and sweet brown eyes. Adam inherited his build and height from his dad as well. Richard was broad at the shoulders and had the same green eyes that made Grace catch her breath when she looked into Adam's, only Richard's had more smile lines around them. Looking at Richard and Paul was a little like looking at Ethan and Adam in another twenty or thirty years. The thought of looking into their eyes for that many years or more made her heart throb with joy.

Sue's mother, Rose, was a tiny little thing, also. White-haired and wizened with age, she was still well in control of her faculties, although her eyesight wasn't very good. She sat in one of the straight-backed chairs in the dining room and did her best to follow all the conversations. They got her telling stories on the men, both fathers and sons. That was the best part for Grace, besides sitting with Joe, Jack's dad, and holding his hand for a little while. He still had a bandage on one arm and wore a smaller band-aid on his forehead from his fall.

"So we're standing around Barney's grave," Jack said as he told his story. "The three of us are fighting tears because we're gonna miss Barney the beagle. Adam steps up to the grave to say a few words, and he starts crying." Jack tried to keep from crying he was laughing so hard. "And Rose starts *beating on us* all of a sudden, just went to town thrashing on us. Wham! Wham! Wham!"

"Adam is crying and hollering, 'Grandma why are ya beating on us?' Then Mama started beating on me, and Kathleen started whaling on Ethan. We're all crying, thinking this is what happens at funerals, and suddenly Rose starts laughing, hollering. '*Ticks*! You're all covered in ticks!' We came running out of those woods laughing, crying, and carrying on. The mamas stripped us down in the yard and picked them all off. Meanwhile, they had ticks climbing all over them as well."

"I'll tell you those little boys could *wail*," Rose said, laughing along with everyone else. "You'd have thought the world was coming to an end. In retrospect, I suppose they might have thought that's what happened at funerals."

Everyone was gathered in the living room, listening as Rose told another story when her men got up and went into the office. All eyes, including Grace's, turned to them when they returned a few minutes later, looking conspiratorial and a little nervous.

Chapter Thirty-seven

They came to stand in front of her chair. She opened her eyes wide in surprise when they knelt in front of her on their knees. She knew this was coming at some point, just hadn't been sure when. Her eyes welled up, and she blushed, her shaking hands clasped in her lap to hide their shaking. She heard women gasp and a few sobs break forth but was only partially aware of them or the camera flashes. All she really saw were ocean blue eyes and pale green eyes and sparkling blue eyes, all reflecting love for her. Jack was in the center, holding a velvet box. Nervously, she looked down at it and back up at them.

"We already proposed, Grace, but we wanted to do it again. We wanted to do it right this time, with the ring." He opened the box as Adam and Ethan reached out to touch her arm or her leg.

"Will you marry me, darlin'?" Jack took her hand and kissed it.

"With all my heart, Jack. Yes."

"Will you marry me, Gracie?" Ethan kissed her palm.

"Yes, Ethan, I'd love to marry you."

"Will you marry me, baby?" Adam kissed her fingertips.

"Yes, Adam, I want to marry you. All of you. I would love to be your wife."

Rose clapped her hands and laughed out loud. "Wonderful!" Her eyes seemed far away, maybe remembering the day her husbands had proposed to her.

Jack removed the ring from the box and slid it onto her finger as they all three gently held her hand. She looked down at it. It was platinum and gold with three strands braided together, intertwining like vines, with three square, bright white diamonds of equal sizes set side by side in a row. It was perfect, representing each of the three men who loved her, whose hearts were bound to hers.

"It's beautiful! I love it, I love you!" She sobbed and wrapped her arms around all of them, crying, laughing, and kissing them. Everyone else laughed and clapped and cried. The women all hugged Grace, and the men all patted Jack, Ethan, and Adam on their backs.

Erin said, "That is the most romantic thing I have ever seen!"

"Meh," Rose said, grinning, waving her hand nonchalantly. "They did okay. Sweet and simple is good."

Everyone laughed and convinced her to tell how she got engaged in 1936 to Harrison and Jefferson McCloud, her husbands.

She had always wanted to go to Italy, and both Harrison and Jefferson knew this. They wrote her a letter telling her how much they loved her and had an Italian friend translate it for them, then mailed it to her. She ran all over town trying to find an Italian dictionary so she would know what it said.

"Do you remember how it went, Mom?" Sue asked her.

"Of course. I'll never ever forget the moment I finally knew what it said. The Italian version was, *Vi vogliamo bene Tesoro. Vuoi sposarmi noi?* Which in English means, 'We love you, sweetheart. Will you marry us?'" She clutched her little hands to her bosom and said, "What could I say? I was so smitten with those two, and they'd gone to such trouble."

"What did you do?" Grace asked. Everyone laughed because they'd heard the story before.

"I had to purchase that Italian to English dictionary, so I put it to good use. I wrote my response out, translated it, and had it delivered back to them. I wrote, *Ti amo tanto tanto, come potrei dire di no? Si! Lo ti sposero!* Which means, 'I love you both so much, how could I possibly say no? Yes, I will marry you!'"

Erin talked Grace into telling the original proposal story from the Friday before, which was met with glowing approval from all the women, including Grandma Rose.

It was late when the evening was over. The women all left their phone numbers with Grace, and she promised to call once they had a plan and a date.

The women had all pitched in and cleaned up the kitchen and put everything away, so there was nothing to do when everyone was gone but go to bed. Grace went to her bathroom and removed her clothing and turned on the shower. She slipped off the ring and almost put it back in the box but remembered they had told her they were having it inscribed for her. Flipping on the overhead light, she looked inside her ring just as Jack, Adam and Ethan stopped in the doorway.

"Ah, we caught her just in time. We wanted to be here when you read the inscription. Read it out loud," Ethan said, watching eagerly.

*Darlin' * Gracie * Baby * CD*

"What does the CD stand for? Oh! Carpe diem. With all my names you call me by. How sweet. I love it. Y'all, I could not ask for more wonderful, thoughtful fiancés. You are so sweet. I'm overwhelmed by your love, by the acceptance of your family. I love you."

Jack lightly tapped the ring. "There is another narrow platinum band that goes with this. You'll wear the engagement ring for now, if it fits properly, and the day before the wedding, Clay will solder the wedding band to the engagement ring. We're having it engraved also."

"With what?" she asked, curious.

"We haven't decided for sure yet, but we were thinking something scriptural. Do you have any favorite scriptures?"

"I have lots of favorite scriptures, but I'd rather it be something significant to y'all. That would mean more to me. I'm tired. Y'all want to take a shower with me? I may need someone to hold me up, I'm so sleepy." She yawned through the last part. "And I want you all to sleep with me tonight. I miss not cuddling up with you." She pouted just a tiny little bit.

"Of course we'll sleep with you, darlin'. We're just trying to give you a break. We don't want you to wear yourself out trying to make us happy."

"I'll be good and just sleep tonight, okay?"

They showered together, then tucked her in as she yawned sleepily, snuggling all around her. She appreciated the care that they had for her, even though she wouldn't have minded if they'd wanted to make love. She drifted off to sleep, smiling in the dark as Adam sweetly stroked her hip.

* * * *

"Here you go, Gracie." Ethan said, handing Grace the scissors.

"Hips and Curves?" She asked as she looked at the mailing label before she cut the tape open on both ends of the mysterious package that awaited her on the breakfast bar when she got home on Monday afternoon. She squealed when she saw a number of colorful packages inside the box. *Satin!*

Jack was broiling fish in the oven while Adam finished up some paperwork and phone calls at the counter top. Excited, she began opening packages. Starting with the pink packages, she discovered a robe, a lace nightgown, and a naughty pink drawstring nightie. She loved the color and thanked Jack sweetly with kisses when she found out he ordered the pink items, promising to model them for him soon.

Then she opened the champagne-colored packages and found a satin kimono-style robe and matching teddy. Discovering those were Adam's selections, she wrapped her arms around his neck and let him lift her off her feet for a kiss, thanking him. He told her he wanted her to have something that was sexy but also comfortable for her. She could wear it just to nap in if she wanted. She loved his tender heart so much and told him so. He kissed her again and set her down very gently.

She opened the black packages. Ethan's gift was a snug, soft, black, long-sleeved, low-cut T-shirt. It was versatile if she wore jeans with it but earthy and sexy if she wore it with just the black high-cut satin panties and demi bra that came with it. She knew the bra would barely contain her nipples when she tried it on. Even if she wore it with jeans, they'd all be thinking about what was underneath. She kissed him and thanked him, laying her head on his shoulder for a second.

She noted the symmetry in the gifts and their givers. Jack bought her something playful, sweet, and sassy in pink. Adam bought her something soft and luxuriant and sexy in an almost gold color. Ethan's gift was something edgy in black. Every item was damn sexy in its own way but reflected the personality of the giver.

"I love all of it! I hope you didn't spend a fortune. All the fabrics feel so rich and expensive."

Adam spoke up, "We were waiting to see if the quality was good before telling you about the website. We wanted to be sure it was up to our standards. June recommended Hips and Curves to me, saying we'd like what we found there. I think we do. I can't wait to see you model everything."

"They have an incredible selection of bridal lingerie." Ethan grinned as she reacted to his words.

"Really? Show me!" she said enthusiastically.

He grinned, opened the computer, and got online. Pulling up the website, he placed the computer in front of her at the bar.

"Well, my goodness, she's *hot*, isn't she?" Grace pointed at the lovely plus-size brunette on the home page, dressed in a black satin corset and transparent black lace short petticoat. She had a playful little grin on her face as she held her manicured finger to her lips like she was shushing the viewer to secrecy. Very playful and sexy.

"Yeah," Ethan said, "everything on this website is modeled by plus-size models, so you can see what the items will look like on. She's my favorite model."

Pressing her lips together to suppress her smile, Grace placed her hand on her hip, cocked it, and pivoted to face Ethan, one eyebrow arched. She clearly heard Adam snort in amusement as he sat at the countertop, watching Ethan trying to get traction as he backpedaled.

Ethan held up his hands and took a step backward. "Totally not getting off on the lingerie model, okay? I'm just saying it's easy to imagine you in the things she models. She's built a lot like you, only you're hotter."

She dropped the disgruntled look, unable to maintain it as he groveled adoringly. "Aw, you think I'm hotter than her? Damn, I love you!" she squealed, kissing him on the cheek, because Grace thought the model with her long black hair, soft feminine curves and generous derriere was flat-out gorgeous.

Jack and Adam came to see which model he was talking about and agreed. "Yep, tiny waist, luscious curvy hips," Jack said, sliding his hands to said area before sliding up and cupping her breasts gently in both hands. "But your breasts are fuller, and your skin is—*mmm*."

The model was olive skinned, and Grace's skin was more ivory toned, which was evidently more to Jack's liking since he was currently licking and nibbling on her ear-lobe.

Jack released her and returned to the kitchen to remove the fish from the oven. "They have a lot to choose from. But they have a whole section that is nothing but lingerie for the bride. You should definitely order from them."

"I can picture that white satin corset and G-string with those white lace stockings and garters any day of the week, not just on our wedding night," Adam murmured.

She stopped and sighed softly. "I live in heaven. You men are so wonderful, so precious to me." Adam stood behind her barstool and wrapped his big, muscled arms around her, gently squeezed her, and kissed the top of her head.

In keeping with her plan, Adam and Ethan promised to help her pick out whatever she wanted for the wedding, which included foundation garments as well as nightgowns and other naughty things. She laughed and giggled at them when Ethan emphasized the word *naughty* and pointed to a pair of crotchless panties displayed in the bridal section of the website.

After they finished eating supper and cleaning the kitchen, Grace got her legal pad and lists, and the four of them sat down to make a plan. She had already decided to sell the house rather than have the headache of tenants to deal with. They agreed on a day to move everything she wanted to keep to the ranch. She planned to donate the rest of the unusable items to the Goodwill Store and Salvation Army and local food banks. Whatever antiques she brought with her they would make room for in the house.

They agreed on a small church wedding, followed immediately by a private binding ceremony and a reception at a Victorian-era mansion that was available for such occasions in Divine. The atmosphere of the place was so much warmer and cozier than a reception hall. Her men surprised her by hiring a consultant to handle all the details for the wedding ceremony and reception. All she needed to worry about was finding the dress and necessary items she'd be wearing or had a need for.

They set a date for the end of July, a little more than six weeks away. Jack said they were also planning to have the renovations completed on the master suite by then, if all went according to their plans and the furniture was finished and the mattress ready on time. She was flexible on that timeline because she knew things seldom went exactly according to plan with such endeavors.

"It's not something we've talked about yet," Jack said, "but we can have the smaller bedroom upstairs fixed up and painted as a nursery, if that's something you would like us to do, Grace. Or if you'd rather, we can fix it up for an office or study for you."

"Do y'all want to have kids?" she asked Jack and Ethan. She already knew how Adam felt and winked at him across the table. He winked back.

"Because I can imagine a whole passel of kids running around here, wreaking havoc."

"You have no idea how much we'd love to have babies with you, Grace." Jack smiled hugely. "But I want you to remember something. You are our main priority and will continue to be, no matter what. If you have four or five or only one baby, it's fine with us, just so you're healthy and happy doing it. Lord, *yes*, I'd love to make a baby with you."

"Exactly how many is a passel?" Ethan asked quizzically.

"Just a whole bunch." She laughed. "I think I'd probably like to play for a year or two, though, before we settle down to having babies."

"Playing sounds fine with us," Adam replied enthusiastically.

She showed them the list of things she would need to purchase, and even though Ethan and Adam would be with her when she made most of these purchases, they gave her a debit card with her name on it. The card was for a new account in her name at their bank. Weekly electronic funds transfers would move money from their bank accounts and deposit it in hers. They set a very generous budget, excessive, in fact, for the purchase of the things she would want and told her the reception was already handled. With the reservations and arrangements made, all they had to do was make a list of who needed to be invited. Ethan began to compile one as they talked about whom they wanted there.

They surprised Grace by asking her to pose for a formal bridal portrait, which they could hang in the living room. That had been Charity's suggestion to them, and they liked the idea. What they didn't know was that Charity had also talked to Grace about doing tasteful boudoir portraits for her men's bedrooms. Something just a little sexy, maybe in lingerie that she knew the men liked. Grace now planned to use the items from Hips and Curves.

Grace and Charity's first stop Friday would be with a girlfriend of Charity's, a portrait photographer, who would be doing all four portraits and the wedding photography as well. The photographer would work her magic with Grace and have the portraits framed and ready to give to her men as wedding gifts.

* * * *

She had to grin, trying to extricate herself from the slumbering Twister game she found herself in. She'd awakened very early to find that during the night they'd all latched on to a body part, clutched to them if possible. In Jack's case, his face was pressed into her cleavage. They released her, and she took her shower and got ready to go to the photo shoot. The lingerie and everything else she needed was already in the trunk of her car. All she'd have to do was leave her car unlocked so Charity could move them to her car once she got there. So far, Jack, Ethan and Adam had no clue what she was up to, and she hoped to keep it a surprise.

They were all sitting at the breakfast bar finishing the morning meal when Charity walked in the front door. "Knock, knock! Everybody decent?"

"Yeah! Come on in, Charity," Ethan called. "Have you eaten?"

"Yes, thank you. Ready to go, sugar plum?" she asked. "Hey, I love that sundress and those sexy silver sandals. Adam, I'm taking you shopping for me, sweetheart. You have the best taste."

"Thanks, but I can't take any credit for good taste. I know a great saleslady at Macy's that has awesome instincts. She helped me pick everything out," Adam replied.

"You should come with us," Grace said, doing a quick spin. "We're going to take me shopping there sometime soon."

"Just let me know when. Well, let's get this show on the road if you're done," Charity said. Grace grabbed her purse and then soundly kissed each one of her men.

They spent the entire morning at the photography studio, doing hair and makeup, listening to music and getting Grace in the proper mindset, and then the lingerie came out.

After the photo shoot, Grace was feeling particularly brave and daring and asked Charity for help with a quandary she was facing. As Grace explained her need, Charity flashed a big grin, and they made an unscheduled stop at an adult toy store in Morehead. Grace walked out thirty minutes later feeling like a naughty girl, bearing a shopping bag that contained lubricant, an erotic romance novel, and three anal plugs in graduated sizes. Charity coached her on the way home in her usual straightforward irreverent style. When Grace walked in the door back at the ranch house after the day's rather risqué agenda, she had a new sexy wiggle in her walk.

She came home with quite a few shopping bags that afternoon and felt like she accomplished something, even finding a dress in Morehead that might work. She asked the owner of Weddings by Maudie if she would put it on hold so she could bring Ethan and Adam to have a look at it. Maudie told her she would also look for others like it that she might be able to get her hands on and would get back to Grace later in the week.

Grace convinced her men to all make love to her that night, and they took their time stroking and making love to her, sending her into a state of rapturous bliss. During the night, she awoke to find Ethan gently stroking her cheek.

"I'm sorry. I didn't mean to disturb you. I just…couldn't keep my hands off of you." In the dim light, she looked up into his face. The love and desire that radiated there were every bit as clear and obvious to her as the hot, hard erection that rested against her hip.

She reached up to his jaw and tilted her lips to his for a kiss. "Ethan? Do you need me?"

"Always."

He rose from the bed, holding out his hand for her to join him. They went in the living room where he collected two thick blankets from a storage cabinet. He opened the back door and led her, naked, out onto the back porch. Stepping out into the night air bare-skinned, Grace felt every sensual nerve in her body fire to throbbing life. The naughtiness of being outside naked, with the added risk of being seen, had her heart beating a rapid rhythm in her chest, and her pussy pulsed in a corresponding beat. Droplets of her slick, sudden arousal coated her slit and dampened her thighs. The night air was humid and sultry, and the crickets and cicadas provided nighttime music, along with the occasional whinny from the horse barns. Ethan placed a folded blanket on the glider, positioning it so that her knees would be protected from the bare metal.

He took her in his arms, leaned her against one of the porch railings, and kissed her, her body pressed to his from lip to toes. He slid a hand down from her breast to her hip and then curved around to her ass, lifting her thigh and positioning it around his hip as she leaned slightly against the thick support post. In this position, his cock slid along her folds, rubbing against her clit. He bent down to take her nipple into his mouth, sucking on it vigorously, before switching to the other one.

His cock slid back and forth through her slit. One or two strokes and the underside of it was coated with the hot juices that flowed from her as he kissed her, further stoking that fire. His fingers slid over the swell of her ass to her cleft, following it down to her pussy, and brushed his fingers through her drenched slit. She hissed and trembled at the sensation, and a moan escaped her lips when his finger slid, light as a feather, over her clit, setting off tremors in her creamy cunt.

He pressed his lips to her collarbone, whispering, "Gracie, you're wet for me, aren't you?"

"Honey, I *stay* wet for you."

He kissed her again, a long, slow kiss, before drawing her onto his lap after he sat down and wrapped his arms around her hips. He kissed his way to her breasts and licked and sucked on her nipples.

"Would you like to try out the glider?" He smiled when she moaned and nodded because she had been hoping that was his plan.

"I thought you'd never ask, honey."

Making sure there was ample padding for her knees, he drew her onto his lap, facing him. His big hands held her hips as she positioned herself over him while she held on to the back of the glider, which he held steady with his feet on the porch. She settled on her knees and shins, her feet hanging over the curved front edge of the glider, perfectly fitting in that space. Holding the glider with one hand, she reached down and spread her lips for him as he held his cock in position for her. Once she felt the wide head at her entrance, she began a slow, hot descent over him that left them both breathless.

She breathed slow and deep as she reveled in the sensation of his thick cock entering and stretching her to accommodate him. She loved taking him inside her like this. Even though she was poised above his lap, over him, she still felt opened and vulnerable to him. She bowed her head and closed her eyes, experiencing the pleasure as every nerve ending in her body sang for him.

As was so often the case with her men, the sheer size of them and the loving attention they paid to her before entering her had her poised on the edge. She arched her back and tucked her hips as she rose over him. She slid down on his cock again, taking all of him into her, feeling his cock increase in size and hardness as she did.

"Ethan, you're so hot and hard inside of me. I love feeling you inside me." She couldn't speak anymore.

She threw her head back, her hair falling across his thighs behind her as she began riding him in swift short strokes, her breath hitching. Moments away from orgasm, she clasped her hands in his, hard, and leaned back. Relying solely on him to keep her from falling off, she rode him to a long, hard, keening orgasm ending in a wail, unable to control how loud she was. Ethan thrust into her pulsing cunt, growling deeply as he buried himself to the hilt and stilled, holding her to him tightly. He filled her with his cum and then pulled her to him, resting his cheek above her breast as they both tried to catch their breath.

He set the rocker in gentle motion as she lay against him, and her still-throbbing pussy responded to the rocking motion of the glider, with him still inside her. Each back and forth sway made her shudder and tremble over him. Her body felt as if it were under his control and not hers as she writhed and rocked on him with the slow movement of the glider. The leisurely pace continued, but he rocked in shorter strokes, causing his cock to gently rock inside her a little more insistently. It was too perfect and beautiful, and she moaned when she felt her muscles begin to tighten down, and tension filled her muscles. She sat up and looked down into his eyes so he could watch the rapture spread over her face. She came again in a slow, hot wave, her pelvis rocking over him, her body, heart, and soul completely satisfied. A soft moan was the only sound that escaped her lips. He stilled the glider, and she melted in his arms, utterly spent.

He drew the other soft throw over her and covered her so she wouldn't get chilled and sweetly stroked her as she recovered. She listened to the crickets and cicadas as they called, at peace with his arms around her while he caressed her back and hips.

"Ethan, when I imagined it, it was pretty hot, but that was really unbelievable. You are a sweet, sweet lover. You spoil me so much."

"I could say the same exact thing about you, Gracie," he murmured against her throat as he tucked her to him. "You feel so warm, so silky, the way you hold on to me, the way you breathe when you're about to come. I can't get enough of any of it. I'd stay inside you forever, listening to your heartbeat if I could."

* * * *

Her co-workers threw her a going away party, wishing her all the best. Some even brought gifts, treating the occasion like a bridal shower. She'd worked with this wonderful close-knit family for several years and loved them all. She would miss them but relished the thought of having weekends free.

After the party was over, Teresa helped her carry the gifts out to her vehicle. On the way to her house, she stopped and got each of the men a large sweet tea. Parking at the curb, she climbed out of the Honda and tried to not spill any of the Styrofoam cups.

Her men had volunteered to go over to her house and begin loading furniture and packing boxes. She'd given them a list of pieces of furniture and other packable items she wanted in the ranch house with her. Now she would direct them in what pieces needed to go to Goodwill, The Salvation Army, and go through her books and other small items. Luckily, she had never been a packrat.

Jack found her in the closet, placing unwanted items in a box. "Honey, you're not taking much with you to the ranch house. You know we'll make room for whatever you want to keep. Are you sure you want to donate all this furniture? You don't have to part with so many things for us." There were five other boxes already packed that would all go to The Salvation Army sitting outside her closet.

"There is too much here that has sad memories of Owen tied to it." Indicating the boxes, she said, "All these are clothing that was too big for me that I would hide inside of, loose-fitting jeans, oversized T-shirts, and frumpy clothing I'll never wear again. Someone else needs these things that they'll actually fit. It's the same with the furniture and other things. It no longer fits who I am or the life I have now. I need a clean slate. Is there anywhere else on the ranch that we could use the furniture, maybe in the bunkhouse or over at Angel's? Is there any of it that y'all could use?"

"I could call Angel and ask him. Quinten Parks is new in town. There might be something among all these pieces that he could use. I'll let them know if they want it they'll need to come right away to claim it."

"Thank you, Jack, for handling that. Would you also call Goodwill and The Salvation Army to come pick up the rest?" She pushed the boxes out into the empty bedroom, where he stacked them for her. She sealed the last one with tape.

Twenty minutes later, Angel arrived with some of the ranch hands and two pickup trucks. Quinten had arrived five minutes earlier and claimed several pieces he could use. Ethan quickly had him loaded, and he went in to thank Grace.

"You're welcome, Quinten. I hope you like it in Divine." She shook his hand after rubbing hers on her jeans.

"I do, ma'am. Ethan's a good man to work for. Well, I'll get out of your hair. Moving days are always stressful. Don't work too hard."

"Not with these men around. I hardly have to lift a finger." She smiled in relief, grateful again for all the help with packing up the house.

With Angel's direction, the ranch hands loaded up most of the remaining furniture. Grace talked Angel into taking the gas grill as well. He had the hands load it, as he was still recovering. A few minutes later, a truck from the Goodwill Store arrived, then another from The Salvation Army. Ethan and Adam helped them load everything they were taking. When the house was empty, and it was all said and done, the items Grace was bringing with her filled Jack's ten-foot flatbed trailer.

She kept a box of books that truly meant something to her, her CD collection that had been culled rigorously, and an antique oak desk that had belonged to her father. She also kept her solid oak headboard and footboard which had belonged to her parents, as well as her mother's collection of Italian blown glass vases and bowls. Her men had carefully wrapped each piece in bubble wrap for her and then placed them in a box that sat on the front floorboard of Jack's SUV to be carried to the ranch in safety.

They'd checked with her several times, making sure that she was not parting with stuff prematurely, but each time she felt lighter and freer in her explanation. She was good. Having them with her helped keep that in the forefront of her mind. She had what really mattered most. Their love. The rest was just stuff.

The following week, Grace and Jack met with a Realtor and listed the house for sale. The house had been left to Grace because she was unmarried, but Grace had told Charity years ago that after the fees were paid and the taxes settled, the remainder would be split in half between the two of them. Charity told her she didn't have to do it, but Grace insisted and said it could be put into the kids' college fund. She owed Charity a debt of gratitude for convincing her to take a chance on Jack, Ethan, and Adam, and she wanted to bless Charity for her encouragement.

By the beginning of June, they already had a contract signed on the house, and the sale went forward with relatively few hitches. They decided to give an allowance to replace the tub rather than messing with replacing it themselves, and the house sold, as is, for the asking price.

* * * *

One Friday, in the middle of July, Grace was working at the sales counter sorting new orders she'd just received when the doorbell rang, and she looked up to greet the next customer.

Shock made her heart pound when she looked into Owen's eyes. She took out her cell phone. She had never filed a restraining order but instantly regretted never doing it. Then she castigated herself.

The Grace who had allowed him to mistreat her was dead and gone. New and improved Grace was either about to clean his sorry-ass clock or maybe get shot in the head if he was armed. She sincerely hoped he wasn't armed.

She moved out from behind the counter, ice in her heart and steel in her backbone. She heard, "Oh, shit," from one of her partners in the hallway leading out front. She knew Rose would call Jack now.

"Don't call him yet, Rose. Hold on for just a second."

She scowled at Owen with distaste. He looked smaller and weaker than she remembered him. His face was gaunt. As he looked her over, she watched the emotions playing over his features.

His face showed a flicker of fear when he looked in her eyes, as though he might have believed she was about to kick his ass personally. He had not fared well in jail but must have cooperated with the judge because here he was.

"What the hell are you doing here?" she asked in a cold voice.

Chapter Thirty-eight

Owen put up his hands in surrender, and his eyes pleaded with Grace to listen to him. Curiosity won out, and she ceased her advance on him. He stood by the door, his hands still in front of him, sort of afraid. Good for him.

"I didn't come here to ask for anything, okay? Please, just hear me out, and then I promise I'll go and never bother you ever again." There was meekness about Owen that was new. The Owen she knew subjugated everyone around him and placed the blame for his life screw-ups at everyone else's feet. This Owen looked broken-hearted, actually just plain *broken*.

"What do you have to say to me that I could possibly want to hear?" she asked defensively. She was very curious but not willing to let him think he'd just get away with saying his piece and then leaving.

"I came to apologize. I came to tell you I'm sorry I came up here last month and asked for money and threatened you. I accused you of stealing my stuff. I know that my things got stolen from my truck while it was impounded. I was nothing but a drunken son of a bitch and I never held a job and provided for you the way a man should." His voice shook with emotion.

"I allowed you to work two jobs to support my sorry drunken ass. I kept you from going to college like you wanted to after high school. I embarrassed you by being arrested drunk on your front lawn last month. I insulted you all those years and told you that you were fat and ugly. I made you think I'd only…you know, *have sex with you in the dark*," he whispered it softly so no one else could hear, "and let you think it was because I thought you were fat. It was because I didn't want you to see how inadequate I was. I accused you of screwing the repairman to pay for the repair on the AC, and I ruined your laptop computer. I wasn't there for you and I used you." His voice cracked, and he quickly swiped the tears from his face on his sleeve. "I'm sorry. *Sorry* for all those things and because I never loved you the way you *deserved.* And Lord have mercy on me, I'm *so sorry* I hit you, Grace. I'll never be able to forgive myself for hitting you."

"You sorry sack of shit, you can't even remember half of what you're apologizing for."

"Your men paid me a visit after I got out of rehab and got put on probation. I was already going to come and apologize to you, but they paid me a call this morning and told me what I'd done. I've only been out of rehab a couple of days, but I'm clean. I'm staying in a half-way house and going to AA meetings every night. Judge says if I screw up again, he'll go hard on me. I got counseling when I was in rehab and started talking to your old pastor who comes to visit there. We're gonna start meeting at his office every week. There's a new distribution center being built in Waco, and a friend of mine I met in rehab told me there might be a job for me there. If I go, I'll stay in AA and keep getting counseling. I'm not well and healthy, but I know I did it to myself.

"I know you're getting married to Mr. Warner in two weeks, and I wanted to congratulate you and tell you I'm really happy for you, Grace." His eyes overflowed as he looked at her, his voice shaking harder. "Mr. Warner is a good man, I can tell, and I know he's going to take good care of you, just like you always deserved. I feel real bad for making you think you were fat and ugly, but even worse because I know you *believed* me."

"Grace, you're just the most beautiful thing I've ever seen, standing there. You look pretty as an angel, and I never saw it and never told you, and I'm a bastard for it, I know. I know all you'll have of me are sad memories because I hurt you so much, but I want you to know I wish you every joy that life can offer you, and I hope someday you can find it in your heart to forgive me."

He wiped his tears on his shirt sleeve again and shoved his hands in his pockets. He scrunched his shoulders and looked at his feet for a second, visibly trying to pull himself together. "If–if there is something you feel like you need to say to me, whatever it is, I deserve it, and you can say it if you want to," he offered and then seemed to brace himself for whatever she might conceivably say.

She felt impassive looking at him, felt no strong emotion at all, really. Maybe that was because he'd surprised her, both by showing up but also by making a sincere, heartfelt apology, something she would not have expected in a million years. She thought of the last few times she'd seen him. She clearly remembered him backhanding her, then beating on her door in the middle of the night, then standing in the very same spot threatening her for money. As those images flicked through her mind one at a time, she realized they no longer had strong emotions attached to them. They were just old memories. She'd experienced too much love in the interim for them to hold sway over her, and his apology seemed to also play a part in some of the pain leaking from the recollection.

"If you have an opportunity to find love again, ever, in your life, will you treat her with respect and honor her?"

"I doubt there will ever be another woman for me, Grace, not after you, after what I've done. I realized in jail the second time around and even more in rehab how bad what I'd done to you was."

Grace sighed, knowing she had to release him and severe the bond forever. "Owen, I hope in time you will forgive yourself. I appreciate your apology. I'd never have thought you'd own up to your actions. I'm glad you're clean. I forgive you, Owen." He'd quietly started weeping again, trying to hold back sobs that were racking his gaunt frame. She handed him the box of Kleenex tissues, which he thanked her for.

"I forgive you for what you did to me and the things you said. I wish you well, Owen. Please promise me now that you will never, ever, contact me again."

He smiled tearfully at her, and she watched as he accepted her words and nodded, wiping his eyes, then his nose. "I promise, Grace. Thank you. Your forgiveness means a lot. Congratulations on your marriage." He raised a hand in farewell and backed through the door as he pulled it open. She heard the ignition of a vehicle start and drive away quietly.

She walked to her desk and sat down in her chair, trying to sort through her feelings. She felt very...detached, emotionally. Should she be crying? Should she be throwing up? Should she be feeling woozy? All she felt now was relief and closure. The closure felt good. She leaned back in her chair, looking at the doorway to the hall leading to the work room.

"Did you call him?" Grace asked, dryly.

Rose's disembodied voice called from the workroom, "Hell yes, I called him. What did you expect, silly girl?"

"I handled it."

"I know! You were *scary cool*. Feel like throwin' up?"

"Nah, I'm good.

"Dizzy?"

"Not now, give it five minutes."'

"He'll be here in less than that. We're sending you home, sweetie. Ethan's coming with him."

"We have deadlines, Rose. I can stay."

"We're in great shape. You can go, sweet cheeks."

"There is no arguing with you, is there?"

"Nope, resistance is futile," Rose said, laughing, as she finally came in the front room. "Get your purse. I hear him pulling in now."

Jack and Ethan walked in the front door, concern written on their features. She got up and went to them and hugged them both in turn.

"Darlin', you all right?"

"Yes, Jack, I'm *very* all right. Perfect." She kissed and hugged him again, then reached for Ethan, who wrapped his arms around her.

"We were afraid you'd be upset, Gracie. Do you feel shaky?" He looked into her eyes.

"No, not yet at least." She shook her head. "He came to apologize, and I forgave him."

"That's great, honey." Ethan stroked her cheek and looked into her eyes, then guided her to sit back down.

"He told me you paid him a visit." Grace said looking from one to the other.

Jack nodded, stroking her shoulder. "Yes. He told us he was planning on coming to apologize to you. I think he was afraid we were going to beat him up."

Ethan scoffed. "Are you kidding? He looked ready to wet his pants when he saw us at the door. We told him if he was planning on making an apology that he needed to be enlightened about everything he'd done to you, since he was blacked out for part of it. I'm glad he didn't chicken out. If you'll give me your keys, Jack is going to drive you home."

"But I have errands to run this afternoon."

"We'll make you lunch, and you're gonna rest for a while," Ethan told her. "The house is noisy right now, but they can knock it off for an hour to let you eat some lunch and rest, then I'll take you to run your errands after that."

She might have argued, but she felt herself beginning to run out of steam. She tried to hide it. It was only 10:45 a.m., and she had things she needed to get done.

She had a fitting to get to. Maudie had found her the perfect dress, if she was judging by the dreamy look in both Ethan and Adam's eyes when they saw her in it the first time. Maudie had ordered fabric that matched the silken mesh on the skirt of the wedding dress and made Grace's veil herself.

Carrie had called her that morning to let her know the portraits were framed and ready to be picked up. This was her favorite part of all her wedding plans—having those boudoir portraits made for her men. There was no way she'd be able to get them if Ethan was with her.

"I see those sleepy eyes, Gracie. Where are your keys? Lie down at home for an hour and you know you'll feel better. Then we can go do whatever you need to do, honey. I promise. Wait until you see what they accomplished upstairs. You're gonna be very happy." She grinned at him and handed him her keys.

She hugged Rose and Martha and climbed into the SUV with Jack. When they walked in the front door, they were assaulted by the noise of progress upstairs. The renovation was ahead of schedule and would be done by the middle of the week before the wedding. Grace was amazed by how quickly demolition had occurred upstairs and watched in awe as the upstairs transformed into the master, or in her case, *mistress* suite.

The bathroom alone was a work of art, done in coordinated shades of rosy pink. The tub was situated in the center of the bathroom, positioned in front of a two-sided fireplace. A large, glass brick window dominated one whole wall. Talk about sexy. Rosy, earth-toned tiles covered the floor and lined the huge walk-in steam shower. The sinks were large, cut glass bowls with elegant faucets and taps. The counters were a sparkling creamy marble with just a hint of rose, and the walls were the palest shade of creamy rose.

The bedroom was to have wooden floors with large, thick area rugs. Wesley had finished the bed a few weeks ago and was done with all but one of the pieces she'd ordered. He and Evan had worked hard getting the furniture built. Schedules had gotten busy, and they hadn't found the time to get together yet. She hadn't heard anymore from Evan on the subject of her relationship, and she hoped that meant that she'd done an adequate job of answering his questions and not because things had gone sour for him.

The canopy, linens, and mattress, which was *enormous*, had arrived and were in storage at the moment, along with several pieces of furniture and the bed which Wesley had delivered to them, saying he had another big rush order he had to get on right away. Grace was eager to see how it would all look put together, and thought that the closed room in the barn where all the furniture was currently stored was awfully full. She didn't remember ordering that much furniture, but couldn't be sure because it was all draped with heavy cotton drop cloths and packed in there so tightly she couldn't even get in.

* * * *

Grace went upstairs to say hello to Adam and check the progress on the suite. While she was up there, Jack fixed them some lunch. Leftover lasagna, salad, and garlic bread.

"She upstairs?" Jack asked softly as Adam came down the stairs.

"Yeah, just came up. She told me what happened. It seems to me like she handles stress better now."

Ethan nodded. "She was woozy earlier, but she bounces back faster. I think it's because she's happy now."

Jack grinned and continued softly, "I think you're right. Raquel called. Grace's formal portrait and our gifts for Grace are all ready to be picked up, but she said to call before we come get them to make sure the studio is open. They must be in and out a lot."

Ethan said, "I'll take Grace on her errands if you want to go get them while I do that."

"Sure, I'll give Raquel a call and let her know I'm coming. You think she'll like them?" Jack asked, peeking around the corner at the stairs. He sure didn't want to spoil her surprise wedding gift.

"Hell, yeah," Ethan said enthusiastically, "she's going to love them. I can't wait to see Grace's bridal portrait."

"Sure, rub it in."

"Don't worry," Ethan snickered, "you'll see it at the reception."

"Whatever," he said, placing the food and plates on the black and gray granite counter top.

"I'm taking her to her final fitting today. She is going to knock you dead when you see her at the church, Jack."

"That good, huh?"

"That *damn* good, yeah," Adam agreed.

* * * *

Maudie zipped the zipper at the back of the dress and then buttoned the short row of satin-covered buttons. She backed away from Grace to get a good look. "It's perfect on you," she said, getting a little misty-eyed. "Even barefoot with your hair down. It's perfect. Did you bring the clip? Would you like me to pin your hair up before we put on your veil?"

"Yes, I remembered. Let me get it." Grace climbed down from the stair stepped pedestal and got the jeweled clip and twirled her hair up into a quick little twist. She was having her hair done at Madeleine's for the wedding but was going to go in a few days before that to be waxed again.

She'd gotten a bikini wax in June, and the men had reacted favorably, so she was working her way toward a Brazilian wax. She doubted she'd be there in time for the wedding, but the landing strip was narrowing down nicely. Her men enthusiastically voiced their approval, though they had said they didn't want to lose her curls entirely, which to them were womanly.

Maudie brought the veil, which flowed and fluttered with her movement. She pinned it securely at the top of the clip that Grace would wear on her wedding day. Maudie helped Grace strap the bridal shoes on. Grace loved how soft and comfortable they were on but how sexy and stylish as well. Grace nodded at Maudie and then went into the dressing room. She heard Maudie bring Ethan into the room and offer him a bottle of water, thanking him for waiting so patiently while they got Grace ready. Grace had wanted to give Ethan the full effect and gauge his reaction.

Her heart doing little flip-flops, she moved to the doorway as Maudie nodded at her. Grace stepped smoothly from the dressing room and slowly walked across the room into his view. She smiled softly, noticing he dropped the bottled water and quickly retrieved it before any spilled.

She saw the dreamy expression she loved. It told her everything she needed to know. They had chosen well. The waistline was an asymmetrical row of pearl and sequin beading that began under the right breast, passing underneath and creating an Empire waist effect, wrapping around at an angle in the back. The same beading also created the narrow but sturdy shoulder straps. The bodice wrapped simply in the front, overlapping slightly at her cleavage, giving it a Greek goddess look. The skirt was several layers of the same fabric that flowed and swirled with the slightest movement. It was smooth and silken, flowing around her feet, barely showing her sandals. The short train would be pinned up onto a tiny button at the reception, creating a beautiful drape in the back, which would allow her to dance as much as she wanted. She turned for him so that he could see the veil, which mimicked the movements of the skirt.

"Do you think it will do?" she asked him cheekily as she pointed a toe and slowly lifted the skirt, showing off her shoe, her calf, knee, and finally the top of her white lace stocking.

His eyes had a definite dazed look to them. "I think it will more than *do*. Grace. You're a goddess in it." He approached her on the pedestal. He took her hand, bowed over it, and kissed her knuckles. Vaguely, she heard Maudie let loose a tiny sob and excuse herself from the room. "You're so beautiful you made her cry."

"No, I think your sweet words made her cry." Grace leaned down to kiss him from the pedestal. "Why don't you send her back in so I can get out of all these buttons, and then we can get over to Clay's? I'm anxious to see your rings."

They wrapped things up with Maudie, thanking her for her extra help in making the veil. With the gown safely wrapped and all the accessories accounted for, they stopped in to pick up the men's wedding bands and the bridal jewelry her men had ordered for her. Each piece was designed to coordinate with her wedding ring. There was a wide cuff bracelet, teardrop earrings, and a teardrop necklace. Grace was stunned by the expense because this was platinum and diamond jewelry, but they had insisted she have it. The men's wedding bands were a more masculine version of Grace's ring, with a polished platinum outer band surrounding an unpolished braided wire in gold for Jack and unpolished platinum for Ethan and Adam. She'd asked Clay to place a special inscription in each ring.

They had agreed to wait until the morning of the wedding to look at the inscriptions because Grace wouldn't see the inscription in her wedding band until then.

* * * *

That same night, Grace went upstairs to the mistress suite, as they were now officially calling it, to talk to her men, who were working on the renovation at night as well. She asked them to stop for a few minutes so she could talk to them.

"What can we do for you, darlin'?" Jack asked, scrubbing the paint off his hands with a damp rag.

Ethan and Adam came in from the bathroom, carrying caulking guns. They both had their shirts off and grinned at her when she eyed them hungrily. Ethan winked at her, already knowing what she wanted because she had asked him about it privately in the truck on the way home that evening.

"I want all of you." Her cheeks burned as she said it, but she knew she was ready. She'd thought about it all week, desiring to make love with all of them at once. She didn't want to wait for her wedding night. Since falling in love with them, she had gotten a lot better at asking for what she wanted and needed. They told her when she was ready they would try with her, and she didn't want her wedding night to be a "try" kind of night. She wanted to be better prepared for them than that.

They grinned and dropped what they were doing. "Let us shower, and we'll be right there," Adam said.

"I want to make sure you understand what I'm asking for, honey. I want all of you…at one time, now, tonight. I want it for our wedding night also, but I don't want that to be the first time."

"You're sure, darlin'?" Jack asked, his eyes narrowed in concern. Grace went to him and slid her arms about his waist and kissed him tenderly.

"I've never been surer of anything. Finish what you're doing. I'll go pour myself a glass of wine and take a nice long bubble bath." At the doubtful look on Jack's face, she added, "Another night of firsts, right? I'll be fine. I really want this, Jack." She kissed him. "I'll leave y'all to work out the…logistics." She made eye contact with Ethan, and he nodded. "I'll be in the tub soaking, enjoying my wine."

She turned and sauntered from the room.

* * * *

Jack's thoughts were a confusing mix of lust, need, love, and concern. He wanted the foursome experience with her like he wanted air in his lungs. But he also knew the realities of that experience. They were all big men. What if it didn't go well? What if she didn't like it? Part of him wanted to wait a while longer, and other *parts* of him wanted to kick his ass for even thinking it as his cock rose up like a steel pole in his jeans.

Dammit.

"She really does want this, y'all." Ethan said. "She told me in the truck this afternoon that she feels very comfortable with us and is ready to try. Lots of lube and preparation and she'll love it. She trusts us so much." Hesitantly glancing over at Jack, Ethan continued, "Jack, Grace wants you to be the first to take her anally."

"She *what*?" This was not the way he planned it.

"She said Adam was the first to have his mouth on her, the first to taste her. I was the one who took her virginity. She wants for you to be the first to take her anally."

"Dammit, you know I can't do that." All of them were impressively proportioned men. When compared with Ethan and Adam, what Jack might have lacked beyond his above average eight inches, he made up for in very sizable girth. The truth was he was too damn thick for her tiny little ass. "The first time needs to be you, Ethan, just like before. It will be easier and more pleasurable for her. What if I do actual physical harm to her less than two weeks before our wedding?"

"Grace told me she knew you would say that. Because you're concerned about it, she knows you'll be extra careful with her and use plenty of lubricant. Grace said she'd relax for you and let you set the pace. If you agree to take her tonight, she'd be willing to put the foursome off until one night next week. She's been using a set of plugs to make it easier for you."

"Holy crap, she has? And we never knew?" Adam responded admiringly. "Sneaky."

"Dammit."

"I know," Ethan reassured him, "but she has her heart set on it, and we'll be there to help her relax. If she tries to hide that it hurts too much, we'll stop you and put it off for a while. But I think she's ready."

"Dammit. She never demands anything of us, and then she asks for the one thing that kills me to think of doing. I was hoping she would ask me *after* her first time, not to *be* the first."

"Another night of firsts, Jack," Adam said, patting him on the back.

"Dammit."

Chapter Thirty-nine

Grace soaked in the hot water, sipping her glass of wine. She thought about what would happen later, and the throb in her clit increased. She had known for a while that she wanted Jack to be her first in anal sex as much as she'd wanted them all to be first in something. But she knew she'd have to prepare herself, otherwise he'd refuse. So she'd used the plugs as Charity had recommended, gradually worked up to the largest one, using it for a couple of hours almost every day. They were soft jelly plugs, and she'd never had trouble getting it in or out and had grown accustomed to being patient and working it in gradually as she learned to focus and relax those muscles in her bottom. Her asshole tingled with pleasure now just thinking of putting the plug in it. The thought of Jack's thick cock going there had her pussy spasming involuntarily.

She opened her eyes when she heard a noise, realizing Jack was in the bathroom with her, and she looked up hopefully at him. He came and sat on the edge of the tub, his brow furrowed in tender concern. His hand dipped into the warm water at her shoulder, then lifted a handful and trickled it over her damp skin. He traced the backs of his fingers under her jaw. He looked into her eyes, and she could see the conflict there. Ethan had told her this would be difficult for him because his desire to give her what she wanted would war with the notion of the pain she would experience if it didn't go well.

"Grace, darlin', I'm worried I'll hurt you."

"I've prepared myself for this, Jack. I've been using a plug." She gestured toward the bathroom counter where the plug now sat.

"Ethan told me, but my cock is so—"

"Thick? I know. I got a plug that would help me accommodate *your* size. I use it for a couple of hours most every day. I left it out so that you could see." She adopted a lower, more cajoling tone. "We don't have to do the foursome, *yet*, if you'll please take my ass tonight."

The plug sat on the bathroom counter, clean and ready to be put away. He looked at the plug, sighed, and finally nodded.

"All right, Grace, if this is what you really want, I'll give it to you. But if it feels wrong or if it hurts too much you *have* to tell me." His voice and his eyes were completely sincere in his plea. "I can't bear the thought of injuring you. I'll take your ass, but that's *all* we're doing tonight. Adam and Ethan will be there to help make you feel good and make sure you come good and hard, but after I'm done, you're getting Advil and a cold compress, all right?"

"Thank you, honey." She rose from the tub and took the hand he offered her. He wrapped her in a towel and helped her dry off.

"Ethan and Adam are just about done in the showers and should be out any minute. They are massaging you while I take a shower and get this paint out of my hair." He grimaced as he ran his fingers through it.

"A massage? Really? How wonderful." She took the towels he handed her along with a hot wet washcloth. "Rated R?"

His gaze smoldered with desire as he dimmed the lights in the bathroom. He smiled playfully for the first time since entering the bathroom. "Triple X. You have to come twice before I'll slide my cock in your ass tonight."

"Oh! Oh, honey! Where's that massage oil?" She hunted in the cabinet for it and hurried from the room. Adam and Ethan waited on the turned-down bed for her, naked, hard, and ready. She handed them the towels and the massage oil. She clipped up her hair and allowed them to help her onto the bed, lying facedown.

The massage was different this time. They both massaged her, but only one of them was the main focus, where before they had equally covered the same area. Adam hovered and stroked her back and thighs gently, but Ethan gave the first massage. Instead of straddling her, he gently parted her thighs so that they lay on either side of his knees. It sent a thrill to her pussy knowing that as he massaged her he could see her glistening slit, wet with her arousal, parted and ready to be taken.

Ethan began at her ankles and gently kneaded his way up to her ass, rubbing and caressing her flesh into relaxed oblivion.

She knew something different was about to happen when he lifted her hips and Adam slid a pillow under her. Once she settled, he positioned himself between her thighs. She felt his stiff cock at her entrance and tilted her hips to give him full access.

"I'm sliding my cock into you now, Gracie, but you can't come while I massage you. You've got to hold it as long as you can. I'll tell you when you can come. No matter what I do, hold it back, okay?"

"Yes, Ethan." The hum in her cunt intensified at his order not to come, making her want to come *worse*. She felt his cock nudge her clenching pussy and knew this would be a fight for self control. Somehow she'd do it for him.

I totally fail to see how that is going to help me relax.

He spread her lips and groaned as he entered her, sinking in a little at a time. Grace moaned softly and felt consumed as his big cock slid slow, warm, and so very hard inside her. Adam groaned, palming his cock slowly as she watched him beside her on the bed. When Ethan was buried to the hilt inside her, he released her hips. His hands were now free to continue the massage.

She stroked him with the muscles in her pussy and gyrated a bit so she could feel him move inside of her and Ethan growled softly. "You're not obeying me. You want me to pop your sweet little fanny for being disobedient?"

Her pussy spasmed wildly on his cock and she froze. *Holy fucking shit! Did I just come?*

Ethan's voice was a deep steely drawl she barely recognized, "Gracie, *that* did not *feel* like you obeying me either. Stop moving, or I'll have to spank you for not doing as I asked." She detected the barest, tiniest trace of amusement in his tone.

Oh shit! He knows exactly what he's doing!

Grace naughtily growled back, "Stop moving, *my ass*! Stop *talking* before you make me come!"

She saw Adam's mouth gape open and his eyes went wide. He looked behind her at Ethan and grinned at him. Ethan chuckled darkly as he stroked her ass with his hot hands, "Oh you are so getting it, young lady. *But not yet.* Hold still." Rippling contractions shivered up and down the length of his hard cock inside her and her pussy liquefied around him. His words had reduced her to a quivering, shaking mass, ready to come completely apart at his first move. She breathed deep as she tried to get herself under control, wondering if he really intended to spank her.

Oh, don't think about it! She took a couple of slow deep breaths.

"Good girl." Ethan crooned, as Adam poured a little of the massage oil on Ethan's outstretched hand. On top of the arousal she felt, a warm rosy glow at his complimentary words also blossomed inside her. She *loved* being his *good girl*. He rubbed the oil between his hands to warm it and then palmed it onto Grace's back. Slowly, but firmly, his hands began a forward and retreat motion over her back, barely moving his torso.

"Gracie's my good girl, aren't you?" His voice was velvet and steel rolled into one devastatingly effective tool for obtaining her submission.

"Are you getting even with me?" she moaned softly.

The action of his hands rubbing through the oil up and down her spine inched his cock in and out as his hands slid down to her tailbone, then up again. She groaned softly

"For what, sweet Gracie?" Ethan asked in a soft, sensual voice.

"For orchestrating that scene and making you wait to come?"

"That's one of my favorite memories, Gracie. No, I'm not getting even." His voice was deep and even, and his touch was the caress of a lover. She loved playing with him like this.

For a minute or two, he went on like that and then changed his angle and began rubbing her shoulders in shorter, faster strokes. The tremors in her pussy threatened again and she cried out, pleading with him to take longer strokes, or to move just a little bit more.

"If you're not getting even then why are you torturing me?"

Ethan chuckled deeply. "Because I love you so much."

His rhythm increased as his strokes became more forceful but still too short. She began to move with him, and the muscles in her cunt tightened. Whimpering, she said, "Honey, I need to come. Please, please, please?"

"Not yet, Gracie. Hold it just a little longer."

His words didn't help her. They made her want it *more*! Judging by how breathless he sounded, it was becoming difficult for him to stay in control, too. She continued moving on him, unable to stop herself, holding her climax at bay by a thin thread. She arched her back and begged, "*Pretty please*!" as sweetly as she could, and he growled and began to thrust hard as she writhed beneath him.

"That is an incredible sight, Grace. You are so precious, baby," Adam said softly to her. "I wish you could see how your sweet little pussy is taking every single inch of his cock as he pumps into you from behind. You love it, don't you? To be taken from behind, to give up that control?" She was trying to hold off her climax, and Adam's words pushed her closer and closer. He knew it, too. "We love it, too, baby. Do you need to come?"

"So bad! *Please*, honey, let me come!" Her hips flexed until he stopped her with his hands, breathing rapidly.

In a deep, sexy drawl, Ethan asked, "Are you going to be a good girl and do as I say next time? Or are you going to be a bad girl?"

"I'll…" *Huh?* "I'll be *whatever kind of girl you want me to be!"* she screamed. "Oh, please!" Her pussy vibrated and pulsed with barely restrained ecstasy.

"You'd be a bad girl?" he growled.

"Yes, dammit! *Now give it to me!*" she howled. She could feel it barreling down on her and really wasn't even sure why she still asked for it when it was almost upon her.

Ethan leaned down by her ear and said teasingly, "Far be it from me not to give you what you ask for, sweet thing." She knew what she'd earned herself a second before it landed.

"Come hard for me, baby." His cupped palm smacked down on her right ass cheek, in a loud, but not terribly painful, pop. She gasped sharply and his palm came down on the other ass cheek a little harder and her entire body exploded with volcanic intensity.

She sobbed and screamed as he rode every pulse with her. A tremor shook his body as he thrust hard one final time and roared loudly as his cum streamed into her cunt, filling her with every powerful thrust. She felt like she was melting beneath him as he crouched over her, his hair brushing her shoulder as he kissed her temple and her jaw and her lips. She moaned blissfully, relaxed to the utmost.

Jack joined them on the bed, caressing her hand. "How are you doing, darlin'? Feeling relaxed?"

"Oh, yes," she murmured, "very relaxed. But I have a feeling they aren't done with me yet." She giggled and then gasped as Ethan slid his still semi-erect cock from her trembling pussy.

Jack reached out a gentle hand and placed it over her tingling ass cheek and his hand made her ass feel even hotter. "Someone got a spankin', I see. Oh, two pops?" he asked, placing his hand on the other cheek as well.

Grace giggled softly, "I'm a bad girl. I said a bad word, and I didn't obey."

"So she got two little licks."

"They don't feel so *little* right now, but I could do with a little licking," she murmured, then chortled in her euphoric haze. Her ass tingled, as Ethan moved over her on the bed. She was still sprawled on her stomach and she giggled and squirmed when she felt his lips on first one ass cheek then the other as he kissed, then licked, the pink handprints there.

"I promise to be a good girl from now on." She whispered as she wiggled her tush for him to kiss it again.

"Now where would the fun be in that, darlin'?" Jack asked with a chuckle and then said, "I think Adam is waiting for you, Grace, let us help you."

They gently helped her roll over to her back, and Adam took up position between her thighs. She noticed as Adam positioned her languid body to his liking that Ethan's cock still glistened with her juices, and he slowly palmed it with his hand. Her pussy pulsed as she watched him. Jack gave Adam massage oil, which he smoothed over her breasts. He'd positioned his cock at her lips, and as he began spread the oil, he, too, began to press slowly into her, a little at a time, then back out and then in a little more.

"That sight, one of our cocks disappearing in to her pussy, never gets old, does it?" Ethan murmured reverently. She moaned with pleasure at the thought of how it must look but also from the feel of Adam's warm, rough hands on her body. His cock entered her inch by delicious inch as he slid home. "Remember you have to hold off just as long as you can, baby."

Adam stroked and teased her until she once again begged to come, then he brought her to another bone-melting orgasm, only this time without the spanking. She'd be hard-pressed to explain how she knew it, but spanking was part of her play with Ethan, but not Adam. Holding off the climax created tremendous tension in her body. When the tension was finally at her breaking point and she was given the release, the resulting relaxation was deeper and more profound. That may have been what they were hoping for because she was definitely relaxed and ready to try with Jack.

He lay down beside her, naked and very hard. She caressed his hip with her hand and then reached for his cock. He kissed her tenderly, stroking her tongue and the depths of her mouth with his own.

"Are you ready to try, darlin'?" he asked softly. She looked into his eyes and nodded silently, smiling serenely.

"Take me, Jack. I want you to." She gasped when she felt Ethan's warm lips descend on her nipple.

"Lie on your back, darlin'," Jack caressed her ass, "and turn onto your right hip just a little." He helped her into position. He bent her left knee and had her hold the knee up near her chest. In this position, he applied the slippery lubricant to her rear opening, smearing it liberally around, even a little on her cheeks, getting the whole area nice and slick. She held her knee in position, knowing it left her pussy wide open to Adam and Ethan's gaze.

"You sure are a pretty sight, Grace, spread open like that," Adam growled. "While Jack is taking your ass, would you like us to lick your clit and your pussy?"

Blushing, Grace said, "Yes, Adam, I think I would like that. Are you going to help me come?"

"You know we will, baby, and we won't make you wait. We'll give you whatever you want, whenever you want it."

"I love you," she weakly whispered as she felt Jack's thoroughly lubricated cock at her tight hole. "I love you all so much." She felt languid and boneless, nothing but a throbbing mass of desire, needing to feel Jack's heat inside her. His warm hand slid over the back of her thigh in a sweet caress.

"When I press against you, darlin', I want you to breathe in and out slowly and relax your bottom muscles, pressing back against me if you can, all right? I'm going to stop frequently and ask if you're okay. Answer me honestly, darlin', all right?"

She nodded as he scooted in behind her. She laid her head back against his shoulder.

"Adam, help her keep her leg up but don't let her pull on it. I don't want her leg or arms to be sore in the morning."

Adam caressed her ankle. “I’ll help you, baby.”

She nodded again and looked up at Jack above her as he pulled her to him and angled his body around hers, his finger rubbing against her lubed asshole.

Watching everything going on around her, she smiled happily when Ethan returned with a full-length mirror from one of the closets in the house. He positioned it for her until she nodded at him. He leaned it slightly against the dresser opposite the foot of the bed so she could see exactly what Jack was doing to her. She watched through hooded eyes, her breathing deep and relaxed as he began to press on her anus circling it with his index finger. She relaxed for him, allowing him to penetrate her with one finger, breathing out and pressing back, just as she did with the plug.

“Still so tight, but I can tell you’ve definitely been preparing yourself. Half the work is knowing how to relax those muscles. You’ve trained yourself well for me, darlin’. I’m adding another finger.”

He lubricated two fingers and pressed both at the tight ring of muscle at her anus. The muscles gave as she breathed out, relaxed, and let him in. He began a steady slow in and out pumping motion, working more of his slippery fingers into her ass. “Are you all right?”

“Yes, Jack, I’m wonderful. It feels good. It feels naughty. I love it. You’re making it good for me, just like you said you would.” She reached back to palm his cheek. He kissed her hand and then kissed her shoulder, appearing more relaxed now about her ability to handle first time anal sex with him. She really was ready for him. There was no denying it.

“You’re so relaxed and trusting, and we love to make you feel good, darlin’.” He continued to pump into her, carefully adding a third finger, which made her groan and pant. He stopped. “Are you all right? Am I hurting you?”

“Yes. No. *Please* don’t stop now, please.” She backed into his fingers, wanting more. He grinned at Ethan and Adam. They nodded at him, encouraging him.

“Darlin’, I’m going to pull my fingers out and slide my cock in. Are you ready?”

“Oh, yes,” she whimpered. “Please.” His cock slid through the lubricant against the tight bundle of nerve endings in her asshole. “I want you, Jack, now, please.” She laid her head back on his shoulder and breathed deep and slow. She watched in the mirror's reflection as the head of his cock found her lubricated asshole.

The muscles in his back and hips rippled strongly in the flickering candlelight. Her asshole resisted the broad head of his cock. As she breathed in and out, his cock pressed at her ass more persistently. The lubricant and his gentle pressure gained him a little ground. Her pussy quivered and trembled as she felt the telltale burning. She knew he needed to enter slowly, so she did not try to back onto him. Instead, she watched in the mirror and encouraged him verbally.

"It'll feel so good when you're inside me, Jack."

Adam held her leg steady, so she let go and reached out to soothe Jack. She reached a hand back around his neck and gently rubbed as her tight asshole began to burn. The combination of pleasure and a tiny pinch of pain made her go completely still, just experiencing it with him.

"Darlin', you're so tight. Even with the right size plug, you're still so tight." He kissed her neck.

She arched her back and moaned, feeling him stretch her more than she'd ever been before. Having a thought, she looked up at Ethan, asking him with her eyes for what he could do. Of course, her Ethan understood.

Ethan caressed her wet pussy with his fingertips. "He's ready to make it good for you, Grace. You trust him. Now teach your body to trust him in this way, too. Let him in," he commanded gently. With his words, the resistance ended. The muscles stretched slowly, the slight pinch made her gasp a little, and the head his cock suddenly slipped in as she watched in the mirror.

"Oh, look at that. Can you see, Jack? You're inside me. Beautiful." She looked up at him, still resting her head against his shoulder. Breathing hoarsely, he cupped her breast and fondled it, rubbing the nipple until it stood up as he gave her body time to adjust. Both her pussy and her ass felt like they were on fire. It must have been absolute agony for him to stop there and wait for her. His cock was so very large in her ass and she bit her lip, determined for him to see that he could do this without hurting her. She focused on those muscles and willed them to not tighten up in reaction to his entry, bearing down against him a little to help her bottom open up. Her breath came fast and soft, and she closed her eyes for a moment, resting against his shoulder. Just the fact he was doing this for her, despite his worries, made her heart sing with love for him, for all of them.

Ethan came to her and kissed her, murmuring softly. "You look so perfect lying there, Grace, so sweetly opening yourself to him. I'll bet being inside you is like sweet torture for him. Jack will make it good for you, honey. Will you let Adam and me have you like this sometime?" His eyes glittered, and she sighed happily as she glimpsed the caveman inside him.

"You know I will, Ethan. I want you and Adam there soon. Jack, I want you to…I want more." Her clit throbbed as his skilled touch had her juices running from her pussy. The stirrings of lust in her drove her to back onto his cock, wanting to move in a sinuous rhythm. She pressed back against him again, slightly. Oh, it felt so good, so naughty.

"Are you all right? Ready for more?" Jack's hand slid down her torso to her mound. He cupped her gently there, growling at the discovery of how wet she was. He slid a finger between her lips, running the underside of his middle finger tenderly over her clit, making her catch her breath.

She nodded languidly. "Yes, more, Jack." She moaned as he slid another inch of his cock into her ass, then backed out and slid in again in a slow rocking motion, taking a little more of her ass with each thrust. She reveled in the vibrations and strokes to her G-spot and gasped when she felt his fingers spread her lips. Adam came to her mound, lapping at the flood of juices Jack's thick cock inspired.

Adam's warm, callused hand slid up the back of her leg, gently caressing his way to the spot at the back of her knee, holding her leg in place, and continued to sweetly lap at her pussy lips. As she watched in the mirror, Jack's dark, rigid cock slid all the way in, seating him deep inside her. It was a fantasy come true to feel so taken, so claimed. She was consumed by the three of them—Jack's cock deeply embedded, Adam loving her pussy, and Ethan, who now licked and nibbled at her other breast, sucking gently at her nipple. He leaned up and kissed her lips, thrusting his warm tongue into her mouth, stroking hers.

Jack held still. "Are you all right, darlin'?" She looked up at him trustingly and smiled. She laid her palm against his warm cheek and then slid her fingers into his hair.

"You're so big, Jack. It's very tight, but it feels so good, too. I'm so happy you were willing to try, honey." She lifted her lips to kiss him.

"Tell us how you feel, baby." Adam stopped what he was doing with his tongue and gently fingered her cunt, spreading her juices over her lips and her clit.

She shuddered in ecstasy as she replied, "I feel taken, so full and tight. I'm naughty and wicked for wanting you in my ass, and I feel like there's *nothing* of myself I won't give you if you ask it of me."

"Slow and easy, Grace. Are you ready for me to fuck your ass?" Jack asked, pulling out a little, then thrusting back in. She tightened on him and then relaxed as he hissed at the sensation.

"Damn, it's going to be hard to not come until you have. That feels so good when you do that." He pumped into her again before sliding out a little more. Each thrust of his cock sent wickedly erotic sensations to her G-spot, which he must have been rubbing. Adam's tongue and fingers stroked her deliciously, sending tremors through her body as she tried in vain to process each sensation separately.

"You look so sexy and wild, Gracie, lying here as Jack slides his cock in your ass while Adam licks and fondles your pussy." All she could do at Ethan's words was moan, unable to speak. "We promised to make it good for you, honey, but *you* make it look so good. I love the smile on your lips. We love seeing you enjoy what we do for you. Do you want it a little faster, Gracie?"

She nodded, her cheeks flushing.

She watched as Jack began to thrust in swifter strokes, listening as he breathed hard and his cock stroked faster. Her moans filled the room as she felt Adam slide his fingers into her pussy, the sensation of having something in her pussy and ass at the same time was utterly mind-blowing, then he found her sweet spot and began stroking it. *Sweet merciful heavens!* She felt her body quickly careening toward orgasm.

She held on to Jack's arm tightly, watching the ecstasy wash over her own face in the mirrors reflection. "I'm going to come soon, Jack. Oh! I'm going to come." She whimpered as Adam began licking more purposefully at her clit, still stroking her G-spot.

Ethan returned his sweet mouth to her nipple, sucking it gently. She looked down at the mirror. How decadent she looked, lying there among her men. Jack was thrusting his thick cock into her ass, Adam's tongue was at her clit with his fingers stroking deep inside her, and Ethan suckled at her breast. He gradually increased the suction until it was nearly, but not quite painful. That was her ultimate undoing as they loved her body to a majestic crescendo.

She was propelled over the edge into orgasm as she came on a gushing wave onto Adam's talented lips and tongue. She cried out at the sweet assault on her senses and gloried in Jack's loud roar as he came, too. He growled her name as he filled her with his cum, mixing the sounds of her bliss with his own. After several long moments of thrusting his release deep into her ass, Jack finally stilled with his head lying limply next to hers on their pillow.

He shuddered one last time, before asking, "Okay, darlin'?" Her heart throbbed with love for him as she snuggled tightly to him. He pressed his lips to her shoulder and shuddered in pleasure again.

"Incredible."

Carefully and slowly, he pulled his softening cock from her tender ass as a blissful moan came from her lips. It had been *perfect*.

"Y'all made that so good, just like you said you would. I'll never forget this moment."

Jack rose from the bed and went to get a warm washcloth and gently cleaned her. Adam brought her a cold compress and ibuprofen and a glass of water. Ethan helped her with the compress while Jack went to take a quick shower.

Adam and Ethan tucked her in between the two of them and cuddled her close, her legs entwined with theirs. Once Jack returned, Adam settled into his favorite sleeping position and allowed Jack to cuddle up close to her as well.

Jack reached out a gentle hand and caressed her ass where it still tingled from her spanking. "How's your ass?"

"My ass is wonderful." She replied with a sleepy chuckle.

Jack growled softly, "Yes, it is. But I meant your butt. I guess that will teach you to disobey, huh?"

"*Oh, yes it will.* I'm feeling naughtier all the time. You might have to take me in hand, Ethan." Grace said teasingly.

Ethan reached out to caress her shoulder and said softly and sincerely, "I'll play however you want, Grace. But the only kind of spanking I'll ever give you is the erotic kind, okay?"

Grace turned and smiled up at him, "As often as I want?"

Ethan laughed softly and nuzzled her throat, "Yes, you little vixen."

Grace looked over at Jack and stroked Adam's shoulder and asked, "That's all right with y'all?"

Jack kissed her nose and said, "Yeah, we talked about it a while back and we all agreed Ethan could spank you *if* you wanted him to, but that kind of play would have to be initiated by you, and Ethan is the only one you should expect it from. Adam and I won't be spanking you, only Ethan, okay?"

Grace playfully said, "I'd let you spank my heinie."

"I know, darlin', but I don't want to spank that sweet little tush. That's Ethan's kink."

"Same goes for me, baby." Adam added, "Though I might take a *bite* every now and then." To demonstrate he gently nibbled at her hip, making her giggle.

Adam's tongue flicked a ticklish spot and made her squeal and wiggle. "You're a nice nibbler, too," she said.

She was glad they understood each other. Ethan would never actually punish her with a spanking, and she would have to initiate that kind of play. It was on her terms.

Adam caressed her hip as he resettled his head on her abdomen, kissing and licking her there. Snickering, he said, "I'm glad y'all got that settled. But whose gonna spank me?"

Chapter Forty

Grace finished all her preparations for the wedding and needed only to focus on the finish work going on in the mistress suite upstairs. She was supposed to meet with Katie Grasso, the interior designer, the Monday before the wedding to talk about where the furniture Wesley and Evan had made would be placed. In a bedroom as big as hers, she had plenty of options, and she was beginning to think the room might swallow the few pieces she'd ordered. She was used to furnishing much smaller rooms. That was why she had Katie to help her.

Katie turned out to be a real gem, helping her pick the right paint colors and fabrics. She'd also found Grace some beautiful, thick area rugs for around the room and the bed.

Grace shopped with her men for the two overstuffed chairs and the chaise lounge they talked about buying before. Shopping for the chaise had been tons of fun because they had such specific needs. The back rest needed to be plush and padded, and it had to be the perfect height. The only way to know if it was the perfect height was for Grace to bend over it. She'd developed quite a talent for finding a reason—removing a piece of lint, feeling the padding on the cushion—to bend over the back of the chaises they looked at so her men could get an idea if it would work or not. She was sure a saleswoman at one of the furniture stores caught on, but she never said anything, just grinned and pretended not to notice.

The one they finally chose had a curved backrest that mirrored the lines of the sleigh bed. It was covered in a thick, velvety padding in a medium sage color. Grace didn't want rose to be the dominant color because she intended to share this space as much as possible with all three men and wanted them to be comfortable in the rooms as well.

The bedspread and window treatments were done in a heavy floral print fabric with accents in mostly burgundy, sage green, a hint of dark yellow and a little mauve. The hand crocheted canopy, done in a burgundy silk thread, draped over all four posters and hung down, creating a drape on either side at the head board. The bed would be piled with pillows in accenting shapes and colors.

Monday, Katie would hang all the window treatments. They would also bring the furniture upstairs, which necessitated the meeting.

Once they started this phase, Grace was not allowed up there until Wednesday night. The workmen had worked hard to finish on schedule, her men chipping in lots of hours in the evening to make sure each detail was attended to properly. No corners were cut upstairs. They even finished the smaller extra bedroom, which would be perfect for a nursery someday.

* * * *

Her last day of work before the wedding was Wednesday, and she hoped to spend the night in the new bed with Jack, Ethan, and Adam. They surprised her with reservations that night at Tessa's to celebrate the suite being finished and the wedding that weekend.

Katie had told Grace she would hang the boudoir portraits that afternoon once everyone else was gone. They were to be hung in each man's bedroom for them to find when they returned home that evening. Katie knew to leave the formal bridal portrait still in its wrapper in Adam's bedroom closet. It was the only one not to be hung tonight because Jack still hadn't seen her in her dress.

The bridal portrait was shot at the ranch one day while Jack was at work. Ethan and Adam just *happened* to be at the ranch the day they were shooting and wound up helping her with the laces on her white satin corset and the zipper and buttons on the back of the dress. Carrie had shot her standing on the stairs leading to the front door of the house and in the backyard within a shady stand of trees.

In the portrait, she held a bouquet made of bright red, vivid yellow and *perfect* pink roses in her hands. Her bridal bouquet would be the same on her wedding day. She had not been able to help the naughty smile that kept appearing during the photo shoot every time she looked at the bouquet or thought of the private joke surrounding the color of the pink roses. A hint of that naughty smile showed up in the shot they finally chose to be framed for over the fireplace.

Grace was glad Ethan urged her to not throw away the beautiful outfit she'd worn on that fateful Friday night in June. Ethan had completely recovered from the bullet wound, and the outfit had come clean with no problem. The silk stockings had been goners, but were easily replaced. She wore the same outfit that night to Tessa's, from the red and black zebra printed top all the way down to her sexy black high heels.

Tessa greeted them herself at the door and seated them in the same booth as last time, congratulating Grace and the men on their upcoming nuptials. The food was wonderful and the service excellent, just like the first time. They were afforded maximum privacy, as before, communicating with the pager.

This time she sat in Adam's lap and allowed them to feed her, using her hands for more sensual pursuits to please her men. They spoke briefly of making more intimate use of the booth, but when Grace reminded them she still wanted a foursome with her men, they opted to head home. After having anal sex with her the first time, Jack wanted to give her a chance to recover before having them all at the same time. She wanted tonight to be the night, and they agreed enthusiastically.

By the time they left the restaurant, the side tying G-string was already in Adam's coat pocket. He'd untied both sides and removed it with his teeth in the privacy of the booth. Knowing what she had on, or off, underneath the pretty top and skirt was driving her men crazy on the way home. They asked her to leave everything on for a little while after she removed her outer clothing, and she agreed.

Ethan's skilled lips and fingers on her body had her quivering and shaking with desire, ready for him by the time they made it to the driveway of the ranch.

"Ethan has you worked into quite a state, doesn't he, baby," Adam said softly from the front passenger seat.

"You can tell?" she asked softly, the siren song for her men to love her all at once singing in her blood.

"Mmm-hmm, when you're aroused and very wet, I can smell the perfume of your sweet pussy. I notice it even more because you're naked under your skirt. There is no mistaking that sweet scent. Are you excited about tonight?"

"You have no idea how much," she replied as Jack pulled up to the house. Ethan helped her from the SUV, stopping to kiss her as she slid off the seat. She returned his kiss enthusiastically.

"Come inside so you can get those clothes off, baby," Adam murmured as he walked past them. "I can't wait to see you in that bra and garter belt."

They led her inside, but she stopped them when they would have led her upstairs.

"I have a surprise for you first." She giggled excitedly. "Come with me." She led them to Jack's bedroom first.

* * * *

The room was softly lit so they could see as they entered. There, on the bedroom wall opposite the bed, was a large portrait of his beautiful Grace. His reaction was both emotional and visceral. His heart overflowed with adoration for her. At the same time, his cock stood up and started howling like a rutting beast.

Jack was speechless looking at it. That sneaky girl had managed this somehow without them knowing about it. In the portrait, Grace was wearing the pink topaz jewelry, the pink lingerie—the robe, the long, lace nightgown, and feathered mules. She was posed beside a four poster bed. Her left arm wrapped around the poster at the foot of the bed. The pink robe was slipping off one shoulder, and the opposite knee was perched on the bed.

Part of her nightgown showed under the robe, and the position she was in showed all her luscious curves. Just a hint of an erect nipple peeked through the nightgown where the inner slope of her breast was exposed by the robe slipping off. Only her knee on the bed was bare, but the image was powerfully erotic, so intimate. The look in her eyes was playful, almost cheeky, but love glowed there, too. This was the woman he'd watched bloom in the last two months.

She handed him a small carved wooden box. Inside it were a stack of other portraits of her that, while very tasteful, were still very erotic and of too personal a nature to display on the walls. Nothing outright nude, that he noticed, but some were close, with just the robe and nothing else, and some with just the short, flesh-baring drawstring nightie. He looked forward to seeing them all later.

"I don't know what to say, Grace. This is incredible. Beautiful. What an amazing thing to come home to."

"The night's not over yet, darlin'," she replied with a crooked grin, making him laugh as her took her in his arms and kissed her thoroughly.

* * * *

She led Adam to his bedroom next. Katie had left a lamp on in there as well. His heart pounded as he looked at the large portrait hung on the wall beside his bed. The day he'd ordered the lingerie for her, *this* was how he'd envisioned her.

He'd been a little concerned that she might think they ordered that stuff for her because they wanted her to change who she was or make her feel like she needed to dress sexier to please them. He'd ordered what he did hoping she would like it because it was comfortable and sexy to *her*. A passing thought occurred to him that he felt her *appreciation* for his choice of garments with the way she had posed for the portrait.

Dressed in the champagne satin teddy and robe, she was curled up amidst tangled white sheets, in repose, napping. One arm was positioned across her waist, hand against her belly, the other flung behind her head, lying half on her back and on her hip. It was very similar to the position they slept in together with his head on her abdomen.

He turned to look at her as she slipped her arm around his waist. She looked up at him, waiting for his reaction, and the tenderness and admiration in her eyes made his heart well over with love for her. His eyes stung with unshed tears. He kissed her soft sweet lips, delighting in her warm, eager response.

She handed him a similar box to the one she'd given Jack. In it were more portraits. There was one of her in just the teddy, perched on her knees, her arms over her head. Her hands were in her long, loose, flowing blonde hair, her breasts thrust forward invitingly, knees parted. There was another with only the robe on. She held it closed in front over her breasts, but the robe was completely off the shoulders, revealing a lot of skin and some cleavage but leaving what it hid to the imagination. In that one, her hair was pinned up with a few loose locks left flowing down over her shoulders. There was a stack of such poses in his box.

"Thank you, Grace. It's beautiful. I can't believe you went to this trouble. When did you do this?"

"The day of the first shopping trip with Charity. It was a *lot* of fun, no trouble at all." The men gave each other a knowing glance.

* * * *

Ethan's room was last. She led him into the dark, dimly lit interior and turned to show him the large portrait on the wall opposite the bed. She was lying on her stomach, propped up on her elbows, chin on her hands. She was wearing the sexy, snug T-shirt he'd bought for her. The black shirt fit just the way he'd envisioned it, showing lots of her delectable cleavage, the sleeves long enough to extend past her wrists and just barely over the top of her hands.

The low-cut neckline of the top was adjusted so that the cheeky row of ruffles that decorated the upper edge of the cups of her black demi bra peeked out playfully. She also had on the high-cut black satin panties. Lying at an angle, her curvy thighs and calves were visible but in soft focus. Her legs were bent at the knees, her dainty feet crossed at the ankles, her toes pointed. She looked sexy, playful, cheeky, and totally hot. The greedy caveman in him agreed whole-heartedly and pounded on his chest. His ravenous cock seconded the emotion.

She handed him his keepsake box, and he took out the entire stack of pictures. There was a similar pose with the T-shirt slipping off a shoulder, showing the satin strap of her bra, and a generous view of the upper swell of her breasts, her index finger in her mouth, like she was sucking something sweet off it. There was a portrait of her on a chaise lounge, reclining on her back, one knee bent. One arm was positioned over her head, and the other lay relaxed over one hip with her hand on her abdomen. In that one, she wore only the demi bra and the panties and her naughty little grin.

There was a very dim, softly lit one of her perched on a bed amidst tangled sheets. She was on her knees, sitting back on her heels, her sweetly curving back the only well lit thing in the picture. Her hair was pinned up in this one, and her hands were in her lap. Her face was in profile, and her body was angled away from the camera so that her feet and one hip were visible, and the side of one breast was also visible but very dimly lit. In this portrait, she was completely nude.

His jaw and Adam and Jack's had all dropped at the sight of that beautiful image. He was afraid his cock might have a permanent zipper mark on it, it pressed so hard against his fly. There was also a close up portrait of her in the gold jewelry he'd purchased for their first date. The gold rings glimmered in the subtle light from the window she gazed out of, her face in profile, her arms placed artfully to cover her breasts, the look in her eyes distant and dreamy. She was nude in that one as well.

"Wow. Unbelievable, Gracie. You sure know how to surprise us. I love them all so much. I love you." He crushed her to him as he kissed her, overwhelmed by her gift.

* * * *

When he released her, she said, "When you look through all the stack of pictures in your boxes, Adam and Jack, you will find nudes and partial nudes I had shot for you as well. Thank Charity for those because otherwise I don't think I'd have had the nerve to do them. I'm glad you like them so much. It's my wedding gift to you."

"We have a surprise for you, too, darlin'. Why don't you come upstairs with us now? We'll bring the boxes. We can look at the rest later. But right now we have something we want to show you." Jack took her hand and led her up the stairs. She shook with excitement, ready to see her new mistress suite. At the bedroom door, he turned to her and smiled. "Hope you like it, darlin'," he murmured, opening the door.

The suite was everything she imagined it would be and *more*. All the pieces of furniture, including the gigantic, beautiful canopy bed, were there. So were the wardrobe, the rocking chair, and the dresser and mirror. She gasped when she saw there were numerous other pieces in the room as well. A bench upholstered to match the bed linens. An entertainment armoire, a chest of drawers, a cedar chest, a lingerie chest, not one but *two* freestanding mirrors. There was a small round table situated among the chairs and chaise lounge in the sitting area in front of the fireplace. They led her to the doorway, and she got her first look at the finished bathroom with its huge rosy pink tub and giant steam shower. The cut-glass vanity basins sparkled under the lights from the crystal light fixtures.

"Did Wesley build all those extra pieces of furniture for me?"

Jack grinned knowingly. "Yes, darlin', they were *part* of our wedding gift for you."

"Part? What else did y'all do?" she asked curiously.

"Come back in the other room. Have a closer look at the walls. Wesley made all your frames for you. You should see them." Jack drew her attention to the frames.

She gasped and whimpered with unrestrained joy when she saw the framed photographs on the walls. Each large portrait had its own place throughout the room, set in a frame that Wesley made for her at her request and the photographer's size specifications.

By the door was a portrait of Jack, out in the corral by the first barn, a coil of rope in his gloved hands. He was shirtless in the black and white print, wearing blue jeans, chaps and cowboys boots. He had his summer straw cowboy hat on, and his chest glistened with sweat. He was looking down at the coil of rope, but there was a faint smile on his face as though he knew she was looking at him. The sunlight struck his skin in such a way that every muscle stood out in relief, his muscled abdomen and the cut of his hips above the chaps and jeans especially pleasing to her eye. She could make out a trail of sweat running down that hardened abdomen into the waist of his blue jeans. Languir was beside him in the portrait as if he were waiting for Jack to jump on his back. She licked her lips thinking how much she might have liked to lick that trail of sweat off his abs.

She moved to Ethan's portrait next. He was posed in shadow, sitting on top of a stack of hay bales, slouching against the outside wall of the barn. His hat lay beside him on the hay bale. Ethan was shirtless as well in the portrait, running his hands through his shoulder length brown hair. The scar from his gunshot wound was slightly visible on his shoulder. The rippling muscles in his biceps stood out in sharp relief, his chest and abs another work of art, glistening with sweat. She noticed the button on his jeans was undone. He looked directly into the camera, gazing back at her with bedroom eyes. She grew wet just looking into those eyes.

In Adam's portrait, he was in action, walking through barn, down the row of stalls, leading Esperer and Coraggio, the newly named colt, toward the camera. Continuing the theme, he was shirtless, too, which was a good thing. His great broad chest glistened with sweat as sunlight shone in on him through the skylights in the barn. He was wearing faded jeans and dusty cowboy boots. She blushed, noticing the faintest outline of his erection through the jeans. The sunlight illuminated his eyes, making them appear to glow. He had a soft smile on his lips as he gazed beyond the camera with a faraway look in his eyes. He had the look of a man in love, thinking about his woman.

"Charity orchestrated this *whole* deal with Carrie and Raquel," Grace said, gazing again at the portraits of her handsome men. "She used the bridal portrait as a means to get all of us to the photographer to have these portraits done. That sneaky girl, I love her even more! When did you do these?"

"The morning of your first shopping trip with Charity, Carrie's partner, Raquel, came out and shot us. The same morning you had yours done." Grace just chuckled and shook her head. Her sister was an evil genius.

Jack handed her a carved wooden box of her own. She held the box in her hands and opened it, blushing as she removed the stack of prints—a thick stack of other pictures of the three of them, some extra shots, others too intimate to display on the wall. Merciful heavens, her men were *hot*! The fiery stirrings of desire pounded in her heart as she looked through the images.

There was a shot of Ethan, his hair slicked back with water dripping from it, dumping water from a bucket over his head at the tap outside the barn. His blue jeans were partially soaked, the water caught in action sluicing down his chest and torso. The sunlight illuminated the water as it fell, each droplet sparkling. In this one, his blue jeans were still unbuttoned, the zipper partially down, and she could just barely tell he was commando. Because the blue jeans were wet, she could see the partial outline of his cock through the faded denim, erect. She gasped, putting her fingertips to her lips.

There was a back shot of Adam grooming Esperer. His broad, tanned, muscled back was lit so that every muscle stood out in sharp relief, his arms widespread over Esperer's back as he brushed him. His short hair was damp with sweat. The faded denim jeans he wore cupped his ass and the backs of his thighs, clinging to the hard muscles beneath. She felt her pussy quiver, imagining those muscles rippling and flexing as he thrust into her, making sweet love to her, and she felt a little damper between her legs. She had to close her eyes and draw a shaky breath before moving to the next picture.

In this picture, Jack was in one of the horse stalls, light pouring in through one of the barn skylights shining down on his muscled shoulders. He looked out a window so that his face was also lit from under his straw hat, highlighting the beard stubble on his jaw. His lips were unsmiling in this picture, but there was peacefulness about his features. With his arms crossed over his chest, he leaned a hip against the feed trough near the window. The sunlight drew attention to the hard muscles in his chest, shoulders, and arms. His jeans rode low on his hips, and because he was turned in partial profile, she could make out the large bulge at his groin. Her fingertips touched the photograph, savoring every inch of him.

"I was thinking of you, wanting you, when she took that picture." Jack's hand trailed down her spine, causing her to shudder and gasp, gazing at him momentarily. The hunger of desire had to be obvious in her eyes.

There were photos of them in the ranch house, too. There was one of Ethan reclining on his made-up bed, his hand splayed out on the mattress, like he wished she was in that spot. His left forearm was tucked behind his head, his long hair fanned out over his shoulders and collarbones, his bedroom eyes looking directly into the camera lens.

There was a photo of Adam working in the mistress suite while it was still under construction, a tool belt on his hips, wearing faded jeans and a tight white T-shirt. He had a hammer in one hand, a two by four in the other. He was looking directly into the camera lens in this shot. Standing by an open window, the light caught his eyes, illuminating them and making them appear to glow as he looked into the camera.

There was a shot of Jack sitting at his drafting table, his bare feet propped up on a side table, crossed at the ankles. He was wearing denim work clothes. The shirt was completely unbuttoned and open a bit, showing his muscled chest. What she loved about this photo were his hands. One was resting on the drafting table. The other was propped on the arm of his desk chair, holding a mechanical pencil between his fingers as though he had just stopped what he was doing to look up at her. His hands were rugged and callused—working man hands. That was something she loved about all of them. There wasn't a soft palm in the lot. He wore a crooked grin, and she blushed, having a good idea what he was thinking in this picture. With his ankles crossed and propped up, it was obvious his thoughts were communicating with other parts of his body as well, if the semi-erect bulge at the juncture of his thighs was any indicator.

There were similar shots taken all over the house and ranch. There was a shot of Ethan, reclining on the glider, his hat pulled down to cover part of his face, as if he was napping. Even napping, he was sexy as hell. There was one of Adam with Coraggio in the corral with his mother. There was a shot of Jack lifting Grace's saddle onto one of the sweet mares they kept for riding on the ranch, like he was preparing to take her for a ride. Near the bottom, she found several sexy shots.

"Before you look at any of those, honey, you need to know we were not totally nude in any of them," Ethan said quickly. "Raquel positioned us and shot them so that it would look that way. I know I'm probably spoiling the illusion for you, but I didn't want you to think for even a second that we were parading around here naked with a single woman shooting our pictures."

"Thanks for telling me, Ethan."

"I had on my running shorts," he said, pointing at the image she was looking at. It was a shot of Ethan, lying down, the light streaming in through the window over his king-sized bed. The sheets were tangled and twisted, and the bed looked as though she had just risen from it, like he wasn't alone in the room. The sheets were draped artfully over his hips and groin but showed a bare thigh and calf and foot. All of them had such sexy, manly feet. His eyes were closed in that shot as though he were falling asleep after making love to her. If he hadn't told her, she'd have assumed he was naked under the sheet.

"And I had on my swimming trunks," Adam said as she moved on to the picture of him fresh from the shower, his hair still damp, as he reclined on the king-size bed in his bedroom, his hips wrapped in a towel. Adam was so large that even with the swim trunks on underneath the towel, it wasn't hard to tell what was on his mind as he smirked for the camera.

In his shot, Jack reclined on the couch, a thick, soft throw blanket draped over his "nudity." One arm was under his head on the arm of the couch, and the other was draped across his torso, one knee up, and the other cocked to the side facing the camera. He looked relaxed in the photo, his trademark playful grin on his face. The look in his eyes was an invitation for her to climb on top.

"There is a pair of running shorts under that throw, darlin'."

"Thank you for telling me. I wish I were different, but I would have been upset later thinking that you might have been totally nude in these shots with Raquel in the room."

"Don't apologize for the way you are, darlin'. We're every bit as territorial about you. The only difference is that it was a woman shooting your portraits. We'd have felt the same way if a man had been shooting you in the nude."

"And you *know* I was really *nude,*" she said in a sexy seductive voice. "Although Jack and Adam still haven't seen theirs."

They quickly opened their keepsake boxes, looked through the shots, and found the nudes she'd done for each of them. Grace knew Jack had found his when she heard the sudden inhalation from him.

In the nude she'd posed in for Jack, she was lying back in the four poster bed. The camera lens was almost level with the surface of the mattress on her right. Her right thigh was up, her leg bent at the knee, and tilted in just a bit. Her left leg was stretched out straight in front of her. Her right arm was positioned above her head, and her blonde locks were fanned out over the pillow in wild disarray. Her right arm in that position tilted her breasts up more than they already were because her back was slightly arched. Judging by his reaction, the real kicker for Jack was that her left forearm was draped over her hip, her hand positioned over the blond curls at her mound.

Her fingertips reached for what lay just beneath those curls. Her middle and index fingers were not visible to the camera, allowing him to assume they might have found their destination. Judging by her slightly parted lips and half closed eyes, she probably had. He looked up at her with respect and admiration in his eyes.

"This is something I will cherish my entire life, darlin'. I'll guard this image, I promise. I know it wasn't easy for you to get in the proper mindset to shoot this beautiful picture, but you did it for me." He kissed her and shared the image with Adam and Ethan.

"Hot. Holy. Hell," Adam muttered, before showing Ethan. Both of them were wide-eyed.

Ethan growled. "Damn, honey! You are fucking hot!"

"What about yours, Adam?" Grace giggled, having a feeling she was about to have her bones jumped.

He leafed through his and found the one at the bottom. He looked at it, then surprise dawned on his features, and he looked at it again, speechless. He looked up at her with such tender adoration in his features it brought tears to her eyes. The photo had achieved the desired effect. He'd understood what she was going for when she and Carrie had orchestrated the shot.

The photo had been taken from directly above the bed, with Carrie perched on scaffolding above Grace. Grace lay in the same tangled sheets as the portrait hanging on his bedroom wall. The position she was in was the same position she and Adam always slept in. Her blonde hair was spread out over her pillow in flowing waves, a single lock curling down between her breasts, which were completely bared to the camera, the nipples erect. Her arms were at her sides, pushing her breasts up even more, and her wrists rested across her hipbones, her hands resting over her abdomen beneath her belly button and directly above her mound. Her right pinkie and ring fingers strayed into the curls of her mound. Her thighs were slightly crossed over, so her slit was not visible beneath the curls. Her eyes were closed, and her features radiated pure, perfect joy and happiness. Her hands covered the spot where Adam laid his head every night, but also where they both hoped his daughter or son would one day grow and flourish.

Stunned speechless, he reached for her, enfolding her in his big muscular arms, his body quaking. "Baby, that takes my breath away. It's perfect." He handed it to Jack and Ethan to look at.

"She…" Ethan said, stunned. "She takes my breath away."

* * * *

Jack gazed at the image in the photograph, searching for the right words. She needed to know how much this affected them, how much they loved her and appreciated her.

"Grace, you live in our hearts…our souls. We love you more than anything in the world. I keep thinking it just can't get any better between all of us, and then it does. Darlin', I adore you so much."

She'd flitted into their life one day, like a butterfly moving from bush to bush. Gracefully, she'd moved between them, sharing with them, giving and taking, loving them all. Life had been good up until the day they'd fallen in love with her. Everything had been right on track. Business had been good, life on the ranch profitable. They had gotten to grow up best friends together, formed a dream of what life could be like with the right woman, and planned and dreamed of the day when she'd come along.

Despite the doubts their family members had, as they entered their thirties, they still believed the right woman was out there somewhere. Then she'd walked up to his father's porch, dressed all in black, on the day of his precious mother's funeral, like an angel of mercy and compassion, and they had known that very day the waiting was over. They'd seen it in the faces of some of their relatives that they'd found *the one* and were witnessing Jack, Ethan, and Adam falling in love with her that day. Life had been good up until the day they'd fallen in love with her. Now there was contentment, peace, and a joy that made his heart feel like it was being stretched in her gentle hands. He still kept thinking it couldn't get any better. Then it did.

Chapter Forty-one

"I'm going to go brush my teeth and get ready. I'll be back in a few minutes," she said as Adam released her from his embrace. They left the suite to shower and do the same. She got ready for them and then slipped into the black satin robe she'd bought for herself. She walked around the suite, dimming lights and lighting the candles. She returned to the bed, turned down the heavy bedspread, blanket, and top sheet, and smiled. Tonight, Adam could sleep without his feet hanging off the bed and be under the covers. She heard their footsteps on the stairs, and her heart flip-flopped and pounded with love for them. She looked up as they came through the door.

"Our first night in our new bed," she whispered softly.

"Your first night in your mistress suite," Adam replied. "Would you like me to light the fire?"

"Should you do that? It's July, and the mess seems impractical."

"It's a gas log. There's no mess," Ethan replied, "and it's cool up here with the AC running. We don't want you to get chilled while we make love to you. The fire will be nice, and we can always turn it off later before we go to sleep."

"Would you like a glass of wine, baby?" Adam asked while Ethan turned the fireplace on.

"No, I'm fine, and I just brushed my teeth." She giggled. "Thank you."

"You're not nervous, darlin'?" Jack kissed her and removed the clip from her hair.

"With y'all? No, there's nothing for me to be nervous about. I'm in love with you, and this is another night of wonderful firsts," she murmured as she untied her robe. They had already removed theirs and laid them on the chaise lounge before returning to her. "Still want to see me in my lingerie before I remove it?"

"Of course. That's what we were hoping for, honey," Ethan replied as they climbed onto the bed and lay down to watch her. Their cocks quickly hardened as they waited.

She stood before them and slipped the robe from her shoulders, baring her breasts and the black satin and lace shelf bra they seemed to enjoy a lot. She watched their faces and took pleasure in their reactions. She loved the way their eyes gazed at her half closed, the slow exhalations of breath, and a deep growl from one of them. The robe slid to her waist.

"More?"

They silently nodded. She parted the robe in front and let it slide to the end of her fingertips before she caught the slithering material. She turned and strode to the chaise lounge, complimenting herself for having the guts to sashay half naked in this outfit in front of them. She'd seen herself in the full-length mirror in the bathroom before putting on the robe. This outfit was guaranteed to get her jumped by her men. She gave them a seductive grin as she dropped the robe on the chaise and turned to face them before slowly sauntering to the bed. There was no way to walk in those shoes except to saunter. It was good for her self-esteem when she saw that all their jaws had fallen open.

Standing before them clad only in the black shelf bra, the black lace garter belt, lace edged silk stockings, and five-inch platform Mary Janes—no panties on because Adam already had those off of her—she said, "Do you like what I have on?"

They all nodded, enthralled, and Adam said, "Very much, baby."

"I'm wearing a brand-new piece of jewelry tonight." It took a few seconds for it to dawn on them what she was saying, and then they got quizzical looks on their faces.

"Grace, you're not wearing any jewelry," Jack answered, looking at her ears, her wrists and her throat.

"Yes. I am. You'll just need to find it." She giggled, reaching back to unhook her bra, freeing her breasts. They watched her every move, adoration in their eyes.

"More?" Again, they silently nodded as she unhooked each stocking from the garter belt and removed it, her round breasts swaying in the candlelight as she bent to unhook the straps before placing the garter belt with the bra. The fireplace had warmed the bedroom slightly, taking the edge off of the chill in the air conditioned room. The flames crackling in the fireplace was a comforting sound. She looked forward to making love in front of the fireplace some day.

She stood before them in the stockings and high heels. All three of them were dazed, their cocks standing straight up and rigid at their bellies. They stared at her, admiration, desire, and lust warring on their faces. She reached up and ran her fingers through her hair and asked, "Are you ready to play hide and seek?"

"What do you mean, beautiful?" Ethan asked he reached for her. He slid a hand around her waist and pulled her to him at the edge of the bed, laying his warm, open lips over a nipple. She gasped and sighed at the delicious feel of his mouth suckling her.

"I'm wearing a new piece of jewelry. Don't you want to see it? If you do, you're going to have to look for it. But first these heels and stockings will have to come off. Would someone like to help? Or should I remove them myself?" she asked seductively.

Adam hopped off the bed and knelt at her feet, looking up at her with adoration and desire in his green eyes. His warm fingers reached out for her hands and placed them on his broad shoulders as she placed her sexily shod foot in his hand. He bent and kissed her ankle as he slid the shoe from it, then placed that foot on the floor. She put the other in his hand, and he paid it the same loving attention. Once the shoes were off, he slowly slid his fingers up her calf and thigh to the top of her silk stocking and then slowly slid each one back down her leg, kissing her flesh as he went.

The loving attention he paid to her was torturously effective, rendering her wet and aroused. Her clit throbbed incessantly, begging for his attention, and she felt fresh moisture rush to her sex as she thought of what they'd find there. He looked up at her, letting her know he knew she was wet and ready with his eyes but not touching her there, which was good. She wanted to be on the bed for that.

"Darlin', now that you're naked, I don't see any jewelry on you anywhere," Jack said.

She smiled and raised her arms and turned slowly for them. Nothing.

"That's why it's called hide and seek. I *hid* it, and you get to *seek* it. Fun?" she asked, giggling.

"Damn, she is full of surprises," Adam said. "She's in full bloom, ready to be made love to, but I didn't see anything."

She gave them her hands, and they helped her up into the bed, settling her among them, helping her to lie back on the piled up pillows. Her clitoris throbbed, and her pussy quivered, she wanted them so bad. She loved the way they played together. They checked her toes, her ankles, her nipples, and even nuzzled in her hair. Nothing.

They must have liked the game, too, knowing there was only one place they hadn't looked yet. "We don't see anything, yet. Why don't you help us out?" Jack asked playfully.

"All right," she whispered softly.

Jack and Ethan were on one side of her, Adam on the other. She drew her knees up, her thighs still close together, and gestured for Ethan to kneel in front of her. When he was in position, she slid her feet down and placed one in each of his waiting hands. The heat in his eyes consumed her, making her heart beat hard in her chest. Her breath came in little pants as a growl came from deep in his chest. In a slow, sensuous move, holding her feet at the delicate arches as he pushed, she began to bend her knees.

"Baby, oh, baby, what did you do?" Adam asked breathlessly. She was nearly brought to orgasm right then by their obvious reactions and being slowly spread open like that.

"Darlin', what—Oh, no! Oh, Grace. You didn't!" Jack had jumped to the conclusion she'd gotten herself pierced. Judging from the strident quality of his voice and the way his eyebrows had drawn up in concern, she'd done well in naysaying Charity's suggestion. Grace was all for trying new things, but she was still a chicken at heart. Luckily, there were less invasive options available.

"No, it's not what you think, honey. You'll see, just look." She laid a placating hand on Jack's thigh.

Ethan pushed her feet until her thighs were pressed against her breasts, which laid her completely bare before them, opening her pussy to their view.

Three pink, sparkling crystals and a heart-shaped iridescent crystal were suspended over her clitoris.

"Does it hurt?" Adam asked, reaching out to finger it, touching her wet clit in the process. Her lips parted on a gasp at the unexpected touch to that very sensitized bundle of nerve endings.

"No, baby. In fact, it feels very good. It's a little tricky to get on but totally worth it once it's in place. I'm too chicken to get that place pierced but Googled non-piercing jewelry of this type and got lucky. What do you think?"

"I think that's the hottest damn thing I've seen since we looked at your pictures!" Adam smiled lustily as she gasped when he stroked her again.

"I think it's absolutely beautiful on you," Ethan said with a grin. "I didn't know you'd be open to genital jewelry, or I'd have had Clay make you something, Gracie." He rubbed her clit, making her moan again.

"Grace, you are full of surprises," Jack said, touching it also.

"The evening's not over yet, darlin'," she replied, whimpering when his fingers dipped into the moisture dripping from her open slit.

"Honey, how do we get it off of you?" Ethan asked. "I think your little imprisoned clit needs some loving attention. Wouldn't you like that?" He bent down as Jack and Adam each took a dainty foot from him and flicked her clit tenderly with the tip of his tongue. It was like a searing flame rocketing through her clit. Once he slipped the clip off, the blood would come rushing back to her clit and—

His tongue flicked her again. "Oh! Oh! Don't, you'll make me come too fast."

"Oh, I'm planning on making you come several times, honey. Fast or slow, it's all good. Now how do you want me to remove it? I don't want to hurt you."

He slid a finger into her dripping wet entrance as he continued evilly flicking with his tongue. She replied, "Take the largest jewel and lift straight—Oh!—up toward my belly button. Don't pull out, pull up." He captured the jewel between his lips, gently sliding the sterling silver clip off of her inner lips and the hood of her clitoris. The blood came rushing back to her deprived flesh, and she went straight over the edge. "Oh! Ethan! Oh, no! I'm—I'm coming, I'm coming!" she wailed. He dropped the clip from his lips onto her mound as she came, applying gentle soothing pressure to her clit with his warm tongue, laving her throbbing flesh. She sighed softly, shuddering as she felt his tongue flick into her wet entrance. Jack and Adam lay at her sides, kissing her throat and her breasts, whispering their encouragement and love to her as she came down from the powerful climax.

"Baby, was that good?" Adam asked.

"Mmm, so good." She sighed, stretching like a contented cat.

"Man, I love it when you do that, darlin'. Stretching like a little kitten, about to start purring."

"Oh, I'd definitely purr if I could right now. That was wonderful. Did you like my new jewelry?" She removed it from her mound where it had stayed while she had ridden out the orgasm. She laid it over on the night table in a crystal dish.

"You say you found that online?" Ethan asked, grinning wickedly.

"Uh-huh. Why?"

"It looks like we have more shopping to do, boys." Ethan chuckled.

"Oh, hell yeah! What else did they have, baby?" Adam asked.

"Besides the clit clip? They had all kinds of nipple jewelry, cock rings, pussy dangles, and something called a bottom teaser." She giggled at their surprised expressions. "They're all non-piercing, in either sterling silver or solid gold, which would be heavier and, *oh, my goodness* that would feel good. They also had heavy beads that add more weight to their pieces. Mmm. Y'all are going to spoil me!" She giggled and had a feeling they were going to be paying that website a visit, soon.

"We live to spoil you, Gracie." Ethan murmured, then grinned devilishly as he slid the tip of his tongue over her pussy lips again. "Now we've found something that pleases you, we'll have to get some more. I'm also going to check in with Clay."

"You're not worried he'll think I'm a deviant?"

"Clay would never think that about you, darlin'," Jack replied, nuzzling her breast. "He handcrafts and sells that sort of jewelry all the time. We just didn't know you'd like to *go there*, that's all. You're just more and more fun all the time."

She settled back on the pillow, looking at the men she adored most in the entire world and asked, "Don't you think it's time we all made love together?"

Adam helped her up and switched places with her, lying back on her pillow. He drew her on top of him so that she straddled his hips. Adam drew her to him for a long, searing kiss. He stroked her tongue with his and she sucked gently on his bottom lip. Jack and Ethan moved around the room, arranging things and getting ready.

She lost herself in Adam's kiss. Gone were the fun and games. The teasing and playfulness from earlier was replaced by the tenderness and warmth they each bestowed on her in all their movements and murmurings. She felt a warm hand down her back and gentle fingers in her hair.

She heard someone moving something around and opened her eyes to find the source. Jack was moving one of the freestanding mirrors beside the bed so that now she could see herself straddled atop Adam, her gentle giant. The mirrors were a very generous size and adjustable on carved rolling frames. She would never grow tired of being able to watch as her men made love to her. She looked down at Adam, his eyes brimming with love for her.

"Ready?" he asked softly.

"Yes," she whispered back. She felt a warm hand at her backside as Ethan applied a generous amount of the lubricant to both her pussy and her tight rear opening. He massaged his lubricated fingers around her opening, pressing inward. She breathed slowly and relaxed, allowing him access.

"Yes, honey, that's good, let me in. I'm just going to stretch you a bit and make sure you are ready for me. Feel all right?"

"Yes, Ethan. Thank you for being so gentle and careful with me," she whispered, but she addressed all three when she said it.

Ethan pressed in and fucked her with his fingers for a minute, spreading them apart a little to help her stretch and let his cock in, applying more of the lubricant to the opening. After a minute, he removed his fingers, and she groaned in frustration just as her body had begun to sing with arousal at the feel of him there.

Ethan chuckled. "You want my cock to fill your ass, honey?"

"You know I do, Ethan. I want all of you so much."

Jack had moved into position at Adam's shoulder. Adam was too tall for her to lean forward over him to reach Jack's cock with her mouth, so he was kneeling, sitting back on his heels at Adam's left shoulder.

Adam stroked her hips and held her as he slid his cock right into her pussy. Adam growled, "Baby, you feel good. So hot and smooth." Adam was still a very tight fit for her. Ethan was thoughtful to use plenty of lubricant at both openings. Otherwise, she wasn't sure how she would be able to take two of them.

Jack smoothed a hand over her shoulder, leaning into her to kiss her. “Darlin’, you’re going to have to be still on Adam now so he can stay in control, and Ethan is going to slide into your sweet little ass. Once they have a rhythm established, you’re going to take my cock in that hot sweet mouth of yours, all right?”

“Jack, what if I can’t concentrate with it all going on at the same time and I don’t make you come?”

“Darlin’, this is your first time doing this. It doesn’t have to be perfect, but trust me when I tell you all I’ll have to do is look at you. With Ethan’s cock in your ass and Adam’s cock in your pussy at the same time and my cock in your sweet little mouth, I’ll come with no problem at all. Don’t worry about me. Just enjoy yourself. You’ve been looking forward to this.” He kissed her gently again.

“Gracie, lie down on Adam. Let him hold you for me, all right?” Ethan murmured, pressing a large warm hand on her back. She rocked down on Adam and settled against him willingly, resting on him as he wrapped his warm arms around her back, grounding her.

Ethan tilted her hips up and slid his hand up her spine to her shoulder, and she felt his cock at her rear opening. She breathed out and willed herself to open when he whispered, “Slow and easy, honey.” He pressed against her and, after a momentary resistance, was able to ease into her tight opening. She slammed her eyes shut and pressed her forehead against Adam’s pectorals. Her pussy started quivering as Ethan began to slide in.

Adam held her and whispered, “Slow and easy, just like Ethan said, baby. Damn, you feel so good. Fuck. So tight. Tighter. Damn.” They both growled at the tight sensation.

Ethan’s voice was deep and gravelly, “Oh, damn, Jack, you were right. She’s feels so good.” He rocked into her in the same rhythm Jack had used the first time, gaining a little more of her ass each time until he was thrusting all the way into her and pulling nearly all the way out before pumping into her again. “Ah! Adam, ready? Once you start moving and we get the rhythm right, this won’t last long. She feels way too damn good and so tight! Look, Grace, did you see? You’ve taken us both, honey. I’ll bet Jack would love for you to suck his cock right now.”

She lay still and breathed deep, watching in the mirror. She quivered as Ethan stroked his beautiful cock into her ass, overwhelmed by the sensation of two cocks filling her at one time. The burning was not as sharp this time around, so there was more pleasure and less pain, the blend of the two sensations making her body buzz and throb.

The position Ethan had tilted her pelvis to applied maximum pressure on her clit against Adam's pubic bone. Every thrust of Ethan's cock sliding into her rubbed her against Adam. She was sure he could feel how wet she'd gotten him already, and she hadn't even come yet. The other night, she'd felt taken and claimed when Jack had fucked her ass the first time. Now she felt conquered, overwhelmed by a greater force. She watched as they made love to her in a concert of motion. She felt tiny, sandwiched between them, their cocks thrusting in and out, their muscular bodies so virile and strong as they loved her. She wouldn't last long if she watched. When Ethan suggested she suck Jack's cock, she smiled and looked up at him in bliss, her lips parting as she licked them.

"Is it that good, darlin?" Jack asked.

"Oh, yes," she moaned. Ethan and Adam were now taking turns thrusting in so that she was always filled, and the in and out motion was doing lovely things to her G-spot. The sensation sent her on a tight upward spiral, and she opened wide for Jack, certain this was going to be over too soon. There was no way she could hold this orgasm back for long. He slid his cock between her parted, wet lips, stroking into her mouth in short, gentle thrusts. She reached out one hand and wrapped it around the base, causing him to growl and hiss, then she began to stroke his thick cock with her hand as she loved him with her mouth.

She swirled her tongue around the head of his cock, sucking him into her mouth, gently stroking his length with her lips. She began gradually increasing and then releasing the suction she created with her mouth. He moaned and cried out as her mouth brought him to the very edge. Dimly, she heard Ethan and Adam begin to pant.

She glanced at them in the mirror, the sexy and erotic image implanted in her memory for all time. Her back was arched, and her mouth around Jack's cock was sucking him into blissful agony judging by the look on his face. His head was thrown back, and his lips parted. Adam gazed up at her, licking her neck as his powerful body arched under her, his muscles rippling and flexing as he pumped his cock into her wet cunt. Ethan knelt behind her on his knees, pulling his cock out and thrusting back into her ass in perfect timing with Adam's thrusting. She was in a constant state of fullness, her clit and G-spot receiving tender, constant care from their cocks.

Ethan grasped her hip with one hand, the other stretched out and holding her shoulder, pulling her back onto his cock, which set the rhythm for her stroking motion over Jack's cock. It occurred to her that he was dominant in this moment, controlling with his motions how she moved, pleasing them all, including her. He made eye contact with her in the mirror, his face a picture of rugged, male ecstasy as he whispered to her, "We're going to come soon, Gracie. When you're ready, let go for us." His sweet, gentle words were not ordering or commanding, but *releasing* her.

Her body began to shudder uncontrollably, but she had the presence of mind to begin swallowing and continue sucking as Jack growled loudly. "Yes. Grace, Yes. Oh, fuck! That is so good." His cum streamed into her mouth, and she swallowed every copious jet.

She finally released him, unable to hold back the long, rapturous wail that flew from her lips. She struggled to contain the wild, convulsive movements of her body as she rode both their cocks at once.

She collapsed on Adam's chest as he came hard, groaning in ecstasy, sobbing her name. The muscles continued to convulse in her pussy over and over until she saw stars. Her cheek lay on Adam's chest, and she heard his heart pounding rapidly. Ethan finished a few seconds later, howling rapturously as he grasped her to him tightly. His seed streamed into her ass as he flexed over and over against her, filling her completely. His head finally fell forward, his hair hiding his face from her view. She closed her eyes with a moan, trying to lift her head unsuccessfully. She was completely limp, unable to move, so she lay there and listened to the four of them breathe.

After catching his breath, Ethan gently pulled out of her and went to the bathroom to shower quickly. Jack followed him and returned with a warm washcloth. He helped Adam carefully lift her from his cock. Jack laid her back on the mattress and gently cleaned her, making sure to remove all he could of the lubricant. A minute later, Ethan returned from the bathroom.

They were all still a bit unsteady as Ethan brushed her hair from her cheek while she lay there quietly. "Gracie, how do you feel? Did we ride you too hard?"

She looked at them through hooded eyes and smiled softly, sighing deeply. "N–n…" she began but couldn't get it out.

"Was it that good, darlin'?" Jack asked with a chuckle, grazing her flushed cheek with a knuckle.

Her breath hitched in her chest, and her lip quivered as she finally said, "So good…better than my fantasy."

"I could say the same thing, baby. That was heaven," Adam murmured.

Jack propped the pillows back up at the head of the bed, and they helped her crawl to them and lie back down. "I'm glad y'all lit the fireplace. That was nice," she said, yawning.

They pulled the top sheet and blanket up and got comfortable. Ethan was tucked in at her back, his arm around her shoulders as she reclined against him, softly caressing a breast with his fingertips. Jack was cuddled to her, facing her, his hand resting on her ribcage. Adam snuggled into his favorite spot, with his cheek resting on Grace's abdomen, his hand caressing her hip and the top of her thigh as she drifted, falling into a deep, sweet slumber that lasted all night long.

* * * *

Early Saturday morning, the four of them got to read the inscriptions inside their wedding bands. They let Grace look at hers first.

Her worth is far above rubies. Proverbs *31:10.*

"I will cherish this always. I love you," she whispered with tears in her eyes as she returned it to Jack's hand. She handed his to him.

Jack's ring was pure platinum, polished brightly, with three braided strands of unpolished gold wire inlaid in the center. Jack turned the ring and read the inscription aloud, as well.

*My joy * My rock * My love*

Jack sighed and cried a little bit in happiness as he held her to him.

She wiped his tears and handed Ethan his ring next. Ethan and Adam's rings were also brightly polished platinum, but the braided wire inlaid into theirs was unpolished platinum. Ethan read it aloud.

*My soul * My first * My love*

Ethan's voice shook as he read. He was speechless as he took her in his arms and kissed her tenderly.

She gave Adam his ring, her hand shaking just a tad as she looked into his brimming, pale green eyes. Adam read aloud, his voice cracking, tears streaming down his cheeks unashamedly.

*My heart * My gentle giant * My love*

"I'll never get over falling in love with you," he murmured simply. She threw herself into his arms as he lifted her off the floor, wrapping her legs around him like she did the first time they kissed. She sobbed happily into his neck as they all patted her and whispered their love to her.

Chapter Forty-two

Valerie entered the dressing room. "It's time, sweetie." Her features were lit with excitement.

"Are you staying, Valerie, or heading over to the mansion?" Grace asked as she was led to the foyer where Justin waited, darkly handsome in his black tuxedo.

"I'm staying for most of the ceremony, honey. I wouldn't miss this for the world. Then I'll see you in a little while at the reception. The room you requested upstairs at the mansion is all set up. Just go in the private servant entry, and it will lead you straight upstairs, so you won't be waylaid by guests. I'll see you there. Break a leg!" She giggled and adjusted the platinum and diamond scrollwork necklace at Grace's throat. "Perfect!"

Grace looked down at her bare ring finger as Teresa handed her the bridal bouquet made up of red, yellow, and pink roses. Once again, the pink roses were all handpicked by her husband-to-be. Grace had a feeling that Charity suspected but kept her mouth shut because of Teresa, not wanting to shock her. Grace's wedding ring was currently residing in either Ethan's or Adam's coat pocket, waiting for the right moment.

Valerie opened the doors to the sanctuary silently as the soft piano music accompanied by an acoustic guitar and violin began to play an instrumental version of "I Know How the River Feels" written by Amy Powers and Steven Dale Jones.

Teresa stepped through the doors, her flowing gown in a deep burgundy duplicating the soft movement of the fabric in Grace's dress. Her long ebony hair was done up with curling tendrils falling to her shoulders. A charming blush spread on her cheeks, and her eyes were downcast until she began her walk. She had promised Grace that she would hold her head high.

Charity winked at Justin, then blew Grace a kiss as she waited on her brother-in-law's arm. Charity stepped through the doorway, sashaying a little as if she felt Justin ogling her ass with his eyes. Her long blonde hair tumbling down her back in thick chunky curls,

Justin chuckled darkly, and Grace grinned up at him. “She’s reading your mind right now, isn’t she?” She giggled softly, watching Charity make her way into the sanctuary.

He nodded and groaned. “That dress. Mmm.”

As Charity disappeared from sight, Grace looked up at Justin expectantly.

“In a hurry, sweetheart?” he asked, chuckling.

“As a matter of fact, yes. You’re going to have to hold me back, Justin. I may run to them when I see them.”

“Don’t worry. I’ll help you keep it stately and dignified. Just hold on to me.” He smiled down at her, patting her hand with his callused palm. “Those are good men, Grace. You’ve chosen well. They’ll take good care of you.”

She nodded, unable to speak over the lump in her throat at his sweet words. He guided her to the doorway, and she got her first look inside the sanctuary and her men. Justin had held her back, angled from the door so they could not see her until this exact moment.

* * * *

Jack inhaled softly at his first sight of Grace. He dimly heard similar, barely perceptible reactions from Ethan and Adam. He knew it must be hard for them not to react more the way a bridegroom would, but the crowd in the church sanctuary was mixed.

They were surrounded by people who loved them and cared about them, regardless of whether they knew about or understood her attachment to all three. Justin and Charity and their two preteens, Justine and Beau, were Grace’s only close family. It was not a huge gathering but filled the small chapel nicely.

All the ranch hands were there, as well as everyone from the club. Wesley and Evan were there and between them sat Rosemary Piper. Rachel Lopez and their good friend Hank was also there. All of Jack, Ethan, and Adam’s families were there, and that filled the chapel to capacity.

Grace moved with fluid motion down the aisle on his future brother-in-law's arm, looking like a lovely Greek goddess in her wedding gown. Ethan and Adam had been right. It was perfect for her. The fabric swayed and fluttered with each graceful movement, accentuating her curvaceous hips and tiny waist. Her lush breasts swelled so sweetly from the dress and were tantalizing to behold. Her golden hair was swept up on top of her head with stray curls falling down around her soft shoulders, and her veil fluttered behind her from its clip in her hair. He was glad she'd decided to wear the veil back in her hair rather than over her face because then he could enjoy the triumphant joy that was etched across her features as she made her way slowly down the aisle.

The music continued to play as Justin made his way to the designated spot and stopped with her. The pastor approached, smiling broadly. "Who gives this woman to be married?" he asked.

"Her sister and I do," Justin replied clearly, smiling at Grace, then up at Charity near the altar.

Jack came forward as the pastor backed away slightly, and Justin laid Grace's hand in his waiting one. Justin then backed away from her before turning to go sit with his son and daughter. Grace held on to Jack as he helped her up the stairs to the altar, where Ethan and Adam also waited. They looked positively enthralled by her beauty.

"This is the happiest day of my life, Grace," he whispered softly to her as he helped her.

She looked up at him adoringly and said, "The day's not over yet, darlin'."

* * * *

She looked over Jack's shoulder to Ethan and Adam lined up behind him. They carefully positioned themselves beside Jack so that when they turned to her and she repeated her wedding vows she'd be able to see all three of them, but no one would be able to tell from the pews.

The music ended, and the ceremony was performed. Rings were exchanged with vows as their friends and family looked on. As she repeated the standard wedding vows, she gazed in turn at each of them, loving them with her eyes. After the ceremony, everyone was invited to the Victorian mansion on the other side of little Divine. A brief round of traditional wedding pictures was taken, and then Jack, Ethan, and Adam escorted her from the church to the waiting, already cooled SUV.

Jack pulled around to the old servant entrance on the side of the Victorian mansion. Using this entry point, they avoided being delayed by all the guests who waited for their arrival. They helped Grace up the steep old-fashioned stairs, wary of her tripping on her skirts. They stopped at the top of the stairs so she could catch her breath. Inside the largest suite in the mansion, a small party of guests waited for them.

She looked at the three of them standing there, so solicitous of her, and couldn't help but beam with joy.

Jack caressed her upper arm with his knuckles. "You doin' okay, darlin?"

"Oh, so much better than okay. I can't believe my good fortune. I'm just blown away."

"We're so happy you're ours now, baby," Adam replied softly then leaned down to kiss her.

"Ready to do this, Gracie?" Ethan lifted her hand and pressed his lips to her knuckles.

"Yes, I'm ready."

The group in the suite consisted of all their immediate family members and Angel and Teresa. Many others downstairs were aware of the binding ceremony going on upstairs but were not in attendance because of space limitations.

The man who would perform the binding ceremony was a friend of Ethan's. In the ceremony, they spoke of their commitments to one another and a desire to share their lives and love in harmony. Each man in his turn got on one knee and kissed her hand, vowing his love, protection, and provision for her as their female family members blotted tears. Repeating the vows the officiate spoke, she took each one by the hand, kissed his palm and placed his ring on his left ring finger, then kissed each in turn on the lips. Erin took pictures for each part of the ceremony at Grace's request, and Angel shot a video for them with Jack's camera.

In the dining room downstairs, Grace knew all the guests were waiting for the happy couple to arrive. She struggled for a moment with having to assume the façade which excluded two of the men she loved. Their close family members silently went down the front stairs and formed two rows for the officially wedded couple to enter the dining room through.

The entrance was hard for her as the guests stood and clapped. Adam and Ethan took it in stride and kissed her cheek as she passed them, then blended in with the other guests. Shortly thereafter, they were all seated together again at the head table. Charity orchestrated that by sitting down with Justin and their children, Angel, and Teresa all at one end of the table, leaving the rest of the seats available in a group for Grace and her men to occupy.

Ethan and Adam received plates for the four of them, and Grace amused the guests by sitting in Jack's lap and allowing him to feed her by his own hand. She traded hot caresses with Ethan and Adam under the table cloth, wishing they were back at Tessa's place. Tessa was in attendance with her partner, Yolanda. Grace happened to look up and catch Tessa's eye across the room, and they raised their wine glasses in toast to each other. Tessa winked as Yolanda looked on smiling, raising her glass as well.

Later, Adam and Ethan were able to feed her a bite of the wedding cake, which was already cut and served, according to her plan. Grace eliminated many wedding reception traditions that required excluding Ethan and Adam. Erin promised to take a picture of the four of them cutting the top tier of the cake later.

After the caterers finished serving the evening meal, the DJ began to play music in the ballroom and Grace and Jack followed everyone else in. The moment the DJ saw the bride and groom enter the room, he played their song. It was the vocal version of their wedding march song, "I Know How the River Feels," sung by Ty Herndon. Nobody else danced while Grace and Jack had their first dance, moving gracefully around the dance floor alone, lost in their own little world with each other. It was difficult to maintain the illusion because she also wanted to dance with Ethan and Adam now. Next, Joe came and took her away from Jack and had a dance with her while Jack danced with Charity. Justin danced with Grace after Joe and then the next dances were claimed by Richard and Paul, Adam and Ethan's fathers.

"You look lovely this evening, Grace," Richard said sweetly as he held her hand and twirled her to the music, "and you sure can dance, little lady! Adam told me that about you, and he was right."

"Why thank you, Richard, I really appreciate that," she replied, blushing.

"You're welcome." He smiled down at her with the same pale green eyes Adam had. "When it's permissible, if you'd like, you can call me Dad."

"Thanks, Dad," she whispered, her lip trembling. Joe had told her the same thing earlier, and it had brought tears to her eyes, surprising her. She hadn't had anyone to call Dad in years.

"You're welcome, sweetheart. Now don't cry. You'll get me in trouble with Sue and Adam." He smiled down at her as she grinned back through her tears.

"Y'all are so sweet to me. I'm so happy to be a part of your family." She hugged him around his waist because he was so tall, just like Adam.

She had a similar conversation with Ethan's father, Paul. She fell in love with their families as well for making her feel so welcome.

The next two songs the DJ played were the songs Grace had requested to dance with the three of her men. Her prayers were answered when no one cut in during those songs. The first was "It's Your Love" by Tim McGraw and Faith Hill. The second was "Must Be Doin' Somethin' Right" by Billy Currington. She was positive one song would not be enough and had picked those two especially for her men. The first was danced with Jack so that it would appear that Ethan cut in on them, and then Adam would follow Ethan during the second song. Jack kissed her as he released her to Ethan.

"I have never wanted to press my lips to you more than I do right now," Ethan murmured passionately as he smiled down at her congenially. His expression, carefully neutral, was belied by the desire woven into the velvety texture of his husky voice in her ears.

She smiled demurely up at him and whispered, "My lips wish yours were pressed up against them, too. Either set would be happy to return your kiss."

"You don't make it easy for me, do you?" He groaned, his fingers twitching at her waist. "My fingers ache to draw you closer."

"How much longer, sweetheart?" she whispered huskily, stroking him imperceptibly with her fingertips.

"At least another hour. It didn't seem like that long, but this is torture. Jack will let you know when it's okay."

"I love you like crazy, Ethan," she whispered, unable to keep herself from looking into his eyes, knowing that they radiated love for him.

"I'm your slave, Gracie," he whispered back. "I'm going to make up for this vanilla dance a little later, I promise."

"I wanted this dance, even if it is a little more restrained than we're used to. I can't wait to cut loose with you later, honey."

Adam cut in a moment later, and Ethan kissed her cheek and released her to him. She smiled up into his gleaming green eyes and squeezed the hand that held hers gently.

"How are you doing, baby?" she asked.

"Patiently waiting for the go ahead from Jack so I can lay a kiss on you that is so hot they have to crank down the thermostat. How about you, gorgeous?" His fingers caressed her softly through the back of her dress.

Grace giggled deliciously at the thought and softly replied, "You let me know the moment you get the okay, and I will enthusiastically assist you in that endeavor. Your fingers are so warm through my dress and my corset."

"Oh, Lord, don't remind me about the corset." He groaned, rolling his eyes. "You are so beautiful in your wedding dress, baby. Now thoughts of what you look like in that corset will be on my mind the rest of the evening."

Grace drifted closer in the dance and whispered, "I utterly adore you, my handsome husband."

"You're the queen of my heart, baby," he whispered back, his voice a deep, husky drawl, full of emotion.

As the dance ended, she allowed herself a soft, gentle hug around his waist and then released him chastely, reluctantly.

"Soon, baby," he whispered.

* * * *

Valerie brought her several small bouquets, and the DJ called for all the single women to come to the center of the ball room. She handed each one of them a bouquet made of silk flowers that matched the live ones in her bouquet, which she planned to keep and have dried and preserved.

Surreptitiously, she handed Teresa a slightly larger bouquet made from real live flowers. When Teresa noticed the difference, her cheeks blushed, and her eyes widened, as she sniffed the fragrant roses.

"Honey, you just won the bouquet toss. You'd never have fought for the bouquet, but you were the one that deserved it. I love you." Grace kissed Teresa's cheek. She turned Teresa so she faced the direction where Angel was standing nearby, talking to Ethan. She whispered, "Seize the day, baby!" Teresa blushed and laughed, then took the hint.

Grace watched as Teresa moved through the crowd. Angel's eyes lit up as she made a beeline straight for him. He asked her for the next dance, and she accepted. He spoke softly in her ear as he escorted her to a corner of the dance floor. She blushed again, looking over at Grace, smiling in gratitude as Angel taught her how to dance.

Jack mingled with Grace, introducing her to their family members, his as well as Ethan and Adam's. She did as Jack had suggested and assumed that they knew about the four of them and were not in a place where they would discuss it openly. Later in the evening, they could converse more openly with her, after the last of the wedding guests who were not aware of the true nature of the marriage had gone home.

Grace felt large warm hands slide around her waist from behind. She placed her hands over them and knew instantly it was Jack.

"Dance with me, wife?"

"Always, husband."

"You are stunning tonight, darlin'. You hold my heart in your hands, you know that?"

"The same goes for you, my handsome husband," she replied and kissed him slow and deep.

He returned her kiss. Gentle tenderness was replaced with desire and need as his warm tongue stroked hers. The lights on the dance floor dimmed considerably, giving them a little breathing room from watchful eyes. As "Steam," also by Ty Herndon, played, they flowed over the dance floor, kissing and never missing a beat. They ended the song in the middle of the dance floor to thunderous applause. Grace blushed, and Jack bowed, grinning. By the end of the kiss, Grace's entire body was simmering with arousal, ready to be taken.

Once the dance floor filled again, everybody dancing to "Getting You Home" by Chris Young, Adam came and claimed her from Jack. As they settled into the dance, Adam said softly, "Look around. Lots of people have gone home now. It's just family and close friends left. *Oh, hell yes!* I just got the go ahead from Jack and his dad if you want to act like you're *really* married now."

She looked around excitedly, watching for Jack and finding him standing with his father. They both grinned at her, and Jack nodded, blowing her a kiss. She blew one back and threw herself into Adam's arms, giving him a wedding kiss hot enough to steam the chandeliers. He squeezed her tight and spun her around. She heard soft laughter from around the ballroom, but didn't mind. They finished their dance with a long, searing kiss before Ethan claimed her from Adam.

"I've been watching you, my wife," he said softly, seductively, pulling her into his arms and onto the dance floor as the DJ played Faith Hill's "Let's Make Love." He held her to him snugly, and his very hard, insistent erection pressed against her abdomen.

"And I've been *wanting* you, my husband." She kissed him deeply, turning into his kiss, getting as close as she could to him, rubbing her pelvis against his erection. She heard him groan as he released her lips.

"The temptress has been unleashed I see." He chuckled as she nodded and looked into his eyes with all the adoration she'd had to hide for the last three hours. He whispered love words in her ear as they danced, setting her body on fire, stoking the flames as only Ethan could.

* * * *

Jack stood beside Adam and watched in admiration as Ethan danced with Grace. Her head was on his shoulder, her face tilted toward his neck. Anyone else watching would have thought they were sharing a quiet dance as Ethan whispered pretty sweet nothings in her ear. It was a good thing they couldn't hear what he was saying to her. Jack had a pretty good idea, though, and he knew Adam did, too. Knowing her body the way he did, all the telltale signs were there. He could see the almost imperceptible tightening in her torso and the way her hands held on to him, but she never missed a step. They watched his hand stroke down her back, ready if she needed the support. Jack was thankful for the tuxedo jacket that hid his enormous erection from public view as he knowingly watched Ethan's hand indiscernibly catch her around her waist.

"Damn, how does he do that?" Adam muttered in awe.

"Part of their connection, I guess." Jack grinned as he noticed the faint blush above the neckline of her gown.

Her head had fallen momentarily against Ethan's shoulder, her face hidden in his long hair. His face was a picture of male satisfaction. He glanced up and made eye contact with Jack and Adam, and they saluted him. He grinned cockily, realizing they knew what he'd been up to on the dance floor.

"She sure does love to dance," Erin stated happily as she came to stand next to them. "The cake is set up with a clean knife if y'all still want to take cake pictures. Good luck getting her off the dance floor." She walked away to find a dance partner herself.

When their song ended, Ethan smoothly escorted Grace to the ladies' room down the hall. Jack and Adam danced with their moms and the other ladies still in attendance, cutting in on each other just for the fun of it. When Grace returned with Ethan, he passed her hand to Jack and went in search of refreshment for her, coming back with ice water. She told him she hadn't had much to drink all day, too caught up in the wedding buzz. She drained the whole glass when he gave it to her.

After taking the cake-cutting pictures in the dining room, they returned and visited with some of the guests, including Wesley, Evan, and Rosemary. She danced with Ethan again, cutting loose to "Hot Mama" by Trace Adkins, which was fast becoming one of Jack's favorite songs, just for getting to watch her dance with such complete abandon. The dress didn't slow her down at all. "It Did" by Brad Paisley was the next song up, and Ethan brought her back to Jack so she could dance with him to that song. It mirrored what he'd told her about thinking things couldn't get better, then they did.

* * * *

"My Best Friend" by Tim McGraw played as Grace danced with Adam, holding him tightly, letting him lead. He palmed her cheek and she looked up at him. "My wife."

Her eyes slid closed, and she shuddered slightly. "Those are the most beautiful words I've ever heard," she murmured. "I love you, my husband. I can't wait for you to make love to me." He bent down to kiss her thoroughly. "I want you, Adam. I want you all."

He held her to him. After the song ended Charity brought the bag that had her regular clothing and shoes. Grace gave her bouquet to Charity to deal with and then pulled her aside.

"I need to thank you for everything you did, Charity. Thank you for encouraging me to take a chance with these men and for orchestrating those boudoir portraits. Honey, you're my best friend, and I love you so much." She started to tear up. Charity waved her hands in her face.

"Oh! Stop crying, you're messing up your mascara, sweetie!" Charity wiped her fingers gently under Graces eyes. "Come on, raccoon eyes are not sexy, except on raccoons. You should be smiling. You're going to get laid!" She giggled risquely. That worked because Grace smiled and laughed.

Rachel Lopez gave Grace a big hug and said, "You looked so gorgeous today, Grace. Congratulations, honey."

"Thank you, Rachel. What are y'all gonna do now? You look too good to go home this early."

"Well, since The Pony is shut down for the wedding, Wes and Evan are going to take Rosemary to a club in Morehead. I'm going to go with them, and I think Hank, Eli, and Rogelio are going to go, too."

Grace smiled appreciatively as Eli strode toward them across the room. "Mmm, Eli is looking particularly delicious tonight, Rachel. You should see the way he is looking at you right now while your back is turned. Are you sure you're not interested in dating him? He is really into you."

Rachel rolled her eyes. "Please, don't go there, honey. I am way more trouble than that poor guy needs right now. He is so sweet, but I'd probably only make him miserable." She turned to look his way, based on the direction of Grace's gaze, growled softly, and turned back to Grace.

"*See*? There is a very good reason why I tell him no," she muttered as Grace watched not one, but two very pretty wedding guests approach Eli and begin flirting with him.

"No, I *don't*, honey, because it's still you he's watching right now," Grace murmured, hugging Rachel.

"I can't compete with that, Grace. I'm a realist. I like being his friend," she muttered unconvincingly.

"Just wait and see. Maybe things will work out. You never know. I just hate to see you miss an opportunity like that. I have a feeling you may regret not taking that chance. Jack's mom always said to live life with no regrets. Have fun tonight," Grace said, giving her another hug.

She blew Eli a kiss, and he waved back at her, still watching Rachel's back as she turned and walked away. Grace had a good feeling about those two, despite the way Rachel struggled against the attraction she felt for Eli.

Angel and Teresa came and hugged them, as did Wesley, Evan, and Rosemary. Grace thanked Wesley and Evan again for the beautiful workmanship on her new furniture and turned to Rosemary. "Rosemary, we didn't have much of a chance to talk tonight, but I know that Wesley and Evan have wanted us all to get together sometime. After we get home from our honeymoon, I'll call you and we'll plan on doing that. Maybe you and I could have lunch sometime."

"I would really like that, Grace."

Everything was loaded up in the SUV, and the remaining guests prepared to give them their traditional send off. This time the four of them ran out to the SUV together amidst the flying handfuls of birdseed. They would leave in the morning to drive to the airport in San Antonio. They were honeymooning on Grand Cayman Island in the Caribbean. Grace had her heart set on snorkeling and playing with dolphins.

Tonight, they were spending at the ranch house in their own bed, making love until they couldn't move anymore. The SUV had been decorated by well meaning pranksters, but the interior was safe and sound.

They lost the last of the tin cans about three miles down the road from the mansion. Back at the ranch, they helped her down from the back seat of the SUV and led her up onto the porch. At the door, Jack swept her into his arms, carrying her over the threshold, then up the stairs, followed by Ethan and Adam, not placing her back on her feet until she was at the door to her bedroom. She opened the door and was greeted by the sweet odor of scented candles, lit and burning in votives all over the room. The fireplace was on also.

"Katie came back and lit everything for us," Jack explained. The air was warm and fragrant, the light softly dancing in at least a hundred flames.

"It's like a fairy tale, y'all," she whispered.

"A naughty one, maybe," Ethan replied, placing the bags on the floor by the door.

"I'd like to take a quick shower, if y'all don't mind, but I'm going to need help with this wedding gown first. If y'all want, you can join me."

Jack came up behind her and began to unfasten the buttons. They helped her out of the dress and then hung it in the closet. She turned slowly so they could see her lingerie, loving the admiring, lustful looks in their eyes lit by the dancing flames.

"Darlin', are those pearls?" Jack asked as he smoothed his hand over the cleft of her ass.

"They sure are. Help me get this corset unlaced and I'll show it to you." She turned her back to Ethan, and his long fingers made quick work of the laces at her back. Soon, she was out of the white satin corset, and the garters were unsnapped from her sheer white stockings. She stood before them in only the stockings, her high-heeled sandals, the white pearl G-string, and her bridal jewelry. She had never felt more beautiful or desirable.

"Well, that is a pretty little pearl G-string you have on, isn't it, baby?" Adam's voice was husky with desire. His warm hands slid over the satin covered, elastic strings at her hips, pressing her against his big erection.

"My goodness, Adam. You're so hard and big. Gracious, you *all* are." She reached out to stroke them through their clothes. "Do you think you can wait while I clean up a bit, or should you take me right now?"

"Let's all shower together, and then we can get dirty and shower again later," Ethan said, offering a compromise, sort of. They all won, either way.

"For right now, I think we need to help Grace out of all this clothing." Jack kissed her and backing her up against the bed.

She held out a dainty foot, and Ethan removed the high-heeled sandal and then slowly slid the stocking down with great care, kissing her inner thigh as he did. Adam paid her the same loving care and attention on the other foot and leg. Jack continued to kiss her, pressing her up against the side of the bed. She arched her back. His splayed fingers slid down her abdomen, finally finding the waist band to the G-string. She stopped him when he started to push it down and said, "Take a closer look. Pearls aren't the only special thing about this G-string." Her voice was soft and shaky with emotion and desire. She didn't think she'd ever been happier than she was in this moment.

Jack knelt in front of her and gently stroked the white satin over her mound. What looked like a single piece of satin were actually two halves, trimmed in pearls and held together by little satin bows. He looked up at her, hunger and expectation in his eyes, and she smiled and nodded. He pulled gently on the first bow, then the second, as they listened to her quick breathing. He slid one finger inside the panty and then parted it with another.

He grinned and said, "Grace is playing peek-a-boo with us."

He leaned forward and slid his warm, wet tongue into her slit as she cried out in pleasure. With her elbows propped behind her, she watched him as he slid two fingers slowly into her pussy while pressing his thumb against her sensitive clit. He began stroking her sweet spot.

"I love this little G-string, darlin'. It's very naughty, but very convenient, too. Can you see Adam, Ethan? I love this sweet little pink pussy. I could feast on it all night, darlin'." He kissed her abdomen, continuing the slow, torturous strokes, gradually increasing the speed and the intensity. Adam and Ethan helped her up onto the bed as Jack continued to stroke her. They whispered loving words of encouragement to her as her orgasm loomed close. They whispered naughty words to her, too, like only her dirty-talking cowboys could, making her even hotter and wetter.

"Mmm, Grace is sweet as sugar, but she loves it when we talk dirty to her, don't you, Gracie?" Ethan asked.

"You know I do, Ethan. You make me come every time you do, like on the dance floor tonight." The memory of what he'd said to her earlier set off that involuntary tightening in her pelvic floor, signaling a fast approaching, deep orgasm.

"What did Ethan talk about doing to you to make you come, baby?" Adam asked as he leaned down and took her nipple in his hot mouth and suckled while he stroked her belly. She whimpered her need, knowing why Ethan brought it to mind as they played with her. It would set her off like a rocket again.

"He told me all about how—Oh! He'll bend me over the chaise lounge and fuck my pussy from behind. Oh! Then he'll slide into my ass and fuck my ass as well. He said he might even tie me to it first, if I've been bad." She giggled and then gasped as Jack flicked her clit with his tongue.

"Are you planning on being bad, darlin'?" Jack asked, glancing at Ethan, who was currently teasing her other nipple into quivering submission.

"If being fucked from behind while I'm tied up is my punishment, I may have to be very bad, so bad I might even need to be *spanked*, isn't that right, Ethan, honey?" She reached out for him, his lips parting over hers in a deep kiss while he stroked her breast.

"I'd be just as likely to do it if she was good or bad. As long as Gracie is happy and satisfied, who cares?" Ethan said softly. "Let go for Jack, Grace, give him your sweet cream." Ethan's soft voice in her ear as he nuzzled her, combined with Adam's suckling and the deft strokes Jack delivered to her sweet spot, created an intense storm inside her.

Ethan whispered, "Give it to him, Grace. Come for Jack," and her eyes flew open, and the tension snapped like a rubber band stretched too tight. She screamed as a raging fire exploded through her body, and her orgasm gushed from her over his hand. She rode each pulse in their arms, shuddering and shaky. Jack slowly withdrew his fingers and licked the sweet cream from them, then gently licked her pussy, sending aftershocks though her body when he touched her clit with his tongue. A sigh of pure, unadulterated delight slipped from her tingling lips.

"Feeling good, baby?" Adam asked, kissing her.

"I've never been this happy," she murmured, nuzzling Adam's cheek.

Jack looked up at her, a haze of desire and male satisfaction written in his eyes and on his face. "The evening's not over yet, darlin'. Now how about that shower?" He held out his hand to her. Adam and Ethan growled in agreement. She smiled, thinking it just couldn't get better than this, being with her men. Then it did.

Epilogue

Three Years Later

Adam entered the bathroom to find Grace already standing in the tub. He helped her rinse the bubbles from her skin, squeezing the water from the washcloth over her shoulder and enjoying the sight as it splashed over her now fuller, lovely pink-tipped breasts. She was just over-the-top gorgeous to him.

"How was your soak? Are you feeling a little more relaxed?" He gently lifted her from the tub and set her on the bath mat. He wrapped the towel around her and patted her dry.

"I think the nap and bubble bath were just what I needed to help me unwind. Tomorrow I go for my six weeks follow-up. You know what that means, right?" She pressed up against him. He leaned down and kissed her. The banked passion inside him raged forth, and he hardened quickly. He cupped the back of her head in his hand and slid the other down her spine before gently squeezing her ass.

"If Dr. Guthrie says it's all right, that is." He'd missed her sweet body something fierce these last few months. From the beginning of the ninth month she'd been too uncomfortable to enjoy making love. She'd needed to be held and comforted more than she needed sex. Then she'd been off limits for the six weeks since the baby had been born.

All three of them had been there with Grace through her labor with Dr. Guthrie's approval and stayed right beside her through the delivery. They'd taken the classes and learned to be good coaches for her, helping her to relax and stay focused. Rose Marie Warner was born just as the sun had begun to rise. Grace had looked out on a new rosy day as her baby daughter nursed at her breast for the first time, her proud fathers looking on. Her tiny little rosy lips parted so sweetly, suckling from her mother's breast was a sight that reduced all three of her tough daddies to tears.

Adam had thought to himself that that was the happiest moment of his life. The thought that there would be even happier moments yet to come made his heart feel like it was being stretched near to bursting.

As he kissed Grace, he felt her relax against him and sighed. Then abruptly, she giggled. He looked down to see she had leaked all over him. She pressed the damp towel against her nipples to stop the let-down reflex. She giggled again. "I guess that's what I deserve for getting turned on by you. I wouldn't have minded getting wet, but I definitely didn't mean like *that.*"

"I miss those sweet nipples." He chuckled as he caressed her shoulder and kissed the top of her head.

"Well, after tomorrow, you won't have to miss them anymore. You can lick, but don't suck. That's all I can say, unless you want to see what my milk tastes like, that is."

"I'll bet it's sweet tasting, just like everything else about you." He slid his long robe on her and turned up the sleeves a bit for her, and she tied it at the waist.

"How is Rose Marie?"

They've been taking turns rocking her. She fell asleep on Jack's chest earlier. We took pictures for you. She's the sweetest thing, just like her mama."

"Except when she screams."

"Seems I recall her mama screaming being one of the *sweetest* sounds my ears ever heard," he replied as he slid his arms around her shoulders.

Grace giggled. "Maybe so, but she screams at the first hunger pang. My screams were because I was in absolute ecstasy. Big difference." She chuckled and slid a hand towel into the front of the robe, pressing against her nipples. "Oh, there I go *again*. I should probably feed her now. Sorry, your robe is a little damp now."

They found Ethan and Jack out on the back porch. Ethan held little Rose Marie in his big, muscular arms, crooning to their sweet little baby girl as he leaned against the porch railing. He smiled tenderly at Grace when she padded out barefoot wrapped in Adam's robe. She peeked at Rose Marie, who was gazing raptly up at one of her handsome daddies, wide awake. Sensing her mother, she squawked hungrily.

Ethan rose from the railing as Grace turned and sat down on the glider. She opened the left side of Adam's robe, and Ethan laid Rose Marie in her arms. It didn't bother Adam in the least for her to nurse openly in the privacy of their home. As a matter-of-fact, he felt a sort of primitive male pride in seeing her tending to their baby in such a natural way. Plus, he did love the sight of her fuller breasts these days. There was no denying it. He knew without a doubt that Jack and Ethan shared his feelings.

Adam stood against the porch rail, gazing down on one of his most cherished fantasies coming to life before him—Grace wrapped in his robe as she sat on the glider, one foot tucked under her, the other pushing the glider to rock. Their daughter wrapped in a fuzzy pink blanket against the slight chill in the evening air, little tufts of blonde hair wafting in the evening breeze as she nursed at her mother's lovely breast. Grace nuzzled her little head with her lips, singing softly to her.

Adam joined her on the glider, putting his arm around Grace's shoulders, watching as Rose Marie looked up at him, her baby-gray eyes studying him seriously while he watched over them both. He reached out a gentle finger and lightly brushed her cute little nose. His mom swore it was the Davis family nose. Time would tell.

"It couldn't get any better than this moment, right now," she whispered, laying her head on Adam's shoulder and looking up into Jack and Ethan's adoring eyes.

But it did.

THE END

www.heatherrainier.com

ABOUT THE AUTHOR

Heather Rainier lives and writes in South Central Texas. Her stories offer up the content of her fantasies, with autobiographical humor, triumph, and tragedy mixed in.

Heather believes that life doesn't always present love to us in neat little sanitized packages. We have to seize the day, live life with no regrets, forget the past, never give up, learn to trust, and dare to live, even in outrageous circumstances.

When not happily typing at her keyboard, Heather is usually busy corralling her kids, volunteering at local schools, or loving on her smokin' hot husband, who thankfully loves to cook.

Also by Heather Rainier

Everlasting Classic: Divine Creek Ranch 2: *Her Gentle Giant, Part 1: No Regrets*

Everlasting Classic: Divine Creek Ranch 2: *Her Gentle Giant, Part 2: Remember to Dance*

Available at
BOOKSTRAND.COM

Siren Publishing, Inc.
www.SirenPublishing.com

LaVergne, TN USA
18 March 2011
220729LV00004B/57/P